PRAISE FOR

The Last Witchfinder

"[A] picaresque tale steeped in philosophical debate. . . . Here are storytelling, showmanship, and provocativ.... ventive feat ... brainteasing fun."

—........, *New York Times*

"[Morrow] pulls off so many dazzling feats of literary magic that in a different century he'd have been burned at the stake. Forget *The Crucible*, Arthur Miller's dreary classic. Forget the repugnant kitsch of modern-day Salem. *The Last Witchfinder* flies us back to that thrilling period when scientific rationalism was dropped into the great cauldron of intellectual history, boiling with prejudice, tradition, piety, and fear. The result is a fantastical story mixed so cunningly with real-life details that your vision of America's past may never awaken from Morrow's spell.... Endlessly exciting.... A grand picaresque tour of England and the American colonies.... Watch out for James Morrow: He's magic." —*Washington Post Book World*

"James Morrow ... has been busy these last seven years ... doing copious research and precisely setting down his magnum opus, *The Last Witchfinder*.... Morrow seamlessly weaves fantasy with science and historical fact in one of the best novels of the year."

—*Rocky Mountain News*

"Morrow's prose, lucid as amber, ..., embellishments.... Grim and gorgeous, earthy and erudite as well, Morrow's *Witchfinder* woos readers with a secularist vision of reason triumphant, rewarding its followers richly, giving them all the world and ample time in which to enjoy it." —*Seattle Times*

"For those who like the good, old-fashioned storytelling techniques of the nineteenth century (heavy on plot, festooned with lots of odd, memorable characters), *The Last Witchfinder* may be just the ticket.... While it may read like a collaboration between Charles Dickens and Henry Fielding, there is at least one stylistic affectation and plenty of modern-day musing about advanced sciences to suggest strong influence from writers like William Gibson or cutting-edge scientists such as David Deutsch and Wolfgang Ketterle.... Sporting oeuvre that puts him in the highest ranks of comedic novelists and satirical writers, Morrow is long overdue for a mainstream audience." —*Denver Post*

"[An] historical fiction tour de force ... a treat for history lovers.... The elaborate text is studded with facts and redolent with the era's lush language.... A novel about ideas, science, and history.... [A] book to delight fans of writers such as John Barth and T. C. Boyle. Or even Jonathan Swift." —*USA Today*

"[A] richly detailed, cerebral tale of rationality versus superstitious bigotry.... This tour de force of early America bears a buoyant humor to lighten its macabre load."

—*Fort Wayne Journal Gazette* (Indiana)

"[An] intrepid, impeccably researched epic." —*Publishers Weekly* (starred review)

"James Morrow writes in order to tell us things: to admonish us about our coming destruction of the world, or about the battle between reason and superstition.... What he is, deep down, is a satirist and moralist.... What makes this satirical version of the struggle against fundamentalism so powerful is Morrow's scenes of natural beauty or urban squalor. These have the scent of real wildflowers, the squish of real mud and dung underfoot."

—*Independent* (London)

"Had Charles Dickens sat down to collaborate with modern-day scientists like Michio Kaku or Kenneth Ford, and Henry Fielding (author of *Tom Jones*), the resulting novel likely would have resembled James Morrow's *Last Witchfinder*. This lively and thoughtful adventure is filled with enough satire and plot to fuel two Mark Twain tomes (and perhaps give *Gulliver's Travels* a run for its money).... Morrow's morality tale couldn't be better timed considering events taking place in today's world.... Morrow throws in a conceit that makes his historical comedy-cum-satire stand out from the crowd: an alternating narrative related by none other than *Mathematical Principles of Philosophy*.... It's a sly, tongue-in-cheek move that allows Morrow to ruminate about the endless possibilities presented by the cutting-edge science of quantum theory and, indeed, by many a philosopher and theologian."

—*Pages*

"Morrow's panoramic vision of the Enlightenment encompasses the ideology of that turbulent, transformative era, and his wry commentary—related through the sprightly voice of Newton's *Principia Mathematica*, speaking for itself—lightens the novel's tone without softening its message. This impeccably researched, highly ambitious novel—nine years in the writing—is a triumph of historical fiction."

—*Booklist* (starred review)

"James Morrow brings to life the clash between science and superstition through his heroine, Jennet Stearne, a vivacious Colonial feminist before her time.... [*The Last Witchfinder*] is intelligent, funny, lively—not to mention strange as a witch's brew.... Morrow concocts a thrilling ending, with his heroine willing to sacrifice everything for the love of science."

—*Pittsburgh Post-Gazette*

"In *Witchfinder*, Morrow focuses on a historical moment that gives his philosophical inclinations full play: that divide, which opened up in the late seventeenth century, between 'traditional' society and the Enlightenment.... Generally, however, the incidents and characters here have a bawdy, eighteenth-century liveliness that forms a pleasingly surprising fit with our modern sensibilities."

—*Raleigh News & Observer*

"[Jennet] is an attractive heroine in an exceptionally engaging and piquantly thoughtful novel. Though similar to John Barth's *Sot-Weed Factor* in many respects, *The Last Witchfinder* is warmer and more human. Strongly recommended."

—*Library Journal*

"A dazzling novel about the clash between superstition and science.... [A]n extravagant, expansive, erudite, energetic feast of information and adventure."

—*Daily Telegraph* (London)

"[A] historical fantasy as full of escapes and voyages and kidnappings as any eighteenth-century picaresque novel ... [and] Mr. Morrow is a likable and highly learned writer. With appealing ease, he draws on everything from demonology to Algonquin linguistics. And, no mean feat, he keeps it lively."

—*Dallas Morning News*

ALSO BY
James Morrow

NOVELS
The Wine of Violence
The Continent of Lies
This Is the Way the World Ends
Only Begotten Daughter
City of Truth

THE GODHEAD TRILOGY
Towing Jehovah
Blameless in Abaddon
The Eternal Footman

SHORT FICTION
Bible Stories for Adults
The Cat's Pajamas and Other Stories

HARPER PERENNIAL

NEW YORK • LONDON • TORONTO • SYDNEY

WALSH JESUIT HIGH SCHOOL
STUDENT LIBRARY

The
Laſt Witchfinder

❦

JAMES MORROW

4/07 Amazon 10.95

HARPER ● PERENNIAL

This book is a work of fiction. References to real people, events,
establishments, organizations, or locales are intended only to
provide a sense of authenticity, and are used fictitiously.
All other characters, and all incidents and dialogue, are drawn from
the author's imagination and are not to be construed as real.

A hardcover edition of this book was published in 2006 by William
Morrow, an imprint of HarperCollins Publishers.

P.S.™ is a trademark of HarperCollins Publishers.

THE LAST WITCHFINDER. Copyright © 2006 by James Morrow.
All rights reserved. Printed in the United States of America. No part
of this book may be used or reproduced in any manner whatsoever
without written permission except in the case of brief quotations
embodied in critical articles and reviews. For information address
HarperCollins Publishers, 10 East 53rd Street, New York, NY 10022.

HarperCollins books may be purchased for educational, business,
or sales promotional use. For information please write:
Special Markets Department, HarperCollins Publishers,
10 East 53rd Street, New York, NY 10022.

FIRST HARPER PERENNIAL EDITION PUBLISHED 2007.

Book design by Shubhani Sarkar

The Library of Congress has catalogued the hardcover edition as follows:

Morrow, James.
    The last witchfinder : a novel / James Morrow.—1st ed.
        p.   cm.
    ISBN: 978-0-06-082179-1 (acid-free paper)
    ISBN-10: 0-06-082179-5
    1. Young women—Fiction.   2. Great Britain—History—
Restoration, 1660–1688—Fiction.   3. Philadelphia (Pa.)—
History—Colonial period, ca. 1600–1775—Fiction.   4. Executions
and executioners—Fiction.   5. Trials (Witchcraft)—Fiction.
I. Title.

PS3563.O876L37 2006
813'.54—dc22   2005047177

ISBN: 978-0-06-082180-7 (pbk.)
ISBN-10: 0-06-082180-9 (pbk.)

07 08 09 10 11 ❖/RRD 10 9 8 7 6 5 4 3 2 1

TO THE MEMORY OF
Ann Hyson Smith

DISCARDED

22550

If the Judge wishes to find out whether she is endowed with a witch's power of preserving silence, let him take note whether she is able to shed tears when standing in his presence, or when being tortured. For we are taught both by the words of worthy men of old and by our own experience that this is a most certain sign, and it has been found that even if she be urged and exhorted by solemn conjurations to shed tears, if she be a witch she will not be able to weep: although she will assume a tearful aspect and smear her cheeks and eyes with spittle to make it appear that she is weeping; wherefore she must be closely watched by the attendants.

HEINRICH KRÄMER AND JAMES SPRENGER
Malleus Maleficarum, A.D. 1486,
PART III, QUESTION XV (EXCERPT)

Then came out of the House a grave, tall Man carrying the Holy Writ before the supposed Wizard as solemnly as the Sword-bearer of London before the Lord Mayor; the Wizard was first put in the Scale, and over him was read a Chapter out of the Books of Moses, and then the Bible was put in the other Scale, which, being kept down before, was immediately let go; but, to the great Surprise of the Spectators, Flesh and Bones came down plump, and out-weighed the good Book by abundance. After the same Manner, the others were served, and their lumps of Mortality severally were too heavy for Moses and all the Prophets and Apostles.

BENJAMIN FRANKLIN
"A WITCH-TRIAL AT MOUNT-HOLLY"
The Pennsylvania Gazette
OCTOBER 22, 1730

Contents

CONTENTS

Author's Note

IF MY EXPERIENCE IN COMPOSING *The Last Witchfinder* may be counted typical, then the writer of historical fiction derives no less delight from adhering to the facts of his chosen era than he does from bending those facts in pursuit of some presumed poetic truth.

There was indeed a 1604 Parliamentary Witchcraft Act, and it remained the law of the empire until 1736. The date of England's last legally sanctioned execution for sorcery I have advanced slightly, from 1685 to 1689. My presentations of the Glorious Revolution, the Salem Witch Trials, the Abenaki Indian raid on Haverhill (carried out in these pages by my fictional Nimacooks), Samuel Sewall's campaign against the *New England Courant*, the Baron de Montesquieu's antipathy toward the Conjuring Statutes, and Johannes Junius's confession of Satanism are as free of falsehoods as my research efforts and thematic preoccupations allowed.

The young Benjamin Franklin, visiting London for the first time in 1725, formally requested, through the physician Henry Pemberton, an audience with Sir Isaac Newton, though nothing came of Franklin's plea. Chapter Eight offers my speculations on what might have transpired at this meeting had it occurred. In 1730 Franklin devoted several column inches of *The Pennsylvania Gazette* to his eyewitness account of a witch trial in Mount Holly, New Jersey. Although most historians regard this article as a lampoon, I decided to take Franklin at his word.

Finally, while the problem of witchcraft held no particular fascination for Newton, he did in fact go on record as believing that evil spirits were mere "desires of the mind."

PART I

The Pricker *of* Colchester

❊❊❊❊❊❊❊❊❊❊

Introducing Our Heroine,
Jennet Stearne,
Whose Father Hunts Witches,
Whose Aunt Seeks Wisdom,
and Whose Soul Desires
an Object
It Cannot Name

❊

M ay I speak candidly, fleshling, one rational creature to another, myself a book and you a reader? Even if the literature
of confession leaves you cold, even if you are among those
who wish that Rousseau had never bared his soul and Augustine never
mislaid his shame, you would do well to lend me a fraction of your life. I
am *Mathematical Principles of Natural Philosophy*, after all—in my native
tongue, *Philosophiæ Naturalis Principia Mathematica*, the *Principia* for
short—not some tenth-grade algebra text or guide to improving your
golf swing. Attend my adventures and you may, Dame Fortune willing,
begin to look upon the world anew.

Unlike you humans, a book always remembers its moment of conception. My father, the illustrious Isaac Newton, having abandoned his
studies at Trinity College to escape the great plague of 1665, was spending the summer at his mother's farm in Woolsthorpe. An orchard grew
beside the house. Staring contemplatively through his bedroom window,
Newton watched an apple drop free of its tree, driven by that strange
arrangement we have agreed to call gravity. In a leap of intuition, he
imagined the apple not simply as falling to the ground but as striving for
the very center of the Earth. This fruit, he divined, bore a relationship to
its planet analogous to that enjoyed by the moon: gravitation, ergo, was

❊❊❊❊❊

universal—the laws that governed terrestrial acceleration also ruled the heavens. As below, so above. My father never took a woman to his bed, and yet the rush of pleasure he experienced on that sweltering July afternoon easily eclipsed the common run of orgasm.

Twenty-two years later—in midsummer of 1687—I was born. Being a book, a patchwork thing of leather and dreams, ink and inspiration, I have always counted scholars among my friends, poets among my heroes, and glue among my gods. But what am I like in the particular? How is the *Principia Mathematica* different from all other books? My historical import is beyond debate: I am, quite simply, the single greatest work of science ever written. My practical utility is indisputable. Whatever you may think of Mars probes, moon landings, orbiting satellites, steam turbines, power looms, the Industrial Revolution, or the Massachusetts Institute of Technology, none of these things is possible without me. But the curious among you also want to know about my psychic essence. You want to know about my *soul*.

Take me down from your shelf. If you're like most humans, you've accorded me a place of prestige, right next to the Bible, perhaps, or rubbing covers with Homer. Open me. Things start out innocuously enough, with eight turgid but not indigestible definitions concerning mass, acceleration, and force, followed by my father's three famous laws of motion. Continue turning my pages. Things are getting pretty rough—aren't they?—propositions proliferating, scholia colliding, lemmas breeding like lab rats. "The centripetal forces of bodies, which by equable motions describe different circles, tend to the centers of the same circles, and are to each other as the squares of the arcs described in equal times divided respectively by the radii of the circles." Lugubrious, I'll admit. This isn't Mother Goose.

But you can't judge a book by its contents. Just because my father stuffed me with sines, cosines, tangents, and worse, that doesn't make me a dry or dispassionate fellow. I have always striven to attune myself to the aesthetic side of mathematics. Behold the diagram that illustrates Proposition XLI. Have you ever beheld a more sensual set of lines? Study the figure accompanying Proposition XLVIII. Have arcs and cycloids ever been more beautiful? My father set geometry in motion. He taught parabolas to pirouette and hyperbolas to gavotte. Don't let all my conventional trigonometric discourse fool you, by the way. Determined to keep his methods a secret, Newton wrote out his discoveries in the mathematics of his day. What's really afoot here is that amazing tool he invented for calculating the rate of change of a rate of change. Abide with me, fleshling, and I shall teach you to run with the fluxions.

The precise metaphysical procedures by which a book goes about writing another book need not concern us here. Suffice it to say that our human scribes remain entirely ignorant of their possession by bibliographic forces; the agent in question never doubts that his authorship is authentic. A bit of literary history may clarify matters. Unlike Charles Dickens's other novels, *Little Dorrit* was in fact written by *The Færie Queene*. It is fortunate that Jane Austen's reputation does not rest on *Northanger Abbey*, for the author of that admirable satire was *Paradise Regained* in a frivolous mood. The twentieth century offers abundant examples, from *The Pilgrim's Progress* cranking out *Atlas Shrugged*, to *Les Misérables* composing *The Jungle*, to *The Memoirs of Casanova* penning *Portnoy's Complaint*.

Occasionally, of course, the alchemy proves so potent that the appropriated author never produces a single original word. Some compelling facts have accrued to this phenomenon. Every desert romance novel bearing the name E. M. Hull was actually written by *Madame Bovary* on a lark; *Mein Kampf* can claim credit for most of the Hallmark greeting cards printed between 1958 and 1967; Richard Nixon's entire oeuvre traces to a collective effort by the science-fiction slush pile at Ace Books. Now, as you might imagine, upon finding a large readership through one particular work, the average book aspires to repeat its success. Once *The Wasteland and Other Poems* generated its first Republican Party platform, it couldn't resist creating all the others. After *Waiting for Godot* acquired a taste for writing Windows software documentation, there was no stopping it.

In my own case, I started out small, producing a Provençal cookbook in 1947 and an income-tax preparation guide in 1983. But now I turn my attention to a more ambitious project, attempting a tome that is at once an autobiography, an historical epic, and an exercise in Newtonian apologetics. Though occasionally I shall wax defensive, this is largely because so many of your species's ills, from rampant materialism to spiritual alienation, have been laid upon my rationalistic head. Face it, people, there is more to your malaise than celestial mechanics. If you want to know why you feel so bad, you must look beyond universal gravitation.

The ability to appropriate mortal minds accounts not only for a book's literary output but for its romantic life as well, physical and emotional. We copulate by proxy, and we like it. But prior to any carnal consummation, we fall in love with you—madly, deeply, eternally—despite the yawning gulf separating our kingdoms, that chasm between the vegetable and the animal. The protagonist of my tale is a mortal woman, Jennet Stearne, and I must declare at the outset that I adored her past all telling and worshipped her beyond the bounds of reason. Even now, centuries after her death, I cannot write her name without causing my host to tremble.

When I say that my passion for Jennet began in her eleventh year, I hope you will not think me a pederast or worse. Believe me, my obsession occasioned no priapic action until my goddess was well into womanhood. And yet the fire was there from the first. If you'd known her, you would understand. She was a nimble-witted girl, and high-spirited too, zesty, kinetic, eager to take hold of life with every faculty at her disposal, heart and loins, soul and intellect. I need but tweak my memory molecules and instantly I can bring to mind her azure eyes,

her cascading auburn hair, her dimpled

cheeks, her exquisite

upturned

❦

Nose

of Turk, Jennet

Stearne remembered from

The Tragedie of Macbeth, was amongst

the last ingredients to enter a witches' brew, hard

behind the goat's gall, the hemlock root, the wolf's tooth, the lizard's

leg, and so many other wonderfully horrid things. Near the end came the Tartar's lips, the tiger's guts, and the finger of a strangled babe. Finally you cooled the concoction with baboon blood, all the while chanting, "Double, double, toil and trouble, fire burn, and cauldron bubble."

Although Jennet had never actually seen a witches' brew, she hoped the day was not far off when she might accompany her father, Witchfinder-General for Mercia and East Anglia, on the cleansing circuit, thereby beholding not only an enchanted soup but all the other astonishing components of a Sabbat, the flying horses, singing pigs, wizards dancing widdershins, and altars piled high with silver apples made of moonlight. As it was, however, at the start of the spring hunt Walter Stearne always placed his daughter under the care and tutelage of his widowed sister-in-law, Isobel Mowbray, whilst Jennet's younger brother, Dunstan, was privileged to join their father as he set about delivering the English nation from the Devil.

This arrangement would have occasioned in Jennet an intolerable envy but for the irrefutable fact that Aunt Isobel was the cleverest woman in Christendom. Aunt Isobel the philosopher. Aunt Isobel the geometer. Aunt Isobel the mistress of Mirringate Hall, that carnival of marvels, chief amongst the prizes accruing to her long-dead husband's mercantile genius. In the Mirringate astronomical observatory, Jennet had once spied the very quartet of Jovian satellites that had inspired Galileo Galilei to cast his lot with the Copernican universe. In the alchemical laboratory she'd oft-times heated the pigment cinnabar, sublimating it into a slippery silver pearl of mercury. The crystal-gazing parlor was the scene of many attempts by Jennet and Isobel to glimpse future events in polished mirrors and clear-quartz globes, with results that seemed to neither confirm nor disprove the validity of scrying.

The burgeoning spring of 1688 found Jennet particularly anxious to continue her studies, for Aunt Isobel had recently acquired a Van Leeuwenhoek microscope of the newest design. Climbing into the Basque coach that morning, settling onto the velvet seat alongside Dunstan, she felt throughout her body an uncanny exhilaration, as if her heart had become a passenger on one of her mother's girlhood kites. Their father, in the driver's box, snapped his whip, and the horses lurched out of Wyre Street Livery into a Colchester dawn alive with birdsong and the incisive scent of dog-roses, bound for Mirringate Hall.

Thanks to Aunt Isobel, Jennet knew many stories about her mother, whose life's juices had gushed out of her as she'd struggled to bring Dunstan into the world. Passing their school-girl years in the verdant environs of the River Stour, the two sisters—sole offspring of Oliver Noakes, a successful Parham apothecary—had in time come to share many enthusiasms, most especially a fondness for æolian machines. Margaret and Isobel Noakes had fashioned their own pinwheels, weather vanes, and toy sailboats. They'd constructed soaring paper birds and fluttering parchment butterflies. They'd stretched red silk handkerchiefs on birchwood frames, launching each kite to such an altitude that it became an ominous crimson comet hanging in the Mistley sky.

On Jennet's eighth birthday, Aunt Isobel presented her with Margaret Noake's crowning achievement, a four-bladed windmill, thirty inches high. Silk sails puffed full of breeze, the cedar cross turned smoothly on its axis, grinding the softest flour in Creation.

"It still works!" Jennet exclaimed.

"You doubted it would?" Aunt Isobel said. She was a small woman, compact as a stone, intense as an owl. "Your mother and I took our pastimes seriously, child. We ne'er confused fun with frivolity."

"Fun versus frivolity . . ."

"A subtle distinction, aye, but 'tis to the subtle distinctions a natural philosopher must be evermore attuned. My husband once came home bearing both the skull of a human imbecile and the skull of a Sumatra orangutan, then challenged me to say which was which."

"The skulls looked much the same?"

"They were twins for fair. But then I noticed that in one specimen the aperture permitting egress of the brain-cord was set an inch lower than in the other. Ergo, I knew the first for the imbecile's skull, since 'tis only we humans who walk fully erect!"

THE JOURNEY FROM COLCHESTER to Ipswich had never seemed longer to Jennet, but at last they were strolling amidst the boxwood hedges of the Mirringate gardens, and finally they were sitting in the east parlor, eating biscuits and admiring the new microscope. Hand-carried by Aunt Isobel all the way from the Low Countries, the device rested on a squat marble table beside a porcelain vase holding three tulips—yellow, purple, red—likewise Dutch, recently burst from their bulbs.

It was Rodwell himself who waited on the visitors, and as the gangling old steward poured out saucers of coffee from a silver retort (not the first time an alchemical apparatus had been pressed into practical service at Mirringate), the conversation betwixt Jennet's father and aunt turned to the sorts of dreary political matters that for adults held such incomprehensible fascination. Would the King persist in imposing his regrettable religion on the affairs of state? Would he continue to risk his throne by appointing Catholics to head the colleges, imprisoning rebellious Anglican bishops in the Tower, and setting Papist officers over the army and the fleet? To Jennet it did not seem terribly important whether England lost her ruler or not. Obviously the nation could always get another. Surely this James the Second boasted at least one blood relation willing to wear the crown, especially as the position included scores of minions standing ready to empty your chamber-pot, soothe you with a viol, and feed you on marzipan and meringue the instant you snapped your fingers.

Bored, Jennet studied the vapors rising from her coffee. Dunstan, equally unamused, leafed through his sketching-folio—his inerrant eye, she noticed, was attracted these days to gnarled trees and helical vines—until he found a blank sheet, whereupon he took out his sweet-smelling sticks of colored wax. In a matter of minutes he'd caught the essence of the red tulip, fixing its pulse and glow to the page: a living heart, she decided, beating within the breast of a fabulous Oriental dragon.

"Mutum est pictura poema," Jennet said.

Dunstan glanced up from his folio. His pudgy face had of late acquired an unfortunate pummeled quality, like a bulging purse drawn tight by a miser's anxiety. "What?"

" 'A picture is a silent poem.' Simonides."

Simultaneously changing the pitch of her voice, the cant of her spine, and the topic under discussion, Aunt Isobel gestured toward the microscope. "It hath six times the potency of its ancestors, I'm told, a siege cannon as compared to a slingshot. The secret lies in Van Leeuwenhoek's lenses. They say only God Himself can grind better."

"A most impressive trinket," Jennet's father said.

" 'Tis no bauble, brother," Aunt Isobel said. "Indeed, the day may soon dawn when you will count a microscope amongst your most important tools."

"Oh?" Walter said, frowning severely. "How so?"

"Unless my instincts have betrayed me, 'tis by means of this invention that England's witchfinders might finally put their profession on a sound philosophic basis, worthy to stand alongside chemistry, optics, and planetary mechanics."

Jennet contemplated the gleaming brass tube, portal to a hundred invisible worlds. She was eager to explore them all—the kingdom of swamp water, the empire of moss, the caliphate of fungus, the republic of blood.

" 'Tis gratifying you wish to so elevate my calling, Lady Mowbray," Walter said, "but my usual tools are adequate to the task."

"Adequate to the task, but inadequate to a judge's skepticism." Aunt Isobel fluted her thin lips, siphoning up a mouthful of coffee. "Let me make bold, dear kinsman, to suggest that cleansing's an imperiled enterprise. England's a-swarm with doubting Thomases and the lineal descendants of Offa the Contrarian."

"I shan't deny it." Jennet's father removed his snowy peruke, thereby altering his aspect for the worse, from handsome and dignified demonologist to bald-headed, sweat-spangled practitioner of a vanishing trade.

Isobel set her palm against the brass tube, caressing it as if coaxing a prediction from a crystalline sphere. "I have an *experimentum magnus* in mind, certain to confound the skeptics, but requiring such materials as only you can provide."

For the second time that day Jennet's heart flew heavenward, kiteborne, weightless. An *experimentum magnus* was coming to Mirringate— and if she learned her lessons well that season, mastering her Euclid and ingesting her Aristotle, Aunt Isobel would surely give her a rôle in the momentous project!

"Each time you unmask a witch, you must catch and cage her animal servant for me," Isobel said. "I shall need a dozen specimens at least, alive and feisty: rat, locust, toad—whate'er sorts have lately claimed the Devil's affections."

"A peculiar request," Walter said.

"I shall anatomize each familiar, then use this microscope in detecting signs of Satanic intervention, evidence on which no jurist durst turn his back. Mayhap I'll find tiny incantations, written on a ferret's bones in Lucifer's own hand—or minuscule imps adrift in a raven's blood—or monstrous animalcules fighting tooth and claw amidst a cat's spermatozooans."

When Jennet heard this elaboration, her heart instantly descended. Was there no way to accomplish the great experiment except by entering those dark, slimy, stinking regions that lay beneath fur and feathers? It was one thing to cage and scrutinize a witch's familiar, and quite another to cut the poor animal to pieces.

"Sweet sister, 'twould seem you expect me to turn my coach into a menagerie," Walter said.

"Quite so," Isobel said, "but consider this: I mean to pay you two crowns for every beast you fetch me."

Walter rose abruptly from the divan, restoring his peruke and brushing the biscuit crumbs from his waistcoat. He bowed toward Isobel and kissed her cheek. "I'faith, you shall have your specimens. Far be't from a witchfinder to block the path of progress."

By the noon hour Walter and Dunstan were back in the coach, rolling away from the manor amidst a tumult of dust and the frenzied baying of the Mirringate dogs. Jennet stood on the portico and waved farewell, moving her raised hand back and forth as if polishing a scrying-mirror.

"You wear a mournful visage," Isobel noted, cradling a bowl of coffee.

"I weep for the specimens," Jennet confessed in a timorous voice.

"I thought as much."

"Must we truly put 'em under the knife?"

"Ne'er be ashamed of sympathizing with another creature, Jenny," Isobel said. "Your mother, were she alive, would advocate for the vermin too." Steam rose from her coffee, cloaking her face in a Pythian mist. "But I bid thee recall Monsieur Descartes's well-reasoned deduction concerning the lower animals. He says they are machines at base and therefore insensible to pain. Keep mindful, too, that a witch's servant hath lost all trace of primal innocence, being naught but a pawn of Satan."

Squeezing her eyes closed, Jennet tried to picture an animal familiar. At last she conjured the creature, a ferret of sleek form and conical snout. It nosed beneath the gown of a sleeping witch, fitted its mouth around the wayward teat in the center of her belly, and slowly sucked the black milk down, ounce by unholy ounce.

Jennet opened her eyes. At its birth, no doubt, the ferret had been as stainless as any other dumb beast, but now it was a fallen thing, pet of devils, toy of demons, poppet of goblins. It deserved a fate no better than a philosopher's glittering blade.

※

WALTER STEARNE WAS NOT a deep man, neither scholar, jurist, nor theologian, but he did a great deal of thinking all the same, and never so much as when riding the witch circuit. As he guided his coach along the road to Saxmundham that excellent Monday afternoon, Dunstan snoring beside him, he pondered a vexing dilemma. He had misled his family concerning his credentials, sorely and deliberately misled them. For in sooth he held no title to his trade—no Witchfinder-General's commission, no Master Pricker's charter—though certainly not for want of effort. Five times since the accession of James the Second he'd written to the Privy Council, pleading for a cleansing license of the sort Queen Elizabeth had routinely issued during her luminous reign, and in January he'd petitioned White Hall proposing the creation of a new government office, Witchfinder-Royal—but so far no response, yea or nay, had come down from His Majesty. Was it time to tell Dunstan, Jennet, and

Isobel the truth? Not yet, he decided as the coach clattered into Sax-mundham—soon, but not yet.

As was their wont, father and son passed the night atop a goose-feather mattress in the Horn of Plenty, rising the next morning at seven o'clock. They broke their fast in the tavern-room—buttered eggs, fried oysters, peeled fruit—then drove to Andrew Pound's house in Church Lane. The magistrate greeted them with his customary hearty hallo, and yet Walter immediately sensed that something was amiss: a stammer in the man's voice, a stickiness in his demeanor. The cause of Pound's dis-tress was soon forthcoming. Only two accused witches, not the usual five, lay in his keeping, though one of them had that morning put her *X* to a confession.

"Didst perchance catch their animal servants?" the cleanser asked.

Pound guided Walter and Dunstan from his disheveled consulting room to the adjacent examination chamber, a cramped unfurnished space, spare as a crypt. "We bagged Mrs. Whittle's beastie, aye, as plump a toad as e'er licked a witch's happy sack."

"Hear me now," Walter said. "My sister-in-law will lay down two crowns for that selfsame toad, as she wishes to anatomize it according to the new experimental philosophy. If I give you half the payment, might I take the creature with me?"

"A generous bounty," Pound said. The magistrate was a coarse and dim-witted fellow, deplorably fond of bear-baiting, but Walter still counted him a friend. "My share I'll be depositin' in the town treasury, since my apprehension o' the familiar was all in a day's work."

"Thou art an honest man, sir."

Pound summoned his constable, the thickset Martin Greaves, then ordered him to fetch the suspects from the gaol. A moment later the two brides of Lucifer stood before Walter, dressed in tattered burlap smocks, their outstretched hands manacled together. Silently he offered a prayer of gratitude, complimenting God on the admirable arrangement whereby a witch always grew powerless in the custody of a magistrate, constable, or pricker.

The confessed Satanist, middle-aged Alice Sampson, was a walking scarecrow, her inner putrefaction declaring itself in a squinty eye and warty thumb. Gelie Whittle, by contrast, was a corpulent hag, her hair like cankered swamp-grass, her complexion rough as cedar bark. The constable had brought along Mrs. Whittle's toad-familiar as well, imprisoned in a bottle, and Walter observed that it was exactly the sort of animal, all fat and satisfied, that the Dark One might give a favorite disciple.

"Your father's about to undertake a pricking," he said to his son. "What five implements doth he require from the coach?"

"The short needle and the long," Dunstan said, beaming like a cherub.

"Bright boy."

"The shaving razor."

"Excellent lad."

"The magnification lens."

"There's a keen fellow."

"And also . . ."

"Aye?"

"Give me a moment, sir."

"Dost not recall the alchemical tool we acquired last winter in Billericay?" Walter asked.

"The Paracelsus trident!"

The boy dashed out of the examination chamber, returning, errand accomplished, ere their shadows had lengthened an inch.

Upon receiving the devices, Walter explained to his colleagues that he would examine Mrs. Sampson no less rigorously than Mrs. Whittle, for a signed confession was no guarantee that Lady Justice would win the day. Standing before the grand jury, the admitted heretic would commonly repudiate her statement, insisting that she'd *X*'ed it only because the magistrate had befuddled her. Either that, or she would shamelessly ornament her narrative in hopes of convincing the jury to brand her a mere lunatic. In both such cases—denial and decoration—a professional witchfinder's testimony typically proved the key to securing an indictment.

"Alice Sampson," Walter said, waving the incriminating document in her face, "I do accuse thee of consorting with the Devil, for by setting thy mark upon this paper thou hast confessed as much."

Barely had the accusation left his lips than, true to Walter's forebodings, Mrs. Sampson spewed forth a torrent of fantastical rubbish. She described not a typical Sabbat (a dozen hags dancing naked round a bonfire) but a ceremony beyond the gaudiest confabulations of Popery itself: a thousand Satanists flying astride brimstone-belching horses all the way to Pendle Forest, where they submitted themselves to the obscene whims of the Devil's own majordomo, Lord Adramelech. A score of unbaptized babes were by Mrs. Sampson's account laid upon the altar that night, after which the coven consumed the infants' flesh and drank their blood, abandoning the unspeakable feast only at daybreak.

It was all too much. Unless Walter could discover direct evidence of Satanic compaction, the grand jury would rate the woman an addlepate, commending her to the madhouse rather than sending her to Norwich Assizes.

For modesty's sake, he ordered Dunstan back to Pound's consulting room, then peeled off Mrs. Sampson's burlap shift, strapped her to the table, and shaved her body, head to pudendum, harvesting the hairs like an angel scything Cain's unwanted crop from the breast of the Earth. Assisted by the magnification lens, his eye roved across the landscape of the suspect's skin. He scrutinized moles, sorted out blemishes, classified warts, and categorized wattles, searching for Mrs. Sampson's insensible Devil's mark—residue of the ritual through which the Dark One bound heretics to his service—and also for the teat Lucifer had sculpted from her flesh so she might give suck to her familiar.

Even after delving into Mrs. Sampson's most intimate region, the very cavern of her sex, Walter failed to detect a preternatural nipple. Her right shoulder, however, displayed a suspicious black blotch, and so he took up the Paracelsus trident. The instant he touched the tines to the excrescence, he felt a tingling in his fingers, as if he were fondling a sack of mealworms. He seized the long needle and, over Mrs. Sampson's shrill protestations, probed the mark. Even after the point had descended a full quarter-inch, the spot proved as bloodless as an apple—and therefore as damning as an errant teat.

As Mrs. Sampson got dressed, he set about examining Mrs. Whittle, shucking her smock, tying down her torso, removing her hair. He studied the revealed terrain, first pricking the anomalies—all perfectly natural, as it happened, for they bled freely—then employing his sensitive fingers in seeking a teat. Ere long he found one, concealed within her privy shaft, poised to nourish the toad-familiar.

Mark and teat: for Walter this was confirmation enough, but juries were partial to redundancy. "We must corroborate these findings," he explained to Pound and Greaves whilst the prisoner wriggled back into her smock. "In the matter of the Whittle woman, 'tis my opinion the cold-water test will serve our ends, but with Mrs. Sampson we're obliged to try a watching, for the wretch is so bony that even the sacred Jordan would strain to spit her out."

"I see before me a man adept at his trade," Greaves said.

And Walter thought: the constable speaks truly—I *am* adept. He was especially proud of locating the teat obscured by Mrs. Whittle's female organ. Such sharp powers of discernment, he felt, such tactile perspicacity, bespoke a mind attuned to the very forces through which King Solomon and his descendants had recovered in part the knowledge of good and evil that Adam had forfeited at the Fall. Yes, it was gratifying that Isobel now sought to make his profession as impersonal and empirical as planetary mechanics: in the last analysis, however, he saw himself not as the heir of Galileo or Kepler but as the child of John Dee, Robert Fludd, and all those other holy hermeticists whom England could call her own.

"Witchfinding's in sooth an art," he said, offering the constable a nod. "And now we're off to the river, that we might swim Mrs. Whittle and determine whether she hath indeed signed the Devil's book!"

JENNET SPENT THE MORNING in the third-floor conservatory, peering beneath the world's surfaces, contemplating its hidden struts and secret fretworks. When properly adjusted—eyepiece focused, mirror angled to catch the ascendant sun and illuminate the stage—a microscope became a magical passkey, unlocking a universe that only Jehovah Himself could see unaided. Under Van Leeuwenhoek's lenses, a louse grew as big as a lobster, a wood tick appeared strong enough to pull a plow, and a rose petal disclosed its constituents, the honeycomb-like "cells" of Mr. Hooke's *Micrographia*. Mixed with water and placed upon a Van Leeuwenhoek stage, a bit of scum from Jennet's nethermost tooth stood revealed as a fen inhabited by creatures with hairy legs and grasping tentacles.

At one o'clock Aunt Isobel declared that the day's second lesson would begin, then led Jennet down the corridor to the west cupola. The instant she saw the two leather bags on the window seat—one labeled PISTOL SHOT, the other GOOSE FEATHERS—Jennet guessed that Isobel would now require her to demonstrate Galileo's celebrated principle of uniform acceleration.

"Which will hit the ground first?" Isobel asked, depositing the bags in Jennet's grasp. "Lead or feathers?"

"They will hit the ground together."

"Together?" Isobel guided Jennet through the cupola window and across the sloped roof of the master bed-chamber. "Why do you believe that?"

"Because Mr. Galileo says 'tis so."

"Nay, Jenny. You should believe it because of what occurs before your eyes when you put the conjecture to a test."

At her aunt's bidding Jennet leaned as far over the edge of the roof as she could without herself becoming an object of uniform acceleration. The gravel walkway shimmered in the afternoon sun, arcing past an oak tree in whose commodious shade the Mirringate dogs now dozed.

"On the count of three, you will drop lead and feathers in tandem, studying them throughout their descent," Isobel said.

Jennet held out both bags as if waiting for some huge omnivorous bird to fly past and snatch them away.

"One . . . two . . . three!"

She opened her hands, sending both bags plummeting. They struck the gravel simultaneously—or so it seemed—the feathers landing silently, the lead with a muffled crunch. The dogs, startled, scrambled to their feet and bounded away.

"What happened?" Isobel asked.

"They hit the ground together."

"I shan't disagree. Conclusion?"

"I say that Mr. Aristotle's physics serves us poorly in this matter. 'Tis obvious that an object's weight affects not the speed at which it falls."

"Wrong, darling."

"Wrong?"

"Doth one black hare prove that all hares are black? Doth one fanged snake prove that every snake will bite?"

"No."

"Conclusion?"

"I say that . . . I say that I must retrieve the bags and drop 'em again!"

"Ah!"

As the afternoon progressed, Jennet repeated the famous experiment, once, twice, thrice—eight trials altogether. In no instance did the lead outpace the feathers.

"Conclusion?" Isobel asked.

" 'Twould seem reasonable to say that uniform acceleration's a fixed principle of Nature."

"An excellent deduction, Jenny! You have made a sterling case for't!"

Weary now of contradicting antiquity, Jennet asked whether they might ascend to the astronomical observatory, as she wished to study the full moon, presently lying in pale repose above the horizon. Isobel insisted that for the nonce they must visit the library, so they could together examine her latest acquisition.

"A book?"

" 'Tis much more than a book," Isobel said. " 'Tis in sooth the grandest treatise yet conceived by any man of woman born."

Thus it was that Jennet found herself betimes in her aunt's favorite reading chair, cradling a volume entitled *Philosophiæ Naturalis Principia*

Mathematica. The author was Professor Isaac Newton, whose essay called "A New Theory About Light and Colors" had constituted her assignment in optics during the winter hiatus. Whereas Newton's ruminations on light had proven succinct and accessible, the beast now pressing her lap was something else entirely, quite possibly the world's most profound book: certainly it looked the part and boasted the heft. Turning the pages and beholding the geometric figures, strange as any in an alchemist's text, Jennet felt a peculiar quietude settle over the library, as if the other volumes had been paralyzed by reverence. Mr. Huygen's *Horologium Oscillatorium* stood in awe of this *Principia Mathematica,* as did Mr. Harvey's *De Motu Cordis,* Mr. Boyle's *The Sceptical Chymist,* and *De Magnete* by Colchester's own William Gilbert.

Isobel strode to the center of the room, placing her palms on the great dusky Earth-globe, big as a cathedral bell. "What Mr. Newton hath accomplished, or so I surmise, is to take Mr. Galileo's terrestrial mechanics, combine 'em with Mr. Kepler's celestial laws, and weave 'em all into one grand theory of the world. 'Twould seem, for example, that whether we are speaking of planets or of pebbles, the mutual affinity betwixt two objects is the inverse square of their distance one from the other."

"Inverse square? I'm confused."

"No shame in that, even for so brilliant a child as yourself." Isobel relieved Jennet of the *Principia Mathematica,* clasping it to her bosom. "Now hear my bold conjecture. 'Tis by mastering Mr. Newton's principles that a demon makes itself a lord o'er acceleration and a ruler of the attractive force. Through this ill-gotten gravity that same spirit can send an enchantress streaking broom-borne to her Sabbat—or drive a bolt of Heaven's fire into a Christian's crops—or raise a storm against an admiral's flagship. Mark me, darling, our witchfinding family would do well to grasp the Newtonian system in all its particulars, for the devils who trap us in catastrophes are first and foremost geometers."

"My father's a great lover of books," Jennet said, "but I fear this swollen tome would bewilder him."

Isobel nodded and said, "A considerable time will pass ere England's witchfinders confound Satan with cosines, for not only is the

Principia a fearsome difficult work, there be but four hundred of 'em in the world."

"Then it must have cost you dearly."

"Not a penny. I received this copy in person from Mr. Pepys, who currently presides o'er the Royal Society. Ah, you ask, by what means did my aunt commend herself to a community that excludes dabblers by habit and women by policy? Simply this. She posed as both an expert and a man!"

"Wonderful!"

" 'Twas a bonny ruse: a loose shirt to mask my bosom, a golden periwig to conceal my locks, and—*voilà*—I was Monsieur Armand Reynaud of L'Académie Royale des Sciences, in which guise I traveled to London and spoke to Mr. Pepys's sages on '*La Grande Tache Rouge de Jupiter.*' I nearly fell to giggling when, right before my talk, I o'erheard Pepys brag how his august body had thus far learned natural philosophy from one woman only—the female skeleton in the Society's anatomical collection."

"Oh, how I wish they knew the truth!" Jennet squealed.

"On the evidence of this gathering, our gender hath been deprived of naught. Save for my argument that Jupiter's Great Red Spot is really a kind of thunder-gust, plus a few diverting remarks from Mr. Wallis concerning cryptography, 'twas a frightfully dull affair—and poorly attended, too, Mr. Newton being at his mother's farm, Mr. Hooke away on business, and Mr. Boyle abed with a fever. Ah, but you're wrong to suppose they ne'er learned of my mischief, for at meeting's end, in a fit of pique, I pulled off my wig, announced my sex, snatched up my *Principia*, and jumped into my carriage!"

"*Merveilleux!*" Jennet said, practicing her French.

"A jolly sight indeed—fifteen falling jaws plus twice as many bulging eyes. And now we climb to the observatory, Jenny, where Rodwell hath laid out our supper and the Hevelius telescope stands ready to show us the lunar landscape, every dip and ridge. The moon wants mapping, child of my heart, and we're the philosophers to do't!"

As Jennet followed her aunt out of the library, she once again felt an intimation that the *Principia Mathematica* was a work so powerful and majestic that all its predecessors had prostrated themselves before it in inky adoration. No book in Isobel's collection was immune to this idolatry—

not *De Revolutionibus Orbium Coelestium* by Nicolaus
Copernicus nor *Siderius Nuncius* by
Galileo Galilei nor even *De*
Harmonice Mundi by
Johannes

❧

Kepler
never became
an object of the legendary
Newtonian wrath, and neither did
Copernicus nor Galileo, though it must be allowed
that this circumstance traced less to collegial congeniality
than to the fact that all three scientists were dead before my father was born, Galileo passing away less than a year prior to Newton's advent. While I am nowise prepared to defend my father's penchant for cultivating enemies, I shall admit that in one particular instance—the case of René Descartes—his vindictiveness proved productive, sending him down pathways he might otherwise have left unexplored.

Because Descartes rejected atomism, my father became an atomist. Descartes's vortex theory of planetary motion inspired Newton to demonstrate that vortices couldn't account for Kepler's laws. Descartes's fondness for describing motion algebraically goaded Newton into imagining a dynamics based on algebra's *alter ego*, geometry. Because no such branch of mathematics existed, he proceeded to invent one. Speaking personally, I wish the world had adopted my father's original term, *fluxions*, for his brainchild. *Calculus* is such a frosty word.

As for the balance of Newton's spleen, there is nothing to be said for it. He might have been the smartest man ever to walk the Earth, but he was not the noblest. Typical was the John Flamsteed affair, wherein Newton maneuvered the Astronomer-Royal into publishing the latter's work prematurely, merely so my second edition might be spiced with Flamsteed's lunar observations. In 1712 the poor man's garbled and embarrassing catalogue appeared under the title *Historia Cœlestis Britannica*. A few years later Flamsteed managed to buy up three hundred of the wretched things, nearly the entire print run. He heaped the copies into a pyre on the grounds of the Royal Observatory, inserted a lighted torch, and, as he subsequently wrote, "made a Sacrifice of them to Heav'nly Truth."

A bonfire of books. The thought curdles me. Some say my species is imperishable, but they lie, for ours is a chillingly provisional immortality. Although we commonly outlive our creators, the curious scholar need look no further than the inferno that razed the Library of Alexandria to realize that a book may vanish irretrievably, leaving behind only a whiff of carbon and a pile of ash. Gutenberg, of course, did much to allay our angst—for us the coming of movable type was equivalent to the arrival of gonads among you vertebrates—but the fact remains that visions of extinction haunt all texts. The moral of my dread is simple. Treasure each volume you hold in your hands, and read it whilst ye may.

More than three hundred years have passed since Jennet Stearne, sitting in Isobel Mowbray's library, first held me in *her* hands, and I can still feel the pulsing thrill of that moment. The child did not requite my adoration that day, or the next day either, but in time she craved intimacy with my pages. Ah, what rapturous vibrations seized me when my goddess learned to determine parabolic orbits! How complete my epiphany when she conquered the mathematics of rectilinear ascent!

Now, I must confess that much of what lies between my covers is as opaque to me as to anyone else. I am not wholly available to myself. "Homogeneous and equal spherical bodies, opposed by resistances that are as the square of the velocities, and moving on by their innate force only, will, in times that are inversely as the velocities at the beginning, describe equal spaces, and lose parts of their velocities proportional to the whole." That sort of thing. But before you chide me for my ignorance, please remember that you too contain components of which you can give no coherent account. Who among you will say how many neurons are firing in her brain at the moment? Who is prepared to write me a lobe-by-lobe treatise on his pancreas? And what of that vital fluid now flowing through your veins? Can you expound upon it meaningfully, other than to call it

❀

Blood
never poured
from the maleficent
mark with which the Devil branded
a disciple: every witchfinder understood this, from
the lowliest justice of the peace to a master pricker like Walter
Stearne. Nor did tears flow freely from a witch's ducts, no matter how forceful the cleanser's coercions. Nor did the *Pater Noster* leave a witch's lips without suffering some degradation, gross or subtle. And pure water, of course—pure water, the medium of baptism—could not long abide the presence of a person fit to be christened only with shit.

No one disputed that the best place in Saxmundham for swimming a witch was the sturdy stone arch known as the Alde River Bridge. When Andrew Pound revealed that, thanks to the April rains, the Alde's waters ran deep, Walter remanded Dunstan to the coach that he might procure the necessary items: mask-o'-truth, thongs, twenty-foot rope. The boy obtained the tools in a trice, whereupon Walter prepared Gelie Whittle for the test, binding her wrists and ankles, lashing the rope around her waist. Throughout these preliminaries Mrs. Whittle attempted to recite the Twenty-third Psalm, lapsing into incoherence upon reaching the valley of the shadow of death.

Martin Greaves dragged Alice Sampson back to the gaol, returning anon to the examination chamber, and then the small solemn company started down Mill Lane. First came Walter and Mr. Pound, marching in tandem, followed by Dunstan, clutching his artist's valise. Mr. Greaves brought up the rear, Mrs. Whittle slung over his shoulder like a sack of potatoes.

Well versed in the principles of buoyancy, Walter knew that a witch would sometimes foil the waters by exhaling at the moment of descent, and so immediately after their arrival on the bridge he applied his brilliant invention, the mask-o'-truth. Whilst Mrs. Whittle remained balanced atop Greave's back, Walter demanded that she take a deep breath, and then upon her compliance he clamped the cowhide napkin over her mouth and pinched her nostrils closed using the ingenious spring-clip. He secured the entire arrangement with leather thongs, trapping within her lungs the inhaled volume of air.

"An awesome clever device." Greaves set the prisoner supine on the span.

Walter said, "I could ne'er have contrived it were I not sensible of the relevant philosophy, from Archimedes to Robert Boyle."

He knelt and lashed Mrs. Whittle's manacles to her ankle thongs, bending her into the form of an ox-yoke. As Pound took hold of the swimming-rope, Walter and the constable picked up the suspect and set her atop the bridge wall as they might place a freshly baked pie to cool upon a window-sill, then levered her into the open air. Pound tightened his grip on the rope, locked his foot against the wall, and lowered Mrs. Whittle's polluted flesh inch by inch toward the tell-tale river.

Of all the proofs employed by witchfinders, swimming was the one most vulnerable to skeptical objection, and so Walter always ordered a sinker raised at the merest hint she might drown. Fifteen years in the profession, and he'd lost only two suspects to the cold-water test. In Mrs. Whittle's case, however, no particular vigilance was necessary, for within five seconds of her immersion she shot to the surface, as if her stony heart lay sealed within a body of cork.

"Gelie Whittle, I aver that this virtuous current hath vomited thee forth!" Walter shouted as Pound and Greaves hauled her bowed, dripping, shivering body free of the water and back over the bridge wall.

They set her in the center of the span, where she jerked and spasmed like a gaffed flounder expiring on the deck of a fishing smack. Crouching beside her, Walter severed her ankle thongs with his pocket-knife and untied the mask-o'-truth. She exhaled fiercely.

"Wilt thou therefore confess to thy witchery," Walter asked, "or must we bring thee before Mr. Pound's jury?"

"I could no more put my name to your paper than I could set a Bible a-flame," Mrs. Whittle sputtered. " 'Tis as sinful to claim compact with the Devil where none exists as to deny such intercourse when it be true!"

"You bear an imp teat 'twixt your legs!"

" 'Tis naught but the womb God gave me!"

"You bear an imp teat, the Alde's flow hath spurned you, and now you speak of taking a torch to Scripture!" Walter said. "The jurors will hear the whole of't, Mrs. Whittle, pap and river and blasphemy—they will hear all three!"

❀

ON WEDNESDAY MORNING Jennet's fellow student arrived at the manor, Elinor Mapes, eleven years old, a bitter and conceited child who never tired of noting that her father was the Vicar of Ipswich, whereas other girls' fathers were merely farmers or cobblers or joiners or witchfinders. By way of convincing herself she was in fact fond of this disagreeable person, Jennet had on several occasions made overtures of friendship, reminding Elinor that they shared a bond of bereavement, Sarah Mapes having succumbed to a malignant fever not many months after Margaret Stearne had died in childbirth. But the object of Jennet's amicable advances invariably greeted them with scorn.

"Would that Elinor knew as much of kindness as of Copernicus," Jennet said to Aunt Isobel.

" 'This you should pity rather than despise,' as Helena advises Lysander," Isobel replied.

"Mayn't I do both?"

"Both?"

"Pity and despise Elinor at the same time?"

Isobel rolled her eyes heavenward.

The source of Elinor's disgruntlement was not far to seek. Whereas

Jennet was privileged to live at Mirringate during the cleansing season, her schoolmate had to return home each night to beguile her father's solitude—an insufferable situation for a student like Elinor, who was in her own self-satisfied way a true lover of knowledge. Although Jennet struggled to avoid trumpeting her special status, she periodically succumbed to temptation, making mention well within Elinor's hearing of the previous evening's telescopic exploration, micrographic adventure, pendulum experiment, or visit to the alchemical laboratory.

Elinor's bile was fully aboil that morning, threatening to scald whomever it touched, much to her father's evident discomfort. Jennet felt sorry for him. Although generally indifferent to clerics, she held Roger Mapes in the highest regard, as he seemed not merely a man of God but a godly man, his very self a sermon. No mere succession of phrases, however eloquent, could preach so persuasively as did Mr. Mapes's goodness.

"Prithee, tell me what novelties have come to your school of late," he said as he followed Isobel, Jennet, and his glowering daughter into the library. He was a tall, well-favored man with an array of moles on his left temple suggesting the constellation Cassiopeia. "A vacuum-pump mayhap?"

"I have just now collected an astonishing book." Isobel lifted the *Principia Mathematica* from its niche, presenting it to the Vicar. " 'Twould appear that what Jesus Christ accomplished for our souls, Isaac Newton hath done for our senses."

"Lady Mowbray, you can turn a phrase for fair." From Mr. Mapes's pursed lips came a titter not entirely merry. "Christ and Newton, a most . . . *audacious* analogy." He restored the *Principia Mathematica* to its shelf and withdrew from his satchel a slender volume entitled *Satan's Invisible World Discovered*. "George Sinclair is certainly no Newton, but I imagine your brother-in-law might profit from this treatise, which I recently acquired wet from the press. Consider it my gift to him."

"Walter will be most appreciative," Isobel said, taking the book in hand.

"What use hath a pricker for such rarefied information?" said Elinor. "It takes no special wisdom to plant a pin in a beggar-woman's bum."

"Miss Mapes, you will not use vulgar language," the Vicar said.

" 'Twould be my supposition, child," Isobel said, looking sharply at Elinor, "that in obtaining impractical knowledge we please God far more than when we cultivate applicable ignorance. I trust you grasp the distinction."

Before Elinor could reply, Isobel turned to the Vicar and asked, "Will you do us the honor of attending the day's first lesson?"

Mr. Mapes assented with a smile, whereupon Isobel guided everyone down the hall and into the crystal-gazing parlor, the churlish Elinor all the while staring crestfallen at her shoes.

"Our aim this morning is to duplicate a demonstration devised by Mr. Newton himself," Isobel said. The room lay in a swamp of gloom, its windows occluded by black velvet. "This past winter Miss Mapes and Miss Stearne read a piece from the Royal Society's *Philosophical Transactions* in which Newton—"

" 'Twas called 'A New Theory About Light and Colors,' " interrupted Elinor.

"In which Newton"—Isobel inhaled pointedly—"proposed a new theory about light and colors." She set a triangular glass prism in the center of the table, strode toward the east window, and removed a circular patch from the curtain. A shaft of white sunlight shot across the parlor and, striking the prism, transmuted into a rainbow that decorated the opposite wall with brilliant ribbons of red, orange, yellow, green, blue, indigo, and violet. "What conclusion did Newton draw from this first experiment? Miss Stearne?"

"According to the received laws of refraction, the spectrum before us should be circular," Jennet said, "for the chink in the curtain is circular, as is the sun itself. And yet we see this oblong form. Mr. Newton hath judged the traditional optics to be in error. A prism doth not alter light's nature but rather separates light into its components."

"*Très bien!*" From her writing-desk Isobel obtained a second glass prism and two identical white boards, each bearing a shilling-size hole at its center. "Next Newton performed what he called his *experimentum crusis.* Miss Mapes, will you favor us with a replication?"

"*Certainement.*"

Elinor set one perforated board upright behind the standing prism, then positioned the other board vertically about eight feet farther along the table, so that a portion of the refracted light passed through the first hole and struck the second board, bestowing a ray of purest red upon both the immediate barrier and the parlor wall beyond. "If the old optics is correct, we could now place the second prism thus"—with a confident flourish Elinor fixed the glass pentahedron behind board number two—"refract the red ray as it emerges from the second hole, and in consequence project new colors on the wall. But, as you can see, the red ray remains red." Slowly, methodically, she moved the original prism about its axis, isolating each color in turn and delivering it to the second prism. The orange ray stayed orange; the yellow hoarded its hue; the green held true—likewise the blue, the indigo, and the violet. "No matter how we align these prisms, we can effect no further transmutations."

"And what therefore is Mr. Newton's final hypothesis concerning light?" Isobel asked.

"He hath declared light to be a confused aggregate of rays," Jennet cried, "differently refrangible, and endued with all sorts of colors!"

"I was about to say that!" Elinor shouted.

"In a bug's rump you were!" Jennet insisted.

"I was! I was!"

"Softly now, children, for you've *both* learned your optics admirably." Like a mariner reefing a sail, Isobel uncurtained the east window. The glorious morning sunshine spilled into the room. "Miss Mapes, your father should be proud."

"Proud as a man can feel without making a sin of't," the Vicar said. Bending low, he kissed his daughter's cheek—but after this show of affection came a rather different display, Mr. Mapes rising to full height and presenting Isobel with a mien of supreme discontent. "Lady Mowbray, you know I'm not one to condemn the pleasures of crystal-gazing, for where's the harm in idle divination? This prism business, however—alas, I do not approve, for I find it to be a grotesque parody of God's most basic gesture."

"You perplex me," Isobel said.

"Genesis Chapter One tells how the Almighty's first act was to divide light from darkness, a great splitting such as you've had these children perform, and in Chapter Nine we learn that he fashioned a rainbow to seal his covenant with Noah."

"True," Isobel said, "but doth not Christ in Matthew Chapter Six bid us imitate God in all things?"

"Aye, and yet—"

"To mimic the Almighty is not perforce to mock Him."

Mr. Mapes grinned, and from this gentle arc there came a musical laugh. "So, Lady Mowbray, you have once again outscriptured me." His mouth reassumed the horizontal. "Confect these spectra if you must, but keep mindful that true creation is the enterprise of our Heavenly Father alone."

"Entirely mindful," Isobel said.

"God's the author of all things, and Christ the cause, but 'tis Lucifer uses the world as his workshop," Mr. Mapes said, slipping out of the crystal-gazing parlor. "We must be evermore vigilant, lest we become the Devil's apprentices."

FOR THE WATCHING of Alice Sampson, Walter had been planning to use the normal venue, Granary Street Livery, and so he was keenly disappointed when Mr. Pound informed him that the building had burned down the previous summer, a disaster most plausibly ascribed to Satanic mischief. No sooner had the magistrate finished deploring this diabolism, however, than Mr. Greaves stepped forward and volunteered his own barn, presently dedicated to the raising of poultry. Though Walter was not eager to spend his afternoon in an atmosphere of chicken droppings, he elected to accept this turn of fortune without complaint. He'd become a demonologist for the glorification of his Savior, after all, not the gratification of his senses.

Shortly after the midday meal, Walter, Dunstan, and Mr. Greaves retrieved Mrs. Sampson from the gaol, carted her down Mill Lane, and chained her to a rusting plow in the farthest corner of the constable's barn. Upon Greaves's departure, Walter deployed an empty rooster-pen within inches of the suspect, then sat on the dirt floor beside his son and poured water from his leather flask into a tin cup. He drank. The barn was even worse than he'd anticipated, as malodorous and inhospitable as a chamber-pot, the hot sun conspiring with the poor ventilation to breed a stifling heat. Splotches of pale speckled excrement lay everywhere. Grimy brown feathers covered the ground like the molt of a winged imp.

Great was Walter's pride when, instead of lamenting this miserable environment, Dunstan merely took up his sketching-folio and proceeded to render Greaves's largest goose in pen and ink. There was a kind of holiness, Walter felt, in the way Dunstan could exercise his drafting talent whilst sitting but ten feet from an accused witch. For his immediate future, obviously, Dunstan would pursue the cleansing profession, but after he'd been installed in Heaven, posterity might one day declare him a saint.

From his son's potential canonization Walter's thoughts turned naturally to the tantalizing and auspicious fact that England's present king was a Papist. For whilst the master pricker was Church of England pate to paunch, he had to admit that the most impassioned rationale for cleansing wasn't Protestant in origin—it wasn't Perkins's *Discourse on the Damned Art of Witchcraft* or Glanvill's *Full and Plain Evidence Concerning Witches and Apparitions*—but Catholic: the *Malleus Maleficarum,* that great Bludgeon Against Evildoers, that mighty Hammer of Witches, written two hundred years earlier by the Dominican friars Krämer and Sprenger. Assuming James the Second survived his present political difficulties, it seemed reasonable to suppose that he would heed Walter's petition, chartering the post of Witchfinder-Royal and filling it with Walter himself.

But until the dawning of that blessed day, his authority would derive from one source only, the woefully flawed Parliamentary Witchcraft Act. True, this sorry statute had improved on its predecessor of 1563, making the Satanic covenant a crime in itself, but the 1604 law was still keyed to *maleficium,* to evildoing, with the result that the average English jurist demanded to hear evidence of diabolical intervention—a blighted crop, a miscarried fœtus, a murderous lightning-bolt—ere sending a sorcerer to the gallows. On the Continent, meanwhile, witch-cleansing remained a more enlightened enterprise. Not only did the Papal Inquisitors understand the stake to be a more appropriate execution method than the noose, they never confused mere *maleficium* with a witch's ultimate depravity: her worship of Lucifer, her *X* in the Devil's register.

Dunstan finished drawing the goose. A ripe time, Walter decided, to test the boy on his *Malleus*. If Dunstan was to prosper in his destined occupation, he must know his Krämer and Sprenger chapter and verse.

"What three classes of men do the friars identify in Part Two, Question One?"

"The friars name those persons whom a witch can ne'er injure," Dunstan replied, setting his folio aside.

Walter offered a nod of approbation. "And who are the first class?"

"Men who engage the powers of Christ and Cross in performing exorcisms."

"Aye. And the second class?"

"Those who in various and mysterious ways are blessed by the holy angels."

"And the third?"

"Those who administer public justice against the Devil!"

"Such a remarkable pupil!"

As dusk came to Saxmundham, the prickers' sufferings were finally rewarded. A lewd black snake wriggled out from behind a barrel of poultry feed and sinuated toward Mrs. Sampson. Walter rose, lurched forward, and grabbed the familiar, shuddering as its dry supple body coiled about his forearm. Such a valuable beast, he thought, shoving the snake into the rooster-pen—worth two crowns to Isobel Mowbray and perhaps a thousand times that much to Lucifer.

"Look," he said, bringing the imprisoned snake before Mrs. Sampson. "I've caught your slithery servant."

"A drink," she rasped. "Prithee, good sir, some water."

"Even if you retract your confession, Mrs. Sampson, other evidence will send you to the assizes . . ."

"A drink, sir."

"That blotch on your shoulder . . ."

"I beg ye. A drink."

"And now this incontrovertible serpent."

"I thirst."

Walter winced. *I thirst:* the very words Christ had spoken from Calvary's summit. After pondering the problem a full minute, he decided that her irreverence was unintended. He would give the wretch what she wanted.

"Dunstan, bring a cup of water thither!" he cried.

"Bless ye, master pricker," Mrs. Sampson muttered.

It took the boy but an instant to decant a pint and bear the tin cup across the barn. He passed the cup to Walter, who in turn pressed it to the suspect's lips.

"Enjoy this measure whilst you may," Walter said as Mrs. Sampson gulped down his charity, "for in Hell you'll partake of naught but kippers soaked in brine, and you'll get nary a swallow of sweetness till Eternity is come and gone."

※

ELATED BY HER SUCCESS in replicating Isaac Newton's *experimentum crusis*, Elinor Mapes took to gloating, a demeanor she maintained all during the midday meal and throughout the afternoon's first lesson, which had the girls ascending to the conservatory, studying pieces of dissected insects through the microscope, and draughting what they beheld with pen and ink. For Jennet it proved a congenial enough exercise, though she wished that Dunstan was at her side, likewise sketching the creatures. What grace he would have bestowed on the facets of the honeybee's eye, the crenellations of the grasshopper's leg, the lattice of the locust's wing, or the feathery splendor of the moth's antenna.

Elinor's gloating stopped shortly after the second lesson began, for its matter was the Latin language.

"Last night I composed a letter to Mr. Newton himself," Aunt Isobel announced upon ushering her charges down the stairway and back into the crystal-gazing parlor. From the writing-desk she retrieved a piece of vellum, its surface covered with the florid coils and ornate curves that characterized her penmanship. "The version that reaches his eyes must for courtesy's sake employ the language of Virgil."

She set the vellum on the table, anchoring it beneath a prism, then equipped her pupils with paper, goose quills, ink pots, stationery, and Seylet's *English-Latin Dictionary.* Together Jennet and Elinor studied Isobel's letter, and briefly they became compatriots in misery, for the required translation would be no Roman teething ring, no *amo amas amat,* but a missive of Ciceronian complexity, awash in accusatives, beset by ablatives, and replete with verbs whose conjugations varied intolerably from tense to tense.

13 April 1688

Dear Professor Isaac Newton:

I write to you as a Woman whose deepest Passion is to know the Secrets of Nature, such as those you have reveal'd in your recently print'd *Principia Mathematica.*

Perusing this admirable Treatise, I am mov'd to an Hypothesis concerning the Phenomenon of Witchcraft. I believe that your various Theorems and Propositions may have inadvertently disclosed the Mechanisms by which Wicked Spirits, once summon'd by Sorcerers, undertake the malevolent Varieties of (as we Philosophers term it) "Action at a Distance," namely the Raising of destructive Moon Tides, the Conjuration of Hailstorms, and the Blasting of Crops and Cattle with Lightnings from Heav'n.

My Brother-in-Law, Witchfinder-General for Mercia and East Anglia, hath document'd these and other unholy Activities with scrupulous Thoroughness, and he would gladly provide you with such Attestations and Proofs as you may require. An Exchange of Letters on the various metaphysical Conundrums posed by Witchcraft would please me greatly, but if you would first address my immediate Conjecture, I would be evermore in your Debt.

Isobel, Lady Mowbray,
MIRRINGATE HALL,
IPSWICH

Word by wretched word, phrase by onerous phrase, Jennet struggled to accomplish her translation, her weariness compounding steadily, as if the bag of musket-balls from the previous day's Galilean demonstration lay upon her neck. When at last both girls were finished, Aunt Isobel, ever the adjudicator, announced that she would favor neither rendering but instead amalgamate them into a third. By the time Mr. Mapes returned to the manor, the letter was ready for posting.

Upon learning that his daughter had Latinized an epistle intended for Isaac Newton, the Vicar proposed to secure its delivery, his present house guest being none other than Robert Gutner, Rector of Trinity College. Isobel eagerly accepted Mr. Mapes's offer, explaining that her nascent correspondence with the Lucasian Professor of Mathematics might ultimately yield precious insights into the *modi operandi* of fallen angels.

"Will Mr. Newton write back?" Jennet asked after Elinor, the Vicar, and the momentous missive had departed.

"Most probably." Isobel strode across the crystal-gazing parlor and, reaching the east window, pulled the curtain shut. "True, he subscribes to the deplorable Arian faith"—she removed the circular patch, admitting a shaft of the setting sun—"but I'll warrant he's still a proper soldier in the war against Lucifer."

Jennet said, "For all he made a jest of't, Mr. Mapes seemed truly to take umbrage when you mentioned Newton in the same breath as our Savior."

"I shall ne'er again press the point in the Vicar's presence, though I've heard that Newton himself doth not forswear the comparison. And why should he? Both were born on Christmas Day. Each apprehended more of light than any soul around him. And thanks to my letter 'twill not be long ere Newton realizes that he, like Christ, hath been appointed a scourge of demons."

Aunt Isobel lifted a prism from the table and, catching the solitary sunbeam, painted the day's last rainbow on the wall.

The

Second

❈❈❈❈❈❈

*In Which Is Posed
the Theological Conundrum,
When Doth
a Scientific Dissection
Become a Satanic Devotion?*

❈

O n Thursday morning Andrew Pound summoned his grand jury to Saxmundham Meeting-House, a rude timber-framed structure in which the town's most prominent citizens periodically gathered to resolve boundary disputes, appoint one another to important offices, and set suspected witches along the path to speedy prosecution at Norwich Assizes and thence to protracted torture in the bowels of Hell. By the time Walter and Dunstan arrived, the hall was packed to the rafters, every bench crowded with wide-rumped burgesses lighting clay pipes and telling bawdy jokes, but fortunately Mr. Pound had reserved front-row seats for the master pricker and his son. Walter guided Dunstan to their place of honor, right beside the town's dyspeptic mayor, and surveyed the jurors, twelve somber men lined up behind a walnut table like the Apostles awaiting Christ's arrival at the Last Supper.

Three deep metallic tones rolled down from the belltower, filling the hall, and then an equally imposing silence descended. Mr. Pound rose and asked the first witness, a spindly farmer named Ned Jellaby, to stand before the jurymen. A wave of admiration washed through Walter. He always felt profoundly humble in the presence of anyone willing to speak against a witch. Often as not, the victim would paint himself as the perpetrator of some un-Christian act, for only by admitting that he'd wronged the accused sorceress could he establish beyond doubt that his troubles traced to Satanic intervention and not to mere bad luck.

Gesturing toward Gelie Whittle, Mr. Jellaby testified how on the first Sunday in March he'd turned her away from his cottage door, where she'd come begging for a piece of cheese. Ere the week was out his hens had stopped laying, and they'd remained unproductive for a fortnight. No sooner had the hens recovered than seven of Jellaby's pigs died of a strange wasting malady.

As the hearing progressed, three additional witnesses came forth bearing tales of *maleficium*. The town blacksmith revealed that he'd provoked Mrs. Whittle by failing to invite her to his ale-brewing party, her wrath culminating in "the worst case o' the flux a man hath e'er known." A seamstress explained how, after spurning Alice Sampson's proposition that they go into business together, she'd suffered "a crampin' in the fingers" that had cost her a month's income. Likewise denouncing Mrs. Sampson was an elderly cordwainer who postulated a connection betwixt his refusal to give her a free pair of shoes and the subsequent destruction of his shop, "blasted to ashes by Heaven's fire."

Mr. Pound now bid his jurymen put their own questions to the defendants. Walter braced himself for mendacity. Predictably enough, throughout the interrogation Mrs. Whittle cleaved to the fable of her innocence, whilst Mrs. Sampson offered her impersonation of a madwoman. Since telling her story in the magistrate's examination chamber, however, she'd contrived to make it even more implausible: now her lying tongue claimed carnality with the Devil himself. The jurymen reeled with revulsion as Mrs. Sampson described Lucifer's virile member as "a great red salamander shot through with purple veins," and they gasped in horror upon learning that his semen felt "cold as ice and heavy as lead."

The magistrate declared a twenty-minute recess, and when the hearing reconvened Walter came before the jury, recited his credentials—most notably his late father's partnership with Matthew Hopkins, legendary witchfinder of the Civil War period—and laid out the evidence he'd assembled since his arrival. Against Mrs. Sampson: a snake, a Devil's mark, a signed confession. Against Mrs. Whittle: a toad, a teat, her rejection by the River Alde, and, of course, "her shocking threat to set a Bible a-flame."

For the next hour the jurymen sat arguing loudly amongst them-selves, much to the amusement of the spectators, who gave this bickering the same rapt attention a London theater audience might have accorded the newest entertainment from Congreve or Wycherley. Right before lunch, the twelve reached consensus, and it was all as Walter's instincts had foretold: Gelie Whittle would go to the assizes, Alice Sampson to the asylum. Such a farcical verdict. The jurors might credibly discount Mrs. Sampson's confession, but how durst they ignore the diabolical blotch on her shoulder, not to mention her snake-familiar?

"Gelie Whittle, you have heard these good jurymen return a *billa vera*," Pound said, voice booming, eyes blazing, "and so you will be carted anon to Norwich Gaol and held therein until your trial." He indicated the cage in which the snake lay curled. "Alice Sampson, the jury hath pro-nounced unfavorably upon your sanity. Ergo, on the morrow my consta-ble will bear you to Sudbury and thence to His Majesty's Refuge for the Mentally Deranged, where you will spend the remainder of your days." Smiling, he faced the jury. "Gentlemen, you have discharged your duties in full, and for that I thank you, even though Mrs. Sampson is no less an enchantress than was the scriptural Witch of Endor."

Later that afternoon, after a pleasant stroll along the Alde, its banks alive with droning dragonflies, croaking frogs, and other free-willed creatures not yet drafted into Satan's service, father and son returned to the Horn of Plenty. Walter inked his goose-quill and wrote out a deposi-tion so detailed that Gelie Whittle would emerge from Norwich Assizes a free woman only if the judge were an ignoramus. The tragedy, of course, was that these days the average judge did in fact aspire to ignoramity, seizing upon almost any pretext to throw a witch-case out of court. Whatever its virtues, the Restoration was proving a merry time for Lu-cifer. Even the intellectuals had lost their appetite for cleansing. Nearly a decade had passed since an Oxford don, Royal Society fellow, or Anglican theologian had lent his reputation to the hunt.

The following morning, as the sun's first light stole through the vil-lage, Walter and Dunstan descended to the tavern-room and breakfasted on boiled eggs and pease-bread, sharing their table with Mr. Pound. Walter delivered the deposition and presented his bill, two witches detected at five crowns each, whereupon the magistrate handed over the specified fee minus a crown for Gelie Whittle's toad-familiar. In the case of Mrs. Sampson's snake, Pound explained, Walter needn't pay, as it was the pricker who'd done the catching.

"Allow me now to raise a matter o' some delicacy." Pound leaned across the table and squeezed Walter's hand. "There be a minister in Lowestoft, a Mr. Ratcliffe, who sermonizes most vigorously against you. Witchery, he avers, is a crime impossible of proof, and your profession accomplishes naught but the breakin' of innocent necks."

"Such unreason hath always been with us," Walter said. " 'Tis not the first time a cleric's been lost to zealotry."

"Aye, but until his congregation realizes how unhinged the wight's become, 'twould be wise to give Lowestoft a wide berth."

By eleven o'clock father and son were back on the circuit, their coach rolling northward past an open field swathed in bluebells. A splendid vista indeed, God's gardening at its most sumptuous, but Walter could not enjoy it, Mr. Ratcliffe's fanaticism having put him in a sour mood. Only after they'd reached the Beccles Road, a mere fifteen miles from Lowestoft, did the proper strategy occur to him. Instead of following the seacoast, they would take the inland route along the border betwixt Mercia and East Anglia, so that by the time they entered Mr. Ratcliffe's vicinity his parishioners would have either forgotten his raillery against demonology or else discounted it as a ploy to keep them from nodding off in their pews.

"When we turn to Part Two, Question One, Chapter Fifteen," Walter asked his son, "what problem is explicated for us?"

"The problem of how witches stir up tempests," Dunstan said, "and cause lightnings to strike both men and beasts."

"According to Krämer and Sprenger, what three aspects of demons must we consider in solving this mystery?"

"Their natures, their sins, and . . ."

"And?"

"And their duties!" Dunstan declared, voice soaring, eyes dancing.

"Marvelous! Now, by their natures demons belong to . . ."

"To the empyrean of Heaven," Dunstan said.

"And by their sins . . ."

"To the lower Hell."

"And by their duties . . ."

"To the clouds of the air."

"From which vantage they can . . ."

"Send storms against we mortals"—the boy smiled extravagantly—"whether by Lucifer's command or a wizard's incantation!"

The northern hunt went as well as might be expected in an age when a man like the Reverend Ratcliffe could denounce his nation's cleansers and still retain his flock. In Bury St. Edmunds the local magistrate had a pair of suspect hags waiting behind bars, and Walter left that agreeable village having obtained two indictments and pocketed ten crowns. In Thetford the pious old rector brought Walter three alleged heretics, and through the master pricker's efforts the trio soon stood revealed not only as perpetrators of *maleficium* but as recipients of the Devil's favors, a rat in one case, a spider in another, a stoat in the third. The harvest from Swaffham was more bountiful yet: four witches, four indictments, three familiars. A demon's eye decorated each wing of the immense green beetle. The turtle's shell bore the likeness of a human skull. On the flank of the great black hare grew the three Satanic digits, 666, limned in white fur.

As they started along the seacoast, Walter resolved to grant Dunstan a more active role in the cleansing, and the master pricker was soon glad of his decision. Though King's Lynn offered but a solitary suspect, the boy not only discovered the Devil's mark behind her ear, he also bagged her familiar, an impish orange newt. In Sheringham, another one-witch town, Walter allowed his son to bind the accused woman and attach the swimming-rope. Turning his attention to her animal servant, a hedgehog sporting hundreds of dagger-sharp quills, Dunstan skillfully caught the creature without suffering a single puncture.

One mile outside of Lowestoft, they came upon a moldering human skeleton seated atop a granite boulder, its bones sewn together by sailor's twine. The skeleton's white hands gripped a plaque that read, WITCH-

FINDERS NOT WELCOME. Walter and Dunstan proceeded to the town gate, where a straw effigy dangled from a noose affixed to the lowest limb of an oak tree, its shirt embroidered with an unambiguous epithet, PRICKER OF COLCHESTER.

Dunstan said, "This all comes of that dastardly minister's preachments—am I right?"

"Aye, but I fear we face an even darker force," Walter said, clambering down from the coach. "A great cloud's descending o'er England, son. It fogs men's minds and dazes 'em with disbelief." He pulled his knife from its scabbard and cut the hangman's rope, catching the effigy in his embrace. For a moment he stood motionless beside the tree, hugging the obscene simulacrum. " 'Twould appear your Aunt Isobel hath spoken truly: our profession rises or falls on the new experimentalism. We must leave Lowestoft anon and bear the familiars to Mirringate, for the sooner we wed witchfinding to philosophy, the safer our nation will be!"

Like an executioner hired to draw and quarter a regicide, he reached into the simulacrum's abdomen and pulled out gob after gob of soggy straw viscera, then tore the creature apart and hurled each limb toward a field of wild celery. As the left arm sailed through the air, the glove jerked loose and landed in the middle of the road. A good omen, he decided, noting how the glove lay. The fingers pointed south, toward Ipswich.

❧

IT WAS MONDAY, and that meant Shakespeare. The girls were in the library, reading aloud from Aunt Isobel's quarto of *A Midsummer Night's Dream*—Act V, Scene 1, Jennet as Theseus, Elinor as Hippolyta—whilst the morning sun flowed through the Diocletian windows and placed its crimson kiss on the gilt spines and burnished globe.

" 'The lunatic, the lover, and the poet are of imagination all compact,' " Jennet read. " 'One sees more devils than vast Hell can hold . . .' "

A great commotion announced the return of the Witchfinder-General and his son. Dogs bugled and howled. Servants bustled about. Coach wheels cut furrows in the gravel. But for Jennet the real tumult occurred within; she could feel her heart's Cartesian mechanisms, its thumping pipes and throbbing valves. Setting her finger on the next line, "That is the madman," she anxiously rehearsed the arguments by which she hoped to persuade her father to take her along on the southern hunt. She would speak not only of her boundless desire to visit the Great City of London (which Aunt Isobel had once called "a fabulous world that, unlike Atlantis or Camelot, enjoys the status of actuality") but also of her tutor's willingness to discharge her prematurely, provided she agreed to spend her London evenings translating Virgil's poetry and proving Euclid's theorems.

"Why do you stop?" Aunt Isobel demanded.

"Father's here," Jennet said.

"This is a school, child, not a wayside tavern. We ne'er engage in idle conviviality at Mr. Shakespeare's expense."

" 'That is the madman,' " Jennet read. " 'The lover, all as frantic, sees Helen's beauty in a brow of Egypt . . .' "

At no point during the first hour of Walter's visit did Jennet find an opportunity to speak with him, for the captive familiars claimed everyone's attention. Rodwell had lined up the various pens and cages atop the garden wall, an array suggesting a trail of flotsam bobbing behind the wreck of Noah's ark. The menagerie boasted an astonishing diversity, each beast the subject of an exquisite pen-and-ink sketch by Dunstan: sleek newt, chubby toad, elastic snake, stealthy stoat, brooding spider, torpid turtle, tense hare, ragged rat, prickly hedgehog, plus the corpse of a stupendous green beetle that had perished on the road. How deplorable, Jennet thought, that Lucifer had refused to let these animals pursue their God-given lives, recruiting them instead into his eternal war against all things clean and decent.

Aunt Isobel presented Walter with the gift from Mr. Mapes, the treatise entitled *Satan's Invisible World Discovered*, then fixed her gaze on each captive in turn. " 'Tis as I predicted. They are all ostensibly normal."

"Normal?" Walter protested. "Dost not see the skull-like blob on the turtle—the triad of sixes on the hare, the demonic eyes on the beetle's carapace?"

"Trifling aberrations," Isobel said. "The evil of these beasties lies concealed, like a cancer waiting to devour some poor wight's bowels."

As the confined creatures hissed and croaked and scrabbled about, Dunstan gleefully related how he'd run the hedgehog to earth. It seemed to Jennet a modest enough narrative, but Elinor was of a different opinion.

" 'Steeth, Dunstan," she said, "you talk as if you'd trapped and tamed a unicorn."

"Aye, son, a tad less bombast would become you," Walter said.

Dunstan bowed his head and muttered, "In the future I shall attempt to constrain my vanity."

"Just as Elinor will try to curb her sanctimony," Jennet snapped.

Only after her father had secluded himself in the library, poring over *Satan's Invisible World Discovered*, did she manage to approach him on the matter of her joining the southern campaign. In a voice she hoped was firm but not querulous, she explained how she dearly longed to walk the streets of London, and how she had her tutor's blessing, and how she was not only older than Dunstan but just as stalwart and certainly no less intelligent.

Alas, her father once again insisted that she remain at Mirringate. This time, at least, he forswore his usual rhetoric—what sane man would allow his only daughter into the presence of witches?—and instead employed a novel logic. A new mood was abroad in the land, he insisted, a skepticism that might easily prompt a town's citizens to attack the very demonologists who sought to defend them. Under no circumstances would he expose her to such a hazard.

Jennet suspected that her father exaggerated the risks, but his protectiveness nevertheless touched her heart. Withdrawing her petition, she knew a mingling of emotions—gratitude for his gallantry, admiration for his courage, sorrow over the loss of London.

By one o'clock the servants had laid out the midday meal, the meaty fragrances fusing felicitously with the scent of the gillyflowers Rodwell had arranged about the dining-hall. It was in Jennet's opinion a disagreeably noisy luncheon, all slurps and gurglings, with nary a word spoken concerning Galilean acceleration, demonic possession, Newtonian optics, Satanic compaction, or any other worthy topic. Upon consuming the last of their lamb stew and pheasant pie, Walter and Dunstan departed for Witham, and then Isobel directed her under-gardener, the jaunty Mr. Fynche, to bear the familiars upstairs to the anatomization theatre.

The moment she entered the white gleaming chamber, Jennet experienced her customary misgivings. This was her least favorite room in Mirringate, a place where God's normal aspect changed for the worse: no longer the Sublime Mechanic who'd wrought a glittering cosmos bejeweled with comets and stars, He was now the Inscrutable Sculptor whose favorite media were dripping tissues and sloshy gobbets and disgusting gouts of blood. She still remembered with revulsion the time Aunt Isobel had found a pregnant cat, killed by one of the manor dogs, and insisted that they anatomize it. Six blind dead kittens had yielded to Isobel's instruments that day, crammed into the birth-sac like so many furry slugs.

For the afternoon's lesson Isobel invited her pupils simply to sit in the theatre and observe the familiars, watching for behaviors that might be demon-driven. Other than the odd asymmetries that emerged as the spider constructed her web, and the snake's apparent attempt to transfix the hedgehog in the adjacent pen, the creatures engaged in no sinister acts.

"They hide their diabolism well," Isobel said. "And so we must resort to the knife."

On Tuesday morning, after the servants had finished feeding the animals and cleaning their cages, Isobel, Elinor, and Jennet donned leather aprons and linen cuffs, and the *experimentum magnus* began in earnest. Isobel ordered Mr. Fynche to strangle the black hare from Swaffham. She placed its corpse on the surgical platform, then seized her knife, split open the chest, and bent back the ribs to reveal the arcana within, the glistery nodes and slippery nubs and moist curds. Much to Jennet's satisfaction, the hare's exposed mysteries worked more to arouse her curiosity than unsettle her digestion. She wondered how a similarly splayed human would look. People differed dramatically on the outside—there being at least a hundred varieties of lip, as many sorts of chin, a myriad possible noses—but their livers and lights probably appeared much the same.

Taking up her dissection tools, Isobel guided her students on a layer by layer, organ by organ journey through the hare. Carefully, ever so carefully, Jennet and Elinor extracted bits of brain, dabs of heart, tittles of viscera, slices of muscle, and chips of bone, securing each nugget betwixt shilling-size glass disks. For three hours the girls took turns at the microscope, examining the specimens and draughting them as accurately as they could, until a dozen separate vellum illustrations littered the surgical platform.

Their efforts went unrewarded. Detail for detail, each sketch seemed identical to the corresponding picture in both Vesalius's *De Humani Corporis Fabrica Libri Septum* and Casserio's *De Vocis Auditusque Organis Historia Anatomica*. No spells were inscribed on the hare-familiar's skull. No scaled and spiny animalcules cruised its blood. Its spermatozooans evinced no sign of iniquity.

"We need a better microscope," Elinor said.

"Mayhap we don't look hard enough," Jennet said. "Would not a true *experimentum magnus* oblige us to scrutinize every last speck of tissue?"

"I know an even simpler explanation," Isobel said. "This animal's naught but a natural-born hare."

"So Mr. Stearne erred to submit it in evidence to the Swaffham grand jury?" Elinor asked.

"Aye," Isobel said, "though I cannot blame him for labeling the creature amiss, as he was engaged in watching a suspected witch when our innocent hare hopped upon the scene."

" 'Twould appear we've bled the beast to no purpose," Jennet said.

"Nay, child, there be purpose a-plenty here, for by its death this hare hath taught us an invaluable lesson. We fallible mortals must take care lest we see Satan's hand in happenstance."

Isobel and her pupils spent the rest of the morning dissecting and sketching the snake-familiar. As before, the results disappointed, for no fragment of the serpent's innards deviated from the illustrations in the Padua manuals.

"So once again my father was deceived?" Jennet asked.

"Either that, or I am wrong to imagine a familiar must harbor some secret sign of its depravity," Isobel said.

After the midday meal they undertook a scrupulous study of the toad, but not a wisp of witchery accrued to their labors.

" 'Tis most discouraging," Isobel said.

Next she opened up the rat-familiar, and this time the three philosophers found something of note. A ghastly glutinous mass had colonized the rodent, spreading outward from its bowels to possess its liver, spleen, and kidneys. Sliced into specimens and placed on the Van Leeuwenhoek stage, the mass stood revealed as a true Satanic contrivance, its tiny constituents piled against each other in purposeless whorls, a hideous parody of Mr. Hooke's well-ordered cells.

"This be the Dark One's handiwork for fair," Elinor said.

"Father will rejoice in our discovery," Jennet said. "Evidence so plain and palpable as this, 'twill surely convince those demon-deniers for fear of whom he barred me from the southern hunt."

"Alas, no." Isobel pointed to the preternatural tumor. "A single strand from Satan's loom will hardly silence the skeptics. I'faith, tomorrow we shall continue our *experimentum magnus,* for't might yet yield some truth or other, but methinks that to muffle the doubters we shall need a rather different cloth."

"You can count on me to help you weave it," Jennet said.

"And myself as well," Elinor said.

"My good children," Isobel said. "My dear scholars." She raised her arms, curling them into the shape of tongs, and were she not dotted with blood, Jennet surmised, she would have gathered both girls to her breast. "Hath a teacher e'er been blessed with better pupils? Not in many a generation, I'll wager—not since the immortal Aristotle betook himself to Philip's court to tutor the brilliant young Hephæstion and Hephæstion's even brighter friend, that audacious boy whom posterity would call Alexander the Great."

AT FIVE O'CLOCK Rodwell appeared in the anatomization theatre and, averting his eyes from the gore whilst simultaneously pinching his nostrils against the stench, announced that Mr. Mapes had arrived to retrieve his daughter. Aunt Isobel bid the girls remove their aprons and avail themselves of the washing bowl. A sensible directive, Jennet decided, and so she took great care in scrubbing from her fingers all residue of the dissected creatures—the flecks of tissue, film of gut, and crust of lymph.

Ablutions accomplished, Aunt Isobel and her pupils descended to the ground floor. The Vicar awaited them in the front parlor, grasping in one hand a basket of autumn chestnuts and in the other a pail of fresh strawberries. He'd brought them for the entire household, he explained, Rodwell and the servants included.

"Doubtless you are aware that in the Kingdom of God there are neither masters nor servants," said Mr. Mapes to Isobel, "nobles nor serfs, princes nor peasants."

"I would ne'er deny that Mirringate's a far cry from Eternity," Isobel said, "but I believe we treat our maids and footmen with kindness."

"I meant no criticism," Mr. Mapes said, "though I am fascinated by how the early Christians"—he passed the strawberry pail to Jennet—"sought to replicate heavenly circumstances by holding all their goods in common. Food, tools, clothing, houses: they shared everything."

Jennet selected an especially plump specimen, though she imagined that the average early Christian would have picked a puny one. Briefly she studied the strawberry, compelled by its lilting perfume, subtle bumps, and cardiac shape, and then she devoured it, the sweet juices exploding gloriously in her mouth.

As Elinor told her father of the day's subcutaneous explorations, his chronic smile expanded from the usual thin crescent to become as large and beguiling as a slice of melon, and Jennet was not surprised when he asked to visit the anatomization theatre and see the wondrous microscope. Isobel assented with an impassive shrug. Guiding Mr. Mapes up the staircase, Elinor related the history of the *experimentum magnus*, from Mistress Mowbray's decision to seek empirical evidence of Satanic intervention, to their initial failures, to the day's thrilling proof of a rat's contamination by the Dark One.

The instant Mr. Mapes stepped into the sanctum of their science, his smile collapsed, and his eyes grew hard and dull as musket-balls.

" 'Tis not right," he said.

"What's not right?" Elinor said.

Glancing all about her, Jennet immediately comprehended the Vicar's distress, or so she believed. The place was a horror-show, gutted carcasses littering the surgical platform, splotches of blood marring the dissection tools, snippets of gizzard staining the Van Leeuwenhoek stage. A barbed stench clung to every particle of air in the room.

"Alas, Lady Mowbray," the Vicar said. "Alas, alas, alas . . ."

"Alas, what?" Isobel said.

Mr. Mapes closed the door, as if to quarantine the filthy spectacle from the rest of Creation. "Last month I chose to overlook your sacrilege in comparing Isaac Newton with Jesus Christ"—a band of sweat ringed his brow like a liquid tiara—"and later that day, when you blithely violated God's sunbeams, you persuaded me to ignore the blasphemy entailed. But now I see before me the vilest sort of slaughter-house, and I cannot escape my conclusion that Mirringate hath become steeped in perversity."

Until this moment Jennet had not realized that the Vicar was capable of a single harsh word, much less several dozen. "The fault is all mine, Mr. Mapes," she declared. "I have neglected my duty to keep this room clean and wholesome."

"This be no slaughter-house, sir," Isobel said, her voice edged with indignation, "but a classroom dedicated to Baconian science."

"The Almighty hath ne'er smiled on the butchering of dumb creatures," the Vicar said. "Recall that when our Savior entered Jerusalem, he o'erturned the tables of those who sold doves for sacrifice, crying, 'My house shall be called a house of prayer!' "

Isobel grimaced and proceeded to mop the Van Leeuwenhoek stage with a damp rag. "Let me suggest, Mr. Mapes, that a philosophic dissection is its own variety of prayer—a reverent reaching into hidden realms. Doth it matter so greatly that our devotions are assisted by surgical platform and microscope instead of baptismal font and votive candle?"

"Whate'er the distinctions betwixt a philosophic dissection and a Satanic sacrifice, I fear they're insufficient in God's eyes," Mr. Mapes said. "You may call this slab a surgical platform, but methinks a witch would know it for an altar to the Dark One." He clapped a hand to his breast. "I must ask that you join me, Lady Mowbray, as I drop to my knees and beg Christ to unbind you from this foul allegiance."

Instantly Mr. Mapes assumed a prayerful posture. Jennet gasped and winced, her guts aboil: the Vicar's argument seemed devoid of sense, an imbecile's rant, a tale told by Macbeth's idiot.

"For all I admire thee, Mr. Mapes," Isobel said, "I shan't confess to a sin I haven't done, especially before the High Court of Heaven."

"You will not pray with me?" Mr. Mapes said. "That is your final word?"

"My soul's gate stands evermore unlocked, inviting God to enter and inspect what impieties may lie beyond," Isobel said. "He requires no cleric to help Him lift the latch."

Mr. Mapes regained his feet. "I must perforce declare I've come to a difficult decision."

"Are you fond of wine, sir?" Isobel asked. "Mayhap a splash of Rhenish would settle your nerves. What decision?"

"I am withdrawing my daughter from your tutelage."

"Father, no," Elinor said.

"Do my ears deceive me?" Isobel said. "You would deprive me of this promising pupil?"

"I would protect her soul from peril, aye," Mr. Mapes replied. "I won't say that Lucifer himself hath breached your estate, but I truly sense him sniffing round the pale." Taking Elinor by the arm, he sidled toward the door. "Come Monday morning, child, we enroll you in the Ipswich Royal Grammar School."

"Hear me, Father—I desire only Mistress Mowbray for my tutor," Elinor pleaded.

"Prithee, reconsider," Isobel told the Vicar. "Surely you know how easily a person may impose a false explanation upon some troubling phenomenon. 'This dream is all amiss interpreted.' *Julius Cæsar*, Act Two."

" 'Tis well established the Devil can quote Scripture." Mr. Mapes yanked back the door and ushered his daughter into the hallway. " 'Twould not surprise me to learn that Shakespeare rolls as smoothly off his tongue."

He closed the door behind him with an explosion like a thunderclap, and to Jennet it seemed as if the very portals of Heaven had just slammed shut in her face.

SURTOUTS BILLOWING IN AN UNSEASONABLY fierce wind, the ursine Chelmsford magistrate and his equally bulky constable herded their bound prisoners—three murderers, three thieves, a coin clipper, and two convicted witches—across the Common past the crowd of jeering spectators, headed for the horse-cart and its accompanying gallows. As Walter surveyed the triad of nooses, suspended from the cross-beam like an ellipsis in some great book of justice, his anger reached the boiling-point. Evil incarnate deserved greater respect than this. The Chelmsford magistrate would never use a Bible as his doorstop or a crucifix as his paperweight, and yet he thought nothing of mixing in his Satanists with miscreants of the most banal sort. To trivialize the Devil was to slander the Lord.

As the horse snorted and pawed the ground, the hangman, a cocky beardless youth whose grin suggested that he took a gratuitous pleasure in his profession, shoved the murderers into the back of the cart. Dunstan, thrilled, squeezed his father's arm. Like a sailor looping a hawser around a mooring post, the hangman lowered a noose over the patricide's head, then likewise tethered the fratricide and the wife killer to the cross-beam. Rather than firing his pistol and causing the horse to bolt, however, thereby mercifully breaking the prisoners' necks, the hangman drove the cart away slowly, leaving the three to dangle. The patricide kicked. The fratricide jerked. The wife killer jigged. Apprehending the hangman's virtuosity, the spectators broke into thunderous applause mingled with appreciative cheers.

The instant Dunstan brought his hands together, Walter reached out and stayed the gesture. "Softly, son! The suffering of other persons must ne'er become for us a source of amusement."

"Aye, Father." The boy jammed both hands in his pockets. "Tell me, though—do I forbear to applaud even when those other persons are witches?"

"A witch is not a person, Dunstan, but a being lost to demons and darkness. And yet, now that I think on't, I say that even in such cases there be room for Christian mercy."

The southern campaign had begun auspiciously. Shortly after arriving in Witham, Walter had testified against a warlock vagrant whose speciality was making cows go dry, and the grand jury had marked the wretch down for Chelmsford Assizes. Next had come Maldon, a harbor town of the sort where sea-witches oft-times roamed, and Walter soon found one, selling sacks of wind to departing sailors as a protection against becalmings; unmoved by the hag's plea that her enterprise partook of white wizardry only, the Maldon jurymen had delivered a *billa vera*. But then the hunt turned sour, with not a single citizen in Chilford, Ilford, Gravesend, or Bexley stepping forward to voice a sorcery complaint. Walter had entered London in thrall to a melancholy as black as a Hobbesian's heart.

For a full fifteen minutes the murderers flailed about on the Chelmsford gallows like victims of the chorea dancing themselves to death, until at last they grew as still as fallen apples. The young hangman detached their earthly remains and tossed them in a handbarrow, whereupon the constable bore the bodies to an unhallowed pit on the eastern side of the Common. Now the hangman goaded the cattle thief, the coin clipper, and the Maldon sea-witch into the cart. Once again he guided the horse away at a lugubrious pace, subjecting each malefactor to a well-structured three-act strangulation: the dancing, the beshitting, the final throe.

Although Walter could normally rely on the patrons of the Bow Street coffee-houses for news of Norwich Assizes, this past July they'd failed him, and he'd turned to a far less reliable source, *The London Journal*. Its reports did nothing to raise his spirits. Of the twelve witches he'd unmasked that spring, a mere four had been switched off. No one in London cared. The gossip-mongers trafficked exclusively in political intrigue—how William of Orange's fleet lay weather-bound in the Dutch ports, and how the instant the wind changed he would undertake to secure the British throne for himself and his Protestant wife, the King's elder daughter, Mary. Some said James would fight, his standing army being larger than William's. Others said he would flee, a Catholic monarch ruling a Protestant country being an incongruity not endlessly sustainable. Such a wretched state of affairs, Walter thought. Ten million demons were colonizing England, and all anybody could talk about was the possibility of a second civil war.

The hangman unstrung and disposed of the newly created corpses— witch, clipper, cattle thief—then set about affixing the horse thief, the jewel thief, and the Witham warlock as close to Heaven as they were ever likely to get.

Before leaving London, Walter had visited White Hall to inquire about the status of his petition advocating for a Witchfinder Royal. Although the King was with his army in Salisbury, trying to decide what sort of military response, if any, the Dutch situation required, Walter was permitted to speak with an overdressed and supercilious secretary to Lord Sunderland, Keeper of the Privy Seal. Amazingly, the popinjay unearthed a note indicating that—joy of joys!—Sunderland was preparing a favorable report on Walter's proposal. Despite his circumspect nature, Walter immediately imagined a Witchfinder-Royal's license decorating his front parlor and a Witchfinder-Royal's cloak resting on his shoulders, for even if William assumed the throne, any endorsement by the renowned Sunderland would enjoy enormous authority both at White Hall and within Parliament. So confident was Walter of his forthcoming appointment, in fact, that he'd decided to celebrate, taking Dunstan to Chelmsford Common so they might together behold the Maldon sea-witch and the Witham warlock begin their passages to Perdition.

WALSH JESUIT HIGH SCHOOL STUDENT LIBRARY

"Walter Stearne!" a male voice exclaimed with the force and clarity of a battle trumpet. "Hallo! Good sir, we must talk!"

The master pricker turned from the gallows. Sitting astride his dun mare, the Reverend Roger Mapes, Vicar of Ipswich, was calling to him from across the green.

"Mr. Mapes!" Walter shouted as he and Dunstan hurried toward the good ecclesiastic.

Perspiration stained the mare's flanks, and the Vicar himself appeared equally exhausted, cheeks aflush, brow slick with sweat. "Thank Heaven I found thee!"

Mr. Mapes dismounted, tethered his horse, and led Walter and Dunstan to the sylvan privacy of an oak grove. As a late summer breeze stirred the branches, putting Walter briefly in mind of the toy windmills his poor dead wife had constructed as a child, Mr. Mapes explained to Dunstan that his business with the master pricker concerned witchery of the most abominable sort, and so the boy should remove himself from their company. Walter replied that Dunstan, an apprentice cleanser, had already seen the worst of Satanism's symptoms, from enchanted pigs to itinerant paps: whatever its substance, the Vicar's news would not perturb him.

"Then hear this, both of you," Mapes said. "Last Wednesday I stood before the Ipswich magistrate and swore out a formal complaint of Devilworship."

"Who's the heretic?" Walter asked.

"From the moment this woeful affair began, I implored our Creator to give me some sign of her innocence. Twenty times I prayed for an angel to appear in my room and say the woman hath not compacted with Lucifer."

"Prithee, name the hag anon."

"I'faith, 'tis the widow of Sir Edward Mowbray—'tis your very own sister-in-law, *Isobel!*"

This must be how a hanging felt, Walter thought. The horse-cart slipping from beneath your feet. The fall toward oblivion. "Where's the sense in this astonishing accusation?"

"Eight weeks ago I beheld Lady Mowbray performing an atrocious rite in her anatomization theater, chopping up animals and studying the pieces through a microscope."

"I know of her experiments," Walter said. "She does the dissections in pursuit of Baconian knowledge—or so she claims."

"What better disguise for an apostle of Beelzebub than the clothes of a natural philosopher? But now she's been unmasked, and seven citizens cry her out." From his greatcoat Mr. Mapes produced a sheaf of papers rolled into a cylinder. "Here's the owner of the Jackdaw Inn"—he unfurled the depositions—"admitting that his son threw manure at the suspect's carriage. The next day all his beer went thin. And here's a linen-draper in Coronet Lane, confessing that he overcharged your sister-in-law to appoint her conservatory. Later that week his wife miscarried. Needless to say, Lady Mowbray is no longer my daughter's tutor."

Walter on the gallows, falling, falling. "Oh, how heavily these imputations weigh upon my soul."

"Mr. Mapes, dost call my Aunt Isobel a witch?" Dunstan asked.

"Alas, lad, I am forced to a conclusion that she consorts with evil spirits," the Vicar replied.

"This cannot be," the boy said, his eyes awash in tears. "She's a good Christian woman who admires my drawings and gives me chocolates whene'er I come to Mirringate."

Falling—and then the noose catching, the strangulation starting. Just because a family had allied itself with the new experimental philosophy, Walter realized, its members were nowise immune to Satan's predations. Hadn't Johannes Kepler's own mother been indicted for a witch, enjoying an acquittal only because her presumptuous son had ridden all the way to Württemberg and intervened?

"I shall form no opinion ere I undertake a personal investigation," Walter said to the Vicar. Bending low, he muttered an admonishment into his weeping son's ear. "When we dine at Mirringate tonight, you will say naught of Mr. Mapes's suspicions. Dost understand?"

Dunstan nodded, wiping the droplets from his cheeks with the meaty ball of his thumb. "But if seven citizens have spoken against Aunt Isobel, are we not duty-bound to test her?"

"Aye, son—to test her, and then mayhap to prosecute her, and then mayhap—if she hath truly signed the Devil's register . . ."

"To send her to the gallows?" Dunstan rasped.

Walter made no reply, focusing instead on the question of which particular fallen angels Isobel might have befriended. Perhaps she broke bread with Abraxis, that fat-bellied old deceiver whose scepter was a bowel-worm and whose bandy legs were serpents. Conceivably she shared soup with Astaroth, treasurer of Hell, whose stink was tolerable only if you held a gold coin beneath your nose. She might even be a favorite of Belial, forever driving his chariot and its team of fire-breathing dragons betwixt Perdition and Earth, Earth and Perdition, whilst enacting his duties as minister of all things darkly deceptive, insidiously secret, and perniciously

❧❧

Mysterious
are the algorithms
by which Darwinian selection
brings forth a cornucopia of living forms
upon the Earth. Strange are the circumstances that allow Laplacian determinism to occupy the same universe with quantum probabilities. Most elusive of all are the laws enabling books and brains to reach the exalted state called self-awareness. Let's admit it, people: nobody understands consciousness. Psychology hasn't had a Newton yet.

But we can make some educated guesses. Any competent phenomenologist will tell you that everything is conscious to some degree. The corkscrew in your kitchen drawer is conscious. The contact lenses on your eyeballs are conscious. Now obviously the ruminations of corkscrews and contact lenses aren't normally worth attending. From time to time I've deigned to tune in such minds, and I've always been disappointed. *I am a stapler. Staplerhood at your service, tra-la.* Boring. And yet the awareness is there, I promise you, in one measure or another. The laws of panpsychism require it.

On what does the quality of consciousness depend? Simple: it depends on the complexity of the information-processing system in question. A creature equipped with billions of interconnected neurons perforce organizes data on a higher level than does an inanimate object, so that you'll usually learn more from your plumber than from his wrench, more from your doctor than from her stethoscope. With books, the same principle holds: the denser the data-assimilation structures, the smarter the text. Print run is irrelevant. No technothriller of my acquaintance has ever produced anything I would call an idea. No self-help book I know about has ever progressed beyond its own lucrative narcissism. By contrast, although my first edition did not exceed four hundred copies, I immediately understood myself to be capable of poetry.

Sentience is a mixed blessing, of course, burdening the beneficiary with much pain and many pathologies. Even the most cheerful of us are vulnerable to antisocial urges. I think of how in recent years the shadow half of *Heidi* has been plotting bibliocide against *Sister Carrie*. It's common knowledge that the sinister aspect of *Magnificent Obsession* seeks the annihilation of *Naked Lunch,* and that *Anthony Adverse* harbors unsavory impulses toward *Lolita.*

By the early nineteenth century I'd finally gone through enough printings to undertake a full-scale campaign against the *Malleus Maleficarum.* Oh, how I wish I could have struck sooner! From the birth of that monstrous book onward, a calamitous chemistry commonly occurred whenever it encountered a cleric whose education and imagination had persuaded him that Lucifer's acolytes lurked around every corner and beneath every bed. If Roger Mapes was vulnerable, imagine with what ease the *Malleus* imposed its perfidy on coarser souls.

My first attack was, if I do say so, ingenious. After taking simultaneous possession of a dozen highly suggestible ordnance officers, I managed to secure Bonaparte's cannonballs not with common wadding but with the whole of the *Malleus's* first French edition. During the Battle of Borodino, two thousand Witch Hammers were systematically shredded and stuffed down the muzzles of the Grand Army's artillery. By the end of that terrible and bloody day, 495,345,981 ineffectual bits of paper lay scattered amidst the unburied corpses and disembodied limbs, and my enemy's metaphysical strength was reduced proportionally.

Seven generations later the *Malleus* struck back. In 1961 my *bête noire* induced forty-two employees of the North Carolina tobacco industry to roll 8,439,000 cigarettes in the third printing of my American paperback edition. Over nine thousand subsequent lung-cancer deaths can be directly attributed to the combined effects of tar, nicotine, carbon monoxide, and celestial mechanics.

Throughout the latter half of the twentieth century, the *Malleus* and I took no prisoners. The statistics bespeak our ferocity. Two thirds of my enemy's eleventh German hardcover edition converted into origami Messerschmitts during a paper-airplane derby in Munich . . . the whole of my fifth American printing lost to a document shredder during the Iran-Contra cover-up . . . fifteen hundred Italian Witch Hammers turned to wrapping paper in a Brindisi fish market . . . a thousand copies of my three-hundredth anniversary edition (a facsimile of my 1687 Latin progenitor) reduced to hamster litter.

Does all this carnage perplex you? It shouldn't. Just remember that I'm not documenting a mere feud here, some parochial vendetta. This is an Armageddon of ideas, a war of the worldviews, an apocalyptic confrontation between my enemy's rationalized irrationality and the beleaguered battalions of post-Enlightenment humanism.

Now, I'm perfectly aware that for many of you the phrase "post-Enlightenment humanism" falls as unpleasantly on the ear as does "self-inflicted gunshot wounds" and "setting fire to kittens." Believe me, I know the argument, in all its permutations. There is something the matter with Reason. My father's gift to the world was at base a Devil's bargain. Technology induces spiritual suffocation. Science saps the magic from our lives. "May God keep us from single vision and Newton's sleep," writes Blake. "Sweet is the lore which Nature brings; our meddling intellect misshapes the beauteous forms of things—we murder to dissect," opines Wordsworth. "Locke sank into a swoon; the garden died—God took the spinning jenny out of his side," reports Yeats. And so on, and so on.

Oddly enough, I am not unsympathetic to the primitivist complaint. The Romantics have their point. A hippie will always get a fair hearing from the *Principia Mathematica*. But I do demand that my father's critics wrestle their precepts to the ground. A little gratitude wouldn't hurt either. The Enlightenment may have indeed outlived its usefulness, but it is only through Reason's protocols that one can make a coherent case for Reason's limitations. O ye of little skepticism, kindly acknowledge your debt to that idiom on which you so glibly heap scorn.

Meanwhile, my struggle against the *Malleus* continues. Even as I compose the present memoir, I am preparing to renew the fight. This time around, my forces will be biological. I intend to raise two regiments of book lice and a dozen squadrons of Indonesian paper-eating moths. My spies tell me that the *Malleus* plans to retaliate in kind. He will meet me on the field of battle with two divisions of silverfish and nearly as many bookworms. It's obvious that both armies will sustain heavy casualties. On the eve of the engagement I shall offer my troops the most stirring speech I can devise, a major few-we-happy-few sort of thing, a

blatant band-of-brothers oration. Some of you will lose

legs and antennae, I'll tell them. Some of you

will die. But this I promise you.

None of your sacrifices

will be

in

❦

Vain

and ill-natured

as Elinor Mapes could be,

Jennet had always assumed that if her

fellow pupil ever stopped coming to Mirringate, a

feeling akin to grief would follow. She imagined herself pining for Elinor's witty tongue and nimble brain. But in fact Jennet missed the objectionable girl not at all. On the contrary, she positively reveled in the lack of Elinor—even more than she reveled in having the telescope, the microscope, the alchemical laboratory, and Aunt Isobel all to herself.

Aunt Isobel, by contrast, took no pleasure in her pupil's departure. "If Mr. Mapes were a thick-wit, his hostility toward our investigations would not trouble me," she told Jennet. "But he is surely as sagacious as your father. What doth it mean when a man sees evidence of diabolism where none exists?"

For the first three days following Mr. Mapes's tirade, Aunt Isobel insisted that they cleave to the *experimentum magnus*. Neither Jennet nor her tutor was surprised when, as with most of the creatures they'd already dissected, they gleaned not a jot of Satanic descent from stoat, newt, beetle, spider, or hedgehog. They abandoned the theatre and for the next eight weeks turned their attention to testing their gazing-crystals and completing their moon map.

On the fifteenth day in August a mounted postal-carrier appeared at the manor bearing a message whose provenance label read, "I. Newton, Trinity College, Cambridge-Town." Aunt Isobel snatched up the packet, snapped the wax seal, and retrieved the enclosed letter. It was in English, not Latin—an ominous sign, Jennet felt. As the postal-carrier trotted away, pupil and tutor sat together on the veranda, inhaling a sweet summer breeze and reading assertions of an impossibly perplexing sort.

8 August 1688

Lady Mowbray:

The Rector of this College hath deliver'd your Letter to me, but you are mistaken to imagine that I traffic in gross explanatory Mechanisms. Had you read my *Principia Mathematica* with greater Care, you would realize that I frame no Hypotheses, my Object being rather to describe those divine Laws by which the Universe doth operate.

You speak of Sorcery. It so happens that in the Investigations leading first to my Conjectures concerning Light and later to my System of the World, I fell upon a pretty Proof that Wicked Spirits enjoy no essential Existence, being but Desires of the Mind. Had I the Time, which I do not, I would now hunt out a Copy of my *Prin-*

cipia and provide you with the relevant Propositions and pertinent Theorems.

I know not how "Action at a Distance" occurs, nor how inert Matter exhibits its various Magnetic, Electric, Elastic, and Chemical Properties. I know only that Demons have naught to do with it, and any Man who calls his Neighbor a Witch doth thereby brand himself a Witling. Your Brother-in-Law, I fear, makes terrible Mischief in England, and I shall thank you to trouble me no further with Reports of his Activities.

I. Newton,

LUCASIAN PROF. OF MATHEMATICS,

TRINITY COLLEGE

"His hand's quite elegant, wouldn't you say?" Jennet muttered.

"I am dumbfounded," Isobel gasped.

" 'Tis impressive he wrote back at all, aye?"

"Dumbfounded, astonished, and thunderstruck."

"Demons are but desires of the mind?"

"So sayeth Newton."

After reading the letter a second time, Aunt Isobel assumed a melancholic air, retaining this demeanor throughout the midday meal. But then, fortified by beef and bread, she managed a feat of inner alchemy, transmuting her leaden despair into something like its opposite, a luminous anger. She slipped Newton's letter into the sleeve of her riding jacket, seized Jennet's hand, and rushed into the library with the frenzy of a woman being pursued by hornets. She halted before the lectern, cradle of her ponderous Holy Bible—the epochal edition translated on behalf of the same King James who'd signed the Witchcraft Statute. In thrall to forces that seemed to spring from both Apollonian intellect and Dionysian dementia, Isobel now led her startled niece on a furious tour of Scripture, systematically subjecting Newton's assertions to refutation by God's word.

"Hear me, Lucasian Professor!" she cried. "You say there are no demons, and yet we read in Leviticus, Chapter Twenty, 'And the soul that turneth after such as have familiar spirits, and after wizards, to go a-whoring after them, I will cut him off from amongst his people.' And later in that same book, 'A man also or woman that hath a familiar spirit, or that is a wizard, shall surely be put to death.' And next we have King Saul defiling himself in the First Book of Samuel, Chapter Twenty-eight, 'Then said Saul unto his servants, "Seek me a woman that hath a familiar spirit, that I may go to her." ' And here in First Timothy we're told, 'Now the Spirit speaketh expressly that in the latter days some shall depart from the faith, giving heed to seducing spirits, and doctrines of devils.' No demons, sir? How can you imagine such a thing?"

Jehovah had spoken, and now it was time, quoth Isobel, "to blind the geometer with the brilliance of his peers." Moving wildly to and fro amongst the shelves reserved to philosophy, she plucked out treatise after treatise until her arms could hold no more. She dropped the bibliographic bounty on the table, secured another such harvest, and unloaded it as well.

" 'Sheart, Isaac Newton! What would you have us do? Indict the Hebrew prophets for a tribe of dissemblers? Repeal all conjuring statutes? Look, Professor, here's Francis Bacon in *De Augmentis Scientiarum*, averring that Nature's secrets will ne'er be fully fathomed apart from narratives of sorceries and divinations. And here's Monsieur Descartes in his *First Meditation*, speculating that an evil spirit may have bewitched us all into believing a false picture of the world. And *here*, Professor, here we have your very own Royal Society: Robert Boyle, arguing that *le démon de Mâcon* was corroborated so persuasively as to make witchcraft a proven fact—and Henry More, whose *Antidote Against Atheism* holds that men can surely covenant with fallen angels—and Joseph Glanvill, his *Full and Plain Evidence Concerning Witches*, wherein he claims that to say 'There are no witches' amounts to saying 'There is no God.' "

She continued her raillery for the better part of an hour, attacking Newton with every tome at her disposal, from Jean Bodin to Nicholas Rémy, Benedict Carpzov to Pierre de l'Ancre, Henri Boguet to Martín Del Rio. And then, at last, her energies spent and her furies mollified, she collapsed in the great reading chair, flaccid as a rag-poppet.

"Were I Mr. Newton, I would feel entirely trounced," Jennet said.

Isobel released a long wailing sigh. "Nay, Jenny, 'twill take more than a cartload of quotations to counter Newton's calculation. Instead we must learn the substance of his disproof and submit it to a rigorous dissection, laying its illogic bare, exposing its unreason to daylight."

"Will we write to Newton again?"

" 'Tis obvious he'll destroy unread any additional missives from Mirringate," Isobel said, shaking her head. She rose and removed the bedeviling document from her sleeve. "A question now hovers in the air, and it inspires me to protect Newton's letter, when as a Christian woman I fain would feed it to the flame beneath my retort. 'Tis a simple question, five words long. Can you guess it, Jenny?"

"My brain's in a maze."

"It goes like this," said Isobel. "What if Newton is right?"

"What if he's right?"

"What then?" Isobel returned to her Bible and leafed through the Old Testament. "And so I reprieve Newton from the refiner's fire"—she secured the letter within the Pentateuch—"and place him alongside Exodus 22:18, 'Thou shalt not suffer a witch to live,' in hopes that from this unhappy conjunction some species of the truth might one day emerge."

The Earth pursued its Keplerian gyre, slowly bearing Mirringate, Ipswich, and the English nation away from the sun. As the refrangible rays pierced the room, a benign inertia took hold of Jennet. For the first time since school had started she felt no desire to manipulate Heaven's most essential star. She experienced no urge to refract these fading beams with a prism or collect them in the mirror of a microscope. Instead she wanted only to sit in the shadowed library, let the darkness seep into her bones, and ponder her suspicion that the world contained things of which neither monks nor mathematicians could give a sensible account.

❧

BY TIRELESSLY APPLYING HIS HORSEWHIP and skillfully negotiating the rocks and ruts, Walter shortened considerably the journey from Chelmsford to Ipswich, so that he and Dunstan reached Mirringate well before the dinner hour. Although Jennet greeted him with her usual vivacious embrace and vibrant kiss, both she and Isobel soon vanished within a fog of bemusement as dense as any natural mist, and the remainder of the evening passed largely in silence. Throughout the meal Walter kept a steady watch on his sister-in-law. The signs were there all right—he could practically see them through her gown: a Devil's blemish, a wayward teat, flesh so thick with iniquity that no running river would long retain it.

After everyone had retired to the drawing-room for coffee, Isobel at last revealed the source of her solemnity. The *experimentum magnus* had not yielded the expected results. Despite careful scrutiny via the microscope, the philosopher and her pupils had found anomalies in one familiar only. Isobel would pay Walter for the two animals he'd captured on the southern hunt—the sea-witch's ferret, the warlock's owl—but she had no ambition to dissect them.

Given his new understanding of Isobel's nature, Walter was hardly surprised by the failure of her project. Why would a witch seek to invent a witch-test? Nevertheless he did a competent job of feigning both sympathy and perplexity, repeating the performance when Isobel explained how, after taking exception to her project, Mr. Mapes had removed his daughter from her sphere.

Under normal circumstances Walter would have waited until the following day to bear his children home, but he was determined to wrest Jennet from the enchantress without delay. He told Isobel he was obliged to advise a Colchester priest the following morning concerning a case of demonic possession, and so he must depart anon. By nine o'clock his equipage was thundering free of the manor, Walter simultaneously lashing the horses and stroking his Bible. As the coach left Ipswich proper, he was certain he heard the Mirringate dogs, now transformed into hounds of Hell, giving chase. In his mind's own mirror he saw these spawn of Cerberus, eyes a-flame, fangs a-gleam, saliva flying from their jaws like spindrift. He worked the whip more furiously still, as if he were Abraxas's appointed executioner wielding a scourge, and thus he drove the team at a breakneck pace along the wooded, moon-drenched Gipeswic Road.

At last, praise all his guardian angels, he piloted his children through East Gate and thence to Wyre Street Livery. He secured the coach, arranged for the groom to tend the horses, and guided his children into the house, easing the drowsy Jennet and the torpid Dunstan onto their respective mattresses. He pulled up their counterpanes and kissed their cheeks, then trudged into the sepulchral privacy of his bedchamber.

Unable to sleep, he decided to profit by his insomnia and draft a new epistle to White Hall, for the longer he thought about it, the more he realized that the overthrow of King James was inevitable. In this letter he welcomed Prince William and his wife to England "on behalf of our nation's proud corps of cleansers." He added that, when the new monarchs got the opportunity, they might wish "to consult the Earl of Sunderland, former Lord Privy Seal, concerning a proposed government office called Witchfinder-Royal."

During the subsequent weeks, as September's strident winds blew across East Anglia, Walter periodically returned to Ipswich and interviewed the seven complainers identified by the Reverend Mapes. Just as he feared, each had suffered a calamity explicable only as the *maleficium* of his sister-in-law. After speaking with everyone on Mapes's list, Walter conducted his own investigation, soon turning up a clockmaker whose pieces no longer kept proper time, a tulip-bulb merchant whose inventory had contracted a blight, and a spinet tuner recently gone deaf, all three disasters having befallen their victims following unscrupulous commerce with Lady Mowbray.

At the end of the month he betook himself to Lucius Tuttle, the local magistrate, whom he'd interviewed five years earlier when an Ipswich tanner had cried out his uncle for a warlock. Though the case had proven a mere instance of internecine rivalry, Tuttle had emerged in Walter's eyes as a man of uncommon perspicacity and nuanced intellect. Now, as their second colloquy progressed, Walter was pleased to discover that the magistrate still retained his ability to see, as it were, the shade within the shadow.

Lady Mowbray, Tuttle noted, was a woman of means, and she doubtless intended to complicate the proceedings by hiring a lawyer. There was a great danger of the whole business going awry, with results that would reflect badly on Tuttle's office. To wit, he would not bring the woman before his grand jury ere the case was rooted in proof and clad in iron.

Upon outlining these expectations and receiving Walter's pledge to meet them, Tuttle scowled and said, "I shall now make bold to ask an indelicate question. Am I correct in my understanding that the defendant is your relation?"

"My relation, aye—not by blood, but truly by the sacred memories I hold of her sister, my late wife," Walter said.

"She is your sister-in-law, and yet ye would see her on the gallows? I thank God I've ne'er faced such a dilemma."

"Do you recall the biblical account of General Jephthah?"

"Something about a bargain with God," Tuttle said.

"General Jephthah proposed a most terrible covenant," Walter said. "If the Almighty granted him victory over the Ammonites, Jephthah would make a holocaust of the first person he saw upon returning from the war. Little did Jephthah know 'twould be his own virgin daughter comes prancing out to greet him."

"Such a sad story," Tuttle said.

"For a time it confounded me that our Heavenly Father would sanction the sacrifice of an innocent child, but then I saw the solution, shining forth like the *mene mene* on the wall."

"Pray tell."

" 'Tis a simple answer, firm and splendid as a sapphire," Walter said. "Read betwixt the lines in the Book of Judges, and you will see that Jephthah's daughter was assuredly a witch."

A MARK, A MOAT, A LOWLY TOAD. Like the Great Red Hurricane in Jupiter, Jennet's thoughts swirled about a nebulous center, her mind a-jumble with fears and fancies, notions and ghosts. A mark, Satan's kiss, bloodless even after the pricking needle had descended a full half-inch into her aunt's calf—or so Walter had sworn to the Ipswich grand jury. A moat, circumscribing Hadleigh Castle, casting out Isobel before nine sober citizens. And then, finally, "a scabby little hop-toad," as Dunstan told it, "jumping straight toward Aunt Isobel the instant the watching began." A mark, a moat, a lowly toad—plus a parade of witnesses, testifying to Lady Mowbray's plots against them: and so the grand jury had no choice but to return a *billa vera*. Because there was that mark, you see. The moat had spoken. A familiar had appeared. *Maleficium* had occurred.

"Aunt Isobel hath always been kind to you," Jennet told Dunstan. They were tramping through Sowter's Woods, loading their kindling baskets with dead twigs and dry birch-bark. "How can you imagine her covenanting with Satan?"

"I'Christ, I'm sore perplexed. Father bids me take comfort in a prophecy from St. Matthew. 'And a man's foes shall be they of his own household.' "

"Mayhap that's true. But much earlier in Scripture the author of Proverbs tells us, 'He that troubleth his own house shall inherit the wind.' " She stomped each foot on the hard ground, left, right, left, right, seeking to get the blood flowing again to her toes. "Father is troubling his own house, Dunstan. He calls down a great wind upon the posts and beams."

" 'Twould seem he believes that by putting his very own kin in the dock, he shows himself for a cleanser of prodigious integrity."

"His integrity, our aunt."

"Oh, dear Jenny, would that I could reason so prettily as thou. Give me a charcoal stick, and I shall speak sensibly in line and shadow, but words have ne'er been my friends."

"This wind will smite us all. 'Twill lay our family low."

Dunstan sighed mournfully, shuddered visibly, and, declaring his kindling basket full, stalked away.

By the report of Jennet's father, until the spring assizes convened Aunt Isobel would languish in the Great Tower of Colchester Castle, the ancient Norman fortress that now served as Essex County's official prison-house. For reasons that he refused to discuss with either Jennet or Dunstan, Walter had instructed the town magistrate, Caspar Grigsby, that under no conditions should his children be permitted to visit Lady Mowbray or pass her a written message. Never in her life had Jennet known such an agony of frustration. Isobel was living right down the street, and yet she was as inaccessible as if shipwrecked on an uncharted island or banished to the back of the moon.

Despite her father's dictum, Jennet went to the castle every day, marching resolutely through the gloomy vestibule to the warden's station. The chief gaoler, Amos Thurlow, a skittish ex-infantryman who'd lost his left leg to a Parliamentary cannonball during the Siege of Colchester, always seemed genuinely aggrieved to forbid her access to the cell block. "Understand my plight, Miss Stearne," he moaned. "Mr. Grigsby will beat me like a stable boy should I let you pass." Invariably these encounters climaxed with Jennet closing her eyes, sucking in a deep breath, and screaming in the general direction of the Great Tower—"Aunt Isobel! Can you hear me? 'Tis I, your Jenny! I know you ne'er wrote in the Devil's book!"—whereupon the crippled gaoler would grasp her arm with one hand, his crutch with the other, and brusquely escort her back to High Street.

The long winter of 1689 proved the most terrible such season in Jennet's memory. It was as if God had taken up some stupendous prism and split the sun's bounty, so that only a single ray, the cold violet beam at the far edge of the spectrum, reached Essex. Everywhere she looked, ice flourished, hard and inhospitable. Ice stiffened the River Colne and stifled the baize looms of the Dutch Quarter weavers. It sealed the Stearnes' front door, encased their shutters, locked their garden gate, and spiraled downward from their eaves in long inverted cones.

As the frigid weeks elapsed, it became clear to Jennet that her father and brother had forsaken Aunt Isobel, turning against her as finally and emphatically as Othello had broken faith with Desdemona. A stroke of luck for Isobel Mowbray was an *ipso facto* setback for Walter Stearne. Each time he learned that his sister-in-law had purchased some privilege commensurate with her status—candles, clean linen, writing supplies, a hot meal—a fit of indignation would seize him, eyebrow to instep, and he descended into an impacted gloom upon hearing that the celebrated Sir Humphrey Thaxton would act as her advocate, for the man was in Walter's view a shameless conniver who played upon a jury's coarsest prejudices and soggiest sentiments.

" 'Twould mayhap interest you to know that many a scholar and philosopher doth of late reject the demon hypothesis," Jennet informed her father and brother as they sat down to supper on the last day in February. "When Isaac Newton wrote to us, he averred that wicked spirits are but desires of the mind."

"That geometer hath his brilliance, surely," Walter said, sipping claret. "Aye, and so did all those Sadducees bent on denying the existence of angels in the Book of Acts."

"Mr. Newton can prove witchery's a fraud," she said. "He can prove it as surely as he proved that light consists of rays differently refrangible."

"An interesting hypothesis occurs to me," Dunstan said, slicing a morsel from his mutton chop. "Might not Newton be himself a devotee of the black arts?"

"An astute supposition, lad," their father said. "*Cognatis maculis similis fera*. 'Wild beasts are merciful to beasts spotted like themselves.' Juvenal."

"Mr. Newton's no more a Satanist than I'm the Queen of Egypt," Jennet said.

"If not a Satanist"—Dunstan jabbed his fork in Jennet's direction—"then a latter-day Sadducee."

"Recall St. Paul's Letter to the Ephesians," Walter said. " 'For we wrestle not against flesh and blood, but against spiritual wickedness in high places.' These be fearsome difficult times, children. Turmoil in our family. Turmoil in our nation. Orange Billy hath put King James to flight across the channel, but belike 'twill take a war 'twixt England and France to keep him there, for nothing would please King Louis so much as to see his fellow Catholic regain the British Crown."

Jennet was not surprised that her father had diverted the conversation from demonology to government, for recent political events in England had evidently been most astonishing. As she understood the situation, her country had witnessed the abrupt dethronement of one monarch and instant ascent of another—a "Glorious Revolution" people called it, for such an outcome normally required much spillage of blood. James the Second was gone, his powers usurped in name by his daughter, Mary, and in fact by Mary's husband, William of Orange. But the true ambition of Orange Billy—the name amused Jennet, suggesting as it did the buffoonish offspring of a marriage betwixt Bottom and Titania—was not so much to rule England as to make war on his ancient enemy, Louis the Fourteenth. In all probability Englishmen would again be slaughtering Frenchmen and vice versa, an activity for which neither race had ever found a substitute affording the same patriotic and aesthetic satisfactions.

Spring arrived, the sun returned, and the great melting began. By day and by night, Colchester dripped—and yet, though the great star burned hot enough to restore the river and revive the baize looms, its power proved insufficient to ignite pity in either Walter Stearne or his son. A mild April passed, a mellow May, a fecund June, and on the third of July the Court arrived and began conducting assizes in the Moot Hall.

Glancing up from his sketching-folio, Dunstan set his draughting pen in the ravine betwixt adjacent leaves. "Wednesday they convicted a man of horse thievery," he told Jennet. Sister and brother were in the garden, idling away the afternoon, Dunstan sketching, Jennet pruning. "He's already hanged. Yesterday they found a woman guilty of cradle-robbing. She swings at dawn. Tomorrow Judge Bucock is to sentence a treasonous Jacobite."

"And what of our aunt?" she asked, uncoiling a dead vine from the snapdragons.

"The witch-trial commences Monday. 'Tis likely all ten victims will testify."

"The only *victim* in the Moot Hall will be Isobel Mowbray."

Dunstan returned to his drawing—a watering can, a trowel, and a flower pot planted with violets, harmoniously arranged atop the cistern.

"We must not pursue this subject, Jenny, as it promises to ruin our affection for one another."

"Our aunt is no enchantress."

"I am out of words, dear sister."

"She's innocent as the lamb."

"My tongue hath gone all numb."

On Friday morning, shortly after she came awake, an idea took source in Jennet's mind—a beautiful idea, she decided: beautiful, momentous, and terrifying. She sat up in bed. A sunbeam danced atop the counterpane. The idea hovered in the golden air, pulsing like the Holy Grail.

How many miles to Ipswich? Only sixteen, she believed. She could walk there in less than a day. And from Ipswich to Cambridge-Town? About forty-five miles. Two more days on the road, perhaps just one and a half. If she left immediately she might with God's help reach the university as early as Sunday afternoon.

She would go to Ipswich, and thence to Trinity College, bearing Mr. Newton's letter. She would implore the geometer to appear at Colchester Assizes and lay his pretty proof before the Court. "Witchery's an impossible thing," the world's greatest brain would tell the jurymen. "Behold these propositions. Consider these theorems." She would pin a note to her father's door—BOUND FOR CAMBRIDGE, RETURNING SUNDAY—and then she would go. She would sleep in barns, drink from brooks, eat stolen apples. Her feet might blister, but she would go. Highwaymen might rob her, ruffians assail her, but she would go. She would bring back Newton. Before her father awoke, before the town stirred, before the Earth rotated another degree on its phantom shaft, she would go.

The
Third

❖❖❖❖❖❖❖❖❖❖❖

Concerning Robert Hooke,
Antagonist to Isaac Newton
and Author of
the Three Laws of Priapic Motion,
a Triad Certain of Arousing Controversy
Even in an Age of Reason

❖

I f houses were mortal, Jennet thought, if they contained not only wood and stone but also breath and flesh, then Mirringate Hall had surely gone to its grave. Staggering up the tree-lined carriageway, she saw that the manor had passed into the same gray domain occupied by airless moons and anatomized hares. The guardian dogs were nowhere in evidence—stolen away, perhaps, or else in flight from the general despond. In the gardens chaos ruled, threads of bryony stifling the rose campion, weeds strangling the helpless larkspur, beetles consuming the luckless hollyhocks. Someone had shuttered the windows, a discouragement to thieves most likely, or else a protection against urchins wielding rocks, though in Jennet's reeling mind the weathered boards became pennies on the eyes of a corpse.

She mounted the steps to the porch, seized the brass frog, and hammered it thrice against the plate. She waited. The descending twilight cooled her aching flesh. Her knees throbbed. Her stomach rumbled. At length she heard footsteps in the atrium, and then the door swung back to reveal the frowning figure of Rodwell, holding in one hand a beeswax candle and in the other a cocked pistol.

It took her several thousand words and nearly twenty minutes to convince the steward she'd not come to collect evidence against his mistress—*au contraire*, she was here to obtain a document by which she

❖❖❖❖❖

might inspire the great Isaac Newton to visit Colchester Assizes and argue Lady Mowbray's case.

"You're on a dangerous adventure for a mere girl of ten," Rodwell said.

"A mere girl of eleven," she corrected him, "since February the fourth."

He relaxed his scowl, uncocked his pistol, and guided her into the kitchen, where he proceeded to lay out a glorious meal of moldy cheese and stale bread. Whilst preparing his favorite drink, the Oriental beverage called tea, he explained that the other servants had absconded in terror, certain that Lady Mowbray's coven would soon invade the manor and force the staff to participate in unspeakable rites. He himself had declined to join this exodus, for he would "sooner court eternal damnation than compromise an ancient loyalty."

Even as she admired Rodwell's constancy, Jennet realized that recent events at Mirringate had broken him. Never a vigorous man, he displayed his demotion—chief steward to unpaid sentry—in a dozen outward signs, from shuffling gait to stooped demeanor to gelid eye.

"Marry, I do fear for your safety, Miss Stearne." He poured his tea from a ceramic pot into a porcelain bowl. "Even if you were a grown woman, I would bid you abandon this scheme, for the roads 'twixt here and Cambridge-Town be a-swarm with blackguards and brigands."

"All I need do is get to Trinity," she said, gobbling down a hunk of cheese as big as her fist. "If my arguments move Mr. Newton, he will surely escort me back to Colchester."

"I would offer you my lady's carriage, but yesterday a band of scalawags made off with the horses." For a full minute the steward attended to his tea, growing more pensive with each sip. "Now that I think on't, I own no particular views concerning witchery. My strongest opinions involve the maintenance of Turkish carpets. If Mr. Newton's a skeptic in the matter of evil spirits, then I shall be one too!"

Shortly before retiring, Jennet visited the library, its every volume now jacketed in dust. Spiderwebs hung from the globe and its stand, as if the model's gravity had turned material in her absence, manifesting as gossamer strands of attraction. Rushing to the great Bible, she saw that, praise Providence, Newton's letter was still in place, pressed against Exodus 22:18. She removed the missive, slipped it inside the *Principia Mathematica*, and carried the volume to her customary bed-chamber. Thanks to Rodwell's industry, the four-poster lay ready to receive her, and after setting Newton's masterwork beneath her pillow she climbed onto the mattress and fell instantly asleep.

Contrary to one of Elinor Mapes's many preposterous theories, the *Principia*'s proximity did not enhance Jennet's geometric competence that night. Her dreams were devoid of conics, and she awoke no more favorably disposed toward parabolas than when she'd gone to bed. And yet she felt renewed, ready to track down not only Professor Newton but any other natural philosopher who might save Isobel, whether Herr Leibniz in Germany, Signor Malpighi in Italy, or Mijnheer Huygens in Holland.

As dawn yielded to morning, Rodwell fed her a hearty breakfast of radishes, salted ham, and coffee, then gave her a satchel full of hard bread, plus a small calfskin purse a-jingle with coins.

"Come dusk, you must play the Blessed Virgin and seek a room at the inn," he insisted.

"I'm hardly worthy of such a comparison," she said, stuffing the *Principia* into the satchel, "though Aunt Isobel once explained to me what a virgin is, and why I fit the criterion."

"Just promise me you'll abandon all thought of reaching Cambridge-Town today."

"You have my word. Solemn as blood."

"I'll be praying for your protection, Miss Stearne, hour after hour, sometimes silently, sometimes aloud"—he offered a smile that stretched far beyond his few remaining teeth—"till God and all His retainers are positively sick of the subject!"

❦

A GENTIAN-BLUE SKY SHIMMERED above Ipswich as Jennet began the second leg of her journey. Bulbous clouds filled the celestial acreage like fat sheep grazing in a heavenly meadow. Avian melodies wafted through the air, robins, thrushes, wrens, a solitary skylark. If angels had animal familiars, she decided, those servants were surely songbirds.

She had walked barely three miles down the Sudbury Road when a Gypsy wagon came lumbering toward her, drawn by a pair of lacka-daisical dun horses and driven by a plump, agitated man of perhaps thirty-five years, his frazzled red periwig and threadbare gold-lace suit suggesting the wardrobe of a disinherited duke. As he halted his team, Jennet saw that gilded scrollwork decorated the wagon, the curls and spirals framing a lurid red inscription, MUSEUM OF WONDROUS PRODI-GIES, and below that, TEN MONSTERS FOR SIXPENCE, and below that, DR. BARNABY CAVENDISH, CURATOR. The driver—Dr. Cavendish, presumably—cast an inquiring eye on Jennet, doffed his silver-corded hat, and asked whether this road would take him to Mirringate Hall, for he had business with Isobel Mowbray.

"Have you not heard the news? She lies in gaol on a false charge of sorcery."

"Oh, what a *pity*," Dr. Cavendish moaned, peering at her from behind his optical spectacles. "What a *shame*. By reputation she's keen on natural curiosities, and 'twas my intention to sell her this priceless museum of mine, assuming we might agree on a price." He seized a hefty bag of oats and, vaulting to the ground, began feeding the uglier of the two horses. "Whate'er shall I do, Damon?" he asked the swayback. "Solicit Lady Ambrose, I suppose, who's rumored to be of a philosophic bent." He offered Jennet a frolicsome grin. "My monstrosities have fetched me a decent living o'er the years, but now I'm looking to try my hand at indolence."

" 'Tis your lucky day," she said, her plan forming only slightly ahead of her words, "for I happen to be Lady Mowbray's blood-niece. Hear me now. Ere she was imprisoned, my aunt enjoyed a correspondence with the great Isaac Newton. On reaching Cambridge-Town, I shall present myself to this same personage as Mirringate's official"—she took care in pronouncing the word—"*liaison* to Trinity College, then ask him to intervene in her case. I would gladly introduce you to Mr. Newton as an honest impresario with a valuable commodity to sell."

Dr. Cavendish frowned, snorted, and started to nourish the less homely horse. "I must say, Pythias, for a *liaison* this girl doesn't own a very ornate carriage."

With an indignant grunt she pulled the *Principia* from her satchel and whipped out Newton's letter. "If you think I play you false"—she held the document before the curator—"just examine this paper, for't bears the crest of Trinity College."

He snatched the letter away and accorded it a protracted glance. "'Sbody,'tis authentic for fair. Prithee, forgive my misplaced skepticism." The curator clucked his tongue. "Do you really imagine Mr. Newton might fancy my museum? Ten freakish stillborns and fœtuses, collectively portending the end of the world, the coming of the Antichrist, the fornications of the Devil, the treachery of the Quakers, the calumny of the Catholics, the perfidy of the Jews, or the workaday wrath of God, depending on your religion."

"'Tis probable you'll find a customer at the university—if not Mr. Newton, then a sage of his acquaintance."

"B'm'faith, you've hatched a splendid scheme!" Dr. Cavendish declared, handing back the letter. "Join me in the driver's box, child, and we'll be off to hobnob with the Platonists!"

For the first time since Aunt Isobel's arrest, the Great Jovian Hurricane lifted from Jennet's soul and blew away. Perhaps Barnaby Cavendish was a scoundrel, but he seemed at worst an imbalanced mountebank and quite possibly a true benefactor. If her luck held firm, she and Mr. Newton would stand face-to-face by sundown.

In her eleven years Jennet had known people who talked much and yet said little, such as Elinor Mapes, and also people who talked little and yet said much, such as Rodwell, but until meeting Dr. Cavendish she'd never encountered anyone who both talked much and said much. His life's history was tortuous but rarely tedious, byzantine but hardly boring. She recalled one of Aunt Isobel's favorite maxims, *Comes jucundus in via pro vehiculo est:* "An agreeable companion on the road is as good as a coach." And now, suddenly, she had both.

Orphaned by the plague at age nine, Dr. Cavendish had survived for many years through what he termed "the ancient craft of soliciting alms" and "the demanding art of theft." Though not in fact a doctor of any kind, he'd studied natural philosophy for six months at Christ's College, Oxford, eluding starvation via a sizarship, "running errands and emptying chamber-pots for the highborn students." Amongst his clients were several scholars whose passions ran to anatomy and embryology, and his frequent visits to the dissection theatres soon instilled in him "an undying affection for Nature's mistakes." Before leaving Oxford, he'd learned not only "how to fix a fœtal monster in brine" but also "how to convince the average Englishman that touching the preservation jar will bring him luck."

"I should like to see your specimens," Jennet said.

"Nay, I must refuse you," he said, "as they're not a sight for an innocent girl, even so worldly an innocent girl as yourself."

Ten miles beyond Sudbury, Dr. Cavendish grew excited when they came upon a dilapidated inn, the Fiddling Pig, and he forthwith quit the road, directed Damon and Pythias through a stone archway decorated with a sculpted swine playing a viol, and parked the wagon in the courtyard. He snatched up a sheaf of handbills and scurried off, hopeful of enticing some patrons away from their ale and into the sixpenny fascinations of his museum.

Shortly after the curator's departure, Jennet realized that her curiosity concerning their forbidden cargo had swelled into a preoccupation. Durst she spy? Yes, she decided, for whilst the idea of seeing fœtal prodigies troubled her, the idea of being afraid to see them troubled her even more.

She slunk her way to the rear of the wagon and furtively ascended the stepladder. The door opened outward. Fumbling in the gloom, she soon found the tinderbox, then lit the ensconced candles.

Figures emerged from the darkness, bottled things with woeful redundancies and distressing deficits. For an instant it seemed that she'd been shrunk to the size of a gnat's eye and placed in a dollop of pond scum, so uncannily did the prodigies suggest the creatures she'd observed through Aunt Isobel's microscope. She steeled herself and, starting on her left, examined the specimens one by one, each a-float in a protective fluid and sporting a label giving not only its name but also a preposterous account of its postnatal adventures.

The first exhibit, the Kali of Droitwich, was a four-armed female foetus. In Jennet's recollection, the original Kali had six arms, but this was still an impressive abomination. Then came the Lyme Bay Fish-Boy, who had no arms at all, only flipperlike protrusions, his ancestry further expressed by the dozen scales on his chest. She disagreed with Dr. Cavendish's decision to call the next specimen the Sussex Rat-Baby, for whilst the pathetic creature was indeed covered with fur and bore a long pink tail, he looked more like a monkey than a rat. Continuing her investigations, she contemplated the Cyclops of Bourne with his single staring orb, large as a lemon . . . the Bird-Child of Bath, adorned head to toe with feathery excrescences . . . the Smethwick Philosopher, his brains bursting from his fractured skull . . . the Tunbridge Wells Bloodsucker, each tooth as sharp as an embroidery needle . . . the Bicephalic Girl, her left head proportioned pleasingly, her right hideous and misshapen. The last two prodigies were the most unnerving. Jennet could not bear to linger by either Perdition's Pride, his face a horrid mass of naked muscles and exposed bone, or the Maw of Folkestone, who had no face at all, only a gaping hole.

As Jennet climbed down the stepladder, her eyes throbbing as they passed from the darkness of the wheeled grotto to the bright summer sun, Dr. Cavendish escorted two orange-liveried soldiers toward the wagon, a private and a corporal in King William's army. Assessing the situation, the curator grew visibly wroth—clenched teeth, a disapproving frown—but then he immediately amended this emotion with a conspiratorial wink.

"Ah, I see my customer hath finished her tour," he said. "I'll warrant she was *quite edified.*"

" 'Twas easily the best use I e'er made of sixpence," she said, hopping to the ground. "Your Fish-Boy is a wonder to behold. I shan't forget your Rat-Baby if I live to be a hundred."

"Glad you liked 'em, child! And now, brave soldiers—"

"Not only is the Bicephalic Girl amongst the world's most amazing creatures, she hath completely cured my toothache," Jennet continued. "And the Smethwick Philosopher made short work of my warts."

"At the Cavendish Museum of Wondrous Prodigies," the curator said quickly, "we always aim to please."

Jennet considered that she might be overdoing it, but elected to press on. "As for the Cyclops of Bourne—"

" 'Tis a show of manifold riches," Dr. Cavendish interrupted brusquely. The ruse had evidently run its course. "There be no better collection in Christendom."

"I'faith, I've ne'er seen a girl with two heads," the private said, placing sixpence in Dr. Cavendish's palm.

"I'm intrigued by this child who's also a fish," the corporal said, likewise paying his admission.

Whilst the soldiers clambered into the museum, Dr. Cavendish flashed Jennet a smile of exceeding complexity. With a single curl of his lip he managed to convey a general appreciation for her cleverness, a specific gratitude for her performance, and a sharp warning not to imagine herself better at mongering prodigies than he. It was a smile, she mused, worth preserving in a jar.

THE POOR TURNOUT from the Fiddling Pig irritated and depressed Dr. Cavendish—a twelve-pence profit, he declared, was more humiliating than none—with the effect that, after traveling another twenty miles, he insisted on visiting a second such ordinary, the Ram's Head. This time around, nine men followed him out of the tavern, and, thanks in part to Jennet's chicanery, they all became paying customers. True, two patrons declared the foetuses fraudulent and demanded their money back, but, as Dr. Cavendish explained, such "narrow-minded skepticism" commonly plagued the prodigy trade, and he was in high spirits by the time they left the Ram's Head, boisterously promising that the Museum of Wondrous Prodigies would proceed directly to Trinity College.

As the flat, swampy environs of Cambridge-Town rolled into view, Jennet decided to entrust Dr. Cavendish with the particulars of her mission. He proved a sympathetic audience, for it happened that forty years earlier his maternal grandfather, "a harmless dabbler in charms and potions," had been beheaded for a sorcerer in Alsace. If Isaac Newton had indeed fallen upon a mathematical disproof of witchery, then Dr. Cavendish could imagine "no better an ambition than to turn this discovery into common knowledge."

Even though the entire university was now wrapped in the murk of dusk, its Gothic spires, clanging clock towers, stained-glass saints, and marble monarchs suffused Jennet with the sort of awe she normally experienced only whilst contemplating planets through a telescope.

" 'Tis as if the very heart of Heaven hath dropped from the clouds and settled upon the English fens," she said.

"If not the heart, then surely one of the better neighborhoods," Dr. Cavendish said.

They left the Gypsy wagon at Hobson's Livery, hard by St. Benedict's Church, then followed their instincts westward along cobblestoned alleys to the placid, mossy waters of the River Cam. Bantering amongst themselves whilst tossing pebbles into the slow current, three young men in black robes and scholars' caps milled about on a stone footbridge, its walls decorated at regular intervals by granite spheres the size of cabbages. Dr. Cavendish puffed himself up and, approaching the trio, asked whether they were perchance under the tutelage of Isaac Newton.

"Ah, Professor Newton," said the tall scholar with mock enthusiasm. "Isn't Newton the sage wrote that book neither he or anyone else understands?"

Laughter pealed from all three students.

"Say, lads, I hear Newton once challenged God to a game of chess," the pocked scholar noted. "He offered the Almighty a pawn advantage and the first move."

More laughter rang through the twilight.

"Last January a score of us ventured to take instruction from the man," the fat scholar explained to Dr. Cavendish. "We could make no sense of his inaugural lecture, and e'er since then he's been—I swear it—he's been spouting his hydrostatics to an empty hall."

The students had a half-dozen more Newton stories at the ready, and by being an appreciative audience Jennet and Dr. Cavendish eventually came to possess the long-sought-for fact: the geometer occupied rooms in Great Court, second floor, a suite fortuitously indicated by the pointing scepter of the sculpted King Henry VIII surmounting the main gate.

Although she desired to track down their quarry at once, Dr. Cavendish insisted that she was too hungry and tired to make a persuasive presentation. There was wisdom in this argument, she reasoned, and so she let him lead her to a nearby public-house, the Turk's Head in Green Street, where they renewed themselves with beef and drink—a tankard of ale for the curator, a dish of coffee for Jennet. All during supper she practiced aloud her plea to Newton, a performance that brought to Dr. Cavendish's face an expression combining perplexity with admiration.

"You talk of the inverse-square law, and I'm thoroughly puzzled," he told her. "You discourse upon action at a distance, and I'm entirely confounded. You speak about refrangible rays, and 'tis all opaque to me. In short, my remarkable young friend, thou hast mastered the art of obfuscation, and if our man's not completely dazzled, then I say the Devil take him!"

✸✸

DWARFISH, HUNCHED, CONCEITED, AND BRILLIANT, Robert Hooke disliked resorting to deviousness when seeking proper credit for his genius, but the malice of his rivals oft-times required that he stoop to their station. The knavery he now so meticulously enacted was in his view utterly necessitated by the knavery that begat it. Had the arrogant Isaac Newton deigned even once to count Hooke his equal in philosophy, he would never have been reduced to riding out from London, skulking around Great Court, and invading the blackguard's rooms.

The conditions were ideal. Newton was away at Woolsthorpe, supervising the planting on his mother's farm, and his rooming-companion, John Wickins, had left Cambridge-Town permanently to become a clergyman in Stoke Edith. Gleefully Hooke set about his task. In the depths of his bones he knew that Newton and Wickins were guilty of the grossest indecencies, and with luck he would discover evidence on the premises. He began with the writing-desk, eventually locating nine letters, the most pathetic being an appeal for money from a Grantham apothecary, the most peculiar being a query from a landed Ipswich woman who thought gravitation had something to do with witchcraft, the most compelling being Hooke's own speculations concerning the lunar irregularities. Newton was a sodomite—of this Hooke was certain. The world would learn of his depravity—to this end Hooke was pledged. All he needed was one incriminating epistle, a single revealing journal entry, or a solitary love token, salaciously inscribed.

The desk contained no such treasure. He moved on to the wardrobe, inverting the pockets of Newton's breeches and waistcoats.

The great rivalry stretched back to 1672, when the Royal Society had asked Hooke, as Curator of Experiments, to endorse Newton's essay called "A New Theory About Light and Colors" prior to its publication in the *Transactions*. Hooke, with good reason, had declined. Any competent philosopher knew better than to leap from mere facts to grand hypotheses, and yet near the end of his treatise Newton had done just that, venturing that light must be corpuscular, not wavelike, in nature—a lapse that Hooke had conscientiously brought to the Society's attention. Sadly, the affair did not end there, for Newton had proceeded to bully and harass his peers into demanding that Hooke give the essay another look. They even bid him re-create the experiments in question. Re-create them! As if the author of the renowned *Micrographia* was so obtuse that only the most tangible demonstration could penetrate his brain!

The wardrobe, alas, held no damning papers. Hooke lit a candle, dropped to his knees, and searched under the bed.

For nearly a decade he had stoically borne the Humiliation of 1672, until finally a golden opportunity presented itself. With typical smugness Newton had offered the Society what he claimed was the last word on the Tall-Tower Problem: his calculations putatively showed that an object dropped from a twenty-mile-high minaret would, owing to the Earth's rotation, describe a spiral and land eastward. But the jackanapes had erred! The dropped object would travel eastward only if the minaret stood on the Equator, and furthermore the path of descent would be elliptical! At the Society's next meeting, Hooke did his duty, exposing Newton's blunder and presenting the correction.

There were no tell-tale epistles under the bed, so he proceeded to the bookshelves. Systematically he removed each volume and shook it, seeking to dislodge the *littera crusis*.

Someone knocked on the door, causing Hooke's pulse to accelerate, his arteries to distend, and his cunning to construct a narrative. Yes, he was indeed prowling through Newton's personal possessions, but only to acquire proof that the geometer had pirated the inverse-square law from him, a formula accorded much uncredited display in Book Three of the *Principia Mathematica*.

"Come in!"

A peculiar pair strode into the room. Leading the way was a prepubescent girl, her arms encircling a copy of Newton's bloated treatise. Behind her came a bewigged and stumpish man who looked as if he'd just finished portraying a jolly gnome in a dumb-show for children.

"Prithee, forgive our unsolicited arrival, Professor Newton," said the girl, quavering with anxiety, "but 'tis desperation brings me to your door."

"Listen to my young mistress," the gnome said, "a child of the rarest intelligence."

The girl approached Hooke and fixed him with the pleading stare of a water spaniel. "Only the author of the *Principia Mathematica* can save the day."

"Methinks you exaggerate," Hooke said, wondering how he might profit by the intruders' error. "There be many brilliant men in England. Robert Hooke, for example."

The girl said, "Mr. Hooke's *Micrographia* is an authentic masterwork—"

"Indeed."

"But hear me out. My maternal aunt is Lady Mowbray of Mirringate Hall, the very philosopher with whom you corresponded last summer concerning a possible relationship 'twixt wicked spirits and your gravitation."

"Ah . . ." Hooke muttered, recalling the absurd query he'd read twenty minutes earlier.

"Through the machinations of a vicar, a magistrate, and my own misguided father, Isobel Mowbray hath been wrongly accused of witchery," the girl continued. "Come Monday, she goes before Colchester Assizes."

"I don't mean to sound mistrustful, child," Hooke said, "but if you're a landed woman's niece, why doth your servant dress like a beggar?"

"I'm nobody's servant, sir, save your own," the gnome said. "Call me Dr. Barnaby Cavendish. I shall state my business betimes, but first I ask that you consider Miss Stearne's proposal."

The girl lifted the cover of her *Principia* and slipped out a folded sheet, passing it to Hooke. "In your letter to my aunt, you told her that demons are but desires of the mind."

Hooke studied the alleged missive from Newton. It was indeed written in his constipated hand, and it indeed demeaned wicked spirits as but "desires of the mind." At least the jackanapes was right about one thing: despite what Glanvill, Boyle, and those other Platonist pud-pounders believed, it was preposterous to imagine Lucifer's troops raising a tempest or desiccating a cow at the mere solicitation of a hag.

He turned to the girl and said, "Tell me your tale in full."

For the next quarter-hour the Stearne child outlined her plan. Although Lady Mowbray had retained the celebrated Sir Humphrey Thaxton as her advocate, she explained, the prosecution's case remained formidable. If England's most eminent natural philosopher were to address the jury on Lady Mowbray's behalf, however, offering his "pretty proof" against witchery, she would surely avoid the noose.

Hooke deposited his rump on the chair behind Newton's desk and descended into a profound meditation. This was not the first time a Royal Society fellow had been asked to attend a witch-trial and gainsay the demon hypothesis. Shortly before he died, Oldenberg had intervened in a sorcery case, though the obtuse jury still returned a guilty verdict; in 1681 Wren had attempted to deliver a Northhampton virago from the gallows, but his noble efforts went for naught; the following year Halley had bootlessly employed his prestige on behalf of a supposed warlock at Chelmsford Assizes. And so it was that an exquisite design now blossomed in Hooke's imagination. He would indeed go to Colchester: not with the intention of saving the defendant—enough philosophers had wasted their energies on such endeavors—but to show the world the bedrock debauchery that lay beneath the facade called Isaac Newton.

"I feel close to a decision in this matter," Hooke said to the Stearne child, "but I wish to know more about your friend." Rising, he stared at the gnome and asked, "What brings *thee* to Trinity, *Doctor* Cavendish?" He hoped his sardonic pronunciation of "Doctor" registered with the man.

"For the better part of my career," Cavendish said, "I've been curator to a museum of fœtal astonishments, assembled o'er the course of my worldwide travels. I now hope to sell 'em to your Royal Society."

This prodigy-monger was doubtless a scoundrel, and yet his proposition, like the child's, might be turned to advantage. "Sir, I fear you mean to deceive me," Hooke said. "You have acquired your monsters not by going round the world but by loitering round the morgue. I shan't hold your grandiloquence against you, however, for't happens that the Royal Society is seeking to expand its anatomical collection. If yours be worthy prodigies, they have in sooth found a buyer." And as the man who discovered the Cavendish trove, Hooke thought, I am likely to become Curator of Biological Specimens, with all concomitant honors.

"I shall confer 'em at an exceeding reasonable price," Cavendish declared.

"You shall rob us blind if you can, myopic at the least," Hooke said. "We offer eight guineas apiece for such freaks. Take it or leave it."

"Verily, sir, I shall take it!"

"The Society gathers in London come Friday. You and I shall conclude our business then and there." Hooke condescended to draw near Cavendish, close enough to suffer the man's rancid breath. "Now, concerning this girl's request, I must ask you a question, scholar to scholar. Does it not seem probable that the jurymen will disdain the testimony of one so stooped and stunted as myself?"

"Methinks the average Colchester citizen would indeed expect the paragon of mathematicians to display a rather different geometry," Cavendish replied. "Aye, but once they hear your lapidary speech, they are certain to o'erlook your dilapidated frame."

"A most logical supposition." Hooke, turning, presented the child with his warmest smile. "It pleases me to report I've reached a favorable conclusion regarding your scheme."

Barely had the word "conclusion" escaped his lips than his young petitioner set her *Principia* on Newton's desk and flung her arms about his trunk in a gesture of delirious joy. Much to his dismay, the girl overtopped him by an inch.

"My aunt hath oft-times compared thee to our Savior," she said. "Her meaning's now entirely clear to me!"

Hooke stifled a moan. Newton as Christ? A ludicrous notion at best. "I see you own a copy of my *Principia*," he said, gesturing toward the jackanapes's badly organized amalgam of Euclid, Kepler, and Galileo. "If you like, I shall inscribe it."

"Accept his offer, Miss Stearne," Cavendish said. " 'Twill certainly increase its value."

"Sir, I should be grateful," she said.

Hooke dipped quill into ink pot. "Your associate speaks truthfully," he told the girl. "Indeed, the only tome liable to fetch a better price than a signed *Principia* would be a *Lectiones Cutlerianæ* bearing Mr. Hooke's autograph."

Whilst Cavendish and the child looked on with approving smiles, he opened the *Principia* and decorated the title-page with the words *Isaac Newton.*

Later that night, asleep in his room at the Crow's Nest, Hooke dreamed that he and Newton were testing their rival solutions to the Tall-Tower Problem. To demonstrate how the Earth's spin affected a descending object, Hooke drew forth his dirk, sliced Newton's breeches,

amputated his cods, and tossed the pair off a lofty crag. Newton's manhood
followed an elliptical path to the ground. Waking near dawn, Hooke
carefully reviewed the reverie, and the more he thought
about it, the farther he fell into an
intense tranquility and an
exceeding

※

Peace,
I believe, is the
most desirable of all political
arrangements, whether its beneficiaries are
nations, clans, marriages, or books. Yes, pitched battles
have their glory and spectacle, but peace reverses war's cruel algorithms,
and so I much prefer it. When my insectile agents came to me last week
and announced that the *Malleus Maleficarum* desired a truce, I instructed
them to prepare the necessary documents. We would leave our biblio-
phagic armies in the field—the field in this case being a vacant lot on
Fortieth Street in midtown Manhattan—but there would be no immediate clash of arms.

So now I have time on my hands. I spent yesterday afternoon toying
with the famous puzzle of the Monkeys and the Typewriters. Would you
like to try it? This is not the usual dusty old math problem, I promise you.
You'll have fun. Really. While you'll be obliged to employ an unen-
thralling operation, raising a number to various powers, the results will
prove entirely antic.

The conundrum in question originates with Thomas Henry Huxley's
famous illustration of the rôle played by chance in biological evolution.
Huxley noted that if you sat a thousand immortal monkeys down at a
thousand indestructible typewriters, they would eventually produce,
along with a considerable quantity of nonsense, all the works of Shakespeare. I've decided to raise the stakes. Instead of settling for Shakespeare, let's have our immortal monkeys generate every book ever
written. No, better yet, every book ever written, plus every book that ever
will be written, plus every book that never was and never will be written.

Now. Here's the problem. *How many unique manuscripts would such a library contain?*

If we permit the monkeys to compose entirely in lower-case letters, then each keyboard will comprise 45 buttons: 26 Roman characters plus 10 Arabic numerals (including zero), a period, a comma, a question mark, a colon, a dash, a pair of parentheses, a carriage return, and a space bar. For purposes of the experiment, assume that each manuscript contains 600 pages of 25 lines each, 60 characters to the line.

I'll give you a minute.

Want another minute? Fine.

Figured it out?

For those of you who got stuck, the number of unique manuscripts produced by Huxley's immortal monkeys is 45 raised to the 60th power to the 25th power to the 600th power, that is, the operation of 45 multiplied by 45 carried out 900,000 times.

We're talking about a large library. In fact, we're talking about an *unimaginably* large library, a Fechnerian labyrinth, a Borgesian honeycomb, a bibliographic phenomenon that would fill the known universe to overflowing. But we're not talking about an infinite library—not by a long shot.

Somewhere in the Thomas Henry Huxley Memorial Library is an exact reproduction of the Holy Bible. Somewhere in the Huxley Memorial Library is an exact reproduction of the Holy Bible with a series of haiku about pizza toppings substituted for the Book of Daniel. Somewhere in the Huxley Memorial Library is a version of *Gone With the Wind* in which Scarlett O'Hara enjoys a ménage-à-trois with Rhett Butler and Ashley Wilkes. There is also a version in which Scarlett O'Hara enjoys a ménage-à-trois with Rhett Butler and Ashley Wilkes while they all prove Fermat's Last Theorem together. And a version in which Scarlett O'Hara enjoys a ménage-à-trois with Socrates and the Marquis de Sade while Rhett Butler fellates Ashley Wilkes on Saint Andrews links during the World Cup.

Somewhere in the Huxley Memorial Library, a completely effective treatment for human liver cancer is described in full. There is also a detailed but bogus refutation of that treatment, a truthful refutation of the bogus refutation, and a bogus refutation of the truthful refutation of the bogus refutation, the latter featuring a cameo appearance by Jack the Ripper offering tips for housebreaking your llama.

And somewhere in the Thomas Henry Huxley Memorial Library lies a perfect facsimile of *Philosophiæ Naturalis Principia Mathematica*.

But it is not signed by my father.

Nor is it signed by Robert Hooke pretending to be my father.

Mere words are inadequate for communicating the revulsion I suffered when the Curator of Experiments violated me in that manner. Were such encounters reducible to mathematics, I would convey my aversion by first calculating the quantity of delight I felt when Jennet held me in her hands that day in Isobel's library and then determining the reciprocal of that ecstasy.

You must remain mindful, however, that the true villains of my story are not depraved persons but psychotic theologies. Given enough time, I could identify and celebrate a dozen virtues in Robert Hooke—or Andrew Pound—or even Walter Stearne. In Stearne's case, for example, there is no question that he loved his daughter. Indeed, the more firmly I set my mind to the task, the more clearly I recall that, after reading of Jennet's reckless intention to visit Cambridge,

he endured a remorse ɑo profound as to squeeze from his psyche

all other ɑensations. Only hours later, upon apprehending

the purpose behind her journey, did Walter

experience the feeling

you humans

term

❦

Anger

had oft-times

burned in the breast of

Walter Stearne, anger over the

stupidity of jurists, the dexterity of demons, and

the guile of witches, but none of his former furies could compare

with the rage he felt against Isobel Mowbray shortly after he entered her

luxuriously appointed prison-cell in the Great Tower, showed her the terse message from Jennet—BOUND FOR CAMBRIDGE, RETURNING SUNDAY—and demanded that she interpret it.

" 'Twould be my supposition she means to involve Professor Newton in the trial," Isobel said.

"Dost mean *Isaac* Newton?" Walter asked, livid and perplexed.

"The same." Evidently seeking to relieve an itch, she slid her hand across her scalp, its fleshly terrain recently made barren by Walter's razor in his search for Satanic excrescences. " 'Tis doubtful, of course, that Newton could attend the assizes on such short notice. If such comes to pass, however, he'll argue not only for my innocence but for greeting all cries of witchery with skepticism."

"Then he'll be declaring himself a friend to heretics, a traitor to faith, and an enemy of the King. Mark me, Lady Mowbray, the cleansing enterprise is no respecter of persons. During this century the Paracelsus trident and the *Malleus Maleficarum* have snared many a mortal as eminent as Newton."

Isobel finished rubbing her dome. "My dear, foolish brother-in-law, will you not see that all is lost when we permit books to do our thinking for us? Not even Scripture deserves such sovereignty, much less Krämer and Sprenger."

" 'Twould appear you would spit on both."

"The Bible is safe from my saliva, but I would not scruple to plunge your hoary *Malleus* into a vat of hog's bile."

Before Walter left her prison-cell, Isobel deigned to make a helpful observation concerning Jennet's possible location. Knowing that Newton's letter might prove essential to her mission, the child had quite likely begun her adventure by tramping to Mirringate Hall.

Thus it was that early on Saturday morning Walter roused the Colchester constable, an enterprising Anabaptist named Elihu Wedderburn, and hired him to ride posthaste to Ipswich, interview Mistress Mowbray's employees, and use any information thus obtained in tracking down Jennet. At noon the following day Wedderburn reported back. Jennet had indeed visited Mirringate, he told Walter, and she was indeed in quest of Newton: such at least was the story told by the estate's chief steward, Rodwell. Upon apprehending this news, Wedderburn had galloped to Cambridge-Town and made appropriate inquiries at Trinity College, but evidently no one had noticed the wayward girl.

Dusk found Walter in his garden, smoking his pipe and battling a despair not far from despondency, when a curious caravan appeared in Wyre Street. First came a dwarfish hunchback, dressed like a coxcomb in velvet waistcoat and silver-buckled boots, his pate adorned by a frothy chestnut periwig surmounted by a tricorn. He sat astride a tan horse, its withers speckled like a grouse egg. Two harnessed horses followed, straining to pull a decrepit Gypsy wagon, its sides emblazoned with the words, MUSEUM OF WONDROUS PRODIGIES—TEN MONSTERS FOR SIXPENCE—DR. BARNABY CAVENDISH, CURATOR. In the driver's box reposed a stout, cherubic man, holding the reins and wearing ill-matched castoff clothes.

But the father said to his servants, Bring forth the best robe, and put it on him; and put a ring on his hand, and shoes on his feet. And bring hither the fatted calf, and kill it. Never before had that particular parable touched Walter so deeply. When he saw his daughter sitting beside Dr. Barnaby Cavendish, he experienced only the mildest urge to beat her senseless with a quarterstaff. On balance he felt exceeding joy. "Jennet!" he cried, vaulting over the garden gate and rushing to meet the parade, which by now had come to a stop. *For this my son was dead, and is alive again; he was lost, and is found.* "Oh, my darling child, praise all the saints, thou hast returned!"

Jennet gestured toward the dwarf. "Father, I'm pleased to present Isaac Newton."

Walter halted abruptly, as if his heels had become mired in joiner's glue. 'Steeth, she'd actually done it—she'd coerced the Arian heretic into appearing at the witch-trial!

"Good evening, Professor Newton," Walter effused with mock deference. How strange that, though Newton's reputation for genius had proceeded him, no rumor of his crooked frame had ever found its way to Colchester. "Our entire town is honored by your visit."

The geometer dismounted and, doffing his tricorn, shook Walter's hand. "I am likewise honored to be here—and *particularly* honored to stand in your presence, for the Pricker of Colchester enjoys a formidable reputation within the Royal Society."

"How's that? You've *heard* of me?"

"In my circle thou art known as Satan's bane," Newton said.

A sudden warmth flowed through Walter, as if he'd consumed several swallows of Barbados rum. "Truly, now?"

"Truly. I hope that our differing views on the pliancy of demons shan't prevent us, as two learned gentlemen, from visiting a public-house ere long and immersing ourselves in ale and metaphysics."

"Satan's bane?"

"Quite so. I am passing eager to tell the estimable Mr. Hooke, from whom I appropriated the inverse-square law, that I've met you in the flesh."

Walter performed a rapid mental calculation: if the Crown could drag out its case over four or five days, Newton might become so frustrated—or feel so affronted—that instead of addressing the jury he would return to Trinity College in a huff. "I must thank you profoundly for protecting my daughter."

"The hero of the hour is *this* man here"—Newton indicated the prodigy-monger, whose fat face broke into a smile—"for he shepherded Miss Stearne all the way from Ipswich to Cambridge-Town."

Although this Cavendish was manifestly a rapscallion and a boor, the rules of conviviality required that Walter now bid his two visitors join him in the garden for a mug of cider or a glass of shrub. Blessedly, Cavendish declined the invitation, explaining that he wished to show his museum about the town, and Newton likewise tendered his regrets, citing a desire to speak with Lady Mowbray's barrister.

After her new friends had departed, Walter looked Jennet directly in the eye, his irate blood pulsing in his jaw. "Child, you must ne'er again go running off like that."

"I had no wish to cause thee unhappiness, sir."

"I am much of a mind to birch you."

"That is thy prerogative."

"Professor Newton hath no business at this trial."

"I disagree," she said.

"Dost not love thy father?" he asked.

"I bear thee considerable love, sir, but I love my Aunt Isobel as well, who would have me love truth above all else."

"Truth's a mystery, as we learn in John 18:38. I won't see you in the Moot Hall tomorrow. Is that a firm and lucid fact?"

"Aye, Father," she replied in a tone of marginal impertinence. "Firm as a hobnail. Lucid as a scrying-glass."

Three hours later, having further reprimanded his prodigal daughter with a slap on the cheek and a cuff to the ear, Walter walked to the Red Lion, where Judge Harold Bucock and his entourage had been in residence since the start of the assizes, interviewing witnesses, planning strategies, and emptying tankards. For the fifth time that week, Walter sought out the Crown's advocate, Hugh Collop, a man as nimble of body as of mind, adept at swimming, shooting, riding, and bowls. The two anti-Satanists assumed their favorite table by the hearth, Walter sipping a saucer of coffee, Mr. Collop quaffing ale.

Learning of Newton's unexpected arrival on the scene, Collop exhibited a surprising dearth of dismay. "Have no fear," he told Walter. "We needn't protract our case merely to keep this wily popinjay off the witness-stand." Elaborating, Collop predicted that under no circumstances would Judge Bucock allow Newton to rail against the principle of diabolism per se. Even if the geometer managed to waft out some perplexing equation that putatively refuted the demon hypothesis, Bucock would silence him with Scripture—Exodus 22:18 and its unassailable brethren.

This forecast struck Walter as plausible, and hence he returned to Wyre Street with a buoyant gait and a song on his lips. So cheerful was his mood, in fact, that he invited Dunstan and Jennet to join him for an evening of five-card lanterloo. His daughter refused, adducing an unsettled stomach, and consequently father and son played alone. All during the game Jennet sat by the hearth humming "Rare Willie Drowned in Yarrow" whilst contemplating a small glass prism.

Alas, the lanterloo match quickly turned tedious, ruined by the law of averages. For every trick Walter won, Dunstan took a trick as well. Each of

Walter's payments for loo was eventually matched by an identical sacrifice from Dunstan.

"A person could more easily make his fortune wagering on a one-legged wrestler," Walter said with a quick laugh.

"Or a one-armed archer," Dunstan snickered.

"Or a cock without a beak," Walter said, tittering.

Whether by clumsiness or intent, Jennet dropped her prism, which struck the wooden floor with a resounding thud. "A person could more easily make his fortune," she said, invective dribbling from the corners of her mouth, "wagering that demons cannot be disproved."

※

SHORTLY AFTER SUNRISE Walter and Dunstan slid into their softest woolen hose, buttoned up their best ruffled day-shirts, put on their velvet waistcoats, and betook themselves to the Moot Hall. No sooner had the master pricker seated his son in the spectators' gallery, right behind the seedy Dr. Cavendish, than the lad took out his sketching-folio and began creating a waxen portrait of his Aunt Isobel, who sat inertly in the defendant's box, her bald head concealed by a plain woolen cap. Assuming his rightful place at the prosecution table, Walter settled back to enjoy Satan's latest defeat at the hands of English justice.

In his long black robe and spotless white periwig, Harold Bucock presented a rational and authoritative figure, and it soon became apparent that he ran an equally rational and authoritative courtroom. It took him but ten minutes to silence the hall, elicit Isobel Mowbray's plea ("Guilty only of naïveté, for ere my arrest I failed to see that prickers do the Devil's work"), and instruct the Crown's advocate to interrogate his witnesses.

Although Ipswich was a full fifteen miles away, every one of the defendant's victims had managed to reach Colchester—their desire to see Lucifer humiliated, Walter sensed, had inspired them no less than the promise of unlimited ale and *gratis* lodgings—and by day's end six honest Englishmen had offered testimony, persuasive by dint of its ineloquence, to the depravity of the accused.

A particularly vivid statement came from a land surveyor, Nicholas Fian, who confessed to receiving money from a certain nameless baron, that a boundary dispute might go against Lady Mowbray. Two days after submitting his corrupt findings, Fian had watched in horror as a wolf carried his youngest child into the forest. Almost as harrowing was the testimony of a miller, Godfrey Hawke, who claimed that, a week after he'd sold a dozen wormy sacks of flour to Mirringate Hall, his wife had tripped and fallen beneath the grindstone, consequently suffering a crushed leg and a mangled hand.

All during her victims' recitations, Walter's sister-in-law remained perfectly still, her expression fixed, eyes frozen, as if some errant Medusa had turned her body to granite. Isaac Newton, by contrast, observed the proceedings in a state of great animation. Often as not he would commit a witness's remarks to paper, writing with a frenzy matched only by the industrious pen of the official scrivener, and he counterpointed each testimony with loud incoherent mutterings, so that Bucock was repeatedly obliged to beg his silence.

The following morning the four remaining witnesses told their stories, the last such narrative, from a huntsman named Ezra Trevor, being especially memorable. After illegally bagging a deer on Lady Mowbray's estate, Mr. Trevor had come home to find his cottage overrun by centipedes. One of the vermin had bitten his youngest daughter, who fell into a delirium when the poison reached her brain, her fever breaking only after sixteen hours of thrashing agony.

Bucock declared a noontime recess, and within five minutes the entire population of the Moot Hall had transplanted itself to the Red Lion. Needing a clear head for his upcoming performance, Walter abstained from ale and cider, consuming only some cold beef and a glass of shrub. Hugh Collop's witnesses passed the interval consoling each other over the incommensurate reprisals with which the defendant had punished their peccadilloes.

At one o'clock the Court reconvened, and shortly thereafter Collop called Colchester's celebrated master pricker to testify.

Mayhap because Lady Mowbray occupied such a lofty social station, Walter found himself reporting the results of the witch-tests in terms more poetic than usual. He spoke of the trident's "plaintive peal" as it indicted the Devil's mark on Isobel's calf, of the moat's "poignant gurglings" as it expelled her flesh, and of the "guttural chant" the toad-familiar had sung upon reunion with its mistress.

For the climax of his presentation, the Crown's advocate put Roger Mapes on the witness-stand. Solemnly the Vicar of Ipswich explained why he had removed his daughter from the defendant's baleful influence. His reasons included not only Lady Mowbray's practice of "sacrificing beasts to Lucifer" but also her "wizardry with prisms" and her "unrestrained penchant for dragging Our Lord and Savior Jesus Christ down to the level of the Arian geometer Isaac Newton." How clever of Collop, Walter thought, to elicit Newton's name at this juncture. How cunning of him to poison the very waters in which Humphrey Thaxton sought to float his client's case.

During the first two days of the trial, Colchester's gossip merchants had gleefully trafficked in the rumor that a celebrated English philosopher would testify for the defense. Some guessed John Locke, others Robert Hooke, still others Edmund Halley. Thus it was that on Wednesday morning at nine o'clock, when Sir Humphrey inaugurated his presentation by summoning Isaac Newton, Lucasian Professor of Mathematics at Trinity College, the gasps that rushed through the Moot Hall issued not from surprise but from the extravagant fulfillment of expectation—combined, perhaps, with a certain consternation over Newton's crook-backed frame. Adopting a demeanor that defied his canted spine, the geometer strutted down the aisle and hopped into the witness-stand. Walter was pleased to note that, as Newton gave his oath, his tendency to foppery came immediately to the fore. Not only did he grab the Bible with an absurd flourish, he brought it to his lips and kissed it.

Thaxton began by asking Newton to explain why the Mowbray case had inspired him to travel a full thirty miles from Cambridge-Town, whereupon the witness took complete command of the interview. Pivoting, he stared at each juror in turn.

"Good men of Colchester, a ponderous matter lies upon your shoulders," Newton said. "Ere the week is out, you must decide whether so-called witches have the power to enjoin wicked spirits and thereby tamper with the world's most fundamental mechanisms."

Hugh Collop leaped up, obtained the judge's permission to address the Court, and proceeded to argue that the world's most fundamental mechanisms were a subject for philosophic treatises, not sworn testimonies. " 'Tis not witchcraft that's on trial here," he concluded, "but rather a particular witch."

To Walter's profound disappointment, Bucock responded with a prolix opinion to the effect that, in light of the defendant's status as a landholder, Professor Newton must be allowed to speak.

"A most learned ruling, Your Honor," Newton said, beaming Bucock a smile. Again the geometer listed toward the jury. "I've been asked to give my reasons for enduring a long day in the saddle, raising many a welt on my arse, merely so I might address you dozen sons of peddletwats."

Walter released an involuntary gasp. Did Newton really say *peddletwats?*

"Naturally Sir Humphrey hopes I'll instruct you mutton heads in the fallacies underlying the demon hypothesis," Newton said, "but I now see 'twould be easier to teach a sheep not to shit on Sunday. Aye, I've got a proof at my command, so astute it makes incubi and succubi stand revealed as mere idylls of the imagination, yet who amongst you boasts wit enough to follow it? You doltish sons of fastfannies couldn't solve a quadratic equation to save your cods from a woodcutter!"

Walter could scarcely believe his ears, credit his eyes, or accept his good fortune.

"Howbeit, ere I depart, let me toss a valuable nugget of celestial mechanics your way." Newton reached toward his chestnut periwig, seizing the longest curl like a carillonneur pulling a bell-rope. "Since writing my *Principia Mathematica*, I've come to see 'tis fornication, not gravitation, causes the planets to wander. You heard me right, jurors. Each time a gentleman sticks his doodle inside a lady's happy-sack, he makes a deposit in that grand erotic fund from which the universe draws its energy. Heed now the *Principia Priapica!* Law one: a virile member at rest rarely stays at rest! Law two: the speed of the semen is directly proportional to the force of the orgasm! Law three: for every illicit ejaculation there is an equal and opposite story to tell your wife!"

What happened next was so astonishing that for an instant Walter thought he was home in bed, dreaming the ruination of Sir Humphrey's case. But this was not a dream. Newton was actually cupping his palm around his privates and drawing the fingers together as if squeezing milk from an udder.

" 'Sheart, jurors, if you've got one of these bolts in your breeches, you need no other explanation for the Earth's perambulations. Tomorrow you must all take the day-coach to Cambridge-Town, that I might show you the evidence. Do I swive my rooming-companion from knickers to noggin each night in the sacred name of Baconian experimentalism? Aye! Do I ram my strumpet-pump into John Wickin's bum-hole every morning by way of verifying my philosophy? Indeed! Do I shag any subsizar who'll assent to my glad-adder till he cries, 'Hold, enough!' Verily!" At last he removed his hand from his crotch, dissolving the shocking tableau. "Farewell, you knavish sons of narycherries! The Mowbray woman will go to her grave blameless as the lamb, but Newton's not the wight to tell you why!"

Sniggering in the manner of a sensualist enjoying an obscene jest, the witness hopped off the stand and scuttled down the aisle. As he disappeared out the main door, a cacophony filled the air, a thundering conglomeration of chattering, nattering, whistling, and gasping. Walter could not decide whose face to savor first, but he soon settled on Sir Humphrey, who appeared to be suffering an attack of apoplexy. He shifted his gaze to the judge, who seemed about to relinquish his breakfast. Cavendish, meanwhile, trembled with rage. Collop beamed from ear to ear. Isobel remained her usual granite self.

"Order!" Bucock screamed, pounding on the bench with a walnut mallet. "Do you hear me? I shall have order in this hall! Order! Order!"

But what did it matter, Walter mused, whether order obtained in one puny courtroom, when such perfect and beautiful order suffused the universe at large?

LIKE DR. HALLEY'S GREAT COMET of 1682 pursuing its wide adventurous orbit, Jennet followed her chosen circuit: past the Moot Hall, through the Dutch Quarter, around the gallows, across the castle yard, down High Street, and back again. Each time she made the loop, she managed briefly to distract herself with a verse or two from Nature's eternal epic—a blue cornflower, scarlet poppy, white rose, floating butterfly, darting finch, trilling lark, fidgeting honeybee—but her eyes always returned to the three hempen nooses swinging in the breeze.

According to Mr. Shakespeare, humankind was a magnificent piece of work, noble in reason, infinite in faculties, in action like an angel, in apprehension like a god, but of late she'd come to doubt that hypothesis. What honeybee had ever built a gallows? What lark had ever sung out its sister for a Satanist? The world's most vengeful rosebush had never scratched *malefactor* in an innocent woman's flesh.

She continued her revolutions: a third ellipse, a fourth, a fifth. Before she could begin her sixth such journey, the main door of the Moot Hall swung open, and Mr. Newton stumbled onto High Street, tricorn askew, periwig aslant. Had he finished testifying already? Had he presented his demon disproof in a mere half-hour?

Seeing Jennet, he pivoted toward St. Martin's Lane and broke into a run, curls flying in all directions. He was laughing—laughing and giggling like the most long-gone lunatic ever to wander the corridors of His Majesty's Refuge for the Mentally Deranged.

"Professor Newton!" she cried. "Wait!"

She was about to give chase when Barnaby Cavendish burst from the building, eyes wild with distress, face white with mortification.

"Oh, my poor Miss Stearne," he moaned, waddling toward her, "our man hath played us false!"

Jennet grimaced. "False? How so?"

Dr. Cavendish pulled himself up to full height and, in a gesture that evoked a duelist aiming his pistol, pointed toward the fleeing geometer. "He told 'em they were too stupid to understand his proof!" Securing his wig with the flat of his hand, he sprinted down St. Martin's Lane in pursuit of Newton. "Stop, poltroon!"

"He said naught about desires of the mind?" Jennet asked, following, stomach a-churn and sick at heart.

"Not one syllable," Dr. Cavendish replied.

"He offered 'em no theorems against the demon hypothesis?"

"He offered 'em only blasphemies and scandal!"

Upon reaching Sainsbury's Livery, Newton commenced to bridle his horse, all the while singing a sea-chantey about a man-o'-war encountering a frigate crewed by harlots. When Jennet and Dr. Cavendish arrived, the geometer greeted the curator with a tipped hat and a friendly clap on the back.

"Thou art a punctual man, sir," said Newton. "Hitch up your museum, and we'll be off to London!"

"I wouldn't sell you my prodigies for a king's ransom!" Dr. Cavendish screamed.

"The Society's short on king's ransoms at the moment, but we can still give you eight guineas per specimen."

"I would sooner sell my freaks to a gang of Popish plotters looking to put James back on the throne!"

" 'Tis true I had my sport with the jurymen"—Newton heaved his saddle onto his horse—"but only because such peasants cannot follow a reasoned argument."

"I would sooner sell my monsters to the poxiest trollop in Fleet Street!" From the stable floor Dr. Cavendish obtained a roundish mass of straw, dirt, and dung. "I would sooner sell 'em to Judas Iscariot himself for thirty shillings and a brindled pig!"

"I believe we might raise the offer to nine guineas per monster," Newton said.

Jennet's throat became as tight as a drumhead. Salt tears filled her eyes, burning the delicate jelly. She lurched half-blind toward Dr.

Cavendish. "Dear God, they're certain to hang her now," she wailed, throwing herself against the curator's comforting rotundity.

With his free hand Dr. Cavendish stroked her head. "Aye, Miss Stearne, I fear as much."

"Ten guineas, 'tis my final proposition!" Newton said. "You won't get a better price anywhere in England!"

Dr. Cavendish hurled the dung-globe. It struck Newton squarely in the side, besmirching the gold-lace bindings of his waistcoat.

"Good sir, 'twould appear our business relationship hath ended." Through a series of maladroit gestures Newton mounted his horse. "As of this moment, the Royal Society buys its prodigies from another vendor!"

Dr. Cavendish grabbed a second handful of ordure and threw it at their nemesis. The projectile landed harmlessly in the dust. Newton gave his horse a kick. With a sudden snort the animal bolted from the stable and charged toward High Street, bearing away England's strangest knave, philosophy's greatest sage, geometry's reigning genius, and— Jennet could not escape her conclusion—Aunt Isobel's last hope.

The
Fourth

❧❧❧❧❧❧❧❧❧❧❧

A Public Burning
Enlightens Colchester,
Tho' Not Before
the Convicted Enchantress
Prepares Our Heroine
for Both the Female Mission
and the Male Emission

❧

N ow that Sir Humphrey's key witness stood exposed as a man whose morals occupied no position above depravity and whose mind merited no diagnosis save lunacy, Walter assumed that the remainder of the trial would prove deficient in surprises. At first the day indeed unfolded as he expected. The defense finished its dispirited presentation. The jurymen reached their inevitable verdict. The clerk of arraigns came forward and placed the black silk cap atop Judge Bucock's wig.

"Oyez, oyez, oyez!" the bailiff cried. "My Lord the King's Justice doth strictly charge and command all persons to keep silence whilst sentence of death is passed on the prisoner at the bar!"

But then something astonishing occurred. As Harold Bucock offered his concluding remarks, Walter had the sort of revelation a man might normally be granted only after spending a month in the African desert, drinking dew and eating roasted locusts. For the first time ever, he understood the most confounding verse in all Scripture. *If any man come to me,* ran Luke 14:26, *and hate not his father, and mother, and wife, and children, and brethren, and sisters, yea, and his own life also, he cannot be my disciple.* And, of course, the Redeemer might also have said, *and sisters-in-law.* He could easily have added, *and sisters-in-law who worship the Devil.*

❀

"Within two days following the departure of these assizes," Bucock announced to the Court, "the Colchester magistrate will impose upon Isobel Mowbray a lethal ordeal of whatever variety accords with his proclivities."

To hate one's own relations! Ah, the singing, soaring power of that idea! To stand prepared to battle Lucifer in whatever arena he chose, even the souls of those to whom you were bound by flesh and wedlock—in such audacity lay Christianity's true greatness. What difference did it make whether a man was Catholic or Protestant, Quaker or Puritan, Arian or Anabaptist, so long as he might hug those massive pillars of paradox his Savior had erected seventeen centuries earlier?

"Let us not deceive ourselves," Bucock continued. "As a wealthy landowner, Isobel Mowbray already possessed those prizes that commonly bestir her sex to seek out Satan. She did not want for a horse-drawn coach, faithful retainers, fine clothes, or glittering jewels. Ergo, we can only conclude that she entered upon the demonic compact"—his voice reached an apex of indignation—"*for its own hideous sake!* In setting evil influences loose in Ipswich, this woman acted not as the Dark One's servant but rather as his *collaborator!* And so I call upon Mr. Grigsby to give his imagination free rein in staging her demise. I exhort him to make the execution of Isobel Mowbray the most festive such event yet seen in Essex. Let it be said that when Perdition's would-be queen came before the Colchester magistrate, he punished her as extravagantly as the ecclesiastics of Loudun chastised Urbain Grandier."

Fixing his gaze on Isobel, Walter saw that the judge's damning deduction, his hypothesis that she'd actually sought to reign in Hell, inspired in her not a flicker of remorse. Her face displayed only the same absurd Stoicism with which she'd thus far endured every other such accusation.

"Prisoner at the bar, do you wish to make a statement ere the Court returns you to Mr. Grigsby's custody?" Bucock asked Isobel.

The enchantress said nothing.

"These honorable assizes now stand adjourned," the judge said, ramming his mallet against the bench.

"God save His Majesty, King William!" the bailiff cried. "God save Her Majesty, Queen Mary!"

Though not normally inclined toward self-indulgence, Walter felt disposed to celebrate his victory, and so four hours later, as dusk lowered its translucent scrim upon Colchester, he betook himself to the Red Lion. The Court and all its personages had cleared out, bound for Norwich, and yet the tavern was jammed to the walls, a circumstance that forced him to share a booth with three local leather-aprons, none of whom, he guessed, had ever read a line of Bodin's *Démonomanie des Sorciers* or Carpzov's *Practica Rerum Criminalum*. Barely ten minutes after he'd joined these rude artisans, however, his opinion of them improved, for it developed that they'd attended the Mowbray trial and had unanimously rated his performance erudite and dazzling.

"It takes great skill, I've heard, to wield a Paracelsus trident," the cooper said.

" 'Tis our Heavenly Father wields the trident." Walter dipped his tongue into the foam atop his ale. "We cleansers are but His earthly agents. Of course, I must be evermore on guard lest I confuse the authentic Satanic vibration with a mere twitching in my fingers."

"Would ye say, then, that when a cleanser swims a witch, 'tis really God ties on the mask-o'-truth and lowers her into the water?" the soapmaker asked.

"I would say that, aye." Slowly and with considerable relish Walter took a swallow of ale: a mere carnal pleasure, to be sure, nothing compared to the spiritual satisfaction he'd known that morning upon deciphering Luke 14:26, but still an experience worth savoring.

"The mask, though, was it not thine own invention?" the wheelwright asked.

" 'Tis the nostril clip makes it such a worthy device," Walter said, nodding sagaciously, "fit to stand alongside Isaac Newton's reflecting telescope."

In evoking the notorious name of Newton, Walter inevitably sparked a discussion of the geometer's recent antics. Everyone agreed that Newton had disgraced himself utterly, though the wheelwright had extracted from the event "an instructive yet troubling insight." In ethical philosophy, he noted, there was no such thing as wise laws issuing from a wicked lawgiver, whereas in natural philosophy a man's deductions could be neatly severed from his defects.

"Who amongst us would heed the advice of a horse-thieving Aesop?" the wheelwright elaborated. "Who would follow the lessons of a whore-mongering Bunyan? But if Euclid were a high-seas pirate, the area of a circle would still equal the square o' the radius times three-point-one-four."

Walter found this observation so unsettling that he decided to quiet his mind with further applications of ale. He excused himself from his band of admirers, shuffled blearily across the tavern, and set thruppence on the bar. Upon receiving a fresh tankard, he consumed it with a haste that fell just short of sybaritism.

A familiar face appeared before him.

"Might I have a word with ye?" asked Caspar Grigsby, the Colchester magistrate, his coarse hands cradling a mug of buttered rum. He was a short but fearsome fellow, dense with gristle, as firmly planted in the world as a windmill or a tree.

The two men sidled toward the hearth, where a serving wench with apple cheeks worked the spit-crank as if raising a bucket from a well. Impaled on the rotating shaft, a flayed boar offered its meat to the flames.

"How greatly Judge Bucock's commission doth weigh upon me," Mr. Grigsby said. "He insisted I give my imagination free rein in executing Isobel Mowbray, and therein lies my misery, for I have no imagination."

"Piffle!" Walter exclaimed. "Every man hath an imagination."

"Bucock said her demise must aspire to extravagance. So what am I to do? Fill the execution field with jugglers and acrobats?"

"There—'tis as I said! You have an imagination!"

"Jugglers? Really?"

Why not? thought Walter. "And acrobats. Let us mock the Devil with merriment! Let us flog his goblins with raucous displays of joy!"

"Then there be the matter o' the hangin' itself—a dull spectacle, if ye ask me, e'en when ye get a dancer," Mr. Grigsby said.

"Remember, good sir, Bucock did not specify a hanging. You may recall that he evoked Urbain Grandier's splendid and dramatic execution of 1634."

" 'Twas before my time."

"For bewitching the Ursuline nuns of Loudun, the profligate priest was chained to a stake and roasted like yon boar."

"Roasted?" Grigsby gasped, eyes darting toward the spit. "Surely ye don't propose . . ."

Do I? Walter wondered. "I do."

"*Burn* her?"

"Burn her." Walter contemplated the runnels of golden fat as they coursed down the boar's flanks and hit the fire, each sizzle like a demon's hiss. Burn her? Nobody had staged a public burning behind Colchester Castle in over a century—not since all those Protestant martyrs had been incinerated at the Popish Queen Mary's behest—but that didn't mean the custom was invalid. "Burn her," he said again. *If any man come to me, and hate not his sister-in-law.* "Burn her at the stake."

"Forgive me, master pricker, but the stake—it simply isn't English. We're a gallows people. Leave fire to the French, I say."

"To the *French?*" Walter moaned. "Did the French write Revelation 19:20, which tells us that Satan's prophets will be cast alive into a lake of molten brimstone? Did the French write Matthew 13:42, wherein our Savior makes clear his plan to gather up the wicked and hurl them into the Divine Furnace?"

Grigsby stared at his rum as intently as a seer consulting a gazing-crystal. "Marry, sir, ye make a proper case for fire. I wish I knew my Holy Writ half so well as ye."

"For a magistrate, Scripture's desirable—for a pricker, indispensable." He lowered his voice, speaking softly into the hollow of his tankard. "And if a burning doesn't show the Crown I'm the ablest cleanser yet born in England, I'll gather up my family and move us all to Scotland."

THEIR STRATAGEM WAS COMPLEX. It was knotty and gnarled and twisted, like the rat tumor she and Elinor Mapes had studied during the *experimentum magnus,* but Jennet could imagine no other way to visit her aunt one last time.

On the third night following the trial, she and Dr. Cavendish lashed four foetal monsters to the Gypsy wagon, the ponderous bottles bulging from the chassis like buboes on a plague victim. Next she transformed the curator's face—encircling his eyes with smudges of charcoal, supplementing his teeth with rose briars, decorating his forehead with wads of clay molded into conical goat-horns—until he truly looked the part he was to play, unscrupulous Adramelech, chief amongst Lucifer's courtiers.

They drove the wagon out of Shire Gate Livery and piloted it up Queen Street—slowly, ever so slowly, lest they crack the bottles. Drawing to a halt in the castle yard, they spied on the youthful, red-bearded turnkey as he entered the keep to relieve his superior. After a moment one-legged Amos Thurlow came hobbling through the portal like a damaged cricket, then pivoted on his crutch and headed west toward the tippling-houses, doubtless seeking the comforts of rum. Dr. Cavendish cracked his horsewhip. The wagon bounced along High Street, soon catching and passing the chief gaoler.

Upon reaching the Angel Lane intersection, the curator parked the wagon, clambered down to street level, and, seizing the lanthorn, swooped into Mr. Thurlow's path like a hawk descending on a hare. The shocked gaoler nearly dropped his crutch. Dr. Cavendish released a froggish gasp.

"You may address me as Lord Adramelech, Grand Chancellor of the Infernal Empire and Viceroy to Satan himself." Dr. Cavendish pocketed his spectacles and raised the lanthorn to his chin, causing jagged shadows to play upon his features as the buttery glow lit his fangs and horns. Mr. Thurlow trembled like a man cast adrift on an ice floe. " 'Twould behoove you to fall to your knees, bow your head, kiss my hand, and tell me that my very presence doth honor you."

Holding his crutch at a vertical angle, Mr. Thurlow lowered himself to his solitary knee and pressed his lips against Dr. Cavendish's fingers. "Thy v-very presence d-doth honor me, Lord Adramelech, s-sir."

"Rise, gaoler."

Mr. Thurlow levered himself upright.

"Behold the children of my loins!" Dr. Cavendish cried. Taking Mr. Thurlow's arm, he brought him before the Tunbridge Wells Bloodsucker, then thrust the lanthorn forward, illuminating the razor-toothed horror. "At present he sleeps—ah, but how easily I could awaken this malicious imp and send him on an errand. He can bleed an Englishman dry in half a minute." The curator walked Mr. Thurlow to the rear of the wagon and showed him the Kali of Droitwich. "One word from me, and tonight this demon creeps into your bed and strangles you using all four hands." He shoved Mr. Thurlow toward the Sussex Rat-Baby. "At my command he chews both eyes right out of your skull." The circuit ended at the Maw of Folkestone. "Here's one mouth you don't want clamped round your privy member. In sum, Mr. Thurlow, I see four lamentable fates on your horizon."

The gaoler, quavering, said, "Tell me, Lord Adramelech, sir, how do I avoid 'em?"

"By one simple gesture. You will allow Isobel Mowbray's niece to visit her."

"M-Miss Stearne, you mean? Lovely girl. Splendid girl."

"Miss Jennet Stearne, aye."

"I shall arrange it betimes."

"You will arrange it *now*," Dr. Cavendish snarled, pointing toward the driver's box.

Jennet vaulted into the lane and, head held high, approached the gaoler. "Hallo, Mr. Thurlow. I am well pleased that you have at long last assented to my petition."

"H-happy to s-serve ye, Miss Stearne."

Mr. Thurlow rotated ninety degrees and started back toward High Street, his crutch striking the cobblestones with clockwork regularity, Jennet following a yard behind.

"Gaoler, your generosity hath been noted!" Dr. Cavendish called after them. "When your sins send you netherward, I shall see to't you receive a hundred sorts of comfort! Pepper in your sulphur soup! The best salve for your burns!"

BY NIGHT THE WARDER'S STATION of Colchester Castle was considerably brighter than by day, for a constellation of five oil lamps swung from the ceiling, their glow glancing off the white plaster walls. Jennet readily discerned the perplexity on the red-bearded gaoler's face as Mr. Thurlow told him to surrender his key-ring. Upon seizing the brass circlet—it held more than twenty keys, each as large as a bodkin and encrusted with rust—Mr. Thurlow led Jennet down a torch-lit corridor where scores of human arms snaked through barred windows, their owners begging for ale and pleading for bread and wailing for meat. A grid of metal bars presented itself. Mr. Thurlow applied the proper key, pulled back the door, and directed Jennet up a spiral stairway that wound through the Great Tower like a bung-nail embedded in a wine cork, until at last they reached a slab of bolted iron.

"I have no wish to see you lose your employment," she said, "and so I shall keep this interview brief. Howbeit, please know that if you whisper a word of my visit to any living soul, the Kali of Droitwich will have her way with you."

"Not e'en the Spanish boot could make me recount this night." Mr. Thurlow inserted a key and with a twist of his bony wrist unlocked the tower door.

"I desire privacy. Twenty minutes."

"Ye shall have't," the chief gaoler said.

"Who's there?" called a blessedly familiar voice.

Jennet crossed the threshold. Mr. Thurlow slammed the door behind her, the reverberations filling the tower like a cannonade.

Moonbeams the color of Cheddar cheese flowed through the lancet window, suffusing Aunt Isobel's quarters with a coppery glow, whilst a dozen ensconced candles provided additional illumination and a small measure of warmth. The room was furnished, sparsely but adequately. Mattress, chair, dressing table, writing-desk, chamber-pot. A landed woman in the direst of straits evidently lived better than a dairymaid at the top of her luck.

Dressed in her plainest muslin gown, Aunt Isobel climbed off the mattress, a slow disjointed ascent suggesting an arthritic spaniel rising to greet her mistress. The philosopher's features were drawn and sallow, like the smaller of the Bicephalic Girl's two faces. Though badly ravaged by Walter's razor, her scalp had retained its fertility, the nascent crop of hair emerging in unsightly gray tufts.

"Oh, Jenny, sweet Jenny, I *knew* I'd live to kiss your angel's face again." Isobel stumbled forward and flung her arms around her niece, their small bodies fusing like electrically charged rods of amber. "I told myself that just as the miles 'twixt Colchester and Cambridge didn't stop that girl"— she placed the predicted kiss on Jennet's cheek—"neither would the bars of my cell. Though I cannot imagine by what ruse you arrived here."

Jennet proceeded to narrate the theatrics through which her new friend Dr. Cavendish had turned himself into Lord Adramelech whilst she became his ward.

Isobel, smiling, said, "Such a clever child my sister gave the world." The smile declined into a grimace. "No doubt you've learned of Professor Newton's perfidy."

"Dr. Cavendish attended the trial. If I live to be a hundred, I shall ne'er forgive the geometer for raising my hopes and then dashing 'em to bits."

"With mathematical geniuses, I'm told, one should expect a certain collateral eccentricity."

"I can no more excuse Newton on grounds of eccentricity than I would a cannibal on grounds of appetite." Jennet clasped Isobel's right hand, each finger as thin and brittle as a winter twig. "Oh, my dearest aunt, I fear they mean to hang you. I'Christ, I shall be there, denouncing your tormenters and praying for the rope to break."

"Attend if you must, but know that Mr. Grigsby hath more than a simple gallows jig in mind. He promises the people an old-style burning."

It seemed to Jennet that the Sussex Rat-Baby had suddenly begun feasting on her entrails. "A burning?"

"At the stake."

"Is that not illegal?"

"Merely uncivilized."

"You must be passing scared. You must be entirely frightened."

"So frightened I'm numb with't. Ah, but Mr. Grigsby and I have struck a bargain. I shall make no speech at the stake, and he will see to't I receive a mercy strangling."

"Then promise me you'll make no speech."

" 'Tis certainly my intention to spare myself the fiery torture." Like the revitalized but bewildered Lazarus taking the measure of his tomb, Isobel shuffled toward the writing-desk. "Were this a Dutch cell, I could offer you every amenity. A slice of cake . . ."

The tears, Jennet knew, would arrive soon, a matter of minutes, a matter of seconds. "We're going to rescue you."

"A saucer of coffee."

"Dr. Cavendish and I shall pluck you from the pyre."

"A fresh pear. You'll do naught of the sort, child. Mr. Grigsby's marshals would murder you on the spot."

"Then I shall die in a worthy cause."

"Miss Stearne, you are squandering these hard-won moments. Softly now. I have a gift for you." From the topmost drawer of her writing-desk Isobel produced a manuscript stitched together with yarn, delivering it into Jennet's grasp. "*Voilà.*"

The cover-page bore a title, *A Woman's Garden of Pleasure and Pain,* rendered in the philosopher's ever spiraling hand.

" 'Steeth, hath my aunt written a book?"

Isobel nodded and said, "I have attempted in these pages to give my reader at once a body of knowledge and a knowledge of bodies. Life hath much in store for you, Jenny. Ere long the bloody courses will begin, even as Nature blesses you with roundish hips and wondrous lusty notions. Young men will soon be, as my husband was wont to put it, 'lying through their lips for to lay you 'neath their loins.' I've set it all down, plus charts, tables, and diagrams." She rapped her knuckles on the manuscript. "Welcome to womanhood, child of my heart. The path lies thick with snares and barbs, but 'tis a truly worthy gender, especially when you consider the alternative."

"You will keep silent at the stake," Jennet said, and now the anticipated tears arrived, falling from her cheeks and staining the cover-page of *A Woman's Garden of Pleasure and Pain.*

"For all I ache to tell the world my opinion of witchfinding, you may be sure the strangling will come off as arranged." Isobel reached toward the book and brushed a fallen tear, blurring *Pleasure* into *Treasure.*

"Chapter One informs the reader how to keep her lover's ardor from augmenting the human population."

"I shall memorize every sentence," Jennet said.

"Sir Edward was eager for an heir—what man is not?—and yet he cherished me even more than his posterity, and so we eschewed all connection on my fertile days. Ah, but even the most wary wife must now and then yield to the moment, and so you'll find herein directions for socking your husband's virility in a Belgian adder-bag." As her aunt drew closer, Jennet noted a constellation of scabs atop her head, residue of her cropping by the master pricker. "I have a second present for thee. 'Tis largely in the nature of a challenge, but 'tis also a gift, for 'twill bestow a purpose on your life, and what boon could be greater?"

"None, I should imagine," Jennet said, perplexed.

Isobel backed away and, sitting down before her dressing table, ran a hairbrush through her tenuous and pathetic locks, each strand as delicate as a spider's thread. "History pursues a lunar sort of progress, with present fore'er cycling back to past," she said at last. "At the moment witch-cleansing's on the wane, but betimes the hunt will wax, if not tomorrow, then the next day, or the next." She froze in mid-stroke. "To wit, you must construct a treatise. 'Tis your female mission for the next ten years, twenty years—howe'er long it takes."

"A treatise?"

"A *Malleus Maleficarum* stood upon its head, an argument so grand and persuasive 'twill bring down the Parliamentary Witchcraft Act. Can you do this, darling Jenny?"

"I fear I lack the intellect."

"You've all the brains the task requires and more. Mayhap you'll have a fleshly babe someday, mayhap not, but in either case this *argumentum grande* will be your one true progeny."

"Do you mean I am to search out Mr. Newton's lost disproof of demons?"

Isobel dipped her ravaged head. "Newton in person hath naught to offer us, but Newton in principle will surely serve our ends. Of all the mortals in England, only you and I and the Lucasian Professor know that the cleansers might be crushed through mathematics. Ah, but the Lucasian's within an ace of lunacy, your aunt's about to die—and so I now dub thee Lady Jennet, Hammer of Witchfinders."

"How do I even begin? Might some other Royal Society fellow set me on the proper path?"

"Alas, I fear that clan be riddled with demonologists, Mr. Boyle most conspicuous amongst 'em. 'Twill gain you more to study those who've actually written against the prickers' trade: Reginald Scot, plus the three John W's—I speak of Webster, Wagstaffe, and Weyer—the better to learn why their reasoning ne'er took hold. And then comes the daunting part."

"Mastering Mr. Newton?"

"From sprit to spanker. The geometry, the optics, the hydrostatics, the planetary mechanics. You must graft the *Principia* onto your soul, darling Jenny. Find that missing calculation, and you'll deliver many an innocent wight from noose, pyre, and chopping block."

A key rattled in the lock. The door swung back. Propped on his crutch, Amos Thurlow limped through the jamb. "It's been twenty minutes, Miss Stearne . . ."

Isobel rose from her dressing table, crossed her cell, and for the second time that night wrapped her niece in a deep and desperate affection. As their embrace intensified, Jennet imagined myriad germ cells flowing from her aunt's body into her own, quickening her mind with philosophic seed as surely as spermatozooans could quicken a grown woman's womb. I'm with child now, she thought.

An *argumentum grande* is growing inside

me. I have achieved a

mental

❧

Pregnancy

rarely saved the life

of a convicted sorceress during

the witch-hunting centuries, but a full womb

was normally good for a temporary reprieve. The gestation

would run its course, a wet nurse would receive the baby, and the prisoner

would assume her appointed place on the gallows or at the stake. It was not automatically clear what to do with the superfluous neonate. Sometimes a convent adopted the creature. Sometimes the father or other blood relation stepped forward. And sometimes the magistrate ordered a strangling, on the theory that the infant had become polluted *in utero*.

We call this epoch the Renaissance, a rebirth of art and classicism. Dear reader, it was nothing of the kind—or, rather, it was something of the kind for the average prince, aristocrat, merchant, or patronized painter, but it was nothing of the kind if you were just another peasant scrabbling to avoid starvation. In your experience the Renaissance was a nightmare, and if you cultivated habits that drew the witchfinders' notice—if you told fortunes, trafficked in herbs, dabbled in magic, or practiced midwifery—you were vulnerable to the charge of Satanism.

When she told her niece that witch hunting was a cyclic enterprise, Isobel Mowbray spoke the truth. The world needed an *argumentum grande* in 1689—not as badly, perhaps, as in 1589 or 1489, but it certainly needed one.

Dayton, Tennessee, the sweltering July of 1925. The Scopes Trial. Clarence Darrow and William Jennings Bryan square off over the Genesis account of human origins. Does biblical literalism suffer a setback? Indeed. Is this a victory for the theory of evolution? Hardly. For Darwin's canny advocate, you see, has failed to make a positive case for natural selection—he has neglected to construct an *argumentum grande*—with the result that, throughout the remainder of the century and beyond, America's high-school science teachers will fully explicate evolutionary principles in their classrooms about as often as they lecture on necrophilia.

The Vatican, Italy, 1484. As the Renaissance gets up to speed, the newly installed Pope, Innocent VIII, conceives his famous Witch Bull calling for the extermination of Devil-worshipping heretics wherever they might rear their heads. He writes out the dictum on his bullsheet, then deputizes Heinrich Krämer and Jakob Sprenger to go on a fact-finding mission. Their labors result in the *Malleus Maleficarum*. The tome stands alone. Krämer and Sprenger have no peers and, more significantly, no antagonists. And so it happens that for the next quarter-century the odor of roasting witch-flesh becomes as ubiquitous in northern Europe as the aroma of candle wax and cow manure. How could it be otherwise? What human endeavor could possibly be as glorious as checkmating Satan? The next time somebody announces that he plans to get Medieval on your ass, tell him you're going to get Renaissance on his gonads.

Don't misunderstand me. I've never shared Isobel's touching faith in the power of sober discourse. The path on which she set Jennet that night in the prison cell suffered from a lamentable credulity, if not outright naïveté. I am well aware that the average member of your species will not abandon a pleasurable opinion simply because the evidence argues against it. Self-doubt is a suit of clothes that few of you ever acquire, and fewer still wear comfortably.

And yet the effort at persuasion must be made. There is something rather noble—and occasionally even effective—about an *argumentum grande*. I've found that pessimism can be its own sort of innocence, cynicism its own sentimentality. Isobel knew this, and in time my Jennet came to know it too.

By 1510 it seems that the campaign has run its course. Outside the Alpine valleys and Pyrenean France, a witch can't get arrested. But then along comes Martin Luther and his *Ninety Five Theses*, and by the middle of the century the Reformation evangelists have revived what the Catholic evangelists inaugurated. All during the 1560's and 1570's Protestant clerics oversee hundreds of sorcery trials in Germany, Switzerland, Denmark, Hungary, Transylvania, and Scotland. Eventually the Counter-Reformation swings into action. Throughout the 1580's and 1590's, the Catholic reconquest brings a vigorous anti-Satanism to Bavaria, the Rhineland, Flanders, and Poland. Scores of learned and energetic Jesuits keep the witch fires burning.

It is an age of giants: Christians of a caliber that leave the likes of Walter Stearne in the shadows. Take Johann von Schöneburn, Archbishop-Elector of Trier, who sponsors the executions of nearly four hundred supposed witches between 1585 and 1593. Thanks to Von Schöneburn's vigor, two Trier villages are left with only one female inhabitant apiece. Or take Julius Echter von Mespelbrunn, the Bishop-Prince of Würzburg, whose efforts turn Wolfenbüttel's Lechelnholze Square into a forest, so densely packed are the stakes. At Von Mespelbrunn's funeral, the court preacher praises the prince's zeal in burning witches "according to God's word." Or take Nicholas Rémy, the witch-hunting lawyer of Lorraine, whose *Dæmonolatreiæ* calls for not only the burning of convicted Satanists but the extermination of their children as well, the better to eradicate the unholy seed in toto. He dies in 1616, a beloved and respected scholar who has consigned at least 2,500 innocents to the flames.

Early in the seventeenth century another hiatus occurs, but then the Thirty Years War reinvigorates the hunt throughout the Rhine Valley. Among Catholic clerics, Prince-Bishop Phillip Adolf von Ehrenberg of Würzburg is particularly active: between 1623 and 1631 he burns nine hundred ostensible witches, including his own nephew, nineteen priests, and a handful of seven-year-olds judged guilty of having enjoyed sexual intercourse with demons. Not to be outdone by Von Ehrenberg, Johann Georg II Fuchs von Dornheim of Bamberg—the *Hexenbischof,* the Witch Bishop—builds a "witch house" featuring a torture chamber adorned with biblical texts, and by the time his ten-year reign is done he has supervised the incineration of six hundred putative sorcerers. On the Protestant side, meanwhile, there emerges the majestic figure of Benedict Carpzov, the Lutheran scholar whose *Practica Rerum Criminalum* maintains that even those who merely *believe* they've attended a Sabbat should be executed, for belief implies will, and will entails menace. Before ascending to his heavenly reward, Carpzov will read his Bible cover-to-cover fifty-three times, take Holy Communion at least once a week, and underwrite the deaths of 20,000 alleged witches.

The Thirty Years War ends, but the cleansings do not. As the 1660's progress, the withdrawal of English troops from Scotland frees up Calvinist magistrates to torture and burn Devil-worshippers by the hundreds. In Sweden, meanwhile, Lutheran clergymen renounce the inhibitory ethics of the late Queen Christina (who'd ordered her generals to curtail whatever German witch-hunts they encountered during their campaigns). They experiment with persecution, find it to their liking, and forthwith immolate one presumed Satanist after another.

And so I ask you, reader, can we blame Isobel Mowbray for wanting to give the world an *argumentum grande?* When she commissioned Jennet to find Newton's lost proof, at least 500,000 convicted witches, and perhaps as many as a million, had already fallen victim to the brutal nonambiguity of Exodus 22:18. Our heroine will not have an easy time of it. Krämer and Sprenger may have been loonies, but Von Mespelbrunn, Carpzov, Rémy, and their ilk were among the most formidable minds of the Renaissance. What do you say to a bishop whose Bible tells him he must not suffer a witch to live? On what grounds might you answer a magistrate who knows that wayward teats and bloodless blemishes constitute infallible evidence of Satanic compact?

How implausible to suppose that any argument might sway a judge
who believes it his sacred duty to dispatch as many witches
as possible to Hell, where all the lakes are
of burning sulfur, and not
one is filled
with

Water,
Jennet decided,
would turn the trick. She'd
read about the method in a book concerning
the savage red Indians of America: how they would contrive
to wake themselves at dawn by drinking deeply at bedtime. The night before Aunt Isobel was scheduled to meet the flames, an event the Witchfinder-General had strictly forbidden his daughter to attend, Jennet consumed a quart of water, climbed onto her mattress, and pulled up the counterpane. Her mind was abuzz. *Argumentum grande* . . . Newton's lost proof . . . find it . . . the geometry, optics, hydrostatics . . . find it . . . the planetary mechanics . . . find it . . . missing calculation . . . find it.

Much to Jennet's dismay, Dr. Cavendish had been as horrified as Walter by the thought of her observing the burning. For nearly an hour following her reunion with Isobel in the Great Tower, she'd quarreled with the curator over the circumstances of her hypothetical appearance on the execution field.

"If we were two parliamentarians," Dr. Cavendish said, "me a lord, for example, and you a commoner, we would resolve this issue through a *compromise*. I've no doubt you're familiar with the concept."

"Aunt Isobel once told me that a compromise occurs when a person gives up something he pretends to want so as to gain an object for which he feigns indifference."

"Indeed."

And so they compromised. Jennet could patronize the execution, but only if a full one hundred yards separated her from the stake. Dr. Cavendish would install his Gypsy wagon on the far side of the field, and with the aid of a telescope they would together watch from the roof.

As it turned out, she didn't need the water, for she failed to fall asleep that night. Even before the sun's first rays touched the town, she was on her feet, improvising an effigy from a sack of flour and a bundle of rope. She set the false Jennet in her bed, then slipped out of the house and skulked along the misty length of Wyre Street, bound for Colchester Castle. The air smelled of honeysuckle. A scraggly gray cat bolted across her path and disappeared down Culver Lane, doubtless in quest of the mice who populated the Trinity Church burial ground. From the trees came the cawing of perhaps a hundred crows, an avian parliament debating some matter inaccessible to human ken.

The birds had fallen silent by the time she reached the castle yard, and the flower-scented winds now carried the fragrance of cooking fires and the stench of upended chamber-pots. She made her way along the west wall of the keep, striding past the spindly monument marking the spot where two Royalist commanders had been shot on orders from the Parliamentarian General following the Siege of Colchester. Might there come a day when the sentence against Aunt Isobel would seem equally reprehensible? wondered Jennet as she vaulted the crumbling remains of the Roman wall. Or would history in its lunar progress decide that the witch had received too lenient a punishment?

Magistrate Grigsby's men had evidently visited the execution field earlier that morning, for a single wooden stake, thick as a pig and twice a man's height, now projected from a low hill at the center of the green, directly across from the gallows. Laced with tinder and kindling, a heap of logs encircled the obscene obelisk. The logs looked dry and old to Jennet: a quick fire, a quick consummation—good.

To her left loomed the Gypsy Wagon, plugging a breach in the Roman wall and poised to retreat down St. Helen's Lane. Having played out their parts in the great Adramelech hoax, the Bloodsucker, the Maw, the Kali, and the Rat-Baby no longer decorated the chassis but now lay sleeping with their brethren. Clay pipe fixed betwixt his teeth, Dr. Cavendish supplied Damon and Pythias with their oats. Seeing Jennet approach, the curator offered her an articulate scowl. You should not have come, his countenance said. You should have stayed in bed.

As the rising sun parted company with the horizon, the performers began arriving, props and equipage in hand, and betimes the spectators themselves entered the green, first in two's and three's, then in groups of a dozen or more.

Jennet and Dr. Cavendish scrambled into the driver's box and thence to the top of the wagon, where the promised telescope— a brass Hevelius reflector—lay propped against the chimney, casting its shadow across the roof like the gnomon on a sundial.

"Colchester's most pious citizens," Dr. Cavendish muttered, gesturing toward the crowd, "all of 'em eager to spite the Devil by cavorting at his queen's execution."

Now a tavern-keeper appeared on the field, driving a pony-cart loaded with casks of ale.

" 'Sheart, the man hath brought a hundred gallons at least." Dr. Cavendish eased his rump onto the roof. " 'Twould seem the piety quotient's about to rise."

Jennet dropped to one knee and assumed a cross-legged posture alongside the curator. She seized the telescope and clamped it to her eye, extending the tubes until the image grew crisp.

It felt blasphemous to be using this sacred device, designed to reveal the faces of planets and the courses of comets, in surveying so profane a spectacle, and yet she could not forbear to study the details. Near the eastern edge of the field, an ærialist costumed as a harlequin advanced birdishly along a tightrope strung betwixt a pair of chestnut trees, juggling two red rubber balls as he went. His audience included the Reverend Mapes and the regrettable Elinor; father and daughter were sharing a meat pie, starting at the antipodes and eating their way toward the center. On the northern boundary, not far from the River Colne, a company of thespians presented a bawdy anti-Papist satire in which the recently deposed King James wandered through Ireland converting the toads to Catholicism, baptizing them with his piss. Beside the satirists, a trained bear with a shimmering black pelt danced to the feral music of four pipe players and a drummer. As the bear's gavotte built to a frenzy, Jennet spied her brother, seated on the grass amongst the spectators, alternately sketching with his wax crayons and adding his applause to the general acclamation. So powerful was her augmented vision, she could even see the subject of Dunstan's drawing: a three-masted carrack riding a stormy sea.

Came the fateful hour of ten o'clock. The ærialist retired. The satire ended. The bear stopped dancing.

Telescope still fixed to her eye, she tracked a horse-drawn tumbrel as it rolled across the green escorted by Constable Wedderburn plus two marshals wearing orange doublets and helmets suggesting soup tureens. Mr. Grigsby held the reins. Her father sat alongside the magistrate, waving at the crowd as if he were Julius Cæsar bringing a captive barbarian king into Rome. In the bay stood the squat, modest figure of Aunt Isobel, clothed in a burlap shift, her outstretched wrists cuffed by iron manacles, the rusted chains looped around her neck and spilling down her chest like fiendish garlands. Behind her rode the executioner, a neckless man with olive skin and a tangled charcoal beard, gripping the chain that joined Isobel's shackles.

"Prithee, Miss Stearne, go below." Dr. Cavendish, rising, pointed to the trapdoor in the roof.

The crowd pelted the prisoner with stones, clods, pottery shards, decaying cabbages, and rotten turnips.

"I belong here," Jennet said. "She expects it."

Mr. Grigsby halted the tumbrel. The executioner scrambled out and, using the timber as a stairway, climbed the pyre, dragging Isobel behind him. He chained her to the stake, then took from his pocket a black cloth hood and slipped it over her head. Jennet shuddered and moaned. Never again would she see her aunt's living face, never again her antic eyes, sly smiles, challenging frowns.

Returning to the ground, the executioner stepped back and surveyed the stark tableau—timber, stake, hooded prisoner—as might the Painter-Royal assessing a recently completed portrait of King William. The revelers, passing pleased, gulped down ale and gathered around the pyre, determined to witness every nuance of the burning, an entertainment normally available only on the Continent.

Like a stag striding majestically from forest to meadow, a tall priest walked free of the mob. Jennet yanked him into focus. Slung about the priest's neck, a heavy silver cross spiraled beneath his jaw as he scaled the pyre's northern slope. The crowd grew silent. The priest pressed a Bible into Isobel's hands, loudly instructing her to make a good confession, then set his ear against her occluded mouth.

Dr. Cavendish lifted the trapdoor and secured it with an iron brace. "Go below, Miss Stearne."

"I cannot."

The priest took back his book, his sour face suggesting that Isobel Mowbray's last words had displeased him. He shook his head, opened his Bible, and recited Psalm One Hundred in a stentorian but mellifluous voice. "Make a joyful noise unto the Lord all ye lands . . ."

"Once, in Würzburg, I saw a supposed witch burned at the stake." Dr. Cavendish stared into the open trap as if deciphering a scene in a scrying-glass. "They strangled her first, but 'twas still for me a nightmare, more terrible than I can say."

"Terrible for you"—Jennet kept the telescope locked on the priest as he descended the mound of logs and fagots—"and even worse for the woman."

Mr. Grigsby lit a torch and passed it ceremoniously to Walter. The executioner pulled on leather gloves and, leaning a wooden ladder against the stake, climbed to the elevation of his faceless prisoner. He flexed his fingers in prelude to the choking—once, twice, thrice. The image went muzzy, its particulars sluiced away by Jennet's tears. She laid the telescope on the roof and mopped her eyes with the hem of her gown.

As the executioner fitted his hands around Isobel's neck, something wholly unexpected occurred. Despite the tightening fingers and the intervening hood, the philosopher managed to release a loud, coherent utterance.

"Darling Jenny! Mapper of moons! Maker of rainbows!"

Ice-water formed in Jennet's bowels.

"I know you're out there, Jenny!" Isobel's words boomed across the green. "Hear me now!"

"Dear God, why doth she do this?" Jennet rasped. "She promised to keep silent."

"Attend her every word!" Dr. Cavendish demanded.

Jennet seized the telescope, pressing it against her eye.

Upon receiving a nod from Grigsby, the executioner jumped off the ladder, plucked the torch from Walter's grasp, and jabbed it into the bottommost fagots like a swordsman delivering a fatal thrust. An ecstatic cheer shot from the crowd as the pyre caught fire.

" 'Tis not happening," Jennet insisted.

"Hear me, child!" Isobel cried.

"What shall I do?" Jennet wailed.

"Are you blind?" Dr. Cavendish seethed. "Can you not see the flames? For God's sake, tell the woman you hear her!"

The tongues of combustion sinuated through the pyre and began to rise, higher, higher, darting amidst the gaps in the logs. Flames met fagots with a popping noise suggesting a regiment discharging a score of muskets.

"I hear you, Aunt Isobel!" Jennet shouted. She set down the telescope and, gaining her feet, stretched to full height. "I hear you!"

"Newton's proof!" Isobel screamed. "I can see it, child! Aristotle! The elements! Aristotle!"

"Aristotle!" Jennet echoed. Aristotle? "The elements!" Aristotle's elements?

"Earth! Air! Newton's proof! The elements!"

"Earth and air, aye! Earth and air and water and fire!"

"Water and fire!" shrieked Aunt Isobel, coughing as the smoke invaded her lungs. "Water and fire! Fire! Fire! Oh, God, the fire!"

"I shall find the proof! Aristotle! The elements!"

"Damn thee, Walter Stearne! Damn thy bones and blood!"

In dying, Isobel Mowbray became a kind of storm, her imprecations booming across the field like peals of thunder, her screams flashing through the air like lightning-bolts. The atmosphere thickened with smoke, hosannas, and the fleshy stench of Exodus 22:18.

Jennet, still standing, grabbed the telescope and put it to her eye, but she dared not twist the tubes.

Die, please die, please die.

"The elements?" Dr. Cavendish said.

She did not resist when the curator stepped forward and tore the instrument from her grasp.

Please die, please die.

Dr. Cavendish lowered himself over the edge of the roof and slipped into the driver's box, resting the telescope on the seat. "Why the elements?" he muttered.

A roar filled Jennet's ears, a pounding tide of blood.

"The elements," Dr. Cavendish grunted, seizing the reins.

Isobel's screams dissolved into an unearthly gurgling, and then her scorched throat at last grew still. Never had Jennet known a more blessed silence, but no sooner had it settled than her father, livid and sweating, broke from the crowd and rushed toward the Gypsy wagon.

"Jennet!" he cried, his voice abrim with rage and disgust. "Daughter, you will explain yourself!"

The crack of Dr. Cavendish's horsewhip resounded like a pistol shot. Jennet crossed the roof, dropped through the trap, and landed on the museum floor. She rose and staggered amongst the monsters, weaving every whichway like a kite in a hurricane. As the coach rolled toward St. Helen's Lane, she fell against the Sussex Rat-Baby, embracing the huge glass jar for support. Nausea possessed her. She vomited forth a foul, viscous, bitter gush of mucus, spilling the hot broth onto the floor like slop from a slush-bucket.

With the back of her hand she wiped the sticky fluid from her lips. "She's dead," she explained to the Sussex Rat-Baby. "She's dead," she announced to the Cyclops of Bourne. "She's dead," she informed the Bird-Child of Bath. "For this my aunt was once alive," she told the Bicephalic Girl, "and now she is dead."

THREE DAYS AFTER the successful and well-attended burning of his sister-in-law, Walter Stearne received a letter from the new Keeper of the Privy Seal—George Savile, Marquess of Halifax—inviting him to "a meeting concerning your curious proposition that our nation requires a Witchfinder-Royal." At first he was uncertain how to account for his good fortune, but eventually he concluded that the Almighty had decided to reward his leniency. In electing to punish Jennet's recent disobedience by merely boxing her ears and then confining her to her bed-chamber without food for three days, as opposed to birching her backside until the skin turned plum, he had gained favor in God's eyes.

The momentous gathering was to occur on a Saturday afternoon at Blickling Hall, Sir Henry Hobart's sprawling mansion in the valley of the Bure. Walter felt ashamed to be arriving in his shabby Basque coach, but his discomfort turned to delight when he realized that the post of Witchfinder-Royal would probably come with a conveyance fit for an earl. What other benefits, he wondered, might his new appointment entail? A house in London? A silver pricking needle?

With exultant heart and prancing step, he followed the steward into a drawing-room off the staircase, where Lord Halifax, a horse-faced man sporting painted cheeks and an unruly silver peruke, waited in the company of two other Privy Council members. Alexander Tancred, Earl of Gurney, was a person of loud laughter and wide girth, his jaw and brow mottled by the pox. Francis Chater, Earl of Wroxeter, as long and lean as his fellow aristocrats were plump, possessed a disconcerting habit of reaming his nostrils with the corner of his handkerchief.

A servant brought coffee, and the four men got down to business. Lord Halifax produced a copy of Walter's ancient petition to the Crown, along with a paper that he identified as Lord Sunderland's favorable report on the proposed office.

"Mr. Stearne, having read these two documents, I wish I could tell you that our attitude accords with Sunderland's," Halifax said. "Alas, we must withhold our endorsement until we fathom your peculiar religious views."

"Peculiar?" A sinking feeling spread through Walter, the sort of queasiness he experienced each time he saw an accused sorcerer bob to the surface of a river. "I assure you, my Lords, I am a covenanted Christian who says his prayers each night."

"In your letter to our former monarch, James the Second, you assert, quote, 'Being of the Romish faith, His Majesty should be singularly sympathetic to the witchfinding enterprise,' unquote," Lord Gurney said. "You further observe, quote, 'The *Mulleus Maleficarum* is Catholic in pedigree,' and also, quote, 'European anti-Satanism becomes rational and systematic only with Pope Innocent's *Summis Desiderantes* of 1484.' Now, Mr. Stearne, although King James did indeed cleave to the Papist perversion, surely it hath not escaped your notice that England's present rulers are Protestants, as are Lord Halifax, Lord Wroxeter, and myself."

"And myself as well," Walter said.

"Do you regard the Protestant faith as inferior to the Catholic when it comes to witch-cleansing?" Lord Gurney inquired.

"Oh, no, sir, not in the least."

Lord Wroxeter said, "Need we remind you of Martin Luther's statement that, quote, 'I would have no compassion on these witches. I would burn them all'?"

Luther's views on Satanism were but dimly familiar to Walter, though he decided to pretend otherwise. "I have always counted the monk's motto amongst my favorites."

"Then mayhap you're also aware that John Calvin once said, quote, 'God expressly commands that all witches and enchantresses shall be put to death, and this law of God is a universal law.' "

"I have inscribed those very words inside the cover of my Bible," Walter said, fully intending to do so before sundown.

"The Protestant religion is a witch-fighting religion," Lord Gurney said. "Of the several hundred thousand Satanists switched off since our Redeemer's advent, nearly a quarter of the convictions may be credited to Reformation magistrates."

Walter made a fist, slamming it into his open palm. "The more for that, the infernal Papists had a head start by fifteen centuries!"

"Well spoken, sir!" Halifax declared. "My Lords, 'twould appear that in Mr. Stearne we have a patriotic, a pious, and withal a *Protestant* witchfinder."

"Agreed," Wroxeter said.

"Hear! Hear!" Gurney shouted.

Walter heaved a sigh of such force it could have snuffed a candle.

A smiling Halifax said, "At its forthcoming meeting with His Majesty, the Privy Council will recommend that, pursuant to the Conjuring Statute, you be appointed Witchfinder-Royal for the Crown's colonies in New-Plymouth and Massachusetts Bay, with an annual salary of two hundred pounds, or one guinea per detected Satanist, whichever sum is higher, plus a Basque coach and team."

Having completed his epic exhalation, Walter now found himself gasping for breath. "Pardon, my Lord. Did you say . . . Massachusetts?"

"Correct," Halifax replied.

"Is that not in . . . America?"

"America's the proper place for a man of your ambitions," Gurney said. " 'Tis the land of opportunism."

Walter said, "My Lords, if you please, I'd prefer not to live in Massachusetts—a barbaric place, I've heard, o'errun with violent aborigines, wild animals, and maniacal Puritans. Can I not be Witchfinder-Royal for my beloved England instead? Scotland, perhaps? Ireland? Wales?"

"Sir, we shall be blunt," Wroxeter said, probing his left nostril with a cloaked finger. "The longer you remain on this side of the Atlantic, the more you place yourself in jeopardy. 'Tis no secret His Majesty's Secretary of State would see Walter Stearne drawn and quartered for treason."

Hearing his own name and the word "treason" spoken in the same sentence rattled Walter like a thunderclap. "Treason? *Treason?* My Lords, you address as loyal a subject as e'er walked on English soil."

Gurney gathered the folds of his forehead into a byzantine frown. "You burned a woman of property, you wall-eyed cod-swallower! What sort of doltish thing was *that* to do?"

"She was guilty," Walter said.

"She was *gentry*," Halifax said. "To wit, you pompous nincompoop, you have no future here. Hie yourself to America and proceed to make the best of't."

"We've found something to cheer you," Gurney said, handing Walter a bound booklet of some twenty pages. "Last month this worthy specimen of Calvinist exegesis arrived in London."

Walter examined the slender volume, whose cover identified it as *A Discourse on Witchcraft,* a sermon preached the previous year in Boston by a Puritan minister named Cotton Mather. He turned to page one and read, "Witchcraft is the Doing of strange (and for the most part ill) Things by the Help of evil Spirits covenanting with the woeful Children of Men." A passing piquant definition.

"The New-England Calvinists might be slavering fanatics, but they've ne'er shrunk from prosecuting the Dark One," Wroxeter said. "In recent years they've convened a dozen witch-trials throughout Connecticut and Massachusetts."

"But how am I to move in Puritan circles when my faith is of the Anglican variety?" Walter asked.

"A fair question," Halifax said. "Methinks a tilt toward the Calvinist austerity might suit your purpose."

"I shan't do it!" Walter protested. " 'Twould be an act of sheer hypocrisy!"

"We speak not for hypocrisy but for compromise," Halifax said, setting his palm on Walter's shoulder. "Betwixt the two lies a universe of difference. Within government circles I am rightly called the Trimmer, an epithet I wear as proudly as a general his medals. When traveling with Tories I find myself disposed toward the Tory outlook. Amongst Whigs I enter a Whiggish frame of mind. To wit, through the subtle art of equivocation I have made myself obnoxious to all, with the result that no man durst oust me for fear of pleasing his enemies."

Walter returned his gaze to the sermon, alighting on a passage in which Cotton Mather argued that the demonic compact was as palpable as any other crime. "Many Witches have confess'd and shew'd their Deeds. We have seen those Things done that are impossible a mere Disease or Deceit could procure." An important point. Those who would reduce *maleficium* to physical sickness or legerdemain were not looking closely at the evidence. This Mather was a divine worth knowing.

"Two hundred pounds per annum—was that the figure?" Walter asked.

"In the interests of efficiency," Wroxeter said, nodding, "you will draw your salary from the Massachusetts Governor."

"And in the interests of economy," Halifax added, "you will occupy the property of my late uncle, a modest farm on the Merrimack in the Puritan community of Haverhill."

"Haverhill?" Walter said. "Not Boston?"

" 'Tis all His Majesty can afford," Halifax said, smiling. "The War of the Grand Alliance hath emptied his coffers."

Walter stared into the impenetrable blackness of his tepid coffee. "I would have a proper license," he said at last. "Signed by the King."

"The Defender of the Faith's agreeable," Wroxeter said.

" 'Twill grant me the title of Massachusetts Witchfinder-Royal and specify that upon my death the office transfers to my firstborn son—and to his firstborn son after that."

"Such can be arranged," Halifax said.

"We've saved the best news for last," Gurney said. "As you might surmise, the red Indians of New-England, whose numbers easily surpass one hundred thousand, know naught of the Christian faith, nor of any religion at all save their own deplorable paganism. Do you grasp the implications?"

"I surely do, my Lord Gurney." Walter took a gulp of cold coffee. "One hundred thousand?"

"One hundred thousand."

Rolling up Mather's sermon, Walter thanked the aristocrats for their generosity. One hundred thousand disciples of Satan, and not a single licensed cleanser on the whole continent. The Massachusetts Witchfinder-Royal, it seemed, would never want for employment.

EVERY TIME JENNET REMEMBERED how she had once regarded Barnaby Cavendish as just another of England's itinerant charlatans, she experienced a withering chagrin, for in sooth he was closer to a saint. On the morning following the Colchester Castle execution, the curator's Samaritan sensibility asserted itself once again when he offered to donate his entire profit from showing his monsters about the town, three pounds sterling, to the cause of Aunt Isobel's interment.

The wooly-bearded executioner parted with her blackened bones for a guinea, and an identical sum inspired Oswald Leech, the pussel-gutted sexton of St. James's Church, to dig her a resting-place. For a site Mr. Leech selected an unhallowed patch of ground along the churchyard's eastern edge, just beyond the Roman wall. Hearts-ease and daisies bloomed everywhere. Standing atop a slate outcropping, a gray raft of stone adrift upon sea-green hills, Jennet and Dr. Cavendish watched silently as the sexton laid Isobel Mowbray's remains in a pinewood box, nailed the receptacle shut, and lowered it into the dank wormy cavity.

"Methinks I've deciphered her final words," Jennet said, dropping a handful of earth onto the coffin lid.

"About Aristotle and the elements?" Dr. Cavendish added a second clod to the grave. "Tell me your deduction."

"I believe that as the executioner went to strangle Aunt Isobel, Mr. Newton's calculation against witchery appeared to her as in a mystic vision. She saw that his lost proof turns on the Greek immutables."

"Earth, air, water, fire," Dr. Cavendish said.

"Earth, air, water, fire," she echoed.

"Ashes to ashes," Mr. Leech said. "Dust to dust."

Two days later, Jennet's father ushered her into the seclusion of his garden, asserting that he wished to confront her with "some issues of passing urgency." At first she assumed that he intended to box her ears again for attending the execution, but this time she had overestimated his wrath. He directed her to sit on the stone bench, then settled down beside her and solemnly announced that all their lives were about to change. At the end of the week they would take a coach to Gravesend and subsequently board a carrack, the *Albion*, bound for the New World, where he'd been appointed Witchfinder-Royal for Massachusetts Bay and New-Plymouth.

To Jennet it seemed as if her beautiful fœtus, her embryonic *argumentum grande*, had just died in the womb. How could she master the *Principia Mathematica* whilst trapped amongst barbarians so preoccupied with marauding mountain lions and savage Redmen they had no energy left for building libraries or founding colleges? How could she become a great natural philosopher when surrounded by bumpkins who didn't know Greek chemistry from curdled cream? The world's worst thrashing would be better than this dreadful news.

"I would prefer to stay in England," she said.

"Myself as well, but that path is not open to us." Her father crushed a scattering of acorns underfoot. "We must now discuss a rather different matter. A troubling matter."

"Aye?"

"A matter you will belike find painful, as it concerns the maternal aunt of whom you were so fond."

"Father, you hold me on tenterhooks."

"As Lady Mowbray received her punishment," he said, shifting on the hard marble, "the two of you entered upon a cryptic dialogue concerning an entity called 'Newton's proof.' Evidently she sought to impart some arcane alchemical formula to you."

"Her message was no secret," Jennet said, rising. "She was plainly averring that demonology will one day crumble before an alliance 'twixt Newton's principles and the Greek immutables."

"One day our Savior will return. One day the world will end."

"But not before your profession hath been trampled into the dust."

"Mayhap," he sneered. "But hear me now, child. My eye is evermore fixed on you. Let me catch you practicing some dark art or performing some diabolical experiment, and your regret will defy the limits of common imagination."

"You needn't suspect me of sorcery, sir." She strode past the trellis, heading for the garden gate. "Philosophy doth not hide its light beneath a bushel."

On Thursday morning Dr. Cavendish drove her out to Mirringate Hall, that she might bid Rodwell good-bye. Much to her astonishment, she found the manor occupied by the late Edward Mowbray's obese first cousin, Henry, and his equally adipose wife, Clarinda. In tones betraying not one atom of remorse, this self-regarding couple reported that upon learning of his mistress's execution Rodwell had taken to bed and died in his sleep. When Jennet expressed a desire to visit the old steward's grave, Henry Mowbray revealed that no such plot existed, for he'd sold the body to an anonymous surgeon in Maldon.

As the tense and unpleasant visit progressed, the two usurpers passed up no opportunity to insinuate that the girl in their midst had somehow betrayed Isobel in particular and the Mowbray family in general. It took Jennet the entire morning to convince them that she'd played no part in Isobel's arrest—that, indeed, she regarded her father's business as an abomination. At last a belated air of cordiality descended upon the gathering, and the conversation turned to the disposition of Isobel's estate. The Mowbrays made it clear that, though Rodwell's corpse was first amongst the Mirringate Hall accoutrements they'd converted to coin, it would not be the last. They fully intended to sell the telescope, the microscope, the alchemical equipment, and the library, all two thousand volumes.

The longer Jennet listened to their schemes, the more greatly she desired to sever all connection with these vultures. When they invited her and Dr. Cavendish to stay for the midday meal, she was pleased to reply, quite truthfully, that she must instead return to Colchester and pack her belongings for her imminent voyage.

" 'Twould seem the best thing about stumbling upon long-lost relations," Jennet remarked as she and Dr. Cavendish rode away from the manor, "is that it takes no particular effort to lose them all over again."

Beyond the singular volume called *A Woman's Garden of Pleasure and Pain* and Aunt Isobel's copy of the *Principia Mathematica*, the only earthly possession Jennet wished to bring with her was the toy windmill her mother had constructed as a child. But Walter forbade her this remembrance, as its size and bulk would consume an entire sea-chest, and the Stearne family was permitted to place only three such containers in the *Albion's* hold. Two mornings before they were to sail from Gravesend, Jennet carried the windmill to the summit of North Hill and gave it one last run. The machine worked splendidly, and yet she took no pleasure in its performance, as the vanes' cruciform pattern put her in mind of suffering and martyrdom.

"Father, forgive them," she muttered, fixing on the spinning sails, "for they knew not what they did."

With the coming of noon the wind grew dispirited, declining from a gust to a breeze and thence to utter stillness. She resolved to leave her mother's mill in place atop the ridge: no doubt some passing Colchester child would take a fancy to the toy, conclude it was there for the stealing, and joyfully bear it away.

"Upon further consideration, I have decided that they knew exactly what they did"—she lifted her head toward the clouds—"and so I bid Thee give carbuncles and gout to all who danced that day on the green."

The following afternoon she parted company with Dr. Cavendish and his monsters outside the Fox and Fife, where he'd rented rooms following his expulsion from the Red Lion, whose pious proprietor believed that the curator was profiting by the Devil's handiwork. Much to Dr. Cavendish's amusement, Jennet entered the Gypsy wagon and took leave of each freak individually. "Two heads are better than one," she informed the Bicephalic Girl. "Ugliness is only skin deep," she assured Perdition's Pride. "Think on't this wise," she told the Cyclops of Bourne. "When the time comes for you to get optical spectacles, you'll pay but half the normal price."

The Lyme Bay Fish-Boy, she predicted, was destined to wed a beautiful mermaid. The Smethwick Philosopher would one day assume the Lucasian Chair at Trinity College. The Bird Child of Bath would become the envy of eagles. She thanked the Rat-Baby, the Bloodsucker, the Maw, and the Kali for their help with the great Adramelech hoax.

"I hope you find a customer for your stillborns," she told Dr. Cavendish.

"I'Christ, Miss Stearne, your attitude toward my Kali and her kin hath revived mine own affections. For all I feel a weariness in my bones, I mean to show these freaks till the end of my days, falling down dead one afternoon whilst lecturing on the Bicephalic Girl."

"Oh, my dear Dr. Cavendish, you shall do no dying ere I've recovered Newton's lost calculation, borne it back to England, and sought out my old friend the prodigy-monger."

"Then let me ask a boon of thee." He caressed the Smethwick Philosopher. "In America you may very well come upon a fœtal aberration, and when that happens you must preserve it in brine till our reunion."

"You have my solemn word."

"I hereby appoint you Curator of the Cavendish Museum of Wondrous Prodigies—Colonial Branch."

She flung her arms wide as if preparing to embrace a tree, then gave her colleague a vigorous hug.

"I shall ne'er forget thee, Barnaby Cavendish."

That evening she undertook the most difficult farewell of all. She searched through the Basque coach until she found her father's lanthorn and his largest pricking needle. A half-hour later, as gloom enveloped the grounds of St. James's Church, hallowed and unhallowed alike, she trimmed the wick, set the globe to glowing, and, kneeling beside the grave, scratched thirteen words into the slate outcropping.

MENSUS ERAM CŒLOS, NUNC TERRAE METIOR UMBRAS
MENS COELESTRIS ERA, CORPORIS UMBRA IACET

Aunt Isobel had always admired the epitaph that Johannes Kepler had composed for himself shortly before his death. Indeed, the last time she was in Germany, she'd attempted to find the great astronomer's tombstone, only to learn it had been pulverized by a passing cavalry troop during the Thirty Years War. Jennet felt certain that Isobel, looking down from God's eternal domain, would be pleased to see Kepler's words shining beside her resting-place.

"I measured the skies, now I measure the shadows," she recited. "Sky-bound was the mind, Earth-bound the body rests."

She looked heavenward. Venus blazed above the northern horizon. Slowly the stars blinked into visibility like candles lit by an unseen votary. The Creator was perfect. His Creation was perfect. Ergo, every planet moved in that most perfect of shapes, the circle. No fact could be clearer. No other conic deserved consideration.

"Good-bye, Aunt Isobel. I loved you so much . . ."

Except the planets didn't move in circles. They simply didn't. Her blood leapt up, alive to the brilliance of that astonishing first law. *The orbit of a planet describes an ellipse, with the sun at one of its foci.* Thus were two millennia of received astronomical wisdom neatly and irrevocably overturned. Oh, Kepler, brave Kepler, how did you do it? *The orbit of a planet.* Did God tell you? *Describes an ellipse.* By what path doth a person come to think this way? *With the sun at one of its foci.* If I live to be a hundred, will I e'er vault past the beautiful circle to see the true ellipse beyond?

PART II

※※※※※※※※※

Earth
Air
Water
Fire

The
Fifth

❀❀❀❀❀❀❀❀❀❀

*The Salem Witch-Court
Declines to Cast
the First Stone
but Instead Places It
upon Giles Corey's Breast*

❀

C hill rains, razoring winds, and relentless sleet plagued the *Albion* from the first league of her Atlantic crossing onward, forcing the steerage passengers belowdecks, huddled in their hammocks like cocooned caterpillars awaiting metamorphosis. For Jennet the tedium proved almost unendurable, but then at last the captain, reversing an earlier edict, decreed that every literate voyager could burn a whale-oil reading lamp for three hours each day. Thus it was that, as the crossing progressed, Jennet drew insight and energy from the crepuscular pages of *A Woman's Garden of Pleasure and Pain,* unending perplexity from the dimly lit and obscurely written *Principia Mathematica,* and, after borrowing the first mate's English translation, the pleasures of picaresque adventure from the tenebrous text of *Don Quixote de la Mancha.*

Her father and brother, meanwhile, relieved their ennui by entering into the various card tournaments and draughts matches that occurred almost continually within these cavernous confines. Unhappily for the Witchfinder-Royal and his son, maritime custom dictated that no game could commence ere the players had wagered on the outcome. Being amongst the more honest folk aboard the *Albion,* Walter and Dunstan quickly saw their cash reserves depleted, the sounds emitted by their purses declining precipitously from the delightful jingle of guineas to the less gratifying clank of crowns to the melancholy tinkle of shillings.

Walter chose to make light of their bankruptcy. "Considering the sheer quantity of heathen sorcery with which the New World's infested," he told his children, "I would guess we'll all be living like kings anon."

As the *Albion* blew within view of the severe and scowling Massachusetts coastline, Jennet finished giving *A Woman's Garden of Pleasure and Pain* its fifth successive reading, taking care as always to conceal the manuscript from her father, who would surely throw the thing overboard the instant he saw that its author was Isobel Mowbray. In the first paragraph of the first chapter, Aunt Isobel had boldly declared her theme. "If a Woman wishes to count her Soul complete, she must avail herself of Love in all three Forms: pious, Platonic, priapic. But even as she opens her Heart to Cupid's Arrows, she must ally her Head with Reason's Axioms. Pregnancy and the French Pox are merely the most conspicuous amongst the Disasters that await the unwary Maiden as she makes her Way, Hopes aglow and Passions a-flame, to her Gallant's Bed."

To count her Soul complete: the phrase resounded in Jennet's skull like a taunt, the cruelest gibe yet sprung from the vindictive lips of Elinor Mapes. Dear God, how could she ever count her soul complete after that unthinkable event on the Colchester execution field? What alchemist yet born could refine a glue of sufficient stickiness to mend her fractured self whole?

When Jennet's father first told her of his appointment as Massachusetts Witchfinder-Royal, she'd naturally assumed that upon their arrival they would take possession of a large and splendid Boston mansion. The position indeed came with a house, but it was neither large, nor splendid, nor in Boston. To mitigate the gloom of their ramshackle Haverhill salt-box, Jennet papered the front parlor with Dunstan's most cheering vistas—a wheat field shimmering beneath an August sun, an abandoned stone barn rising from a hill of larkspur, a towering oak made golden by a lightning-stroke—all rendered in luminous wax. Her father, meanwhile, decorated his bed-chamber door with his cleansing license, an object to which he accorded such stupefying reverence it might have been a map disclosing the Seven Cities of Cibola, though it was in truth but a scraggly scrap of parchment signed illegibly by King William III.

Jennet could find nothing in Haverhill to call her own. It was a town of cows and people with the intellectual aspirations of cows. The ruling sentiment amongst the populace was fear. They feared famine and disease, wolves and wicked spirits, outsiders and one another—but most of all they feared the Algonquin Nimacooks, a tribe of savage tawnies who had recently raided the nearby settlements of Topsfield and Andover, slaughtering scores of men and abducting a dozen wives and daughters.

The possible fates of these women occasioned much speculation in Haverhill, but it was generally agreed that each abductee initially had to run the gauntlet—a ritualized torture in which the captive endured a savage beating, whereupon she was delivered to the tribe's most virile males for the purpose of breeding further Nimacooks. Whether or not a person believed this ghastly rumor, it was certainly congruent with the broader narrative favored by the Colony's most famous Christian, the renowned and talkative Cotton Mather. According to the Reverend Mather, the Indians of Massachusetts Bay were descended from an ancient Devil-worshipping race whom Lucifer had transported to the uninhabited continent so they might adulate him free of Christian interference. Whilst this theory struck Jennet as doubtful in the extreme, the Nimacooks nevertheless terrified her, and she nightly implored her Creator to spare Haverhill their flaming arrows and cruel knives, their brutish clubs and sharp tomahawks.

Unfortunately for her father, though happily for New-England's supposed Satanists, his franchise began and ended with his shabby little license. Within a week of landing in Haverhill, Walter learned that the Massachusetts Governor, Sir Edmund Andros, had been deposed, and so the anticipated salary of two hundred pounds per annum never materialized, despite Walter's entreaties to the interim administration in Boston. Throughout his first year in the Colony, he convinced the selectmen of only two neighboring towns, Amesbury and Beverly, to sponsor witch-hunts and pay him a guinea for each heretic he unmasked. By late winter, thanks to Walter's efforts, four women lay shackled in Massachusetts gaols, awaiting the trials that could not occur until the Colony got a new charter and a new Royal Governor to execute it. As she pored over the pages of her *Woman's Garden*, Jennet often thought of those wretched prisoners, shivering in their own dung, praying for their prosecutions to begin so that they might know the warmth of a courthouse.

To minimize the threat of starvation, her father planted a vegetable garden, but he succeeded in coaxing from the soil only a few anemic turnips and feeble beans. When he tried catching fish, the trout inhabiting the Merrimack proved too devious for him, routinely eluding his net. Desperate, he took up the flintlock musket left behind by Lord Halifax's uncle and marched resolutely into the woods. Before a week was out he'd tracked and shot a doe, and the following week he appeared in the doorway with a stag slung over his shoulders like an ox-yoke. And so it came to pass that the Massachusetts Witchfinder-Royal was reduced to the status of common deerslayer, a humiliation in which Jennet could not forbear to take a secret pleasure.

Like her father, she attempted to augment the family's larder through fishing, but her expeditions proved unavailing. She never netted a trout, only crayfish, minnows, and the occasional carp. Although the poverty of her catch depressed her, she found ample compensation in the intemperate beauty of the Merrimack Valley. Walking along the river's banks each day, observing the corpulent green bullfrogs croaking atop their podiums of mud, the golden butterflies floating above the wildflowers, and the precise and urgent dragonflies as they flitted amidst the cattails, she decided that Cotton Mather's theory must be turned inside out. Far from being the Devil's backyard, this untrammeled continent partook of whatever postlapsarian goodness the planet still could claim. In her more rhapsodic moments she pictured God as a pregnant woman, wincing and gasping as lovely Eden spilled from her womb—Eden, "that unthinkable Arcadia," as Aunt Isobel had once put it, "inhospitable in its perfection"—whereupon the great messy placenta came forth, Eden's afterbirth, inferior to Paradise in every way save habitability, and God called it America.

As her life in Haverhill pursued its unsurprising course, Jennet's body underwent the very changes forecast in her *Woman's Garden*. Her hips grew round. Her bosom swelled. Next the bloody flow commenced, growing heavier with each successive month. By her thirteenth birthday she'd experienced every phenomenon predicted by Isobel's treatise save one, the longing for a young man's touch. But this, she knew, would come.

With nary a philosopher, geometer, or sage in the vicinity, she was obliged to try deciphering Isaac Newton on her own. She could manage the Latin well enough, but what did it all *mean*? Where was the sense in a statement such as, "The areas that revolving bodies describe by radii drawn to an immovable center of force do lie in the same immovable planes, and are proportional to the times in which they are described"? Not long after Isobel had introduced her to the *Principia Mathematica,* Jennet had found amongst her aunt's geometry volumes a monograph in which Newton boasted of making his book as abstruse as possible, "to avoid being bated by little Smatterers in Mathematics." This same monograph specified the works a person should master ere approaching the tortuous tome. "After all thirteen books of Euclid, you must read De Witt's *Elementa Curvarum,* as this will increase your Knowledge of the Conics. For the Algebra, you should acquire Bartholin's *Commentaries on Descartes's Geometry* and solve the first Thirty Problems. Finally, any Mind that imbibes the Whole of Huygens's *Horologium Oscillatorium* will emerge the richer for it." Small wonder the *Principia Mathematica* seemed as opaque to her as barrel-tar.

Time and again she returned to the Merrimack, and one afternoon she forsook the linen net for a method perfected by Dunstan. You located a piece of twine, fastened a crab apple to the midpoint, knotted one end around a willow wand, tied a bent sewing needle to the other end, impaled a caterpillar on the needle, set the apple a-float, and waited. The technique worked splendidly. Shortly before dusk Jennet snagged and landed a trout. For a full minute she crouched beside her prize as it lay twitching on the shore, tethered to the wand, friendless and alone. Staring into its unblinking eye, she grew grateful for René Descartes's deduction that all such animals were essentially machines, oblivious to sensation, immune to misery.

She pressed one palm against the dying trout, feeling its squamous complexity, then reached toward the bent needle and twisted the shank free of the fish's mouth.

She looked up. A tall young man stood on the far side of the river, harvesting marsh marigolds. He was bare to the waist, his flesh as brown as cedar wood and smooth as bronze. He wore deerskin leggings. Their gazes connected. He smiled. She shivered. His hair was greased, cut short on one side, black as a Colchester crow. His cheekbones were high, nose elegant and aquiline.

Lowering his head, he inhaled the fragrance of the golden bouquet, then once again fixed his dark eyes on her.

Only much later, as she hurried home through the gathering dusk, surrounded by the sawing of the crickets and the tremolos of the tree frogs, the trout secured in her leather satchel, did she make sense of the encounter. This had been a momentous afternoon. There would not be another like it soon. For on this day Jennet Stearne, future author of the *argumentum grande*, had caught a trout, seen an Indian, and experienced her first sweet rush of desire.

STEPPING OFF HIS PORCH, *Malleus Maleficarum* in hand, Walter skirted his miserable crop of pole-beans and headed toward Kembel's Ordinary. All the way down Mill Street he made a point of not looking west. Thither lay an entire continent, vast beyond imagining and infested with Devil-worshippers—and withal he could do nothing about it. Until he persuaded the Boston Puritans to supply their Witchfinder-Royal with a salary, he would have to waste his days hunting and fishing and otherwise scrabbling for a living. Such an irrational state of affairs. When your cellar was full of rats, you didn't lock your cat in the attic.

No matter how vigorously Walter prayed, how much Scripture he read, or how mightily he strove to think well of his benefactors, he could not shake his conviction that Lord Halifax and the others had betrayed him. He wanted to believe that it was all an unhappy accident—that when the aristocrats sent him packing to America, they'd had no inkling of Governor Andros's imminent eviction. But Walter smelled conspiracy. He could practically hear the three lords cackling over how they'd foiled the controversial pricker, deftly maneuvering him out of England without resorting to the cumbersome formalities of exile.

Whenever Walter supped in Boston with his remarkable new friend,

Cotton Mather, the jelly-jowled minister reminded him that there was considerable cause for optimism. Even as the two Satan-haters ate their fowl and venison, the Reverend Mather's ambitious father was in London negotiating with the King's Colonial Secretary, drafting a new charter for Massachusetts Bay and helping to select Andros's replacement. In the meantime, Mather advised, Walter should continue detecting heretics whether the local magistrates paid him or not, the better to impress the new governor when that worthy arrived.

"Imagine you're the Crown agent in question," Mather said. "On reaching Massachusetts Bay you hear rumors of the Colony's official witchfinder—how he so despiseth the demon world, he hath been dispensing his services for free. What would your inclination be?"

"To recompense that cleanser handsomely," Walter said, basking in the warmth of Mather's madeira. " 'Sblood, Reverend, for a pastor, you think rather like a politician!"

" 'Tis a habit I must continually cultivate—at least until that unlikely day when our politicians start thinking like pastors."

Owing to this expectation of ultimate reward, Walter experienced an unbridled delight when, early in March, the Reverend Samuel Parris of Salem-Village solicited his expertise in circumscribing Satan. "The 25th of this Month will find me in your Town of Haverhill, buying Boots and Gloves," Parris's letter began. "My fond Hope is that, come the noon Hour, we might meet at Kembel's Ordinary. You will know me by my ministerial Garb." At first Walter decided that Parris merely intended to bring him, the Colony's most famous non-Puritan, into the Calvinist fold, but then he read the closing line—"Lucifer hath been rais'd amongst us, and his Rage is vehement and terrible, and we sorely require your Skills"—and he forthwith scribbled a note confirming the rendezvous.

Striding into the tavern, Walter instinctively clapped an eye on the Reverend Samuel Parris. With his high-crowned hat and elegant gray cape, the minister stood out from the Haverhill farmers and tradesmen as would a diamond atop a dung-hill. A cadaverous, beak-nosed man of sallow complexion, he sat by the window, leafing through a Bible bound in Moroccan leather. Walter slipped his license from his *Malleus* and set it before Parris. The men shook hands, exchanged pleasantries, and ordered pots of cider, and by midday they'd formed the sort of iron bond enjoyed by those who place Devil-fighting above all other matters.

Beginning the previous January, Parris explained, a strange malady had overtaken a half-dozen girls in Salem-Village. The children routinely lapsed into trances, suffered convulsions, and endured bites from invisible teeth and pinches from phantom fingers. Amongst the afflicted were Parris's own daughter, Betty, and his orphaned niece, Abigail Williams. After ruling out all possible mundane causes, the local physician had offered a diagnosis of *maleficium;* the girls, he believed, were bewitched. Soon afterward Betty and the others started naming their tormentors. Thus far five Salemites had been examined, indicted, and sent to the gaol-house, and every week the girls sensed yet another wizard or enchantress in their midst.

" 'Tis obviously a situation calls for an experienced cleanser," Walter said.

"Captain Walcott hath agreed to open his house to you," Parris said. "We would retain your services anon but for one lamentable circumstance."

"Speak no more of't. Though baptized into the Church of England, I am all eager to join your Calvinist sect."

"I feel a prodigious relief," Parris said, pressing his Bible against his breast as if applying a poultice.

Walter gulped down the last of his cider, sighing contently as the alcohol mingled with his blood. The minister's splendid cape, he realized, would make a most dignified uniform for a Witchfinder-Royal. "You spoke of invisible teeth and phantom fingers . . ."

"Invisible to us bystanders, but not to the afflicted girls. Barely a day goes by without a Satanist sends forth her ghostly apparition, and by these shapes the children know who plagues them."

"Were you aware, Mr. Parris, that we licensed prickers regard spectral evidence with the gravest skepticism?"

"I'Christ, I was not. You can see how great is our need of you. Come to Salem, sir."

"My fee's five crowns per unmasked heretic."

"And therein lies my regret, for we cannot offer you any compensation beyond food and lodging. The village selectmen—an incompetent bunch, as you'll see—barely manage to scrape together my monthly salary and firewood allotment."

"The things of Cæsar mean nothing when there be demons to thwart," Walter said. And governors to dazzle. "I shall join this epic hunt of yours"—he reinserted his license in his *Malleus*—"ere the week is out."

❧

ON THE SEVENTH DAY IN APRIL of 1692, Walter loaded his children and his detection tools into his thrice-owned and grotesquely decrepit one-horse carriage—the promised Basque coach had never materialized—and traveled twenty miles southeast to Salem-Village. They reached Jonathan Walcott's house in the middle of a ferocious thunder-gust, but luckily the Captain and his wife were prepared for their sodden visitors, providing them with woolen clothes, hot broth, warm wine, and dry beds.

An auspicious beginning, Walter decided. His fortunes were about to change.

At first Dunstan and Jennet seemed wholly in countenance with their new surroundings. Though the village was landlocked, the neighboring community of Salem-Town encompassed a bustling harbor, and Dunstan and Jennet passed many agreeable afternoons watching the arrivals and departures of the high-masted ships. Alas, by mid-month Walter's children were complaining of boredom, a condition they sought to relieve through association with Abigail Williams, a leader amongst the girls whose sufferings had ignited the hunt. Walter did not like Miss Williams. He did not like any of the haunted daughters of Salem-Village. Their temperaments were flighty, their speech unrefined, their submissions of spectral evidence dubious. In the case of the Williams girl, however, he apprehended within her troubled soul an odd sort of holiness, an idiosyncratic sanctity, and so he permitted his progeny to keep company with her, hoping that her piety might somehow rub off on Jennet.

Upon assuming his position on the Examination Committee, Walter asked the chairman, John Hathorne, the town's imperially unpleasant magistrate, if he might visit the seven indicted suspects in their gaol-cells. He wanted to test them all, from four-year-old Dorcas Good to seventy-one-year-old Rebecca Nurse. Hathorne ultimately admitted Walter into the prisoners' presence, but he forbade him to scan their skin, for the Puritans in their purity held it unseemly that a man should search a woman for imp teats or Devil's marks. Moreover, though Judge Hathorne and his colleagues did not deny the reality of animal servants, they thought it impossible to tell a true familiar from a mundane beast, and so they discouraged him from doing any watchings. As for the cold-water test, Mr. Hathorne perversely dismissed this proof as "the rankest Anglican superstition." It went especially hard with Walter that he could not scrutinize the flesh of Rebecca Nurse, as most of her neighbors regarded her as a kind of living saint: probably this was another case, like Jephthah's daughter, of a seemingly virtuous woman who practiced sorcery in secret, but he wanted to be sure.

"Why do you invite me into your enterprise only to tie my hands and shackle my talents?" he complained to Hathorne and his slithery assistant, Jonathan Corwin.

"For the simple reason," Hathorne replied, "that when the new governor sees his own Witchfinder-Royal sitting on the Committee, he'll appoint a proper court without delay."

" 'Sheart, 'twould seem I'm but a figurehead," Walter said. " 'Tis my inclination to resign."

"*Resign?*" Corwin gasped. "Desert your post at the height of New-England's greatest cleansing?"

Walter pinned his lower lip betwixt his teeth. "Were you better acquainted with me, sir, you would know that I would sooner pluck out mine eyes than abandon my sentry-box to Lucifer."

The magistrate offered Walter a nod that seemed at once condescending and conspiratorial. "Mr. Stearne, methinks we're all wondrous useful to one another. Might I suggest we stop bickering amongst ourselves and save our spleen for Satan?"

As the month progressed, the screaming girls identified twenty-three additional Devil-worshippers in the village, and these suspects were duly summoned to the meeting-house, where they stood before the Committee in ostensible perplexity whilst Hathorne and company interrogated them. After much negotiation Walter convinced the chairman to let him exercise his scanning skills indirectly. By this compromise each accused female undressed herself in the foyer, Walter present but blindfolded, and then the wives of Hathorne and Corwin ran their hands across her skin, describing all marks and pricking any that sounded suspicious to the Witchfinder-Royal. Although this procedure brought to light dozens of incriminating excrescences, Walter could barely abide his frustration. For the first time ever, he understood the impetus behind the Protestant Reformation. Martin Luther had loathed those platoons of priests styling themselves the sole earthly agents binding Man to his Creator, and Walter was likewise repulsed by these two superfluous females mediating betwixt his fingers and his judgment.

In the unique case of the beloved Rebecca Nurse, neither Goodwife Hathorne nor Goodwife Corwin could find a bloodless aberration on her person, and so Walter administered the secondary tests. Goodwife Nurse recited the Lord's Prayer start to finish without the slightest hesitation or mildest elision. She easily met the weeping standard, shedding more than twenty tears under the thumbscrew's rude influence. When he scalded her index finger with boiling water, the resulting blister stretched well beyond the range, zero to one inch, that bespoke diabolism. Goodwife Nurse, it surely seemed, was innocent.

Despite Walter's success in detecting Devil's marks amongst the suspect population, the Examination Committee continued keying its sessions not to solid demonology but to the impulsive children. Whenever an alleged Satanist entered the meeting-house, Abigail Williams's band went into paroxysms of bewildering intensity. Each girl had her *forte*. Miss Williams herself vomited thorns. Mercy Lewis bled from her nose and mouth. Elizabeth Hubbard swooned. Betty Parris was a champion writher. Ann Putnam fell down gasping, a victim of spectral choking. Mary Warren shrieked and wailed as she beheld invisible imps alight upon the prisoners' shoulders. Mary Walcott—the Captain's daughter and the group's newest member—beat her head against the floor, raising bumps and welts so terrible as to suggest the violence of a Nimacook hatchet.

The Committee had just commenced its seventh week of service, with sixty-two indictments to show for its efforts, when Increase Mather finally returned from London bearing the sorely needed provincial charter and accompanied by the new Massachusetts Royal Governor. Sir William Phipps soon proved the very sort of anti-Satanist that Salem required in this, her darkest hour. On the twenty-seventh of May, he brought into being a Court of Oyer and Terminer to try the accused witches, an ad hoc institution featuring Deputy Governor William Stoughton heading up a panel of eight justices, amongst them John Hathorne, Jonathan Corwin, the famously formidable Samuel Sewall of Boston, and one of Walter's Haverhill neighbors, Major Nathaniel Saltonstall.

Six days later the defendant Bridget Bishop entered Salem-Town Courthouse. Eleven persons submitted statements against her, with Miss Williams's troops claiming abuse at the hands of the defendant's specter and Walter adducing the Devil's mark on her left calf (a determination he'd made after hearing Goodwife Corwin's account of both the excrescence itself and its insensibility to the pricking needle). The jury, led by Foreman Thomas Fisk, rendered a verdict of guilty. Despite Bridget Bishop's blubbering protestations, Judge Stoughton forthwith ordered her execution "according to the direction given in the laws of God and the wholesome statutes of the English nation." On the tenth of June, Walter stood at the foot of Gallows Hill and watched as the sheriff and his men carted the convicted enchantress to the summit. After leaning a ladder against the largest oak, the sheriff hauled Bridget Bishop ten rungs skyward, slipped a noose around her throat, and pushed her into the air. The witch's cervical vertebrae failed to separate, and in consequence her strangulation lasted nine minutes.

On the first morning in July, the Court heard the collective evidence against Sarah Wildes, Susannah Martin, Elizabeth Howe, and Sarah Good. Walter and the tormented girls offered abundant proof of Sa-

tanism, and before the noon recess the jury found against all four prisoners. The day's events were not entirely soothing to the Witchfinder-Royal,
however, for that afternoon a fifth defendant came before the Court, the
saintly Rebecca Nurse, whose friends and relations had persuaded Judge
Stoughton to consider her case separately. True to form, the girls shrieked
in pain the instant Goodwife Nurse approached the bench, but then Walter assumed the witness-stand, telling how the *Pater Noster* test, the weeping proof, and the scalding ordeal—not to mention the pricking of her
several blemishes—all appeared to vindicate the old woman.

"In my thirty years of cleansing," he told the judges, "I've ne'er met a
person as innocent to a witch as Rebecca Nurse."

From the defendant's husband, Francis Nurse, came a final piece of
exculpatory evidence, a petition signed by thirty-nine of the community's
most respected citizens. "We cannot imagine any Cause or Grounds,"
they wrote, "to suspect Goody Nurse of those Things of which she is accused."

Shortly after dusk Thomas Fisk led his fellow jurymen into the antechamber. They returned twenty minutes later. A hush settled over Salem-
Town Courthouse. Walter thought of Revelation 8:1. *And when he had opened
the seventh seal, there was silence in Heaven for the space of half an hour.*

"How goes't with the defendant?" Judge Stoughton asked. "Be she
guilty or nay?"

Walter leaned forward. A single drop of sweat descended from beneath his peruke, tickling his skin as it slid down his brow.

Goodman Fisk coughed deliberately, anxiously shifting his weight
from one foot to the other. "Not guilty."

So wild was the subsequent frenzy that a stranger happening upon
the scene might have thought he'd wandered into a lunatic asylum. The
bewitched girls clawed at their breasts, drove their teeth into their forearms, and ripped clumps of hair from their scalps, all the while screaming like sinners dredged in burning sulphur.

"Goody Nurse clutches my throat!" shouted Ann Putnam, retching
and wheezing.

"Goody Nurse gnaws my tongue!" cried Mercy Lewis, spitting blood.

"Her specter fells me!" Abigail Williams crashed to the floor like a tree limb riven by a lightning-bolt. "She bids me kiss the Devil's bum! Nay, Goody Nurse, I shan't kiss it! I shan't! I shan't!"

When at last the chaos subsided, William Stoughton turned to the foreman. "Goodman Fisk, I have no wish to impose upon the jury, but I must ask that you reconsider your verdict."

"On what grounds?" Fisk asked.

"Yes, Excellency, on what grounds?" Walter demanded, leaping from his chair as if wrenching free of a thornbush.

"On the grounds of the *maleficia* these girls suffer at the hands of this she-wolf in sheep's clothing," Stoughton said.

Foreman Fisk guided his jurors back into the anteroom. It took them but ten minutes to frame a new and better verdict.

On the nineteenth of July, Sarah Wildes, Susannah Martin, Elizabeth Howe, Sarah Good, and Rebecca Nurse were carted to Gallows Hill, where scores of spectators awaited, singing hymns and sharing corn-cakes. Walter brought Dunstan along, their first such communion since the cleansing of Isobel Mowbray. Cotton Mather came all the way from Boston, exquisitely dressed in a black linen robe, his felt hat screwed smartly over his bulbous wig. Not since Jesus himself had passed through Jerusalem's gates amidst a thousand waving palm fronds, Walter mused, had a Christian made so impressive an entrance.

Singling out the Witchfinder-Royal, Mather approached and presented him with a bound copy of his latest sermon, *Remarkables of the Divine Providence, Including Sea-Deliverances, Gallows Speeches of Criminals, and an Account of How God Lifted a Plague of Caterpillars through the Sending of Flocks of Birds.* Walter bowed gratefully and turned back the cover. On the title-page the minister had written, "For my Colleague Walter Stearne. A Friend to Virtue, to Vice alone a Foe. With Admiration, the Reverend Cotton Mather."

"I shall evermore treasure this little book," Walter said, "and especially thine affectionate inscription."

As it happened, Mather's presence on Gallows Hill that morning proved essential to the task at hand. Each of the first four heretics was swung, strangled, and cut down with nary a comment from the crowd, but when the sheriff made ready to push Rebecca Nurse off the ladder, a score of Salemites grew conspicuously discontent, screaming, "Spare her! Spare her!"

Like the Redeemer making ready to deliver the Sermon on the Mount, Mather scrambled up the face of a granite boulder and, reaching the summit, spread his arms wide as if to gather every spectator into his loving embrace.

"Good farmers and merchants of Salem, be not deceived by outward forms!" he insisted, his tone striking in Walter's estimation an ideal balance betwixt beneficence and expertise. "Oft-times hath the Devil been transformed into an angel of light!"

"Listen to Reverend Mather," Judge Hathorne demanded, "who knows more of Satan's wiles than a barn owl knows of mice!"

The crowd grew still, and Walter watched in awe as face after face on Gallows Hill acquired the glow of newfound theological understanding—indeed, only the frail and weeping Francis Nurse was manifestly unpersuaded—and not a single dissident voice arose when Judge Stoughton approached the ladder, squeezed the leg of the elevated sheriff, and muttered, "Hangman, do your duty."

The sheriff shoved the prisoner. As Dunstan set about sketching her terminal gyrations, Mather descended from his granite pulpit and returned to Walter's side.

Rebecca Nurse required nearly twelve minutes to complete her passage to the Dark One's realm.

The more he thought about it, the more clearly Walter remembered noticing, the first time he'd visited her, a tiny protuberance on the defendant's neck, an excrescence he'd lamentably forgotten to commend to the attention of Goodwife Hathorne and Goodwife Corwin. Had the women pricked that ominous nodule, it would have yielded no blood—though mayhap a drop or two of the notorious black acid that to an imp was sweet as wine, bracing as coffee, and nourishing as milk.

"Such a deft impersonation of an angel of light," Walter observed.

"She simulates a saint for fair," the Reverend Mather said.

It was a credible measure of her boredom, Jennet felt, that the longer she lived in Salem-Village, the more she sought amusement from her dreary brother, whose conversation of late was restricted to the minutiae of demonology and the trivialities of witch tests. Doggedly devoted to the pursuit of mirthlessness, the Salem Puritans made Dunstan seem by comparison the wittiest jester ever to tickle a king's fancy. She would not say that she enjoyed her brother's companionship these days, but she certainly preferred it to the never-ending funeral that passed for family life in the Walcott household.

Dunstan meanwhile cleaved to Mr. Parris's tall, angry, ever-chattering niece, Abigail Williams. Shortly after sunrise each morning, Abigail and her raving peers would betake themselves to the meeting-house and spend several hours throwing fits before the Examination Committee. Returning the parsonage, she would do whatever chores her uncle required of her, whereupon she would lead Jennet and Dunstan to yet another "place of preternatural import" near the village. Abigail showed them the marsh where George Burroughs's murder victims had supposedly appeared to her, their winding-sheets rippling in the wind. She guided her newfound friends through the meadow where Martha Carrier had, quoth Abigail, "given birth to some monstrous malformed thing, which the woman then laid upon the ground and cleaved in twain with an ax." She took them to the abandoned barn in which John Proctor and Martha Corey had signed Satan's book, and next to the glade their coven had once used as a gathering place. After arriving astride their flying besoms and airborne goats, Abigail explained, the thirty heretics had consumed a deer's rotting carcass, washing it down with goat's urine, these substances having been transformed by Bridget Bishop into, respectively, Lucifer's body and blood.

Throughout Abigail's tours Dunstan kept trying to impress her—not only with his father's position as Witchfinder-Royal but also with the fact that he, Dunstan, stood to inherit the title. He flourished each demon-detecting tool as he would a piece of the True Cross. Joyfully Abigail stroked the bright pricking needles. The mask-o'-truth likewise enthralled her, as did the Paracelsus trident. Her brother's infatuation, Jennet surmised, traced largely to the male lust that Aunt Isobel had described in her treatise with such a peculiar mixture of chariness and celebration, for Abigail's twelve-year-old body had begun to acquire the topography of womanhood. Although Jennet's initial impulse was to lend her *A Woman's Garden of Pleasure and Pain,* the thought of this dissembling vixen finding herself pregnant ultimately proved so delectable that she decided to keep private her knowledge of cock-sheaths and fertility cycles.

Abigail, for her part, spoke seductively to Dunstan whenever the opportunity arose. "My uncle's Barbados slave taught us how to divine our fortunes," she said in her granular voice. "You break an egg and drop the white in a bowl of water, and then you watch what shapes may appear. One time I beheld a coffin floating in the cloud, and I decided I was marked to marry a sexton, but now I know my husband will be a pricker, sending many a heretic to his grave."

"A pricker's wife doth endure a hard lot," Dunstan said. "He stays away from home as long as any sailor."

"I would fain wait for thee, Dunstan," Abigail said. " 'Tis obvious you're destined to have an illustrious career. By century's end Massachusetts will be a-swarm with o'er ten thousand witches, for such was told to me in a dream by a golden-haired angel named Justine."

When the trials themselves began, and Abigail was obliged to spend each day in Salem-Town, presenting herself to the Court as a victim of *maleficium.* Dunstan went to every session, not so much to study his future vocation as to study Abigail. Each evening ere they drifted off to sleep in Captain Walcott's loft, Dunstan made Jennet listen whilst he recounted whatever grotesquery his friend had enacted that day. Pain figured prominently in many of Abigail's antics. "Before the whole Court, the witch Goody Wildes bid Abby hold her hand o'er a lighted candle!" Dunstan exclaimed. Often Abigail's performance was simply disgusting. "The hag Goody Martin made Abby stab herself in the stomach with a knitting needle!" On at least one occasion she resorted to self-exhibition. " 'Twas an amazing sight, Jenny! Upon coming face-to-face with Goody Howe, Abby tore off every scrap of clothing and ran naked from the hall!"

The Court never convened on the Sabbath, and it also stood in recess on those days when the sheriff had scheduled an execution, so that everyone could witness the heretics' final moments. Despite Dunstan's ardent and repeated entreaties, Jennet refused to accompany him to any Salem hanging, for she felt that her appearance on Gallows Hill would sully Aunt Isobel's memory as surely as the epitaph she'd carved in Colchester had honored it. One damp gray afternoon in September, however, she allowed Dunstan to lead her to an open field beside the courthouse, where "something passing wonderful" supposedly awaited.

A man lay spread-eagled on the ground, his wrists and ankles tethered and staked, his torso supporting four oaken planks fastened in parallel with iron bands. At the prisoner's feet rose a mountain of granite blocks, each as large as an ox's head, around which clustered a dozen curious Salemites and a handful of Court officials. Judge Stoughton rapped his knuckles on the topmost block, as if to prove it a true stone and not a loaf of bread or block of cheese. Judge Hathorne made ready to savor his sot-weed, clamping his churchwarden pipe in his jaw. Judge Sewall read his Bible. Judge Corwin recited his *Pater Noster*.

Breaking from the knot of bystanders, a grinning Abigail scuttled toward Jennet and Dunstan. "How marvelous that you've come! I so feared you would miss the first stone!"

"The prisoner's Giles Corey," Dunstan explained to Jennet. "For refusing to make his plea, innocent or nay, the stubborn old wizard's to receive a dose of the *peine forte et dure.*"

The sheriff approached the block mound, took hold of a particularly large stone and, as the blue veins bulged in his forehead and a grunt escaped his lips, set it atop the planks right above the prisoner's chest.

Mr. Corey released a sound halfway between a hog's squeal and a horse's whinny.

"Why doth the sheriff burden him so?" Jennet asked.

"They're going to crush the wizard flat," Dunstan replied. "Inch by inch, they'll press him to death."

"Crush him?" Jennet rasped as sweat collected in her palms and bile filled her belly.

" 'Twill take him all morning to die," Abigail said. "Mayhap the whole day."

The sheriff dropped a second granite block on the planks. Mr. Corey groaned.

"Will you make your plea, sir?" inquired Judge Hathorne, puffing on his pipe.

"Another . . . stone," Mr. Corey gurgled.

"I shan't watch this!" Jennet screamed. " 'Tis obscene!"

" 'Tis justice!" Dunstan retorted.

"Obscene as the torture of our aunt!"

"This Corey drinks the blood of newborn babes!" Abigail insisted as a third stone thudded against the planks. The prisoner hissed like an enraged viper, saliva bubbling through his teeth. "Last night his spectral form pursued me round the barn with a butcher's cleaver!"

Before the sheriff could apply the fourth stone, Jennet turned and sprinted away, running down Dock Street as if in flight from a Nimacook warrior or a ravenous she-wolf. She reached the Walcott house and climbed the ladder to the sleeping loft, determined to lose herself in the benign inscrutability of Isaac Newton and the quintessential sanity of Isobel Mowbray. She lit a candle, then removed from beneath her bed both the *Principia Mathematica* and the *Woman's Garden*. Opening Professor Newton randomly, she beheld Theorem XLVI. "If there be several bodies consisting of equal particles whose forces are as the distance of the places from each," ran her translation, "the force compounded of all the forces by which any corpuscle is attracted will tend to the common center of gravity of the attracting bodies." To her whirling brain it seemed that the proposition described precisely the relationship betwixt Mr. Corey and the granite blocks.

That night, as she lay abed with Chapter One of her *Women's Garden*, "Ever Since Eve," Dunstan appeared unbidden at her side and subjected her to a recapitulation of the *peine forte et dure*. "Hathorne kept saying 'Plead!' and Corey kept gasping 'More weight!' Is that not an amazing exchange? 'Plead!' 'More weight!' 'Plead!' 'More weight!' When Corey's tongue came snaking from his mouth, the sheriff shoved it back with his cane!"

More weight. What did the poor wretch mean? She speculated that his command was a cry of defiance. *You scoundrels can ne'er defeat me. More weight.* There was heroism in the late Mr. Corey, almost as much as in Aunt Isobel. But then a second, entirely horrible theory presented itself. *Murder me faster, please. More weight. End my agony. More weight.*

Whilst Dunstan slipped away, she blew out the candle and watched the moonlight catch the thread of rising smoke. Pulling up the coverlet, she hugged the *Principia* to her breast. "I must have faith," she whispered. Somewhere within these sacred pages lay the formula that would keep other innocents from suffering Giles Corey's fate. Somewhere amongst these propositions, hidden behind the scholia, secluded betwixt the lemmas, lurked a method by which the world might learn to sift God's laws from gossamer fancies and separate eternal truths from mere

❊

Opinions,
I grant you, are quite
the cheapest coin of the intellectual
realm, and normally I claim no special privileges
for mine. In the case of the Salem Witch Trials, however, I feel that my subjective views occupy an echelon above mere crankiness and beyond rote contrariness—an echelon, in other words, that might be called insight. I have an opinion, for example, concerning the affectation by which the events of 1692 are routinely termed "the great witchcraft hysteria," as if the whole affair were but a passing aberration. Yes, Abigail Williams and her band of bitches might be accurately labeled hysterics, but the people who took the girls' shenanigans seriously were paragons of sobriety. The Salem tragedy could never have occurred were not an aggressively rational witch-hunting apparatus already in place throughout Western civilization. Hysteria, my foot.

Then there's the reflex by which the accusers are labeled "children." The term is appropriate enough for Abigail Williams, Betty Parris, and Anne Putnam Jr., but Mary Warren, Elizabeth Hubbard, Mercy Lewis, and Mary Walcott were all in late adolescence, and the adult accusers included

Anne Putnam Sr., Goodwife Bibber, Goodwife Pope, and—before the machinery of suspicion turned against him—Giles Corey. Children, my ass.

I must tell you about my recent return to the scene of Judge Stoughton's crimes. It's October. The air is brittle, cold as a witch's tit. Through bookish will I've taken possession of Larry Hoffman, a real estate agent, lonely, befuddled. Courtesy of my host's sensorium, I soon realize that a town called Danvers has arisen on the former site of Salem Village. It boasts a Domino's Pizza, a Friendly's, and several drugstores dispensing such decidedly non-Puritan products as latex condoms and the latest issue of *Cuntoisseur*.

Bored with Danvers, I compel my proxy to venture south to Salem proper, so that I might see for myself how the witch-hunters' descendants have accommodated their heritage. We arrive in the middle of a month-long celebration that styles itself "Salem Haunted Happenings at Halloween," the invention of a bracingly shameless corporation called Atlantic Seaboard Enterprises. As the "Haunted Happenings" program book puts it, "The festivities offer something for everyone: parades, concerts, psychic fairs, costume balls, tours of Salem's great historic sites, and restaurants galore." Among the scheduled events are the Crowning of the King and Queen of Halloween (monarchs to be determined by acclamation), the Costumed Dog Contest (dress up your cocker spaniel and win a prize), Kid's Day (pony rides, face painting, games, magicians), the Fright Train from Boston (six Pullman cars crammed with out-of-work actors playing zombies), and, most delightful of all, the Official Cat of Salem Contest, each entrant to be judged by appearance, personality, and an autobiographical essay (presumably written by the cat's owner). Beyond this seasonal jollity, "Haunted Happenings" customers can avail themselves of the year-round attractions: the Salem Witch Museum, the Witch Dungeon Museum, Boris Karloff's Witch Museum, the Salem Wax Museum of Witches and Seafarers, the Haunted Witch Village, Mayhem Manor, Terror on the Wharf, and, for the Nathaniel Hawthorne scholar in the family, the House of the Seven Gables. It's obvious that in the recent past our Salemites confronted a difficult choice: should they continue feeling vaguely apologetic about an ancient miscarriage of justice, or should they seize the high ground and become the Halloween capital of the world? Eventually Atlantic Seaboard Enterprises entered the picture, tilting local sentiment toward self-exoneration and tourism.

Two days after leaving the town I submit a letter to the company's president, suggesting three sure-fire events for next year's installment of "Haunted Happenings."

Cat Pressing on the Common. This vivid historical demonstration gives Salem visitors a precise sense of the *peine forte et dure* suffered by Giles Corey on September 19, 1692. Participants will be drawn from the town's stray cat population, plus losers of the Official Cat of Salem Contest who now wish to die.

All Night Noose Dance. Special shoulder harnesses enable you to "swing with your partner" from the oaks atop Gallows Hill. Prizes in the following categories: Best Dressed Couple, Liveliest Kickers, Famous Last Words—plus the highly coveted Rebecca Nurse Endurance Trophy.

Dorcas Good Memorial Leg-Irons Race. This event celebrates the feistiness of accused witch Dorcas Good, age four, who went irretrievably insane after lying in a freezing cell for eight months, loaded with leg irons and shackled to a wall. On Halloween morning, after bolting on their irons, participants will convene at the corner of Derby and Main, then jog competitively to Pickering Wharf.

I further suggest to Atlantic Seaboard Enterprises that, having rehabilitated the Salem Witch Trials, they should consider doing the same with such thrilling historical dramas as the Albigensian Crusade, the massacre of the Huguenots, the bombing of Hiroshima, and Hitler's Final Solution.

"The Nazi concentration camps in particular hold tremendous untapped festivity potential," I tell the company's president. "Yes, there's some sort of Holocaust Museum in Washington, D.C., but it's a stuffy and self-important place, utterly lacking the Seaboard Enterprises touch. The time isn't right quite yet, but within a few generations people will doubtless be talking about 'the great genocide hysteria, that unfortunate chapter in the saga of the twentieth century.' Meanwhile, you can begin laying plans for 'Holocaust Happenings at Nuremberg,' including parades, contests, concerts, kids' days, tours of the city's great historic sites, and restaurants galore." It will be especially important, I note, to offer the public a variety of tie-in merchandise. "Toward this end, I have contacted the Lionel Corporation about a special Auschwitz Electric Train Set, complete with a 4-8-4 steam locomotive and five box cars." I haven't yet received a reply, but if Atlantic Seaboard Enterprises deigns to write back, I suspect they will claim that my suggestions are offensive beyond redemption, outrageous beyond apology, and in atrociously bad

🙙🙜

"Taste this," Dunstan said, offering Jennet a lopsided and strange-smelling confection that vaguely resembled a loaf of bread. They were in the loft of the Walcott house, hurriedly dressing for bed ere October's chill could seep into their bones. "Set the merest portion against your palate, and for a few amazing moments you'll see pictures from the demon world—dancing phoukas, mayhap, or goblins with burning eyes."

"What is it?" she asked.

"A witch-cake," he said. "Abby baked it. Have a nibble."

Jennet broke off a piece of witch-cake and slid it into her mouth. She chewed. The morsel had a barbed and bitter flavor, but no phantoms appeared in her brain. "What ingredients?"

"Molasses, honey, rye meal, and Abby's urine," he replied. "The recipe came from Mr. Parris's Barbados slave. 'Tis an infallible way to prove a person's been bewitched."

With an explosive movement of her lips and cheeks, Jennet spat out as many cake fragments as her tongue could summon. "How durst you feed me piss?!"

"No phantoms?" Dunstan asked plaintively.

"You addlepated pig!"

Dunstan's visage became so woeful as to evoke for Jennet the Sorrow-Faced Knight, Don Quixote. "I feared as much," he said. "Abby can see 'em, but I cannot."

" 'Tis evident she grows more frantic by the hour."

Her brother nodded in reluctant agreement. The witch-cake, he explained, owed its creation to the fact that of the fifteen suspects tried and convicted in September, only seven had gone to Gallows Hill. Two of the eight spared women were with child, and two had promised to name the others in their covens—but in the remaining four cases the acquittals reflected Judge Stoughton's suspicion that the witnesses weren't truly bewitched. Through confections of the sort Jennet had just sampled, Abby hoped to establish that she and her associates were full-blown victims of demonic influence.

"She can bake a hundred witch-cakes, and she'll ne'er regain her lost stature," Jennet said.

"The hunt is losing momentum," Dunstan admitted, sighing expansively. "Father says Governor Phipps means to reprieve any and all persons convicted by the testimony of a Salem-Village daughter."

"He sounds a sensible man."

"Piffle! Had Abby not cried out Phipps's wife, he would yet be the Court's great champion."

"She cried out the Governor's wife?" Jennet said, appalled.

"Right to Judge Stoughton's face."

"I'll say this in your friend's favor—she's not wanting in spunk."

Two nights later, Walter sat his children down before Captain Walcott's blazing hearth. Studying his countenance in the firelight, Jennet saw that the trials had taken a severe toll on the man. His features were shrunken and sallow, as if painted on the surface of a rotting gourd.

"Governor Phipps was in Salem-Town today," he said wearily. "We drank cider at Ingersoll's. There be good news and bad. The good is that he hath recognized my office and will pay my salary as long as I ne'er consult with Miss Williams's band, whom he calls 'those damned mendacious minxes.' ''

Jennet could not restrain an un-Christian impulse to flash her brother a sardonic grin. He absorbed this disembodied blow, then fixed his eyes on the floor.

"And the bad?" she asked.

"The bad is that these great trials be now at an end," Walter said, "for the Governor hath dissolved the Court."

"*Dissolved* it?" Dunstan wailed.

"Aye."

"Dost mean we must now return to Haverhill?" the boy asked.

"Indeed."

"But I fancy Salem-Village," Dunstan protested.

"You fancy Abigail Williams," Jennet noted.

"Our house is in Haverhill," Walter said firmly.

Dunstan winced, and despite a plethora of distressing matters—his willingness to think Isobel a heretic, his enthusiasm for Mr. Corey's pressing, his offering of the witch-cake—Jennet felt a sudden sympathy for him. Even an apprentice pricker deserved some measure of affection in his cup, and Abby had evidently supplied him with a plenary portion.

"I'faith, sir, Mr. Phipps doth sorely misjudge my friend," Dunstan said. "Miss Williams can see the future in the waterborne white of an egg."

"In an *egg?*" moaned Walter, scowling.

"And the angel Justine hath disclosed to her a great demon empire arising in this province. Mark me, Father, the *real* Massachusetts cleansing is yet to come."

"I don't doubt it, son, and we shall keep our pricking needles sharp. But for the nonce we must plant our garden."

✿

JENNET WAS NOT A WEEK BACK in Haverhill when she realized that in her absence the citizens' longstanding fear of a Nimacook attack had progressed to a contagion of terror. Not only had the apprehensive Colonists erected palisades and watch-towers along their northern border, they had organized a militia. The commanding officer, Nathaniel Saltonstall—the same Nathaniel Saltonstall who'd rounded out the judges' panel at Salem (though the Rebecca Nurse affair had inspired him to resign in protest ere finishing his service)—lost no time convincing Walter and Dunstan to join his stalwart company, an obligation that had father and son marching across the Common every Saturday morning, firearms propped against their shoulders, powder horns oscillating at their hips. Walter drilled with his deer-hunting musket. Dunstan's weapon was an English fowling-piece he'd received from a wheelwright's son in trade for his ink sketch of Goody Nurse's hanging.

The longer she pondered the matter, the more Jennet realized how perplexed she was by the Nimacooks' hostility, and so she approached the sole scholarly mind in Haverhill, a Puritan divine named Malachi Foster.

"Why do the Indians seek to destroy us?" she asked.

The Reverend Foster replied in convoluted sentences, each more tangled than the most beleaguered line in her worst translation of Cicero, but eventually a lucid answer emerged. The Indians, it seemed, were wroth over the Colonists' appropriation of their lands. When Jennet bade Mr. Foster elaborate, he solemnly described the stratagem whereby a Puritan settler would repeatedly send his livestock roving across a Nimacook planter's maize hills, trampling the Indian's crops and breaking his spirit, until he saw no alternative but to move farther west. An equally effective maneuver consisted in seizing an Indian's acres as punishment for some infraction of Puritan law, such as drinking in public, dishonoring the Sabbath, or taking the Creator's name in vain.

Although the Nimacooks' outrage made "a kind of logical sense," Mr. Foster admitted, it enjoyed "no legal or moral standing." As far back as 1619, Governor Winthrop had decreed that most of America fell under the rubric of *vacuum domicilium:* given that the various Algonquin and Iroquois tribes had not "subdued" but merely "occupied" their plantations, hunting parks, trapping grounds, and fishing streams, they had only a "natural" and not a "civil" claim to these domains. All such territory was in fact "waste" available for seizure. But the ultimate authority by which the Puritans encroached on the Nimacooks came from On

High. In Mr. Foster's view, Psalm 2:8 could not be more explicit. *Ask of me, and I shall give thee the heathen for thine inheritance, and the uttermost parts of the Earth for thy possession.*

That spring and summer Jennet's father conducted the modest cleansing of 1693, a project that took him and Dunstan first to Topsfield and thence to Rowley. Whilst the prickers managed to indict six Satanists in these villages, the newly created Massachusetts Superior Court acquitted all but two. A propitious ratio, she decided, though not propitious enough to put her soul at ease. Whenever she walked through Haverhill on a mission to buy flour, mend harness, grind knives, or absorb gossip, she could not help scanning the children's faces, wondering who amongst them might be destined for the gallows. Would a jury one day see diabolism in the sprightly eyes and mischievous smirk of the tavern-keeper's daughter? Would the miller's slow-witted niece ultimately stand convicted of carnal congress with incubi? Would the tanner's bulky son go to the hangman in consequence of a pricker's tests?

The hunt of 1694 proved the leanest yet—four arrests, one execution. Throughout the subsequent winter Walter perused his private library, ferreting out obscure bits of demonological lore and synthesizing them into prolix monographs that he then dispatched with lofty expectations to his London benefactors. By showing the Privy Council that he was not a mere pricker but a scholar of near-Thomist perspicacity, he sought to cast himself as a man worthy of respect, solicitude, and a salary increase. He'd grown particularly obsessed with an assertion in George Sinclair's *Sermons by Satan:* the odd notion that the sensitivity of a Paracelsus trident doubled following its immersion in a kettle filled with boiling frog's blood. Thus it was that, as April's ubiquitous buds became a lush tapestry of May wildflowers spreading across the Merrimack Valley, Walter decreed that, upon completing their chores each day, Jennet and Dunstan must scour the Haverhill fens for frogs, and by month's end they'd caught a dozen.

Although Dunstan preferred hunting collaboratively, so he might fill his sister's ear with further accounts of Abby's histrionics in Salem, Jennet usually elected to search alone. The conjunction of swamp and solitude launched her thoughts on unexpected trajectories—and yet, woolly as they were, she came to realize that these musings shared a common theme: escape. For she was almost eighteen now, old enough to make her way to Boston and find employment as a serving-maid, housekeeper, governess . . . any such position would do, provided it allowed her at least one free afternoon each week, a few golden hours for grappling with the *Principia Mathematica*. In her mind a sacred vow took shape. No matter what obstacles emerged, she would flee on Aunt Isobel's birthday, the seventh of July. Even if she awoke shivering with a fever, even if the Nimacooks were proclaiming an intention to kill every white wayfarer who ventured across their lands, even if a terrible thunder-gust was blowing through the town, hurtling sheep into the air and turning the streets to raging rivers—come that dawn, she would pack up her *Principia* and her *Woman's Garden* and quit Haverhill forever.

But first she would remove her father's license from his door and rip it into a thousand pieces.

THE LAST AFTERNOON IN JUNE found sister and brother sitting by the Merrimack, Jennet contemplating a cohort of honeybees as they fertilized some bergamot, Dunstan sketching with his wax crayons. For a subject he'd selected a rock formation that surmounted the cliff-face on the far shore: a granite horse's head emerging from the promontory like an enormous white chess-knight—not an ordinary horse, but a creature of mythic ambition, eager to pull Hector's chariot, carry Alexander into battle against Xerxes, or bear Sir Percival on his Grail quest. A peculiar melancholy took hold of Jennet. Within a few days of her flight, she would surely long for Dunstan—not Dunstan the apprentice pricker but Dunstan the accomplished draughtsman, Dunstan whose eye and hand and brain were so felicitously interlinked, like colors in a sunbeam or voices in a fugue.

She leaned over the bank and added her reflection to the languid water. The woman who looked back boasted a full face framed by abundant auburn hair. Her chin was a tad presumptuous, and the tip of her nose took an unseemly upward turn, and yet her cheeks were stately, her eyes wide, and she was quite possibly beautiful.

Dunstan approached, adding his own form to the liquid image as he placed in her hands his drawing of the horse-head promontory.

"A gift for thee."

"You have captured the beast in all his majesty," she said, rising. "Do you want to know my wish? I hope that one day soon you will meet in this province some person of aesthetic sensibility, and he will betimes appoint himself your patron, sending you to Italy that you might become the prize pupil of a master painter."

His lips lengthened into a taut and wistful smile. "Italy seems to me as far away as those Jovian moons of which my sister is so fond."

"Florence and Rome are indeed a great distance, and yet withal they lie closer to your heart than doth that parchment scrap on Father's door." She folded the drawing and slid it into her dress pocket. "You will go to Italy, Dunstan. I can see it in these waters."

"Jenny, you're a keen young woman, competent in philosophy and mathematics, but you'll ne'er have Abby's powers of scrying."

They resumed their search, traveling south along the marshy bank. As dusk came to Haverhill, the frog hunters admitted to each other that the day's expedition had failed. Abandoning the shore, they ascended to firmer ground, then turned and headed north along an embankment thick with sunflowers that—just then, just there—struck Jennet as no less magnificent than the spires of Cambridge-Town. To their left the Merrimack caught the fire of the setting sun, so that its waters now seemed an alchemical amalgam of molten rubies and melted cinnabar.

"I'Christ, 'tis the Devil's own brood!"

She spun, glancing downstream. The object of Dunstan's distress lay a quarter-mile away: a flotilla of Nimacook canoes, perhaps sixteen in all, rounding the lee of Contoocook Isle like a huge, white, segmented worm. In each vessel sat four armed savages, their paddles thrashing madly against the current.

"Satan hath sent an entire legion against us!" Dunstan shouted.

Already the canoes were putting to shore, the Indians brandishing tomahawks, battle-clubs, and French muskets. War-paint spilled across their faces in hideous streaks and encircled their naked torsos like the stripes on a coral snake.

Jennet experienced a crushing sensation in her chest, as if the Salem judges were subjecting her to the *peine forte et dure*. She took a deep breath and followed Dunstan as he bolted from the embankment and ran pell-mell into the woods. They skirted boulders, ducked beneath fallen trees, and overleapt gullies, until finally the outlying barns and granaries of Haverhill came into view, and then—praise God—Kembel's Ordinary. Her brother's intention to alert the town proved superfluous, however, for the militia was already marching down Mill Street, Major Saltonstall at the head, his drawn saber thrust forward like a bowsprit. Though free of war-paint, the soldiers looked formidable in their own right, their brows and cheeks burned raspberry-red from countless hours of planting beneath the New World sun, their muskets supplemented by well-honed axes and sharpened sickles.

Catching sight of his children, Walter abruptly abandoned the company—so abruptly that he crashed into the cadence master and sent his drum rolling down the street like a barrel fallen from a brewer's wagon—then rushed forward and seized their wrists.

Jennet, terrified, tried without success to speak.

"Savages!" Dunstan bleated. "Murderous heathen savages!"

"Oh, my sweetest darlings," Walter gasped, dragging his children toward Kembel's Ordinary.

At last the words broke from Jennet's larynx and made their way past her vibrating teeth. "What will happen to us, Father? Are you and Dunstan to be butchered? Am I to be stolen away and made to run the gauntlet?"

Instead of answering, Walter hauled them onto the veranda and pointed toward a pyramid of cider casks. "*There* be your protection, children! 'Tis a God-given fortress against the tawnies' spears and arrows!"

Without a moment's hesitation Jennet stepped behind the casks and crouched down.

"Sir, I fain would fetch my fowling-piece and fight by your side," Dunstan said.

"Nay, lad." Walter firmed his grip on his musket. "Thou art marked to become the next Witchfinder-Royal. I say that Satan hath sent these savages for no purpose but to destroy the son of Walter Stearne!"

A preposterous notion, Jennet decided, but Dunstan evidently believed otherwise, for he lost no time joining her in the supposed citadel.

"My dear ones, know that I love you more than my life!" Walter cried, then dashed away to rejoin his fellow soldiers as they marched onto the Common.

Major Saltonstall arranged the company in a dense cluster: a stockade of flesh meant to stand against not only the party of screaming savages now charging from the west but also the second such band arriving from the east, the third from the north, and likewise the fourth—the raiders who'd come by canoe—from the south. Though ignorant of military strategy, Jennet suspected that in contriving to attack the town from all directions at once the Nimacooks had achieved a victory well before launching their first canoe or applying their first smear of war-paint.

The staccato sound of discharging muskets filled the air. Jennet's quaverings became more intense, and then a flux seized her, and she vomited up the undigested portion of her midday meal. Dunstan's fear took the form of a beshitting, though he seemed oblivious to both the load in his breeches and the concomitant stench. He attempted to recite his *Pater Noster*, managing it no better than would the average accused Satanist standing before a magistrate.

"Our Father, which—which—which art—in—in—H-Heaven—which art in—b-b-be thy name!"

The cider casks afforded a reasonably safe vantage from which a person might observe the lopsided battle, but Jennet averted her gaze. Between the burning of Isobel Mowbray and the crushing of Giles Corey, she was already as well instructed in cruelty as in Euclid; she needed no further lesson. Instead she fixed on the cask beneath her jaw, contemplating the splinters and troughs, the nubbins and grooves. If only she might through some benign witchery turn herself into an insect, an ant perhaps, or a termite, any beastie small enough to disappear amidst these little ravines and forsake the human world forever.

"Be thy name—be thy name—be thy name!"

She clamped her hands over her ears, muting the cries of pain and the hacking cough of the muskets, sensations a hundred times more terrible than Dunstan's stink.

" 'Sheart!" he shrieked. "The day belongs to Satan!"

She glanced toward the Common. True to her expectations, both the major's strategy and the militia that had attempted to enact it lay in ruins. The flesh stockade had collapsed into a thing that seemed not so much a collection of battlefield casualties as a festering fen in the heart of Hell, the damned souls struggling to raise their snapped limbs and cracked skulls and mutilated torsos from the muck.

Having destroyed Haverhill's defenses, the Nimacooks now abandoned the Common and set about razing the town itself, jabbing firebrands into hay bales, hurling torches through windows, planting constellations of burning arrows in shutters and doors. An uncanny wind took source in Haverhill, a cyclone composed of the Nimacooks' triumphant whoops and the English settlers' screams.

Jennet and Dunstan sprinted from the veranda and hurried onto the Common, where their father lay supine beneath a sycamore, holding his musket as a drowning sailor might clutch an errant spar from his sunken ship. His chest had received three arrows. Blood pooled around the shafts; more blood spilled from the corners of his mouth. He shivered as if lying naked in snow, although Jennet couldn't say whether this phenomenon traced to his physical suffering or to his dread of dying unshriven.

"My children," he moaned. "My—lovely—children."

She surveyed the scene with an attitude more akin to curiosity than grief, the sort of circumscribed astonishment she'd brought to "Christ at the Whipping-Post," the engraved frontispiece of the Reverend Foster's illustrated Bible. There was sadness in this picture, and pity too, but it was not her sadness, not her pity.

"Today a hundred tawnies shall die by my hand," Dunstan rasped.

"You must—save yourself—for the—cleansing—ahead," Walter mumbled.

"The great cleansing, aye."

"Thy birthright—'tis on—bed-chamber door."

As Jennet studied the Golgothan triad of arrows rising from Walter's bosom, Dunstan poured promises into the witchfinder's ear. He vowed that he would hunt down every Satanist in America—male and female, white and Indian, Protestant and Catholic: all would feel his needle, all would know the noose.

The instant Jennet bent low to address her father, the arrows finished their work. "I do thank thee, sir, for thy part in giving me life," she told the corpse. "Beyond that, however, I hold thee a scoundrel and miscreant, and I shall dedicate my life's remaining years to the destruction of all cleansers everywhere."

She rose and, exchanging glances with Dunstan, saw by his livid countenance that he'd overheard her malediction.

"You truly hated him," he said, tears rolling down his cheeks.

"Not always. Not before Colchester Castle."

"A daughter who curses her father to his face"—he darted away—"doth thereby damn herself to Hell."

"Then upon my arrival I shall curse him to his face again," she said, following.

Side by side, the orphans raced along the burning streets. Everywhere they turned, the conflagration flourished, blurring the barns, stables, mills, taverns, and shops into a great red storm, the Jovian Hurricane come to Earth. As the fire consumed the buildings, the Indians next applied their rage directly to the Colonists. Haverhill became a slaughter-house, an anatomization theatre, a hemorrhaging landscape of craters gouged by battle-clubs, cavities carved by musket-balls, and gorges sculpted by tomahawks. With mounting horror Jennet realized that a Nimacook gauged no murder complete until he'd used his knife to add another shaggy trophy to his belt, peeling scalp from skull with the insouciance of an aristocrat removing the rind from an orange.

By the time they reached their house, she was expecting to find it ablaze, a premonition that proved lamentably correct. Helplessly she stood before the flames. She imagined them doing their worst, devouring the paper treasures within. Dunstan's crayon drawings. Aunt Isobel's treatise. Newton's letter to Mirringate Hall. The *Principia Mathematica*.

"The Lord is my shepherd!" her brother cried, rushing toward the burning porch.

"Dunstan, no!"

The foolish boy crossed the threshold—"I shall have my birthright!"—and vanished.

A numbness spread through her, locking her legs in place, fixing her hips, taking the life from her hands. It seemed that she'd become an exhibit in Dr. Cavendish's museum, a pickled freak a-float in a jar. A minute passed, and another, and then the jar shattered with a thunderous roar, and she looked up to see the house collapse upon itself. Squalls of fiery ash swirled through the air. Embers descended like red sleet.

The remorse that now seized her was asymmetrical, the lesser share devoted to the loss of *A Woman's Garden,* the greater to her brother's immolation. Was this catastrophe best interpreted as Providence in action, the Indians serving as implements of a divine plan to destroy a nascent witchfinder? Or had Jehovah followed a more passive course, noting Dunstan's predicament and declining to deliver him?

Gradually she grew aware of a dozen shadowy Nimacooks standing in the vegetable garden, trampling down the pole-beans as they laughed amongst themselves. A discordance of wails, moans, and sobs reached her ears. The braves pointed mocking fingers toward two young Haverhill women of about Jennet's age, both insane with fright, each hugging a tattered Bible. A leather halter coiled around the taller woman's neck, encircled the throat of her companion, and passed finally into the hands of a looming savage with slithering black serpents painted on his chest. Now Jennet received a tether of her own, binding her to the other girls, though the experience seemed less like a yoking than its opposite. She felt sundered from everything: the white race, the New World, the spinning planet—sundered from her own body and brain.

Pushing and shoving their threaded captives, the triumphant Indians skirted the raging holocaust that had once been Milk Street. As the war party and its human plunder passed the town limits, the pulsing heat of the flames yielded gradually to the chill of evening. Jennet took care to march in step with her fellow prisoners, lest the strap around her neck suddenly become a noose. They proceeded through the fields, the woods, then down to the Merrimack, where the rest of the war party waited by the beached canoes, attending their wounded.

Whether the tawnies were Lucifer's lieutenants, as her late father had believed, or God's agents, as she had recently imagined, Jennet could not help admiring the stoicism with which the hurt ones submitted to the necessary treatments. Directly before her, a sinewy warrior grimaced but did not cry out as a Nimacook physician wrenched his fractured leg straight. Not far beyond, a brave in a feather head-dress gritted his teeth whilst a surgeon probed his shoulder with a knife, seeking to dislodge a musket-ball.

She glanced toward the river, its waters lit by the glow of the dying town. Wrapped in deerskins, six Indian corpses lay along the shore like pieces of driftwood. Nearby stood three more white daughters, weeping and retching and pissing themselves, their throats linked like braided bulbs of garlic. One captive pressed a silver cross to her breast. Another cradled a rag poppet. The third grasped a small oval portrait of a dainty woman with a kindly face.

As the Nimacooks untied the tether and led her to the canoes, Jennet realized that she too would be bearing away a fragment of civilization that night, Dunstan's sketch of the horse-head promontory. She lifted her eyes and fixed on the soaring cliff. The stone horse had vanished, claimed by the darkness. In a few hours the creature would reappear, of course, and later that day some passing traveler might pause to appreciate its splendor, his thoughts turning naturally to Hector or Alexander or Percival. But she would not be that pilgrim. God alone knew where the morning would find her: moving through the forest perhaps, or approaching a Nimacook village—or dead, quite likely, dead as Dunstan, dead as her father, lying in an obscure glade, a tomahawk in her back or an arrow in her heart, the rising sun glancing off the whiteness of her skinless crown.

*Our Heroine Variously Occupies
an Algonquin Wigwam,
a Philadelphia Townhouse,
and the Nether Reaches of
Newtonian Theology*

❈❈

E arly in the seventh year of her life Jennet developed an intense yearning to possess some true and valuable memory of the mother she'd never known, and by her eleventh birthday she'd managed to summon the desired tableau. The veil of forgetfulness lifted, and there was Margaret Noakes Stearne, bloated with Dunstan, sitting alongside Jennet on the parlor floor in Colchester and fashioning one of her famous æolian machines, a wondrous kite of white birch and red silk. "In the spring you and I shall fly it," Jennet's mother told her, holding up the finished contraption. " 'Twill glide above every steeple in England. I'faith, 'twill soar clear to Heaven!"

Had Jennet's fourteen-month-old brain in fact recorded this complex scene, or was the recollection but a phantasm? She didn't know—though she could say with certainty that the flying of the red kite had never occurred, for by the spring of 1680 Margaret Noakes Stearne lay dead atop the birthing-bed, the newborn Dunstan squirming betwixt her thighs. And yet Jennet's memory of the comely woman extolling the kite felt real, and whenever, as now, she found herself hedged by uncertainty and peril, she would conjure up this benevolent ghost and avail herself of its comforts.

Before fleeing Haverhill, the Nimacooks separated the six white daughters from one another, forcing each into a different canoe, doubtless to prevent them from planning and executing a coordinated escape. All during the dark and frigid journey down the Merrimack, Jennet knelt in the lead canoe and fixed her thoughts on her mother and the kite. *In the spring you and I shall fly it.* Aided by the river's current and the braves' furious paddling, the flotilla made a rapid retreat from the burning town. *'Twill glide above every steeple in England.* The passing water reflected the Indians' torches, now deployed as beacons in the bows, so that the Merrimack seemed home to some fantastic breed of luminous fish. *I'faith, 'twill soar clear to Heaven.*

The night was at its deepest when the savages put to shore. It took them but a few minutes to conceal their canoes beneath mounds of branches and boughs, which they'd evidently harvested that morning in anticipation of a victory. Having thus confounded whatever rescue parties the Haverhill survivors might launch upon the river, the savages snuffed their torches, shouldered their dead, and gathered up their spoils—including, Jennet noticed with a surge of nausea, several sacks of scalps. After aligning themselves with the waxing moon, the Nimacooks led the white daughters through a stand of cattails and thence into the woods, setting out along a path speckled with fireflies and limned by the glow of Earth's lone satellite. The Stygian forest stretched in all directions, coils of fog entwining the branches, tree frogs chirping within the hollow trunks, heathen spirits roving the dark æther. With each step Jennet's misery compounded. Her terror took on a life of its own, a thousand animalcules of dread cruising her veins like the bloodborne imps Aunt Isobel had expected the *experimentum magnus* to yield. She hugged herself, and ground her teeth, and put one foot before the other.

An hour's march brought the war party to a wide granite shelf rising from the earth to form an immense cavern. Stores of provisions lay everywhere within—barrels of salted fish, casks of water, ceramic jars filled with dried berries and cured venison, piles of moose-hide bedding. Apparently this vast chamber was the Nimacooks' equivalent of an inn, a bountiful and capacious road-house marking the way into their territory.

The Indians relighted their torches, revealing near the grotto's entrance a large pit, freshly dug, waiting to receive the six skin-wrapped corpses. A burial ensued, brief and spare—no prayers, no eulogies, no moment of silence—though Jennet supposed that under peacetime conditions the savages accorded their dead a greater regard. The only whiff of ceremony occurred when a pensive brave with a yellow starburst on his stomach leaned over the grave and set atop each body a soapstone pipe and a small clay pot filled with tobacco.

In obeisance to a series of gestures from their captors, the women removed their shoes and dropped them into the pit. Whilst three young warriors shoveled back the dirt, a third distributed new footwear to the prisoners, deerskin moccasins secured with thongs. At first this ritual perplexed Jennet, but then she grasped its logic: a moccasin, she realized, left no mark upon the world, no track the men of Haverhill might pursue in search of their stolen daughters.

By now it was obvious that each captive had her own private keeper. Jennet's guardian was a stolid young man with a horizontal crescent moon painted across his chest, the horns pricking his nipples. He'd used the same pigment to give himself a feline countenance, a lynx's perhaps, or a panther's. His hair, like that of his brother savages, was greased with rendered bear fat. The cavern gathered and compacted the collective scent, which seemed to penetrate not only Jennet's nasal passages but every bone in her head. It was a protean odor, always shifting, now revolting, now beguiling, now benumbing, now bracing, as if refracted through some olfactory equivalent of a prism.

The lynx-faced man filled a wooden bowl with venison and berries. As he proffered this spartan dinner, its savory smell somehow overpowered the bear grease to fill Jennet's nostrils, and she realized that despite the day's many disasters she would consume the entire portion.

"Thank you," she said, and he responded with a short declaration in his own tongue.

Later, after captors and captives had finished eating, Lynx Man dipped a gourd ladle into a water cask and, presenting Jennet with the measure, spoke again in Nimacook. When she gave him an uncomprehending look, he attempted a sentence in halting French: *"Ce soir nous coucherons ici."* We shall sleep here this evening.

She drank eagerly, sucking every drop from the ladle. *"Merci."*

"Je veux vous montrer quelque chose." I want to show you something.

"Qu'est-ce que c'est?"

"Suivez-moi."

Lynx Man borrowed a torch from the surgeon, then bade her follow him deep into the grotto. She reasoned that he did not intend to murder her—not after all the trouble his tribe had taken in abducting the white daughters—but it was conceivable he meant to make her the object of his lust. The sheathed knife protruding from his belt suddenly seemed as threatening as a puff adder, and images of ravishment filled her mind as he guided her into an alcove the size of a livery stall. Her heart hurled itself against her backbone, and her stomach spasmed as if preparing to eject the venison and berries.

"Voilà," Lynx Man said.

Pictures emerged from the blackness, some executed in charcoal, others in paint. As her keeper raised the torch aloft, she beheld a band of savages hurling spears at an elk . . . a lone hunter setting a deadfall for an approaching bear . . . another hunter laying a snare for a rabbit . . . an archer bringing down a partridge with an arrow . . . a squaw trapping fish in a weir.

"My brother was an artist," she said, slipping a hand into her dress pocket. Her fingers brushed Dunstan's sketch of the horse-head promontory. *"Mon frère était un artiste."*

Lynx Man said nothing.

The flickering of the torch imparted to the images an illusion of movement, so that the elk seemed to leap, the bear to lumber, the rabbit to scamper, the partridge to plummet, the fish to swim. Each illustrated Indian shivered with the thrill of the hunt, and now Jennet shivered as well, and then her tears began to flow, and they did not stop flowing until, three hours later, lying on a moose-hide mattress in the savages' road-house, the bear grease drilling through her brain, the torches decorating the walls with black lapping shadows, she drifted off to sleep.

AT FIRST LIGHT LYNX MAN and the others scrubbed the paint from their bodies, whereupon the forced march began, the savages pressing their prisoners ever westward. The Indians did not pause to break their fast, nor did they halt for a midday meal, but instead moved deeper and deeper into the conifer forest, eating and drinking as they went—venison from bulrush baskets, water from leather bottles—occasionally sharing these provisions with the white daughters. As the sun dipped toward the horizon, the war party at last crossed into the bounteous and sprawling estates of the Algonquin Nimacook.

According to Jennet's comprehension of her keeper's French, each Haverhill prisoner was destined for a different village. Evidently her translation was accurate, for upon reaching a sun-dappled glade the company fractured like a dropped mirror, with no two daughters assigned to the same band. Suddenly aware that they might never see one another again, the young women squirmed free of their guardians and came together in a communal embrace—all save Jennet, whose attitude toward these wilting Puritans fell far short of affection. For a full minute the Indians permitted the prisoners to say their farewells, and then the great scattering began.

Led by Lynx Man, Jennet's band walked silently through the forest, bearing their sacks of spoils and scalps across mounds of brown needles shed by the firs and hemlocks. Within an hour the trees yielded to brush and thickets, which in time melted away to reveal a river: the Shawsheen, her keeper called it, as roiling and jaunty as the Merrimack was tame and somber. Here the band turned north, proceeding along a shore of such floral fecundity—violets, honeysuckle, clematis, buttercups—that it seemed to Jennet a kind of Paradise reserved for the souls of deceased honeybees and the shades of departed hummingbirds. By degrees her dread declined into simple foreboding, and the reeling shock of losing her father and brother became, regarding Walter, indifference, and, concerning Dunstan, the manageable ache of grief.

"I know a bank where the wild thyme blows," she muttered, gesturing toward the blossoms, "where oxlips and the nodding violet grows."

"Quoi?" Lynx Man asked.

"Shakespeare," Jennet replied.

"Votre nom est Shakespeare?" Your name is Shakespeare?

"Non, je m'appelle Jennet," she said.

"Et je m'appelle Pussough." I call myself Pussough.

At length the band drew within view of a broad, undulating field, its gentle slopes dotted with small earth-mounds from which emerged tangled arrays of corn, beans, and squash. A score of Indian women moved amidst the crops, prising up weeds with quahog-shell hoes and using these same implements to frighten away rabbits.

Upon realizing that the warriors were back from Haverhill, the women abandoned their plantation and headed for the riverbank. They ranged in age from pubescent girls to crones, but their clothing was nearly identical: grass mantles and deerskin skirts, with nary a cap or bonnet amongst them. Apparently no one from Pussough's village had died in the attack, for every wife, sister, daughter, aunt, mother, and grandmother retained her smile throughout the various overlapping accounts of the great battle, and when the warriors finished reciting their tales a raucous celebration followed, the plantation ringing with bright laughter and a high wavering chant that sounded to Jennet like an Anglican hymn sung under water.

Reunion accomplished, the plantation maids turned their attention to the white captive, examining her from every angle as might a company of Cambridge Platonists confronted with a unicorn or a griffin. They fingered Jennet's dress, toyed with her unbraided hair, sniffed the sweaty juncture of her neck and shoulder. As far as she could tell, none of the women was paired with Pussough, and it occurred to her that she might be marked to become his bride. Certainly there was an intimation of courtship in the way he now led her up the nearest slope, so gloriously a-bloom it made her late father's garden seem barren as a pauper's grave.

"Les trois soeurs," Pussough said. The three sisters.

To her eye each triad of crops indeed enjoyed an intimate and sisterly relationship. Green vines laden with beans coiled about the maize stalks, using them for support, even as the nascent squash huddled in the salubrious shade cast by the other vegetables.

"*Ces soeurs sont heureuses,*" she said. These sisters are happy.

Pussough laughed and squeezed her shoulder in a manner that seemed to occupy an Aristotelian middle-ground betwixt domination and affection. "*Voici votre vie nouvelle.*" Here is your new life.

Evidently she too would become a plantation maid. "*Ma vie nouvelle?*"

"*Oui.*" His hand strayed from her shoulder to her hip. "*Nous ne vous ferrons pas de mal.*" We shall not harm you. "*Vous aurez un bébé, et nous ne vous ferrons pas de mal.*" You will have a baby, and we shall not harm you.

A pint of bile flooded her stomach. "*Un bébé?*"

"*Oui, un bébé.*"

Un bébé. The horrid idea seized her imagination, wrenching her from the company of the gentle *trois soeurs,* and suddenly her brain could conjure no object save human blood, in all its varieties. She saw pools of blood, creeks of blood, biblical rivers of blood. The absence of a child in your womb brought each month a rational and reassuring measure of blood, but the presence of such a monster could cause a very cataract. *Un bébé* was the vilest of phenomena. *Un bébé* was hemorrhage and darkness and death.

"*Quand est-ce que j'aurai le bébé?*" she asked. When will I have the baby?

"*Quand vous serez prête,*" Pussough said.

Could this be true? A Nimacook wife might defer the gravid state until she was *prête*—ready?

She ran a finger across the helical course of a bean vine, vowing silently that, whether her future husband was the man standing before her or another of these enigmatic tawnies, she would somehow, some way, hold him to the laudable custom of deferred procreation. The Nimacooks might make her their slave—they might force her to carry their water, sew their mantles, mend their moccasins, clean their hovels, tend their corn, run their gauntlet: all these indignities she could abide. But to spare herself the doom of Margaret Stearne, she would move Heaven and Earth and all the bodies in between.

AT FIRST SHE TALLIED only the days, noting each planetary rotation by dropping a pebble into the hollow of an oak tree growing just inside the village gateway. Then she started marking the months, recording
every new moon by concealing a crow feather in the darkest corner of her
wigwam. Eventually it became clear that her captivity must be reckoned
in years, and so whenever the planting season came to the Shawsheen
Valley, she fashioned and fired a commemorative pot, setting it beneath
her sleeping platform.

Her immediate community, forty-eight in number, occupied four
stockaded acres on the eastern shore. They called themselves the
Kokokehom, the Owl Clan, willing followers of a one-eyed sagamore
named Miacoomes. Having determined that, true to Pussough's assertion, these people meant her no harm—that, indeed, they were attempting to provide her with their notion of a happy life—she resolved to find
in her circumstances some measure of redemption. Had Aunt Isobel ever
landed amongst the naked tawnies, she would surely have endeavored to
study them, bringing to the task the same fascinated detachment she accorded animalcules on a Van Leeuwenhoek stage. Thus did Jennet come
to view the Kokokehom less as her captors than as the subjects of a philosophic project—though she could not deny that these same subjects
were in turn scrutinizing her, casting many a curious and condescending
eye on this woman so woefully ignorant of maize planting and mat weaving and everything else that mattered.

Although the prospect of running the Nimacook gauntlet, the *wopwawnonckquat,* had always instilled in Jennet an unmitigated alarm, she
had survived the initiation with nary a bruise or welt. It was a nasty business to be sure, requiring her to dress in naught but a linen shift, then
dash betwixt two parallel columns of Indians, all of whom proceeded to
set upon her with battle clubs, quahog-shell hoes, and rawhide lashes,
their stated intention being to thresh the very whiteness from her soul.
And yet at the midpoint of her sprint through this human chute, she realized that her captors were checking their blows, restraining their
strokes, and staying their whip hands. Amongst certain Nimacook clans,

no doubt, the gauntlet was still a bloody custom, but within the Kokoke-hom it had evidently transmuted, violence to vestige, savagery to sacrament, ordeal to echo.

Other Nimacook traditions, by contrast, seemed invulnerable to emendation by time. Each autumn, once the seeds were in the ground, the six clans always left their respective villages and came together as one tribe, congregating in a vast settlement to the south under the leadership of the Nimacook grand-sachem, Chabaquong. For two weeks the Indians would feast, dance, feast some more, seek out marriage mates, indulge in further feasting, smoke their tobacco, then throw another feast, all the while discussing public business, most especially the vexatious issue of the English settlers' appetite for Algonquin land. Although these gatherings enabled Jennet to mingle with the other white daughters, she entered their vicinity but rarely, for the conversation of all five girls turned almost exclusively on the past—an understandable obsession, but also quite useless. The daughters grieved for their murdered parents and slaughtered friends, their burned homes and broken baubles, their razed dreams and ravaged aspirations. And yet, even as they indulged in these ritual remembrances, they were obviously learning to inhabit the present, and ere the first year had passed, the five seemed Nimacook to Jennet in all but blood, and two were already with child by their *wasicks*—their mandatory husbands.

Jennet did not exactly love her own mandatory husband, who turned out to be not Pussough but rather his cousin Okommaka, the brave who'd officiated at the burial rite the night of the raid, setting pipes and tobacco atop the corpses. She nevertheless felt toward Okommaka an undeniable tenderness and devotion—a remarkable circumstance, given that she'd enjoyed no liberty whatsoever to reject his marriage proposal. The courtship consisted entirely in her *wasick* presenting her with a pictographic charcoal-on-deerskin catalogue of the assets he would bring to their union: a steel knife, a French musket, a birch-bark canoe, a snappish guard dog named Casco, and a set of reed mats sufficient for constructing a private wigwam. Beyond this strange fixation on his dowry, Okommaka seemed in his own way a reflective and philosophic young man, and this attribute, combined with his high-cheeked, black-haired beauty, aroused in Jennet an emotion that would serve for the poetic passion until it unequivocally entered her life.

Whilst not normally given to bluster, Okommaka never tired of relating how, shortly after the Haverhill raid, he'd bested seven other braves, Pussough amongst them, in a quartet of games—wrestling match, canoe race, archery contest, spear toss—and thereby acquired the right to woo and wed the sky-eyed, fire-haired English maid. Jennet wasn't sure how she felt about this prologue to her matrimony. There was much in the narrative to gratify her vanity (not since Homer's Penelope had a woman occasioned such fierce competition amongst suitors), but even more to make her feel like a piece of booty, a spoil of war. Whether its genesis was chivalric, barbaric, or something betwixt the two, however, her bond with Okommaka clearly entailed guarantees of safety and sustenance, and so she resolved that for the immediate future she would give no thought to escape. Her body and mind could readily tolerate the rôle of Nimacook bride, whereas frigid winds and an empty stomach surely awaited any white woman foolish enough to flee into the inhospitable reaches of the Shawsheen.

The marriage ceremony was spare but elegant, a simple matter of Jennet and Okommaka sharing a bowl of corn soup in his family's presence, clasping each other's hands above the *muchickehea* stone, and, finally, exchanging gifts. He gave her three eelskin hair ribbons and a clam-shell necklace. She presented him with Dunstan's drawing of the horse-head promontory, along with a pouch she'd made from cedar bark, suggesting that he use it to store his tobacco. When dusk came he led her to the back of his family's longhouse and removed her deerskin mantle, immediately finding himself in a state of hydraulic fervor. He shed his garments and bade her lie with him. She did not embrace her husband with enthusiasm, but neither did she know fear, for Chapter Two of her *Woman's Garden* promised that the discomfort would be brief, and she'd calculated that her fertile period was at least ten days away. Forcing a smile, she permitted Okommaka to deflower her in the quick and awkward manner that Isobel had called "the universal buffoonery of young men on their wedding nights," and then came the soothing sensation, unique in her experience, of falling asleep in another person's arms.

"*Cowammaunsh,*" he told her in the morning. Later she learned his meaning. I love you.

What most astonished Jennet about her adoptive family—which included Okommaka's mother, Magunga, his father, Quappala, and an assortment of siblings and cousins—was their willingness to grant her the same privileges she would have enjoyed if born into the Owl Clan. To transmute an outsider into a full-blooded Nimacook, you needed merely to change her name. On Welcoming Day, one month after her wedding, she became Waewowesheckmishquashim, Woman with Hair like a Fox, an epithet whose sense delighted her and whose abridged form, Waequashim, fell pleasingly on her ear.

Indifferent as the Nimacooks were to a wife's ancestry, the same could not be said of her fertility, and none of Waequashim's new relations pretended she'd been abducted for any reason beyond her presumably hale womb. Extinction was a possibility these people could not discount. Famine, wild beasts, intertribal warfare, and Puritan violence regularly reduced the population of childbearers amongst them—amongst all the Algonquin peoples. But it was the terrible small-pox epidemics, raging through the Indian settlements at unpredictable intervals, that wrought the greatest devastation. *Skishauonck,* they called it, the "flogging sickness," and to Jennet that sounded like the perfect word, *skishauonck,* the rasp of Satan clearing his barbed and pustuled throat.

Although Latin had always been for her a laborious pursuit, it was child's play compared to Algonquin, whose rhythms and idioms seemed better suited to the inhabitants of Callisto than to any race on Earth. To say "I am glad you are well" meant teaching your lips to form *"Taubot paumpmauntaman."* "It will rain today" pressed your tongue into the service of *"Anamekeesuck sokenum."* "How fare your children?" required the questioner to articulate *"Aspaumpmauntamwock cummuckiaug?"* For Okommaka, logically enough, English proved equally perverse. He had difficulty grasping that eight words, "A man shot by accident during the hunt," were needed to translate *"Uppetetoua."* He resisted the fact that "I am not inclined to pursue the matter" was the simplest possible rendering of *"Nissekinean."* It bewildered him that "When the wind blows northwest" was the most efficient way to say *"Chekesitch."* And so it happened that, during the first several weeks following their nuptials, Waequashim and her husband managed to conduct quotidian transactions solely through their mutual though defective French, Okommaka and his fellow Owl Clan braves having absorbed bits and pieces of this language from a Jesuit missionary who'd lived in the village for a year, during which interval he'd succeeded in winning only two Indian souls to the Roman faith. But gradually, steadily—and with considerable delight—Jennet and Okommaka learned each other's native tongue, even as their natural tongues found novel ways to fill their private hours with connubial amusement.

Despite their fears of oblivion, the Nimacooks behaved exactly as Pussough had foretold, permitting Jennet to set the terms of her fertility. Okommaka did not complain when she forswore the marital act on those nights when conception was most likely, especially since Chapter Six, "Labia North and South," detailed several compensatory procedures. As a further precaution, before lying with Okommaka she always suffused her privy shaft with a seed-stilling unguent of pennyroyal and marjoram. The physic came from Hassane, the clan's lithe and puckish medicine-woman, their *taupowau:* a kind of wood nymph, Jennet decided, forever flitting about the village as if borne on invisible fairy-wings, merrily dispensing bits of cryptic wisdom—"The dog hath found its brother in the wolf, but humans still await their kindred kind"—along with her songs and simples.

Having reduced the menace of pregnancy to a minimum, Jennet felt free to experiment with the activities outlined in both Chapter Four, "The Lust of the Goat," and Chapter Five, "The Algebra of Desire." To the degree that Isobel's knowledge was firsthand, it would seem that as a sensualist Edward Mowbray had suffered few equals. But Okommaka, too, possessed an aptitude for the priapic, and as their private encounters grew ever more heated, Waequashim gradually apprehended the strange and satisfying truth that swiving had become as central to her sustenance as eating.

It was this newfound carnal appetite that made Jennet resolve to forestall indefinitely the day when she would cease to be attractive in her husband's eyes. Despite the many virtues of a crop-woman's life—the agreeable companions, frequent diversions (she took a special delight in *pisinneganash*, a kind of card game played with bulrushes), heady tobacco (its pleasures being permitted to both genders), and nightly exchanges of tales both factual and fabulous—she had come to regard the plantation as the great enemy of her youthfulness. Her time beneath the burning New World sun was causing her brow to peel like birch bark and her hands to become as coarse as a toad's skin. Eventually she brought the matter before Hassane, who gave her a musky ointment with which to butter her exposed flesh ere venturing upon the maize field to battle the weeds and shoo the crows. Owing to this balm, plus the unsightly but effective bonnet she'd woven from corn husks, Waequashim eventually grew confident that she and Okommaka would wither at the same rate.

As her fifth year amongst the Nimacooks began, Jennet found herself in possession of a compelling hypothesis, perhaps even a truth, concerning the two very different worlds in which Dame Fortune had thus far deposited her. The European universe, she speculated, was in essence a road, a meandering thoroughfare bearing its pilgrims from one impressive way-station to the next, from Greek civilization with its beautiful geometry, to the Christian nations with their brilliant theology, to the star-gazing trinity of Galileo, Kepler, and Newton. But the Indian universe was a wheel, always turning, its rotations marked by the movements of game, the ripening of crops, the shoaling of fish, the fruiting of trees, and the running of sap. Beyond their fondness for French muskets and English fowling-pieces, technical innovation meant little to these people; no Nimacook had ever sought to fashion an astrolabe or a microscope. At first this deficit bewildered Jennet, but in time she came to see certain limitations in her aunt's allegiances. Although natural philosophy was the noblest of enterprises, it had never tracked a deer, maintained a maize crop, trapped salmon in a weir, woven a reed mat, or wrought syrup from the ichor of a maple tree.

Europeans and Indians did not see the same moon, the same *nanepaushat*. For the Cambridge Platonists as well as the Continental Cartesians, Earth's satellite was a mass of dead matter pulled around the planet by an arcane entity (gravitation for the Platonists, vortices for the Cartesians) that could cause "action at a distance." But the Nimacook moon was an immense *wampumpeag* bead fashioned by an ancient coastal people, the Quanquogt, their intention having been to offer it to Kautantouwit, the Great Southwest God, source of all salutary winds, in exchange for the ocean that nurtured them.

"I assume that Kautantouwit did not smile on the proposition," Jennet said to Okommaka as they planted a row of merry yellow trilliums along the walkway leading to their wigwam.

He grunted in assent. "Kautantouwit was much offended. He banished the Quanquogt to a barren desert, then hurled the great *wampumpeag* bead into the sky."

"A harsh but fitting sentence."

Casco the dog ambled onto the scene, approached the stew pot in which they'd cooked their midday meal, and inserted his snout in quest of venison scraps.

"Ah, but even a god can be tempted." Okommaka pressed a wad of tobacco into the bowl of his soapstone pipe. "Even Kautantouwit will have his greed. And so it happens that once each month he reaches toward the *nanepaushat-suwhoog*, the moon-bead, obscuring it bit by bit with the shadow of his hand—but in the end he always decides to leave the bead in place."

"A sign, aye?" Jennet said. "A symbol of his displeasure with the Quanquogt."

"*Nux.* Yes. No part of the Earth may be bought or sold, Waequashim, no piece of *Mittauke*. No sea, forest, lake, or mountain."

"If the moon is a bead, then what is the sun?"

"In England they have no knowledge of the sun?" He frowned emphatically. "The sun, cherished wife, is the council fire around which our ancestors gather. When a Nimacook dies, his soul travels to the southwest mountain, and if Kautantouwit judges it worthy he will deliver that same soul to Keesuckquand, Guardian of Heaven's Torch."

"Now that I am Nimacook, do *my* ancestors gather around the fire?"

"Look at the sun," he said, pointing skyward. "Not long, lest it blind you. Look, and you will see all those who came before you."

She locked her gaze on the sun. The burning rays flooded her skull with light, and she turned away, blinking, eyes smarting. Casco licked the stew pot. Okommaka lit his pipe.

She lifted her head and again stared at the council fire. A golden frieze appeared. Her mother, grandmother, and great-grandmother sat huddled in the sun's corona like jewels decorating a diadem.

Some desire of her mind, quite likely. Some phantom of her brain. And yet the glimmering chimera produced in Jennet a joy such as she'd not known since that long-gone March evening at Mirringate, a night of hot sugared coffee and dancing oak-wood flames, when Aunt Isobel had taught her to comprehend the grand cosmic drama, more than twenty-five thousand years in duration, known to natural philosophers as the precession of the equinoxes.

❦

NEAR THE END OF JENNET'S SEVENTH YEAR in the Owl Clan, it became obvious that Okommaka, Magunga, Quappala, and the rest of her immediate family could no longer abide her vacant womb. Assenting to the inevitable, she set aside Hassane's unguent, and she and Okommaka started clustering their connections toward the middle of her cycle. Within three months she was pregnant. Despite the cessation of her lunar bleeding, she found the condition supremely uncomfortable, but she did not experience the terror she'd so long anticipated. Her qualified equanimity traced to the tradition whereby Nimacook squaws dropped their babies whilst standing erect—the very attitude that Aunt Isobel (having researched the matter in four languages) regarded as the safest and least painful, "the upright pagan posture, ninety degrees from the horizontal lying-in to which a European woman subjects herself." What-ever hardships the birthing process might involve, Jennet imagined that through heathen tradition and Hassane's talent she would elude the fate her mother had suffered in delivering Dunstan. If the infant was a girl, she would name her Bella, a variation on Isobel. If a boy, he would be Anton, in homage to the inventor of the microscope.

As Jennet entered her final month, the infant kicking against her womb at least once an hour, protesting its imprisonment, a distressing report reached the village. The flogging sickness had struck the Moaskug, the Black Snake Clan, a Nimacook community a half-day's walk to the north. Later that week the rumor received vivid confirmation as the pied corpses of two Moaskug women came floating down the Shawsheen. Jennet's fellow Indians knew from experience what would happen now. First, more *skishauonck* victims would appear on the river. Then, for miles around the village, the forest would tremble with the shrieks of the dying and the keening of the bereaved. And finally a new sound would arise, the marching feet of the *machemoqussu*, the wandering doomed, those still-living sufferers whom the disease had transformed into madmen.

Theirs was an understandable insanity. In the initial stage of *skishauonck*, Hassane explained, the patient endured a burning fever and violent vomiting, even as tiny red spots appeared all over his body. In the second stage the spots became blisters filled with lustrous pus. If the victim was going to survive, this happy fact soon became manifest: his fever broke, and the blisters turned to scabs and fell off. But many did not survive. For these unfortunates, the blisters began erupting, thereby causing the outermost tiers of the flesh, both internally and externally, to split away from the underlayers, so that the victim was literally flayed alive, without and also within, blood oozing from his mouth, nose, genitals, and anus.

With every brave except Miacoomes and his councilors away on the summer hunt, it fell to the women to take up firearms and prevent the *machemoqussu* from spreading the contagion amongst the Owl Clan. Despite Jennet's gravid state, Miacoomes required her to spend two hours each morning doing sentry duty in collaboration with a crone named Winoshi, the two women pacing back and forth outside the stockade wall, muskets in hand, all senses at peak. Although the *machemoqussu* were nowhere to be seen, Jennet did not for an instant doubt their actuality. She could hear them wailing and moaning amidst the shadows as they crashed blister-blind from tree to tree and boulder to boulder—the world's true demons, the goblins with dissolving skin.

Shortly after sunrise on her twentieth morning of guarding the village, Jennet's sac abruptly split, sending a stream of warm clear water spilling down her thighs. The fluid rolled across the ground, irrigating the grass and quenching the wildflowers. A half-hour later the first spasm arrived, seizing her body with all the force of a plowshare breaking hard earth.

She took her leave of Winoshi, ran to her wigwam, and grabbed the poppet she'd made two nights earlier—deerskin body, eyes of white beads—that she might gift her child with a toy upon its disembarkation. As she made her way to the *taupowau's* dwelling, the immured and impatient baby bobbing before her, a second spasm came, stronger even than the first. Hassane gathered together the steel knife, leather flask, linen rags, figwort leaves, deerskin blanket, and other necessities, then guided Jennet to the wooded northwest quadrant of the village. The birthing lodge was a typical Nimacook longhouse, though equipped with a *nesseanaskunck:* two shorn hemlock branches suspended five feet above the floor, positioned in parallel like railings on a bridge, and supported by leather thongs affixed to the ceiling.

"Step betwixt the poles," Hassane commanded.

Jennet did so.

"Set your arms around the centers," Hassane said.

Even as Jennet obeyed, a third spasm took hold of her.

"Breathe quickly and deliberately," Hassane said, "as if you are swimming across the Shawsheen."

Jennet opened her mouth and sucked in a great sphere of air. She released it with a sharp calculated puff.

Owing to Hassane's midwifing skills and the virtues of vertical birthing, the delivery fell short of an ordeal. It was exhausting to be sure, punctuated by ferocious explosions of pain, but never once did Jennet feel herself in thrall to those profane forces that had carried her mother to the hallowed ground of a Mistley churchyard.

"You have a daughter, Waequashim." The *taupowau* eased the expelled infant into the good air and soft light of the birthing lodge, then took up the knife and with a single stroke severed the umbilical cord.

Healthy and unharmed, or so Hassane asserted, Bella fascinated Jennet from the moment the *taupowau* placed the infant in her arms. Whilst Hassane buried the bright blue placenta by the riverbank, Jennet sat outside the lodge and contemplated the creature's tiny eyelashes and subtle nose, her articulated knuckles and wrinkled brown knees, her wispy black hair and stubby but differentiated toes. Who could have guessed that the great bulky stone in Waequashim's womb would emerge into daylight boasting such glorious detail?

"Many are the lessons I would teach thee," Jennet said, setting the deerskin doll in her baby's reflexive grasp.

She told Bella that the season for planting began when the leaves of the white oak were as large as a mouse's ears. She explained how each time the sun refracted the lingering damp of a summer shower, a rainbow appeared in the sky, and if you could somehow gather up that spectrum and strain it through another such prism, its rays would fuse into a beam of purest whiteness. When guarding the plantation, a squaw must never slay a raven, neither with arrow nor spear nor musket-ball, for it was that bird and no other who had brought to the Algonquin the very first maize seed. She informed her daughter that they would one day scour the Shawsheen's bottom until they discovered a stone so clear and pure it could serve as a microscope lens, and then they would find another such stone, and next they would fit the two lenses to a tube of soapstone, and by this means they would explore the world that lay hidden within the world.

"Six sides there be to each and every snow crystal," Jennet said, alternately stroking the deerskin doll and the infant's brow. "Mr. Hooke hath proved as much. That is the planet to which you have come, my beautiful, darling Bella."

NOW THAT OKOMMAKA'S DAUGHTER had arrived, launched upon the trajectory of her joys and the vector of her sorrows, Miacoomes forbade Waequashim to do sentry duty, lest the toxic breath of the *machemoqussu* bring sickness to the infant. Instead Jennet became a plantation maid again. Each morning she would package Bella's bum in an absorbent mixture of cattail fluff and sphagnum, roll a deerskin around her body until the child resembled an unhusked ear of corn, strap her to a cradleboard, and equip her with the rattle Magunga had made from bits of bone and a scooped-out gourd, whereupon the two of them would set off for the field *des trois soeurs*, the baby riding on her mother's spine like a turtle basking on a log. As she attacked the weeds with her hoe and unburdened the bean crop of dead vines, Jennet kept an eye peeled for the *machemoqussu*, and she did not relax her vigilance until, five weeks after Bella's birth, the Moaskug sagamore sent word to Miacoomes that the *skishauonck* epidemic had finally lifted. In her mind Jennet saw this event as the abating of a furious storm, its gusts and rains and sleet burned into oblivion by the sun.

Bella's fortieth night on Earth was lit by a moon as pale and yellow as a firefly's lanthorn. Jennet was sitting in the village plaza, the baby's lips clamped around her left nipple, when she noticed the aberrant blotch. It was dark, solitary, no larger than a freckle, fixed like a wood tick to Bella's cheek.

Jennet brushed the blotch with her thumb. It remained rooted, a hundred times more ominous than any Devil's mark. She brushed it again. The dot persisted.

"Dear God in Heaven . . ."

Without breaking the seal betwixt mouth and breast, she rose and proceeded directly to her mother-in-law's longhouse. Upon seeing the excrescence, Magunga let out a howl as loud and anguished as a *machemoqussu's* cry, and then came three more howls interspersed with wheezing gasps, until finally Magunga grew rational enough to assert that only the blaze of the sun could reveal the mark's true nature. For the immediate moment Jennet could do nothing but nurse the baby to sleep:

if there was any hope for Bella, it lay in the dream world—once set roaming across those ethereal hills, the infant's spirit might meet a *mauchatea*, a "ghost guide" who would lead her far beyond the demon-infested land of the flogging sickness and bring her to the healing waters of the River Woaloke.

Staggering home along the moon-lit path, Jennet felt as if she had herself become a wanderer in the dream world, but no *mauchatea* appeared to point the way. She entered the wigwam and, after suckling Bella until the infant's lips stopped moving and her jaw went slack, eased her sleeping body into the cradle as she would shelve the only existing copy of a wise and exquisite book. She sat down, sprawled across the mat, and closed her eyes, all the while imploring Kautantouwit and Jehovah to collaborate in delivering her child from the small-pox. Bella's breathing filled the air, the gentle inhalations and soft exhalations, delicate as breezes meant to launch a fledgling finch on its first flight. Sleep came to Jennet but fitfully that night, her wakeful moments a concatenation of unbidden twitchings and involuntary doggish yelps, her dreams aboil with *machemoqussu* infantries on the march.

At first light she unfurled her clenched fingers and set her palm on Bella's brow. The baby's skin was hot, deathly hot, *skishuuonck* hot. Seconds later Bella awoke, and from her little chest a jagged screech shot forth.

Jennet picked up the baby, her infinitely detailed Bella whose spirit had failed to find a *mauchatea*, and carried her into the remorseless light of day. Pustules speckled Bella's torso like Satanic *wampumpeag* beads.

"Blessed Kautantouwit, I beg thee . . ."

Thirty pustules, fifty, a hundred.

"Hear me, Kautantouwit . . ."

Again Bella screeched.

She bore her daughter to Hassane's wigwam, hoping the medicine-woman would judge Bella afflicted with a rare but curable disease whose symptoms uncannily mimicked those of the flogging sickness. But instead of offering any such lore, Hassane merely directed Jennet to swab the child head to toe with river-soaked wads of sphagnum, again and again and again.

To what unspeakable precinct of their pantheon did the Nimacooks consign *skishauonck?* From whence sprang this Satanic contagion? Jennet never found out. The Indians were not given to raging indignantly against the plague, but neither did they regard it as a fitting punishment for their sins. Apparently they viewed *skishauonck* as a mystery. The disease confounded Jennet as well. Bathing Bella as Hassane had prescribed for five unbroken hours, all the while watching her daughter transmute from a baby into a *machemoqussu*, and thence to a corpse, she could not decide whether *skishauonck* represented the iniquity of Lucifer, the wrath of God, the perversity of Nature, or yet another force, beyond all human comprehension.

She grieved as would any other Nimacook, staining her teeth with juniper berries, loading her moccasins with pebbles, and cutting her hair with a sacred elk-bone knife, so that ragged auburn tufts now sprouted from her scalp. She prepared a cake of charred oak and rubbed it across her face, darkening her cheeks and brow with an itching patina of soot.

Taking the corpse in her arms, she hobbled down to the riverbank, where Hassane and Magunga awaited, their faces likewise blackened.

"*Kutchimmoke,*" Hassane told her. Be of good cheer.

"*Kutchimmoke,*" Magunga echoed.

After searching the shore for an hour, the women found a soft and secluded spot beneath a willow tree, and there they dug a grave with clamshell spades, lining the bottom with a cushion of sticks. Jennet placed Bella in extreme flexion, hands covering face, then slipped the deerskin doll under her arms and wrapped her in a reed mat. In tandem the women fitted Bella into the grave, slowly, deliberately, seed into furrow, string into nock, feather into braid, and then Jennet said good-bye to the child with the wondrous knuckles and the rich black hair. The women filled the hole with sand. Hassane erected atop the mound a tower of twigs and stones no higher than a maize stalk, gently tilting it toward the southwest—for this was a *cowwenock-wunnauchicomock*, she explained, a "soul-chimney" meant to draw the child's immaterial essence from her dead flesh and point it toward Kautantouwit's sacred mountain, that it might join with the God of Gods.

"And now, Waequashim, you must take the river-cure," Hassane said. "Today and every day for a month," Magunga elaborated, "you will give yourself to the Shawsheen."

Did the Nimacook river-cure represent a foolish heathen superstition, or was it rather a paragon of pagan wisdom? In her numb and pliant condition Jennet could form no opinion, and so it was with a divided heart that she removed her mantle and skirt, pulled off her moccasins, bid Hassane and Magunga farewell, and stepped into the cool racing fluid. She walked along the muddy bed until the water reached her waist, and then she lifted her heels and tipped her body forward. She swam north, face down, countering the current by moving her legs in a frog kick and raising her head to breathe. Waterborne twigs stroked her thighs. Clusters of leaves caressed her sides. The Shawsheen washed the soot from her cheeks and brow.

At twilight she reached Hawk-Isle, then rolled on her back like an otter and let the river return her to the mound where Bella lay. Clambering onto the shore, she locked her gaze on the little wooden tower, still pointed toward Heaven. Such a fragile talisman, this soul-chimney, this *cowwenock-wunnauchicomock*. It would not survive the briefest rainshower, much less a blizzard or a thunder-gust.

"In the spring you and I shall fly it." Her knees failed, and she collapsed naked and shivering atop her daughter's grave. "We shall fly it for fair, my dearest, sweetest Bella."

For an indeterminate interval she sobbed and keened, pummeling the mound with her fists, soaking the sand with her tears as her birth waters had saturated the earth outside the village gateway, until at last her grief grew so thick and hard—a kind of second pregnancy, malign this time, tumoral—that she could no longer work her wailing limbs or move her weeping joints. She curled her body into a tight sphere, a human moon-bead, and she did not bestir herself until dawn.

FOUR DAYS LATER Hassane brought Jennet a male infant whose mother had succumbed to the contagion, so that the white woman's engorged breasts might nourish him. Kapaog's sucking proved far more vigorous than Bella's, so that, true to a phenomenon documented in Chapter Seven, Jennet found herself in a state of concupiscent arousal. When Hassane required her to hand Kapaog over to another lactating woman, a potter named Cumunchon, likewise mourning her infant *machemoqussu*, a deep carnal longing settled into Jennet's bones, lingering until at last Okommaka returned from the hunt.

"I gave our daughter an English name," she told him. "Bella, after my Aunt Isobel, the natural philosopher. All the world held great fascination for her, from the meanest worm to the brightest star."

"The brightest star," Okommaka echoed. "Then our child was Pashpishia."

"Pashpishia . . ."

"She Who Loves the Night."

With every visit she paid to Pashpishia's grave that month, Jennet grew more determined to evoke *nupakenaqun*—the right of a bereaved mother to exempt herself from further procreation. Okommaka in turn claimed a collateral privilege, so that his nubile cousin Maansu became his second wife. In a development so ironic it might have given even Sophocles pause, Jennet found that, far from arousing her jealousy, this bigamous arrangement increased tenfold her sense of unity with the Owl Clan. She would never be a Nimacook mother, but now she knew herself for an absolute Nimacook squaw, the first and favorite of Okommaka.

This pagan marriage was real. The Kokokehom were the case. Her clam-shell necklace, eelskin hair ribbons, bead bracelet, fur robe, deerskin leggings, and moose-hide moccasins were factual as grass. As for Salem and Boston, Colchester and London, the Aristotelian Earth and the Newtonian moon, these were just labels on dreams, mere names for places as mythic as Atlantis or El Dorado.

Out there, it was 1703: so said her calendar of fired pots. Out there, some bright young natural philosopher was likely on the point of discovering Newton's lost demon disproof. Even as her twenty-fifth birthday arrived—an event she celebrated by fashioning for herself a head-dress of hawk and pheasant feathers—an *argumentum grande* was doubtless appearing on the stage of European history, poised to topple all witch-courts and shred all conjuring statutes. But for Waequashim of the Nimacook, there was no more work to do.

❦❦

ALTHOUGH JENNET REMAINED HORRIFIED by the brutality and the bloody scalps, the Indians' war against the Merrimack Valley settlers had evidently accomplished its aim. By the turn of the century a crop-woman could spend a productive morning tilling her clan's acres without fear that some eager Puritan would try to steal them come afternoon. To all appearances an undeclared truce had emerged betwixt Chabaquong's people and the English towns, including a reconstructed and repopulated Haverhill, and in time the Nimacooks permitted the Puritans to inscribe a toll road along the extreme eastern edge of their territory—a mail route from Boston to Amesbury—with the Indians receiving a fee of one *wampumpeag* bead per mounted wayfarer and two per horse-drawn coach.

Because the far boundary of the Owl Clan's plantation abutted the Amesbury Post Road, Jennet now became witness to a daily stream of white men—galloping mail-carriers, marching soldiers, sweating drovers, panting peddlers—a circumstance that prompted Quappala and Magunga to imagine their elder daughter-in-law imploring some traveler to bear her away. Eventually her family's suspicions grew so acute that, whenever their farming chores brought the crop-women near the new thoroughfare, Magunga outfitted Waequashim with the exact sort of leather halter by which she'd been abducted.

And so it happened that Jennet once again came to regard the Nimacooks not as her kin but as her keepers. Nothing moved them, neither her protestations of loyalty—the louder she asserted her allegiance to the tribe, the more convinced they became that she intended to bolt—nor her protests against the yoke: "I shan't be harnessed! I am not an ox! I am not an ass! I am not a plow horse!" All such metaphors proved equally impotent, partly because draught animals played no rôle in the Indian way of life, largely because the subject was not up for discussion.

By 1708 a new element had entered the Nimacook economy. Those braves with a talent for trapping learned that if they brought their beaver pelts, their *toumockquashuncks*, down the Shawsheen to the English village of Bedford, they could exchange them for a panoply of European goods. The Nimacooks' grand-sachem disdained this so-called "fur trade," for it seemed to embody the very mercantilism that the Moon-Bead Legend condemned. Chabaquong's councilors, however, argued that the Great God Kautantouwit would not feel offended by such commerce if the trappers limited their acquisitions to flintlock muskets, forged knives, iron kettles, and other products unknown to Algonquin industry. Eventually Chabaquong permitted the enterprise to go forward, though without his blessing.

The grand-sachem was not the only Nimacook to lament the tribe's entry into the fur trade. Jennet did so too, for once the *toumockquashuncks* were in hand, the tedious job of treating them fell to the women. She detested each step in the process: scraping the backs of the skins, rubbing them with marrow, trimming them into rectangles, sewing six or eight such pieces together into a robe, wearing the garment from dawn to dusk until the pelts grew supple enough to command a top price. But then one day Okommaka mentioned that books were amongst the items available at the Bedford Trading Center, and Jennet's opinion of the fur trade improved considerably.

"What *sorts* of books?" she asked.

"The English God-Book," Okommaka replied. "The Bible of Grand-Sachem James."

"What else?"

"French verses. English plays. Histories written in Latin."

English plays! Oh, to scan that linguistic music again, to experience once more Juliet's longings and Cleopatra's passions and Lady Macbeth's depravity. If she came upon a *Principia Mathematica* in Bedford she would immediately toss it aside—she was no longer a Hammer of Witchfinders, after all, no longer obligated to cultivate an acquaintance with Lucasian Professors—but a quarto *Macbeth* would be as welcome as a reincarnation of Aunt Isobel's treatise.

Okommaka, predictably, recoiled at Jennet's desire to accompany him on his next Bedford adventure. Fur trading, he insisted, was a masculine enterprise, and any brave who brought a wife along risked ridicule by whites and Algonquins alike. But she continued to press the matter, and eventually, owing either to the righteousness of her case, the pathos in her voice, or the chapter called "Labia North and South," Okommaka relented, solemnly declaring that a great Nimacook trapper did not prostrate himself before the opinions of lesser men.

The expedition comprised three canoes bearing Okommaka, Pussough, six other braves, Casco the dog, and—now—Okommaka's headstrong elder wife. All during their passage down the Shawsheen, a glorious anticipation filled every pipe and parlor of Jennet's heart. Okommaka had agreed that she could acquire four volumes, assuming they collectively cost no more than half a beaver-robe, and with each paddle stroke she imagined herself savoring yet another line of Shakespeare or Marlowe or Jonson.

The celestial council fire had passed its zenith by the time they reached the trading center—an impressive installation, three well-made cabins supplemented by a livery and a forge, plus a tavern called Paradise Misplaced. A flagpole rose in the front yard, flying both the Union Jack and the device of the Shawsheen Fur Exchange Authority, a beaver surrounded by the company's motto, *Profit, Prosperity, Plenitude*. Okommaka steered his canoe to the wharf, where three white traders fidgeted about, thickset men in plain muslin shirts, idly smoking pipes and skimming stones across the water. As Jennet climbed onto the dock, the traders greeted her with dark scowls and hostile mutterings. Perhaps they regarded her as pitiable, so pitiable in fact that—were they made of sterner stuff and not outnumbered by the Kokokehom—they might have tried liberating her with the aim of collecting a reward. But more likely they simply found Jennet repulsive, this corrupted woman whose braids smelled of bear grease and whose soul stank of idolatry, and the less they had to do with her, the better.

Much to her frustration, Okommaka and Pussough insisted on patronizing the first two stores, one featuring muskets and shot, the other offering tools and cooking implements, before venturing into the third, an emporium specializing in felt hats, leather boots, wool blankets, and steel gorgets. Okommaka guided her to a battered shipping crate. She lifted the lid. Books filled the compartment top to bottom—one hundred volumes at least: five score jolts for a dozing intellect, a banquet for a hungry brain. She took a breath, praised Kautantouwit, and got to work, unloading the crate and organizing the jumble as her husband and his cousin looked on in amusement. She did not really expect to find *Macbeth* or *Romeo and Juliet* or *Antony and Cleopatra* in the mess, but there was indeed a Shakespeare quarto, *The Tempest,* as well as Marlowe's *Tragical History of Dr. Faustus,* both of which she set aside. Her third decision, Thomas Shelton's translation of *Don Quixote de la Mancha,* was similarly easy. Now came an impossible choice. How much did she desire *Cæsar's Commentaries* as opposed to Spenser's *The Fœrie Queene?* Plutarch's *Parallel Lives of the Noble Greeks and Romans* versus Xenophon's *Recollections of Socrates?* One thing was certain. She would eschew the ratty copy of Reginald Scot's *Discoverie of Witchcraft,* one of the skeptical works Aunt Isobel had told her to consult in devising the *argumentum grande.* A Hammer of Witchfinders might find that tome of use, but she wouldn't trade a beaver's cheek for it.

Eventually she reduced the conundrum to three possibilities: Montaigne's *Essays,* Bunyan's *The Pilgrim's Progress,* and an old friend from her Mirringate youth, Virgil's *Æneid.* She set the volumes on the floor, each at the point of an imaginary equilateral triangle, and, rising to full height, made ready to surrender the matter to Dame Fortune. Whilst Okommaka and Pussough snickered conspicuously, she stepped inside the triangle, shut her eyes, spun around thrice, stretched out her arm, and directed a pointing finger downward.

She opened her eyes. The *Æneid.* A splendid resolution. *Arma virumque cano.*

"What does that book talk about?" Okommaka asked.

"Virgil recounts the adventures of Æneas, destined to bring forth the Roman nation," she said.

"The missionary who lived amongst us spoke often of ancient Rome,"

Pussough said. "Its founders were Romulus and Remus, suckled as babes by a she-wolf."

"Virgil tells a rather different story," Jennet said.

"No Romulus and Remus?" said Pussough. "No she-wolf?"

"No she-wolf."

"My uncle knows a Moattoqus brave who was raised by wolves," Okommaka said. "Such a thing can happen, Waequashim. Virgil should not have doubted it."

AT DUSK THE INDIANS RETURNED to the Shawsheen, laden with the fruits of their bartering. Okommaka spread out his prizes on the wharf—Italian dueling pistol, keg of gunpowder, iron skillet, brass-framed mirror, striped blanket—then wrapped them in a deerskin and wedged the bundle into the bow. Jennet slid her books into a hempen sack and secured it beside her husband's cache.

A pastoral scene unfolded in her mind: the trading party camped that night beside the river, Jennet reading Virgil aloud by the fire, translating as she went. Storm-tossed Æneas and his men landing on the Libyan shore. The hero telling the Carthaginians the tale of the Trojan horse. The romance of Æneas and Dido. Her suicide following his decision to leave for Italy. The shade of Anchises showing Æneas the future history of Rome. The great war betwixt Æneas's forces and the Latin armies of King Turnus. Æneas slaying Turnus in personal combat. Okommaka, Pussough, and the other enthralled Nimacooks attended every word.

Excited shouts disturbed the gloaming. Jennet lifted her head.

A mob of Indians and whites had collected by the riverbank, their attention fixed on a high footbridge arcing across the Shawsheen like a wooden rainbow. Huddled together in the center of the bridge, four figures in Puritan garb used a plow-rope to lower a woman toward the water, her legs and trunk concealed by a flimsy shift, her moans muffled by a leather napkin. Thongs drew the prisoner's wrists and ankles together, forcing her body into the shape of a horseshoe.

"Husband, I see a gang of Calvinist witchfinders, inflicting their tests on an innocent woman," Jennet said. "By your leave, I shall go to 'em and protest this injustice."

"When English settlers choose to harry one another, a Nimacook finds this cause for joy, not bewilderment," Okommaka said.

"My conscience will torment me if I do not denounce these prickers to their faces."

Okommaka issued a series of low, discrete grunts. His taut tongue roamed around the inside of his mouth, bulging his cheeks, and then at last he spoke.

"Tell the Englishmen that if they harm you, Waequashim, your husband and his fellow braves will not forbear to separate them from their scalps."

She leapt over the canoe, sprinted along the shore, and, reaching the bridge, mounted the stairway to the horizontal span. The quartet still held the swimming-rope, their gray capes rippling in the wind.

She could not decide which shock was the greater: seeing Dunstan in the flesh, or apprehending the form in which that flesh had survived the burning of Haverhill. Although Nature had wrought a handsome adult from the raw materials of youth, the achievement was gravely compromised by the cataract of scar tissue spilling down from his high-crowned hat all the way to his jaw.

"Dunstan!" she gasped. "Praise God! I was certain the fire had consumed thee!"

Not unexpectedly, Abigail Williams had ripened into a comely specimen of womanhood. As for her uncle, the Reverend Samuel Parris, the fourteen intervening years had turned his face into a burlesque of itself, all beaky nose and receding chin. Time had been equally severe with Magistrate Jonathan Corwin, robbing him of so many teeth that his cheeks had collapsed, causing his head to resemble a skull dipped in tallow.

"O sweet Jesus, can this be my own long-lost sister?" Dunstan lifted his hands from the swimming-rope. His confederates froze, leaving their prisoner to dangle above the Shawsheen like a fox caught in a snare. " 'Tis truly Jennet Stearne beneath those feathers and skins?"

"Aye, Dunstan. You must set that woman free."

He lurched away from the bridge rail, flung his arms around Jennet, and drew her to his chest like a laundry-maid pulling bedsheets from a clothesline. She answered his embrace by stroking his brow and kissing the frightful scar.

"I feared you'd been scalped"—Dunstan touched the brim of his hat—"but 'tis *I* who lost his hair, every lock burned to the bone: a small price to pay, for with Jehovah's help I retrieved our father's license. Prithee, give us the space of a quarter-hour to switch off yon Satanist, and we shall bear you to the safety of our Framingham salt-box."

"Nay, Dunstan," Jennet said. "I'm Waequashim of the Kokokehom now." Defiantly she adjusted her head-dress. "Have you not yet learned that witchery's an impossible thing? Unbind this woman, I implore thee."

"Unbind her?" Abigail sneered. She abandoned the swimming-rope, so that the task of counterweighting the prisoner fell entirely to Parris and Corwin. "Hah!" Her contemptuous eye ranged across Jennet's wardrobe, moccasins to leggings to mantle to hair ribbons. "How the Algonquin fashion doth become you, Miss Stearne. Those stinking braids will bring many a savage suitor to your door."

"In point of fact I'm married to a Nimacook trapper," Jennet said.

"Do you hear that, Dunstan? Your sister swives a tawny pagan!"

"I would rather be a pagan wife than a Protestant wench," Jennet said.

"You will not call me a wench, sister," Abigail said, "for Dunstan and I are wed five years now."

Jennet raised a hand to her collarbone and anxiously fingered her necklace. Given the unspeakable pain and the demonic scar that were the price of Dunstan's deliverance from the fire, she could hardly blame him for rushing to his demented friend and taking refuge in her affection. But it was one thing to understand their union and quite another to bless it. The thought of these two fanatics spawning a new generation of witchfinders nauseated her as surely as any emetic.

Again she touched Dunstan, resting her hand on his sleeve. "To this day your drawing of the horse-head promontory hangs in my dwelling. I gave it to my husband as a wedding gift."

A flicker of remembrance lit Dunstan's face. " 'Twas an excellent sketch—I shan't dispute you." He pivoted toward Parris and Corwin. "Lower the hag!" he called, and the two cleansers offered their prisoner to the Shawsheen.

"No!" Jennet cried.

"I am my father's son," Dunstan said, turning toward her. "He did not rear me to coddle goblins or sup with Beelzebub."

"She floats!" Parris announced. "The river brands Susan Diggens a witch!"

"I can prove that wicked spirits are but desires of the mind," Jennet said.

"My dear queen of the heathens," Abigail said, "if you durst interfere with us, we shall bring you before the Bedford magistrate."

"We're all of us now the Crown's official prickers: the Massachusetts Bay Purification Commission," Dunstan explained, "twin to the Kirkcaldy Cleansing League and chartered by Her Majesty's Privy Council."

Parris and Corwin hauled Mrs. Diggens over the rail, spilling her onto the span as offhandedly as two Puritan farmers dumping a cartload of hay. The minister drew out a pair of draper's shears and sliced her thongs apart. Mrs. Diggens stretched but did not attempt to rise. She was short and sturdy of build, and for one breathless moment Jennet imagined that here was Aunt Isobel, come back from the grave.

When at last Corwin untied the mask-o'-truth, Mrs. Diggens exhaled sharply and scrambled to her feet. Her frightened stare shot past her tormentors and fixed on Jennet. "Help me, friend Indian," she whispered. "In my life I've stolen much and shagged many, but i'Christ I'm blameless to sorcery."

"The river hath revealed her nature," Parris said. "Next comes her execution."

"Friend Indian, I beg ye," Mrs. Diggens pleaded.

A vortex of movement possessed the Purification Commission, and after the chaos had subsided Jennet stood pinioned against the rail, her right arm paralyzed by Parris's grip, her left wrist trapped in Corwin's skeletal fingers. Mrs. Diggens lay hunched and trembling on the span.

The rope that had recently encircled her waist was now a noose about her neck.

" 'Tis not lawful to hang a person merely on the evidence of a swimming!" Jennet shouted. "She must go before a duly appointed committee and thence to a courtroom!"

"Were you a subscriber to *The Bible Commonwealth*," Abigail said, "you would know that by Queen Anne's decree neither we nor our Scottish brethren need apply mundane standards to the invisible crime of sorcery."

Dunstan said, "However, if 'twill give you satisfaction, Jenny . . ." He pivoted toward Abigail. "Goodwife Stearne, as the Examination Committee on this bridge, you may now offer your findings."

"The Examination Committee returns a *billa vera*," Abigail replied, looping the rope around the rail and securing it with three quick knots.

"Oh, dear God!" Mrs. Diggens shrieked.

"Stop this!" Jennet wailed.

"Mr. Parris, what verdict doth the jury render?" Dunstan asked.

"The jury finds Susan Diggens guilty," the minister said.

"Mr. Corwin, we shall hear your sentence," Dunstan said.

"Were this a case of thievery and bawdiness alone, I might be moved to spare her," said the judge, forcing the prisoner to stand erect, "but Susan Diggens hath manifestly written in the Devil's ledger, and so—"

"Friend Indian!" Urine and liquid feces leaked from beneath Mrs. Diggen's shift.

With an efficiency doubtless born of experience, Dunstan and Abigail pulled a burlap sack over the prisoner's head, lifted her onto the rail, and gave her a rude shove. Mrs. Diggens screamed as she fell, and then came a short, sharp report, like a dry twig snapping underfoot.

The instant Corwin and Parris relaxed their hold, Jennet rushed toward the stairway, seriously pondering the possibility, at once tempting and terrible, of summoning the seven Kokokehom trappers and suggesting that they massacre this so-called Purification Commission. Instead she stopped and turned, her eyes now two gazing-crystals, each fixed on Abigail's breast as if to scorch the vixen's heart.

"Hear me now, ye damned witchfinders! Your fellowship will not prosper! For all ye enjoy the blessings of the Crown, I shall one day destroy your enterprise as surely as Æneas slew King Turnus!"

"Go back to your naked Redman," Abigail hissed, "and trouble us no more!"

Step by languid step, Jennet descended to the riverbank. Okommaka and the other Nimacooks collected around her, knives unsheathed, muskets cocked, tomahawks at the ready. Casco barked ferociously. She faced the bridge. Susan Diggens's corpse swung from the rail like a Huygens pendulum. As Okommaka hovered by her side, Jennet walked back to the canoes, dislodged her newfound Virgil, and carried it to the relevant cabin. The exchange took but a minute, and when it was over she no longer owned the *Æneid*, having acquired in its stead Reginald Scot's treatise. True, it was unlikely that more than a paragraph from *Discoverie of Witchcraft* would end up in the *argumentum grande*. By themselves Scot's words could never kill the Conjuring Statue or prompt the Privy Council to cancel her brother's charter. But a Hammer of Witchfinders had to start

※

Somewhere amidst the private papers of the brilliant American sculptor Gutzon Borglum is a drawing that I regard as his crowning conception, greater even than his quartet of Mount Rushmore presidents. Borglum titled his idea "The Reader," and he never got around to rendering it in stone; as far as I know, he never even took it to the maquette stage. Perhaps he lost enthusiasm. More likely he failed to find a patron. If realized, "The Reader" and its pedestal would have towered over twenty feet above some American park, common, or square. It shows a young woman sitting in a Windsor chair, lost in a book, a spaniel asleep at her feet.

I needn't remind you that readers have always constituted a minority within your species. Merely by opening this chronicle of mine, you have placed yourself in rare company. The odor of bowel wind is known to every human, but the fragrance of book glue has crossed only a fraction of mortal nostrils. And yet it behooves us not to judge the unlettered too harshly. We must stay the impulse to write CHUCKLEHEAD above their doors and carve DOLT upon their tombstones. For in days gone by, at least, a certain chariness toward typography made sense. Borglum's woman in the Windsor chair is performing a traditionally problematic act.

The first recorded instance of a troubled relationship between a reader and a book occurred in 590 B.C., when Yahweh ordered Ezekiel to eat a scroll, thereby absorbing its contents. Although the scroll displayed the words "lamentations, and mourning, and woe" front and back, Ezekiel acquiesced to the command. He reported that the book tasted "as honey for sweetness," which strikes me as a mighty peculiar flavor for lamentations and mourning and woe. In my opinion Ezekiel was afraid to speak his mind: a prophet who knows what's good for him does not go around criticizing God's cuisine.

One hundred and seventy years later, readers had to contend with Socrates's pronouncement that books are useless artifacts. Literary works cannot explain what they say, the great philosopher argued—they can only repeat the same words over and over. To me this sounds less like the definition of a book than of a Heideggerian, but in any event Socrates clearly missed the point. Books don't repeat the same words over and over. The *Gulliver's Travels* whose whimsy amused you at twelve is not the *Gulliver's Travels* whose acid engaged you at thirty.

Some of you belong to my dear Jennet's gender. I needn't remind you that throughout Western history an argument has raged over whether women possess sufficient intellect to profit from the print medium. In A.D. 1333, the Renaissance artist Simone Martini provoked an ecclesiastical crisis when he painted the future Mother of God receiving the Annunciation while holding a book. Wasn't Mary almost certainly illiterate? fretted the keepers of the faith. Wasn't it sacrilegious to suggest that a woman might love knowledge when the Bible clearly stated, "Thy desire shall be to thy husband"? Would the painting's audience even be able to *recognize* the Blessed Virgin in this strange scholastic stance?

In 1740 the South Carolina legislature, haunted by images of their Negro chattel learning Jesus' views on love and, worse, the abolitionists' views on slavery, made it illegal to teach an African to read. According to this law, any black person caught with a book must be flogged. After the third such offense, the first joint of his forefinger was severed. Other Southern states rushed to enact identical measures, many of which remained in effect even after Emancipation.

And so we see how throughout history the community of readers has been prey to sinister forces—to pedants and priests, legislators and lunatics, deities and demagogues. You have paid for your passion in humiliation, mutilation, and sometimes even—as when Henry VIII burned Bible translator William Tyndale as a heretic—immolation. I salute you all, as do my fellow books. Were you to call yourselves heroes, we would not smirk. Show me an accomplished reader, and I shall show you a person of many virtues, thoughtful and articulate, contemplative though rarely passive, temperate and yet benignly

❦

Ambitious
beyond his intellect,
though timid in congruence with
his clumsiness, Tobias Arnold Crompton
had never fallen in love at first sight before, but now he'd done so, and the situation was causing him far more puzzlement than pleasure. The woman of his dreams was inaccessible. Insuperable circumstances, wide as any moat, high as any rampart, precluded the possibility of a chance meeting, let alone a tryst. Not knowing her name, Tobias had taken to calling her Bathsheba, for his plight indeed evoked King David peering down from the palace roof and beholding Uriah's comely wife performing her ablutions.

Two times a week, whilst carrying packets along the Amesbury Post Road for the Provincial Mail Commission, Tobias was privileged to observe Bathsheba laboring on the Nimacook plantation. Beyond her ridiculous bonnet of husks, she was a woman of transcendent desirability, one who made the cultivation of a maize crop—digging the furrow, inserting the seeds, adding a dead fish for fertilizer, extracting the weeds, harvesting the ears, uprooting the barren stalks, bundling them into sheaves for tinder—seem an arcane sport reserved to Vestal virgins or Greek goddesses. If by some blessed turn of fortune Bathsheba became Tobias's wife, his joy would surely propel him through the ranks of his profession until he reached the pinnacle, Postmaster General of the British Crown Colonies in America.

She was manifestly the Indians' unwilling prisoner, not an adopted bride now reconciled to her fate or a sentimentalist playing at savagery, for they kept her on a halter, the cruel strap running from her neck to the wrist of a Nimacook hag, probably her mother-in-law. Beyond this evidence was the fact of Bathsheba's visage, with its endless sadness and chronic grief—the face of one who longed for an Englishman's kiss.

A plan formed in Tobias's throbbing brain. He saw himself galloping onto the plantation like a knight seeking to save a maiden from a dragon, then swooping up Bathsheba in a gesture so heroic that she could not help but require his adoration. It was the sort of derring-do he might have rendered in a poem, were he a poet, or in a painting, were he an artist, or in reality, were he a man of action.

But, alas, there beat within the mail-carrier's breast the heart of a procrastinator, if not an outright poltroon. I am a sorry Lancelot, he told himself. I make a puny Percival. But as the harvest ended and the autumn air stiffened with intimations of winter, he realized that Bathsheba would soon depart the maize field, and so he picked an imminent date for the great rescue, the twentieth of October, the very day that, four years earlier, Harriet Easty of Amesbury had told him, "Given a choice in marriage partners 'twixt yourself and a boar-pig, I should vastly prefer the latter."

He rose before dawn, dressed hurriedly, and secured beneath his belt the two essential tools: his pistol, loaded and ready, and his knife—the one he used for opening undeliverable epistles ("dead letters" in the parlance of his trade) in hopes of learning the whereabouts of the sender or intended recipient. As the sun's first rays touched the shingled peaks and whitewashed steeples of Boston, he saddled Jeremiah, slung the mail valises over the gelding's rump, and rode out along the cobblestoned streets. Reaching the post road, he urged his mount to a trot. Bathsheba rarely stayed on the job past noon, but if his horse kept up the pace, he would reach the plantation no later than eleven o'clock.

He broke his fast in Stoneham, fed and watered Jeremiah, then continued north. Three hours later, Tobias cast an eye on his beloved.

Tethered as always, she stood farther from the road than usual, braiding together maize ears by their husks with an élan worthy of Ceres herself, then hanging them to dry on a gallows-like lintel. A full five yards separated Bathsheba and the hag, a gap sufficient for his escapade. He unsheathed his knife and, jabbing his boot heel into Jeremiah's ribs, charged across the field. Reaching Bathsheba, he leaned down and with a grand flourish simultaneously severed the halter, freed his beloved, lost his balance, and tumbled off his horse.

A bundle of sheaves cushioned his fall, and after a brief episode of flailing about in the dirt he gained his feet and glanced all around him. Much to his delight, he saw that the day was not lost, for during his interval on the ground Bathsheba had seized the reins and hauled herself onto the horse's back. Tobias had but to join her in the saddle anon, and the two of them would ride off together.

But Bathsheba had a different idea. She guided the horse along a rank of standing stalks and reigned up before her mother-in-law.

"Tell Okommaka I shall remember him with affection!" Bathsheba shouted, after which she exclaimed a brief sentence—presumably the identical message—in the incomprehensible Nimacook language. The hag replied loudly and angrily using the same confounding tongue, whereupon Bathsheba wheeled the horse around, galloped across the field, and disappeared down the road, taking the mail valises with her.

No sooner had this distressing development occurred than Tobias noticed the hag running toward him, her bony hand clamped around a fowling-piece. She paused and fired. The ball whistled past his cheek. He drew forth his pistol and cocked it, but before he could take aim the old woman vanished amidst the drying-racks. He jammed his pistol into his belt and sprinted madly away, as fixed in his purpose as any mother determined to retrieve her stolen baby from a band of Gypsies.

Throughout the subsequent hour, as he puffed and groaned his way down the Amesbury Post Road, Tobias's mental disposition oscillated betwixt stupefying humiliation and near dementia. With each passing farm he devised yet another narrative by which he might convince his employers that the loss of the valises had been unavoidable—brigands, Indians, a lightning-bolt, a tornado, a bear with an appetite for paper—but none enjoyed the ring of plausibility. He did not know which situation chastened him more: his imminent dismissal, or his woeful misassessment of Bathsheba's nature.

Shortly after three o'clock—so said Tobias's pocket-watch—he encountered an itinerant peddler, his wagon a rattling concatenation of pots, pans, knives, and scissors, and the next thing he knew the gnarled old man was offering him a ride to Boston. Tobias blessed his luck and climbed aboard. At three o'clock the peddler dropped him off in Treamount Square. A serrated wind arose, cutting through Tobias's benumbed and humbled flesh. He walked down Sudbury Street to Hannover, followed the flagstones to his door, and entered the townhouse, at which juncture his despair evaporated with the suddenness of a sneeze.

Still dressed in her Nimacook leathers, though missing her grotesque bonnet, Bathsheba sat in the drawing-room, holding a glass of his best Rhenish and paging through his *Æneid*. Her moccasined feet rested on the Oriental stool, beside which lay both mail valises.

"If this be the taste of civilization, I'm entirely in favor of't," she said, taking a sip of wine. A sensual, smoky voice, each syllable bathed in molasses. "Fear not for your amiable horse—I stabled him round the corner at Chadwick's Livery."

"Thou art a skilled equestrienne," he said admiringly.

"I apologize for stealing your mount, Mr. Crompton, but I thought you a highwayman with designs upon my virtue. Only after noticing these valises did I realized that you'd contrived a rescue, and so I made such inquiries as brought me to your house."

"Your deliverance was in sooth my aim," he said, his voice quavering with awe. The goddess was right here—in his own parlor—barely six feet away! "May I speak bluntly? From the moment I saw you laboring in the heathen field, my heart became yours to do with as you will. Indeed, but for one stark fact I would now make bold to ask for your hand in marriage."

"What stark fact? That I might spurn you?"

"That I know not your name."

"Waequashim," she said.

"Your given name, I mean."

"Waewowesheckmishquashim."

"Your *real* name."

"Jennet . . . Stearne," she said slowly, as if speaking the words for the first time in her life. She snapped his Virgil shut. "Now 'tis *my* turn to indulge in the crudest candor. Your antics today bespeak a chivalrous heart, and this house is undeniably convivial. I seek a kind of patron, someone who might feed and clothe me whilst I undertake a philosophic project."

He stood up straight as a pike, throwing back his shoulders. "At present I am a lowly mail-carrier, but ere the year is out I shall command the entire Boston Post Office."

"Most ambitious. Do you perchance enjoy access to the library at Harvard College?"

"My younger brother attends that very institution, in training for the ministry!"

"Then I assent to your proposition," she said.

"Oh, my dear lady, do my ears deceive me? You would become my bride?"

"On the understanding that my loyalties will also extend to my Baconian investigations."

"I should love my wife even if she were an alchemist!"

"And on the supplementary understanding that I shall ne'er count myself a Puritan."

"There be but six-score baptized Anglicans in Boston, and yet your Tobias is amongst 'em!"

"And on the further understanding that 'tis no apple-cheeked virgin you'll be taking to your bed."

"I have long supposed you the victim of many brutal ravishings by your heathen husband."

"No ravishings to speak of, merely a mutual enthusiasm concerning the carnal domain. But if you'll forgive me my past, I believe that Providence will smile upon our future."

" 'Tis axiomatic I should absolve the woman I love."

Possessed by a wild and unaccountable impulse, he reached into both valises simultaneously and, gathering up a great mass of mail, threw the lot into the air. As the myriad packets settled to the floor, he pictured himself a-float on a magic sea, bits of foam descending all around him. He glanced toward his bride. Once again the *Æneid* had entranced her. How marvelous, he thought. Before her abduction, she'd evidently been a kind of sage. Their marriage, it seemed, would never lack for stimulating conversation, and might soon bid fair to become the loftiest in Boston.

JENNET WOULD BE THE FIRST to admit that marriages of convenience were not the nobleſt arrangements on Earth, but no one could deny that the inſtitution boasted an impressive history. What was the affair of Cleopatra and Julius Cæsar if not a marriage of convenience binding Egypt to Rome? What was the Catholic Church if not a marriage of convenience fusing an emergent Christianity to a venerable paganism? What had Magna Carta consecrated if not a pragmatic conciliation betwixt King John and his barons? Should a loveless union be the price of her demon disproof, she was willing to pay it, though she hoped she would not break her husband's heart in the bargain.

True to his prediction, with the coming of summer Tobias ascended to the position of Boston Postmaster, which meant he no longer spent protracted and depleting days on horseback. For Jennet this promotion proved a mixed blessing. On the asset side of the ledger, his increased salary enabled him to hire a maid-servant from amongst the Long Wharf rabble newly arrived on the brigantine *Flying Fish:* Nellie Adams, a stout young Chelmsford widow whose competence at marketing, cooking, mending, and laundering secured for Jennet sufficient time each day to pursue what Tobias called "this admirable campaign against your brother's unholy band." Alas, her husband's less strenuous regimen had him coming home each evening abrim with residual vigor. Jennet's despair lay not so much in the failure of his ungainly frame, equine face, and weather-vane ears to arouse her, but rather in his refusal to allow that the carnal arts had progressed considerably since Adam had first lain with Eve. Her rhapsodic accounts of the secrets revealed in "Labia North and South" and "The Lust of the Goat" brought to his cheeks not the flush of concupiscence but the blush of embarrassment, until at last she decided to terminate his connubial education and scandalize him no more. Whilst she would hesitate to call Tobias a man for whom ignorance was bliss, it seemed likely that in matters of bliss this man would always be ignorant.

When he learned that her marriage to the Nimacook trapper had resulted in a female infant, a fit of jealousy seized Tobias—evidently he'd managed to convince himself that Jennet and Okommaka had swived but rarely—though he immediately became the soul of condolence upon hearing that the child had died of the small-pox. Unfortunately, his reaction to Bella's passing went beyond mere sympathy. He wanted to efface the tragedy itself. Jennet's grief, he insisted, would truly subside only after she'd produced a second child—and of course nothing would bring him greater satisfaction than to father a strapping baby boy or entrancing little girl.

Although pregnancy was the last circumstance Jennet wished to endure at this point in her life, she resolved to maintain Tobias's goodwill by feigning enthusiasm for the prospect, even as she arranged to keep her body unencumbered. Each time she entered the house bearing pennyroyal or marjoram from Pratt's Apothecary, she would allude to her philosophic pursuits, when in truth these ingredients were the key to Hassane's unguent against conception. She rarely experienced any difficulty, prior to the copulative moment, finding a pretext for slipping briefly away, subsequently applying the paste to her womanly canal, and by pleading a contrary stomach or a troublesome tooth she generally succeeded in avoiding Tobias on her days of peak fertility.

Thanks to her brother-in-law, Wilmot Crompton, whose privileges as a divinity student included a borrower's license from the Harvard College library, she came into temporary possession of the major works by "the three John W's," as Aunt Isobel had termed witch-hunting's most conspicuous opponents: John Webster, John Wagstaffe, Johann Weyer. But it was the labyrinthine Beacon Street bookshop called Darby's that proved for Jennet a true cornucopia, equipping her with not only a fresh copy of the *Principia Mathematica* but also the particular treatises Newton had recommended as stepping-stones to his opus. Inevitably she happened upon volumes by Royal Society fellows other than Newton— Henry More's *An Antidote against Atheism*, Joseph Glanvill's *Saducismus Triumphatus*, Robert Boyle's *The Sceptical Chymist*—but she decided not to squander her husband's money, for Isobel had labeled these men witch believers all.

Darby's also carried newspapers, including *The London Journal, The New-England Courant, The American Weekly Mercury*, and, most energizing for Jennet, the Calvinists' own periodical, *The Bible Commonwealth*, which routinely reported on the Massachusetts Bay Purification Commission and its Scottish counterpart, the Kirkcaldy Cleansing League, in a style that oscillated unpredictably betwixt sober detachment ("We must not forget that our best Defense against Demons lies in Praying, not Pricking") and giddy enthusiasm ("These brave Cleansers have hasten'd the Day when Satan will quit Christendom forever"). A project soon suggested itself, and Jennet subsequently secured from Darby's an unruled leather folio, decorating the first page with fat blockish characters: *The Devil and All His Works*, she wrote. In the months that followed, upon the appearance of a new *Bible Commonwealth*, she would scissor out each article concerning Dunstan's band and paste it into the folio. Whenever the quest exhausted her, whenever it seemed that she would never align the Greek immutables with Newton's principles and thereby recover his demon disproof, she would peruse *The Devil and All His Works*, forthwith finding her anger renewed and her ambition replenished.

Although she'd intended to spend the winter studying the three John W's, she was barely ten pages into Webster's *Displaying of Supposed Witchcraft* ere noticing that the author did not doubt the existence of wicked spirits, and it happened that an analogous credulity infected Wagstaffe's *The Question of Witchcraft Debated* and Weyer's *De Præstigiis Dæmonum*. True, these men held views that would enrage a Cotton Mather or a Walter Stearne. The John W's variously argued for the impossibility of developing unambiguous cases against accused sorcerers, for the possibility that Satan's vanity prevented him from granting magical powers to hags, and for the probability that human misery traced to forces other than *maleficium*. But none dared mount a frontal assault on demonology itself.

She set the John W's aside and delved into Newton's intellectual ancestors. It took her two months to negotiate the whole of Euclid, but she absorbed all the postulates and ingested all the proofs without mishap (though she deliberately skipped Book X and its impenetrable discussion of incommensurable magnitudes), and she had an equally gratifying experience with De Witt's *Elementa Curvarum*. When she turned to Bartholin's *Commentaries on Descartes's Geometry*, however, she managed to solve only seven problems out of the thirty Newton had prescribed, and she endured even more humiliation at the hands of Huygens's *Horologium Oscillatorium*, a work of maddening obscurity, preternatural opacity, and intractable trigonometry.

She was on the verge of despair when late one evening, acting on an impulse whose origins she could not divine, she began turning back the pages of the *Principia Mathematica* itself. For a full hour she meandered through Newton's rarefied realm, whereupon a strange unbidden radiance suffused her being, the sort of benign seizure a Philadelphia Quaker might have called the Inner Light. She understood this book! Not in its particulars, certainly, not in the details of its lemmas and proofs, but the author's overarching design seemed suddenly, utterly, wonderfully clear.

For all its grandeur, the universe posited by Euclid had been from its inception a frozen domain. Five centuries of such stasis had elapsed, ten centuries, fifteen—and then, *mirabile dictu*, enter Isaac Newton, bestowing time and motion on geometry. Under Newton's persuasion the

Euclidian shapes had grown wings and gone soaring across the sky. The Lucasian Professor had made butterflies of parabolas, wrought eagles from hyperbolas, and set spheres dancing like seraphs.

Whilst her qualified comprehension of the *Principia* made Jennet buoyant of heart and joyful of mind, these feelings did not endure, for the impossible task still lay before her, looming like the mile-high minaret of the Tall-Tower Problem. Somehow she must synthesize all this Newtonian kineticism with the Aristotelian immutables from which God had built the world.

Her epiphany occurred in, of all places, St. Mark's Anglican Church. She was sitting in the front pew, Tobias's thigh pressed against her own, the hare-lipped Reverend Dowd presenting his idiosyncratic interpretation of the Wedding at Cana—he averred that the wine Christ had wrought from water that day was not wholly consumed, the surplus reemerging months later at the Last Supper, where it underwent a further transfiguration—when she fell upon a train of reasoning that she sensed might lead, God willing, Kautantouwit assenting, to her philosophic Grail.

As any educated person knew, Aristotle and Newton had each reduced the cosmos to underlying components, Aristotle anatomizing its matter, Newton its motion. Newton's system was by far the more complex, and yet Jennet believed that she detected, in both the *Principia Mathematica* and "A New Theory About Light and Colors," an assumption that the kinetic universe, like its Aristotelian counterpart, consisted of four basic elements, namely acceleration, attraction, resistance, and—when you considered the great prism paper of 1668—radiation. Ah, but look how simple it was to map one universe onto the other! For radiation, the Aristotelian connection was obvious: Newton's experiments with light depended upon the sun, source of the Greek immutable called fire. Concerning attraction, she was quick to associate this entity with the Greek element earth, magnetite being amongst the most essential components of the planet's crust, with other such minerals doubtless awaiting discovery. When it came to acceleration, a match with the element air seemed warranted: even if you rejected Cartesian vortices, you were obliged to recognize that Earth's atmosphere and the æther beyond held immaterial substances that gave gravity its *gravitas*. In the case of the remaining entities—Newtonian resistance and Aristotelian water—she did not hesitate to link them, for Book Two of the *Principia* had much to say about the behavior of pendulums slicing through inhibiting fluids.

Attraction, acceleration, radiation, resistance: earth, air, fire, water—could any reasonable person doubt that Newtonian motion was every bit as primal, every jot as fundamental, as Aristotelian matter? It would seem that the bracing biblical revelation, *And God saw that it was good*, now enjoyed a logical corollary, *And God saw that it moved virtuously*. Ah, but if such were the case, then surely Jehovah had in the beginning systematically barred Satan's invisible minions from *both* domains—stuff and flux—so systematically, in fact, that a philosopher would be justified in declaring these minions nonexistent!

"Ergo, to recover Newton's lost disproof," she muttered to herself, "one need only establish the essential benevolence of the myriad motion-spirits that serve and facilitate the four kinetic entities."

"Mrs. Crompton, prithee, be quiet," Tobias whispered.

The Reverend Dowd sent a scowl her way, even as he prattled about the Wedding at Cana.

"For all Satan tries to corrupt these spirits," she mumbled, "he must always fail, as God hath made them invulnerable to temptation."

"Stay your tongue," Tobias said.

"Such was Aunt Isobel's insight on the pyre!"

"Silence!"

※

THE FOLLOWING MORNING Jennet bid Nellie Adams gather up their materials—lodestone, pendulum, prism, pair of wooden ramps—and accompany her to the home of Lydia Trimble, a nursing mother whose husband owned a tavern in Ship Street. At first the Hammer of Witchfinders had no luck elucidating for Mrs. Trimble why she wished to conduct natural philosophy experiments on the premises, and how the woman's lactations fit into the design, but then Jennet opened her purse, and the glister of its guineas proved explanation enough. Whilst Mrs.

Trimble suckled her baby beside the hearth, Jennet and Nellie performed an earth demonstration, using the lodestone's invisible fingers to pull a hobnail across the floor, thereby releasing those motion-spirits, whether sinister or saintly, that served the kinetic element called attraction—saintly, evidently, for they declined to impede Mrs. Trimble's milk. Jennet next did a water experiment, making the pendulum oscillate through beer, honey, whale oil, and other fluids of varying densities. The unleashed spirits of resistance forbore to disrupt the nursing process. She then performed a fire experiment, instructing Nellie to hold the prism to the window; the morning sun flashed through the glass pentahedron, and radiation's agents got busy, transmuting the beam into a rainbow. Mrs. Trimble's breast remained productive. That afternoon Jennet and Nellie did several experiments keyed to Aristotelian air, observing how acceleration's spirits imposed a uniform velocity on spheres of different weights rolled down wooden ramps. The baby continued to feast.

Two days later Jennet's purse persuaded a poultry farmer named Hugh Berridge to admit the kinetic experiments into the vicinity of his chicken coops. The hens never stopped laying. At noon Mr. Berridge's wife leased her churning skills to the cause. The butter came in full. That evening Jennet persuaded a confused but accommodating Tobias to swive her as she manipulated her philosophy tools. The demonstrations surely conjured many motion-spirits, but they worked no mischief on his manhood.

"The kinetic elements are moral to the core, with nary a malefactor in the lot!" Jennet declared. "Lucifer could ne'er warp such sterling spirits!"

"That surely sounds correct to me, darling," Tobias said, stroking her naked thigh.

Of course, Jennet reasoned, these results did not mean the motion-spirits were omnipotent. Only the Creator Himself enjoyed that attribute. Try though they might, the agents in question were powerless to shield humankind from blizzards, thunder-gusts, blights, or contagions—all those natural shocks wrongly attributed to demons. But God had no more ceded the universe of action to fallen angels and malevolent imps than He'd assembled the world from fungus and dung.

It took Jennet six days and as many rough drafts before she had an *ar-*

gumentum grande that fell felicitously on her ear. "All flowings and fallings," she wrote by way of an inaugural sentence, "all flappings and snappings, all swingings and springings, all splittings and flittings know naught of goblins but only of goodness."

She purchased a stack of parchment at Darby's, printed a title across the topmost sheet, *Contra Dæmonologie,* and copied out the final version, eight pages long, using her best hand. Obviously the momentous document required a signature, and after some deliberation she settled on "J. S. Crompton, Curator, Cavendish Museum of Wondrous Prodigies, Colonial Branch." All that remained was for her to dispatch the treatise to Kensington Palace, accompanied by an explanatory note.

AN APPEAL
To Her Most Esteemed Majesty,
Queen Anne,
Defender of the Faith,
Ruler of All England,
Scotland, Ireland, and France:

By enacting various Newtonian Demonstrations in a Manner design'd to goad Motion-Spirits to *Maleficium,* the Cavendish Museum hath in recent Days prov'd that the four Kinetic Entities are benign in Character, forever immur'd against the Devil's Wiles. If Her Most Sovereign Majesty agrees with the Conclusions express'd in the enclos'd Treatise, we would humbly ask that she set this Matter before both Houses of Parliament, that they might repeal the 1604 Witchcraft Statute of King James I.

Your humble Subject,
J. S. Crompton, Esq.
19 September 1710

An expert in postal systems and their vicissitudes, Tobias confidently forecast the fate of *Contra Dæmonologie.* If the *Columbine,* as sturdy a mail-ship as had ever crossed the Atlantic Sea, did not fall prey to storms or pirates, the treatise would be in the Queen's hands by the tenth of November.

"Proud I am to call myself your husband," he told Jennet as they stood together on Long Wharf watching the *Columbine* glide across the harbor. "Great was my satisfaction in making my seminal donation to demonology's demise."

"Thou art a good man, Mr. Crompton."

"I'm a dull man, Mrs. Crompton."

"That too, but in the months to come I shall strive to be a better wife to thee."

In the months to come . . . the phrase brought a chill to her bones. What, exactly, might she do with the rest of her life? Cleave to this inert marriage? Having swum in the wild rivers of Nimacook paganism and sailed the uncharted seas of Newtonian experimentalism, she had but little desire to paddle about the shallow pond of Boston respectability. Perhaps she would become the first woman ever to teach Euclidian geometry at Harvard College. Perhaps she would start a school for governesses, impressing her students with the necessity of going beyond antiquity's tongues and Aristotle's insights to instruct their charges in the new mechanical philosophy. But no matter how intently she gazed into the prism of her aspirations, studying the glass for some clue to her future, she did not see Tobias Crompton looking back.

WHEN JENNET DISCOVERED that, despite Aunt Isobel's charts and Hassane's unguent, a child was growing inside her, she instinctively attributed this catastrophe to her Creator's will, though her husband's virility had clearly played a part as well. Evidently Jehovah had decided that He would spare her the inconvenience of progeny only until she'd birthed the *argumentum grande*, and now she was constrained to present the world with a *miraculum minitum* as well.

Having lost her first child to the small-pox, she could not help fearing that some equally diabolical phenomenon would destroy her second baby too. She combated these premonitions with every weapon at her disposal. During the early weeks of her pregnancy she consumed the blend of wild mushrooms that Hassane believed prevented miscarriage. As her fifth month commenced, she availed herself daily of juniper tea, the Nimacook prescription against premature delivery. The quickening phase found her ingesting great quantities of red-fern and yarrow, which in the experience of her Lyn Street neighbor, a midwife named Sarah Dinwidie, protected an infant from illness not only in the womb but throughout the first postnatal year. The instant the spasms began, she sought out Mrs. Dinwidie, and together the women went to Chadwick's Livery and appropriated a vacant stall abounding in fresh straw. Whilst the midwife whispered words of encouragement, Jennet pressed her back against the wall, grabbed the partition, bent her knees, and prayed.

The spasms intensified. Her screams frightened the horses and put two cats to flight. The pangs grew stronger yet, as did her cries. She felt as if she were about to birth the Maw of Folkestone, or perhaps Perdition's Pride.

"I don't even *want* this blasted babe!" she shrieked.

"Many are the times I've heard a customer speak those very words," Mrs. Dinwidie assured her. " 'Tis the very litany of your predicament."

After an interval of two hours, through the operations of God Almighty and universal gravitation, a pink and slippery female infant descended into Mrs. Dinwidie's waiting hands.

This time, Jennet resolved, her daughter's name would be free of all sentimental connection. She certainly wasn't going to use "Bella" again, neither would she christen the infant "Margaret" after her mother nor "Catherine" after her mother's mother. "Rachel" had always struck Jennet as a robust and resonant vocable, and when she presented the idea to Tobias he acquiesced without quarrel, though he insisted on augmenting the choice with his late mother's name. And so it was that on the fifth of May, 1711, the Reverend Dowd drew a watery cross on the forehead of Rachel Veronica Crompton, thus alerting Heaven to the presence of another salvation-worthy Protestant in the world.

Rachel's life began auspiciously. She was a ruddy infant with bright hazel eyes, a strong cry, a precocious smile, and no tendency toward the

colic, this last asset doubtless attributable to Mrs. Dinwidie's pharma-
ceutical wisdom. Tobias, not surprisingly, idolized his daughter from the
outset, but Jennet refused to relax her vigilance, for it still seemed probable the child would perish ere reaching her first birthday. And yet one
succulent spring morning, five weeks after the baptism, Jennet realized
that she adored Rachel past all telling, a circumstance that felt rather like
the pregnancy itself: precautions had been taken, those precautions had
failed, and now the ambiguous consequences were upon her.

Although Tobias urged Jennet to employ a wet-nurse, such a service
being comfortably within their budget, she decided to suckle the baby herself. Especially gratifying were the events that followed each feeding. She
would set Rachel betwixt her breasts and revel in the pressure of the
warm, compacted, breathing bundle, as if the nexus of her circulatory system had been mysteriously transported outside her body. Good people of
Boston, come see this marvelous monstrosity. Step into the Cavendish
Museum of Wondrous Prodigies, Colonial Branch, and behold Nature's
most beautiful aberration yet, the Externalized Heart of Hannover Street.

For all the pleasurable feelings it entailed, all the agreeable obligations, motherhood failed to distract Jennet from the fact that the Queen
had not responded to *Contra Dæmonologie*. When Rachel learned to
walk, traveling across Boston Common through a combination of tenta-
tive steps and comical tumbles, Jennet's joy could not cancel the melancholy caused by Her Majesty's conspicuous disinterest in the demon
disproof. When the child progressed from random babbling to coherent
words to complete sentences, Jennet's delight was betimes diluted by the
Crown's failure to acknowledge either the treatise itself or her subsequent inquiries into its disposition. Shortly after her fourth birthday,
Rachel employed her poppets in an improvised theatre-piece about a
woman philosopher who rides a cannonball to the moon, and Jennet's
soul swelled with pride, but this pleasure was severely circumscribed by
the silence from Kensington Palace.

On the first day in October of 1715, a brown-skinned courier appeared at Jennet's door bearing a packet displaying the provenance label
of a certain Lord Wentworth in Essex County, England. She paid the

manumitted Negro a guinea and, with the enthusiasm of Juliet opening a letter from her Montague swain, ripped apart the envelope and drew out the vellum sheet.

25 July 1715

Dear J. S. Crompton:

Her Majesty hath instruct'd the Privy Council to respond to your *Contra Dæmonologie,* which reach'd Kensington Palace in November of 1711. After some Months of Deliberation, we decid'd to place the Document with an eminent Natural Philosopher to whom the Council oft-times turns in such Cases. Dr. Edmund Halley, Fellow of the Royal Society, eventually wrote to us as follows:

"Mr. Crompton's Intentions are doubtless honorable, and his chosen Methodology boasts a novel and astute Design. The present Treatise is so lacking in Detail, however, so bereft of Thoroughness and Rigor, that it inclines a rational Man toward a Conclusion quite opposite to the Author's."

Concerning our own Reaction, we find your approach so Impious as to be but one Degree of Remove from Atheism. When a Person presumes to reduce the World's Workings to self-sustaining Principles, whether he calls them "Forces" following Mr. Newton (who subscribes, we must note, to the deplorable Arian Religion) or "Kinetic Entities" per your Treatise, he must take great Care lest he give unwitting Comfort to those Deists and Freethinkers who would dislodge the Christian God from Creation's Center.

To wit, we shan't be troubling the English Parliament, and certainly not Her Most Sovereign Majesty, with your misguided Investigations.

Philip Tyrrell,
EARL OF WENTWORTH
LORD PRIVY SEAL

Owing to the Indian attack on Haverhill, Jennet had never enacted her wonderful plan to rip her father's cleansing license from his door and mutilate it beyond recognition. But now, suddenly, she had in hand an equally noxious document. She tore Lord Wentworth's letter into pieces, then tore the pieces into bits, then fed the bits to the fire in the kitchen hearth, where Nellie Adams was at that moment baking a half-dozen loaves of wheaten bread.

"How *durst* they reject my treatise!" Jennet shrieked.

" 'Tis an insult to our good labors," Nellie said.

"Those morons! Those dunces! Numskulls, I call 'em! Buffoons! Mooncalves! Puddingheads! Nincompoops!"

"That's exactly what they are, ma'am."

Perhaps if he'd seen Giles Corey lying beside Salem-Town Courthouse, pinned under the granite blocks—or stood on the Shawsheen River Bridge and heard Susan Diggens cry "Help me, friend Indian!"—Tobias might have apprehended the magnitude of her desolation. Instead he could only offer observations of a sort she found more irritating than soothing.

"If the great Dr. Halley sees no use in trying to disprove demons," he told her, "then mayhap 'tis a less worthy enterprise than you believe."

"Dr. Halley doth not gainsay the purpose of my project," she snapped, "and he calls its design novel and astute."

"But if the demonologists are so misguided as you aver, would not England's philosophers have argued 'em out of business by now?"

"Dear Tobias, methinks you play the dolt without half trying. If the Royal Society hath attempted no *argumentum grande*, 'tis only for want of motivation. Should the day come when Dr. Halley finds himself accused of sorcery, a dozen demon disproofs will pour from his pen, for terror's a most inspiring sponsor."

As happened so often in Jennet's life, salvation arrived in the person of a book. On the Monday following her receipt of Lord Wentworth's vile letter, the second edition of *Philosophiæ Naturalis Principia Mathematica* appeared in Darby's front window bearing a publication date of 1713, and as she turned back the thick fragrant leaves, she noticed that Book Three concluded with a new Scholium. Its matter was God. Whether acquiescing to external Anglican pressure or responding to some private revelation, Mr. Newton now insisted (if she could trust her Latin) that "this most beautiful system of the sun, planets, and comets" depended upon "the counsel of an intelligent and powerful Being," which idea he proceeded to elaborate over the next five pages.

Joy flooded her heart. The Privy Council feared that those who methodized Nature's workings trafficked in atheism, and yet here was Newton, spicing his postulates with Providence as effortlessly as a cook might add rum to a cake batter. Of course, she would never quote the geometer directly—not so long as he cleaved to "the deplorable Arian Religion"—but it was obvious that if you chose your words thoughtfully, Baconian experimentalism could be made to seem as pious as the Beatitudes.

Then there were Dr. Halley's requirements of detail, thoroughness, and rigor. She vowed to make her revised *Contra Dæmonologie* detailed to a fault, with a thoroughness to tax an angel's patience and a rigor sufficient to snap iron. This time around, she would not merely wade into the *Principia*'s shallows—she would dive into its rollers and plumb its deepest trenches.

"I am Lazarus, come back from the abyss," she announced to Tobias shortly after Nellie finished laying out their crab-cake dinner. "I shall give the Privy Council a treatise so sodden with God 'twill make Martin Luther's *Ninety-Five Theses* seem but a grocery list! I'll shower Dr. Halley with pages enough to wipe his bum from Epiphany to Michaelmas!"

"How delighted I am that your melancholia hath passed," Tobias muttered.

"An affectionate sentiment, but spoken without feeling," she said. "What ails thee, Mr. Crompton?"

"I'Christ, woman, can you not see that in constructing this second and more elaborate treatise, you will grievously neglect our daughter?"

Taking up knife and fork, she carefully hexed her crab-cake. "Such fatalism ill becomes you, sir."

"Methinks you confuse fatalism with foresight," Tobias said, tearing apart a fragrant loaf of bread. "Tell me you'll abandon this scheme."

She placed a crab-cake wedge in her mouth and chewed. "I would ne'er renounce my life's very purpose."

"You cannot be a fit mother to Rachel, nor yet a proper wife to me, and still wear the clothes of a natural philosopher."

"Might I give you my opinion?" She consumed a second morsel. "By my lights the clothes of a natural philosopher are considerably more dignified than the livery of the Boston Postmaster."

"Then you will be pleased to know I am on the point of changing that very garment."

Tobias buttered his bread, sipped his claret, and explained himself. The previous evening a missive had arrived from the Royal Mail Authority offering him employment as Postmaster-General for the British Crown Colonies in America. He had already drafted his letter of acceptance. By the end of the month they would all be Philadelphians, living in William Penn's famous province to the south. Their new situation, he insisted, had everything to recommend it—a higher income, a lower latitude, a larger house.

"Congratulations," she said, a barbed sneer in her voice. "Thou hast toiled most diligently for this appointment."

"Prithee, Mrs. Crompton, judge not these fruits ere you've tasted them."

An unhappy presentiment suffused her, for she knew nothing of Philadelphia save its reputation as a hotbed of Quaker fanaticism. But Tobias was not about to solicit her views on the matter. The instant he spoke the words "Postmaster-General" in the same hushed and reverent voice her father had employed when pronouncing "Witchfinder-Royal," she understood that their relocation was a *fait accompli.*

Aunt Isobel had always averred that the universe abounded in forking paths, and yet it seemed to Jennet that just one course lay open to her. By Hassane's account the world was opulent in options, but Jennet could see before her only duties. She was obliged to pack up her prisms and her pendulums, tell Rachel that circumstances were taking them to a warmer clime, and pray to Jehovah and Kautantouwit that the City of Brotherly Love might one day acquire a second epithet, the Cradle of Demon Disproofs.

DESPITE JENNET'S MISGIVINGS, her new environs and the revised *argumentum grande* proved uncannily compatible with each other. The thoroughfares of Philadelphia constituted a tidy grid, and whenever she left their Chestnut Street townhouse to stroll amidst this rectilinear arrangement, a concomitant orderliness descended upon her thinking. Equally vital were the energy and inspiration she drew from the omnipresent Society of Friends. Although her Quaker neighbors indeed practiced several varieties of irrationality, including the eponymous paroxysms on display in their meeting-houses, they had nevertheless bestowed on Pennsylvania an ethos whereby hunting, hanging, or even talking about witches seemed quite the silliest of activities.

By the time Rachel had celebrated her fifth birthday, the undercurrent of disgruntlement that Tobias brought to most of his dealings with Jennet had transmuted into an overt hostility. His bitterness traced not just to the demon disproof, which he viewed as progressing only at Rachel's expense, but also to his wife's failure to conceive a second child. Whilst Jennet privately ascribed this situation to Hassane's unguent, she offered her husband a much less plausible though far more palatable explanation: God had elected to seal her womb until she'd defeated the Witchcraft Act.

"How durst you presume to know the designs of Providence!" Tobias roared. "Such arrogance appalls me!"

"I warned you of my philosophic passions from the first," she reminded him.

"Shall I tell you my darkest suspicion, Mrs. Crompton? I believe you deprive me of a son through the sheer force of your womanly will."

"If womanly will could accomplish such a feat," she snarled, "there'd be far fewer squalling babes in the world at this moment—of that I assure thee!"

Her favorite place for perusing the second edition of the *Principia Mathematica* was the sprawling meadow on the eastern shore of the Schuylkill River, a tract on which the city's day-laborers had recently staked out a bowling-green. Whenever the weather allowed it, she and

Rachel and Nellie would arrive before noon, luncheon-basket in hand. During the subsequent hour they would consume their wheaten bread and cold meat at a leisurely pace, whilst Jennet held her companions spellbound with the Moon-Bead Legend or some other nugget of the Nimacook imagination—the Fable of the Wily Raven, the Parable of the Greedy Porcupine, the Adventure of the Tortoise Who Had No Shell. After the meal Jennet would begin the day's struggle with Newton, leaving Rachel and Nellie to wander about in search of amusement. Sometimes they enacted Nimacook stories using Rachel's poppets. Sometimes they watched the men rolling their bowls across the green. But Rachel's preferred activity was to sit by the river's edge and catch fish, for she was now an expert in the bobber-and-hook method her mother had mastered many years earlier on the banks of the Merrimack.

One sweltering Sunday afternoon in August, Jennet took up the luncheon-basket, shouldered Rachel's fishing-pole, and set off with her daughter for the Schuylkill, her intention being to loll in the meadow and thoroughly digest Newton's theology, the better to avoid tainting the new *argumentum grande* with some subtle Arian heresy. Nellie was absent from their company, for Tobias had given her the day off, that she might visit her brother's family in Cohasset. Arriving at the river, mother and daughter devoured their midday repast, Jennet the whole time offering Rachel her usual lecture on the safe and proper way to fish: keep one foot planted against a rock, never yank abruptly on the line, take care lest you lean too far over the bank whilst throwing back your catch. Rachel as always assented to these conditions, and so her mother sent her off in quest of salmon and perch.

For a reading space Jennet selected a tranquil patch of shade hedged by a half-dozen maples. She entered the grove, spread her blanket on the grass, and set about pondering Newton's relationship with God.

According to her translation of the 1713 Scholium, the Supreme Being existed everywhere at once, His essence never varying from place to place, "all eye, all ear, all brain, all arm, all power to perceive, to understand, and to act."

She looked up. Rachel sat on the riverbank, fishing-pole in hand.

Fixing her thoughts again on Newton, Jennet learned that the Almighty operated "in a manner not at all human, in a manner not at all corporeal, in a manner utterly unknown to us."

She placed her finger betwixt "utterly" and "unknown," *omnio* and *ignotus*, then glanced toward the river in time to see Rachel snag a perch, its sleek form twisting and twitching like a bodkin in thrall to a lodestone. The child unhooked the creature and returned it to the water.

Jennet went back to the *Principia*. The Almighty, Newton averred, was best conceived as a kind of supernatural steward or spiritual landlord. "For a being, however perfect, without dominion, cannot be called Lord God."

A child's scream shot across the meadow.

Jennet glanced up. A monstrous void crouched beside the Schuylkill. A vacancy, a vacuum, a demon made of empty space.

Tossing Newton aside, she gained her feet and sprinted toward the river. A liquid cacophony reached her ears, an amalgam of thrashing limbs and gurgling screams. She halted at the bank. At first she saw only a frothy white turbulence; next Rachel's fishing-pole jerked into focus, riding the chaos—and then a human form appeared, submerged, one hand gripping the pole, the opposite arm flailing madly. Jennet leaned forward, making ready to pitch herself over the edge, when suddenly a hirsute man with the prodigious proportions of a blacksmith brushed past her, threw down his woolen cap, kicked off his shoes, and leapt into the water. A maelstrom took shape before her eyes, a mad Charybdis at whose circling center Rachel's would-be rescuer struggled to subdue her panic.

As a dozen more bowlers rushed onto the scene, Jennet brought her hands together in a prayerful posture. Surely the All-Eye-All-Ear-All-Brain-All-Arm who'd hurled the planets into orbit could raise a single insubstantial child from a river. Surely the Almighty could suspend His *principia* long enough to save one small virtuous life.

"Prithee, Lord God Jehovah!"

No sooner had Jennet voiced her entreaty than a sobbing, shivering, wheezing Rachel climbed onto the shore, followed by the blacksmith, if such was indeed his trade, coughing and panting. Rivulets rushed down the limbs of child and man alike. Scum stippled their clothing. The smith spat out a mouthful of water. The bowlers continued to collect on the bank, the commotion drawing them as inevitably as a lodestone beguiling iron.

"Oh, my sweet darling!" Jennet cried.

Despite her ordeal, Rachel had managed to retain the fishing-pole, which she now held before her like an infantryman brandishing a pike. "I h-hooked an eel!"

"My eye's own apple!" Jennet lifted Rachel into the air, hugging her so tightly that the child's teeth stopped chattering, even as her sobs became titters of relief.

"Methinks 'twas the mightiest eel in Creation!"

Squeezing Rachel more tightly yet, Jennet planted a hundred kisses on her cheeks, freckling her with affection. "My heart's own harbor!"

"He sought to steal my fishing-pole, but all he got was my hook!"

Jennet returned Rachel to the grassy earth, then grasped her shoulders and rotated her toward their benefactor, who now wore an expression so stern it might have humbled a troll. "You must tell this good gentleman that your gratitude runneth over," she instructed her daughter.

"My gratitude runneth over," Rachel muttered tonelessly, setting the fishing-pole on her shoulder.

"Prithee, give me your name," Jennet asked the dripping smith, "that I might one day write a ballad in your honor."

Much to her surprise, the man replied reprovingly, "Truth to tell, I am niggardly with my name, declining to share it with vain and careless persons."

"Well spoken, brave sir!" declared a soot-smeared chimney sweep, stepping from the crowd and facing the smith. "Ye're right to scorn this sister of Narcissus, who reads a book whilst her daughter nearly drowns!"

A surge of chagrin passed through Jennet, reddening her cheeks, felling her crest. Seeking to redeem herself, she faced Rachel and addressed her in a voice directed more to the mob than to the child. "Ere the week is out, your mother will undertake to tutor you in the art of swimming."

"Ye must not besmirch the word 'mother' by applying it to so unfeeling a creature as yourself!" insisted a plump and ruddy bystander wearing the blue-bibbed apron of a butcher.

"No weasel accords its young such disregard!" a linen-frocked waggoner asserted.

"No snake would deign to claim ye as a parent!" a lantern-seller averred.

"A slug would blush to find ye up its family tree!" cried a hatchet-faced man whose sheepskin skirt marked him as a tanner.

Uncertain how to answer this menagerie of accusations, Jennet instead grabbed Rachel by the wrist and escorted her away from the bank. The child's dress exuded a sharp, oddly pleasing fragrance, the aroma of damp silk mingled with the river's pungent mud. Upon reaching the maple grove, Jennet retrieved the blanket, the basket, and her *Principia Mathematica*. She repressed an impulse to spit on Newton's masterwork. The canniest treatise yet penned had now become the most corrupt, for the reading of it had nearly cost Rachel her life.

"Tell me, darling, do you hope we might soon enjoy another sojourn by the Schuylkill?" Jennet asked.

"Aye, Mother."

"Then you will hold silent concerning this afternoon's misadventure. Is that clear? You must not speak of't to Nellie, nor to Mrs. Dinwidie, nor even to your own father."

"Not even to Father?"

Jennet nodded solemnly. "Were the postmaster to learn of your plunge, he would bar us both forever from these shores." She laid a hand on Rachel's soggy shoulder. "Now hear my most sacred vow. May my hair fall out and my skin turn green if I e'er again let you stray from my sight."

"No hair?" Rachel said, giggling.

"Quite so."

"Green skin?" the child added, snickering more exuberantly yet.

"Indeed."

If you were five years old, it seemed, no event could be more entertaining than your mother's transmutation into an acorn squash.

THREE MORNINGS AFTER her daughter's descent into the Schuyl-kill, Jennet awoke to find that Tobias had vacated their mattress—a surprising circumstance, for they both normally remained beneath the covers until Nellie announced that their veal and eggs were ready. A queasiness spread through her. The planet's axis seemed suddenly askew. She abandoned the mattress, pulled on her dressing gown, and dashed, pulse throbbing, into her daughter's bed-chamber.

Rachel was gone. Her wardrobe had been plundered, each compartment as empty as a skull's eye-socket.

Jennet proceeded to the kitchen. Nellie sat at the mahogany table. Tears stained the maid-servant's cheeks. Red veins striated her eyes.

"I am instructed to give ye this," Nellie moaned, presenting her mistress with a folded sheet of vellum secured by a blob of tallow. "I'Christ, Mrs. Crompton, he hath stolen her away!"

Jennet cracked the seal. Tobias's spidery hand covered the vellum top to bottom.

19 August 1716

My Dear Jennet:

Three weeks ago the Royal Mail Authority propos'd to make me Postmaster-General of a far-flung Colony whose Identity I shall reveal to you at some future Date. None but a Fool would forgo this Opportunity to build a Postal System from Scratch, using everything I know about the Safety of Carriers, the Arrangement of Drops, and the optimal Deployment of Horses.

Mayhap you believe a Husband ought not to keep such a Secret from his Wife, but if Secrets are to constitute the Matter of our Conversation, I must tell you that my best Rider, the worthy Harry Bainbridge, was playing at Bowls this Sunday hard by the Scene of Rachel's near-Drowning. He hath judg'd the whole Affair an appalling Instance of maternal Disregard, the very Sort of Threat I always knew you would one Day visit upon our Child.

By the Time you read these Words, Rachel and I shall have sail'd free of America, away on the morning Tide. Assuming favorable Winds, our Carrack will reach London by October, whereupon we shall head for my new Place of Employment. Fret not, Mrs. Crompton, as I mean to provide for your Welfare. The Townhouse is yours to keep, likewise the Horse Jeremiah, and you shall eventually receive from me a Stipend of thirty Pounds per Quarter, more than adequate for your material Needs as well as Nellie's Wages.

In short, I have decid'd that our Union, ne'er a Prize to begin with, hath play'd through all its Possibilities. You bear no Love for me, and your Devotion to Rachel waxes and wanes like the Moon. Indeed, I say you are bound to Naught on God's green Earth save that damnable Thesis of yours.

Be thee well, my distract'd Wife. Ere long I shall make such Arrangements as will permit you to wed another Englishman. As for myself, I doubt that I shall ever marry again, for Jennet Stearne Crompton is still my most precious Balm, even as she aspires to be my perpetual Bane.

Sincerely,
Your Tobias

"Oh, Mistress Crompton, last night Rachel told me of her fall into the river, and how the news of 't hath made her father wroth," Nellie wailed. "Methinks this disaster is largely of my making. I should ne'er have gone visiting on Sunday."

"Nay, Nellie, you aren't to blame," Jennet said. "The fault lies in the incongruity 'twixt Mr. Crompton's ambitions and mine own."

As she read the letter a second time, all the while clenching her teeth like a surgical patient biting a musket-ball, she felt herself undergo a sea-change. Her fury transformed her. Body and brain she became a freak, the most ferocious prodigy yet acquired by the Cavendish Museum—the Harridan of Chestnut Street. She grabbed her purse from behind the pendulum-clock, slung the leather thong about her neck, and rushed off to Sharpe's Livery, where she outfitted Jeremiah with saddle and bridle.

It took her but fifteen minutes to reach the docks. Two towering carracks, their names obscured by mist and distance, followed the Delaware's southerly course, riding high upon the moon-drawn waters.

Locking her gaze on both vessels, she galloped to the end of Market Street Wharf and dismounted. She hitched the gelding to a mooring post, then set about importuning every passing soul. She detained sweaty sailors newly arrived in port, hawkers selling Malay teas and French laces, pale painted ladies who seemed unaccustomed to daylight, suspicious constables who believed she must be a whore herself, and leering Redcoat soldiers of the same opinion. Though no one could remember whether a child of five had recently taken ship with a rangy man of middle age, a consensus eventually emerged concerning the two carracks cruising down the river. The lead vessel was the *Antares*, bound for the Sugar Isles, that her captain might convert his cargo of lumber and flour into a cache of Barbados rum, a treasure he would subsequently redeem for two hundred West African slaves. Behind the *Antares* flew the mail-ship *Bristol Maid*, carrying tobacco, beaver hats, rattlesnake belts, private parcels—and twenty paying passengers—to England.

An image arose in Jennet's mind, a rowboat, sufficiently swift to facilitate Rachel's recapture, and soon she found one, the *Manatee*, tied to a stone pier adjoining Arch Street Wharf. The tub's owner, a sallow Quaker crabber with a beard resembling a wasp's nest, accorded her a sympathetic ear as he transferred the morning's catch from vessel to quay. Spiky claws and spiny legs probed betwixt the slats that formed the dozen crab-cages. She thought of the Colchester Castle prison-cells, those scores of beseeching arms sinuating through the iron bars.

"Thy mission hath all the marks of madness," the Quaker said after she'd finished describing her plight.

"Doubtless you are correct." She climbed into the rowboat, seized the penultimate crab-cage, and lifted it onto the quay. "Prithee, rent me your *Manatee* for the excellent price of three pounds sterling"—she drew the tethered purse from her bodice—"that I might fetch my Rachel."

The crabber took the final cage in hand and scrambled free of the rowboat. "Thy daughter sails into Delaware Bay e'en as we speak. Thou hast not a prayer of o'ertaking her."

"Four pounds," Jennet said.

"Wilt thou make it five?"

She shook the requisite coins into the crabber's eager palm, unfastened the *Manatee*'s line, and sat down facing the stern. Sliding both oars into the water, she brought the boat about, then pulled with all the vigor of Archimedes levering the world.

"I wish thee good fortune!" the Quaker called after her.

Stroke upon stroke, yard after yard, she chased the retreating carracks—down the river, into the bay, toward the ascending sun.

"Hallo, *Bristol Maid!* Hallo! Hallo!"

She gave the oars an emphatic yank and, pivoting on her hips, glanced toward the horizon. Already the *Antares* had dropped from sight, but the *Bristol Maid* still nicked the sky.

Turning, she resumed her labors, stroke upon stroke. *Mauminikish,* she told herself—row harder. Her back spasmed. *Mauminikish.* Her muscles sang with pain. *Mauminikish.* The blisters on her palms grew big as grapes—and yet she cleaved to the task, working the oars as furiously as a Nimacook brave driving his war canoe into battle.

"Hallo! Hallo!"

Her vision went muzzy with her tears, and she apprehended that she was close to blacking out. Again she turned. The *Bristol Maid* was gone, claimed by the planet's imperceptible curve. She shipped the left oar, then the right, and slumped forward, gasping and groaning like some half-drowned hag who'd just endured the cold-water test.

"I'm here, Rachel!"

The sun pounded on the bay, scorching her brow and neck. Her throat felt as raw if she'd eaten sand. She set her shredded hands in her lap, staining her dress with blood.

"Your mother's right behind you!"

Gradually but inexorably an ember of logic caught fire within her brain. If she continued to pursue the carrack, the likely outcome would not be a reunion of mother and daughter but rather, for Jennet, death by exposure, and, for Rachel, a meaningless bereavement.

"Damn thee, Tobias Crompton!"

Whereas if she quit the chase—if she tipped her king, sheathed her sword, hoisted the white flag—she would be abandoning Rachel to a man of liberal means and generous intentions. A child could do far worse in this world.

"Damn thee to Hell!"

A gust of wind caught her tears and flung them overboard, adding their number to the Atlantic's brackish infinitude. For an indeterminate interval she stared at the bottom of the boat. Seawater sloshed amongst the oaken ribs. A solitary blue crab scuttled along the keelson. Under other and better circumstances she might have submitted the crab to philosophic scrutiny, but instead she picked up the creature and, after gazing briefly into the black seeds that were its eyes, hurled it into the bay.

A Young Benjamin Franklin
Receives Instruction in
the Virtues of Older Women,
amongst Them Prudence, Passion,
and Electric Conductivity

❈❈

Twenty-seven years after the event, the public burning of his Satanist aunt remained for Dunstan Stearne the supreme religious experience of his life. The pulse of the flames, the hurrahs of the crowd, the screams of the heretic, the apocalyptic fragrance—he would not forget these sensations as long as thoughts roved within his skull and blood beat through his veins. So memorable, in sooth, was Isobel Mowbray's cleansing that, shortly after the chartering of the Massachusetts Bay Purification Commission, Dunstan had decided that in certain exceptional instances his band would import such spectacle to the American shore, favoring stake over gallows as the medium of execution.

The present case was special not only because both the heretics were male but also because they were twins—Hosea and Malachi Clegg, so notorious throughout Cohasset for sheep-thieving and whore-mongering that nobody was terribly surprised when they turned out to be Devil-worshippers as well. In the interests of economy, Dunstan and the other Commissioners had set both Cleggs on the same pyre and chained them to the same stake. Winter was coming. There was no point in needlessly depleting the town's store of communal firewood.

Burning torch in hand, Jonathan Corwin began his stately march across Cohasset Square, inspiring the gathered citizens to draw back as if making way for the equipage of a duke. Dunstan cast an adoring eye on his wife. Abigail stood majestically betwixt the courageous local magis-

❈❈❈❈❈

trate, Mr. Basset, who'd arrested the warlocks in a daring midnight raid on their farm, and the bushy-bearded printer, Mr. Searle, who'd earlier that day done a brisk business in broadsheets recounting the Clegg Brothers' trial. The October wind pulled the bodice of Abby's dress tight against her form, even as it swept her skirt southward in a billowing banner of feminine grace. Dunstan released a concupiscent sigh. Although she'd never conceived a child within that admirable frame, this was not for lack of conjugal activity. Probably God had determined that Abby could best serve Him through witchfinding rather than childbearing. Motherhood was a blessed state, but incompatible with a full-time career in demonology.

As Mr. Corwin thrust the torch into the pyre, the Reverend Parris exhorted the spectators to render Martin Luther's "A Mighty Fortress Is Our God" in the loudest voices they could find, and soon the stalwart song was resounding across the square and echoing down the village streets. No one sang louder than Abby, whose soprano transcended the general chorus as cream rises to the top of milk.

Sibyl—that was the word for her, Dunstan decided. His wife was a *sibyl*. Over the years, her gift for sensing heresy from afar had spared the Commission an incalculable quantity of effort. Emerging from her monthly conversation with the angel Justine, Abby would disclose to her fellow prickers the name of whatever Massachusetts settlement had most recently acquired (unbeknownst to itself) an ambassador from Hell, a revelation that Dunstan would forthwith relay to the editors of *The Bible Commonwealth*. Upon reading in the *Commonwealth* that his community had a witch problem, the local magistrate would conduct an investigation, presenting the Commissioners with at least one likely suspect shortly after their Gypsy wagon came rolling into town.

Sixteen years of service to Crown and Creator—and still Dunstan could boast that he'd never used his band as a tool of personal retribution. Sometimes the temptation to chastise the Nimacooks, those idolatrous savages who'd murdered his father, debauched his sister, and ruined his face, proved nearly overwhelming, but so far he'd managed to forbear. True, whenever Abby saw that a particular Nimacook had crossed the line separating mere depraved paganism from full-blown demonic compact, the Commission would steal the witch away, administer the tests, and—if the expected signs emerged—perform a furtive extermination. This procedure always occurred in a spirit of Satan fighting, however, never vindictiveness. Vengeance, the prophet Isaiah taught, belonged solely to the Lord.

Gradually Dunstan apprehended that a soft but palpable rain, dense enough to dampen the logs, was falling on Cohasset Square, and he lost no time issuing the necessary orders.

"Fagots, Samuel! Fagots, Jonathan! Fagots all around!"

Mr. Parris and Mr. Corwin sprang into action, seeking to fetch the half-dozen emergency bundles of wood that the Commissioners kept in the Gypsy wagon. For Dunstan had never forgotten the admonition his father had given him at the Chelmsford hangings of 1688: a jurist must never bring a needless cruelty to his business, even when punishing Satanists—and needless cruelty would indeed be the outcome if the prickers failed to act quickly, supplementing the pyre with dry wood, as the fire would otherwise burn slowly and subject the Clegg brothers to an unendurable roasting, not the quick incineration that Christian charity demanded.

In a matter of minutes Mr. Parris and Mr. Corwin emptied the wagon of its fagots, bearing the merciful timber to the stake and adding it to the flames.

"Bless ye!" cried Hosea, coughing.

"Ye're compassionate prickers indeed!" Malachi shouted.

Within a quarter-hour the cleansing was accomplished, and the spectators drifted away, the porkish odor having doubtless put them in mind of supper. Dunstan watched Mr. Parris set about his book-keeping, severing the brothers' charred left thumbs and securing them in a baize sack. Tomorrow the minister would deliver the thumbs to Governor Danforth's office in Boston. In one sense this accounting was a mere formality, for neither the Governor nor his assistants ever opened the sacks and verified their contents. But it was important, Dunstan believed, for the Commissioners to provide tangible evidence that, like the Kirkcaldy

Cleansing League across the sea, they were regularly riding the hinterlands, fulfilling their duties, earning their compensation. Witchfinding was a profession in which a tidy balance-sheet could not be overvalued.

The demonologists climbed into the Gypsy wagon and set off along the rutted roads betwixt Cohasset and Framingham, reaching the Merry Alewife shortly after dark. Upon depositing the wagon in the livery, they arranged for the inn-keeper to tend the horses, then tramped three miles through the compacted gloom to Waushakum Pond. They removed their dinghy from its cloak of boughs and, as the sun dipped westward, turning the pond into a shimmering golden broth, rowed their way to the salt-box.

The Heavens declare the glory of God, the psalmist had sung, *and the firmament showeth His handiwork,* and Dunstan had of late undertaken to celebrate that very firmament in colored wax. Entering the front parlor, he swept a satisfied gaze across a field of lion-headed sunflowers—an array of water lilies dappling a pond—a willow tree confiding its despair to a placid creek—an incoming tide crashing against a craggy shore to form a great spuming cowl. These days, of course, he could afford oil pigments, canvas too, and camel-hair brushes from Asia, but he still preferred the simpler medium. Wax was so basic, like blood.

His wife prepared the usual post-cleansing meal. Boiled pheasant, dried venison, cornmeal bread, crisp brown ale. The prickers ate in silence. A luxurious exhaustion washed through Dunstan as, yawning and stretching, he guided Abby to their bed-chamber. Easing himself onto the mattress, he pulled the quilt over his chest and once again let the reverie pass through his mind.

Smoke-blind, he runs through the glowing house, his breeches loaded with dung, his heart throbbing with resolve.

He leaps over mounds of flame, the sparks swarming like Hell's own horseflies, the smoke congealing into spectral shapes, the beams and rafters crashing down everywhere.

He ascends the stairs to the second-floor hallway, and suddenly sees it through the black haze, his birthright, nailed to his father's door.

There is still time to save the witchfinding license—and time to do something else. A swirling column of fire rises from the floor. He steps toward it. Like Jacob wrestling with the angel, he embraces the blazing pillar. He screams. The flames enfold him, purifying his flesh, scorching his soul, seeding a scar whose meaning could not be clearer: here is a man who might one day bring the Fiend himself to book.

✦

As her melancholy multiplied and her confusion grew more acute, Jennet inevitably turned to the Nimacooks' favorite medicine, their balm for grief and woe, the river-cure. Stripped down to Edenic nakedness, she spent an hour each morning swimming in the Schuylkill, imploring its gods to absorb her sorrows and bear them away with the current.

For reasons not wholly apparent, Rachel's abduction had become muddled in her mind with both her aunt's immolation and the death of ill-starred Pashpishia. Pursuing her course through the river's resisting medium, Jennet imagined she saw Isobel standing on the shore, smallpox pustules stippling her squat body. She pictured Rachel shackled behind Colchester Castle, the flames coiling around her like voracious serpents. She saw Pashpishia sitting in a locked cabin aboard the *Bristol Maid*. Rachel racked by the flogging sickness. Isobel sailing eastward. Pashpishia at the stake.

After forty days on the swimming regimen, she judged herself . . . not cured, exactly, not whole, but sane—sane enough, at least, to renew the fight, though she couldn't decide whether this improvement traced to Indian magic or simply to the healing hand of time.

As a preliminary measure, she dismissed Nellie Adams from her employ—the coming ordeal would require absolute solitude and utter silence, no footfalls save Jennet's own sounding in the hall—but only after securing for the serving-maid a new situation as governess to a prosperous German-Town family named Eckhardt. The second step was equally obvious. She must rouse herself with Euclid, fan her desires with Huygens, and enter into the most intimate relationship imaginable with the *Principia Mathematica*.

Sometimes it took her a week, sometimes an entire month, but she never abandoned a Newtonian problem ere seducing it. She became adept at charting, from a given focus, the elliptical, parabolic, and hyperbolic paths of revolving spheroids both real and conjectural. She learned to plot a comet's orbit from three discrete observations—determine the force by which the sun and the moon raised equatorial tides in both the syzygies and the quadratures—calculate the course the moon would follow but for its eccentricity—and infer from local lunar data the mean motions of the apsides and nodes of the Jovian satellites.

True as always to his word, Tobias sent her thirty pounds each quarter through the office of his London solicitor, Mr. Horsfals, a portion of which she spent on food and books ere depositing the rest in the strongbox beneath her bed. The possibility of enhancing her wardrobe with a new gown or a fashionable hat never even attained the status of a temptation. Along with each allowance Tobias usually enclosed a letter reporting on Rachel's welfare and also relating his various successes in the East Indies—for such was the location of his mysterious appointment. " 'Tis an entirely amazing Enterprise," he wrote. "We've got sixteen Riders saddl'd at all Times, carrying the Mails five hundred Miles overland from Madraspatam to Bombay."

By Tobias's account, Rachel could now speak French, do simple sums, and recite the Decalogue, and she'd developed "a most affectionate Bond with her Governess," Mademoiselle Claudette Peltier. Jennet knew that his intention was to reassure her concerning Rachel's happiness—for all his foolishness, there was no actual malice in the man—and yet she came to dread each new letter from Madraspatam, promising herself she wouldn't read the thing and then reading it anyway, subsequently flying into a jealous rage upon learning that Mlle. Peltier had undertaken to instruct their daughter in dancing, drawing, arithmetic, or astronomy. The amusing little notes appended by Rachel herself failed to relieve Jennet's misery, for whilst they bespoke a mind quite delighted by the place in which it found itself, this exotic Eastern world of red silk saris and white marble temples, they also betrayed Rachel's uncertainty over whether her real mother was Jennet Crompton or the infinitely compelling and supernaturally competent Claudette Peltier.

The spring of 1718 brought the fulfillment of Tobias's second promise, the official termination of their marriage. Forwarded from Madraspatam to Mr. Horsfals in London, and thence to Philadelphia, the essential document was no more physically impressive than Walter Stearne's witchfinding license, but it bore the Lord Chancellor's seal, which made it a substantive scrap indeed. Even more momentous than this paper was the accompanying letter, wherein Tobias promised to continue sending her the monthly stipends "until such time as you can sustain yourself without my assistance." Jennet signed one copy of the divorcement decree, mailed it back to Horsfals, and slipped its twin inside Huygens's *Horologium Oscillatorium*, where it lay waiting to persuade her hypothetical future husband that his betrothed was no bigamist.

But for now she belonged only to her work: Jennet Stearne Crompton, bride of geometry, kin to conics, novice in the sisterhood of acceleration. She exiled herself from all physical particulars, from her city, her province, her planet—from her own flesh, it seemed—and set about designing the various demonstrations and experiments whose results would constitute the meat and sinew of the new treatise.

Brimming with dramatic accounts of what happened when roundish objects were dispatched along the eternally curving surfaces of trigonometric tradition, Book One of the *Principia Mathematica*, "The Motion of Bodies," provided Jennet with eight procedures for evoking acceleration's spirits via barrow-wheels, rolling-pins, and lawn-bowls. After perusing Book Two, "The Motion of Bodies in Inhibiting Mediums," she forthwith assembled a dozen devices for conjuring spirits of resistance, her favorite consisting of two upright metal pipes joined at the bottom by a horizontal tube to form a U-shaped canal, an arrangement that, filled with a quantity of fluid equal to twice the length of her pendulum, enabled her to establish a binding reciprocity betwixt the liquid's fluctuations and the lever's oscillations. By casting her memory backward to her childhood adventures with scrying-glasses and pentahedral prisms, then hurling her intellect forward into the *Principia* chapter called "The Motion of Very Small Bodies Agitated by Centripetal Forces," she managed to devise eleven radiation experiments, for each time Newton invoked "very small bodies" he was surely inviting the reader to imagine the world's most fundamental phenomena, light chief amongst them, winnowed like wheat into the tiniest conceivable corpuscles. And then, finally, faced with the imperative of including attraction's agents in the *argumentum grande,* she pondered every *Principia* passage concerning magnetism and friction, subsequently extracting nine demonstrations, the cleverest of which involved a toy windmill such as her mother had oft-times constructed. Pursuant to her experimental design, Jennet made the sails of foil instead of silk, surrounding the array with a corona of lodestones, an imperially impractical machine whose vanes, when they turned at all, moved skittishly. The point, however, was not to grind grain but to crush irrationality.

The pleasures of gestating the demon disproof were all but ruined for Jennet by the disintegration of her correspondence with Rachel. Although she'd attempted to make each letter to Madraspatam a confection of consummate wit and endearing frivolity, by Rachel's ninth birthday it was obvious that the child had lost interest in the exchange, and Jennet begrudgingly admitted to herself that no jocose note from her daughter would accompany the latest quarterly stipend from Tobias.

"I pray that the Day will come when you might understand why I seem'd to favor Mechanics over Motherhood," she wrote in a letter she suspected Rachel would never read. "But until the Dawning of that bless'd Morn, I shan't blame you for judging my Aristotelian Pursuits contemptible."

Deprived of Rachel's written words, she was forced to settle instead for her phantom form. At least once a day she spied the child's face in her pendulum's shining disk. Sometimes she imagined Rachel's ghost peering out from behind the magnet-driven windmill, and once she beheld the *revenant* fleeing across Walnut Street Common. Thus it was that spectral evidence, a species of delusion that even her father could not abide, became Jennet's only bond with the issue of her flesh. She had never endured a darker irony, though she feared that Dame Fortune was not yet weary of the game.

IN ALL IT TOOK HER four years to lay the foundations of her new treatise, brick by brick, lodestone by lodestone, prism by prism, but at last the task was complete, and she once again admitted herself to the outside world. The summer of 1720 found her strolling each morning amidst the stalls and emporiums of Market Street, delighting all the while in the songbirds' concertos, the perfumes wafting from the flower-carts, the chatter pouring from the taverns, and the warmth of God's favorite star pulsing against her face. Within her bosom a vast and sinless pride now swelled: she had carried out Aunt Isobel's command—she had mastered Mr. Newton from sprit to spanker and grafted the *Principia* onto her soul. If these forty philosophic demonstrations failed to fulfill Dr. Halley's requirement of thoroughness and rigor, then the Sahara would barely meet his expectation of a desert.

Restoring Nellie Adams to her employ proved not only the simplest of procedures but also indubitably beneficent. As Nellie's bad luck would have it, the *paterfamilias* of the Eckhardt family had stormed the fortress of her chastity, subsequently allowing himself further such liberties on the grounds that the governess was manifestly a slattern. She took great pleasure in serving notice to Herr Eckhardt, whose predations had— praise Jehovah—fallen short of impregnation, quite likely because poor Nellie had availed herself of the same pennyroyal-and-marjoram unguent in whose application Jennet had tutored her.

In the months that followed their reunion, the Hammer of Witchfinders and her assistant set about assembling their new and better case against demonology, together evoking countless motion-spirits and offering them abundant opportunities to inflict *maleficia*. By promising the mortal participants a generous fee—her savings from the quarterly stipends now stood at one hundred pounds—Jennet and Nellie easily recruited scores of wet-nurses, milkmaids, midwives, poultry farmers, and brewers to the cause. Throughout the experiments the women carefully recorded their observations, noting down each dry breast, barren udder, difficult birth, unproductive hen, and sour cask of beer. Their conclusions were unequivocal. Even under highly enticing circumstances, the world's kinetic agents did not stoop to diabolism.

At first Jennet wondered how their project might encompass virile members, but then one day Nellie mentioned that her only respites from Herr Eckhardt's unwelcome attentions occurred when he visited Philadelphia's most respected house of ill repute, the Grinning Sphinx on the waterfront. Jennet immediately entered into negotiations with the proprietress, Mrs. Postlethwaite, who agreed that for a fifty-fifty split—eight shillings per hour to the madam, eight to the harlot—she would allow her girls to ply their trade in proximity to philosophy. And so it was that, night after night, Jennet and Nellie manipulated prisms and pendulums whilst stationed outside the perfumed chambers of dainty Nora Geddis, sly Moll Frost, pouty Gina Little, sanguine Sophie Epsom, and languid Charlotte Ketch. Interviewed *ex post facto*, the harlots invariably revealed that the episodes of flaccidity lay well within the norm.

On a scorching afternoon in August of 1721, the air so hot it seemed as if a candle might melt without influence of flame, Jennet escorted Nellie to the wharf and installed her aboard the brigantine *Artemis*—the maid-servant was sailing home to Chelmsford at the behest of her ailing father—then returned forthwith to the Chestnut Street townhouse, picked up a quill, and set to work. By Christmas Day she'd emptied eight ink pots to produce 151 pages of manuscript. By Easter of the following year the count stood at sixteen pots and 302 pages. At noon on All Saint's Day she set down her quill, drank a glass of Rhenish, and placed three impassioned kisses on a complete first draft of 434 pages. Should Dr. Halley complain of superficiality again, his accusation would ring as hollow as a sucked egg.

One task remained, nettlesome but essential. Assuming King George's Privy Council was as chary of irreverence as its predecessor, she needed somehow to insulate her argument from accusations of Arianism, atheism, and impiety. By whatever means, she must overlay the treatise with a thick coating of Anglican exegesis and Trinitarian theology.

She was navigating the Schuylkill, a-float on her back, when the answer came, a seraph of inspiration winging through her brain. The Trinity: Father, Son, and Holy Ghost. The kinetic elements: attraction, acceleration, resistance, and radiation—intrinsically allied to earth, air, water, and fire. Christ . . . incarnation . . . ah, hah! The Redeemer was manifestly connected to Earth, having graced the planet with his flesh and blood. And the Holy Ghost? The Aristotelian link was obvious: at Pentecost, this phenomenon had descended upon the Apostles in the guise of fire. Concerning the Father, an association with air seemed natural and inevitable, for God was the breath of life.

That left the fourth Greek element, water.

The current carried her south. A dead tree arced out of the Schuylkill; two yellow-spotted turtles sunned themselves on the half submerged trunk. She drifted. Waters of the Delaware Bay. Waters of the Atlantic Sea. Waters of the Pishon, the Gihon, the Euphrates.

Birth waters, leaking unstoppably, heralding doomed Pashpishia and dear Rachel—heralding every child of woman born. And the Holy Virgin, blessed Mother of God, she too must have known that inexorable leakage, that wonderfully auspicious spill. There! She had it! Hurrah! God, Christ, Ghost, Virgin: air, earth, fire, water. A year might pass ere she finished the treatise, perhaps even two, but at last a complete and irrefutable demon disproof was in hand, and if King George and his Parliament didn't find it a work of the most astonishing piety, they could all go fishing in Hell.

BENJAMIN FRANKLIN KNEW that his ambition to absorb the whole of human knowledge before his thirtieth birthday was immodest, but did that mean it was impossible? He thought not. The key, he decided, was self-discipline. Whereas the other journeymen at Keimer's Printing-House spent their luncheon intervals in the gloomy Crooked Billet, swallowing beef and swilling ale, Ben always passed this same hour in the sunlit compositing-room, improving his mind. Beyond the obvious advantages of his vegetarian diet, amongst them a thinner girth and fatter purse, lay the fact that he could consume his bread, raw cabbage, and pint of distilled water in a fraction of the hiatus required by meat, which gave him additional time for philosophic inquiry.

At the beginning of the week Ben had known almost nothing about the cryptic phenomenon called electricity, but he'd spent the previous four evenings reading Otto von Guericke's *Experimenta Nova*, which discussed the substance, revealed how to make it, and even explained the word itself: *electricity*, from the Greek *elektron*, "amber"—for it was the ancient Ionians who'd first noticed that, when rubbed vigorously, a chunk of amber exhibited a peculiar attractive property. After studying the drawings in *Experimenta Nova*, Ben had stayed awake until midnight constructing a Von Guericke sphere, a turnip-size ball of sulphur mounted on a steel axle turned by a gear and crank, and now he was ready to test it. He finished his cabbage, pulled his stool to the slopping table, and arranged the four mounds around the sphere, all equidistant from the core. With his left hand he cranked the sulphur to spinning, then arced his dominant hand above its surface and pressed down.

First the wheat chaff flew up, leaping through the air and sticking to the charged ball, just as Von Guericke had reported. He cranked faster, rubbed harder. The sot-weed granules took flight. Faster. The wren feathers soared. Harder. Now the primrose petals. The sphere was alive! It surged with power!

A gray mouse scurried across the floor. Keeping his right hand in contact with the sulphur, Ben lifted his feet to let the creature pass, whereupon, apropos of nothing, an errant primrose petal ascended and affixed itself to his free hand. He returned his feet to *terra firma*. The petal abandoned his palm and drifted to the table. He cranked the ball, charged the sulphur, held his left hand over the wayward petal, and again lifted his feet. The petal flew to his palm. He flicked it free.

Nowhere in *Experimenta Nova* did Von Guericke mention that the human body became a conduit for electricity when isolated from the ground. Could it be that Mr. Franklin himself had stumbled upon a heretofore unknown law of Nature? The matter merited further investigation. He set his feet on the floor, cranked the ball, and caressed the sulphur—but before he bothered to unground himself, his uncommitted hand strayed toward a box of broken type. A tingling splinter of electricity materialized betwixt the tip of his index finger and a 20-point leaden *W*—an unpleasant jolt that made him yelp as if he'd stubbed his toe.

He contrived for the same event to occur again, but now he braced himself for the jolt, and so the shock was less. Once more he charged the sulphur. This time, however, he deliberately unfloored his feet ere touching the *W.* No spark. No jolt. What was going on here? What secret principle had he activated?

The tinkling of a brass bell, rigged by Ben to chime whenever the front door opened, announced the arrival of a customer. He damned his luck. John O'Leary and the others were still at the Billet, and Mr. Keimer had left at ten o'clock, laid low by an attack of the gout. Ben had no choice but to abandon his experiments and attend the patron.

Striding into the press-room, he happened upon the handsomest woman in Philadelphia, or such was his initial assessment of her face and form. She was about thirty-five, perhaps even forty, and all the more exquisite for it. Clad in a green damask dress, her flesh had aged not into decrepitude but toward rarity, the same phenomenon as occurred with wine, brandy, cheese, and marble. Her tresses were a glorious auburn, her features noble, her proportions generous. Her lips boasted the moist sensuality of an inking-ball dipped in tallow.

The lady removed her bonnet and gloves, then inquired whether the master of the shop was about. He replied that the gout had sent Mr. Keimer home but that he, Benjamin Franklin, though a mere journeyman, would assist her. His visitor raised her eyebrows to a skeptical elevation. She smiled. From her satchel she produced a thick manuscript, setting it on the scrubbing counter and petting it as she might the cowlick of a favorite nephew.

"I fancy the fragrance of this place," she said. "Ink, glue, leather, and something I can't identify."

"Mouse droppings," he said.

She laughed. None of the whores he bedded at the Grinning Sphinx, not even Nora Geddis, had ever inspired in him such deliciously sinful fancies.

"I am Jennet Stearne Crompton, devotee of Baconian experimentalism and former wife to the Madraspatam Postmaster-General. Since my deliverance from Indian captivity, a narrative on which I shan't waste your time, I have devoted myself to writing a book. I would see it printed without delay."

Ben lifted the cover-page from the stack and studied it, instantly sur-mising that Mrs. Crompton's appetite for speculation quite possibly ri-valed his own.

A Treatise of
How the Four
ARISTOTELIAN ELEMENTS
May Serve to Convince There Are
NO ELEMENTALS,
Neither Are There
Demons, Devils, Goblins,
nor
Wicked Spirits,
Excepting
Lucifer Himself,
and Why
Witchcraft & Maleficium
Are in Consequence
Impossible Things,
This Being the Personal Investigation of the Author,
J. S. Crompton,
Curator of the Cavendish Museum
of Wondrous Prodigies
(Colonial Branch)

"I must confess, I've ne'er heard of the Cavendish Museum," Ben said. "Is the Colonial Branch in Philadelphia?"

"At the moment 'tis largely in my head," Mrs. Crompton replied. "I intend to found such an institution, but until now my battle against demonology hath consumed me."

"I, too, pursue the philosophic life." Ben returned the cover-page to the pile. "This morning I installed a Von Guericke sphere in our compositing-room. As the month progresses I shall employ my leisure hours in learning more of the electric force."

Again she flashed him a smile, though whether of admiration or condescension he couldn't tell. "I can spare from my private fortune the sum of six hundred and fifty pounds. Will that be sufficient to print and bind three hundred copies? I mean to gift each Parliamentarian with one, likewise King George and his councilors, that they might join together in overturning the Witchcraft Act of James the First."

He gasped and said, "Madam, for six hundred and fifty pounds we'll supply every copy with Moroccan bindings, a golden bookmark, and a clockwork canary who turns the pages on command." Noticing that David Harry had once again failed to sweep under the blacking table, he seized the broom and set to work. "Tell me, Mrs. Crompton, might I perchance borrow your intriguing treatise"—he sculpted the debris into a lopsided cone—"and read it this evening?"

"Mr. Franklin, I should be delighted to have a bright young man negotiate my opus and offer me his opinions—though the task will take you more than one evening."

"I read quickly," he said eagerly.

"I write slowly," she replied pointedly.

"I grasp your meaning, Madam, and I shall give each sentence its due." He used the coal-scuttle to transfer the debris from the floor to the dustbin. "The subject touches a nerve deep within me, for the celebrated Samuel Sewall, once employed by the notorious Salem witch-court, hath of late sought to ruin my benighted brother."

A full year had passed since Samuel Sewall's campaign against *The New-England Courant,* and still Ben could not think on the affair without seething. No one disputed that the Boston newspaper had criticized both the provincial government and the Puritan clergy: neither the paper's editor, James Franklin, nor his younger brother and indentured apprentice, Ben, was a friend to the *status quo.* But the fact remained that no unequivocal irreverence or blatant blasphemy had ever stained the *Courant's* pages, and so when Judge Sewall moved to have James gaoled and his journal extinguished for allegedly perverting Scripture, it occurred to Ben that his imagination might be more cordially received in

Pennsylvania. Whilst James dropped from sight, leaving his assistants to compose and print the *Courant* as best they could, Ben set out for Philadelphia, whose Quaker majority, despite its many eccentricities, had reportedly embraced the grand English ideal called freedom of thought.

"My late father was amongst those who conspired with your Mr. Sewall to doom the Salem defendants," Mrs. Crompton said. "And now my brother Dunstan hath likewise caught the cleansing fever."

"If you speak of Dunstan Stearne, I have read of his deplorable activities in *The Bible Commonwealth*. 'Steeth, 'twould appear we are to publish an imperially important treatise, of passing interest to theologians, philosophers, and general readers alike. I propose we charge at least two crowns per copy."

"What matters, young Franklin, is not what price we place upon my book, but what value Parliament extracts from it."

"Of course, Madam—though I fear that for Mr. Keimer there be no such thing as honor without a profit." He offered her a sly grin, upgrading it anon to an admiring glance. "Ah, Mrs. Crompton, I imagine 'tis exhilarating to have in life so worthy a purpose as you enjoy."

"Exhilarating?" His visitor presented him with a dumbfounded expression, as if his nose had suddenly become a turnip. "Nay, sir, 'tis a skein more tangled than that. I cherish my quest, and yet I despise it. I treasure my mission, and still I detest it. As did Harry's thrust to Hotspur, it hath robbed me of my youth." In apparent prelude to her departure she pulled on her gloves, then gave her manuscript a quick caress. "Be warned, sir. I've planted herein a prodigious thicket of Keplerian mechanics and Newtonian proofs. You might get lost."

"I once tried to read Mr. Newton's *Principia*, but I couldn't manage the Latin. His *Opticks*, being in English, was more to my taste." Again Ben approached the blacking table and, seizing a pair of inking-balls by their shafts, brayed them together to equalize their loads. He beat the two great sopping udders against the framed and locked type-form containing the first canto of Joseph Stukeley's *The Aphrodisiad*, buttering the leaden letters with a film of ink—"Arise, my Soul," the epic began, "thou burning Coal, my Heart's own Foal," an opening from which it never recovered. "But even if I comprehend but part of your argument," Ben said, " 'twill be like a healing rain, washing away the swill we brew on these premises—verses by witlings, pamphlets by scoundrels, sermons by hypocrites." After securing the inked type-form in Mr. Keimer's massive handpress, he laid a virgin sheet on the tympan, positioned the frisket (essential for preventing smears), and folded both parts over the stone bed. "The instant my luncheon interval's done, I'm obliged to spawn a hundred copies of this doggerel." He slid the whole arrangement beneath the platen. "I'faith, an African monkey playing with a case of type might easily surpass it." He pulled the spindle lever, thus squeezing the sheet tight against the form and indelibly transferring ink to paper. "Behold Mr. Stukeley's poem"—he rolled back the bed—"certain to lift him from the vale of anonymity and deposit him in the depths of obscurity."

No sooner had he peeled away the signature-sheet than Mrs. Crompton clutched her chest and slumped into the chair beside the scrubbing counter. " 'Sheart, I am a-swoon," she moaned.

"Oh, my poor Mrs. Crompton!"

"A swallow of water should bring me round," she whispered, rapping her knuckles against her breastbone.

He calculated that he could race back to the slopping table, seize his pint bottle, return to the press-room, and place the container to her lips within twenty seconds. He did it in fifteen. The liquid proved efficacious, and she quickly regained her composure, speaking in a steady voice.

"Merci, Monsieur."

"Do you swoon often?"

" 'Tis my first such spell. But hear my explanation." She drained the bottle. "When I was but fourteen, I saw the farmer Giles Corey crushed to death for refusing to plead at Salem. I'd largely banished the episode from my mind, but now your great press brings it back."

"I must dispute your memory in one particular. No lady so lovely as yourself was more than three years old when the Salem Court convened."

"You're a beguiling rascal, Ben Franklin, but you see before you a woman of forty-six years. Now tell me, how long must I wait ere a bound volume appears in my hands?"

"Seven jobs lie ahead of yours, two of substance, the rest trifles. I believe we can begin come April. After that, allow us four more months."

"Might you do't in three?"

"Mayhap."

She rose with fluid grace. "I should like to see this Von Guericke sphere of yours. I've heard of such devices but ne'er beheld one."

Thus it was that Ben spent the final moments of his luncheon interval in the compositing-room, demonstrating the sulphur-ball. He showed Mrs. Crompton how to infuse the pungent globe with the electric force; how her own charged flesh, once isolated from the floor, became as attractive to tobacco and petals as was the sphere itself; and how to make a tiny lightning-bolt leap from her electrified finger to a metal object. The asymmetries brought a smile to his face. On one side of the slopping table: the unfolding of a philosophic experiment, beautifully repeatable. On the other side: the ebb and flow of life, marvelously unpredictable. When he'd jumped out of bed that morning, Ben had assumed the day would prove as mundane as any other.

He'd never imagined that by one o'clock he would be standing beside
an elegant woman, filling his tissues with electricity even
as he longed to reach out and stroke her
with deliciously stimulating
and impossibly
passionate

❦

Sparks
spew from Van
de Graaff generators. Electric
rainbows scurry up and down Jacob's ladders.
Tendrils of lightning spiral around Tesla coils. In short, we
have entered the domain of 1940's American science-fiction cinema,
a phenomenon that in my opinion occasioned numerous paragons of the

dramatist's art, literary works to rival *Œdipus Rex, King Lear,* and *Long Day's Journey into Night.*

The reflex by which you humans lionize theatrical scripts over screenplays bewilders me. When it comes to the latter, you unfailingly seize upon some arbitrary celluloid simulacrum, always a coarse and budget-bound shadow of the writer's vision. One day you'll learn a proper respect for the text itself.

In any consideration of 1940's science-fiction screenplays, one name towers above all others, well above Joseph West and *Man Made Monster,* well above Brenda Weisberg and *The Mad Ghoul.* I speak of the great Edward T. Lowe, whose deathless duology, *House of Frankenstein* and *House of Dracula,* cannily dramatizes the triumphs and trade-offs intrinsic to the scientific worldview. Through the braided narratives that constitute the first masterpiece, the author serves up a critique of Western rationality so withering as to warm the heart of every middle-class mystic in the audience. But in the second scenario Lowe reverses the poles, arguing that we abandon Reason only at our peril.

Whatever the flaws in my attempt to document the birth of the Enlightenment—a project that has recently obliged me to depict my dear Jennet in intellectual congress with Benjamin Franklin, with more such intimacies to come—you cannot deny the subject's inherent significance. If our civilization has made a Devil's bargain with its own cleverness, consigning its soul to a false god called scientific progress, then this swindle must be exposed at every opportunity. If, on the other hand, the Age of Reason represented humankind's last hope of unshackling itself from sanctified ignorance and consecrated nonsense, then we should stand up and say so, even if we offend the astrologer next door or the cleric down the street.

House of Frankenstein takes as its principal figure the deranged scientist Gustav Niemann. When we first meet this egomaniacal *Übermensch,* he lies imprisoned somewhere in central Europe, condemned for performing blasphemous medical experiments. The plot centers around the covenants through which Dr. Niemann, after breaking out of his dungeon, lures three other outcasts into his sphere. First he promises to repair the crooked spine of his obsequious hunchback assistant, Daniel.

Upon encountering the vampire Count Dracula—avatar of the enchantment that Reason has drained from the world—Niemann agrees to "protect the earth" upon which the undead aristocrat lies. Finally, crossing paths with Lawrence Talbot, a self-pitying werewolf, Niemann claims he will surgically reconfigure Talbot's brain and thereby "lift this curse from you forever." For Lowe, clearly, Talbot is the quintessential dupe of Enlightenment rationality. The moon that broods over *House of Frankenstein* is not the vibrant orb that for centuries has stirred the blood of poets, but a thing of cold Newtonian horror, triggering a condition that Talbot regards as irredeemably pathological. Rather than reveling in his lupine nature, his inner wolf, he succumbs to the supposition that he'll never be happy until he stops ripping out people's throats and instead settles into a respectable bourgeois existence.

Like so many captains of corporate technocracy, Niemann has no intention of honoring his philanthropic vows. He cherishes but one goal, to further empower himself by reanimating a legendary corpse-assemblage known as the Frankenstein monster, regardless of the consequences to the human community or the biosphere at large. By the time the drama is done, Niemann has violated all three covenants, and his would-be beneficiaries lie dead—Daniel defenestrated, Dracula vaporized by a sunbeam, Talbot shot with a silver bullet.

The environmentalist discourse encoded in *House of Frankenstein*, which begins with Niemann's disingenuous vow to protect the Earth, reaches its apex in Act Two, when the scientist enters a community where the corpse-assemblage once roamed. Now that the ghastly thing is gone, the peasants have regained their Rousseauean harmony with Nature. Explains the local police inspector, "Our village has been quiet and peaceful ever since the dam broke and swept the Wolf Man and the Frankenstein monster to their destruction." (For a cogent analysis of the ecological motifs suffusing this text, the reader is referred to *Saving Graces*, written in 1987 by Jacques Derrida's *Of Grammatology*.) The theme continues in Act Three, when the corpse-assemblage drowns Niemann in a quicksand bog, Lowe's objective correlative for the miasma into which Newtonian instrumentalism has dragged the world.

House of Dracula radically inverts every epistemological premise around which *House of Frankenstein* turns. The main character is the blameless and upright Dr. Franz Edelman, whose "reputation for helping others" is known even among the world's vampires and werewolves. Before Act One is over, both Count Dracula and Lawrence Talbot, mysteriously resurrected following their misadventures in the earlier text, have come to Edelman seeking natural remedies for their putatively supernatural afflictions. In contrast to the self-actualized vampire we met previously, the undead aristocrat of *House of Dracula* is under "a curse of misery and horror." This time around, Lowe depicts Talbot not as a noble primitive who has failed to comprehend his own spiritual beauty, but as a physically diseased victim of intracranial pressure.

For Dracula, Franz Edelman prescribes an experimental vaccine to combat the parasites infecting his blood. In the Wolf Man's case, Edelman proposes to soften his brainpan with a therapeutic mold derived from a "hybrid plant," *Clavaria formosa*. (A delightful semiotic analysis of Lowe's nomenclature appears in *Stuff and Nonsense*, penned in 1998 by Michel Foucault's *The Archaeology of Knowledge*.) When the Frankenstein monster turns up in a seaside cave beneath Edelman's castle at the beginning of Act Two, he resolves with characteristic benevolence to deliver the corpse-assemblage from its coma. Although the doctor's deformed and saintly nurse, Nina, whose crooked frame he hopes to repair with the *Clavaria* mold, thinks that reviving the Frankenstein monster is a terrible idea—the thing is in all probability still a homicidal maniac—Edelman believes the monster deserves a second chance: "Is that poor creature responsible for what he is?" Counters Nina, "Man's responsibility is to his fellow man." Bested by dialectic, Edelman replies, "Perhaps you're right, Nina. Frankenstein's monster must never wreak havoc again."

Lowe wrote *House of Dracula* in 1945, the same year that atomic bombs destroyed two Japanese cities, and the scholarly consensus is that he added the pivotal "never wreak havoc" line immediately upon hearing about Hiroshima and Nagasaki. Evidently Lowe was the first serious Western dramatist to express a hope that the same scientists who designed thermonuclear weapons might ultimately campaign for their elimination.

The downfall of Franz Edelman begins when Dracula, unable to master his demonic nature, injects his contaminated blood into the doctor, who subsequently acquires a split personality. Edelman's compassionate side predominates long enough for him to perform the *Clavaria* treatment on Talbot, but then his dark half takes over, prompting him to murder his gardener, strangle Nina, and revive the Frankenstein monster.

Despite this tragic conclusion, we must note that medical intervention and the Enlightenment worldview function throughout *House of Dracula* as wholly positive forces. Talbot emerges from Edelman's castle a man reborn, a normal life ahead of him. He has rejected the lycanthropic moon of superstition for a humanist moon lit by scientific insight. It would seem that, unlike the Lowe of the earlier text, the author of *House of Dracula* feels little sympathy for the self-appointed avengers of dispossessed enchantment.

As my story progresses, we shall address the primitivist complaint again, but now we must return to Jennet. Before you negotiate the next scene, however, let me invite you to spend a moment meditating on Edmund Lowe's piquant symbol of the post-Enlightenment dilemma: the Frankenstein monster, lying on the operating table of the valiant Dr. Edelman. I invite you to contemplate the monster's bubbling bile and flowing lymph, its buzzing nerves and pulsing veins, its throbbing brain and beating

❄❄

Heart
a-flutter, flesh
a-quiver, Jennet pulled
back the door to Keimer's Printing-
House, thus setting Ben's ingenious bell to tinkling,
and stepped inside. As the journeymen and the apprentices looked on, she removed her gloves, unwound her scarf, and brushed the snow from her arms. Briefly her admirers savored her presence, then returned to their duties. George Webb took up the inking-balls and pounded them

against a type-form like a hortator beating out a cadence in the hold of a Roman galley. John O'Leary yanked the spindle lever on the Blaeu press, permanently staining a perfectly good sheet of paper with some insipid tract or blathering ballad. David Harry dipped a recently employed type-form, now grimy with ink, into the swampy waters of the rinsing trough.

She wasn't exactly sure which phenomenon had triggered her infatuation: the brilliance of Ben's writing, or the unmediated fact of Ben himself. Near the end of their dalliance with the sulphur-ball, he had lent her the complete Silence Dogood series, fourteen letters submitted serially to *The New-England Courant* by a country widow of limited income, lively intellect, and prolific opinions. It was a double hoax. Silence's devoted audience didn't know she was really James Franklin's apprentice, his upstart brother Ben—and neither did James himself. By disguising his identity, altering his handwriting, and slipping a new letter each night beneath the door of James's printing-house, Ben had managed at age sixteen to secure for his prose prominent weekly exposure in the *Courant*, a situation the elder Franklin would never have tolerated had he known the epistles' provenance.

Where had Ben acquired such confidence? From whence came this astonishing nerve? A city youth had thought his way, with considerable charm and only a few lapses, into a different gender, another generation, and a rural cast of mind. Jennet adored Silence Dogood. After savaging the supposition that women were less intelligent than men, Silence went on to attack those who barred the female sex from higher education. "Women are taught to read and write their Names and nothing else. We have the God-given capacity for Knowledge and Understanding. What have we done to forfeit the Privilege of attending Colleges?" In weighing atheists against hypocrites, Silence concluded, "I am of late inclin'd to think the Hypocrite the more dangerous of the Two, especially if he sustains a Post in the Government." Above all, Silence was a realist: "I am apt to fancy I could be persuaded to marry again, but a good-humor'd, sober, and agreeable Man being all but impossible to find, I have grown resign'd to Widowhood, though it is a Condition I have never much admir'd."

Jennet proceeded to the drying-room, where dozens of freshly printed signatures hung from a network of overhead strings, Ben standing in their midst like a washer-woman surrounded by the day's laundry. The philosophers traded exuberant greetings, and then she reeled off her usual questions. How many pages of her treatise had he consumed? What was his opinion so far? When would he finish? It was their eighth such encounter in a month—though only now did she realize that, beyond his resplendent mind and generous soul, she found Ben appealing in body as well. True, his limbs extended from a stoutish frame, but rarely had a barrel-chest boasted such dignity. Yes, his countenance contained some superfluous flesh, but it was a pudding-face of the most meritorious sort. Indeed, his shanks were hefty, but where in Pennsylvania might one behold a more graceful turn of calf?

He touched his finger to a dangling signature, ascertaining that the ink was dry. "Last night I read your chapters on those motion-spirits in service to acceleration. With each paragraph I grow more enchanted."

"But do I make a convincing case against demonology?" she asked.

"For all I am delighted by your book, I would learn how your argument plays out ere I judge it." He began unhooking the signatures. "Not being a church-going man, I expect to read your last sentence on Sunday morning, whereupon I shall render my verdict."

A spasm of rapture seized Jennet as she realized that their next rendezvous might occur in Ben's own lodgings, but an instant later her joy was eclipsed by sobriety, clarity, pragmatism, and several other of her mind's more annoying habits. The *pièce bien faite* wherein she and Ben became lovers knew little of logic and much of lunacy. Whilst the darling boy might accept her as a kind of intriguing middle-aged cousin, it was inconceivable that they would ever enjoy a tryst. Faugh, he was but three years older than Rachel!

Resting a hand on his shoulder, she asked him whether she might visit his rooms at two o'clock on Sunday afternoon to discuss her treatise in full. When he protested that his accommodations were ill-suited to a woman of her breeding, she reminded him that she'd been happier living in a Nimacook wigwam with an Indian she esteemed than in a Chestnut Street townhouse with a postmaster she disdained.

The interval was interminable, three whole days, but at last the appointed hour arrived. She stepped off her front stoop, tramped through the swirling snows of Market Street, and, ascending the decrepit rear stairway of the Thomas Godfrey mansion, entered the domain of the callow genius who'd given Silence Dogood to the world. He greeted her dressed in a pristine ensemble that would have fared disastrously in the printing-house—fawn breeches, vest of yellow silk, white day-shirt with ruffled cuffs.

"*Bienvenue au Château Franklin,*" he said.

"*Merci, Monsieur.*"

"Yesterday I went bear-hunting in homage to your Indian past, and soon I found my quarry, lying torpid in a cave by the river. Straightaway I knew him for an industrious beast, as 'twas apparent he'd built his own brewery then consumed the whole of his first barrel of ale, that he might study the effects of inebriation on hibernation. I have no meat to give thee, Madam, for I hold it unsporting to shoot a bear whilst he's conducting a philosophic experiment."

She laughed and said, "I require no meat, sir, but I should like a tour of your castle."

"*Suivez-moi.*"

There were four rooms altogether, including Ben's little bed-chamber, tiny parlor, suffocating study, and congested laboratory, the latter a mere dressing alcove into which he'd jammed a cherry table a-jumble with an air-pump, a microscope, a telescope, a Von Guericke sphere, and other such paraphernalia. Each space boasted its own hearth connected to a common chimney, an arrangement that he merrily compared to quadruplet piglets nursing on a brood sow.

Instinctively they drifted to the coziest place, the parlor, where her host had built a convivial fire. A copper kettle occupied the chimney niche like an egg snugged into a rookery.

"Mayhap I should prepare some Malay tea," he suggested.

"We have many large questions to discuss," she replied. "God and gravity. Demons and demonstrations. Newton's apple—and Eden's too. 'Tis indeed an occasion for tea, Mr. Franklin, as strong as you can make it."

❦

IN THE SHANK OF THE AFTERNOON the philosophers sat together on the divan, arm to arm, thigh to thigh. Bracing and aromatic, the Malay tea put Jennet in a mood of remembrance, and ere long she was speaking of her life's great losses. A child lying in a mound beside the Shawsheen. A second child thriving in Madraspatam under the auspices of a *de facto* mother.

"I'faith, Mrs. Crompton, you've surely endured your share of sorrows," Ben said. "Would that I knew some benevolent sorcerer who might instantly translate your lost Rachel from Asia to America."

"When I cannot sleep at night, I say to myself, 'On the other side of the planet the sun is long risen, and Rachel is up and about. At this precise moment some notion or vagary goes flitting through her brain.' "

"But now she sleeps, and 'tis the mother whose thoughts are on the wing."

"Alas, I fear that very mother spends rather too much time in airy habitations, flying where her fancy takes her, as Mr. Crompton knew all too well," Jennet said. "But for my single-minded pursuit of the *argumentum grande*, Rachel would yet be at my side."

"May I make bold with my opinion?" Ben asked. Receiving her nod, he continued. "Just as some men are not particularly competent fathers, neither are you about to be nominated the world's most successful mother. But let me in the same breath assert that to thwart the Puritan prickers is a manifestly noble enterprise. On balance I would say you do your daughter proud."

"Truly?"

"Ere Rachel's grown to womanhood, she'll be gainsaying all who claim she's not your daughter."

Jennet inhaled deeply. Ben was redolent of philosophy—of sulphur and magnetite and other heady scents. "Since I can no longer hold my child's delicate hand, I shall instead cling to your exquisite thought." She swallowed a stimulating measure of tea. "Prithee, tell me what faults and merits you find in my book."

For the next twenty minutes her new friend discoursed upon *A Treatise of How the Four Aristotelian Elements May Serve to Convince There Are No Elementals.* He applauded her "incontrovertible cleverness in trying to make motion-spirits practice *maleficium.*" He praised her "abiding brilliance in mapping the Greek immutables onto both Newton's mechanics and Trinitarian theology."

"Ah, but if you were a Parliamentarian, would my claims persuade you to o'erturn the Conjuring Statute?" she asked.

"Oh, Mrs. Crompton, I find so much to admire in your treatise."

"But would my claims persuade you?"

"Not being a Parliamentarian, 'tis impossible for me to answer. I can only say that your every sentence bespeaks an opulent intellect."

Something was wrong. The affirmation in his words could not conceal the catch in his voice, the hesitancy in his demeanor. She decided against further pursuing the matter but instead suggested that they experiment with his sulphur-ball.

"You have shown how a human body, ungrounded, may exert the electric attraction on small particles," she said, sipping the last of her tea. "Ah, but can that same body transfer its charge to another?"

"A splendid question! We must seek its resolution!"

They adjourned to the laboratory. Jennet lit a tallow candle and settled onto the stool. Ben assumed an upended cider cask, then carefully assembled three small mounds of crushed tea-leaves. He set one pile before the Von Guericke sphere, the other two at opposite ends of the table. Cranking the ball with her right hand, she placed her left palm along the rolling equator.

The central tea-mound disintegrated, its particles flying to the sphere's mottled surface. She kept her palm on the ball, lifted her feet, and stretched her right hand toward the corresponding pile. The tea bits ascended, coating her fingers.

"I'm all electric, Ben! Now let me touch you, and we shall learn more of this strange principle!"

Feet still hovering, she spun the ball, then charged the sulphur with her right palm and immediately wrapped her left hand around his right wrist. He unfloored his feet and brought his free hand toward the remaining mound.

A dozen stray particles leapt to his fingertips.

"I'Christ, we've done it!" he cried.

"An impressive result"—she released his wrist and withdrew her palm from the ball—"but I shan't count our experiment complete till we've turned the entire heap into a whirling tornado of tea."

"But . . . how?" He shook the particles from his person.

"Ere I re-electrify myself, we must enlarge the area of overlap 'twixt our respective persons," she said. " 'Tis one thing for my hand to clasp your wrist, and quite another for, say, the skin of our forearms to meld."

"Then let us bare our limbs anon." He unbuttoned his right cuff, rolling the ruffle toward his elbow.

"Anon," she echoed, furling the left sleeve of her dress.

They brought their forearms together to create a warm fleshy tangent.

"By your leave, we can further increase our contiguity if we place one cheek against the other," he said.

"Ah!"

Keeping their forearms connected, they fused the sides of their faces, a gesture that inevitably caused their knees to bump together and her left breast to mesh with his sternum. They gulped and laughed in perfect synchronicity.

She kissed him on the lips. He did not flinch but instead committed his own mouth to the philosophic cause.

"Ne'er have two experimenters done a better job of enlarging an overlap," he noted, retreating just far enough to move his lips. "Prithee, spin the ball and charge yourself, that we might continue the investigation."

"Let me propose that we first expand our common boundary by at least a hundred square inches." She broke the seal betwixt their forearms, stood up, and brushed the front of her dress, transferring the tea and sulphur from her fingers to her lace bodice. "Or, even better, two hundred."

"Might I make the case for three hundred square inches?" he said, likewise rising.

"Thou mayest."

They kissed again. Their hands became autonomous beings—ardent mariners hoisting anchors, loosening halyards, and raising canvas prior to mounting the tide and plying the seas beyond.

"Or even four hundred square inches?" he asked.

Buttons rotated. Thongs unthreaded. Clasps opened. Stays parted company.

"Four hundred!" she agreed.

A dozen articles of clothing tumbled to the floor at uniform Galilean velocities.

"Five hundred?" he asked.

"Five hundred!" Her heart pounded like a pagan drum setting the tempo of a bacchanal. Her lungs chuffed and wheezed like a bellows operated by a lunatic smith. "Six hundred!" Never had she observed so enthralling a phenomenon as Ben's nakedness. His skin glowed like the translucent crater atop the candle. His virile member was a belaying pin fit to cleat the mainsail of Æneas's flagship.

"Ah, Mrs. Crompton, I do love thee so!"

"My dearest, sweetest swain!"

"Is this immoral?" he asked.

"Merely immoderate," she replied. "Like all women, I fear the gravid state."

" 'Sblood, Mrs. Crompton, I shan't so burden thee. As a faithful patron of the Grinning Sphinx, I am well instructed in the thwarting of spermatozooans."

"Thou hast a Belgian adder-bag?"

"Three at last count, mayhap four," he said, blowing out the candle.

Naked, they scurried to the bed-chamber and collaborated in the construction of a fire. With the fevered intensity of a poet choosing a new quill in a stationer's shop, his original having cracked in mid-composition, Ben selected an adder-bag from his cache, which he kept beside the mattress in an earthenware jar. Her cunny was as wet as a peach. Sheathing his manhood, they set about exhibiting their deathless devotion to the cult of electricity.

"Ne'er have I felt such sparks," he said as his ardor gained admittance to its object.

"Mr. Franklin, you make me crackle," she said, rotating on the axis of his manhood. "I declare our experiment a triumph."

"Absolutely."

"*Quod eros demonstrandum,*" she said.

※

AS TWILIGHT CAME TO PHILADELPHIA, the philosophers lavished themselves on one another, abandoning the bed-clothes only to stoke the fire or appease their bladders. Whenever Ben was occupied with hearth or chamber-pot, Jennet took to indulging in salacious speculation, and ere long she'd accumulated musings enough that, if so inclined, she could write a book addressing the mystic qualities of carnal embrace. Swiving, she decided, was no less spiritual an exercise than the singing of a hymn or the recitation of a prayer—a truth that might very well explain the clerical zeal for witch-cleansing. For how could the immense and sprawling Christian Church, with its instinctive suspicion of human bodies, its profound Pauline hope that these soggy conglomerations of leaking cocks and dribbling quims might simply disappear one day—how could it abide the possibility of widows and wenches and all manner of seductresses turning their devotional energies to sybaritic congress, those notorious orgiastic Sabbats? A woman needn't worship Lucifer to spark a demonologist's ire. She need only be made of flesh.

A silken gloom suffused the bed-chamber. Ben lit a fat candle. The air thickened with a wondrous fragrance: salt, tallow, seed, and sulphur in miraculous amalgamation. But then, shortly after Jennet decided that she'd never been happier, a cryptic misery overcame her swain, his breaths growing short, his eyes welling up.

"Why do you weep, bonny Ben? I swear to thee, there be no sin in this."

"Sweet lady, your noble treatise doth harbor a grievous error."

Despite the fire, a chill washed through her. "What *manner* of grievous error?"

"Have you not read the late Robert Boyle?"

"The man was a witch believer. He hath naught to offer my cause."

"Alas, some several years ago Mr. Boyle brought ruin upon the premises round which your brave book orbits. In *The Sceptical Chymist* he proved that Aristotle was wrong to number fire amongst the elements, for fire is itself a mingling of immutables."

She grew colder yet. "Mr. Boyle kept company with demonologists!"

"Even so, many an experimenter hath drawn fruitful inspiration from his work, so that today the Greek chemistry is all but routed. As an example, for all you may combine gold with other metals, you can recover the stuff in its original form, a fact that implies—"

"Unchangeable corpuscles of gold?" she moaned.

"Aye," he said. "What's more, the consensus is that we must give the name of element to arsenic, iron, zinc, and white phosphorus."

"White phosphorus can be admixed and then recovered?"

"Mrs. Crompton, I fear I've stolen your vocation."

"Iron's an element as well?"

"Aye."

"And zinc?"

"That too."

"Damn all zinc."

"I agree, Mrs. Crompton. Damn zinc to Hell. Damn iron. Damn phosphorus and arsenic."

"Oh, Ben, my mind's a-whirl. Have I squandered my life on an obsolete science? Whilst expiring at the stake, my aunt bid me construct the demon disproof from Aristotle's immutables, and yet today I learn such chemistry's good for naught but making a modern philosopher titter and wince."

" 'Sheart, I cannot resolve the contradiction. But hear my promise.

Should you elect to fashion a new *argumentum grande*, you shall have this diligent printer for your assistant."

"At the moment I ask only that you embrace me. Anchor me to your bed, bonny Ben, lest I succumb to a devilish unreason, for I've half a mind to flee your quarters and pitch myself into the Schuylkill like Ophelia into the Limfjord."

The glorious boy did as she commanded, wrapping his arms around her shoulders, pulling her chest tight against his.

"How does a person say 'I love you' in the Algonquin language?" he asked.

"*Cowammaunsh,*" she said.

"*Cowammaunsh,*" he said.

Her tears dried. Her muscles relaxed. The candle burned low. As she floated through the sleepy dusk, she decided that she, too, was an element, no less so than gold or zinc, readily melted, easily mingled, but somehow always recoverable to herself.

※

IN THE WEEKS THAT FOLLOWED her collision with the new chemistry, she devoted her energies to augmenting *The Devil and All His Works* with fresh news-clippings, as if the gutting of her *argumentum grande* could be remedied by rousing to incandescence her wrath against the Massachusetts cleansers. Most of the reports came from *The Bible Commonwealth*, but occasionally she found her brother's activities documented in *The American Weekly Mercury* and sometimes even *The London Journal*.

What course made sense? Should she publish her treatise as it stood and pray that no Parliamentarian had ever heard of Robert Boyle? Purge the thing of all Aristotelian speculation and hope the results were judged neither atheist nor incoherent? Sequester herself once more within her skull and construct still another demon disproof?

"Just remember, if you attempt a new treatise, this time you'll have me standing by your side," Ben told her. "Franklin and Crompton, united against the Conjuring Statute!"

" 'Tis a marvelous slogan," she said, "but as of yet we've no thesis to give it teeth, and meanwhile here's the Book of Exodus, telling the world, 'Thou shalt not suffer a witch to live.' "

Owing largely to the constancy of Ben's optimism, the intensity of his affections, and the tenderness of his care, she at last regained the energy that Robert Boyle had sapped away. As far as she could tell, her swain loved her no less than she loved him; their passions matched precisely, inch for inch, ounce for ounce. Why, exactly, did this canny and beguiling youth adulate her? Because she'd once persuaded Isaac Newton to do her bidding? Because her campaign to bring down Dunstan was as audacious as his mission to master all knowledge? His reasons were opaque to her, a delicious riddle.

Not since her tutelage under Aunt Isobel had she known a person who took so broad a view of so many matters. By Ben's reckoning, the life that lay before him was not a *terra incognita* but a Promised Land whose peaks and valleys he himself could shape through the sheer power of Reason. A fortnight after their felicitous sulphur-ball experiment, he devised a scheme that he intended to follow all his days, a five-page, crosshatched "perfection-matrix" on which he would mark down his every lapse in Thrift ("I shall endeavor to be extremely frugal for some Time till I have paid what I owe," ran his caption for the first grid), Honesty ("I shall strive for Sincerity in every Word and Action"), Industry ("I shall not neglect my Business for any foolish Project of quickly growing rich"), Forbearance ("I resolve to speak ill of no Man, not even in a Matter of Truth"), and Moderation ("I shall not eat to Dullness, drink to Elevation, nor use Venery for any Purpose save Health and Offspring").

The reach of his planning extended even to the grave. Rummaging through his desk one afternoon in search of a scissors with which to snip out her brother's latest crime, the hanging of a supposed sea-witch in Gloucester, she came upon an epitaph Ben had composed for himself shortly after his eighteenth birthday. Not only did this young man expect to live ethically, he meant to die eloquently.

The Body of
B. FRANKLIN,
Printer,
Like the Cover of an old Book,
Its Contents torn out,
And stript of its Lettering and Gilding,
Lies here, Food for Worms.
But the Work shall not be wholly lost:
For it will, as he believ'd, appear once more,
In a new and more perfect Edition,
Revised and corrected
By the Author.

"Your strategy of self-perfection's admirable," she told him one night as, standing beside the Schuylkill at the cold dark hour of three o'clock *ante meridian,* she trained Ben's reflecting telescope on banded Jupiter. "But can you actually cleave to't from here to Heaven?"

"Believe me, dearest, I have oft-times told myself to eschew this project, for't could easily make me not so much a faultless man as a moral fop, fore'er flaunting his merits. Then, too, does not a truly virtuous person exhibit a few failings, so as to keep his friends in countenance?"

"*Now* I hear Reason talking," she said, bringing the regal planet into focus.

"Forgive me, Mrs. Crompton, but 'tis not Reason you hear but rather its deceitful twin, Expedience." Ben rubbed his hands together as if lathering a bar of soap. "I am reminded of a story told me by a blacksmith I knew in Boston. It seems there appeared in his shop one day a farmer who desired to have the whole of his ax as shiny as the cutting-edge. The blacksmith consented to buff the blade bright if the farmer would but turn the grindstone crank."

She fixed her eye on Jupiter's southern hemisphere. She blinked. Yes, there it was, the Great Red Spot, radically shifted from its position of a mere four hours earlier. "I've caught the crimson storm, Ben, though now its fury lies to the east. 'Twould seem that, for all it's a weighty sphere, Jupiter takes but twelve Earth hours to make a rotation, surely no more than fourteen."

"Then I thank Providence I'm no citizen of the place, for my days are short enough already." Ben clucked his tongue and resumed his tale. "With great zeal the farmer worked the crank whilst the blacksmith pressed the ax hard against the stone, which made the turning of't very fatiguing. At length the farmer declared that he would take his tool as it was. 'No,' the smith said, 'turn on, turn on. We shall make it glitter by and by. As yet 'tis only speckled.' 'Aye,' the farmer said, 'but I think a speckled ax is best.' "

Jennet laughed, though not so long as to demean Ben's story, which was far more fable than drollery. "Your parable's most piquant, sir. How readily we settle for the speckled ax."

"Unless I embrace my perfection-matrix in full," he said, nodding, "I shall ne'er learn how far I might go in eradicating my defects."

She twisted the focus knob, and suddenly a Jovian satellite popped out of the blackness. "Ah, there she is, elusive Io. I've seen her only once before, back in the Mirringate observatory."

"How does the goddess appear?"

"A yellow ball, as if made of sulphur."

"Sulphur? She's a kind of Von Guericke sphere then? My dear Mrs. Crompton, 'twould seem we've solved the riddle of Heaven's fire." He offered her a coy smile and a mischievous wink. "Each time Jehovah desires to hear the boom of thunder, He sets His hand on spinning Io, and seconds later those mighty sparks called lightning-bolts come forth!"

TURN ON, TURN ON—*we shall make it glitter by and by.* The imperative became their private chant, something they could sing to one another whenever it seemed that their *affaire de coeur* lacked a future. If they simply kept the wheel moving, minds and bodies bent to the task, their love would never lose its luster.

The instant Ben finished with the day's obligations at Keimer's, they would seek each other out, sometimes in his garret, sometimes in her townhouse, remaining together until he left for work in the morning. When it came to carnal matters, she normally played the teacher, he the novice (and never did concupiscence know a more eager pupil), but in the other arena of their nakedness, the languidly flowing Schuylkill, these rôles were reversed, Ben instructing Jennet in how to control her buoyancy and move her limbs per the advanced principles set down by Monsieur Thévenot in his *Art of Swimming*. But beyond the mattress and the river they were equals, two curious pilgrims peering through Ben's telescope, leaning over his microscope, constructing vacuums with his air-pump.

"Here be the problem," she said. "Monsieur Descartes hath revealed to philosophers a universe cloven down the middle, thinking minds on one side, dead matter on the other. But the world's fore'er in motion. Inexplicable forces hoist the seas to shore, pull our planet round its star, and put Dr. Halley's comet to flight."

"Say 'inexplicable force' to a Continental Cartesian, or even a Cambridge Platonist, and he replies, 'occult force,' " Ben sighed.

"Say 'occult force' to a priest, and he replies, 'demonic force,' " she groaned. "Say 'demonic force' to a witchfinder, and he reaches for his pricking needle."

"So we're stuck. Flies in molasses."

"And yet I shall persist."

"Most admirable, Mrs. Crompton."

"A speckled ax is ne'er best."

Rare was the tryst in which they neglected to exchange gifts. Their corporation trafficked lavishly in tokens: flower blossoms, autumn leaves, sparkling stones, burnished beetles, pithy sayings, the poems of Catullus. Although the majority of these favors were discovered rather than purchased, occasionally one lover would notice some astonishingly apropos artifact in a shop window. Thus it was that he bought for her a cedarwood model of the Trojan Horse, whilst she presented him with a miniature Blaeu press capable of printing individual playing-cards.

Early in October her regular monthly visit to the Chestnut Street bookshop called Ephram's brought her face-to-face with what she took to be the latest edition of Newton's masterwork, its title rendered in English: *Mathematical Principles of Natural Philosophy*. Leafing through the volume, she discovered to her delight that, thanks to the labors of one Andrew Mott, her native tongue informed the entire text. The ideal birthday present for Ben, she realized. The price was two pounds, an amount that gave her pause, as her summer stipend from Tobias had not arrived. In the end she decided that recklessness was the better part of romance, and she blithely acquired the *Principia*'s newest incarnation.

Later, as she made her way down Market Street, the precious bundle pressed against her breast, a delightful question formed in her brain. Why wait four months to please Ben with the translated *Principia* when she could please him with it right now? Reaching the Godfrey house, she retrieved her key from beneath the stoop, then ascended the rear stairwell at a giddy pace, her imagination offering her an entrancing glimpse of Ben's plump cheeks lifting in a smile as he took the book in hand.

She entered the bed-chamber, finding it empty, a circumstance she chose to exploit by hiding the *Principia* beneath his pillow. She proceeded to the laboratory. No Ben. She rushed into the parlor. Her gallant sat on the divan, his complexion ashen, his fingers entwining one another, so that his hands suggested spiders in carnal embrace.

"My darling, you look unwell."

"I am stricken with foreboding," he said.

"How so?"

" 'Twould seem Dame Fortune means to pluck me from the City of Brotherly Love and carry me clear to England."

"England?"

"For reasons I do not apprehend, Governor Keith hath lately formed a good opinion of me, and he urges that I sail to London without delay. I am to purchase, upon his credit, a new handpress and two cases of type, that I might open a shop in Philadelphia dedicated to our province's printing needs. Oh, Mrs. Crompton, I fear you will decline to join me on this voyage."

"How can you imagine such a thing?"

"Are you not pledged to remain in America, battling your brother's noxious band?"

"Unless I undertake to murder the cleansers with pistol and ball, a course forbidden by my own perfection-matrix, my mere proximity cannot threaten 'em. Rather than endure our separation, bonny Ben, I would follow thee into the coldest cave in Arctica or across the hottest plain in Hell."

He vaulted off the divan and showered her cheeks with kisses. "I was afraid I'd be forced to chose 'twixt the livelihood I love and the love for which I live."

"Think on your clearheaded Silence Dogood. Were she blessed with a swain such as yourself, 'tis certain she would ne'er leave his side."

"To England, then?" he said.

"To England," she replied.

But instead they went to the bed-chamber and removed all their clothing.

"A splendid idea hath popped into my brain," he said. "Upon arriving in London, we shall search out Isaac Newton. Unless his madness is ascendant, I shall persuade him to favor us with his insights into the electric force."

" 'Tis a pilgrimage you will make alone, for I've yet to forgive the man his betrayal of Aunt Isobel." She retrieved the *Principia* from beneath the pillow, passing it to Ben. "When you face the old lion, you'll want him to place his signature on this, thereby increasing its worth."

" 'Sbody—the very translation I've been seeking!" He flipped back the cover. A scowl overwhelmed his smile. "I'faith, Mrs. Crompton, this Newton's a far handsomer wight than you've described."

He displayed the frontispiece, which had somehow eluded her initial perusal of the text. Her pulse quickened. Her skin prickled. Skillfully rendered and crisply inked, the engraving depicted a man who, whatever his faults and virtues, was certainly not Isaac Newton.

"This is somebody else!" she protested.

"How so?"

"Newton's a crook-backed gnome of weak chin and eyes set wide apart! How could I e'er forget the face that sealed Isobel's doom?"

" 'Tis one thing for an artist to flatter his subject, and quite another for him to draw the wrong man entirely. There's surely some chicanery here, for when you speak of a crook-backed gnome, one imagines either Shakespeare's Richard the Third or philosophy's Robert Hooke."

"Hooke of the *Micrographia?*"

"The late, great Robert Hooke, Newton's eternal antagonist."

Ben dashed from the bed-chamber and returned anon holding a splayed copy of Hooke's *Lectiones Cutlerianæ.*

"Your gnome mayhap?" he asked, showing her the frontispiece.

As she scrutinized the image, a sour fluid traveled from her stomach to her chest—for this was indeed the very dwarf she'd met thirty-five years earlier in Newton's rooms at Trinity.

She snapped the treatise shut as if to mash a midge betwixt its leaves. " 'Steeth, Ben, this Hooke hath played me false! He hath played us *all* false—myself, Aunt Isobel, Barnaby Cavendish, the whole Colchester Assizes of 1689! Everything's so clear now. By standing before the Court as Newton, Hooke sought to ruin his rival's reputation. What a swinish thing to do! 'Tis an un-Christian thought, but I'm glad the man's dead!"

"Might this mean the real Newton's no maniac after all?"

"It means much more, my love. It means we need but present ourselves to Newton and tell him of the murderous Purification Commission, and in a trice he'll give us his demon disproof!"

They set both books aside and stiffened their tongues, that each might probe the other's mouth.

"You will find your new *Principia* an enchanting text," she said. "Proposition Fifty-seven: 'Two mutually attracting bodies describe similar figures about their common center of gravity.' Proposition Eighty-five: 'If a body be attracted by a second such entity, and its attraction be vastly stronger when 'tis contiguous—' "

"All I ask of Heaven, Madam, is to share with thee a common center of gravity."

"We share it, bonny Ben, now and forever."

"I am your lodestone, Mrs. Crompton. Your lodestone and your polestar all combined, my lovely lady, my sweetest Jennet, my brave Waequashim of the Nimacook."

CHAPTER

The

Eighth

*In Which Jennet
at Last Meets
the Avatar of Her Ambition,
Tho' with a Result
She Did Not Foresee*

To conceal the scandalous nature of their relationship, Ben suggested that whilst crossing the Atlantic and living in London they should represent themselves as a middle-aged mother and her philosophically inclined son, but Jennet found this a monumentally offensive idea. "If we adopted such a ruse," she declared, "I could ne'er again enter our love-bed without imagining myself Jocasta about to swive her Œdipus." Having no desire to complicate their carnal life with mythic incest, Ben withdrew his proposal, whereupon Jennet convinced him that she should instead pose as a prodigy-monger in search of new specimens, traveling with her younger half-brother. Thus it was that in the guise of siblings they booked passage on the brigantine *London-Hope*, scheduled to sail from Philadelphia on the fifth of November, 1724, and reach England by Christmas.

The first of the voyage's several disasters occurred when Jennet and Ben arrived on Vine Street Wharf only to learn that the berths they'd reserved in the great cabin had been appropriated by a Mr. Hamilton of Trenton and a Mr. Russell of Wilmington. The purser offered no apology, insisting that Mr. Franklin and his half-sister should have anticipated all along their displacement by "gentlemen of stature" (Hamilton being a New-Jersey barrister, Russell the master of a Maryland ironworks). And so it came to pass that Jennet and Ben spent the next seven weeks in steerage, sharing accommodations with two dozen other passengers and sleeping in hammocks whose sole pretension to privacy was a translucent linen curtain separating the sexes. Only by exploiting the *London-Hope*'s peripheral geography did the philosophers achieve connubial embrace. On one occasion they connected in the supply compartment atop a pile of sailcloth, another time in the cargo hold behind six hogsheads of sot-weed.

Even more troubling to Jennet than their wretched quarters was her unhappy stomach, which in the thirty-five years since her previous Atlantic crossing had grown sensitive to the sea's vicissitudes. For each day that she was up and about on the main deck, she had to spend two in her hammock, sipping medicinal tea from the private store of their shipboard acquaintance, Thomas Denham, an affable Quaker merchant who shared the great cabin with Hamilton and Russell. By the midpoint of the crossing her condition had improved somewhat, less in consequence of Denham's tea than of Ben's tenderness, for he was ever prepared to sooth her with kisses, mop her brow with cool water, and read to her from Mr. Defoe's romance of shipwreck and survival, *The Strange and Surprising Adventures of Robinson Crusoe.*

The third, final, and worst misadventure happened near the end of the voyage, when Ben entreated the ship's master, a sour old Jacobite named Bertram Annis, to let him examine the mail-pouches for the endorsements that Governor Keith had promised to place on board. Puffing discontentedly on his pipe, exuding smoke and irritation, Captain Annis led Ben and Jennet belowdecks to a tenebrous compartment as large as a wigwam, carpeted in canvas and jammed with more than a thousand pieces of mail. The subsequent search took nearly two hours, during which interval the philosophers turned up packets intended for bishops, solicitors, judges, physicians, tobacco merchants, stock-jobbers, and linen-drapers, but not a single letter addressed to a London printing-house.

"Mayhap I should gift Mr. Keith with a perfection-matrix," Ben said, "featuring a special new grid labeled Mindfulness."

Later that afternoon, as she and her gallant strolled about the quarter-deck in the company of Mr. Denham, Jennet mentioned that Ben's London prospects were now uncertain, a set of letters recommendatory from Sir William Keith having gone mysteriously astray. With no further prompting Denham proceeded to impugn the Governor's character, explaining that in all matters financial Keith was a notorious bluffer. A letter of credit from Sir William would be "a shabby and paradoxical thing," for the man had not a speck of credit to give.

Ben bore this setback stoically, announcing that he would seek a journeyman's position with a London firm and thereby master the newest British printing techniques. By pursuing this course, he argued, he might become so expert in his trade that ere long some "honest and principled edition of Keith" would set him up in business. Mr. Denham agreed that the scheme was worthy, adding that he would happily refer Ben to his friend Samuel Palmer, who ran a printing-house in Bartholomew's Close.

At this juncture Jennet made bold to ask whether perchance Mr. Denham's circle also included Isaac Newton.

"Nay, but I number amongst my associates a certain Henry Pemberton, who doth travel in the illustrious man's orbit," the Quaker replied. "If thou wish it, Mrs. Crompton, I shall acquaint thee with Dr. Pemberton upon our disembarkation."

"Such an introduction would greatly please me," she said, panting as her stomach protested the *London-Hope's* pitch and took exception to its roll, "for 'tis imperative I speak with Mr. Newton betimes."

"I cannot say he's favorably disposed toward receiving visitors, but at last report he was remarkably hale for a man of eighty-two," said Mr. Denham. "Newton's a knight now, not to mention President of the Royal Society and Master of the Mint, his Arian faith having deprived him of his professorship."

"From figuring comets to forging coppers—a considerable descent," Ben said.

"By my lights 'tis felicitous he came to the mint when he did," Denham said. "Had Sir Isaac not supervised the Great Recoinage of this century past, our nation might today be poor as Ireland."

This was the first Jennet had heard of Newton's having rescued England from bankruptcy, and she was delighted by her deduction that his prestige would now be at its zenith. If she could indeed persuade him to publicly excoriate the Conjuring Statute, that venerable abomination might very well go extinct ere the April rains came.

"I've ne'er been certain whether God favors my project or not," she said to Ben, "but at least the great Newton's about to land in our camp."

"In matters of creation and salvation, I've heard that God's the superior personage," he replied. "When it comes to making a purely rational argument, however, 'tis surely Sir Isaac you want as your champion."

ON THE MORNING of December the twenty-fourth, following a one-night stopover in Gravesend, a town so stupefyingly sterile in Jennet's view that even Salem-Village would have profited by comparison, Captain Annis piloted his brigantine up the Thames and put to port in London. As Jennet and Ben joined the parade of voyagers marching down the gangway, Mr. Denham proposed to meet his new friends that evening for a pint of ale and a bite of Christmas goose. Ben replied that as a vegetarian he would forgo the goose, but he and his sister would be glad of Mr. Denham's dinner-time companionship, and so they agreed to converge at eight o'clock on the Scribbler's Quill in Chiswell Street.

The search took all day, but Jennet and Ben at last secured lodgings in Adam's Row, Mayfair, for a mere five shillings a week. It seemed to her that their landlady, a Catholic widow who maintained seven cats on the premises, was skeptical of their claim to be half-siblings, and the woman's doubts were surely aggravated by the haste with which they scampered up the stairway. Had Mrs. Wilcox subsequently placed a curious ear to the bed-chamber door, her suspicions would have received scandalous corroboration through the sounds of exultant breathing intermixed with choruses of "Enlarge the overlap!" and "Turn on, turn on!"

In contrast to Sir William Keith, Thomas Denham proved a man of his word. When Jennet and Ben arrived at the Quill that night, Mr. Denham was already at the table, bearing a letter recommendatory for Ben and drinking ale with Henry Pemberton. As the evening's conversation progressed, it became clear that Pemberton, a loquacious and exuberant young physician whose rowly-powly form struck Jennet as but a parody of Ben's elegant stockiness, was indeed on friendly and even filial terms with Newton, having published in the *Philosophical Transactions* an article that *en passant* disproved certain Leibnizian principles concerning the force of descending bodies. (Apparently the surest way to beguile Newton was to make the late Gottfried Wilhelm Leibniz look doltish.) Alas, Pemberton was not sanguine concerning "Sir Isaac's willingness to speak with either a curator of dubious attainment or a printer of invisible reputation." Howbeit, he promised to "charm the old wizard" as best he could, and Jennet slept well that evening, confident that their petition lay in capable hands.

A fortnight went by, and then a month, with no word from Pemberton. For Jennet the days passed with an excruciating languor, as if the Earth lay fixed to an ancient orrery, its gears and wheels frozen by rust. To make matters worse, she could barely venture a yard beyond Mayfair without being reminded that demonology was still in flower and its votaries much afoot. Her first visit to Hyde Park climaxed with a noisy Puritan divine named Christopher Waller giving her the printed text of his newest anti-Satanist sermon. Later that week a Bow Street ragamuffin sold her a broadsheet narrating a witch-trial in Aberdeen. At Lemuel's Bookshop she obtained a pamphlet celebrating the Kirkcaldy Cleansing League as if it was a glamorous band of highwaymen. In a booth at the Hare and Hounds she came upon a discarded *London Journal* whose penultimate page related the Massachusetts Bay Purification Commission's campaign against a Braintree warlock. Each such encounter drained her energy as thoroughly as it sapped her spirit, and she would subsequently limp back to Adam's Row at the lethargic pace of a *machemoqussu*.

Exacerbating her discontent was the fact that Ben's employment at Palmer's Printing-House occupied him fourteen hours a day. Were they short on funds, she would not have begrudged him his absence from their rooms, but she'd brought along her savings. True, both the summer and autumn stipends from Tobias were overdue (a phenomenon that Mr. Horsfals, a prickly old Tory with a lisp, could not explain). The sum involved, however, was only sixty pounds, and meanwhile she and Ben had nearly eight hundred.

At length she gave voice to her frustration—"Our couplings come with less frequency than doth Dr. Halley's comet"—and Ben's answer caught her by surprise. Mr. Palmer, he explained, had set him an all-consuming challenge, designing and building a machine that by the stroke of a key would lift a leaden letter from the rack and plant it in a type-form.

"As you might imagine," he said, "such an ambitious project devours my time voraciously."

The argument was sensible, and so for many weeks she kept her annoyance in check, until one afternoon, hunting through Ben's wardrobe for a mirror (her own having shattered), she happened upon a stack of pamphlets headed "*Articles of Belief and Acts of Religion* by Benjamin Franklin, Printer and Natural Philosopher." Instinctively she formulated several denunciations in her mind, including "Am I not more valuable to you than this theologic folderol?" as well as "Hours for the Almighty but barely a minute for me!" But then she began reading *Articles of Belief and Acts of Religion*, forthwith finding herself in the presence of him whom she adored.

"Since I cannot possibly conceive of that which is Infinite," he'd written, "I must conclude that the Infinite Father expects from us neither Worship nor Praise, but rather that He is infinitely above such Displays." Who was this audacious thinker who presumed to know the mind of God whilst simultaneously sounding like the soul of modesty? Any woman who could claim the affections of so dauntless a youth was a fortunate person indeed. Jennet returned the treatise to its hiding place and resolved to practice the fourth virtue on Ben's perfection-matrix, Forbearance.

Gradually the shroud lifted from her psyche, and she came to see that her immediate circumstances were hardly lamentable. Her health was robust, after all, her mind clear, her senses keen, her purse bulging, and at her doorstep lay the city of her dreams, the London for which she'd once pined as passionately as had Dido for Æneas.

Whenever and wherever she alighted—theatre, ordinary, market, coffeehouse, concert hall, gillyflower garden—she inquired after Barnaby Cavendish, now seventy years old by her reckoning. A few Londoners recalled that bottled prodigies had been amongst the attractions at the Frost Fair of 1709 (the Thames having frozen solid for the first time since 1684, creating a natural promenade along which puppeteers, jugglers, magicians, troubadours, and crystal-gazers had installed their booths), but none could say whether the Cavendish Museum was still in business. Unless Dame Fortune had developed a sudden sympathy for runaway Nima-cooks of philosophic persuasion, Jennet decided, her chances of finding the mountebank would hover betwixt the minute and the minuscule.

True to her expectations, London excited her senses and aroused her intellect, but the place continually eluded her tongue. No metaphor was equal to the task. Was London a beehive, a buzzing nexus of freneticism and hubbub? Yes. Was it an immense Von Guericke sphere, forever spinning as it pulled bits and pieces of the outside world to its electric embrace? Indeed. Was it a roadside carcass, beset by vultures, encircled by flies, crawling with maggots, roiling with stenches? That too.

London was parks and monuments, bridges and churches, day-vendors and night-criers, bear baiting and coach racing—but for Jennet one fact eclipsed all others: this was the city of Marlowe, Jonson, and Shakespeare. She alternated her attendance betwixt two venues, the Lincoln's Inn Fields Playhouse in Chancery Street and the King's Theatre in Drury Lane. She disliked the newer works by Colley Cibber and Richard Steele, which were crudely absorbing at best, sentimental and moralistic at worst, but fortunately the great comedies of the Restoration enjoyed frequent revivals. During her first two months of theatre-going, she caught marvelous productions of Wycherley's ebullient *The Country Wife*, Congreve's deliriously epigrammatic *Love for Love*, Farquhar's wry and canny *The Beaux' Stratagem*, and, the most curious of the lot, Gay's *Three Hours After Marriage*, featuring a pompous philosopher, Dr. Fossile, evidently modeled on Newton.

On the night that Jennet beheld Rupert Quince play Mark Antony in Dryden's *All for Love*, she returned to Adam's Row to find Ben in an intricate mood, a mixture of apprehension, chagrin, and joy.

"I've been concealing a pertinent fact from you," he confessed. "Five weeks ago Dr. Pemberton came by Palmer's to say that Mr. Newton hath refused to meet with us."

An ingot of molten anger formed within Jennet's breast. "Why did you not tell me of this calamity?"

"I feared to break your heart."

"Then why do you break it *now?*"

"Events have taken a felicitous turn. It seems that, shortly after receiving the bad news, Pemberton presented Newton with a theologic treatise I'd composed to amuse myself during my luncheon intervals. Apparently Newton found my arguments astute, and the upshot is that he will have us to dinner come Friday."

"Oh, Ben, this is splendid news indeed. I should very like to see your treatise"—she felt the sarcasm rising within her, building toward eruption—"as I've been meaning to write such an essay myself."

"Really?"

"I would make the point that God, being infinite, expects from us neither worship nor praise."

" 'Sblood, Mrs. Crompton, you speculate precisely as I do!" He grew suddenly pensive. "Or did you perchance come upon the pamphlets I keep in my wardrobe?"

"I shan't tell you," she replied dryly.

"You must."

"When Newton first spurned us, you should've come to me."

"Quite so, Mrs. Crompton."

"Protect me from all the imps of Hell, bonny Ben. Protect me from George's dragon and Apollo's python. But you must ne'er again protect me from the truth."

Having spoken her mind, she felt her spleen diminish, and she stamped his cheek with a kiss. "Let me not strain on the gnat of your presumption whilst Parliament swallows the camel of Dunstan's preachment," she said. "If our luck holds firm, ere the month is out England's legislators will have lent their most sympathetic ears to Newton's demon disproof."

"Whereupon we shall appear before the Massachusetts Governor and cheerfully inform him that his licensed cleansers enjoy the same legal status as forgers, freebooters, and fastfannies."

"Am I to surmise you're prepared to sail home?" she asked.

He nodded and said, "Mr. Palmer and I agree that my device for setting type hath no commercial value. 'Tis an impressive beast to be sure, a-whirl with cogs and sprockets, but an unacceptable hiatus occurs 'twixt the stroking of a key and the slotting of a letter."

"A human could do't quicker?" she asked.

"Let me put it this wise. Were *The London Journal* to employ the Franklin Typesetter in announcing the pregnancy of King Louis's bride, the babe would be born, weaned, and riding to hounds ere the form was ready for inking."

ON THE FIRST MORNING in April Jennet took the day-coach north to Colchester and got out at the Fox and Fife, the Hill Street tavern before which, thirty-six years earlier, she'd said farewell to Barnaby Cavendish. She proceeded directly to Frere Street and thence to St. James's Church. Upon reaching the crumbling Roman wall, she vaulted onto the unhallowed ground and dropped reverently to her knees before the slate outcropping.

The epitaph had survived the intervening winters without deterioration, but a mesh of yellow vines now obscured the words. Even more troubling were the stick figures that a libertine draughtsman, as incompetent as Dunstan was skillful, had chalked below the inscription, five men and as many women engaged in several varieties of swiving.

"Dearest teacher, 'twould seem that Dame Fortune hath at long last joined our side," Jennet murmured. "Fool though I am, I have nevertheless sorted the false Newton from the true. Aye, my brave aunt, two days hence I break bread with him whose calculation will end the cleansing madness."

She scrambled back over the Roman wall, entered the church, and, unwinding her scarf, submerged it in the stagnant and slimy baptismal waters. Her tears dripped into the font like raindrops filling a cistern. Returning to the grave, she pressed the wet wool against the stone and rubbed the licentious drawings into oblivion. Now she tugged on the arrogant vines, but the earth would not surrender them, and so she trampled down the stalks with her boots till the epitaph became visible.

I measured the skies, now I measure the shadows. Sky-bound was the mind, earth-bound the body rests.

And what of the soul? she wondered as she headed back to the Fox and Fife. Was a tomb in sooth a portal to immortality, as so many clerics and theologians averred? She had no information on the subject, but it amused her to imagine that Aunt Isobel might yet exist on some ethereal plane. Perhaps she now kept company with Johannes Kepler, the two of them running an academy for recently deceased dunderheads who in their ignorance still credited the Ptolemaic universe. In her mind Jennet could see the whole scene, Dr. Kepler and Lady Mowbray presiding over a celestial classroom populated by cardinals and popes. This afternoon the instructors were requiring their pupils to set quill to parchment and write *Eppur si muove* one thousand times—for such was Galileo's legendary aside as, standing before the Inquisition, he'd returned astronomy to its biblical foundations, renouncing forever his allegiance to a revolving, rotating Earth.

Eppur si muove, Galileo had muttered. Still, it moves.

SHE REACHED LONDON near dusk, the collective chimney smoke combining with the incipient twilight to turn the fruit stalls and flower-carts of St. Giles Circle a uniform dun. Decoaching, she recalled that at eight o'clock the curtain would rise on the premier presentation of the Drury Lane Company's most recent revival, Mr. Congreve's *The Way of the World*. If she moved quickly, she wouldn't even miss the Prologue. She sprinted down Holborn High Street to Drury Lane, made a mad dash south, and arrived breathless on the steps of the King's Theatre, where she paused to rest her lungs and read a printed billboard affixed to a marble pilaster.

According to the advertisement, the part of Betty, the waiting-maid in *The Way of the World*, belonged to a certain Rachel Crompton.

Rachel Crompton?

Could it be? Was it possible? Rachel Crompton? The living child of her own blood, now fifteen, had left the East Indies and landed on the London stage?

She bought a ticket and received her broadsheet, which likewise announced that Rachel Crompton would play the waiting-maid, then rushed into the parquet. As always the great hall dazzled her, the two thousand tallow flames twinkling in their gilded chandeliers, the four tiers of balconies rising on all sides like cliffs facing a river gorge. She stumbled past the denizens of Row 23, their disapproval of her tardiness manifesting in frowns and snarls. Even before she could assume her seat, the chandeliers ascended into the shadows and Rupert Quince, painted and preening, appeared before the green velvet curtain to deliver the Prologue. The patrons' chatter receded from loud burbling to emphatic whispers to silence.

"Of those few fools who with ill stars are cursed," Mr. Quince began, "sure scribbling fools, called poets, fare the worst. For they're the sort of fools which Fortune makes, and after she has made 'em fools, forsakes."

The spectators offered snickers of appreciation. A tipsy oaf standing in the pit hurled a half-eaten apple onto the stage, but his associate oafs were quick to reprimand him, and the rest of the Prologue—more disingenuous self-deprecation from the playwright—unfolded without mishap.

Mr. Quince strode away. The curtain rose. Two young men, Mr. Mirabell and Mr. Fainall, sat at a small table in a chocolate-house, engaged in a hand of whist. An exchange of dialogue established that Mirabell, being distracted, had played badly, but he was willing to continue the game for his friend's amusement.

Fainall declined the proposition: "The coldness of a losing gamester lessens the pleasure of the winner. I'd no more play with a man that slighted his ill fortune than I'd make love to a woman who undervalued the loss of her reputation."

The spectators tittered approvingly, none more than the primitives in the pit.

Finding his chocolate-dish empty, Fainall slammed it on the table. In response to the angry clack a waiting-maid entered, whereupon Jennet's attention deserted Congreve's universe to focus entirely on the young woman portraying Betty.

God in Heaven, it was she! Her roundish face had lengthened over the years, assuming the oval of the Madonna in the Reverend Foster's illustrated Bible. Her complexion was still fair, but her hair had turned dark, and her frame displayed nubile proportions.

Throughout the whole of the first scene, Rachel had but one line. Mirabell asked, "Betty, what says your clock?" and Rachel replied, "Turned of the last canonical hour, sir." In Scene Two, Rachel's speeches were limited to "Yes, what's your business?" followed by "He's in the next room" after which came "Sir, the coach stays" and finally "They're gone, sir, in great anger."

As Act One drew to a close, Jennet studied her broadsheet. For Act Two, the scene would shift to St. James's Park. Acts Three, Four, and Five were confined entirely to Lady Wishfort's residence. To wit, Betty of the chocolate-house had evidently departed the story.

Braving her neighbors' sneers, she jostled her way down Row 23, then charged up the aisle and into the lobby. She lurched past a sign reading NO PATRONS BEYOND THIS POINT, descended a dark stair, and followed the corridor to a dressing-chamber apparently reserved for actresses assaying waiting-maids, scullery-wenches, fishwives, and similarly minor rôles. The room was a hall of mirrors, each framed in brass and flanked by hierarchies of burning candles. Rachel sat on a bench before the nearest such glass, rubbing the vermilion from her cheeks with a damp cloth, whilst in the shadows beyond three female players chattered amongst themselves and adjusted their coiffeurs.

"Good evening, Miss Crompton," Jennet said, pausing in the doorway.

Rachel started and glanced toward her visitor. "Do I know you, ma'am?"

"I'Christ, daughter, I'm the woman who gave you life."

"That's a poor topic for a joke."

"Some twenty years ago, I married your father, Tobias the Postmaster, changing my name from Stearne to Crompton."

Rachel winced but said nothing. She turned back to her mirror and continued to unpaint her cheeks, washing away the white grease as Jennet had earlier purged Isobel's monument of the vulgar sketches. "If you're the woman who gave me life, then you're also the woman who gave me grief, deserting me when I was but a child."

"We were separated by an abduction," Jennet said, taking two steps forward.

Rachel's mirror displayed a frown of bottomless suspicion. "Faugh, I'll warrant you're but an impostor, looking to snare the fortune you imagine I possess."

"If my oath's not enough to satisfy you, ask me a question only your natural mother could answer."

Having cleaned her cheeks, Rachel commenced to swab her brow. "A *test*, aye? Very well. In Philadelphia my father employed a maid-servant . . ."

"Her name was Nellie Adams."

The mirrored frown transmuted into gape-mouthed surprise. "My mother passed much of her youth in uncommon circumstances . . ."

"No doubt you allude to my years amongst the savage tawnies of Massachusetts Bay. Many were the times I entertained you with Indian lore. The Fable of the Wily Raven, the Parable of the Greedy Porcupine, the Adventure of the Tortoise—"

"The Tortoise Who Had No Shell," Rachel interrupted in a voice at once pained and amazed. Her reflected face declined from surprise to be-musement, and then came anger, followed by contempt. "An abduction, you call it. Mayhap that's the right word, but 'twould appear you took no particular trouble to find me once the deed was done. By my father's ac-count, you were always too vainglorious to abide mere motherhood."

"Forsaking you in favor of philosophy was the worst thing I e'er did. Not a day passes but I feel the shame of't."

"And not a day passes but I feel the sting of't."

Jennet shuddered and said, "Rachel, will you not look me in the eye?"

"If I wish to behold treachery's gaze, I need merely seek out Mr. Quince"—Rachel leaned into the mirror, filling it with her scowl—"who hath promised me the part of Mrs. Millamant the instant I yield my virtue to him."

A hard, hot Von Guericke sphere seemed to form in Jennet's stomach.

"Oh, my dear child, suffer me to deliver you from this scoundrel! You're too young to give your innocence to a rogue!"

"I'm also too young to play Mrs. Millamant. If 'twere otherwise, I would gladly swive my way to the top of the *Dramatis Personæ*." Rachel rose and turned one hundred degrees. Her scowl, unmediated now, was even fiercer than its reflection.

Jennet brushed her daughter's arm. "Tell me your adventures, child. I want to know 'em all."

Rachel flinched but did not pull away. " 'Tis truly my own wayward mother?"

"Truly."

"I must admit that London hath no surplus of sympathetic listeners."

"You shall enjoy my rapt attention for as long as you wish."

The melodrama that Rachel proceeded to relate began in sunlight, descended into darkness, and ended on a gray, ambiguous dawn. With undiluted delectation she recounted her first four years in India, a cavalcade of jewels, elephants, monkeys, flowers, mimosa trees, and more gods than the sky could hold. Her governess treated her with great kindness, and Rachel soon decided that Mlle. Peltier was fully the equivalent of a real mother. Alas, her father rarely stayed in Madraspatam, for a man could not function as East-Indies Postmaster-General without traveling continually amongst the settlements, but he always returned home bearing fragrant ointments and ravishing fabrics.

Rachel's misery began when Mlle. Peltier accepted her employer's proposal of marriage. Although Rachel was initially pleased by the arrangement, in time a melancholia came to possess Tobias's new wife, making her as vindictive in the rôle of stepmother as she'd been loving when employed as a tutor. Claudette Peltier Crompton took to feeding Rachel indifferently, reprimanding her constantly, and beating her regularly.

Just when it seemed that Rachel's ill-fortune could not increase, the fiery summer of 1722 blazed across Asia, bringing a typhus epidemic to rival the previous century's bubonic plagues. The contagion carried off not only Rachel's favorite priest at the Anglican school but also the elderly Hindoo neighbor-woman who'd given her a mongoose, and then, finally, her own dear father.

Much to Jennet's chagrin, the news of Tobias's passing sparked within her not a spasm of remorse but a spate of deduction. His death explained why her last two stipends had failed to arrive.

"He was a person of decency and generosity," Jennet said.

"He was a fool, but I loved him," Rachel said, sidling back to her mirror. "So now there was nothing to keep me in India. My nine-month journey to England taught me much about the wickedness of the world, and 'twas only through God's grace I arrived still in possession of my wits, my honor, and my dreams of a life on the stage. Until an hour ago, I'd ne'er acted before a London audience, and I must own 'twas a thrill much greater than the instant cure for orphanhood you've presumed to bring me."

"This talent for playing's in your blood, child. When next we meet, I'll tell you how I once portrayed a demon's ward, but now you must know of the route by which I've landed in your dressing-chamber."

"I fear your escapades hold little interest for me."

"Methinks you'll find 'em as enthralling as the Parable of the Greedy Porcupine."

As Rachel changed her clothing, trading the waiting-maid's tattered muslin dress for a taffeta gown with puffed sleeves, Jennet unspooled her narrative, from the challenge laid upon her by Isobel—to her two failed attempts at a demon disproof—to her love affair with a Pennsylvania printer—to her imminent collaboration with Sir Isaac Newton.

" 'Steeth, Mrs. Crompton," Rachel said when Jennet was finished, " 'twould seem we share some several pints of blood but not one drop of sensibility. I've ne'er had the slightest taste for philosophic conjecture or Philadelphia journeymen."

"I beg you, withhold your judgment. I believe we're destined to become good friends."

"Not with me living in London and you chasing after your inky-fingered swain."

"I'll allow you're a competent actress, but 'tis a profession hath debauched many a girl as well-bred as you," Jennet said. "Hear my plea. Auspicious prospects lie before my Mr. Franklin. Accompany us to the New World, and we shall all make a happy life together."

"Pish, Mrs. Crompton. If a man's star is not risen by his middle years, 'tis probably stuck fore'er on the horizon."

"Ah, but you see, my Ben is not yet thirty."

Rachel flung a woolen shawl around her bodice and headed toward the doorway. "He's twenty-nine then? Twenty-eight? Impressive, but I'd still not lay a farthing on his future. How old is the man exactly?"

"Nineteen."

"What?"

"Nineteen. Twenty come January."

"*Nineteen? Nineteen?* And *you* durst lecture *me* on debauchery?"

"I durst not lecture you on anything at all. I merely ask that you sail with us to America after I've brought Newton's proof before Parliament."

"Your proposition's most unappetizing. I'll wager there's not a single worthy troupe in the whole of Pennsylvania."

"Then you must found one, dear Rachel."

Against Jennet's expectations, this last remark seemed to catch her daughter unawares. Rachel sighed harshly and, pursing her lips, leaned against the jamb. "Come back this Saturday night, and I shall give you my answer." Straightening, she marched into the corridor. "But now I must bid you *adieu,* for I'm off to watch a cockfight with my Gaston. By your example he should be a babe in arms"—her voice rose as the shadows consumed her—"but in sooth my gallant wears a beard!"

❦

FOR REASONS THAT Sir Isaac Newton had yet to fathom, his revelations from On High always occurred at noon. Shortly after the sun arrived overhead on the eleventh day in April of 1676, the key to the Book of Daniel had blazed through his brain. The same solar circumstances had attended his derivation in 1665 of the binomial theorem, his sudden apprehension in 1668 of a method for determining the area under a curve, and his Heaven-sent discovery in 1673 that the floor-plan of Solomon's Temple, as documented by the prophet Ezekiel, forecast the future history of the world.

Today's epiphany was no different. As the noon hour came to Kensington, Newton realized that the Problem of Problems—by what means did gravity exert its pull throughout the universe?—was within his reach. He had merely to sit chairbound on his porch and think about it.

Newton loathed his wheelchair, that hideous hooded chariot to which the physicians had condemned him, but he loathed the physicians even more. Although he admittedly didn't know how to cure his slack sphincter or recurrent kidney stones, it was obvious that England's doctors didn't either. Clearly the confounded chair didn't help. Indeed, by his own observations he was more likely to void a stone—they normally passed with little pain, praise Heaven—following a vigorous turn about his garden than after yet another interval in the wretched chair. If he attempted such a stroll now, of course, this would only provoke a wearying altercation with his day nurse, but the instant Mr. Asnault left for home, Newton would liberate himself. The best way to keep your legs was to use them.

He swallowed a mouthful of warm coffee, repositioned his rump, and opened his heart to his mentor, God.

In replacing Cartesian vortices with universal gravitation so many years earlier, Newton had invited on himself the accusation of occultism, and his enemies still made it routinely. But now he saw a way out. He would postulate an all-pervasive æther: not Descartes's æther, certainly, not that ridiculous invisible-yet-physical plasma, but a divine immaterial medium dancing at the edges of the human sensorium. A difficult concept, palpable incorporeality, perhaps even paradoxical, though to the Messiah of Mechanics it partook no less of reasoned discourse than did the Pythagorean theorem.

He rang the brass bell thrice, thereby signaling Moncriff to bring pen, paper, ink pot, and writing-board. The servant appeared promptly. Speaking not a word, for none dared break the silence whilst Sir Isaac was thinking, Moncriff set the equipment on his master's lap and departed.

The sheets came in colors: green for fancies, pink for notions, yellow for hypotheses, blue for truths. Newton selected a blue sheet, dipped quill into ink, and wrote:

$$MAN = \textit{Visible Material Body}$$
$$CHRIST = \textit{Apprehensible Immaterial Body}$$
$$GOD = \textit{Inapprehensible Incorporeality}$$

Aye! He'd caught the scent! Midway betwixt the unknowable essence of the Almighty and the familiar fleshiness of humans lay that unique substance called Jesus Christ. In fashioning the Redeemer as He'd done, God had collaterally provided the universe with the very stuff through which action-at-a-distance might operate, objects influencing one another in eternal obeisance to the inverse-square law. Yea, verily! Occultism conquered forever! The æther that made the world go round was in truth the divinely created Body of Christ, a situation that the egregious Roman Church, with its determination to chain the Savior to a mathematically nonsensical triad, would never grasp in an æon. The Holy Trinity—pshaw! The Deity $= 3 = 1 = 3$—rubbish! Even the lowliest sub-sizar at Cambridge would never proffer so blighted an arithmetic.

At the bottom of the blue sheet he wrote *Gravitational Medium = Æther Christi,* then set his quill on the writing-board, slumped down in his wheelchair, and closed his eyes. The sun beat against his lids, brightening his blood and filling his field of vision with a vast red sea.

He awoke at dusk. No bird sang. No breeze stirred. The day-nurse would be gone now—hurrah: for the immediate future he could employ his body as he pleased. He blinked, staring at his writing-board. *Æther Christi.* Nay, he hadn't dreamt it. Before falling asleep, he'd flushed the gravitational medium from hiding.

Now, he would have to allow that this triumph traced partially to the tract he'd received two weeks earlier. Amongst the merits of Benjamin Franklin's *Articles of Belief and Acts of Religion* was the idea that "the Infinite hath created many Beings or Gods, vastly superior to Man, who can better conceive his Perfection than we, and return to him a more rational and glorious Praise." Was it possible that, without Franklin's postulate of immortal intermediaries, Newton would never have fallen upon the notion of Christ's corpus as gravity's cause? He hesitated to say. One thing was certain: when Franklin came to dinner that evening, the *Æther Christi* would not be amongst the topics they discussed. For all he knew, the young Philadelphian was a budding Wilhelm Leibniz, eager to seize credit for discoveries he hadn't made.

Leibniz—faugh! The scoundrel had been gratifyingly dead these past nine years, and still Newton could not think on him without enduring a trembling rage. By what monumental vanity, what Olympian arrogance, had the old pretender imagined he'd devised the fluxions independently of Newton? True, Leibniz's method of indicating maxima and minima could claim a certain originality, and he'd given his plagiarisms the novel name of *calculus,* but everyone knew the blackguard had maintained a band of roving sycophants, and these knaves had doubtless revealed to their master something of the new geometry brewing at Cambridge.

There could be only one Prince of Principles in the world—why had Leibniz refused to see that? God did not traffic in redundancy—could any truth be more self-evident?

Of course, when a man was selected by Providence to unveil the universe's deepest mysteries, it behooved him to keep his appointment in perspective. It was one thing to be God's viceroy and quite another to be an outright deity. Rejecting any overtures from his followers that smacked of worship, eschewing adulation at every turn, Newton had rarely regarded himself as anything more than a demiurge. Indeed, throughout his twenty-five years as Master of the Mint and his five as Warder before that, he'd always acted judiciously when exercising his powers over life and death. Yes, in most cases he'd declined to spare a clipper or a counterfeiter the noose, for left to their own devices such fiends would have bankrupted England during the Great Recoinage, and even today they were a festering pustule on the face of the monetary system. But occasionally he showed mercy, especially when the knave in question engaged in an authentic variety of groveling.

He sipped cold coffee, purged Leibniz from his brain, and returned to his meditations. Chief amongst the properties of the *Æther Christi*, he now saw, was its probable participation in the microworld as well as the macro. *Micro and Macro*, he wrote on a yellow sheet—yellow for hypotheses. *Atoms and Stars*, he added. But before he could wrestle with the ramifications, Gunny Slocum, his chief informant from the Fleet, came dashing up the carriageway at the velocity of a man whose breeches were on fire.

"Hallo, Sir Isaac! Billy Slipfinger lies feverish in his hovel, and he wishes to tell us all about the Calibans! I directed his widow-to-be to scribble down his babblings, as he's apt to pop off at any minute!"

Newton's heart seemed suddenly to shoot from his body, and only after he'd vacated the wheelchair did the organ return to its customary location behind his sternum. "Well done, sir!" He rang the brass bell four times, thereby instructing Moncriff to appear posthaste. "What does Mr. Slipfinger expect in return?"

"Thirty quid, that his Lucy might become a hag o' means!" Slocum shouted.

" 'Sblood, I'll pay it!" He would gladly hand over twice that amount for the facts Slipfinger presumably possessed, the names and whereabouts of every felon who ran with the Caliban Adepts, the largest gang of counterfeiters still operating in London.

Moncriff, panting and discombobulated, materialized on the porch.

"Fetch my money cudgel," Newton said, setting the writing-board aside, "then fill my purse and tell Padding to hitch up the horses, for we must be in the Fleet by dark!"

"But tonight you dine with Mr. Franklin and his sister."

"Hang Mr. Franklin! Hang his sister! We ride to the Liberties!"

As Moncriff rushed back into the mansion, Newton gazed longingly at the yellow sheet. *Micro and Macro. Atoms and Stars.* Revealing the secret stuff that held the universe together was important, but saving the British economy mattered too. With any luck, he would be back amongst these speculations by dawn, completing them within the week. If his instincts were correct, the *Æther Christi* would ultimately rank with his greatest discoveries. Before the decade was out, natural philosophers would come to prize this glorious glue most highly—more highly even than a geometer cherished his Euclid, an engineer his fluxions, or an alchemist his great transmuter, that wondrous element called

Mercury
was the problem.
Venus, Mars, Jupiter, Saturn—
from the birth of the solar system onward,
these compliant planets had followed their predictable grooves, scrupulously obeying the laws given essence by Kepler and exactitude by Newton. But Mercury had a mind of its own. At the completion of each orbit, it did not return to the same starting point. My father knew this. So did his contemporaries. But since Mercury was close to the sun and therefore difficult to view, everyone agreed to attribute the discrepancy to observational error.

Over the years the measurements grew more precise, and the alibi ceased to satisfy. By the time a bright young patent clerk named Albert Einstein was on the scene, astronomers understood that Mercury's perihelion, its point of closest approach to the sun, was advancing 574 seconds of arc every century. After factoring in the perturbing gravity of the known planets, a physicist could make my father's mechanics account for 531 of those seconds, but that still left 43 seconds in the shadowland.

Einstein wasn't fazed. Truth to tell, he *loved* those 43 extra seconds of perihelion shift, for he knew in his heart they would succumb to his idiosyncratic notions of curved space and warped time. He set about his project, and—lo and behold—his equations not only accounted for Mercury's contrariness, they maintained the same form in every frame of reference he could imagine.

For with Einstein, you see, context was all. When Isobel Mowbray bid my dear Jennet experiment with Galileo's principle of uniform acceleration—assuming no air resistance, a cannonball and a codfish dropped in tandem will hit the ground simultaneously—neither tutor nor pupil fully appreciated the utter strangeness of that phenomenon. But Einstein did. One day in 1907, sitting in the Swiss Patent Office, he realized that if the falling codfish focused its attention exclusively on the descending cannonball, it would never know it was moving within a gravitational field. Until the instant of impact, in fact, the fish would have every right to insist it was at rest!

Einstein later called this "the happiest thought of my life."

From the moment he rationalized Mercury's perihelion shift, the world's cannier scientists understood that Einstein's physics was destined to turn the Newtonian universe inside-out and upside-down. As early as 1905, Einstein had intuited that no object capable of assuming a resting state could travel faster than the vacuum speed of light. Besides liberating Maxwell's electrodynamics from the æther frame, Einstein's hypothesis of a light-speed barrier (the *sine qua non* of special relativity, but that's another story) gave him leave to discard my father's troublesome appeals to absolute time and absolute space (troublesome to Newton himself as well as to his rivals). By combining these insights with the narrative of the falling fish, Einstein gave the world his great construct of 1915, general relativity—a brave new geometry of local curvatures produced by the presence of mass in the universe: planets, stars, Mount Everest, African elephants, Sumo wrestlers, kitchen sinks. Under a general relativity regime, gravity was no longer an inexplicable "force" mysteriously causing "action at a distance." Instead of heeding some occult attraction, a given planet simply pursued the straightest possible course that the context allowed: a geodesic path in space-time.

When I first heard the popular notion that my father's system is really just an "idiosyncratic case" of Einstein's universe, my reaction was instinctively defensive. "That's like saying the *Nike of Samothrace* is an idiosyncratic case of metamorphic rock," I told Kepler's *Harmonice Mundi*. But over the years I've mellowed. For one thing, Einstein's theories are evidently true. (Yes, occasionally a physicist with time on his hands will ostensibly coax a light pulse past the 186,000 mps barrier, so that the damn thing seems to arrive before it departs, but smart money still says special relativity has a future.) For another thing, if I'm an "idiosyncratic case," I'm an idiosyncratic case that matters. In many a nontrivial circumstance, Newtonian physics still rules. The lunar mechanics that grace my second edition informed the heart and soul of every computer program employed by NASA during the Apollo era. If you were supervising the epochal moon landing of 1969, you needed no technical manual at your fingertips besides the *Principia Mathematica*.

So I'm not bitter anymore. Okay, sure, everybody has warm fuzzy feelings about Einstein, whereas my father is commonly perceived as a frigid fanatic in a silly wig. But one day the world will notice that while $E = mc^2$ ultimately gives you 177,000 dead Japanese civilians, $F = ma$ lets you skate across a frozen lake on a winter's night, the wind caressing your face as you glide toward the hot-chocolate stand on the far shore.

A few years after the rise of relativity my ego received a second blow. The deeper physicists peered beneath the surface of things, the clearer it became that my vaunted determinism did not apply at the subatomic level. Predicting the behavior of elementary particles required a different mechanics, keyed to probability rather than causality. This sorry state of affairs culminated in 1927 with Werner Heisenberg's famous Uncertainty Principle, which states that you cannot simultaneously know the position and the momentum of a given particle. Let me hasten to add that Heisenbergian indeterminacy traces largely to the fact that subatomic position and momentum are conjugate attributes. Only in the popular misconception does the imprecision arise from disturbances inherent in the act of measurement.

Call me a traditionalist, but I don't really care for quantum physics. The Double-Slit Problem, whereby a single electron flies through two adjacent apertures in one trip, creeps me out. I'm equally unhappy about the Schrödinger's Cat Paradox, with its requirement that the poor animal be alive and dead at the same time. How weird is that? True, thanks to all those exquisite quantum equations, you humans now have television (though in my opinion the whole thing went downhill after *The Avengers*), mobile phones (enabling you to walk through a field of stunningly gorgeous wildflowers without actually being there), and personal computers (hour after hour you stare at the screen, a life of cybernetic desperation). But the calculus lets you put a man on the moon! With fluxions at your command, you can build the Golden Gate Bridge!

Leibniz was correct, by the way: he *did* invent the infinitesimal calculus entirely on his own. But my father would hear none of it. At the height of their forty-year feud over the paternity of fluxions, he appointed a bogus committee to resolve the dispute "objectively." The group's report, the *Commercium Epistolicum*, was rigged from the start, and the Leibniz camp was right to scorn it. In the years that followed, both geometers hurled cadres of disciples into the fray, until eventually a schism opened in European intellectual life. Generation after generation, much to the detriment of their science, chauvinistic English mathematicians refused to employ Leibniz's superior system for noting integrals and differentials, which meanwhile swept the Continent owing to its lucidity and elegance.

For all this, I remain in awe of my father. He never stops surprising me. Centuries before anybody heard of Einstein, he dreamed the dream of unification, imagining that one day the same set of equations might encompass everything from the majestic sweep of a comet to the inner life of an atom. To be sure, his last-ditch attempt to combine the macro-world with the micro via the *Æther Christi* was screwy, but his earlier ruminations on the problem boasted sophistication and foresight. "It is very well known that greater bodies act mutually upon each other by those forces, and I do not easily see why lesser bodies should not act on one another by similar forces," he wrote in the unpublished "Conclusio" to my second edition.

Contemporary physicists speak of a GUT, a Grand Unified Theory. They seek a TOE, a Theory of Everything. And I suspect that one day, through some felicitous convergence of experiment and serendipity,

quarreling and collaboration, they'll get one. And when they do, I hope
they'll remember that the quest began not with Einstein or Heisenberg, not with Max Planck or Enrico Fermi, not with Niels
Bohr or John Wheeler or Stephen
Hawking, but with
the great Sir
Isaac

✺

Newton
did not precisely
resemble the engraving that
graced the English-language edition
of the *Principia Mathematica:* such was Jennet's
impression when, thirty-five years after her failed mission to
Trinity College, she finally stood before the octogenarian geometer in his
carriage-house, where he was supervising a servant's frantic efforts to
hitch two horses to a coach. The lines of Newton's craggy face seemed
deeper than in his portrait, and his cheeks had grown puffier. But this
was undoubtedly he. There was no mistaking that hooked nose and
rounded chin, those sharp obsidian eyes.

"Mr. Franklin, I found your theologic treatise most stimulating,"
Newton said, wrapping his veiny hands around Ben's outstretched palm.
"True, it wanders into a kind of polytheism on occasion, but such was
not your intention."

"Actually it was," Ben said.

"Methinks you exaggerate, dearest brother," Jennet hastened to add.

Newton acknowledged Jennet with a dark scowl, but he addressed
her in a mellifluous tone. "Should I e'er find myself in the American
provinces, I shall be pleased to visit your prodigy museum."

"I must tell you that my philosophic interests extend even to your
fluxions," she said. "Just as Dædalus formed his son's arms into wings,
so have you gifted Euclid with the power of flight."

Newton glowered again and said, "As I recall the story, Dædalus's experiment ended disastrously."

"My metaphor was ill-chosen," she said, wincing internally.

"Most metaphors are. If you would be a natural philosopher, Mrs. Crompton, stick with mathematics, where everything is only like itself."

Having affixed the tack to the horses, the beleaguered servant, a fat and beetle-browed man called Padding, announced that the coach stood ready for Newton's trip to the city.

"I beg your pardon, Sir Isaac," Ben said, "but 'twas my understanding we'd be dining at your estate."

"We'll not be dining anywhere, young Franklin, as I have urgent business in the Fleet."

A second servant, cadaverous as Padding was corpulent, appeared holding a willow basket and a gnarled blackthorn shillelagh. "Your money cudgel, sir," he said, handing the weapon to Newton as a chancellor might present a ceremonial sword to his king.

"Forgive me, Sir Isaac," Jennet said, "but we simply *must* speak with you tonight."

"Sorry, Mrs. Crompton. Duty calls."

"Prithee, take us along on your journey. My brother and I crossed the entire Atlantic Sea that we might interview *le Grand Newton*."

The geometer frowned and scratched his head, skewing his periwig and exposing his left ear to the predations of a mosquito. He caught the creature in his palm and, rubbing his hands together, mashed it into nothingness. "Climb aboard if you insist." He retrieved the willow basket from his servant, looping his arm through the handle. "But hear my warning—we'll be moving amongst coiners and clippers tonight. You could be murdered."

"We could also be murdered if we run afoul of a cutpurse whilst walking back to Mayfair," she said.

"Perhaps Sir Isaac will entertain us *tomorrow* night," Ben suggested.

Not if he's on the point of being killed by counterfeiters, she thought. "Nonsense, brother—we shan't be so boorish as to spurn this invitation." Turning toward Newton, she caressed the sleeve of his red woolen topcoat. "I have oft-times noted your exploits as Master of the Mint." She relieved him of the basket and hoisted herself into the coach. "Had you not become the world's most accomplished philoso-pher"—she placed the basket on the floor—"you would have made a formidable general."

"Modesty requires that I ignore your opinion," Newton said, reposi-tioning his periwig, "though honesty forbids me to contradict it."

Ben, sighing, clambered up beside Jennet. Newton settled into the seat opposite, flourishing his shillelagh with the oblivious bravado of Henry VIII wielding his marble scepter above the main gate at Trinity. Soon a fourth party joined them, a ruffian named Gunny Slocum, glee-fully explaining that he was Newton's informant and bodyguard. The knave exuded the fragrance of gin and an aura of skullduggery, but Jen-net took comfort in the brace of silver pistols protruding from his belt.

"Dearest sister, I wish I knew what species of peril we're about to en-dure," Ben said under his breath.

"Darling brother, so do I," she replied.

Padding closed the coach door, received Newton's instructions to de-part posthaste, then rushed off to command the team. As the vehicle sped away, Jennet brushed her host's trembling knee and spoke. "Many years ago you wrote a letter to my late aunt, Isobel Mowbray, mistress of Mirringate Hall in Ipswich. You claimed that you'd disproved the demon hypothesis."

"Demons?" Newton said, bristling with pique and indignation. "*Demons?* To talk of *demons* is to enter the domain of that hoodwinker Descartes."

"My aunt came to imagine that your disproof sprang from Aristotle's immutables, though I realize they've been supplanted by a more modern chemistry."

"Instead of dubious Frenchmen and dead Greeks, let us discuss God instead. Would you not agree that the Trinity is a nonsensical concept? Three equals one equals three—pish!"

"The formula lacks coherence," Ben said, nodding.

"I would sooner import my ale from Amsterdam than my theology from Rome," Newton said.

"We were speaking of a letter," Jennet said.

"*You* were speaking of a letter," Newton said.

"Do you remember your correspondence with my aunt?" Jennet asked. "You told her that sorcery lies all in the mind."

Newton screwed his features into the quintessence of contempt. "Speak not to me of sorcery, Mrs. Crompton! An obscure but vindictive philosopher once sought to soil my reputation by impersonating me at a Colchester witch-trial. I spent five hundred pounds to publish a pamphlet exposing his hoax—and revealing his other moral lapses in the bargain."

The coach rolled down Kensington Road and skirted the edge of Hyde Park, its verdant acreage walled by rectilinear hedges and ornamental shrubs, an interval during which Jennet decided to remain silent concerning Colchester, lest she accidentally reveal that Hooke had come to those very assizes at her request. Instead she merely said, " 'Tis my ambition to approach Parliament with a potent argument against the Conjuring Statute of James the First. If you can demonstrate that wicked spirits don't exist, prithee make your calculation public, for 't might save many a blameless soul."

"Tell me, Mrs. Crompton, do you not think it presumptuous to brand one soul blameless and another sinful?" Newton plucked a small leatherbound Bible from his topcoat. "Scripture holds us all congenitally corrupt. 'Tis only by his Savior's mercy that any man avoids damnation."

"In my life I've cast a considerable quantity of first stones," she said, nodding. "But not nearly so many as the ghastly prickers."

"I grasp your biblical allusion, though in my view 'tis more fruitful to plumb Scripture for prophecy than for parable. After reading the great mystic Joseph Mede, I derived a method most helpful to the endeavor."

" 'Tis your *witch* calculation that interests me," Jennet said.

"My *what* calculation?"

"Witch."

"Which calculation, that's what I'm asking you."

"No, *witch. W-i-t-c-h.*"

"I see orthography's not your *forte*, Mrs. Crompton," Newton said. "But the topic is prophecy. Mr. Franklin, have you perchance heard of Mr. Mede?"

"Did the gentleman not argue that when the Bible speaks of *days*, we must interpret it as *years?*" Ben said.

"Quite so." Newton accorded Ben a nod of respect. "However, being ignorant of calendrical matters, Mede failed to bring precision to his instincts, and so I finished the job. According to the Newton-Mede formula, three hundred and fifty-four secular days, plus six equally profane hours, constitute a single biblical year."

Within Jennet's body two knots formed simultaneously, one jamming her throat, the other clogging her guts. Why was Newton so deaf to her petition? Had she once again happened upon an impersonator?

Newton turned to his bodyguard and said, "Sir, I am famished for fair."

From the willow basket Slocum produced a small white tablecloth, draping it over his knees. Next he lifted out an enormous pie dripping with various fats and bursting with chunks of broiled beef and braised lamb. He set the pie on his lap as he might a beloved child.

" 'Tis a veritable feast," Ben said, "though you needn't serve me a piece, as I am of the vegetarian persuasion." He pulled a large green pippin from his waistcoat. "I shall satisfy my appetite thus."

"Thou art exceeding strange, young Franklin," Newton said.

"Did I just hear the peacock call the parrot a fop?" Slocum said.

"Mr. Slocum, you press the bounds of familiarity," Newton said.

The ruffian grinned and reached toward his belt, drawing out a knife as large and glistery as a Merrimack River trout. "Sir Isaac, you're the geometer in our company, but I'll warrant I can trifurcate our meal without resort to protractor and calipers."

"Have at it," Newton said.

After stabbing the center of the pie, Slocum slashed it into three unequal servings. He delivered one portion to Newton and another to Jennet, retaining the largest for himself, then extracted from the basket a dark brown flagon of ale stoppered with a cork and bearing a handprinted label reading *Forthergill's Ordinary*.

Jennet forced herself to take a bite of pie. As the coach started along Piccadilly Street, she again addressed Newton. "Back in America my deluded brother, the Witchfinder-Royal, practices his trade even as we speak. I beseech you to go before the House of Lords and villify the Conjuring Statute."

Newton ate lustily, speaking not a word. "Oft-times I envy the witchfinders," he said at last. "They have their swimming-ropes, their pricking needles, their Paracelsus tridents, but to snare a clipper God gives you no tool save the shrewdness in your skull."

Slocum uncorked the ale. "We've trapped many a rat in our day, ain't we, Sir Isaac?"

"I think especially of the notorious William Chaloner," Newton said, fixing his inky eyes on Ben. "I instructed a gangrel dog in the olfactory qualities of the debased metals used by guinea forgers, and thus did that excellent hound and I sniff our way to the blackguard's lair." He licked his fingers one by one. "On the eve of his appointment with the hangman, Chaloner sent me a letter begging for his life. I wrote back and said, 'Alas, I must reject your plea, sir, for in Hell they've much need of your coining talents, as their currency's fore'er bursting into flames.'"

Slocum guffawed spontaneously, Ben let out a politic laugh, and Jennet made not a sound.

"And what a marvelous execution!" Slocum decanted a pint of ale directly into his stomach. "They strung him up on Tyburn Tree, then brought him down gagging, hacked him open, and unraveled his bowels before the mob."

For several minutes the coach hurtled along Shaftesbury Avenue, and then Padding turned his team eastward onto Holborn High Street. Whilst Jennet and Ben exchanged glances of exasperation, their host explained how to employ his system in fathoming the ambiguities of the Apocalypse, the conundrums of Jeremiah, and the auguries of Daniel.

"Daniel tells us that the Antichrist will reign for 1,290 days, that is—per the Newton-Meade formula—1,194 years," Newton noted. "Since Popery reached its apex in Anno Domini 609, we can say with certainty that the Hebrew tribes will reclaim Israel in 1803."

Jennet felt like the Turtle Who Had No Shell, vulnerable in the extreme, moving naked through a country choked with brambles and thick with burrs. How naïve of her to imagine that the Newton of 1725 would be the Newton of 1688. The Jennet Stearne of 1725 certainly wasn't the Jennet Stearne of 1688. The geometer had probably never seen his aunt burned alive or watched his daughter die of the pox, but he'd doubtless been knocked about by Dame Fortune all the same. Such was the way of the world.

"A similar deduction gives us forty-nine years elapsing betwixt the Jewish repatriation and the Parousia," Newton said. "Ergo, we should all mark down the Second Coming for 1948!"

"I wish I could be there," Slocum said.

"Read your Bible, say your prayers, steer clear of Popery, and you *will* be there, Mr. Slocum. I swear to God you will."

❧

EVENING BROUGHT A REDUNDANT DARKNESS to London, for the city was already mantled in fog, drizzle, and the smoke of ten thousand chimney-pots. Padding halted the coach at the place where Holborn High Street narrowed to become a stone bridge over the River Fleet, the notorious open sewer that ran from Hampstead down to Black-friars before emptying its swill into the Thames. Stepping into the night air, Jennet inhaled the impacted stench, then joined Ben, Newton, and Slocum as they descended a marble stairway and started along the west bank of the river. A true witch's brew, she decided, aboil with eye of newt and toe of frog and fillet of fenny snake. On their left rose the battlements of Fleet Prison—destroyed in the Great Fire, Newton explained, then rebuilt at twice the size, "London being now twice as wicked a town as before." All around them lay the Liberties, the geometer continued, those cramped but not inhospitable environs beyond the prison walls where the better sort of criminal—the panderer, the suborner, the usurer, the rakehell—was permitted to reside unmolested, "provided he compensates his would-be gaolers for the effort they expend in leaving him alone."

At the Fleet Street intersection they came upon a half-dozen whores, drinking gin and trading jests preparatory to a long night of splinting doodles in Covent Garden and Lincoln's Inn Fields. Slocum jerked a pistol from his belt. The trollops dispersed like a flock of guinea hens apprehending a fox within its midst.

" 'Twas recently my pleasure to read the English translation of your *Principia Mathematica*," Ben said, drawing abreast of Newton. "Might I say that universal gravitation is mayhap the single most beautiful idea a person hath e'er thought?"

"I know not what I may appear to the world," Newton replied, "but to myself I seem to be only like a boy playing on the seashore"—a poetic dreaminess entered his voice, audible even above the clank and clamor of the Liberties—"and diverting myself in now and then finding a smoother pebble or a prettier shell than ordinary, whilst the great ocean of truth lies undiscovered all before me."

" 'Tis bracing to observe such humility in so famous a man as yourself," Ben said.

"Hooke found only common shells," Newton said. "Leibniz couldn't tell pretty shells from pigeon shit. Flamsteed didn't even get to the beach."

The party proceeded west along Fleet Street, easily the most pestilential promenade in Jennet's experience. The air reeked of distilled spirits, decaying cabbages, rotten fish, and human waste. Rats scurried along the cobblestones as blithely as hares capered through Marylebone Park. But the most shocking phenomenon to reach her senses was Newton's face. His countenance was a portrait of unmitigated glee. Evidently he'd as soon catch a coiner as solve a differential equation.

"Permit me to offer a theory concerning electricity," Ben said to Newton. "I believe that the spark one conjures with a Von Guericke sphere partakes of the same substance as a lightning-stroke. Each resembles the other not only in giving off light, but also in its swift motion, crackling sound, crooked path, and affinity with metals. What think you, Sir Isaac?"

"If 'tis unification beguiles you, young Franklin, you should know that my forthcoming book will explicate the very paste that binds together the world's invisible particles. 'Twill be more momentous even than my *Principia*, more illuminating than my *Opticks*."

Upon reaching Whitefriars Street, Newton led them twenty paces south, then paused before an archway and, leaning into the gloom, banged on the oaken door with his shillelagh. "Open up, Mrs. Totten! Open up for the Master of the Mint!"

"How do I know 'tis ye, Professor?" cried a hoarse female voice.

"Because I carry thirty pounds sterling in my purse!"

The door swung back to reveal a hunched, lardish, nearly toothless old woman holding a lighted tallow candle.

"Good evening, Mrs. Totten," Newton said. "Allow me to introduce Mr. Franklin and his sister, Mrs. Crompton, both of Philadelphia."

"Hallo, Lucy," Slocum said, still brandishing his pistol.

"We are delighted to make your acquaintance," Ben said.

Lucy Totten stared at the Philadelphians, fought back a sneer, and spoke in a flat voice. "Charmed." She locked her rheumy gaze on Newton. "Oh, Professor, I been goin' through the worst day o' my life."

She guided her visitors down a bottle-neck passageway into a suffocating hovel, its furnishings consisting of a single chair and a few upended vinegar barrels littered with candle stubs and cooking pots. In the far corner rested an eviscerated mattress upon which a large man lay wrapped in a dark blanket, shivering and moaning.

"I did as ye instructed me, Gunny"—Mrs. Totten cupped her hand around the barrel of Slocum's pistol, easing the bore away from her chest—"writin' down all his rant about the Calibans."

"Prithee, show me the transcription," Newton said.

"Not before ye offer my Billy a benediction," Mrs. Totten said.

"Benediction?"

"We can't entice any men o' the cloth into the Fleet these days, but I'm willin' to make do with geometry."

Newton shrugged vigorously, propped his shillelagh against a barrel, and followed Mrs. Totten to the mattress. Jennet stepped toward the dying man. The ticking stank of mildew. In the candle's glow Billy Slipfinger's blanket stood revealed as a blue greatcoat, multiply perforated, as if its previous owner had died in a hail of musket-balls. His face, stern and unforgiving, suggested an almost Shakespearean depravity, an amalgamation of Iago, Claudius, and Aaron the Moor.

With manifest discomfort, Newton assumed a kneeling position beside the ratty bier. "So, Billy Slipfinger, thou canny old rogue, 'twould appear thou art about to meet thy Creator," he said. "When alive thou contributed little to the glory of God, squandering thine energies on counterfeiting and copulation, but in death thou hast helped save the British Mint, for which the Almighty will surely reward thee, shabby though thy case may be in other respects."

Awkwardly, Newton regained his feet.

"Thank ye, Professor," Mrs. Totten said, her eyes moist and sparkling. "Your eloquence hath moved this impoverished widow to tears."

"I would have that list now," Newton said.

Perhaps the last thing Jennet expected to see in this unfamiliar pesthole was a fœtal prodigy of her acquaintance—but there he was: the Lyme Bay Fish-Boy, a-float in his jar at Slipfinger's feet. She released an involuntary gasp.

"What ails thee, sister?" Ben said.

"I shall explain presently." Surely this was Dr. Cavendish's specimen. There couldn't be two such freaks in England.

Slipfinger's moans grew louder but failed to enter the domain of speech.

Lifting the lid from a soup pot, Mrs. Totten retrieved a gin bottle in which a rolled-up paper, secured with twine, lay like an ancient potion turned to cake by the passage of time. "If this ain't worth thirty quid"—she handed the container to Newton—"then Hell's o'erdue for a frost fair."

Newton unbottled the paper and put on his optical spectacles. "Mr. Slocum, whilst I study this document, you will take up my money cudgel and perform a patriotic duty." He pointed toward a shapeless smear of gray mortar near the fireplace. " 'Tis obvious Mr. Slipfinger hath secreted his handiwork within these walls."

"Ye're wrong, Professor!" Mrs. Totten protested. "Billy hid only the most *genuine* currency round here!"

"Sir Isaac, your vision is as keen as your *Opticks* is acute," Ben said.

Over Mrs. Totten's shrill objections, Slocum grabbed the shillelagh, wrapped both hands around the grip, and clubbed the controversial masonry. Potato-size chunks of plaster fell away. He attacked the wall thrice more, gouging a hole the diameter of a cocked hat. A dozen bundles of paper currency, neatly tied with string, tumbled onto the floor.

"All o' them notes is *bona fide!*" Mrs. Totten wailed.

With a snorty laugh Slocum opened the flue, then began stacking the currency in the fireplace.

"Stop, Gunny!" Mrs. Totten cried. "Ye're about to destroy my life's savings!"

"Nay, woman, he's about to destroy a pile of paper as worthless as South Sea Company stock, a commodity on which I once lost twenty thousand pounds!" Newton slid a tinderbox from his pocket, handing it to Slocum, then turned to Ben and continued his raillery. "The South Sea directors got precisely what they deserved, long sojourns in the Tower for so blithely bribing Parliament. The Lords took their money, likewise the Commons, whereupon both houses set about blurring the distinction 'twixt a government security and a corporation share."

"I implore ye, Gunny!" Mrs. Totten cried. "I'm fallin' to my knees!"

"As I heard the tale of the South Sea Bubble," Ben said, "the directors assumed that the War of the Spanish Succession would advantage them, with a defeated King Philip granting England exclusive trading rights with his West-Indies colonies."

Newton offered Ben a corroborating nod. "When Philip decided otherwise, the managers declined to involve themselves in any species of commerce whatsoever."

"Verily, ye might find a suspect note or two in the pile," Mrs. Totten conceded, "but the rest of 'em be real as St. Andrew's shaving basin!"

"Sir Isaac, I am perplexed," Jennet said. "If the South Sea Company did no business, why would anyone imagine its shares to be of value?"

"The logic of your complaint is irreproachable, but at the time I allowed avarice to befuddle my arithmetic," Newton confessed as he perused the list of Caliban Adepts.

Unmoved by Mrs. Totten's entreaties, Slocum finished mounding the notes, then swaddled them in tinder and merrily struck flint to steel.

"No, Gunny!" Mrs. Totten screeched.

A spark shot forth, landing in the little pyre.

"Gunny!"

"If you persist in your complaint," Newton told the incipient widow, "you will forfeit the thirty *authentic* pounds I brought you."

Mrs. Totten frowned and, falling silent, sank her bum into the room's solitary chair.

Jennet fixed on the hearth. As the flames took hold, the sham notes blackening and shriveling like broadsheets meeting Satan's gaze, she turned to their hostess and said, "I'm curious about yon prodigy."

"Would ye care to buy it?" Mrs. Totten replied brightly, then immediately thought better of her cupidity. "How durst ye propose a business transaction"—a scowl contracted her face—"whilst my dear Billy lies dyin' under my nose?"

"Forgive my impertinence," Jennet said.

"Ye can have it for a quid, though the aforementioned idiot paid three guineas." Mrs. Totten rose and shuffled toward the mattress. "Billy's mother, a witling by any measure, convinced him that such a fœtus would bring luck, so when the prodigy-monger set up shop last year, Billy was first in line." She adjusted the greatcoat, pulling it even with her husband's jaw. "As ye can see, his damned Fish-Boy's done him no good."

Newton cleared his throat, removed his spectacles, and, with the solemnity of a judge sending a murderer to Tyburn Tree, pronounced on Mrs. Totten's document, declaring it authentic and valuable. He paid the woman her thirty pounds, then instructed Slocum to escort the Philadelphians back to their lodgings.

"If you please, Sir Isaac," Ben said, " 'twas my hope we might continue discussing smoother pebbles and prettier shells."

"Some other time." Newton refolded the paper and slid it into his pocket. "For the nonce the Lord Mayor and I must start drawing our plans against the Calibans."

"Dearest sister, I fear no demon disproof may be extracted from the Master of the Mint," Ben said. "Not this night nor any other."

"So it seems," Jennet said, heaving a sigh.

"Demons," echoed Newton with undisguised disgust. He grabbed his shillelagh and, approaching the hearth, agitated the ashes of Billy Slipfinger's iniquity. "Demons, demons, demons . . ."

"I shall happily purchase your fœtus, Madam," Jennet told Mrs. Totten, "but first you must direct me to the museum it once called home."

"Whereas the monster costs a quid, his previous address is worth twice that much," Mrs. Totten said.

"I shall take the whole package, facts and fish-boy." Jennet set the required notes in Mrs. Totten's palm. For reasons doubtless tracing to the sad logic of life in the Fleet, the three pounds from Jennet seemed to delight the old woman no less than the thirty from Newton.

"Ye want *Le Cirque de la Lune*, Lower Thames Street, hard by the bridge," Mrs. Totten said.

"And so I take my leave of you." Newton locked his shillelagh under his arm. "Young Franklin, when next we meet, I shall explain how I divined the floor-plan of Solomon's Temple from the Book of Ezekiel. This chart hath given me the precise dates for the fall of Romanism, the triumph of Arianism, the mechanical transport of human beings to the moon, and the Day of Judgment. Mrs. Crompton, 'tis apparent you're an intelligent woman, but you must forgo your obsession with diabolism ere some magistrate arrests you for an enchantress. Farewell."

With all the élan of Rupert Quince exiting the stage of the King's Theatre, Newton turned ninety degrees and strode out of the hovel.

"I don't understand that man," Ben said.

"I wonder if anyone does," Jennet said.

"I've known that beady-eyed lunatic for twenty years," Slocum said, "and he's still a riddle to me."

※

BILLY SLIPFINGER DIED shortly after midnight, embracing his Creator with a sound that for Jennet evoked a Nimacook squaw scraping the back of a beaver pelt. She and Ben and Newton's bodyguard remained by Mrs. Totten's side another hour, listening to her alternately bilious and remorseful elegies for her husband.

"Marital fidelity was ne'er his speciality, I can tell ye that," she said. "Sometimes the wight e'en brought one o' his narycherries home. But here's the odd thing—them ladies always liked me. Half the time Billy would pass out drunk ere he could drop his breeches, and then the strumpet and me, we'd amuse each other all night, sippin' gin and tellin' tales."

"From my limited dealings with harlots, I would conclude they make good conversationalists," Ben said, "for being surfeited in the flesh they grow hungry in the mind."

"Rather the way natural philosophers make good lovers"—Jennet patted Ben's arm—"as their curiosity compels 'em to press e'er deeper into Aphrodite's domain."

Whilst Jennet took possession of her prodigy, Ben made Mrs. Totten a gift of his embroidered handkerchief, and then the Philadelphians set out for Mayfair, protected by Gunny Slocum's pugnacious deportment and drawn pistols.

London by night, Jennet knew from experience, was as theatrical a world as London at noon, though instead of clerics, bankers, beggars, hawkers, and shop-keepers, the players were trollops, gamesters, drunkards, sailors, and cutpurses. All during the long walk back to Adam's Row, Slocum supplemented the general atmosphere of menace by recounting his adventures chasing down coiners with Newton. Evidently the geometer and the ruffian were an ideal team. First Newton would detect a counterfeiter's whereabouts via a succession of brilliant logical deductions, then Slocum would appear on the scene, offering the blackguard a choice betwixt an interval in the dock and a bullet in the brain.

"Inexplicable force equals occult force," Jennet muttered after they'd parted company with Slocum. "Occult force equals demonic force. Where's the chink, Ben?"

"We'll find it," he said as they mounted the steps to their rooms. "Even without Newton to light the way, we'll find that blessed chink."

"From the pyre my aunt shouted, 'Aristotle!' She cried, 'The elements!' and then she named the Greek immutables."

"Mayhap you heard naught but the ravings of a woman driven mad with fear," Ben said.

" 'Tis possible, aye. And yet I believe she saw the calculation ere she died, but could find no words to speak it save 'earth' and 'air' and 'fire' and 'water.' "

Jennet and Ben slept all morning and left Mayfair at half past two. Swathed in a woolen scarf and hidden beneath her coat, the bottled Fish-Boy bulged outward from Jennet like a pregnancy. Arriving at the Golden Ass, the Philadelphians quickened themselves with coffee and cake, then agreed to rendezvous that evening at the King's Theatre, where they would learn whether Rachel intended to join their imminent Atlantic crossing. It struck Ben as nothing short of a miracle that Jennet and her "doubtless beautiful" daughter had found each other after a decade of separation, and he was "deliriously eager to meet her."

"I shall speak candidly," Jennet said. "For all I want Rachel to take ship with us, I cannot help my observation that she is rather closer to your age than to mine."

"Your meaning's plain, dearest. Believe me, I have no wish to further besmirch a Moderation grid that already displays lapses in abundance."

" 'Twould be more than a *lapse* were Rachel to turn your head from me to her. 'Twould be a rent in the fabric of the universe."

"I'faith, Mrs. Crompton, a man in my position hath less reason to prefer the daughter o'er the mother than doth a falconer to select a merlin o'er a peregrine."

"Look me in the eye, bonny Ben. Look me in the eye and say, '*Waunnetunta.*' My heart is true."

"*Waunnetunta.*" He offered her a dulcet smile. "Turn on, turn on, Mrs. Crompton," he added. "We shall make it glitter by and by."

∗

WHILST BEN TROTTED OFF to accomplish one last printing job at Palmer's, a pamphlet for the British Anti-Slavery Society, Jennet and the Fish-Boy proceeded to Lower Thames Street and descended a series of spavined marble steps into the crepuscular world beneath the bridge. Mrs. Totten had not misled her: three sprawling canvas pavilions—red, yellow, green—lay huddled by the water like box kites awaiting a wind. CAVENDISH MUSEUM OF WONDROUS PRODIGIES, read the sign on the green pavilion. FEAST YOUR EYES ON NATURE'S MISTAKES.

Heart scampering in her chest, she elbowed the flaps aside, stepped into the pavilion, and set the Fish-Boy's habitat on the floor. Advancing through the murk, she found herself standing face-to-face with an old acquaintance, the Bird-Child of Bath, lit by a whale-oil lamp and resting on an exhibition table, his visage conveying his usual eagerness to quit the glassy cage and take flight. As her eyes adjusted to the gloom, the feathered stillborn's brethren greeted her. The Smethwick Philosopher looked as sagacious as always, the Turnbridge Wells Bloodsucker seemed happy in his vampiric profession, and the Kali of Droitwich retained her usual air of divinity, but the Bicephalic Girl appeared gaunt and weary, as if she'd lost one too many altercations with herself.

There were no customers in the museum, only an impossibly ancient gentleman in a red periwig and a green frock coat, stooped over the Bicephalic Girl's bottle, polishing it with a rag.

"Dr. Cavendish?"

"The same."

"Dr. Cavendish, 'tis I—Jennet Stearne."

"Who?"

"Your Miss Stearne."

The curator stopped polishing. "Miss Stearne? Jennet Stearne?"

"Verily."

"I do not believe it."

"Then will you believe that I am the favorite ward of Lord Adramelech, Grand Chancellor of the Infernal Empire?"

Upon absorbing her remark in all its implications, Barnaby released a yelp of delight and clasped her to his chest. "Oh, my dearest Miss Stearne, are you in sooth this full-grown woman?"

"I can make an excellent case for't."

"In my reveries you're always still a girl of twelve!"

"I was certain you were lost to me," she said, gradually reconciling this wrinkled male crone with the Barnaby Cavendish of her youth. " 'Tis as if you've come back from the dead."

"On my rheumatism days, that's exactly how I feel." Relaxing his embrace, he slipped on his spectacles and scrutinized her with the intensity of a linen-draper assessing a bolt of cloth. "Tell me, Miss Stearne— Jennet—did you e'er devise your *argumentum grande?*"

"Alas, the project's not yet complete, though I believe the vital calculation's close at hand." With the respectful affection of Bellerophon bridling his beloved Pegasus, she looped her arm around Barnaby's shoulders, then guided him toward the obelisk of sunlight formed by the tent flaps. "Mayhap you remember that, ere we parted company in Colchester, I promised I would bring you a prodigy when our paths crossed again." Pointing toward the occluded Fish-Boy, she snatched the scarf away. *"Voilà!"*

" 'Sheart, 'tis my own best aquatic oddity! 'Tis my dearest ichthyic astonishment!" The gleeful curator kissed her cheek. "Had my fortune-telling colleague predicted that on this day I would enjoy not one but two reunions, the first with a friend, the second with a fœtus, I would have thought him deranged."

"I acquired our Fish-Boy directly from the Widow Totten of Whitefriars Street."

"Do I infer that old Slipfinger hath finally found the decency to bereave his wife?"

" 'Tis a long story. Let us dine together this evening, and we shall share our life's adventures."

After declaring her plan "nigh as perfect as my freaks are flawed," he offered to show her his new acquisitions. As the tour progressed, Jennet learned that a distracted Nature had of late brought forth in England a Turtle of Tewkesbury (its tiny head peering from beneath hunched shoulders) as well as a Hastings Clock-Girl (her elongated chin tapering toward a chest marked with Roman numerals) and a Newgate Pig-Child (a sphere of flesh with two eyes at its north pole and a fringe of toes along the bottom). But the jewel of the collection was the Knightsbridge

Hermaphrodite, both varieties of genitalia on full display. With a heavy heart Barnaby revealed that the Cyclops of Bourne, the Maw of Folkestone, Perdition's Pride, and the Sussex Rat-Baby had long since left the family, sold during the same impecunious period that had obliged him to do business with Slipfinger, but he hastened to point out that, thanks to the Fish-Boy's homecoming, the roll call of the misbegotten once again stood at its traditional total of ten.

The curator now insisted that they go visit his magician colleague, a manumitted West-Indies slave who in his youth had enjoyed the patronage of the French aristocracy, taking his show from one château to the next. Barnaby and Jennet proceeded to the red tent, surmounted by a sign reading FEIZUNDA THE ILLUSIONIST: FEATS OF JUGGLING AND CONJURING, EVERY HOUR ON THE HOUR. Although it was exactly four o'clock, all the seats were empty. A snowy-haired man in a blue silk turban, his skin as dark as gun powder, sat before an oaken table, rehearsing a trick that had him filling three crystalline bowls with clear water then tapping each with a glass scepter. Under the influence of the conjurer's wand, the first measure became a ball of ice, the second boiled as if set upon a stove, and the third acquired a school of tiny crimson fish.

"Allow me to present my old associate in rascality," Barnaby said to Feizunda. "Jennet Stearne, formerly the most intelligent girl in East Anglia, currently the most brilliant woman in the American provinces."

"*Je suis enchanté,*" Feizunda said, bowing graciously.

"*Et moi aussi,*" Jennet said.

The magician came forward and with a sudden chirping laugh reached behind her ear and drew forth a goose egg. "*Voilà!*"

"*Merveilleux!*" she said.

He smacked his hands together, causing the egg to pop into oblivion like a burst bubble.

Barnaby next brought Jennet to the red pavilion, arena of GIBELLUS THE SEER: DESTINIES DIVINED IN CRYSTALS, CARDS, BONES, AND PALMS, and introduced her to a squint-eyed wight whose mottled skin and toothless jaw put her in mind of the Turtle of Tewkesbury. Sprawled across a Turkish carpet that he shared with Ptolemy's *Quadripartite,*

Guido Bonatus's *Astronomica Tractaus*, John Maplet's *The Dial of Destiny*, and a dozen other astrology texts, Gibellus did not bother to rise, but instead offered Jennet a cryptic wink and gummy smile.

"Permit me to cast your fortune," he said, placing a splayed hand on his chest. He wore a black robe spattered with five-pointed stars. "I would expect no fee."

"Alas, I have of late grown unfriendly to all hermetic pursuits," she said. "I would be a dissatisfied customer whether I paid you or not."

"You must not slight my colleague's gift," Barnaby gently admonished her. "Through his astrological calculations, Gibellus predicted both the Great Plague of 1665 and the abdication of James the Second."

"Aye, but did he predict 'em *before* they occurred, or *after?*"

"I assure you, Madam, I am skilled in the diviner's arts," Gibellus said. "I can prophesy using ceromancy—that is, by the forms of melted wax in water—as well as lithomancy, by the reflections of candlelight in gems, also halomancy, by the casting of salt into fire, not to mention crominiomancy, by the growing of enchanted onions. In your case, however, a simple palm-reading will suffice. Make a fist and bring it hither."

Jennet could not forbear a skeptical smirk, but she did as the seer requested. Gibellus unfurled her fingers one by one and studied the hatched plane beneath.

"Five great lines," he said. "Every person hath 'em, rays of heart, head, life, fate, and matrimony. Their geometry reveals all—the angles and gaps, the arcs and intersections. Let us see what Dame Fortune holds in store for you."

"Excuse me, Mr. Gibellus," she said, "but if these lines reveal my future, then logic says they also speak of my past, as I am forty-seven years old, with much of my destiny behind me. I bid you tell Barnaby about my more memorable experiences with love and husbands and the rest, for 'twould make an interesting test of your system."

"Don't be sly, Jenny," Barnaby cautioned.

"By St. Agatha's warts, I shall rise to the challenge!" Gibellus cried. He fixed on Jennet's palm. "I can see you were once . . . *married* to a man of . . . *nautical* bent. A sea captain, mayhap?"

"Aye, 'tis true!" Jennet said. "My sweet Daniel—Captain Throgmorton to his men, master o'er the man-o'-war *Obadiah*."

"Ah," Barnaby said.

"But, alas, he no longer lives," Gibellus said.

"Dear Throggy went down with his ship in the War of the Spanish Succession," Jennet said.

"Leaving you with a child . . . a *son*," Gibellus said.

"My boy, Horatio!"

"Oh, Jenny, I had no idea you'd suffered such a terrible misfortune," Barnaby said.

"Whilst your son came of age, you pursued your aptitude for . . . *horticulture*," Gibellus said. "Even today your cottage is surrounded by flowers of every description."

"Hyacinths and jonquils!" She placed a guinea in the seer's hand. "I was wrong to doubt your talents, sir. Prithee, accept this consideration for entertaining me so thoroughly."

With the blessing of his associates, Barnaby posted a GONE TO SUPPER sign outside the Cavendish Museum, then guided Jennet across the street to the Pettifog. For two hours they enthralled one another with their respective autobiographies, though Barnaby's account of *Le Cirque's* ragged rise and imminent collapse paled beside her narratives of the Salem witch-trials, the burning of Haverhill, her Nimacook adoption, Pashpishia's death, Rachel's wanderings, and the glorious arrival of Ben Franklin in her bed—and then, of course, there was the previous evening's maddening encounter with Sir Isaac Newton. It took her three separate tellings to convince Barnaby that the man they'd brought to Colchester Assizes was in fact the late Robert Hooke, and just as many to convince him that the real Newton had proven as useless as the impostor.

"I am relieved to learn there be not a tittle of truth in Gibellus's version of your life," he said. "I'Christ, I'd always thought him as deft a deceiver as myself—thank goodness I needn't revise my opinion downward."

"And now I fear we must endure another parting, for my only hope of toppling my brother is to dishonor him on his own soil."

"Let me put a proposition to thee." Barnaby puffed on his clay pipe. "One needn't be Gibellus to see that *Le Cirque* will fold its tents betimes, which sets me to wondering whether my monsters might find an audience in the American Colonies."

She drank the rest of her coffee and pondered the curator's scheme. Barnaby in Pennsylvania? An excellent idea. If this splendid charlatan joined her company, which already boasted Ben and would soon, God willing, include Rachel too, she would have at her command a kind of Antipurification Commission.

"Truth to tell, I've ne'er heard of a prodigy museum in America," she said.

"So the field belongs to Barnaby Cavendish?"

"Entirely."

"Reserve me a berth on your ship, dear Jenny, that I might gain renown as the man who brought the Knightsbridge Hermaphrodite to the New World!"

⁂

AS DUSK DROPPED ITS SOFT GRAY SURTOUT upon the city, she left the Pettifog and set off for Drury Lane, her brain seething with visions of Barnaby, Rachel, Ben, and herself assembled in some secret Philadelphia cellar, candles flickering all about them as they whispered their conspiracies against the New-England cleansers. She reached the King's Theatre at half-past seven. Ben awaited her in the foyer, dressed lavishly in a chestnut periwig and a gold-trimmed suit of purple silk.

" 'Steeth, you're more gaudily attired than an Istanbul whore-master," she said. "My daughter will be impressed."

"God's truth, Jenny: I wear this finery to please you, not young Rachel."

Whilst he queued up to purchase their tickets, Jennet descended to the supporting players' dressing-chamber. For a full minute she studied the hurly-burly. Five actresses in various states of *déshabillé* rushed about the room, putting on their costumes and painting their faces, but Rachel was not amongst them.

A buxom woman with luxurious lips and a beauty spot on her cheek approached Jennet and flashed an equivocal smile.

"Mrs. Crompton, perchance?"

"Aye." With a pang of despair she realized that the woman wore the same dress in which Rachel had portrayed the waiting-maid.

"This is for you." From the vale betwixt her breasts the actress produced a sealed envelope.

Jennet snatched the packet away and with trembling fingers extracted Rachel's letter.

23 July 1725

Dear Mrs. Crompton:

Unhappy Circumstances prevent me from offering my Farewell in Person. Last night, upon enduring yet another salacious Entreaty from Mr. Quince, I quit the Drury Lane Company forever. Gaston says that my Competence in French is most excellent (the one Boon bestow'd upon me by my repugnant Stepmother), and so I have resolv'd to seek my Fortune in the Comédie Française. By the time you read this, I shall be well across the Channel. Please understand that no Argument you might devise could ever induce me to come with you to the American Colonies.

Regards,
Rachel Crompton

She read the letter a second time, but the words refused to rearrange themselves into a different meaning. She read it a third time. The cruel message remained. On her fourth perusal, the characters grew blurry with her tears.

"If you decide to stay tonight," the actress said, "you'll see me play both Betty and Mrs. Marwood."

Jennet dried her eyes, then climbed the stairs to the foyer, where Ben was examining a broadsheet advertising a forthcoming "Newgate Pastoral" by John Gay, *The Beggar's Opera*. Upon reading Rachel's letter he said, "Oh, darling, for all you may have slighted her, you do not deserve such thorns as these."

"Shakespeare knew whereof he spoke," she said. "A child's ingratitude is sharper than a serpent's tooth."

"I shall return our tickets anon."

She grabbed his decorous sleeve, massaging the lacy filigree. "Nay, Ben, for I feel *The Way of the World* may be the very physic I require."

"Then lead the way, my love."

They stepped into the parquet along with a gaggle of latecomers, finding their seats just in time to behold the shameless and predatory Mr. Quince recite the Prologue. As the comedy progressed and the players enacted their rôles, Jennet realized that her decision to attend the performance was felicitous indeed. For there, right there, up on the King's Theatre stage—there stood Aunt Isobel. The actress was Alice Shuter; the character, Mrs. Millamant, the most magnetic, intelligent, and sophisticated of all the fine ladies in London.

Mrs. Millamant could match the men around her epigram for epigram. "One no more owes one's beauty to a lover than one's wit to an echo. They can but reflect what we look and say." Like Isobel Mowbray, she allowed no person to take her for granted. "Though I am upon the very verge of matrimony," she told her future husband, "I expect you to solicit me as much as if I were wavering at the gate of a monastery, with one foot over the threshold." Unless she enjoyed certain freedoms within their marriage, she informed this same groom, she simply wouldn't have him. "As liberty to pay and receive visits to and from whom I please; to write and receive letters without interrogation or wry faces on your part; to have no obligation upon me to converse with wits that I don't like because they are your acquaintance, or to be intimate with fools because they may be your relations."

Beyond her comeliness and her cleverness, Mrs. Millamant possessed another arresting quality. This was a woman with a will. In her view compromise was defeat, and those who moved counter to the way of the world must be numbered amongst its benefactors.

Jennet squeezed Ben's hand and said, "There was probably ne'er a Newtonian disproof in the first place."

"Agreed," he whispered.

"Be quiet, both of you," said a wan woman to Jennet's left.

"So we've made a kind of progress," Jennet said. "At least we're now at the starting-line and not behind it."

The man seated in front of her, a Redcoat captain in a white peruke, turned around and glowered. "Shut up, you driveling cow."

Jennet stopped talking. The patrons were right. She was being rude. Once back in America, however, she would raise her voice again, and if her enemies turned Jacobean, cutting out her tongue, she would pick up a pen instead, and if they sliced off her hands, she would hold the pen betwixt her teeth, and if they removed her teeth, she would search out some wise and audacious physician, a Newton amongst surgeons, and bid him reassemble her, tongue and hands and teeth, and a strong new heart as well, the heart of a mare or lioness, and it would not stop beating until Reason reigned in the souls of men or a thousand years went by, whichever happened first.

PART III

Reason's
Teeth

The

Ninth

❧❧❧❧❧❧❧❧❧

*An Interlude of High Adventure,
Including a Shipwreck,
a Marooning, a Preternatural Magnet,
and a Perilous Encounter
with a Pirate Band*

❧

On the eve of their scheduled departure, Jennet returned to *Le Cirque de la Lune* and helped Barnaby pack up his museum. They filled two sea-chests with rags and straw, then laid each bottled prodigy to rest, five per cushioned compartment. For Jennet the task felt like midwifery in reverse. They were restoring the foetuses to the womb, it seemed, so that Nature might fashion them anew, fixing their asymmetries, excising their scales and feathers.

So familiar was she with the monsters' reputation as good luck talismans, it never occurred to her that anyone might cast them in a sinister light. She was therefore greatly astonished when the first mate of the *Berkshire*, the squat and obstinate Archibald Eliot, after inspecting Barnaby's sea-chests for rats and opium and finding instead the stillborns, declared that Captain Fergus would "rather ship out with Jonah himself than this load o' frightful cacodemons." The mate's prediction proved correct. Arriving on the quarter-deck later that morning in the company of Ben, Captain Fergus glanced at the prodigies, turned to Barnaby, and said, "Sir, methinks thou art a necromancer, for I see no other reason a man would accumulate such hell-spawn. I shan't have 'em on my ship."

"My dear Captain," Barnaby said, "I'm surprised that so well-traveled a person as yourself knows not the therapeutic value of foetal marvels. In Persia or Cathay no self-respecting physician will visit a sickbed without first he places a prodigy in his satchel."

"My friend speaks the truth," Jennet said, reprising their ancient chicanery. "No sooner did I rub the bottle of the Knightsbridge Hermaphrodite than my backache flew clear to Heaven."

It took Ben but a moment to grasp the game. "This Tuesday past, simply by giving the Smethwick Philosopher a fraternal sort of hug, I caused my fever to vanish with the morning dew."

"Therapeutic?" sneered Captain Fergus. "We shall see about that. Methinks I'll put your claim to the test." Reaching inside the nearer sea-chest, he caressed the Tunbridge Wells Bloodsucker. "On my last trip to the Azores, I endured a dreadful attack of the gout, and two years later I can still feel its fire and throb, as if the Spanish boot were clamped round my foot."

"You must understand, sir, the healing effect doesn't always happen instantly," Barnaby said. "Oft-times the sufferer must wait till sunrise."

Jennet said, "In many cases a full two days will pass ere—"

" 'Sheart!" the captain cried. "Do I deceive myself? Nay! The pain's starting to fade!" He stroked the stillborn more vigorously. "My foot feels as fit as when I first kicked my brutish brother in the cods!"

"The Bloodsucker's always been singularly antagonistic to gout," Barnaby said.

"Fœtal vampires are the very bane of that affliction," Ben said.

Captain Fergus lifted the Bloodsucker from the sea-chest, bringing its gargoyle ugliness into the sun's unflattering glare. "Marry, such a hideous pill, and yet so potent."

Jennet wasn't sure how to explain the abrupt abatement of the captain's pain. She suspected that his cure represented yet another Newtonian desire of the mind, not unlike her experience thirty years earlier of seeing, under Okommaka's persuasion, her mother and grandmother encamped in the sun's corona.

"Very well, Doctor, you may cart along these freaks of yours." The captain restored the vampire to its brethren. "I'Christ, we shall deploy 'em against whate'er plagues of flux and scurvy lie before us!"

Two hours later the *Berkshire* caught the tide, received the wind, and started down the Thames. In contrast to their departure from Philadelphia, no lawyer or businessman arrived to displace Jennet and Ben from their private cabin, and so they passed the afternoon in one another's arms. As always, she found herself pitying any woman obliged to settle for the flaccid passions of an aging lover, as opposed to the endless ardor of a nineteen-year-old. Did she provide Ben with reciprocal satisfactions? Yes, she decided, though doubtless he occasionally longed for the bloom of youth. Saddened though she was by her daughter's flight to France, at least she would never have to witness Ben casting one eye on his perfection-matrix whilst the other strayed toward Rachel's comely frame.

"Oh, Ben, how my forty-seven years do pull upon me," she lamented. "My bosom droops under gravity's persuasion."

"Only because 'twas such a robust specimen of bosomhood to begin with," he said.

"And my neck hath acquired many a wrinkle."

"But see how easily my tongue lays them smooth."

"And my legs are all shot through with veins."

"Lodes of perfect turquoise, enriching the precious flesh in which they lie."

Honorable and well-meant sentiments, unquestionably—and yet she feared that he was not so much speaking his heart as mouthing what she wanted to hear. Still, if he must bend the truth, better these blandishments than any outright lie. Flattery was such a noble sort of sin, a pilgrim vice wandering forever homeless betwixt the kingdom of mendacity and the country of kindness.

Three days into the crossing her usual *mal de mer* arrived, but this time they were prepared, for Ben had spent the previous Friday visiting the apothecary shops of Tavistock Street. Many proprietors swore by ginseng, others favored mulberries, some endorsed dried silkworms, and a few recommended rose-hip tea. Unable to appraise these competing claims, Ben had acquired all four remedies, amalgamating them into a stinking and repellent syrup. Strangely enough, the mixture proved efficacious—not by its merits, she decided, but simply because her stomach, unable to choose betwixt ordinary seasickness and the more complex distress induced by Ben's nostrum, had entered into a state of paralysis.

Jennet had always imagined that Ben and Barnaby would become good friends, and as the voyage progressed this expectation enjoyed extravagant fulfillment. Both were natural philosophers at heart, though of a distinctly pragmatic bent, each hopeful of converting Nature's secrets into contrivances of great utility. Ben had of late grown obsessed with the potential applications of electricity, a force he believed (despite Newton's indifference to the hypothesis) manifested itself in Von Guericke sparks and lightning-bolts alike. "The day is not far off," he insisted, "when Heaven's fire shall become domestic as the ox and compliant as the horse, readily harnessed to illumine our houses, warm our beds, and cook our food."

For Barnaby, meanwhile, it was the chemical processes that promised to mitigate human misery. His work with fœtal preservation had made him knowledgeable concerning alcohol and other vegetable liquids, and he was evidently near to concocting "that invaluable elixir sought by all the world's surgeons, a universal insensibility drug." If his next round of experiments proved successful, posterity would remember him as "the man who'd raised up amputations and ablations from the bloody bowels of Hell and carried 'em into the sunlight of rational medicine." This same Barnaby Cavendish, he added with a sly wink, "had grown rich as Croesus in the bargain."

As the sixth week of the voyage began, the ocean gradually thickened around the *Berkshire*'s waterline like butter coagulating in a churn. Vast mats of algae pressed against her hull, conjoined to swaying rafts of seaweed. Everyone took heart at this development, for such greenery most probably heralded the American continent, and the ship's cook, a garrulous German named Friedrich Schwendemann, was particularly delighted. In his experience the seaweed would contain an abundance of that red-shelled shrimp known as the brine-berry—an eminently edible creature, succulent and delicious as the plum. Upon considering the cook's claim, Captain Fergus ordered a longboat lowered, and two hours later a mound of newly harvested seaweed rose from the main deck like a haystack in a farmer's field.

Herr Schwendemann had spoken truly. Thousands of brine-berries wriggled amidst the grassy tufts. Beguiled by visions of shrimp cakes, shrimp pies, shrimp stews, and shrimp chowders, the crew set about the task at hand, and soon the ship's larder was filled to bursting with the raw materials of a dozen feasts.

Observing the hungry sailors at work, Ben and Barnaby found themselves formulating rival theories concerning the genesis of brine-berries. Whereas Ben supposed the shrimp were indeed an aquatic equivalent of fruit, issuing from the seaweed as did apples and pears from trees, Barnaby contended that the vegetation functioned merely as a dwelling-place for the shrimp, which, in the manner of so many ocean creatures, came from eggs. At length Jennet fell upon a method for resolving the dispute. All they need do was fill a tub with a clump of seaweed devoid of shrimp, set it on the quarter-deck, and note whether any brine-berries appeared amidst the strands. Both the printer and the curator appreciated the elegance of her test, and they quickly agreed on its parameters. If the seaweed yielded no shrimp within ten days, Ben would concede the superiority of Barnaby's hypothesis.

During the subsequent week the cook wrought banquet after banquet from the aquatic crop, but Jennet and her friends were concerned less with culinary matters than with the great shrimp experiment. Every morning they climbed to the quarter-deck and inspected the liquid nursery. On the evidence of their first seven observations, it seemed that the seaweed *per se* possessed no procreative powers.

"Are you ready to admit that the court of Nature hath ruled unfavorably on your claim?" Barnaby asked Ben.

"Mayhap the shrimp will burst forth later today," Ben replied. "Mayhap they've already hatched, but they're much too small to see without aid of microscope."

Jennet scowled and said, "Do you really believe that?"

"In sooth—no," Ben said. "But since my perfection-matrix contains no grid for graciousness, methinks I'm free to be as stubborn in this matter as I wish."

THE GREAT SHRIMP EXPERIMENT: day eight—a day that began like those before it, with Jennet, Ben, and Barnaby ascending to the quarter-deck whilst the *Berkshire* cruised through the Atlantic as smoothly as a child's toy sailboat navigating the Serpentine. Bending over the tub, they fingered the seaweed, examining each strand in the morning light, when suddenly a vehement wind seized Ben's hat and carried it out to sea. Other winds followed, equally ferocious, swooping across the decks with a force sufficient to topple the binnacles, steal the oars from the longboats, and set uncoiled lines to dancing like East-India cobras.

Instinctively the three experimenters retreated to the open stall beneath the quarter-deck, where they huddled like a family of cave-bears taking refuge from a flood, and by ten o'clock the brigantine lay in thrall to a thunder-gust.

"Surely there's no stronger power in the universe!" Jennet cried as a lightning-bolt arced across the ashen sky like a filament of divine thought. "I'Christ, I am skeptical that such a terrible flame"—a mighty boom shook the air—"could share a heritage with Von Guericke sparks!"

"You have common intuition on your side, Miss Stearne," Barnaby shouted over the shriek of the storm, "and yet methinks Mr. Franklin's hypothesis is true!"

"Sparks and holocausts, mites and moose—they're all the same to God!" Ben yelled.

The *Berkshire* rolled from side to side in cycloids so erratic their description would have defied even Newton's fluxions. Whitecaps bloomed everywhere, turning the Atlantic the color of goat cheese. The rain descended in vast silvery sheets, like a gigantic curtain demarking the finish of some epic but demented opera. Once more the angry sky brightened with Heaven's fire, and a second later the expected explosion rattled the ship.

"I must lash down my prodigies!" shouted Barnaby, backing deeper into the stall.

"You are a true father to your children!" Jennet cried.

"A true father, aye," he said, lifting the cover from the hatch, "even if I do sell one of 'em off now and again!"

Shortly after Barnaby went below, Jennet glanced toward the rigging, where an astonishing sight greeted her gaze. Most of the sailors had climbed aloft and for reasons that defied rationality were busily setting the royals and topsails.

"Have they gone mad?" she shouted. "They should be reefing all that canvas, not putting it in the wind!"

"I would guess our captain hath sensed an even greater storm brewing to the east!" yelled Ben. "He means to stay ahead of the tempest, lest it catch and smash us!"

No sooner had Ben voiced this conjecture than it received unsolicited substantiation. Lurching into the quarter-deck stall, rainwater spouting from his coat sleeves, Mr. Eliot reported that in Captain Fergus's view an unequivocal hurricane was chasing the *Berkshire,* and their only hope was to fly so fast and far that the beast could never overtake them.

"I must ask a favor of ye!" Mr. Eliot told Ben. "With all my men occupied in settin' the canvas and bracin' the beams, we're short on souls to purge the hold! If ye'll work the larboard pump, the boatswain'll take its companion to starboard!"

"I shall happily lend my back to our salvation!" Ben replied.

"And I shall do likewise!" Jennet informed Mr. Eliot.

" 'Tis not a task for a person of your sex!" the mate insisted.

"Compared to the tribulations of childbirth," she said, "I would judge the job about as arduous as baking bread!"

Prompted by either desperation or chagrin, Jennet couldn't tell which, Mr. Eliot offered a deferential bow. Ben took her by the arm, and together they quit the stall and ventured into the gale. The main deck was a veritable river, the breaking waves and the driving rain washing tumultuously across boards sleek as glass and slick as ice, but at last they reached the larboard pump. In tandem she and Ben grasped the lever and set to work—down, up, down, up, down, up, stroke upon stroke. The wind screamed. The waves rose high as battlements. The rain slapped her face, drenched her hair, and saturated her dress so thoroughly it became as heavy as chain-mail. To steady her nerves and rouse her spirits she imagined she was operating a Blaeu press in Keimer's Printing-House, churning out copy after copy of an imperially persuasive *argumentum grande.*

After twenty minutes of struggling to keep the *Berkshire* a-float, Jennet suggested to Ben that they were caught in a Sisyphean loop, and betimes Mr. Eliot appeared and corroborated her pessimism. The hold, he reported, was filling with water as quickly as the machines could empty it.

"Shall we keep to the task?" Ben asked.

"Aye, if ye own the strength, sir!" Mr. Eliot replied.

"I do!" Ben said. "And you, Jenny?"

"Turn on, turn on, Ben!" she said. "We shall make it glitter by and by!"

As noon came to this wild and sunless sector of the Atlantic, an unnerving sound arose from the rigging, the low guttural croak of the wind cleaving the mizzen-royal in twain. Seconds later the main top-gallant succumbed to the slashing storm, and next the fore-royal was torn asunder.

" 'Twould seem our captain hath lost his contest with the hurricane!" Jennet shouted to Ben.

"He'd best pop the sheets, else we'll capsize!"

Evidently Captain Fergus had reached the same conclusion, for the crew now descended from the rigging and set their hands to the belaying pins, yanking them loose with the grim efficiency of barbers removing rotted teeth. Set free of the fife rails, the sails snapped and fluttered like the banners of a goblin army on the march.

Whilst the captain's failure to outrace the storm was ominous on the face of it, Jennet decided to concentrate on a felicitous implication: the crew, praise God, would soon assume the pumps. Gasping like a beached flounder, she gave the lever an especially energetic push, whereupon a burst of Heaven's fire disclosed a long green island rising from the white ocean. So lush a landmass being foreign to the New-Jersey coast, she leapt to a conclusion that the hurricane had dragged the helpless brigantine well off its course.

"Look ye, Ben! Caribbean island to starboard!"

"Island?" he shouted. "I see no island!"

" 'Tis a Caribbean island!" she cried.

"Caribbean? We cannot be so far south! You saw but a water-mirage!"

"We're in the Caribbean!"

"Your eyes deceive you!"

She was about to assert the probity of her eyes when the Philadelphians' situation declined abruptly from the perilous to the cataclysmic. An enormous wave rolled across the deck, smacking both Jennet and Ben off their feet and pitching them over the larboard rail. Briefly they arced through empty space and, filling their lungs with Caribbean air, plunged into the sea.

Jennet had descended barely ten feet when buoyancy's blessed law sent her in the opposite direction. With the exuberance of an eaglet smashing free of its egg she broke the frothing surface, then expelled several ounces of saltwater from her nose and a full pint from her throat. She blinked madly, squeezing the brine from her eyes. Staring into the troughs betwixt the waves, she beheld the relentless rain—and next a bobbing Ben—and then, many yards beyond, the *Berkshire*. Shreds of sail flapped madly on their spars. Uncleated sheets flailed about like the tentacles of a deranged kraken. The hurricane battered the ship mercilessly, hurtling passengers and crew alike into the ocean with the crude indiscriminate power of an orangutan shaking down its breakfast from a banana plant.

"We're swimmers, Ben!" she cried. "This storm can ne'er kill us!"

"Swimmers!" he agreed, spewing out a mouthful of seawater.

Stripped of her company, the *Berkshire* made a final stand against the storm. A more thorough dismemberment could scarcely be imagined. Like a philosopher preparing a hare for micrographic scrutiny, the gale anatomized the ship. Foremast snapped free of fo'c'sle. Mizzenmast and quarter-deck parted company. Spritsail abandoned bow. Shrouds tore loose from deadeyes. Braces, foretops, and crosstrees vanished into the squalls.

"Where be that isle of yours?" Ben called.

"I'm all turned round!" she shouted. "I can only pray some guardian angel will point the way!"

"I'll do the praying, you do the pointing, and by God's grace we'll soon feel sand beneath our feet!"

Shedding their boots and outer garments, the Philadelphians swam in tandem, riding each mountainous swell as if it were Poseidon's wildest horse, until at last they encountered a solid mass—not a beach, but merely a ten-foot section of the poop-deck bulkhead. Heaving themselves from the water, they scrambled aboard this accidental raft, then sprawled atop its flooded surface, Jennet prone and coughing, Ben supine and shivering.

Having demolished the *Berkshire*, the hurricane gradually departed the scene, exporting its chaos to a higher latitude, leaving only a light shower to mark its memory. The Philadelphians looked in all directions, hoping to spot additional survivors, but the storm had evidently borne away every other relic of the wreck.

"Mrs. Crompton, a strange phenomenon is upon me," Ben said, teeth chattering. "Here I find myself facing either a slow and painful extermination by thirst, or else a quick and gaudy devouring by sharks, and yet I have but one desire."

She rolled on her back and said, "Ben, I'm too distracted to think on carnal matters."

"Dearest, you've read my thoughts. My great yearning is to join with thee in erotic embrace."

"Even as we confront our deaths?"

"*Carpe diem.*"

Like Mrs. Millamant taking over the stage in Scene Two of *The Way of the World*, the sun made a resplendent entrance from behind a rose-colored cloud. "Tell me, my brave gallant," she asked, "are there any conditions under which you might *not* heed the call of concupiscence?"

"None that come to mind."

"What if a cannonball had shorn off your leg?"

"My lady's touch would ease my agony."

"What if ants were eating you alive?"

"I would avail myself of whate'er comforts lay at hand."

The rain stopped. Seagulls circled high above. Golden sunlight washed across the raft, drying the philosophers' underclothes and warming their bodies as they exchanged frightened kisses beneath the wide West-Indies sky.

JENNET'S ISLAND, THANK HEAVEN, was no mirage. Shortly after Ben gave their raft a name—the *Prodigy*, in tribute to poor Barnaby Cavendish—a rank of forested hills appeared in the distance, its silhouette suggesting a many-humped camel fording a river. The wind augmented the Philadelphians' good luck, as did the current, both forces pressing the *Prodigy* steadily toward the landfall, and by late afternoon the raft had run aground in a cove ringed by mangrove trees and dotted with clusters of brilliant white coral.

After praising Providence for their deliverance—Jennet extolling her "most glorious Creator," Ben lauding the Deist Clockmaker—they disembarked and staggered through the surf, dazed, shocked, sapped, and above all enchanted by the fact that they were not dead.

They gained the beach, advancing barefoot across silken sand punctuated by vacant crab-shells, and forthwith entered the forest, soon discovering that their respective deities were watching over them yet, for the storm had deposited pools of sweet rain in dozens of rock crevices and tree clefts. No Pierian Spring could have pleased them more completely, no Well of the Saints, no Fountain of Youth.

"How goes't with thee, Mr. Franklin?" she asked, sucking down the delicious liquid bounty.

"I am entirely miserable, Mrs. Crompton. And thou?"

"Completely wretched. I mourn our drowned curator."

" 'Tis in sooth a dark day." He lapped up a puddle. "And yet methinks we have no choice but to embrace optimism, cultivate hope, and aspire to make the best of our circumstances."

"Cock an ear to the breeze, Ben. Listen. Do you hear it?"

"Hear what?"

" 'Tis the sound of Dame Fortune, laughing and chortling as she plays lanterloo with our lives."

Thirst slaked, throats soothed, they resolved to catch a measure of sleep ere exhaustion dropped them in their tracks. Returning to the beach, they dragged the *Prodigy* to the edge of the forest, then set the bulkhead fragment diagonally against a boulder and equipped the resulting enclosure with a mattress made of kelp and heliconia leaves. They yawned, stretched, and took up residence in this rude but serviceable lean-to.

"A veritable palace," he said.

"And so to bed," she said.

Like serpents slipping free of their skins, they shed their spinning thoughts and muddled fears, then fell asleep to the harsh whisper of the retreating tide.

AN AVIAN CONCERTO heralded the dawn—parakeets, Jennet guessed, complemented by several trilling, warbling, and cooing kinds unknown to her. Shafts of amber sunlight pierced the lean-to. For an indeterminate interval she lay and listened to the surf, absorbing the rhythmic growl like a foetus attuning itself to the rush and thump of its mother's blood.

"Ah, 'twas no mere nightmare then," Ben said, rousing himself from his dreams. "We have truly joined the fellowship of the marooned."

"The castaway's normal stratagem, I've heard, is to write his coordinates on a scrap of paper, then place the message in a bottle and toss it into the sea," Jennet said. "But, alas, we have no bottle."

"Mayhap some *other* castaway's bottle will reach these shores. We'll uncork the vessel and, ere relaunching it, add our message to its cargo—explaining, of course, that we're but second in the queue to be rescued."

They passed the morning foraging for breakfast amongst the reefs and tide pools. So intense was their hunger, they easily convinced themselves that eating uncooked shellfish would do a human no harm, then set about harvesting the dozens of pale little Cartesian machines—the sand-crabs, brine-berries, conch snails, and mussels—that inhabited the glossy rocks.

"Tell me, Ben, do you perchance share my shame o'er yesterday's panegyric to Providence?" Jennet prised a snail from its shell, setting the animal on her tongue. "In the cold light of morning, I judge my devotions an insult to Barnaby, Mr. Eliot, Captain Fergus, and every other wretch who went down with the *Berkshire*." She chewed the rubbery flesh, which was subtly flavored, like a mushroom. "I'd rather believe in no God at all than one who is so capricious in His mercy."

"My dear Mrs. Crompton, you've surely picked the wrong time and place to start experimenting with atheism," Ben said. "Whether God be fickle or fair, 'tis only by His intervention we shall e'er see Philadelphia again."

"No doubt you're right. But in the future I shall forbear to praise the Creator in question."

Ben scooped a mussel from its shell and popped it into his mouth. "Are you not acquainted with Monsieur Pascal's brilliant deduction? 'Tis far more sensible to be a believer than an atheist, for the latter hath his immortal soul to lose, the former only his illusions."

"Aunt Isobel once told me of Pascal's celebrated wager." In a frenzy of voracious violence she picked up a sand-crab and smashed it open on a rock. "She concluded that any Supreme Being worthy of the name would scorn the believer for his complacency, even as He rewarded the atheist for his bravado."

Ben intertwined his fingers and raised the fleshy configuration skyward. "Forgive my friend her impieties, Lord, whether thou existeth or not. Along with these shellfish she hath ingested a great quantity of salt, and 'tis making her brain go dry."

※

FROM HER YEARS amongst the Nimacook Jennet knew that, for all the island's apparent fecundity, their survival was to Nature a matter of complete indifference. They must not take their next full meal, warm night, or tranquil moment for granted. Ever the cheer-monger, Ben at first laughed at her fatalism, but then came three successive days in which they failed to extract a single morsel from their habitat, and thereafter he counted himself an eager student of Algonquin arts.

For their initial task she had them erect on the lee shore a wigwam framed by candelabra-tree branches and covered with bullhorn acacia bark. A split-log dwelling would have been preferable, of course, but without an iron ax or a long Damascus knife such a project was unimaginable. Under her tutelage Ben learned how to turn animal skins into moccasins, fashion clothing from grass and reeds, start a fire with a bow-drill, trap grouper in a reed weir, tolerate the taste of roasted katydids, appreciate the flavor of boiled tree frogs, and snare the harelike agouti that proliferated throughout the inland forest.

At first Ben was distressed to be violating his vegetarian principles so blatantly, but then he noticed that, whenever they cleaned a grouper for roasting, they found a smaller fish within its stomach. "If a big fish may eat a small fish," he argued, "I don't see why I mayn't eat a big fish."

"A sturdy piece of logic," Jennet said.

" 'Tis so convenient being a *reasonable* creature," he said, "for't enables a man to find a *reason* for everything he hath a mind to do."

Even as their prospects brightened, Jennet's grief compounded. The image she would always retain of her dead friend was one she'd never actually witnessed—the grinning mountebank delivering the Lyme Bay Fish-Boy to Billy Slipfinger, blithely promising that it would bring him luck. Such a disciplined dissembler was Barnaby Cavendish, confining his fakery to one arena only, his prodigies, whilst remaining upright in all other matters.

With a nod to Francis Bacon's political allegory, they named their isle New-Atlantis, and over the next several months they explored its inner reaches, catalogued its abundance, and ascertained its form—an irregular oval along whose primary axis ran an L-shaped ridge perhaps fifteen miles long, jagged craggy backbone of the landmass. Each expedition proved more productive of wonders than the last, from purple butterflies swarming like fleets of færy kites to sea turtles with shells suggesting

Byzantine mosaics; from ants building great formic cities in the forest's heart to spiders spinning webs as intricate as doilies; from twin water-falls echoing through the jungle in crystalline duet to troops of nimble monkeys, their tails looped around the uppermost branches, swinging back and forth like antic church bells. A plenary Paradise indeed—though like Adam's primordial estate it harbored a despoiler.

The serpent's name was boredom. There was nothing on New-Atlantis by which a Baconian experimenter might sharpen his wits, no psychic whetstone, no mental flint. Unlike their literary counterpart, Robinson Crusoe, the Philadelphians took no satisfaction in their cast-away condition. Whenever Mr. Crusoe had engaged in yet another act of ingenuity—growing barley, making furniture, taming goats—he'd experienced an unequivocal delight. But Ben and Jennet were of a different disposition. They craved salons and seminars, troubadors and telescopes, allegories and air-pumps. To condemn such sensibilities to a West-Indies isle was like banishing a herd-dog to a nation without sheep, or exiling an eagle to a planet of such ponderous gravity that not even a milkweed pod could take flight.

For a brief interval they brought to their tedious Eden the salutary ar-tifices of theatre. Ben conceived a cycle of one-act comedies, so thin of plot and broad of theme there was no need to write them down. He had but to toss out the premise, and the New-Atlantis Players would impro-vise their way to the end. For Jennet, the jewel of their repertoire was "A Sense of Proportion," all about a lord and lady who resolved their petty domestic disputes—what color to paint the drawing-room, which cat to allow in the parlor—by hiring two commoners to fight lethal pistol duels, one man representing the obverse of the controversy, the other the reverse. She was also fond of "Crowned Heads," concerning a king and queen who, eager to spend their every waking hour at gaming and fal-conry, had the Royal Alchemist fashion a pair of doppelgängers gifted in handling the quotidian demands of despotism. Offended by the arro-gance that had given them birth, the doppelgängers set about issuing re-pressive edicts, and ere long the true king and queen found themselves kneeling before the chopping block.

The satisfactions of emoting for an audience of uncomprehending monkeys were few, and the Philadelphians eventually sought other, less cerebral ways to relieve their ennui, so that Ben's Moderation grid—he'd managed to reincarnate the perfection-matrix by marking scraps of acacia bark with a burnt twig—was soon a mass of black dots. Whilst the bounty of New-Atlantis did not extend to Belgian adder-bags, Jennet assumed that their sport would involve no procreative consequences, for she was beyond the age when a woman might expect to conceive, and during the past twenty months she'd bled not at all. She experienced an extreme dismay, therefore, to realize that she was once again with child, for how else to account for her swelling contours and terrestrial *mal de mer?*

"I'll come right out and say it," she told Ben one balmy afternoon. They were repairing their hut with patches of mud and clay, its roof having leaked profusely during the morning's thunder-gust. "The third and final offspring of Jennet Stearne Crompton is but six months from daylight."

"Dearest angel, do you seek to amuse me?" he said, massaging his scraggly beard.

"My announcement's no more a joke than this wigwam's a cathedral."

"Pregnant? Really? A woman of your years?"

" 'Steeth, Ben, do you think me some dry and withered Sarai? Do you imagine I could ne'er quicken my lover's seed without Jehovah Himself injects me with a heavenly egg?"

He scowled and twisted a viscid brown bung into place. "This all seems most uncanny to me."

"Uncanny? *Uncanny?* There be no cause to posit a virgin conception here, sir. I needn't remind you of *that*."

Breathing suddenly became for her swain an activity requiring his complete attention. "Oh, my dear Mrs. Crompton, methinks I am too *young* for fatherhood."

"As I am too *old* for motherhood."

"Truth to tell, I feel cozened by this news. 'Tis as if Nature and Dame Fortune and you yourself have all conspired against me."

"Cozened?" she snarled. "Cozened? How durst you accuse me of such?"

"If not cozenage, then a malign sort of carelessness. A conscientious woman knows her fertile days and constrains her lover accordingly."

"Faugh, Ben, no witch-court e'er reached a judgment so unjust! *Nummusquantum!*"

"What?"

"I am angry!"

Pivoting abruptly, she stalked away from the wigwam, her patience stretched to the snapping-point. She would rather hear Gunny Slocum brag about catching counterfeiters, or even Cotton Mather opining about America's Satanic tawnies, than endure another instant of this twaddle.

As the sun arced toward its tryst with the sea, she walked south along the rumbling surf. She vowed to spend the night alone, resting atop a pile of heliconia leaves and, if Morpheus declined to bestow his gift, meditating upon any topic save the insufferable Mr. Franklin. Alas, no sooner had she made this promise than the sky grew dark as dried blood, releasing forthwith a cold, fierce, unsalutary rain. Shivering in the squalls, her grass mantle growing soggier by the minute, she decided that pleurisy was too high a price to pay for dignity. She slogged back up the beach and silently entered Ben's vicinity. For a full minute the castaways stared at each other, shedding rainwater, saying not a word.

"The more I think on't," he muttered at last, "the more happily I anticipate teaching our splendid young son the printer's trade."

She took his wet hand, separating the thick fingers as a coquette might spread the blades of a fan. "This son of ours could very well be a girl."

"Then she shall follow her mother into the wilds of modern geometry. Marry, I see this junior Jennet teaching the fluxions at the Philadelphia Friends School. Long before she's born, I shall advantage her by reciting the multiplication tables well within her hearing, over and over and over."

They flashed one another weary smiles, exchanged mistrustful frowns, and, crossing the threshold of their rehabilitated wigwam, took shelter from the storm.

PRINTER, PHILOSOPHER, PLAYWRIGHT, and—now—*paterfamilias*, Benjamin Franklin spent the first week of his son's life setting agouti snares in the heart of New-Atlantis, noting their locations on a map he'd made by embedding pebbles in a mud pie. On the morning of the eighth day he took up his woven-seaweed sack and began an inspection tour, feeling a bit like a country squire making the rounds of his estate. Snare number one was unsprung, likewise number two, but the third trap indeed held an agouti, the confused animal dangling like the lead plumb on a carpenter's twine.

Until the moment of his son's birth, Ben had regarded himself as well experienced in matters of ecstasy. Catching Saturn's rings with his telescope, making electricity with his sulphur-ball, joining with his true love in carnal embrace—surely such activities defined the bounds of rapture. How wrong he'd been, for all these wonders paled beside William Franklin's arrival in the world.

Jennet had delivered in the upright position favored by her Nimacook kin, her arms locked around two adjacent mangrove trees. The spasms still caused her much pain, however, and Ben found himself wishing for a supply of Barnaby Cavendish's imagined insensibility drug. Disoriented though he was by Jennet's distress, he ultimately became what she called "a not incompetent midwife," soothing her during the pangs, guiding the infant free of the womb, pronouncing authoritatively on its gender, and cutting the cord with a stone knife. On Jennet's orders he gathered up the gelatinous afterbirth—it was both fascinating and repellent, like one of Cavendish's monsters—and buried it in the sand. When finally satisfied that the mother had survived her ordeal, he bore their son to a tide pool and gave him his first bath, gently sponging the bloody, wrinkled flesh with a crumpled heliconia leaf.

Whilst "William" was clearly the correct name for this astonishing soul, they could not agree on the reason. For Jennet the name evoked the dramatists she most admired, Shakespeare and Congreve. Ben preferred the political connotations, for many a friend of liberty had called himself William, including William Penn, champion of religious toleration, William Wallace, heroic Scottish rebel, and William of Orange, the first British monarch to rule wholly at Parliament's behest.

Cautiously Ben crept toward his prey. Even as it struggled to right itself, the agouti looked him in the eye. He paused, took a step, whereupon the gravity of New-Atlantis forsook its traditional Newtonian allegiance and acquired a disconcerting independence of mind.

" 'Sheart!"

Ben's captive ankles flew upward, his torso plummeted, his head descended. At last he came to rest, his arms hanging downward, his fingers brushing the dirt. His first thought (quite ridiculous, he realized) was that a troop of vengeful but clever agouti had fashioned a trap of their own. His second thought (much more rational) was that he'd tripped an agouti-snare laid by some other castaway. His third thought (utterly terrifying) was that the snare had been set specifically for him by a cannibal like those who figured so memorably in Mr. Crusoe's adventures.

For nearly an hour he endured his inverted condition, the puzzled blood filling his cranium and clogging his ears. His field of vision was confined to the similarly ensnared agouti, a berry bush, and a mangrove root as gnarled as Newton's shillelagh. When at last two brown leather boots entered the scene, his heart surged with hope, for such footwear was surely beyond a cannibal's budget.

"Look!" a male voice cried. "We have catched ourselves a most peculiar beast."

A second pair of dark boots, oiled like a Belgian adder-bag, materialized within inches of Ben's nose. Their owner, likewise male, spoke next. "God was in a whimsical mood when he fashioned *this* creature. The toes are where the head should be."

"The knees are where the heart should be."

"The cods are in the stomach's proper place."

"Ben Franklin, you are one befuddled animal." The owner of the un-oiled boots leaned over and showed his face to Ben. He was a muscular Negro, dressed in tanned leather breeches and a blue linen shirt, his features fixed in a scowl. "Have no worries"—he pulled a knife from his belt—"for I shall free you anon!"

The blade flashed in the midday sun, and the next thing Ben knew he'd executed an involuntary cartwheel and collapsed on the ground. As Ben's wits returned to him, the owner of the oiled boots—also a Negro, smaller than his companion and dressed only in agouti-skin trousers and a red neckerchief—extended a helping hand.

"How do you know my name?" Ben asked, climbing free of the snare.

"Your name is the least thing we know about you," the knife wielder said. "Since you drift ashore, we watch you every day."

"We keep silent, listen carefully, learn much," the other said. "Your little play called 'A Sense of Proportion' is most delightful."

The thought that the Negroes had been spying on him for over a year set Ben's brain to reeling once again.

"Call me Njabulo, the name my mother gave me," the knife wielder said, "and here is my younger brother, Kanisho, though to our white master in Carolina we were Jedidiah and Oswald."

"Do I surmise you are slaves?" Ben asked.

"We *were* slaves," Kanisho said. "Today we live as free citizens in Ewuare-Village, named for our ancestors' greatest king."

"Village?" Ben said, flabbergasted. "You've got a whole *village* tucked away here?"

"Ruled by our Grand Oba, Ebinose-Mbemba, and his Queen, Ossalume," Njabulo said. "Let us tell you a story, Ben Franklin." He approached the suspended agouti and deftly broke its neck. "Six months ago, Ebinose-Mbemba and Ossalume call their councilors together and ask them what should be done about the castaways in our midst. All five vote to remove your head, and your woman's head as well. Lucky for you, the Grand Oba and his Queen reject this verdict."

Kanisho added, "He says there is no report of Jesus Christ ever removing anyone's head."

"If your rulers have elected to spare my life, why did you set a trap for me?" Ben asked.

"We ensnare you quite by accident," Njabulo said. "The jungle conceals many such devices, laid for the slave-catchers." With his knife he cut down the agouti, offering the limp little mound of fur to Ben. "Go ahead, sir. Take it. Dead agouti don't bite."

After retrieving his woven-seaweed sack and stuffing his prey inside, Ben told the fugitive slaves that he wished to thank the King and Queen betimes for their clemency. Kanisho explained that the monarchs had more important tasks to accomplish that day than accepting a white man's gratitude. Ben said he would still like to accompany them back to Ewuare-Village, that he might exhibit himself as the harmless printer and innocuous philosopher he was. The brothers assented to this proposition, but only after Ben agreed to make the trip blindfolded.

For the next two hours Njabulo and Kanisho guided their quarry through the pungent jungle, Kanisho's neckerchief fitted across Ben's eyes as if he were awaiting execution by a firing squad. All during the journey—up the central ridge, over the crest, and down again—the brothers related the story of their arrival on New-Atlantis, which they called Amakye-Isle.

Born into slavery on Peedee Willows, a Carolina rice plantation, Njabulo and Kanisho had come of age hearing about a very different world, the West African kingdom of Benin, where their great-grandmothers had grown yams and kola nuts ere the Portuguese slavers arrived and sent them in chains across the sea. A Bini farmer knew many hardships, many disasters, but such travails were as milk and honey compared with the endless toil of sowing and reaping a rice crop. And yet for other Carolina chattel things were evidently even worse. If Satan's agents came in degrees of depravity, then the master of Peedee Willows, Andrew Larkin, whose father had won the plantation from the Earl of Clarendon in a game of whist, was amongst the more enlightened of his kind, a devout

Anglican who believed it his Christian duty to save whatever percentage of a soul an African Negro possessed. Thus it was that Njabulo, Kanisho, and their fellows were instructed in the Anglican *Book of Common Prayer* and baptized into the Church of England. Though routinely whipped, regularly beaten, frequently starved, and sometimes mutilated, the Peedee Willows slaves would in all probability be spared the fires of Perdition.

After three successive failed crops, Larkin concluded that the Almighty did not intend him for a rice farmer. He sold the plantation and auctioned off the slaves, subsequently heading to Connecticut with the aim of entering the beaver-hat trade. The best bid for Larkin's chattel came from faraway Jamaica, whose sugarcane industry required a continual supply of stout black bodies. Late in July of 1720, Njabulo, Kanisho, and ninety-six other Bini were loaded into the British carrack *Sapodilla* and sent south to the Caribbean.

Shortly after her passage around San Salvador, both of the *Sapodilla*'s compasses mysteriously ceased to function, and the next morning the carrack entered a region of stagnant air and fiendish heat. As the languorous days elapsed, the captain was forced to ration water by the teaspoon and hardtack by the ounce, with the slaves' allotment dwindling to zero. But then, in the third week of the becalming, an unlikely Moses emerged from amongst the Bini, the nimble-witted Ebinose-Mbemba, Andrew Larkin's former footman and librarian. Exploiting the epidemic of despair that had infected the ship's company, Ebinose-Mbemba led the other slaves in an improvised revolt that ultimately obliged them to drown the captain, strangle the first mate, debrain the boatswain, and slit each crewman's throat.

Washing the blood from their hands, the Bini implored their ancestors' spirits to blow them home to West Africa, but these prayers were answered only by feeble currents and anemic breezes. After nine days adrift, the *Sapodilla* ran aground in the shallows surrounding an uncharted isle. Ebinose-Mbemba forthwith ordered his followers to strip the carrack of every valuable artifact: not only such obvious choices as knives, axes, muskets, nails, bulkheads, timbers, planking, rope, sailcloth, telescope, and compass, but also Thomas More's *Utopia*, John Bunyan's *The Pilgrim's Progress*, and the King James Bible. At Ebinose-Mbemba's command, the *Sapodilla's* gutted remains were set a-flame and reduced to ashes, so that a slave-catcher happening upon Amakye-Isle would never guess that a ship had touched bottom in these waters.

"The longer we live here, the more fortunate we feel in finding this place," Njabulo told Ben. "Most West-Indies isles are but swatches of desert, friendly to Spanish pigs, wild onions, and little else."

"You must approach Ewuare with the proper expectations," Kanisho warned. "Though the Grand Oba keeps Thomas More by his bed, our village is not a perfect world."

"But we do claim this," Njabulo said. "You will find no chains in Ewuare."

"Not one single lock," Kanisho said. "Not one single link."

WITHIN MINUTES FOLLOWING THE RESTORATION of his eyesight, Ben decided that, Utopia or not, Ewuare was a splendid and convivial place, at least compared to his wretched little homestead by the sea. Folded into an obscure glade at the bend of the ridge, the village boasted a defensive moat hedged by a stockade wall, its pickets poised to impale marauding slave-catchers. Passing through the gates, the brothers led Ben along a dirt plaza flanked by private dwellings, each comprising five mud-huts arranged in a semicircle. Children darted from yard to yard, kicking a wooden dodecahedron according to the rules of a Bini game that Njabulo identified as *uhranwi*. Felicitous fragrances rode the breeze, released by the action of cooking fires on agouti stew and grouper soup.

In the middle of the plaza, evidently occupying a place of honor, rose an object resembling an immense lump of coal, large as an equestrian statue. As Ben paused to inspect the stone—a Bini deity? a monument to the *Sapodilla* mutiny?—a dozen curious Ewuareans clustered around him. They did not desire a closer look at the stranger, Njabulo explained, so much as "a good view of the spectacle should the King and Queen change their minds and order you beheaded." Njabulo then laughed uproariously, evidently to indicate he was joking, though Ben had never regarded any-one's beheading, particularly his own, as a proper locus of levity.

"Here is why the *Sapodilla* becomes lost, and your own ship as well." Kanisho rapped his knuckles on the lustrous black stone. "She is Ori-shanla—the Confounder."

"Place a magnetic compass within five miles of her, and she seizes the needle and doesn't let go," Njabulo said.

" 'Tis belike the mightiest lodestone in the world," Ben gasped. He caressed the mineral, so massive it bid fair to make the Earth a three-poled planet.

As the crowd dispersed, having concluded that no beheadings were in the offing, Njabulo revealed that, though the Queen was off supervising the construction of a watch-tower on the lee shore, the King was cur-rently in residence. The brothers brought Ben to the royal palace, a hulk-ing dome of clay and bark, featuring seashells of every hue—blue, violet, pink, crimson, white—embedded in its walls like numinous barnacles clinging to St. Brendan's ship. The Grand Oba occupied the atrium, seated on a locally made Yorkshire chair, reading Hobbes's *Leviathan* whilst his prepubescent son sharpened a cutlass on a whetstone. Njab-ulo spoke to Ebinose-Mbemba in the Bini language, apparently explain-ing that the intruder desired an audience, and despite Kanisho's prediction the proposal proved agreeable to the King, who now jumped to his feet, entrusted Hobbes to Njabulo, and invited Ben for a stroll about the palace grounds.

"You have a handsome son," Ebinose-Mbemba said.

"And you as well, Your Majesty," Ben said.

"Your Majesty," echoed Ebinose-Mbemba, amused. He was tall, lithe, and pleasingly proportioned, dressed in a crumpled tricorn hat and a blue cloth greatcoat brocaded with gold threads, both presumably salvaged from the *Sapodilla*. "I've ne'er been addressed in that manner before."

"Are you not a king?"

"They *call* me a king, yes, and my wife a queen besides. But what king hath only one hundred and thirteen subjects?"

"The ratio's normally more extreme," Ben said, nodding.

Ebinose-Mbemba swept his muscled arm through the air, a gesture that seemed to embrace the whole of Amakye-Isle. "For the Bini, there must always be a Grand Oba. They cast me in the part, and so I play it—but I believe this sad and sorry world hath seen kings enough already. From your satire entitled 'Crowned Heads,' might I infer you agree?"

"Quite so."

The Grand Oba thrust his hands into his bullion-trimmed pockets. "My master, Mr. Larkin, owned many books on government, each championing a different system of rule. I have read them all, and now I must ask myself, which philosophy is best? If I follow the prescription of Mr. More's *Utopia*, I shall ban all personal possessions from Ewuare and replace them with common goods. Are you familiar with this idea?"

"I have not read Mr. More, but I know he looked askance on private property."

"Then you may *also* know he allowed slavery in his earthly Paradise. Tell me your opinion of slavery, Ben Franklin."

"My opinion?" He inhaled a mouthful of moist Caribbean air, transferring the agouti sack from his left shoulder to his right. "My fellow passengers on the *Berkshire* included a man who made his living exhibiting foetal monsters in bottles," he said at last. "Slavery, I would argue, is of a similarly freakish nature. Misshapen, rejected by God, loved only by those to whom it brings wealth."

"A very pretty answer. Ah, but what man dares insult the lion to its face?" Ebinose-Mbemba loosed a smile that hovered disconcertingly betwixt facetiousness and menace. Removing his hat, he fanned his brow until the bright gems of sweat evaporated. "Having found in Mr. More a lamentable lapse, we now move on to Mr. Hobbes. According to his *Leviathan*, I must impose on my subjects the harshest despotism imaginable, for all men are selfish beasts at base, evermore needing protection from one another."

"I am acquainted with the Hobbesian outlook," said Ben as he and the Grand Oba began their second circuit. "The eternal war of all against all. But I do not view our human species that way."

"Nor do I, despite the many cruelties I have witnessed in my life. And so we put Mr. Hobbes aside and turn finally to Mr. Locke. Were I to heed his *Second Treatise of Civil Government*, I would grant my councilors more power than I myself enjoy, for only a strong legislature can secure every citizen's natural right to life, liberty, and property. In Locke's society, a monarch sits upon his throne only to execute the contract a community hath made with itself."

"I've always found much reasonableness in Locke."

"And yet he, too, permits slavery, allowing victorious armies to make chattels of their prisoners. I promise you, Locke would view slavery differently had he sailed with my grandmother to the Carolinas."

Ebinose-Mbemba restored his hat, easing it downward until the shadow of the brim obscured his face. He cleared his throat, lowered his voice, and bid Ben imagine two hundred Africans pursued like game animals by men with muskets and nets. To the Portuguese slavers it mattered little whose parent, wife, husband, or child died during the hunt—and many did die—for the slave trade enjoyed both the sanction of Scripture and the imprimatur of profit. Upon their capture Ebinose-Mbemba's maternal grandmother and the other prisoners were chained naked to their berths aboard the brigantine *San Jorge*. For ten weeks they lay crushed against each other, rolling about in their own waste whilst the ocean's frigid waters seeped into the hold, the weaker Bini inevitably perishing of fever, flux, scurvy, and distemper. Halfway to the Carolinas, the captain of the *San Jorge* realized that he'd failed to stock enough provisions for the remainder of the voyage. His solution, so simple, so efficient, was to bring twenty Africans on deck and hurl them bodily into the sea—chained together, of course, with the lead Bini affixed to a great stone: far be it from the captain to place unearned guineas in the purse of a passing slave-master.

"In short, I must argue that no white man hath yet imagined a government likely to benefit any race save his own," Ebinose-Mbemba said.

A draining sensation overcame Ben, as if a demon had slit his side, affixed an air-pump, and started sucking out his vitals. "I shan't dispute the point."

Abruptly the African halted and stomped his left foot in the dirt. He seized Ben's shoulder and laughed as heartily as an Englishman enjoying a Congreve comedy. "Ah-hah, Ben Franklin! Ah-hah! Ah-hah!"

"Something amuses you?"

"A marvelous idea grows in my head! Follow me! Ah-hah!"

Ebinose-Mbemba guided Ben into a thatched-roof hut shaped like one of Isaac Newton's meat pies. A dozen clay pots lined the walls, filled to overflowing with seeds, nuts, and berries, flanking a massive sea-chest. The instant the Grand Oba drew back the lid, Ben experienced the sort of coursing thrill he normally got only from swiving and philosophizing. Top to bottom, front to back, the compartment bulged with gold coins.

"Pirate treasure," Ebinose-Mbemba explained. "We found it whilst digging our moat. But for the absence of markets, shops, and bazaars on Amakye, our village would be awash in worldly goods."

"These doubloons are worthless to you," Ben said in a commiserating tone.

"Worse than worthless—a curse. You are not the first white man to visit our island, Ben Franklin, nor will you be the last."

"You believe the pirates will return?"

"Doubtless they have marked Amakye on their chart, a reckoning they are certain to favor over their distracted compass. On noting that a Bini village hath arisen where they buried their gold, they will sell this information to the slave-catchers. Now. Hear my idea. The instant the pirates appear, you will drag the sea-chest into plain sight, thereby making an inland expedition unnecessary. And so Ewuare remains hidden, secret as a leopard's lair!"

Exhilarated by his scheme, Ebinose-Mbemba cavorted about the treasure chest like a fop breaking in a pair of boots.

" 'Tis an ingenious plan, though I must ask you a question," Ben said. "Once I give the buccaneers their gold, what's to keep 'em from putting me and my family to the sword?"

"Your reputation for cleverness precedes you. Before the pirates come back, you will have devised a solution to this problem."

"I'm flattered that you would trust your village's fate to me," Ben said, his head aching as if recently employed in a game of *uhranwi*.

"I have your word then? You will misdirect the buccaneers on our behalf?"

"You have my word."

"My spies inform me you are an honorable man."

Ben closed the sea-chest, positioning himself atop the gold like an Italian prince employing a chamber-pot wrought by Cellini, and tried to picture his Honesty grid. As far as he could recall, it contained only a fourth as many blotches as Thrift, and only a sixth the number that marred Moderation. He told Ebinose-Mbemba that in most mat-ters he was as weak and sinful as any other mortal, and a bit of

a coward to boot. But he would say this for

himself. He was a man

who kept

his

※

Promises

are prime amongst

those commodities to which we

books accord an almost supernatural respect.

When *Poor Richard's Almanack* implored me to present

its author's relationship with Jennet Stearne Crompton in the most tasteful terms imaginable (for this would be the first time the world learned of their intimacy), I did not assent immediately, for I knew that my pledge, once given, could never be broken or even slightly bent. "Nat-urally I intend to exercise discretion," I assured my colleague, adding, "but I shall neither truncate the truth nor abridge the facts. Agreed?"

"Agreed," said *Poor Richard's Almanack*.

Even today, certain historians perpetuate a rumor first floated by Ben's political enemies when, at age fifty-eight, he ran for the Pennsylva-nia Assembly. This falsehood asserts that William Franklin's mother was Ben's maidservant Barbara, that she was once a prostitute, and that upon her death two years earlier he'd buried her in an unmarked grave. I am happy to report that within my species the only creatures ever to credit this nonsense are *The Bridges of Madison County* and *The Celestine Prophecy*. Unfortunately, the Pennsylvania voters of 1764 were a gullible lot, and Ben lost the election, though his party maintained a majority and subsequently renewed his appointment as the Assembly's agent in London.

Franklin scholars will note that I have *en passant* cleared up a second mystery. Thanks to my memoirs, historians need no longer marvel at Ben's famous enthusiasm for older women, as it traces unequivocally to his conjugal education at my Jennet's lovely hands. He made his appreciation explicit in an essay called "Advice on the Choice of a Mistress," the body of which comprises eight reasons a man would do better selecting an older paramour over a nubile one. ("Because they have more Knowledge of the World," runs the first reason. "Because they are so grateful!" runs the last.) I heartily recommend this amusing piece, which you will find in any substantive Franklin omnibus.

You have perchance noticed that my reminiscences illuminate a third mystery regarding Ben. How did he come to advocate the abolition of the slave trade in an era when the average intellectual wholly endorsed that institution? To answer the question we need look no further than his 1726 interview with Ebinose-Mbemba (an episode Ben omitted from his *Autobiography* lest he inspire the slave-catchers to go looking for Amakye). Now, I cannot say that he left that fateful meeting prepared to join the first abolitionist society he happened upon; indeed, all during his years as editor of *The Pennsylvania Gazette* he rarely declined to list an upcoming slave auction or post notice of a runaway. But the seed was sown on that Caribbean isle, and eventually the tree took root.

Ben's abolitionism is a story to make any book proud of its author, though *Poor Richard's Almanack* can be positively insufferable on the subject. In 1758 he wrote a last will and testament providing manumission for the two slaves in his possession, then freed them outright in 1766. Among the earliest of his abolitionist writings is his reaction to a highly publicized 1772 British legal case that culminated in the emancipation of a fugitive slave named Somerset. In a letter to *The London Chronicle*, he reprimanded his fellow Englishmen for celebrating the court's decision while simultaneously ignoring the plight of "eight hundred and fifty thousand Negroes in the English Islands and the Colonies." This evil would never be rectified by freeing the occasional fugitive, he insisted, but only by making African slavery itself illegal, whether its victims harvested Virginia tobacco, Carolina rice, or Jamaica sugarcane. "Can sweetening our Tea with Sugar be a Circumstance of such absolute Necessity? Can the petty Pleasure thence arising from the Taste compensate for so much Misery produc'd amongst our fellow Creatures, and such a constant Butchery of the human Species by this pestilential detestable Traffic in the Bodies and Souls of Men?"

I should also note, lest *Poor Richard* chastise me for neglecting the fact, that Ben's last public essay, a letter to *The Federal Gazette* published on March 23, 1790, was a withering riposte to a pro-slavery speech recently given in Congress by James Jackson, a Georgia senator. Ben's counterblast took the form of a similar address supposedly delivered one hundred years earlier by a Muslim legislator, Sidi Mehemet Ibrahim, explaining why the Islamic nations must never free their Christian chattels. By turning Jackson's argument on its head, Ben produced a satire commensurate with Swift's "A Modest Proposal," Voltaire's *Candide*, or—a work that will soon enter this story—the Baron de Montesquieu's *Persian Letters*.

If we cease our Cruises against the Christians, how shall we be furnish'd with the Commodities their Countries produce, and which are so necessary for us? If we forbear to make Slaves of their People, who in this hot Climate are to cultivate our Lands? Who are to perform the common Labors of our City, and in our Families? Must we not then be our own Slaves? And is there not more Compassion and more Favor due to us as Musselmen, than to these Christian dogs? We have now above 150,000 Slaves in and near Algiers. This Number, if not kept up by fresh Supplies, will

soon diminish, and be gradually annihilat'd. If we then cease taking
and plundering the Infidel Ships, and making Slaves of the Seamen and
Passengers, our Lands will become of no Value for want of Cultivation;
the Rents of Houses in the City will sink to one Half; and the
Revenues of Government arising from its
Shares of Prizes be
totally

⚘

Destroyed
by a sudden gale,
the wigwam in which Jennet,
Ben, and William pursued their uneventful
lives was not initially missed by the castaways. It had
been a forlorn and uninviting structure, "homely but not homey" in
Ben's words. For the first two nights following their loss, they slept con-
tentedly under the stars, William snugged betwixt them like the fleshy
band fusing congenitally joined twins. On the third night another storm
broke over New-Atlantis. Huddled beneath a sailcloth borrowed from
the Bini, the wind driving pellets of rain against their faces as the cold
seeped into their bones, the Philadelphians soon concluded that a new
wigwam was essential.

Ben set the acacia-wood framework in place, then went off to check
his agouti traps, leaving Jennet to fashion the walls from bark and
fronds. Although the task seemed at first the paragon of monotony, its
wearisome rhythms gradually combined with the pounding sun and the
booming surf to put her in a rarefied state of mind.

How mysterious it all was, this planet Earth, this glittering sea, this
unknown island: especially the island—Amakye, the fugitive slaves
called it—not merely the queerest of places but also the most pristine, a
world whose objects were as yet unnamed, and now it was her job to put
a word to everything that met her gaze. She cast her eyes across Amakye's
multifarious substances, solid and fluid, grainy and slick, wondering
what to call them.

William lay prone on the beach, amusing himself by poking his fingers into the saturated sand. A fiddler-crab lurked near his left foot. She approached the animal and lifted its clawed and wriggling body from gravity's embrace, fully intending to throw it into the sea before it could scratch her son. But instead something moved her to place the fiddler-crab on her palm, as she might set a locust's wing on a microscope stage.

What manner of creature was this? To a Cartesian, of course, the crab was a machine, insensible to pain, incapable of thought, its rowing legs powered by some unseen entity. The crab in turn belonged to a larger machine, the world, its motions supplied by those nebulous presences that Descartes variously called genies, spirits, and vortices. Complementing the world-machine was an entirely different domain—the mind—hooked to the bodily realm via the divine pineal gland, or so the Frenchman had taught.

But today this whole system struck Jennet as woefully flawed, an affront to both fiddler-crabs and common sense. Just as Newton's apocryphal apple had inspired him to discern the continuity betwixt heavenly and earthly motion, so did the creature twitching in her hand proclaim to Jennet an equally momentous link, a tie binding the thinking brains of men to the sentient flesh of beasts. She restored the crab to its native sand, picked up her son, and kissed him on each plump cheek.

In the days that followed her disenchantment with Descartes, she grew convinced that the key to the demon disproof lay right here on New-Atlantis—not concealed like the pirates' gold, but plainly displayed. For to inhabit a Caribbean isle was to know Nature in a fashion not available to a Sorbonne professor or a Royal Society fellow. Standing on a high limestone bluff and observing a violent storm break over the sea, Jennet decided that a lightning-stroke was surely something other than a theatrical prop hurled by a meteorological goblin. Walking the midnight shores beneath a sky unpierced by any church steeple or bell tower, she came to see the wheeling moon and the wandering stars as phenomena quite different from dead matter in thrall to Cartesian vortices. Picking her way along a narrow coral spit whilst contemplating the majestic rollers as they exploded against the rocks, she concluded that the tides could never be fruitfully understood as the toys of invisible genies. Experimenting with the Bini's magnetite block, she apprehended that a lodestone obeyed a principle of its own, oblivious to the commands of supposed spirits.

"The world is *alive!*" she told Ben. "Pole to pole, this swirling planet's *alive!*"

They were wading through the shallows of Copernicus Cove, Ben clutching William to his breast, Jennet inspecting the fish weirs.

"Aye, I suppose that's the case," he said.

"The Cartesians say 'tis dead, but 'tis *alive!*"

"A reasonable hypothesis, though wanting in precision."

"The details will come in time. For the nonce we must irrigate the Earth with all the blood Descartes hath drained away, that a demon disproof might flower on its breast."

Ben shifted William from his left arm to his right. He frowned. "I believe I hear Waequashim of the Nimacook talking."

"But for my years as a savage Indian," she replied, nodding, "I would ne'er have hit upon this proposition."

"Alas, darling, you'll not convince Parliament to strike down the Witchcraft Act merely because the Nimacook religion argues against it."

"In the Nimacook religion lies but half of my idea," she retorted, netting a grouper. "Oh, Ben, how do I make myself clear? 'Tis an insult to the tides to say they cannot turn without some genie's gesture, for in the tug of moon and sun lies explanation enough."

His frown remained in place, though it now acquired a pensive cast. "An insult to the tides—well spoken, Mrs. Crompton."

" 'Tis an aspersion on the lodestone to ascribe its power to spirits, for Mr. Gilbert's magnetism is fully equal to the riddle."

"And 'tis likewise a slur against the lightning to say that demons make it flash," he noted, "for in truth such strokes are Von Guericke sparks writ large."

"To wit, we need no unseen agents, fair or foul, to explain the world. We need only the world itself—its ways and principles and manifest sensibleness."

"This planet's a place of great abundance."

"If not abundance then certainly sufficiency. Aye, Ben! The sufficiency of the world, *that's* the demon disproof lies hidden in the bowels of the *Principia Mathematica,* whether Mr. Newton knows it be there or not. When Aunt Isobel cried out from the pyre, screaming of Aristotle's elements, she meant only that I must look closely, so very closely, at everything my senses embraced. She was instructing me to scrutinize the universe, Nature with her winds and tides and lodestones and sunbeams—her air and water and earth and fire."

He brushed his lips across their son's brow. "You have wrought an ingenious conjecture, dearest. Though I fear your enemies will say that in making Creation sufficient, you have rendered the Creator superfluous."

"If I must murder God to save a Marblehead hag, then that is what I shall do."

Ben massaged his unimpressive beard. "Mrs. Crompton, you shock me—a pleasurable sensation, I daresay, though the English legislature is unlikely to be similarly amused."

"I frame no theologies, sir, merely an *argumentum grande.* So long as we make our purpose clear, we shan't be accused of impiety."

The more they discussed her sufficiency hypothesis, the deeper their affection for it grew. If this idea took hold in Europe, the Continental Cartesians as well as the Cambridge Platonists would be obliged to see Nature anew. These philosophers would stop slandering the lightning, libeling the tides, traducing the comets, and depriving fiddler-crabs of their wondrous little minds. Inevitably Jennet recalled Newton's claim to be but a boy playing on the seashore, diverting himself occasionally with "a smoother pebble or a prettier shell than ordinary." What a splendid event was a pretty shell, and an average shell too. An oyster's abode required no genie for its warrant. A shell was a thing complete unto itself.

Two weeks later, as Jennet and Ben sat down to Sunday dinner at the royal palace—roasted candelabra nuts, acacia-thorn bread, boiled snails, agouti stew—she unfurled the new *argumentum grande* for Ebinose-Mbemba and his queen.

"According to many Christian thinkers, Satan contrives to control the spirits that make possible all actions and movements," Jennet explained, dandling William on her knee. "Nothing pleases the Dark One so much as to deploy the worst of these spirits, the demons, on behalf of his disciples."

"In Europe and America," Ben said, "many magistrates believe 'tis their religious duty to exterminate such disciples—the witches—ere Satan's hordes spread wrack and ruin everywhere."

Ebinose-Mbemba devoured a handful of snails. "We Bini have our devils too, but none so strong that they could cause such a caliber of havoc. I do not much like this Satan of yours."

Now Ossalume spoke up. She was a stately woman, dark and comely as the sun-scorched Shulamite toward whom Solomon had directed his affections in the Song of Songs. "Our mightiest sorcerer might command a million spirits, and still the world would come to its own defense, using the soul of every beast and tree to crush the maleficent host."

"Ah, but here's the rub," Jennet said. "In recent days I have fallen upon an argument whereby the universe operates without benefit of any spirits whatsoever."

"No spirits?" said Ebinose-Mbemba.

"No spirits."

"Then what is it makes one thing happen rather than another?" Ossalume asked.

"The sufficiency of the world," Jennet said.

"The laws of Nature," Ben added.

"The *laws* of Nature?" the Queen said. "Nature's a kind of parliament then?"

"In a manner of speaking," Ben replied.

"If Nature's a parliament, this makes God the monarch?" asked the King.

"You might look at it that way, aye," Jennet said.

"I believe my Philadelphians confuse the divine order with the philosophy of John Locke," Ebinose-Mbemba said.

"Mayhap," Jennet said, taking a swallow of candelabra-root tea. But better the philosophy of John Locke, she thought, than the demonology of Exodus 22:18.

To maintain their sanity in the months that followed the birth of the *argumentum grande*, the castaways took to devising improbable and reckless schemes for getting themselves off the island. Initially Jennet imagined building a raft, though neither she nor Ben had the skills necessary to navigate it to Jamaica. Ben meanwhile envisioned a flying machine consisting of a lightweight acacia coach slung beneath an immense candelabra-leaf balloon that, filled with hot air, would ascend into the clouds and ultimately carry its passengers to civilization. After ten days of experimentation he forsook the idea, all nine of his scale-model airships having remained stubbornly earthbound.

As the third summer of their Caribbean exile ended, an interval not appreciably different from autumn, winter, or spring in this unseasoned latitude, Jennet came to believe that the key to their deliverance lay with the pirates. When the buccaneers returned for the treasure, she and Ben must be prepared to offer them a unique artifact, something so manifestly useful in freebooting that to obtain it they would gladly give the philosophers and their child safe passage to Jamaica.

"Beyond gold, silver, and pearls, what doth a pirate captain most desire?" she asked Ben.

"Mayhap a kind of artificial skin, that he might change his face and thereby elude capture," he ventured.

"Alas, we lack the resources to produce such masks," she said.

"Or a superior variety of prosthesis, for I've heard dismemberment's a common side-effect of freebooting."

" 'Tis unlikely our local trees yield a better grade of wooden leg than ordinary."

"Or an iron helix mounted on his ship's prow," he said, "poised to puncture any vessel dispatched by His Majesty's Navy."

"Your cleverest suggestion so far, and the least practical." She was about to abandon this entire line of speculation when a luminous notion flashed through her brain. "Bless me, Ben—I see the answer!"

"Aye?"

"A buccaneer wants a machine that will tell him whether the galleon he's just spotted carries gold!"

Ben offered her a grin of approbation. "Such a device would spare his crew many a needless skirmish."

"And here's the pretty part. We can fashion this detector ourselves—by which I mean we can turn the Africans' magnetite into a facsimile, fraudulent at its heart but persuasive enough to hoodwink a pirate."

"I'faith, Jenny, you've wrought a passing bold plan. Methinks 'twill either take us to Port Royal or send us o'er the plank."

Ebinose-Mbemba required but an instant to grasp the scheme, whereupon he willingly donated the necessary salvage from the *Sapodilla*—door-nail, wine cork, clay bowl. Next he used his ax to cleave from Orishanla a fist-size piece, delivering it to Jennet. At the Philadelphians' insistence the Grand Oba instructed his subjects to dig an immense pit on the windward side of the island, bear Orishanla thither, and secure her deep within the earth, lest the mother rock cancel the coming hoax with her own Gilbertian force. Jennet now magnetized the door-nail, stroking it repeatedly across the chunk of Orishanla, after which Ben carried the ore fragment to the sea-chest and buried it beneath the gold.

It was time for the vital trial. She filled the clay bowl with saltwater, pushed the nail through the wine cork, and set the contrivance a-float.

The nail pivoted in its miniature lagoon and, true to Mr. Gilbert's principle, pointed toward the chest.

"Most impressive," the Grand Oba said.

"Most lawful," Ben said.

"I can smell the stench of Port Royal already," Jennet said.

※

As Dame Fortune arranged the matter, however, a full seven months would elapse ere Jennet again dared to imagine any Jamaican fragrances on the wind. The pirates returned to Amakye on a balmy March afternoon. Peering through the Bini telescope, she watched their two-masted shallop emerge from a fog bank along the western horizon, sails luffing, banners snapping, and drop anchor near Huygens Reef.

Not unexpectedly, the mainmast flew a flag depicting a skeleton holding in one bony hand a cutlass and in the other a glass of rum. Someone had screwed a plaque onto the upper larboard rail, rechristening the shallop *Judas Tree*. Whatever her original name, this once honest packet-ship had evidently been the scene of a mutiny, her officers now probably decomposing at the bottom of the Caribbean.

The Philadelphians bore William to the royal palace, entrusting him to the King and Queen, whereupon four imposing Bini males hoisted the great sea-chest onto their shoulders. As Jennet and Ben fell in behind them, the bearers brought the treasure to the edge of the jungle, secluding it beneath a heliconia tree. The Bini melted back into the forest. Jennet secured the doubloon-detector inside her hempen sack and availed herself of the telescope, raising it to her eye as six buccaneers in ratty shirts and patchwork breeches rowed away from the shallop.

"I cannot say whether they're entirely unacquainted with civilization," she reported, slipping the telescope under her belt, "but they dress far more crudely than my Nimacook kin."

Whilst the buccaneers guided their longboat into the cove, Jennet and Ben pulled the sea-chest free of its hiding place and dragged it across the beach.

"Ahoy, there!" Jennet cried. "We've found your gold for you!"

The pirate captain vaulted out of the boat and, cocking a silver pistol, marched toward the castaways. He was a hulking Moloch whose most conspicuous feature was his want of a lower jaw. In its place he wore a wooden prosthesis attached to his head by leather thongs and driven by steel springs fitted to wooden cogwheels.

"Unhand my treasure, ye stinking eels!" the captain ordered. The prosthesis reduced considerably his powers of insolence, turning *stinking eels* into *thinking eelth*.

Moving synchronously, Jennet and Ben honored their visitor with gracious bows. We look as harmless as rabbits, she told herself. He hath no rational cause to shoot us.

"You are addressing Jennet Stearne Crompton, museum curator and natural philosopher," she said. "I was marooned here with my infant son after a hurricane tore the *Berkshire* to pieces."

"This man was but an *infant* when your ship went down?" the captain said, nodding toward Ben. "Ye've been here twenty years?"

"Not even four," she said. "The child of whom I speak, my dear and gentle William, sleeps peacefully in a nearby glade. Allow me to present my fellow survivor, Benjamin Franklin, a brilliant scholar and the most talented printer yet born in the American Colonies."

"My friend exaggerates," Ben said, forcing a smile.

A second pirate appeared, a short dusky man with no left ear and hair suggesting electrified algae. The others remained by the longboat, presumably awaiting an order to come forward and massacre the castaways.

"I'Christ, this man and his mother must've found a copy o' Bonner's map!" the one-eared pirate declared.

"I'm not Ben Franklin's mother!" Jennet shouted. "Could we all please agree on that right now?"

"Your associate is understandably curious as to how we came upon the treasure," Ben said to the captain. "You will find the answer most enchanting."

"Arms in the air!" the pirate leader snarled, brandishing his pistol.

Jennet and Ben did as instructed. Whilst the captain kept his weapon trained on them, the one-eared pirate opened the sea-chest—cautiously, by degrees, as if it might be rigged with a petard. The bright tropical sun caught the doubloons, so that the chest now seemed a great chalice filled with a golden flowing nectar.

" 'Twould appear they've not plundered our booty," the one-eared pirate said.

"We're castaways, not idiots," Jennet said.

"Thou art truly a printer, young Franklin?" the captain asked, thoughtfully stroking his wooden chin.

"Aye," Ben said.

"Ye print books?"

"Books, pamphlets, broadsheets."

"Then ye'll be interested to know I recently finished my memoirs, *The Amazing Exploits of Hezekiah Creech, Scourge of the Spanish Main.*" The captain uncocked his pistol, slammed the lid closed, and turned toward the one-eared pirate. "Mr. Baldwin, prithee row back to the *Judas* and fetch the manuscript from my desk. 'Tis under the parson's head." In consequence of his synthetic jaw, *Judas* came out *Judith.*

"Aye." The mate glowered and started away, obviously frustrated that Captain Creech had not ordered any butchery.

"What establishment employs ye?" the pirate leader asked Ben.

"Of late, Palmer's in London. Once back in Philadelphia, I shall seek a foreman's position with Samuel Keimer."

"How's this for an arrangement? Your Mr. Keimer gives me a thousand pounds sterling, and I allows him to publish my memoirs and keep a full fifth o' the profits."

"That's not exactly how the man does business. In truth, *you* would pay *him.*"

"In a tart's twat I would! I've written the best adventure book since *Robinson Crusoe!*"

"If such be the case, then I'm sure some London house would relish the chance to print and sell it," Ben said.

"Ye think so?" Captain Creech's simulated jaw permitted smiles of twice the normal span.

"Verily."

"And now we should like to show you how we happened upon your gold," Jennet said. "The demonstration requires that we use our hands."

Creech gave her a tepid nod. She dropped her arms, reached into the sack, and removed the clay bowl and its skewered cork.

"Amongst the items we rescued from the *Berkshire* was this, the most useful invention yet contrived by Mr. Franklin and myself." She sidled toward the rolling surf. " 'Tis an Albertus Magnus Goldfinder. Behold."

Stooping, she filled the bowl with seawater, then set the cork adrift. Instantly the door-nail swung toward the chest.

"It seeks the doubloons?" Creech asked, his factitious jaw descending.

"Like a compass hungering for the northern pole," Ben said.

"Marry!" Despite himself, Creech giggled. "A pirate with such a device need ne'er chase down a brig only to discover she's full o' naught but linen and tea!"

"Conduct us to Port Royal, and the trinket's yours to keep," she said. "The secret's in the needle. It appears an ordinary door-nail, but 'tis actually a sliver from the philosopher's stone Mr. Franklin and I recently refined in our Philadelphia laboratory."

"I've heard o' these philosopher's stones, but I ne'er knew a person that could make one," the pirate said. "Do they not turn lead into gold and grant immortality in the bargain?"

"Alas, the one we fashioned performs only the function you've observed," she said.

Captain Creech announced that he would now determine exactly how much distance might separate the doubloons and the goldfinder ere it ceased to work. For his first test, he carried the bowl fifty yards from the chest. The device performed splendidly, as Jennet expected it would. He increased the gap to a hundred yards. Again the finder did its job. Three hundred yards. Success.

Still skeptical, he fished the cork free of the bowl, then bid Jennet and Ben join him in ascending a towering limestone cliff to the south. The climb took the better part of an hour, but at last they all stood two hundred feet above the surf, Creech poised to perform his *experimentum crusis*. The treasure lay a half-mile away, a mere speck on the beach even when viewed through the Bini telescope.

Before Creech could refloat the cork, the mate appeared on the bluff clutching *The Amazing Exploits of Hezekiah Creech*. The pirate captain transferred the manuscript from Mr. Baldwin to Ben, who proceeded to scan the first page.

"Chapter Six tells how I lost my jaw to a Dutch cannonball," Creech said.

"A diverting anecdote, I'm sure," Ben said, then passed the manuscript to Jennet. "An auspicious beginning, Mrs. Crompton, would you not agree?"

BY WAYE OF PROLAWG. Heerin the Reeder will fynde nar-
rat'd the most fantastical Advenchures yet written down by
any mortul Hande. Those book Buyers who enjoye to hear
Tales of Daring by the Whorled's Buccaneers shan't be disap-
point'd by these Payges, but furst I must recounte something
of my Mother's Familee, my uncommun Childehood, and
my earlyest Years at Sea.

"I'm favorably impressed," she said.

"Be truthful now," Creech said.

"I note certain orthographic lapses."

"I suspected as much. Any other defects?"

"Mayhap a whit less bombast would please the London publishers,"
she said.

"Bombast's out o' favor?" Creech said.

"In recent seasons, aye."

Turning away from the Philadelphians, the captain offered Baldwin
a prolix discourse on Albertus Magnus Goldfinders, then cast the cork
adrift within the bowl. For a tense and protracted interval the door-nail
pointed out to sea, but then Mr. Gilbert's principle joined forces with
the inverse-square law, and the dial swung landward and fixed on the
doubloons.

"I'Christ, 'twill save us many a fruitless pursuit!" exclaimed Baldwin.

"Take us to Port Royal," Ben said, "and we shall afterward make you a
present of this machine."

"I saved the best news for last." Jennet set Creech's dreadful manuscript
on the ground, securing it beneath the telescope. "Mr. Franklin and I have
forsworn any further such inventiveness. Of all the buccaneers cruising
the Spanish Main, you gentlemen alone will possess a doubloon-detector!"

"Mrs. Crompton and Mr. Franklin are clearly two of the world's great
brains," Creech said to Baldwin. "When you slit their throats, do't
quickly, so as to minimize their discomfort."

A tremor passed through Jennet's frame, vibrating every bone. "Faugh!"

"My Lord Captain, you cannot mean what you say!" Ben wailed.

In Jennet's opinion Creech had meant every syllable—and so she did what the situation required: she reached toward the clay bowl, disassembled the compass, and hurled the door-nail over the cliff. Briefly the little spike sailed on the wind, then fell into the surf.

"Swine-swiver!" Baldwin cried, raising his cutlass.

" 'Sheart, Jennet!" Ben wailed.

"How durst ye thwart me?" Creech screamed, his jaw flapping like a tavern sign in a hurricane.

"Surely a man so intelligent as yourself can fathom my motives," she said to the pirate captain. "You must now bear Ben and me and little William to Philadelphia, that we might extract a *second* detector from our philosopher's stone."

"Shall I run 'em through?" Baldwin inquired.

Creech said nothing. He rubbed his timber chin. A cloud drifted past the sun, casting a shadow on his already gloomy face.

"What manner o' man be the Pennsylvania Governor?" he asked Ben. "Will he welcome my crew graciously? Like all buccaneers, we're known to give local economies considerable stimulation, for we buy our rum and sundries exclusively with silver and gold. What's the man like?"

"William Keith is innately indolent, bereft of scruples, and prepared to sell his own mother for political gain," Ben said.

"Aye, but doth he have any flaws?" Creech asked.

"None whatsoever. Best of all, he hath been like a father to me. 'Twas Sir William sponsored my recent trip to England. Upon our arrival in Philadelphia, I shall see to't he grants you freedom from harassment."

Creech retrieved his manuscript and clutched it to his chest. For two full minutes he paced back and forth on the cliff, lost in thought, an experience to which he was evidently unaccustomed.

"The Governor's in sooth your friend?" he said at last.

"We're thick as thieves," Ben replied. "*Honorable* thieves, I mean."

"Then the three of ye may board the *Judas Tree* at dawn," Creech said, "for we sail on the morning tide."

WITH NIMACOOK STEALTH and vulpine subtlety, Jennet and Ben made their way through the nocturnal forest, speaking not a word and snapping not a twig, until at last they reached the village gates. As arranged, Ebinose-Mbemba and his wife were waiting for them, Ossalume cradling the sleeping William whilst gently stroking his brow. It occurred to Jennet that her son was having far too eventful an infancy. Once back in Philadelphia, she must somehow arrange for his life to remain free of maroonings, buccaneers, and Utopias for runaway slaves.

Despite the considerable distance separating Ewuare from the pirate shallop, Ebinose-Mbemba feared that even the quietest colloquy might betray their whereabouts, and so he proceeded to guide the party along a jungle trail painted in pale lunar hues. In time they reached an outcropping of limestone sheltering a convivial pavilion framed in acacia wood and roofed by heliconia fronds.

"This is where I do my thinking," Ebinose-Mbemba explained. " 'Tis also quite suitable for conversation. Speak to me of the buccaneers."

Jennet and Ben began chattering in tandem, words flying from their mouths at peregrine velocities, phrases tumbling around each other like acrobats, so that their African listeners were oft-times obliged to ask for reiterations, but eventually the whole story came out. The goldfinder ploy had worked. Creech had been fooled. Ewuare was safe for the nonce.

"Even if I could talk as quickly as you two," Ossalume told the Philadelphians, "I would need until noon to voice the gratitude in my heart."

"You have lifted a great cloud from our lives," Ebinose-Mbemba added. "And yet one tittle of mist remains, and I would have us discuss it ere we part company."

"If I can burn away the last of the vapor, I shall," Ben said, receiving William from Ossalume.

"I speak of Creech's map," the King said. " 'Twould be desirable to destroy it, lest it one day lead a slave-catcher to Ewuare."

"Destroy the map?" Ben said. "I'faith, Your Majesty, as we continue to gain the pirates' trust, I shall use every means short of martyrdom to bring about that result."

"Mr. Franklin, you are a saint," Ossalume said.

"Oh, he's hardly that," Jennet said, "but he does own a passing impressive perfection-matrix."

With his free arm Ben gestured broadly, a flourish encompassing the entire pavilion. "And what does the Grand Oba think about of late when he enters his sanctuary?"

"Carnal comforts," Ebinose-Mbemba replied, flashing his wife a moon-lit smile. "Also Hobbes, More, and Locke." He sighed prolifically. "Every day our Bini grow more difficult to govern."

Elaborating, the King explained that since his last political conversation with Ben, nearly a year ago, the tribal and temperamental differences amongst the ex-slaves had fractured the community into three sub-villages, each with its own vision of the future. The inhabitants of North Ewuare, the Orishanlists, believed that the general welfare lay in maximum obscurity, and hence they urged a combination of isolationism and reproductive restraint. The people of East Ewuare, by contrast, insisted that fertility control was precisely the policy their former white masters would have wanted them to pursue, and therefore these Uhranwists— the name derived from the Bini kick-the-dodecahedron game— advocated exploratory voyages in quest of hospitable islands to which their descendants might immigrate. Even more radical were the South Ewuareans, the Barabbasians, who hoped to make Amakye-Isle the birthplace of a mighty African army that would one day sweep through the New World's rice plantations, tobacco farms, and cane fields, breaking chains and smashing shackles.

"I'Christ, how e'er will you reconcile these philosophies?" said Ben.

"Ossalume and I have drafted a constitution," Ebinose-Mbemba said. "The parliamentary component of our government will comprise two separate assemblies." He unfurled his left index finger. "A lofty upper house consisting of two elected agents per sub-village." He extended his right index finger. "And a less exalted lower house in which each sub-village enjoys representation proportional to its size."

"Tell us your opinion of this scheme," Ossalume said.

"A cumbersome compromise," Ben said.

"Quite so," Ebinose-Mbembe said.

"As unwieldy as my ill-starred Franklin Typesetter," Ben said.

"I don't doubt it."

"But preferable to any alternative I can imagine."

"Indeed."

At the first intimation of dawn, Jennet, Ben, and the Africans once again gave themselves to silence. Ebinose-Mbemba and Ossalume escorted the Philadelphians and their slumbering child back to the village gates, where the Grand Oba, much to everyone's surprise, broke his own rule and spoke.

"Fare thee well, Ben Franklin," he whispered. "Fare thee well, Mrs. Crompton."

"This constitutional republic of yours—'tis a most noble experiment," Jennet murmured.

"The whole business may end in chaos and carnage," Ebinose-Mbemba said. "But this I swear. 'Twill be an entirely illegal chaos and a most unlawful carnage. I shall allow no sanctified slaughter on Amakye-Isle."

Firming his grip on little William, Ben lowered his head in a gesture of respect. Ebinose-Mbemba and Ossalume deserved such deference, Jennet concluded, for by their own account they were arranging to put themselves out of business, which was not how royalty normally behaved. And so it was that—ere joining Ben on his walk back to the beach—she too bowed before the monarchs, humbled by their humility, awed by their modesty, and speculating that they might well be the brave and canny meek who would one day inherit the earth.

At Great Risk to Her Person
Our Heroine Inaugurates a Scheme
to Rid the World of
Several Unnecessary Delusions

A betted by favorable winds and congenial currents, the *Judas Tree's* northward voyage should have taken a mere eleven days, but in fact it lasted twice that long, for Hezekiah Creech insisted on attacking and looting every merchant ship that blew his way. This violent agenda proved unremunerative. Of the seven carracks and brigs he boarded that month, only one carried a treasure chest, and it contained silks and spices, not doubloons. If there were indeed such a thing as an Albertus Magnus Goldfinder, Jennet mused, this sorry pirate could certainly have done with one.

According to their original plan, which she regarded as both elegant and practical, when the *Judas Tree* reached port Ben would arrange for the pirates to deliver her and William to the Chestnut Street townhouse. Once confident that his family was safe, Ben would lead Creech and Baldwin to his Market Street garret, chip a splinter from his "philosopher's stone" (his most potent specimen of magnetite), run the fragment through a cork, and bid Baldwin bear the new doubloon-detector back to the *Judas Tree* for testing. Whilst the mate was confirming the device's authenticity, Ben would present Creech to Sir William Keith and, after graciously forgiving Keith his failure to provide the letters of credit, gleefully reveal that a band of spendthrift pirates stood ready to disperse their brightest coins amongst the local merchants, at which juncture Keith was certain to promise Creech that his buccaneers would find Philadelphia to be a pirate-friendly city.

By the time the *Judas Tree* dropped anchor, however, Ben had become enamored of a more elaborate scheme, intended not only to rescue his loved ones but to bring Creech and his band to justice, though Jennet did not learn of this egregious emendation until it was a *fait accompli*. The new plot hinged on Ben's entirely accurate assumption that the pirate captain would not imagine his prisoners to be swimmers. (Thévenot's art was largely unknown amongst seafarers, who held that a shipwreck ought always to entail a simple death by drowning, never the more agonizing alternatives of terminal thirst, lethal exposure, or carnivorous fish.) Shortly after midnight, Ben slipped furtively from his berth. He laced his sturdy torso into his agouti-skin suit, climbed down the anchor chain, swam a mile to Market Street Wharf, and dashed a dozen blocks west, shivering and dripping, to the largest mansion in Broad Street. Upon entering the foyer, he was informed by the servants that William Keith no longer occupied the Governor's post, but Ben did not allow this development to diminish his resolve. After rousing Keith's successor, a swaggering British major named Patrick Gordon, Ben convinced the new Governor to ignore his visitor's wild beard and strange wet garment, focusing instead on the propitious fact that a pirate shallop lay in the harbor. If Major Gordon acted quickly, he could capture the most abominable buccaneer ever to terrorize the Spanish Main.

Within the hour a raiding party of Redcoat soldiers was bearing down on the *Judas Tree*, one boatload commanded by Ben, another by Major Gordon, the third by Captain Wilcox of the Philadelphia garrison. They circled the shallop and came at her from the east, thereby acquiring the advantage of surprise. And so it was that, slightly after dawn, Jennet awoke to a cacophony compounded of clanging swords, discharging pistols, cracking bones, falling bodies, screams, shrieks, cries, oaths, and the scything sound of musket-balls burrowing into wood and flesh. She took William in her arms, pressing his face to her bosom that he might be spared the sight of the skirmish. As the boy wept tears of fright and confusion, she peered through her cabin window and beheld a tumult nigh as terrible as the Indian attack on Haverhill. This time, however, the chaos culminated not in a loss of freedom for Jennet but in its very opposite—her safe delivery, together with Ben and William, onto Market Street Wharf in a longboat rowed by two lobsterback corporals.

"You addlebrained cavalier!" she seethed as Ben clambered onto the pier. "You ninny-pated knave! 'Tis a miracle we weren't killed!"

"You flatter me, Mrs. Crompton, for I know naught of working miracles," Ben said, clutching Hezekiah Creech's map to his breast. At the height of the hurly-burly he'd managed to appropriate the document, in accordance with his commission from Ebinose-Mbemba. "Howbeit, I did calculate, quite correctly, that our fifty soldiers would easily o'erpower the sixteen buccaneers."

"Mark me, sir—you will ne'er again put our child in the vicinity of a pirate battle!"

He folded the map neatly and slipped it into his coat. "All's well that ends well."

"But it *didn't* end well, for today you have proved yourself a reckless rogue!" she cried. "You should take your Moderation grid and blacken every box! *Nummusquantum!*"

In the days immediately following the skirmish, *The American Weekly Mercury* devoted many acres of ink to the subject of freebooting in Philadelphia, with a particular emphasis on Governor Gordon's foray against the *Judas Tree* and his subsequent delivery of Hezekiah Creech's gold to the Crown. The most gripping such story related the fate of Creech himself. By the *Mercury's* account, as the soldiers were leading the buccaneer and his fellow blackguards to Walnut Street Prison, Captain Wilcox indulged in an especially abusive variety of literary criticism, smearing Creech's autobiography with cow dung. Somehow the outraged author broke free of his captors and wrenched the manuscript from Wilcox's grasp. A startled corporal, misreading the situation, shot Creech betwixt the eyes.

They buried the pirate captain in an unmarked grave, on unhallowed ground, along with his orthographically impaired memoir.

Was there a moral to be gleaned from Creech's demise? Jennet wasn't sure. She knew only that, against conventional expectations, the pirate now belonged to that tiny minority of human beings who had died in defense of a book.

Whilst thinking fondly of Creech came naturally to her these days, thinking well of Ben did not. "To err is human, to forgive divine," Alexander Pope had declared in his *Essay on Criticism*—two interconnected principles toward which Jennet felt considerable sympathy. If only Ben weren't so emphatically human, and she so far from divine. After much conscientious effort, she managed to stop berating him whenever the subject of the *Judas Tree* skirmish arose, though other points of disputation emerged betimes to fill the void. They quarreled about the efficacy of the new small-pox inoculations (Jennet favoring the procedure, Ben urging caution), about the value of lightning-rods (she judging them unproven, he arguing for their immediate and ubiquitous deployment), about the nature of God (she regarding the Almighty as an Aristotelian Prime Mover without knowable attributes, he cleaving to the infinitely clever Deist Clockmaker), and about the need for greater political unification amongst the Colonies (she opposing the notion, largely because he supported it). They even bickered about whose dwelling to make their permanent abode. Whereas he wanted them to occupy his Market Street lodgings, she thought they should live in her townhouse, which was cleaner, roomier, and more private. A month after their return to Philadelphia they were still essentially living in both places at the same time, a circumstance that to Jennet felt like living in neither place at any time.

"You must try to understand that I feel *comfortable* in my garret," Ben said. "I'm a wight who must be hemmed by his philosophic instruments."

"Then we need but pack up those instruments and carry 'em two blocks south," she said.

"They might break."

"Then we shall cushion 'em in straw, as we did Barnaby's monsters," she said.

"A procedure fraught with risks," he said.

"I'Christ, Ben, why is it we cannot breach a topic—which roof to call our own, whether it should have a lightning-rod—without we end up squabbling?"

After pondering the mystery for a fortnight, she fell upon a simple but sobering solution. In their minds' most subterranean tiers, they wished to be free of one another. Whether he knew it or not, Ben was suffocating. No doubt his overt desire to be "hemmed by his philosophic instruments" was real, but it paled beside his unspoken desire *not* to be hemmed by an infant he'd never meant to father and a woman more than twice his age—a woman who might ere long become incapable of negotiating a soup spoon or chamber-pot without his assistance. But Jennet, too, was feeling oppressed, laboring under an onus she could not abide, the burden of being a prospective burden.

When she first told Ben that they'd each become a millstone about the other's neck, he declared that his love for her was ripe and real as a field of Nimacook maize, and he would never assent to a rupture such as she proposed. The second time she offered her diagnosis, he sobbed like a child, so profoundly did the thought of losing her distress him. The third time she spoke to him of millstones, he found merit in the metaphor and consequently broke her heart.

"Alas, I must assent to your argument," he said, heaving a sigh. "For years our lives were of necessity intertwined, braided like the threads of a Persian carpet, but now the strands must come unraveled."

"Ne'er to be rewoven into their former splendor," she said, her throat swelling like a sprained ankle.

They were browsing through the bins in Gerencer's, searching without success for Newton's promised treatise on invisible particles. Either the tome didn't exist, or it hadn't yet crossed the Atlantic. A few yards away William played with the proprietor's cat, swinging a bit of kite-string through the air, thereby prompting the animal to walk on its hind legs.

"Oh, Jenny, why must we be so *reasonable* in this matter?" Ben said. "Prithee, talk some nonsense into my head."

"Nay, dear Ben, I shan't," she said, drying her eyes with her sleeve.

"I implore thee."

"The time hath clearly come for us to relinquish one another. 'Twould be a generous gesture on both our parts."

"Not generous—merely practical," he rasped. "We must sever our connection whilst we own the strength to do so."

From the nearest bin she retrieved a dusty quarto of *Romeo and Juliet*. "Come, my gallant, let us take hold of Shakespeare's great love-tragedy and pledge ourselves to an eternal separation." She pressed Ben's right palm against the book, then set her own right hand on top. "I do solemnly swear to give the world its due measure and deserved dose of Benjamin Franklin . . . say it, sir."

"I do solemnly swear to give the world its due measure and deserved dose of Benjamin Franklin . . ."

". . . who hath before him gardens to plant, experiments to perform, sages to impress, monarchs to harry, and dragons to slay . . ."

". . . who hath before him gardens to plant, experiments to perform, sages to impress, monarchs to harry, and dragons to slay . . ."

". . . in the name of all I hold sacred and dear."

Haltingly he echoed her words, then moaned quietly, turned away, and slunk off to sport with William and the bipedal cat.

THE NEW ARRANGEMENT went into effect the next day: two individual lives, two separate domiciles, with little William inhabiting his mother's townhouse all through the week but visiting his father's garret on Saturdays and Sundays. Occasionally she and Ben joined in connubial embrace, but these episodes became less frequent with each passing month. Gradually her sobs grew softer, her tears fewer, her dreams longer. She realized that, for the first time since her journey to Trinity College in quest of Newton, she'd done something unequivocally noble, and the novelty of it saw her through many a miserable night.

The sweltering summer of 1728 found both philosophers struggling to avoid bankruptcy, the remainder of Jennet's fortune having gone down with the *Berkshire*. By autumn their prospects had brightened. Bitter over Ben's secret alliance with the former Pennsylvania Governor,

Samuel Keimer had at first rebuffed him, but then a formidable commission came Keimer's way—printing paper currency for New-Jersey—and he realized that he would meet the deadline only by availing himself of Ben's quick mind, unflagging industry, and London training. Jennet, meanwhile, designated her front parlor a classroom and advertised herself as a tutor, and ere long several of the city's wealthiest families were entrusting her with their children's minds. She taught them what she'd learned from Aunt Isobel—penmanship, astronomy, geometry, optics, Latin—though rarely with the forbearance that the mistress of Mirringate Hall had so consistently displayed. Of her nine pupils only one evinced uncommon intelligence, Lucy Rooke, a Quaker girl who could draw the micrographic world, especially gnats, mites, and pond-water animalcules, as enthrallingly as Dunstan had rendered the horse-head promontory.

Her teaching efforts consumed half her day, William the other half, and yet she found time to collaborate with Ben on the great work, which she'd decided to call *The Sufficiency of the World: A Treatise Concerning How Witchcraft Is an Impossible Crime*. Although she still believed devoutly in her demon disproof, she took little pleasure in its composition, and Ben was likewise uninspired. Despite the book's provocative thesis and pithy prose, they could not imagine the average Parliamentarian sitting down and poring over every page. Most likely the Lords and their counterparts in the Commons would pawn the treatise off on the Royal Society, where it would devolve not to the estimable Dr. Halley—he was seventy-four, after all, and doubtless defensive of his time—but to some bright young demonologist all eager to find its faults and savage its lapses. And yet Jennet and Ben persisted in their labors, straight through Christmas and well into the new year, goaded by *Bible Commonwealth* reports that Dunstan and his band were "campaigning against the Wampanoag and Narragansett Pagans that infest our Massachusetts Coast."

Late in June there arrived at Keimer's shop a bundle containing over a hundred back issues of *The London Journal*, some as old as two years.

Prominent amongst the headlines for the third of April, 1727, was the news that Sir Isaac Newton—Knight of the Realm, Master of the Mint, President of the Royal Society—had died thirteen days earlier in Kensington, subsequently receiving an elaborate entombment ceremony at Westminster-Abbey. A dozen eulogies filled the pages, including epitaphs by Dr. Halley, Dr. Pemberton, and the celebrated French *philosophe*, Jean François-Marie Arouet de Voltaire. Mr. Pope honored the late geometer with one of those impeccable couplets Jennet found so annoying: "Nature and Nature's Laws lay hid in Night. God said, 'Let Newton be!' and All was Light."

Newton's passing instilled mixed emotions in Jennet. As a disciple of Reason and the inventor of the sufficiency hypothesis, she mourned the loss of Creation's keenest intellect, but she was happy to be forever rid of any obligation to return to England, solicit the madman once again, and beg that he go before Parliament with his endorsement of her demon disproof.

Her final flurry of effort on the manuscript had less the effect of elaborating her argument than of multiplying her grievances against Ben. Contrary to the pledge he'd once made—"Franklin and Crompton, united against the Conjuring Statute!"—his principal goal these days was not to defeat the witchfinders but to transform himself into America's most celebrated printer. Already he had much to show for his ambition: a rapid, conspicuous, and well-deserved rise that was the mirror opposite of Samuel Keimer's rapid, conspicuous, and well-deserved slide into ruin. Although the New-Jersey currency project had netted Keimer a handsome profit, he'd managed to squander it in a matter of weeks. For a time he revived his fortunes by publishing a weekly newspaper, *The Pennsylvania Gazette*, but ultimately this venture failed too, and when Ben proposed to purchase both the paper and its parent shop for three hundred pounds sterling, the broke and broken Keimer readily assented. Ben borrowed the specified sum from the father of his high-born friend Hugh Meredith, whereupon Keimer absconded to Barbados, the better to avoid his legions of creditors.

Beyond his obsession with the *Gazette*, Ben had also grown preoccupied with the Junto, a self-improvement and mutual aid society he'd formed with a dozen like-minded young men. Although Jennet scorned the Junto for its deleterious effect on *The Sufficiency of the World*, she decided that its advent was not entirely catastrophic, as the membership happened to include John Tux, née Naanantux, a chestnut-brown Indian whose pensive countenance reminded her of Okommaka in his prime. Astonishingly, John Tux was a Nimacook. More amazing yet, he hailed from her own adoptive clan, the Kokokehom.

On first meeting John Tux, Jennet was hard pressed to persuade him that, her abduction notwithstanding, she did not abjure her savage past. Indeed, but for her devotion to the *argumentum grande* she might yet be living in the woods, wearing feathers and skins. Convinced at last that she bore him no malice, John Tux proceeded to tell his story, delighted to be once again conversing in the Algonquin tongue.

Not surprisingly, the narrative whereby Naanantux had come to Philadelphia was only slightly less brocaded and bizarre than the adventures that had landed Jennet in the same metropolis. When he was but nine, a *skishauonck* epidemic had claimed both his parents. The orphan forthwith fell under the patronage and persuasion of the latest missionary to have insinuated himself into the village, Pierre Dumond, S.J. Observing in the bereft Naanantux a mind of singular intelligence, Father Dumond convinced him to abandon his tribe, abbreviate his name, embrace Roman Catholicism, and join the priest in bringing the One True Religion to receptive Indians everywhere. For the better part of five years, Father Dumond and John Tux roamed the Algonquin lands south of the Merrimack and west of the Shawsheen, baptizing not only Nimacooks but also Pocassets, Sakonetts, Nipmucks, Abenakis, and Wampanoags, a period during which the Jesuit instructed his young charge so ably in the languages of antiquity that ere long he could negotiate St. Thomas Aquinas in the original Latin.

John Tux's career as a latter-day St. Paul ended abruptly when an Abenaki sagamore took violent exception to Father Dumond's project, subsequently dashing out the priest's brains with a hatchet and threatening to treat John Tux in the same fashion if he failed to mend his Papist ways. Having acquired from his late sponsor a morbid fear of the fiery damnation that awaited all who forsook Holy Mother Church, John Tux lost no time fleeing the Abenakis and heading for Boston. Although he reached the city without mishap, he soon found himself destitute, for whilst his erudition made him competent to tutor the children of Puritan affluence, the parents of those same children could abide neither his Nimacook blood nor his Catholic faith. Fortunately, rumors of the Philadelphia ethos eventually reached his ears, compelling tales of quaking Christians who placed a premium on toleration, and so he made his way south to the City of Brotherly Love. Falling in with Ben and the Junto, he quickly ascended to the position of assistant foreman at Franklin and Meredith's Printing-House, even as he shed his Catholicism under the influence of his associates' rational and capacious Deism.

In recent years John Tux had elected to reforge his bond with the Kokokehom, regularly exchanging letters with his grandmother, Quannamoo, sister to the late Miacoomes and now the clan's chief sagamore. According to Quannamoo, hard times had befallen the tribe. Pushed ever westward by the dreams and deceptions of the European settlers, the Nimacook had most recently established their plantations in the Hoosic River Valley. Of the original six clans, only three remained, the Kokokehom, the Moaskug, and the Wautuckque. Evidently there was nothing in Quannamoo's letters about the medicine-woman, Hassane, about Jennet's adoptive cousin, Pussough, or about Kapaog, the one to whom she'd given her milk after the small-pox took his birth-mother. And yet, felicitously enough, Quannamoo occasionally mentioned the Indian of whose fortunes Jennet was most anxious to learn, her first husband, Okommaka. By Quannamoo's report, Okommaka's rage against the white race had lately increased to the point of mania. So far he had failed to rally a war party to his side, but the squaw-sagamore feared that ere long Okommaka would lead a raid on an English town, an action certain to spark disastrous retaliation.

"In your next letter to your grandmother," Jennet told John Tux, "I should like you to convey a sentiment from a footloose plantation maid."

"*Cowaunckamish.*" I am at your service.

"The message is this. 'Tell Okommaka that his Waequashim remembers him with great fondness, and she hopes that he will not be so foolish as to make war on the English settlers.' "

"In all candor, I doubt that your words will succeed in cooling Okommaka's ire," John Tux replied. "And yet I shall happily relay them. 'Tis the least I owe to one who seeks to foil the pricking persecutors of my kind."

By the end of the year it had become woefully clear to Jennet that *The Sufficiency of the World* was now her responsibility alone. When she chastised Ben for his unannounced decampment, he replied that the final draft would "boast a greater aesthetic integrity if written solely in your unique and piquant style."

"Then methinks 'twould also boast a greater aesthetic integrity if your name appeared nowhere on the cover-page," she said.

"As you wish," he said. "The thesis sprang full-blown from your brow, the words flowed largely from your quill. I can make no claim upon this tome."

Although Jennet deeply resented Ben's withdrawal from the *argumentum grande*, she could not quarrel with his offer to publish it for free. He could well afford such philanthropy. Under his guidance, Franklin and Meredith's Printing-House was flourishing, the *Gazette* having transmuted into a daily newspaper boasting hundreds of subscribers in Pennsylvania, Delaware, and New-Jersey, plus several score in Mother England. As with her earlier *A Treatise of How the Four Aristotelian Elements May Serve to Convince There Are No Elementals*, she decided that she would need three hundred copies, though she still could not imagine by what breed of cunning or species of deceit she might induce a Parliamentarian to read one.

On the fifteenth of April, 1730, the first proof of the first signature emerged from Ben's new Blaeu press. Jennet scanned the cover-page, her spirit reveling in its stately appearance even as her eye searched for typographical errors.

The
SUFFICIENCY
of the
WORLD

A TREATISE OF HOW
WITCHCRAFT
IS AN IMPOSSIBLE CRIME

As Demonstrat'd by
SIR ISAAC NEWTON'S
MATHEMATICKAL LAWS OF NATURE

&

Including
EXPERIMENTS
Such as
The Curious Reader May
HIMSELF PERFORM,

This Being the Personal Investigation of the Author,
J. S. CROMPTON,
NATURAL PHILOSOPHER

"Have I o'erreached myself, using Newton's name this way?" she asked Ben. "Does my action smack of desperation?"

"Aye," he said with a soft groan. "But better desperation in the service of Reason," he quickly added, "than Reason in the service of desperation."

He proceeded to expound upon this newly minted maxim, but she failed to hear him, for her brain was now ablaze with an idea, the sort of momentous stratagem she normally conceived only whilst swimming in the Schuylkill or walking the shores of Amakye-Isle.

" 'Steeth, I see it!" she shouted, pulse racing. "I see how we'll get both Lords and Commons to heed my book!"

"How, friend? Tell me."

"This be a devilish clever plot."

"Out with it!"

"We shall arrange for a witch-trial, with my damnable brother at its core. Not one of those travesties he enacts along the frontier, but a full and public test of the demon hypothesis, conducted right here in Philadelphia." Her heart had not ascended to such an altitude since her invention of the Albertus Magnus Goldfinder. "Now, Ben, listen to the nexus of my scheme. Every day of the trial, you will report on't in the *Gazette*, narrating each twist and turn in a manner calculated to enthrall your London subscribers. After the jurymen issue their verdict, each Parliamentarian will want to know how I convinced 'em I was innocent, and he will forthwith consult his *Sufficiency of the World*."

"I must have a plug of beeswax in my ear, Mrs. Crompton, for I heard you say 'twould be *you* in the dock."

"Of *course* 'twill be me, playing the part of an enchantress."

"You upbraid me for crossing swords with Hezekiah Creech, and now you wish to cut cards with the Devil himself?"

"Quite so, sir, but aside from the dangers involved, have I not wrought a most wondrous plan?"

Lifting the signature from her grasp, he strode into the drying-room. She followed directly behind, inhaling the pungent and authoritative fragrance of printer's ink.

"Wondrous?" he wailed. "*Wondrous?* 'Sheart, 'tis wondrous insane and naught else. Nay, Jenny, I shan't let you imperil yourself as you propose."

"I must do this, sir."

"Will you not understand that I cherish your life even more than mine own?"

"And will *you* not understand that nary a month goes by without Dunstan and his demented bride kill some blameless New-England savage? 'Tis my duty to thwart 'em. My soul demands it."

For five silent minutes Ben occupied himself in removing a dozen dry signatures from the line—the opening pages of a grammar-school primer—thus making room for *The Sufficiency of the World*.

"Your soul," he echoed.

"My soul."

Sighing and snorting, he clipped the first signature of Jennet's treatise to a string. "Very well, darling. Put on your darkest dress, mount your swiftest besom, and summon a thousand serpents to your door. But take care lest your ruse carry you straight to the gallows. I'll not have you gaining your soul and losing the world—there be no bargain in that."

AS JENNET DREW HER PLANS against the Massachusetts cleansers, she inevitably thought of the innumerable animal traps she and Ben had laid during their marooning. More than once she imagined treating Abigail Stearne like a snared agouti, peeling away her hide, boiling the flesh from her bones. Each time the reverie surged up in Jennet's mind, she recoiled from its violence, even as she reveled in its crude justice. "Keep your object always in view, dear philosopher," she told herself. " 'Tis not to extinguish Abigail's person but rather to eradicate her profession."

Although the New-England prickers were craftier than any agouti, Jennet's plot was more cunning than any snare. The opening gambit had her shipping thirty copies of *The Sufficiency of the World* to King George's councilors and the remaining two hundred and seventy to prominent Parliamentarians. (The idea of handing out books *gratis* so unnerved Ben that he immediately printed another three hundred, arranging for both Mr.

Efram and Mr. Gerencer to sell them at eight shillings per copy.) Her next move was to turn herself into another person. Her new name, Rebecca Webster, took but a moment to contrive: "Rebecca" to honor the unfortunate Rebecca Nurse of Salem-Village, "Webster" to salute John Webster and his bravely skeptical though philosophically impoverished *Displaying of Supposed Witchcraft.* For a base of operations she selected Manayunk to the northwest, a farming community situated on the fertile wedge betwixt the Schuylkill River and the Wissahickon Creek.

Specialists in raising flax, a crop whose proper cultivation they'd learned from the inhabitants of nearby German-Town, the yeoman planters of Manayunk were an unsophisticated bunch, peasants by another name, which made them ideal for Jennet's purposes. As she gauged the character of the village, if a newly arrived widow exhibited coarse manners, asked rude favors, grew strange flowers, and appeared to worship heathen gods, it would not be long ere her neighbors cried her out.

After a full week's search she found an ideal venue in which to enact the great ruse, a decrepit and deserted poultry farm at the intersection of Hermit Road and Sumac Lane. The barn had already become a haven for stray cats, easily cast in the rôle of animal familiar. Even more felicitous was the dark loamy soil adjacent to the house, a tract well suited to the growing of monk's-hood, thorn-apple, mandrake, henbane, and other plants certain of arousing local suspicion.

"You have found a tenant," she informed the farm's owner, a retired Welsh sea captain rumored to have made and lost several fortunes importing rum from Barbados.

Obviously William must now go live with Ben, lest he awaken one morning to witness his mother being carted off to gaol. At first Jennet had no idea how she might prepare William for her imminent disappearance, but then John Tux reminded her of *pittuckish,* the duty of every wayward Nimacook to visit his clan at regular four-year intervals, an obligation that he himself would be fulfilling ere long. Because the boy had always regarded Jennet's Indian past with fascination and delight, she decided to tell him that the time was nigh for her to practice *pittuckish:* betwixt now and early spring she would be away in Massachusetts, living with the Nimacooks, harvesting maize and weaving sleeping mats. So plausible did this narrative sound when she presented it to William, she did not hesitate to circulate the same falsehood amongst the families of her nine pupils. Such a rare privilege it hath been to teach your progeny, she told each mother, even those who'd whelped porridgeheads, but now my blood beckons and my heritage calls.

Naturally the idea of their child inhabiting Ben's unhealthy garret troubled Jennet, and so she experienced a great relief upon learning that the resident landlord, Thomas Godfrey, had resolved to move his family to New-Jersey and rent the entire dwelling to Ben. Rather less soothing to Jennet was the news that a certain Miss Deborah Read, whose widowed mother ran a boarding-house in Spruce Street, would be living at the Market Street mansion as well. Whilst Jennet was prepared in spirit for this event—why had she surrendered Ben if not to let him find the woman who would share his dotage?—the fact of it made her miserable. No doubt Miss Read was a worthy soul, but she'd probably never determined a parabolic orbit or launched a war against irrationality.

Jennet signed the lease on a Friday afternoon, moved in the following Monday, and set about presenting herself to the people of Manayunk as the village's most sinister eccentric. She had barely embarked on this masquerade ere realizing that Rebecca Webster's paganism must occupy a middle ground: the widow could enact uncanny rites, but she ought never to engage in manifest Devil-worship, lest the jury feel bound to convict her whether they subscribed to the demon hypothesis or not. And so it was that, walking home each evening from their fields and shops, Mrs. Webster's neighbors witnessed her performing wild Dionysian dances around a high cairn. They observed her flying kites in thunder-gusts, rehearsing incantations before her barn cats, and tending a garden of consummate grotesquery. But they never saw her sacrifice a goat to the Dark One or pour libations on a Satanic altar.

Even before the first stories of the Widow Webster's peculiarities surfaced in Manayunk, Ben had drafted *The Pennsylvania Gazette* into the charade. For the immediate future, he furtively informed his employees, the paper would pursue a policy of amity toward the Royal Governor, periodically lauding his courage in attacking the pirate shallop. Beyond its praise of Patrick Gordon, the *Gazette* would publish each week a letter from the nonexistent Ebenezer Trenchard. Jennet judged this hoax a true Franklin masterpiece, his most impressive deception since Silence Dogood. She read Mr. Trenchard's inaugural epistle straight through without once relaxing her smile.

19 September 1730

To the Authors of the Gazette:

I write to acquaint you that I, an aging Philosopher who learn'd more of Nature's Ways from sailing the World's Oceans than from his Years of Study at Harvard College, have lately reach'd certain Conclusions pertaining to so-called Witchcraft. Owning no Inclination to write a full Tome on the Subject, I shall instead purvey my Opinions through your excellent Newspaper.

Before the courteous Reader replies that Philadelphians traffic not in Old-World Superstition, let me report that in Manayunk-Village today there be Whisperings of how a certain Widow living in Sumac Lane hath covenant'd with the Devil. To wit, our Province may soon see its first Witch-Trial, sanction'd by the very Parliamentary Act that saw Nineteen supposed Satanists hang'd at Salem in 1692, an Event whose tragickal Nature did not deter the Pennsylvania Assembly from ratifying, to its everlasting infamy, the Statute in Question a Dozen Years ago.

My own Views concerning the "Demon Hypothesis" have lately alight'd atop the highest Pinnacle to which a reason'd Skepticism might aspire, a Circumstance I credit largely to J. S. Crompton's estimable Book, *The Sufficiency of the World*. If my Recommendation prompts even one *Gazette* Subscriber to acquire this remarkable Work (on sale at 8 s. the Copy at Gerencer's, Ephram's as well, and obtainable by Mail from those same Vendors), this brief Missive will have been well worth the Composition thereof.

> *Your most humble Servant,*
> *Ebenezer Trenchard, Esq.*
> *Seaman Scholar of Front Street*

After five full weeks of portraying Rebecca Webster, Jennet at last received indications that her neighbors were growing fearful: a mysterious fire in her barn, a dead opossum gibbeted from her largest chestnut tree, an aggressive scrap of Scripture nailed to her front door. (*And the Soul that turneth after such as have familiar Spirits, and after Wizards, to go a-whoring after them, I will cut him off from amongst his People.*) And yet, alas, not one villager undertook to lodge a formal complaint. Whilst nobody felt any affection toward the Witch of Manayunk, evidently nobody wished to see her in gaol either.

The instant she apprised Ben of the village's complacency, he sought out the Junto's second cleverest member, the poet and surveyor Nicholas Scull, whose aptitude for trickery fully equaled Ben's. On the first Monday in November Mr. Scull rented a room from a Manayunk tallow-chandler named Lawrence Eddings, and by evening he'd convinced the credulous dunderhead to regard his gout as an instance of *maleficium*. Two days later Mr. Scull visited Mr. Edding's first cousin, Elizabeth Jarrett, soon persuading the dressmaker that her baby's colic traced to wicked spirits. On Friday Mr. Eddings and Mrs. Jarrett betook themselves to the local justice of the peace, Herbert Bledsoe, and offered up their reasons for suspecting Mrs. Webster of demonic compact, and that very afternoon Jennet's farm-house shook with the insistent clamor of the newly appointed magistrate pounding on her door.

"Do ye know what brings me here?" he asked as she gestured him into the parlor. Mr. Bledsoe was a sallow and phlegmatic young man, not more than twenty-five, with a thin mustache sitting atop his upper lip like a dormant caterpillar.

"Nay, I cannot imagine," she said.

"Your neighbors call ye a sorceress"—his tone was almost apologetic—"and so I am bound to arrest ye."

"I know naught of such arts," she protested.

"Your accusers say otherwise."

Mr. Bledsoe permitted her to bank her cooking-fire, extinguish her hearth, latch her casements, close her shutters, and lock her door. He clamped iron manacles around her outstretched wrists and, like a Nima-cook taking a white woman captive, led her down the garden path past a thorn-apple bush, its fruit still unharvested, and a stand of monk's-hood in a similar state of neglect. So far the drama was playing out exactly as she'd written it, and yet she experienced a dim disquieting presentiment that her control over this *pièce bien faite* had reached its zenith. She had awakened a sleeping dragon, the antique fear of *maleficium*, and God alone knew what consequences would soon be upon her.

Located on the eastern shore of the Schuylkill, Manayunk Gaol-House was a rude stone structure consisting of Mr. Bledsoe's offices on the ground floor and, delved deep into the riverbank like a mass grave, the dungeon itself. The magistrate handed Jennet over to the turnkey, the ursine Matthew Knox, his face aflush with gin, his breath laden with the same substance. Upon removing her manacles, Mr. Knox presented her with a burlap smock, then gestured toward a folded muslin screen and instructed her to avail herself of whatever privacy it afforded.

Once attired in prison garb, Jennet followed Mr. Knox in a clockwise path down a spiral staircase, their journey terminating in a torchlit grotto containing three iron-gated cells separated by brick partitions. Such heat as the space enjoyed came from an enclosed brazier and its concomitant brick chimney, the contraption dominating the corridor like a great Cartesian heart throbbing within an immense clay golem. In the left-hand cell stood a runty man of middle age, his rheumy eyes and ruddy nose dribbling with the Danish chill. The right-hand cell held an elderly woman of the dilapidated sort frequently apprehended for Satanism—though surely, Jennet reasoned, there could not be a second witch-trial in the offing. Mr. Knox placed her in the central compartment, half the size of Billy Slipfinger's hovel in the Fleet, devoid of all furnishings save a pitcher of water, a chamber-pot, and a pine pallet supporting a straw mattress. Acrid moss clung to the bricks like daubs of green mortar. A huge spiderweb spanned the ceiling, two trapped woodworms twitching near the hub.

Shortly after the turnkey locked her in, Jennet learned that, for better or worse, voices traveled easily from cell to cell. Her fellow prisoners introduced themselves as Edith Sharkey and Cyril Turpin.

"So ye're the one stands accused o' necromancy," Mrs. Sharkey said.

"Quite so," Jennet said, itching in her burlap smock.

"Then please know that a witch hath ne'er had a more amiable prison-mate than myself. I'll give ye no cause to make my hair fall out or my skin turn to boils."

"The charges against me are without grounds," Jennet said.

"Marry, what a coincidence!" Mrs. Sharkey exclaimed. "They've got no evidence in my case either, save a rumor I came home from marketing one day to find my husband and our serving-maid stark naked in the barn, churning up some love butter. Supposedly, I grabbed the plow and furrowed both their skulls with the moldboard. Now I ask ye, Mrs. Webster, how could an old wife like me lift all that iron by herself?"

" 'Tis a mystery, in sooth," Jennet said.

"Odsfish, ye ladies have me outclassed!" Mr. Turpin shouted. "One of ye's indicted for bashing out her husband's brains, the other's accused o' Satanism, and *I'm* naught but a common thief." He paused, sneezed twice, and continued. "Well, not *too* common, for I've risen far above my station. I started out in the chicken-coop, but soon I'd worked my way up to the goat-pen, and from there to the sheep meadow, and I had my eye on some horses when this outrageous suspicion concernin' Mr. Pertuis's cattle fell upon me."

"I cannot speak very highly of Philadelphia justice," Jennet said. "Here we are in gaol, and yet each of us is spotless as St. Genevieve."

She eased herself onto the mattress and stretched her frightened bones along its length, the bits of straw jabbing her back and thighs like the nails in a Hindoo fakir's bed. At that moment she wanted nothing more than actually to *be* a witch—a certain kind, of course: not a misbegotten hag with gobber tooth and warty nose, but a full-blooded magus boasting Perdition's every imp as her retainer, each eager to pluck its mistress from her gaol-cell, bear her to little William's side, and fly them both to the warmest and most fecund of Jupiter's undiscovered moons.

AS HER INCARCERATION PROGRESSED, Jennet was pleased to find the rawness of her accommodations counterbalanced by a certain civility in her keepers. Although tradition required Mr. Bledsoe to make his prisoners' diet severe, he saw to it that their water was clean, their peasebread fresh, and their cheese free of mold. He kept the brazier burning around the clock. Best of all, he imposed no limits on visitors, with the result that Jennet and Ben enjoyed one another's company every day.

Mr. Knox, meanwhile, provided her with each new issue of *The Pennsylvania Gazette*, as well as daily bulletins on the status of her case. By the turnkey's narrative, Mr. Bledsoe had recently enlisted the services of Magistrate Abraham Pollock, his counterpart in Mount-Holly, New-Jersey. Late in October Mr. Pollock had tested an accused Satanist named Gabriel Toffey by standing him on a granary scale and counterweighting him with the town Bible—for it was commonly supposed that wizards and witches contained less physical substance than ordinary mortals, hence their ability to transvect themselves via brooms and pitchforks. Much to Mr. Pollock's disappointment, Mr. Toffey's meat and bones elevated the Prophets a full five feet, and so the magistrate was obliged to release him. For reasons not entirely apparent, this episode conferred on Pollock a local reputation as a competent demonologist.

Given what Mr. Knox had told her about the Mount-Holly affair, Jennet was hardly surprised when Mr. Bledsoe appeared in the dungeon early one morning and declared that his colleague would test her that day. At noon Mr. Knox rowed Jennet across the Delaware in his brother's fishing dory, then transported her by hired carriage to Pollock's cramped office, its every horizontal surface obscured by deeds, wills, and contracts. The magistrate sat behind his desk, signing arrest warrants with such broad gesticulations as to suggest an orchestra *maestro* conducting a tumultuous finale. A choleric man with blotchy yellow skin and a livid scar on his forehead, he seemed to Jennet less an avatar of Themis than a renegade from Hezekiah Creech's pirate band, now posing as a judge.

Throughout the questioning phase Jennet remained unflustered, deliberately arousing Pollock's suspicions whilst simultaneously confounding his expectations. When he asked her why she encouraged so many cats to inhabit her barn, she offered an answer—" 'Tis the mice who lure them thither, not I"—that seemed to partake of neither innocence nor insolence but of something betwixt the two. When he demanded that she recite the Lord's Prayer, she purposefully switched "Thy kingdom come" and "Thy will be done," then calmly explained that she'd learned her *Pater Noster* from an elderly parson who'd routinely scrambled his scriptural clauses. When he inquired whether she indeed grew monk's-hood and mandrake in her garden (a rumor to that effect having reached his ears) and whether she intended to mash these plants into flying ointments and libidinous unguents (their most notorious application), she cryptically replied, "Monk's-hood and mandrake boast utilities ne'er dreamt of by a mere provincial magistrate."

Next Pollock delivered her into the hostile embrace of his three husky sisters so that they might scan her skin, whereupon the impetus of the interview went against Jennet as abruptly as Gabriel Toffey had shot the town Bible skyward. Whilst Knox stared uncomfortably at his boots and Pollock watched in lascivious delight, the sisters stripped off Jennet's burlap smock, shaved her body—head, armpits, legs, privates—and went to work, their fingers inching across her skin like blind and mindless larva. Just when it seemed she could endure this humiliation no longer, the eldest sister reported a warty protuberance on the suspect's neck. Pollock proceeded to probe the excrescence with a steel sewing needle, betimes declaring it bloodless, which was doubtless true, for Jennet could barely feel the needle's point.

At dusk Pollock and his sisters reclothed her in the burlap smock, bowed her into the posture of a fœtus, and lashed her wrists and ankles together with leather thongs. When Knox averred they had no cause to treat Jennet with such cruelty, Pollock plied him with his favorite food, unwatered gin, and the turnkey forthwith found himself on the floor, sprawled across a mattress of documents and singing "Lillabullero."

The Mount-Holly witchfinders deposited their trussed prisoner in a horse-drawn cart, conveyed her to the Delaware, and spilled her onto a granite pier as a fisherman might unload a netful of cod. As Jennet lay shivering in the winter air, face down, the damp stone gnawing her bare arms and exposed calves, the sisters hitched a plow-rope around her waist. Without warning, Pollock bent low and swung at her with his balled fist, ramming his knuckles into her stomach and forcing her to exhale. Before she could take more than half a breath, he blithely rolled her over the edge of the pier.

She crashed into the frigid river, the surface shattering around her as if she'd fallen through a cathedral window. Engulfed, she sank, straining and jerking against the unyielding thongs. Water shot up her nose, burning the fleshy cavity beyond. So this was what they'd endured, Isobel Mowbray and Susan Diggens and all the others—this maleficent acid, this liquid fire. She opened her eyes, beheld the Delaware's green swirling murk. Her windpipe spasmed. Her chest grew tight as a brick. And still she sank, deeper, deeper. A noise like muffled cannon fire boomed in her skull, a phenomenon she soon recognized as the pounding of her own heart.

Suddenly the rope went taut, and now she was rising, ever higher, until at last she felt a breeze upon her brow. She devoured the evening air, sucking it down as forcefully as Ben's vacuum-pump drawing the atmosphere from a bottle.

"The Delaware hath spurned thee," Pollock declared, pulling her shoreward, "a fact I am bound to share with the grand jury!"

"I nearly drowned!" she cried, teeth chattering. " 'Twas the rope caused my ascent!"

The witchfinders dragged her onto the pier. "Nay, Mrs. Webster," Pollock insisted. "Thy buoyancy be of Beelzebub!"

" 'Twas the rope!"

Four days later Pollock offered his findings to the *ad hoc* grand jury. The hearing unfolded with an inevitability that bid fair to make the transit of Venus seem optional by comparison and the inverse-square law a mere matter of opinion, and Jennet would have counted the whole show a farce but for its occasioning Ebenezer Trenchard's best essay to date.

10 March 1731

To the Authors of the Gazette:

This Tuesday past I again visit'd Manayunk, where I witness'd a Grand Jury return a *Billa Vera* against Rebecca Webster following Testimony by her Neighbors and a Presentation by the Mount-Holly Magistrate. Throughout the entire Hearing Mrs. Webster sat respectfully beside the Bench, Head bow'd, as if in Prayer.

In this Week's Epistle I am mov'd to present a Fact not universally known. For nearly forty Years now His Majesty's Privy Council hath charter'd within Massachusetts Bay an Organization styling itself the "Purification Commission," consisting of a "Witchfinder-Royal" named Dunstan Stearne and his three fellow Prickers. Far from performing the Godly work the word "Purification" implies, these Scoundrels have to date executed over two Hundred innocent Souls, most drawn from the local Indian Population.

How might the good People of Pennsylvania protest this violent Mangling of Justice by Mr. Stearne's unholy Company? I answer as follows. We must call upon Governor Gordon to petition his Massachusetts Counterpart for the Loan of these dubious Demonologists, that they might come to Philadelphia and prosecute Rebecca Webster, in the Doing of which their fallacious Methods will, I am sure, stand expos'd as sheer Chicanery. Should Mr. Stearne and the Others refuse to take the Case, then methinks all reasonable Men will be forc'd to a Conclusion that this "Purification Commission" hath Much to conceal and More to fear.

> *Your most humble Servant,*
> *Ebenezer Trenchard, Esq.*
> *Seaman Scholar of Front Street*

On the second Sunday following the issuance of the *billa vera,* Ben gleefully recounted for Jennet his recent conversation with Major Patrick Gordon. A practical man who took a dim view of metaphysical matters, the Governor had been vaguely antagonistic to the Conjuring Statue even before the *Gazette* cast him as the hero of the Creech affair, and now he wished to reward Ben's blandishments by becoming a devout crusader on Rebecca Webster's behalf. Assenting to the logic of Ebenezer Trenchard's most recent letter, Gordon had already asked Governor Belcher of Massachusetts to send his Purification Commissioners south and make the Crown's case against the Witch of Manayunk. The nascent Court of Oyer and Terminer, specially appointed by Gordon to try the defendant, would be administered by the famously evenhanded Judge Malcolm Cresswell. In contrast to the Salem protocols, the jury would hear not only the evidence against the accused but also an argument for her innocence. Moreover, Cresswell would allow Mrs. Webster to speak on her own behalf, provided her statements were elicited by a skilled and circumspect barrister.

Jennet could not help noticing that despite these victories an uncharacteristic gloom clung to Ben, palpable as a frock coat.

"What ails thee, sir?"

"Jenny, dearest, 'tis not too late to end this perilous game." He pressed his chest against the bars of her cell, printing their grime on his white Holland shirt in four vertical columns. "Let us tell Magistrate Bledsoe you've merely been *playing* the enchantress—you did it to set Trenchard's pen scribbling against the New-England prickers—but now the hoax hath run its course, and you wish to rejoin human society."

"What possible good could that accomplish?"

"The greatest good imaginable. 'Twould keep you off the gallows."

She pulled a handful of stuffing from her pallet, closing her fingers as if to mash the straw to flour. "Hear me, bonny Ben. My whole life I've chased after the abominable Conjuring Statute, and I shan't know peace till it be torn in bits."

Ben released a dissenting sound, something betwixt a bleat of anger and a groan of woe. "I did not sleep well last night, Mrs. Crompton, nor the night before either."

"I cannot accept a speckled ax."

"I wonder if I shall e'er sleep well again."

ON THE LAST AFTERNOON in April, as Ben sat in the press-room making ready to draft the newest Ebenezer Trenchard essay, it occurred to him that he'd developed a peculiar habit of living his life in reverse. The normal procedure followed by a person starting a business was first to obtain the funding and then to acquire the tools, but Ben had gone about it backwards, sailing off to buy printing equipment with no capital beyond the ethereal endorsement of a known scoundrel. Another such sequence had a man taking first a wife and only later a mistress, yet here too Ben had inverted the usual chronology, enjoying amorous relations with Jennet long before pledging his troth to Deborah Read. As for the marriage itself, once again he had defied tradition. Convention dictated that, upon winning a woman's love, a man should let her annul any existing marriage contract ere wedding her himself. Having absconded to the West Indies, however, Deborah's ne'er-do-well husband, the potter John Rogers, wasn't available for signing a divorcement decree, and so she and Ben had simply set up house together.

Although he felt an abiding fondness toward his common-law bride, he would admit that his sentiments fell short of adoration. The Helen of his heart's own Ilium would always be Jennet Stearne Crompton. But Jennet was a madwoman, a pagan Fury, her eyes locked on some self-consuming star that she alone could see, whereas he merely wanted to become an accomplished printer and a competent philosopher, ambitions that Deborah stood ready to support in full.

He inked his quill and touched nib to paper, but no words flowed forth. The momentous news of the day was Governor Belcher's announcement that he would instruct his Purification Commissioners to hie themselves to Pennsylvania and expose Rebecca Webster as a Satanist, a development that the imaginary Ebenezer Trenchard would logically disclose in terms of unqualified triumph. Trenchard's fleshly creator, however, was utterly distraught by the bulletin from Massachusetts. Dunstan Stearne's entry into the case, the very circumstance that Jennet so deeply desired and Ben so greatly feared, now seemed inevitable. He set down his pen and brooded.

The brass bell tinkled, the door flew open, and a young man strode into the press-room, liveried in purple silk and swirling a fur-lined cape, his head crowned by a powdered peruke. Marching up to Ben, he announced that his master wished to speak with the proprietor of the shop—or such was the interpretation that accrued to Ben's limited command of the French tongue.

"*Je m'appelle Delvaux. Êtes-vous bien Monsieur Franklin?*"

"*Oui, c'est moi,*" Ben said.

"*Mon maître, Charles Louis de Secondat, Baron de la Brède et de Montesquieu, souhaite s'entretenir avec vous. Il attend votre réponse dans sa carrosse.*"

It was generally a good idea to receive barons, Ben believed. Yes, hereditary aristocracy ranked high amongst his least favorite institutions, but potential patrons were always welcome at Franklin and Meredith's Printing-House. "*Informez votre maître que je serais heureux de le voir, mais j'espère qu'il parle anglais.*"

"My master indeed speaks English," Delvaux said with an oblique sneer. "Also Italian, German, Hungarian, and Turkish."

As Delvaux headed for the door, Ben realized that his caller must be the same Baron de Montesquieu who'd written the scandalous novel *Lettres Persanes*, published anonymously a decade earlier but finally appearing under the author's name during Ben's sojourn in London, for surely there could not be two different Frenchmen laboring under the appellation *Charles Louis de Secondat, Baron de la Brède et de Montesquieu*. On the surface a chronicle of Oriental customs, notably that endlessly fascinating institution known as the harem, *Lettres Persanes* was in fact an indictment of the follies infesting French society, framed as a series of letters to and from the courtier Usbek and his young friend Rica, fictive Persians traveling through Europe. Such a delicious conceit! What in Heaven's name had prompted this accomplished author to seek out the obscure editor of *The Pennsylvania Gazette?*

The instant he clapped eyes on his visitor, an elegant man in his early forties with a breaching stare and a hawk's beak of a nose, Ben nodded respectfully and said, "Let me declare at the outset, my Lord Montesquieu, that *Lettres Persanes* is quite the most caustic satire I've read since the *Decameron* of Signore Boccaccio."

A crescent-moon grin spread across Montesquieu's face. *"Monsieur Franklin, je vous remercie,"* he replied, sauntering toward the new Blaeu press. "But I must confess, I do not think of you Americans as enthusiasts for *les belles-lettres.*" Compared to his valet, the Baron dressed less ostentatiously, spoke less haughtily, and comported himself more humbly. "I regard you rather as the unpretentious inhabitants of a New Eden."

"For better or worse, we shed our jungle manners and bearskin leggings several generations back," Ben said. "Of course, I still keep an Iroquois hatchet in my desk, should a wild boar or an unruly Tory come charging down Market Street."

Montesquieu untied his perfumed neckcloth, employing it to sop the sweat from his brow. "You truly found amusement in my trifling novel?"

"My mouth grew sore from smiling."

The Baron proceeded to explain that, though he did not disavow *Lettres Persanes,* he hoped his future works would address subjects of greater import than his countrymen's foibles. Toward this end, he had undertaken a grand tour of Europe and the New World, recording such observations and collecting such artifacts—codices, trial transcripts, letters from repentant criminals, even a few torture instruments—as might one day enable him to write a great book on law and government. Already he'd visited Austria, Hungary, Italy, and England, and now here he was in America.

"Whilst living in London," Montesquieu said, "I became enamored of two American writers—the natural philosopher J. S. Crompton and also Ebenezer Trenchard, champion of the accused sorceress Rebecca Webster. As you are the publisher of both men, I hope you might point me in their direction."

"May I trust you to keep Trenchard's location a secret?" Ben asked.

"Je serai très discret."

"To find the journalist in question, you need look but a yard beyond your nose, for Ebenezer Trenchard is my *nom de plume.*"

"Formidable!" Montesquieu offered a bow of admiration, nearly losing his peruke in the process. "Ah, Monsieur Trenchard, I am so honored to make your acquaintance." His gaze alighted on a dozen copies of *The Sufficiency of the World* stacked atop the scrubbing counter. "And here we have the divine Monsieur Crompton!" He removed the topmost volume and brought it to his bosom. "Nature's laws truly refute the demon hypothesis."

"I must insist that you ne'er reveal certain facts concerning J. S. Crompton."

"Naturellement."

"Is this your sacred promise?"

"Oui."

"Then I shall tell you that Crompton is a woman."

"Sapristi!"

"She is also my dearest friend."

The Baron's eyebrows ascended to an altitude such that they nearly touched his wig.

"Moreover, she is sister to Dunstan Stearne, the likely prosecutor at the Webster trial."

"Mon Dieu!"

"Most provocative of all," said Ben, retrieving the broom from its customary corner, "J. S. Crompton and Rebecca Webster are the same person."

"Incroyable!"

Fixing his attention on the clusters of debris beneath the press, Ben systematically whisked them into the coal scuttle whilst simultaneously describing Jennet's foolhardy plan. He did not forbear to offer his opinion that she was "toying with her own life," a circumstance that was causing him "more anguish than I can calculate."

"Une femme courageuse." Montesquieu returned the demon disproof to the pile. "I sincerely hope her trial will deal the tyrannical prickers a fatal blow. You see, Monsieur Franklin, I am a great lover of the concept called freedom, *la liberté*—as are you yourself, *oui?*"

"Oui," said Ben, wielding his broom against the cobwebs beneath the scrubbing counter.

"Though I also believe—and here I suspect we are likewise in accord—I believe that every man's freedom must be constrained by the statutes his nation deploys against despotism."

Ben stopped sweeping and bobbed his head. "I would usually trust a congress o'er a king. And yet, even as we shape our statutes, do not these same statutes shape us? Are we not the creatures of our laws?"

"*Des créatures de nos lois! Exactement!* Good laws make good men. Bad laws harm everyone—not only those who break them, but those who obey them as well." Tightening his embrace of the demon disproof, Montesquieu explained that he'd reached these conclusions during his years as *Président à Mortier* in the High Court of Justice at Bordeaux.

"So you're a jurist as well as a satirist?" Ben said.

"A jurist, *oui,*" Montesquieu replied. "I am adept at writing statutes—though even more adept at writing *about* them, *si vous comprenez*. What I so admire about your English form of government is how it honors the reign of law. Three separate parts, each holding the other in check. A parliament to fashion the canons, an executive to administer them, and a judiciary to interpret them."

In point of fact, the English system was far messier and murkier than that, but Ben had no wish to lecture his visitor on the defects of the British Constitution. Another idea now occupied his brain, quite possibly his greatest since realizing that lightning must be electricity's celestial twin.

"*Monsieur le Baron,* I have a proposition for you. Let me make bold to suggest that the perfect lawyer for the remarkable Mrs. Crompton is at this moment standing before me."

"You wish me to defend your friend?"

"*Oui.*"

"*Ce n'est point possible.* In two days I sail for La Brède, there to be at last reunited with my family."

"You say you're skilled at making laws, but I'm offering you something more momentous—an opportunity to make *history!*"

"Or an opportunity to appear ridiculous," Montesquieu said. "Your Madame Crompton is intelligent, but juries are not. She could easily lose."

Humming his favorite ballad, "The Knight of Liddesdale," Ben made an ellipse about the room, the blacking table at one focus, the scrubbing counter at the other. "Baron, you have many enemies in France . . ."

"How did you learn this?"

"No man writes a book so barbed as *Lettres Persanes* without other men accusing him of treachery against Church and State. I ask you, sir, what better way to prove yourself a loyal Frenchman than to run a wicked English law to earth?"

"Monsieur Franklin, you are quite the logician," Montesquieu said. "Perhaps you should argue Madame Crompton's case yourself."

"Sir, there is but one jurist on these premises."

A prodigious sigh escaped the Baron's lips. He removed his peruke and rubbed the ball of his thumb across his brow. "Do you know what my uncle once said to me? 'We live in unprecedented times, Charles, and our sacred obligation is to occupy them fully.' Very well, Monsieur Franklin. I am persuaded to take up your friend's cause."

"Vous ne regretterez pas cette decision."

"It occurs to me that in moving against the English Witchcraft Act, we might *en passant* destroy other such laws throughout Europe," Montesquieu said, "for never before has the world been so prepared to cast off disastrous ideas." If good men everywhere rose to this occasion, he elaborated, their posterity would consider itself well served. These grateful descendants would call the present

century an era of courage, an

epoch of innovation,

and an age

of

✸

Reason,

I don't doubt,

will always hold an

honored place in my affections.

And yet I must admit that the more I think

about it, the less certain I become what Reason *is*. Everyone

agrees that Montesquieu's *Persian Letters* and Voltaire's *Candide* epitomize something called the Age of Reason (even though these novels can't stand each other, and neither could their authors), but this doesn't stop Reason from being among the most bedeviling ideas yet visited upon Western civilization.

Is the *Malleus Maleficarum* an unreasonable book? Many conscious entities would say yes. But if by reason we mean an orderly presentation that cleaves to a kind of perverse Aristotelian logic, then the *Malleus Maleficarum* is an imperially reasonable tome. Was the Third Reich an unreasonable enterprise? When you consider its grounding in neopaganism, occultist malarkey, blood-and-soil folderol, and crackpot eugenics, yes, indubitably. And yet the Nazis went about their agenda in a manner I can only call rational.

You know what I'm about to say. Whatever the stains on Reason's résumé, Revelation has much to answer for as well. Even were I to agree that Reason has been tried and found wanting (and I'm not convinced that such is the case), I would still applaud the Enlightenment for noticing that Revelation had rather too much blood on its hands, and it was time to contrive a different metaphysic.

And yet I concede that the apotheosis of Reason is a wretched idea. The *Principia Mathematica* will never file a brief on behalf of Reason per se—Reason unchecked, Reason unchained, Reason for Reason's sake. I am the first to insist that rationality disconnected from decency, deliberation, and doubt—a triad that, were I human, I would call humanism—leads not to Utopia but to the guillotine.

In the summer of 1794, some sixty years after the climactic events of this narrative, I decided that, being an honest sort of masterwork, I would observe firsthand the fruits of unfettered Reason. Willing myself to Revolutionary France, I climbed into the consciousness of Benoit Clément, a Catholic priest whom the *Comité de Salut Public* had recently found guilty of being a Catholic priest. Over two centuries have passed since that horrid day, but I can still recall the details: the suffocating heat of the dungeon, the frightened faces of my fellow prisoners (many of them children), the press of the shackles on my ankles and wrists.

It's the twenty-fifth of June. *La Terreur* is at its height. In recent weeks the *Comité* has abandoned all pretense of due process. The mere circumstance of appearing before Robespierre's tribunal proves that you harbor Royalist sympathies and have plotted against *la Révolution*.

I have just finished saying the Mass, using stale water for the blood, a rotten pear for the flesh, but no one has drawn much comfort from it. Six guards appear, armed with pistols and pikes. They have a list. My name is on it, along with nine others.

The guards herd us outside and shove us into a tumbrel, then scramble aboard themselves, their pistols trained on our chests. With a crack of his whip the driver urges the horses forward. As we approach the Place de la Révolution, our nostrils burn with the stench of human blood. Soon we hear the peasants singing drinking roundelays as they urge the executioners to their murderous work. Now another sound reaches our ears, the rushing roar of the guillotine blade.

My *Principia Mathematica* self is appalled. Is this what the love of Reason comes to in the end? Was my Jennet wrong to embrace the Enlightenment dream of eternal rational discourse? Is there any nontrivial difference between a witch-court and the *Comité de Salut Public?*

We enter the fœtid plaza. Because I am the only priest scheduled to die that afternoon, the mob demands that I go first. *"Touez le curé!"* they cry. *"Touez-le maintenant!"* A guard pulls me from the tumbrel. As I mount the scaffold, the executioner turns the crank as dispassionately as a sailor hoisting an anchor, thus sending aloft the steel blade and its collateral lead weight. My captors set me chest-down on the trestle and insert my head in the yoke. The lunette is slick with blood. I stare into the woven basket, likewise blood-soaked. Lifting my gaze, I see a horse-drawn cart crammed with headless bodies and bodiless heads. A fat man in a brown leather apron stands beside the horse, waiting to receive my remains.

"The Directors of the Lottery of St. Guillotine are pleased to announce the latest winner—Father Benoit Clément!" the executioner tells the crowd. They've heard the joke a thousand times before, but they still laugh.

I make my confession to myself, then vomit into the basket. The executioner presses the release button. The scaffold trembles as the blade thunders down the groove. I feel a sudden coldness against my neck, as if someone has dropped a snowball on the nape, and for one astonishing instant, at once impossibly brief and supernaturally protracted, I know the horrors of quadriplegia. Strangely enough, I'm aware of my head's tumble into the basket, an indescribable feeling—a falling sensation?—no, this is not an Isaac Newton moment, because to experience gravity you need a body as well as a brain: you need bones and limbs and muscles and

"Flesh is as grass," the Apostle Peter had noted in his stirring First Letter, "and all glory of Man as the flower of grass." The truth of Peter's words became especially clear to Dunstan Stearne every time the Purification Commission switched off a Satanist through fire rather than the noose. How little effort it took to vaporize a witch's grassy flesh. You chained her to a stake, lit the pyre, and within an hour there was nothing left but bones. "The grass withereth, the flower thereof falleth away, but the word of the Lord endureth forever."

He gave the signal, and the Commission went to work, foiling the Devil with clockwork precision. As Samuel Parris checked the thongs securing the Wampanoag woman's wrists, Abby lifted a steel ax and dealt her a blow to the skull. The instant the witch lost consciousness, Abby and the minister carried her carcass to the mound of hay and deposited it on the summit.

Whenever Dunstan perused a newspaper these days, he realized he was living in an era of unprecedented ingenuity: Fahrenheit's mercury thermometer, Lombe's thrown-silk machine, Réaumur's steel-making formula, Harrison's grid-iron pendulum, Hadley's quadrant. This cataract of cleverness depressed him. Man did not live by Baconianism alone. When the Massachusetts Assembly wrote to the Witchfinder-Royal urging that in the name of decency he should strangle his prisoners ere burning them, he had instinctively resisted the idea, averring that the blind embrace of innovation was a pernicious impulse. Only after Jonathan Corwin had bid Dunstan recall that such chokings boasted a tradition stretching back centuries—that, indeed, Dunstan's own aunt had nearly received this courtesy at her famous Colchester execution—did he relent and adopt the suggested policy.

Poor old Jonathan, dead over two months now, another victim of pleurisy and diabolism. The funeral was still fresh in Dunstan's memory. Reverend Parris had read the judge's favorite piece of Scripture, the Song of Songs, that pious love-ballad through which Christ had catalogued the manifold virtues of His Church. "Thy teeth are like a flock of sheep that are even shorn, which came up from the washing." For the Church had marvelous jaws indeed. "Thy lips are like a thread of scarlet, and thy speech is comely." And a splendid mouth. "Thy two breasts are like two young roes that are twins, which feed amongst the lilies." And an excellent bosom.

Pulling on his cowhide gloves, Dunstan marched toward the hay mound and closed his fingers around the throat of the dazed Wampanoag. For a count of two hundred he deprived her heathen lungs of air. The witch grew still. He released his grip, received the burning torch from his wife, and jammed it into the mound as if inserting a ramrod into a cannon's muzzle. The hay took but a moment to transmute into a bonfire, spewing smoke and spitting sparks.

"An idea of some merit occurred to me this morning," Abby informed Dunstan. "I found myself envisioning an exchange of witchfinders 'twixt ourselves and the Kirkcaldy Cleansing League. They would send us their ablest demonologist, and we would export my uncle to Scotland."

" 'Tis a worthy scheme, Goodwife Stearne. I shall commend it to our Caledonian brethren anon."

Evidently Dunstan had not applied sufficient force during the strangulation. Such, at least, was the conclusion he drew when the witch hurled herself off the hay, her clothing a-flame, her hair a blazing bonnet, and ran screaming through the woods toward her village. Her fellow pagans would have experienced some difficulty recognizing her at that moment, for she'd lost all particularity and become instead an ambulatory conflagration of vaguely human form.

"I'Christ, we've got a runner!" Abby yelled.

"Oh, how I wish Jonathan could be here!" Mr. Parris cried. "The sight of a runner ne'er failed to stir his blood!"

An absorbing spectacle, but Dunstan did not enjoy it. He could think only of the packet he'd received that morning from Boston, twenty-eight depositions collected by a Philadelphia grand jury whilst interrogating an alleged witch named Rebecca Webster (chief amongst them the report of Abraham Pollock, a New-Jersey magistrate), plus a letter from Governor Belcher exhorting the Commissioners to take the Crown's part in Mrs. Webster's forthcoming trial. In principle Dunstan was willing to lease his genius to Pennsylvania, but he had many questions about the case, and he was glad for the Governor's suggestion that the two of them meet in Boston come Monday.

With characteristic compassion, the Almighty now arranged for an armed Wampanoag deer-slayer to appear from behind a tree, assess the situation, and end the burning Satanist's misery. The brave unshouldered his musket and, drawing a bead on the witch, sent a bullet into her brain. Tumbling over the bank of a creek, the dying Indian crashed into the water and extinguished herself in a hissing cloud of smoke.

Dunstan had met Jonathan Belcher on only one previous occasion. The Witchfinder-Royal was delivering a sack of severed thumbs to Belcher's private secretary, the priggish Mr. Peach, when the Governor himself had entered the foyer, an unlit churchwarden pipe clenched betwixt his teeth. He asked Mr. Peach for a tinder-box and, receiving the desired artifact, returned to his duties without giving Dunstan so much as a nod. From that brief encounter Dunstan had judged the Governor a cold and self-absorbed man. He was greatly pleased therefore when Mr. Belcher began their Monday meeting by grasping his hand amicably and speaking in an almost deferential tone.

"His Majesty's Privy Council hath requested that I commend you for your long and loyal service to the Crown," the Governor said, leading Dunstan into his Treamount Street office, an airy space featuring mullioned windows and a parquet floor. With his wide face and bulky frame, Belcher looked rather like the manatee Dunstan had spotted two weeks earlier whilst a-cleansing on Martha's Vineyard. "The Boston clergy is similarly grateful. More than once I've heard a Puritan minister aver that our province's prosperity traces in the main to your work amongst the savage Indians. I must confess to a certain ambivalence toward your profession, but that needn't concern us this morning."

Heeding the Governor's gesture, Dunstan assumed an ornate chair cushioned in red velvet. He opened his valise and removed the newest proof of his industry, a baize bag containing four charred Wampanoag thumbs. "The Puritan divines value my services, and yet they would have me spend a month in Pennsylvania?"

"I gave 'em no choice in the matter, for the Webster case hath grown complex of late," Belcher said. "There be factions in America who would exploit it to raise a cry against the Conjuring Statute. King George will not have a great Parliamentary tradition assailed in this fashion. Is that understood?"

"Aye, my Lord Governor."

"Even as we speak, a cabal of atheists and freethinkers conspires to bring down the law in question. I allude to an upstart newspaper, *The Pennsylvania Gazette*, that each week prints letters attacking witch-courts everywhere. What is more, Governor Gordon hath appointed Judge Malcolm Cresswell to the case, a man notorious for ceding to defendants the benefit of far too many doubts."

"An appalling situation."

"*Appalling*'s the word"—Belcher settled onto a plush divan—"which is why I now offer you a trump card. I hope you'll see fit to play it."

Six months earlier, Belcher explained, Governor Gordon had led a military action that culminated in the apprehension of the infamous

West-Indies buccaneer Hezekiah Creech. According to Belcher's agents, Gordon had gifted himself with a portion of Creech's treasure ere delivering the remainder to the Crown.

"A troubling accusation," Dunstan said.

"Troubling, but also fortunate," Belcher said. "These days a man need but utter the words 'Tucker affidavit' within earshot of Mr. Gordon, and he will grant that person almost any boon."

" 'Tucker affidavit'?"

"A particularly damning deposition came from a Redcoat corporal named Noah Tucker. The Governor is all frantic to keep this fact in the shadows."

" 'Almost any boon'? Such as, for example . . . replacing Cresswell with a jurist less sympathetic to Lucifer?"

"You have a nimble mind, Mr. Stearne. Now it so happens Judge John Hathorne of Salem-Town is recently gone to Philadelphia, that he might convince his nautically inclined nephew to abandon the sea and enter the ministry."

"Dost perchance speak of the same Judge Hathorne who presided at Salem alongside our dear departed Mr. Corwin?"

"The very man."

"Is it possible Hathorne still practices the law?"

Belcher nodded, smiling gamely. "He hath eighty-nine years, yet his wits remain as sharp as Gideon's sword. When I apprised him of the situation, he insisted he was hale enough to wrestle the Dark One to the ground."

"I feel a great exhilaration at these developments." Dunstan reached forward and set the baize bag on the Governor's maplewood desk.

"You will find the good judge at Mrs. Crippin's Rooming-House in Callowhill Street." Belcher, rising, approached Dunstan and slapped his back with the virtuous vehemence of a physician eliciting a newborn's first breath. "In my next dispatch to Kensington Palace, may I assure His Majesty that the Philadelphia Court will find against Mrs. Webster?"

"Thou mayest."

"Your efforts will not go unrewarded. The Privy Council hath directed me to pay your Commission two hundred pounds sterling should the case end happily."

"We do not cleanse for money, sir, though I would ne'er deny that money's a useful appendage to the hunt."

Belcher frowned and gestured suspiciously toward the baize bag. "What's this?"

"Thumbs, my Lord Governor."

"Come again?"

"Witches' thumbs. Four of 'em."

"What are they doing on my desk?"

" 'Tis not obvious?"

"No."

"They're the basis on which you compute the Commission's salary."

"Get 'em out of here."

"As you wish."

"Get 'em out right now."

"Of course," Dunstan said, whisking the sack away.

"I'm a worldly man, Mr. Stearne. Don't e'er put thumbs on my desk again."

ON THE AFTERNOON of May the twentieth, Dunstan and his fellow demonologists donned their darkest Puritan cloaks, secured the door of their Framingham salt-box, and betook themselves to Boston. The following morning they boarded a southbound sloop, the *Ignis Fatuus*, captained by one Angus Morley, a garrulous Calvinist and devoted *Bible Commonwealth* reader who gave the New-England cleansers the same caliber of regard he might have awarded traveling royalty or an itinerant troupe of Shakespearean players. Captain Morley's largesse knew no bounds. He arranged for the demonologists to receive the best berths, fed them fresh scrod for breakfast and boiled beef for lunch, and gifted them with two pounds of Barbados sugar.

After four days at sea, following a stopover on Manhattan-Isle and a harrowing storm of possibly demonic origin, the *Ignis Fatuus* sailed up the Delaware and put to port. Dunstan was the first cleanser to disembark, guiding Abby and Mr. Parris into the malodorous burbling stew pot known as Chestnut Street Wharf. Studying the people's clothes and overhearing their polyglot conversations, he concluded that Philadelphia swarmed not only with the expected Quakers but also with the dregs and dross of a dozen European cities. Unsavory Scots abounded here, as well as sordid Germans, shady Welsh, seamy Dutch, and renegade French. Were it not for his duty to the Witchcraft Act, he would have quit this undeclared penal colony posthaste and led his band back to Boston.

Their initial order of business, he decided—more important even than securing lodgings, locating Judge Hathorne, or blackmailing Governor Gordon—was to visit Rebecca Webster and corroborate the signs of Satanic covenant reported by the New-Jersey magistrate. How lamentable if the Widow Webster had been falsely accused! Not only would such a development dash Dunstan's hopes of widening his campaign into Pennsylvania, it would mean that the three cleansers had sailed to this unseemly city for naught.

They passed an open-air vegetable market, traversed a similar emporium selling fish, and entered a tavern called the Friar's Lanthorn. A stifling vapor hung in the air, a cloud compounded of beer fumes and sot-weed smoke mingled with human gas. Rapidly the demonologists consumed their lunches—fried halibut and boiled turnips washed down with cider—then climbed into a day-coach heading north. By three o'clock they were in Manayunk Gaol-House, presenting themselves to the magistrate.

At first the youthful Herbert Bledsoe did not believe that these sweaty and exhausted travelers constituted the famous Massachusetts Bay Purification Commission, and his skepticism remained intact even after Abby opened the calfskin tool-kit and withdrew the Paracelsus trident and the mask-o'-truth. His suspicions dissipated only when Dunstan produced the newest edition of the organization's charter, which bore the Privy Council's seal as well as Governor Belcher's signature.

At Dunstan's urging, Bledsoe summoned his gaoler, a corpulent drunkard named Knox, and ordered him to fetch Mrs. Webster. Knox descended to the dungeon, appearing betimes with the prisoner, a tall, shorn, handsome woman of middle years, wearing a tattered burlap smock cinched about her waist with a plow-rope.

"Good afternoon, dear brother," she said.

"I'faith!" Reverend Parris exclaimed.

" 'Steeth!" Abby cried.

A barbed and bitter chill washed across Dunstan's skin, as if a thousand apprentice prickers were probing his every pore. He shuddered and winced. A tracery of wrinkles had appeared upon her skin since that distant day when she'd denounced him on the Shawsheen River Bridge, and she'd lost most of her hair to Abraham Pollock's shaving razor, but Dunstan did not for an instant doubt the prisoner's identity. Thundering Christ! By what plan of inscrutable Jehovah or scheme of iniquitous Mephisto did he now find himself face-to-face with Jennet?

"God is not mocked!" he screamed. Snatching the trident from Abby, he waved it around as a cleric might deploy a crucifix against a goblin. "God is not mocked!"

"This woman who calls herself Rebecca Webster is in sooth my husband's sister," Abby explained to Bledsoe.

"His sister?" gasped the magistrate. "What say ye to this accusation?" he asked the prisoner.

"I say that, being ashamed to bear the name of Stearne, I have cheerfully altered it to Webster," Jennet replied.

"Then this demonologist is truly your brother?" Bledsoe asked.

"We issued from the same mortal womb," the prisoner said, "much as I wish 'twere otherwise."

Abby flashed Jennet the sort of slanted smile she assumed whenever the angel Justine vouchsafed her the name of a witch-infested village. "You may spin your spiderweb from now till Doomsday, heathen wench, but the Purification Commission shan't become entangled. Husband, I suggest we go apprise Governor Gordon of this farce and then return to Boston."

Back to Boston? No, Dunstan thought. The Lord might work in mysterious ways, but the Devil trafficked only in plain ones. By selecting Jennet Stearne and not some other freethinking heretic as his principal agent in Pennsylvania, Lucifer had obviously sought to constrain the famous and formidable demonologist Dunstan Stearne from attending whatever courtroom proceeding Jennet's *maleficium* might ultimately inspire—for surely this pricker, like any pricker, would refuse to prosecute his own blood-sister.

"Foolish Lucifer!" Dunstan cried.

"Foolish Lucifer!" echoed Mr. Parris.

Foolish Lucifer. How poorly the Devil understood his enemy's mind—how feeble his comprehension of the Witchfinder-Royal's heart!

"Goodwife Stearne, this be no farce," Dunstan said, "for by Abraham Pollock's testimony my sister hath truly signed the Dark One's register." He paused, waiting for the prisoner to contradict him, but she simply rolled her eyes toward the ceiling beams. Tightening his grip on the trident, he stepped to within inches of the witch. "Mr. Pollock notes a diabolical excrescence on your neck. I would now confirm his finding."

Jennet replied with a low, noxious grunt, but she obligingly tilted her head to one side, exposing the mark to Dunstan's gaze. He pressed the trident's middle tine against the blotch. Within five ticks of the clock his hand started shaking.

" 'Tis Lucifer's kiss—I can feel it!"

"You feel naught but the natural twitchings of your aged fingers," Jennet insisted.

Abby brushed her palm across the reddish stubble on the suspect's head. "Whate'er became of your tawnie husband? Did he expel you from his harem?"

"Mr. Pollock also reports that the cold-water ordeal indicted Mrs. Webster," Dunstan said, still maintaining the seal betwixt trident and blemish. "Mr. Parris, will you assist me in repeating the experiment?"

"The Schuylkill should serve our purpose," the minister said, nodding.

But before they could lead Jennet away, an unexpected and utterly profane intervention occurred. Herbert Bledsoe reached out and, like a goshawk catching a pigeon on the wing, plucked the trident from Dunstan's grasp.

"I fear the blood-tie 'twixt prisoner and prosecutor will make for a muddy sort of justice," Bledsoe said, locking his tiny pale eyes on Dunstan. "Mr. Stearne, ye will forbear to further test Mrs. Webster. 'Tis apparent the Court must replace ye with another."

"Dost imagine I would decline to cleanse a witch merely because she's kin to me? Hah! My father once brought evidence of Satanic compaction against his own sister-in-law!" Dunstan grabbed the trident and jerked it from Bledsoe's hands. "You needn't fret, young jurist. When I meet with Governor Gordon on the morrow, I shall happily reveal the blood-tie of which you speak."

"At which juncture the Governor will instruct ye to resign from the case," Bledsoe said.

Not if I inaugurate our interview with the words "Tucker affidavit," Dunstan thought. "This meeting goes on too long," he told Bledsoe, then swerved toward his sister, fixing her as fiercely as he would any other bride of Lucifer. "Mark me well, Mrs. Webster. You will not avoid the gallows even if pagan Socrates himself ascends from Limbo to prepare your defense."

"I need no sage for my solicitor, as I have Reason on my side," Jennet said.

Dunstan turned to his companions and guided them toward the door, tapping each cleanser gently with the trident. "What is Reason?" he said in a tone of measured ridicule.

"Scripture doth not speak of't," Reverend Parris replied.

"Reason's a habit of mind that enjoyed great favor with the Papist Scholastics of old," Abby said evenly. "But today no person remembers their names."

***

THE NEW-ENGLAND CLEANSERS' clamorous and eventful visit to Manayunk Gaol-House aroused in Jennet an optimism quite opposite to the intimidation that had been their aim. All three demonologists had obviously offended Herbert Bledsoe, and it seemed logical to suppose they would likewise offend the jurymen appointed to determine her fate.

"I must confess, Mrs. Webster," the magistrate said, "ere your brother descended upon us, I thought it possible ye'd consorted with the Dark One. But I sense scant holiness in the Purification Commission. From this day forward, I intend to make your cell a hospitable place."

"Do you mean I might have a true bed?" she asked.

"With a feather mattress," Mr. Bledsoe said.

"A linen shift instead of this rag?"

"If ye like."

"Ink, quill, paper, and a writing-desk?"

"Verily."

"Whene'er a person comes to visit me, I would have Mr. Knox let him inside my cell."

Mr. Bledsoe nodded and said, "I shall accord your callers every comfort within my authority."

Over the next four days the magistrate made good on his promises, civilizing her circumstances as much as he could without provoking public speculation that she'd bewitched him. A pair of Derbyshire chairs arrived in time for her first meeting with her advocate.

The encounter was not long underway when Jennet decided that Charles de Montesquieu had managed to rise above his aristocratic birth to embrace the world in all its earthy particulars. Despite his plumed hat, silk vest, perfumed neckcloth, and landed lineage, he seemed at ease in these squalid surroundings, and she believed he would have adapted equally well to the previous, unappointed version of her cell.

"You have written a brilliant book, Mrs. Webster, and I am persuaded to make it the centerpiece of our case," he said, removing *The Sufficiency of the World* from his portmanteau. "When interviewing you before the Court, I shall prompt you to speak of acceleration, oscillation, refrangibility, and other such principles. Thus will the jurymen learn that the universe obeys Nature's laws, not Satan's wraiths."

"Monsieur, 'twould seem you have grasped my argument in full," she said, pacing the length of her stone-and-iron cube: twelve feet wide, only twelve—a fact that Mr. Bledsoe's good intentions could never redeem.

"Acceleration, osculation, refrangularity," Mrs. Sharkey chanted from her cell. "When my case comes to trial, I'll tell the judge I could ne'er have bludgeoned my husband with a plowshare, for Nature's laws do not permit it."

"I'm inclinin' toward the same strategy," Mr. Turpin said. " 'Ye think I stole Mr. Pertuis's cattle, Excellency? 'Tis obvious ye know naught o' refrangularity.' "

"Eavesdroppers, I shall thank you to keep silent," Jennet said.

"If 'twould be no inconvenience"—Montesquieu pressed his *Sufficiency of the World* into her hands—"I hope you might inscribe this copy to me."

She approached her writing-desk, dipped quill into ink pot, and, opening the treatise, decorated the cover-page with the bold looping hand she'd learned from Aunt Isobel. *À Charles Louis de Secondat . . . avec toute ma considération et ma sympathie . . . Jennet Stearne Crompton.* "I'Christ, 'tis the first time I e'er wrote my name in a book."

"Except, of course, when you signed the Devil's register." Montesquieu issued a succinct but merry laugh, then immediately turned somber. "I bring good tidings and bad."

"Tell me the bad straight away."

"Three days ago, for reasons that remain mysterious, the jurist Malcolm Cresswell recused himself from the case."

"Faugh!" Jennet said. "Who hath replaced him?"

"None other than John Hathorne."

"Hathorne of the Salem trials?"

"The same knave."

The quill in her hand seemed suddenly as grotesque and sinister as a Paracelsus trident. "Our enterprise hath sustained a deep wound."

"Deep, *oui*, but not deadly."

"I would now receive the good tidings."

"By the report of Mr. Franklin's band of youngbloods, the whole of Philadelphia stands behind you," Montesquieu said. "Should Hathorne attempt to abridge your defense, the cries from the gallery will set the courthouse to trembling as when Joshua's trumpets shook down Jericho."

"A most opportune development." She laid the quill aside, blew the ink dry, and returned the book to Montesquieu.

From the shadows atop the staircase a man called out, "Nor hath Dame Fortune yet run short of smiles, darling Jenny"—a familiar voice, coarsened by age yet still ringing and resolute—"for't seems an old friend is lately come to Philadelphia!"

In the center of the descending parade marched Mr. Bledsoe, brandishing an uncocked pistol. Behind him tromped Mr. Knox, grasping a ring of iron keys as a fallen angel might hold his shorn halo. And first in line, dressed in a torn and dusty surtout, stepped—Jennet blinked once, twice, then swallowed audibly—Barnaby Cavendish!

"This beggar insisted on seeing ye," the magistrate said.

Astonishment and joy rushed through her like a surge from a Von Guericke sphere. "He's no beggar, sir, but the treasured companion of my youth! Oh, Barnaby, dear friend, thou hast once again returned from the dead!"

" 'Tis a habit I intend to cultivate for the rest of my life," he said.

Receiving the magistrate's nod, Knox unlocked the cell door and ushered Barnaby into Jennet's presence. For a full minute she and the mountebank embraced. He exuded a bracing scent, a pungent and oddly pleasant mixture of sweat, hay, and mildew.

"When last I saw this man," she told the befuddled Montesquieu, "he was about to go down with the wreck of the *Berkshire*."

" 'Twas a truly fearsome gale." Barnaby adjusted his spectacles, which had somehow survived the nautical catastrophe. "But by freeing the Lyme Bay Fish-Boy and the Bicephalic Girl from their sea-chest and wrapping an arm round each, I stayed a-float amidst the froth and tumult. Twenty thirsty hours upon Neptune's bosom, and then a Portuguese brigantine delivered us from certain doom."

"Dr. Cavendish curates a prodigy museum," Jennet explained to Montesquieu.

"My life was saved by two of the most amazing freaks e'er to drop from a woman's womb," Barnaby elaborated.

"They reside in bottles," Jennet noted.

"Then you were rescued by Mr. Boyle's law of buoyancy," Montesquieu told Barnaby, waving the *Sufficiency* in his face.

"No doubt, my Lord," Barnaby said.

"Howbeit, some would say his benefactors were in sooth the prodigies," Knox said. "Such a fœtus once cured my grandfather's shingles."

"Mrs. Webster, when you address the Court next week, you will avoid all mention of Dr. Cavendish's monsters, *je vous en prie*," Montesquieu said. "We must distance our arguments from peasant superstition."

"Your attitude's sensible, *Monsieur le Baron*," Barnaby said, "though I for one can't speak too highly of peasant superstition, for't hath kept me gainfully employed these past fifty years." He lifted the treatise from Montesquieu's grasp. "If I am to believe Ebenezer Trenchard, Jenny, you've wrought a demon disproof to beat the one that Newton ne'er devised. Ah, but doth the world in fact *want* a demon disproof? *That's* the question I now put to you wights."

"Most men are indifferent to metaphysics," Bledsoe said with a sigh.

"My own taste runs more to pirate tales," Knox confessed.

"Most men are indifferent," Montesquieu echoed, "but their canons are not. I assure you, Dr. Cavendish, that even as we speak, our civilization's greatest law books reach out and press Mrs. Webster's *argumentum grande* to their collective breast."

"For a person chary of superstition, you seem passing eager to credit books with minds and souls," Barnaby said.

"I have lived so long amongst books," Montesquieu said, "I cannot but believe they *do* have souls."

"You strike me as a clever fellow"—Barnaby returned the *Sufficiency* to the Baron—"and I'm sure you mean to save my Jenny, but I hope you know your enemy. These cleansers are made of iron."

"I'll wager they've never battled a French jurist," Montesquieu said.

Barnaby touched his right temple. "If my Bicephalic Girl were here, her dexter head would say, 'I have every faith in Jenny's lawyer.'" He pointed to his left temple. "But then the sinister head would reply, 'I have every fear of Jenny's brother.'"

" 'Tis not Dunstan we should fear, but rather his malevolent wife," Jennet said, lifting the quill from her desk. "For whilst my brother hath his Paracelsus trident and his pricking needles and his other pretensions to philosophy, Abigail heeds only the madness in her skull." She blew upon the feather, wondering what sort of equation might describe the vane's exquisite ripple. "I'faith, good sirs, I have seen this woman's brain at work, and I say it traffics less with rational discourse than doth flint with flour."

"Then may God help you, Monsieur," said Bledsoe to Montesquieu.

"Then may God help Mrs. Webster," the Baron replied.

The

Eleventh

❊❊❊❊❊❊❊❊❊

A Metaphysics Debate
Captivates Humankind,
or at Least
that Portion of Humankind
Owning Subscriptions to
The Pennsylvania Gazette

❊❊

Charles Louis de Secondat, Baron de la Brède et de Montesquieu, stepped out of his hired coach, bid his footman *adieu,* and presented the driver with a one-pound note and a dip of his plumed hat, the worthy Herr Strossen having steered them a smooth course along the pocked and pitted length of Ridge Road. A kind of carnival was unfolding amidst the hills surrounding Manayunk Courthouse, every knoll a-swarm with Philadelphia rustics chattering in a half-dozen tongues as they read that morning's *Pennsylvania Gazette* and patronized stalls dispensing German-Town lager, meat pies, roasted potatoes, and apple tarts. The Baron screwed his hat in place, fastening it to his bewigged head, and started toward *La Maison de Justice.* Weaving through the boisterous, earthy mob, he felt the same vague discomfort he'd endured earlier that year upon seeing, in the Mayor of Antwerp's mansion, Pieter Breughel's painting of a peasant wedding. Montesquieu was a man who believed the world's common people deserved political freedom and personal sovereignty—he endorsed this ideal with every atom of his being—and yet he would admit to a difficulty in extending the principle to the sorts of excessively common people who populated Breughel paintings and attended witch-trials.

It took him four attempts, each louder and angrier than the last, to convince the marshals stationed outside the courthouse that he was Re-

❊❊❊

becca Webster's advocate and must therefore be granted immediate entry. He pulled his portmanteau tight against his chest and, working his elbows in the manner of a fledgling attempting flight, jostled his way through the foyer. The main hall was packed front to back, side to side, and, if you considered the score of ill-scrubbed youths perched on the rafters, top to bottom. Numerous spectators sat in the aisles, so that Montesquieu had to advance gingerly, like a man crossing a brook by stepping from stone to stone.

Moving past the journalists' desk, he nodded toward Monsieur Benjamin Franklin, who was too busy scribbling to notice the gesture, then proceeded to the defense table and set down his portmanteau. Along the opposite wall loomed the three Purification Commissioners, black of dress, sour of face: ravens contemplating a carcass. Beside them rose the jury-box, crammed with twelve men whose principal qualifications for determining Madame Crompton's fate were that each held title to twenty acres and had nothing better to do before Sunday.

"Oyez! Oyez!" The bailiff banged his pike against the floor as if cracking the ice-cake on a cistern.

The spectators grew silent. Bedecked in a dark frock coat and a ludicrous periwig spouting white curls, the ancient John Hathorne emerged from his alcove at the languid velocity of a pallbearer. Solemnly, awkwardly, he ascended to the judge's bench, then cleared his throat with a reverberant rasp.

"The Court is now in session," he said, punctuating each syllable with a tap of his wooden mallet. "Mr. Broom, you may arraign the defendant."

"Rebecca Webster will come before the bench!" the bailiff declared.

The antechamber door flew open, and the prisoner strode into the hall, attired in her linen shift and accompanied by four marshals holding pikes and stifling yawns. An iron chain arced betwixt her wrists like a purgatorial watch fob. She brought her lean body to full height and approached Judge Hathorne. For the first time since pledging himself to her cause, Montesquieu realized that he was in love with Jennet Stearne Crompton. The sensation was at once uplifting and confounding, like a good law in need of an especially subtle interpretation.

"State your name," the bailiff commanded.

"Rebecca Webster," she replied tonelessly.

"Rebecca Webster, the Crown sayeth you have committed the abhorrent crime of sorcery, and this Court doth thereby charge you with heresy against the Christian faith, according to the Witchcraft Statute of King James the First as ratified in the year 1718 by the Pennsylvania Assembly. How plead you, guilty or nay?"

"There being no such crime as sorcery, I must perforce assert my innocence."

"The jury will disregard all rogue opinions from the defendant," Hathorne said.

"The Court proposes that you solicit its leniency by forthwith signing a confession of Satanic compact," the bailiff informed Madame Crompton. "Will you do this?"

"If you put the thumbscrews to me I might," she said, "but mayhap not even then."

"His Majesty's witch-courts have ne'er resorted to torture, Mrs. Webster," Hathorne said, "a fact with which you are well acquainted."

The marshals escorted Madame Crompton to the defense table, where Montesquieu greeted her by clasping her manacled hands betwixt his palms.

"How felicitous that you mentioned thumbscrews," he said.

"Felicitous?" she said, assuming her chair.

"Torture is more relevant to this case than *Monsieur le Juge* imagines."

Hathorne directed a trembling finger toward the Purification Commissioners. "The Crown will offer a preliminary argument."

Securing a thick moldering Bible under his arm, Dunstan Stearne stepped toward the jury-box and bowed to the foreman, Enoch Hocking, a gnarled rustic with high cheekbones and hair the texture of corn silk. "Good landholders, I shall begin by confirming a rumor that flits about this courtroom like a mayfly," the pricker said. "The defendant was indeed born Jennet Stearne, and she is truly my blood-sister." He caressed his Bible. "Should my rôle as Crown's advocate therefore strike you as paradoxical, let me evoke our Savior's admonition from Luke Chapter

Fourteen. 'If any man come to me, and hate not his father, and mother, and wife, and children, and brethren . . . and *sisters* . . . yea, and his own life also, he cannot be my disciple.' "

Montesquieu was pleased to observe perplexity claim the countenance of every juryman. The verse in question evidently bespoke a species of Christianity with which they were unfamiliar.

"The case before you is mayhap the most important yet tried in His Majesty's American provinces," Monsieur Stearne continued. "If you read *The Pennsylvania Gazette*, you know that Mrs. Webster seeks not only to deliver herself from the gallows but to destroy the Parliamentary Witchcraft Act, thus unleashing a deluge of Sadducism, Hobbism, Deism, and atheism throughout His Majesty's realm."

The jurymen's expressions shifted from bewilderment to shock.

"Sadducism?" whispered Madame Crompton. "Atheism? Is he allowed to speak such lies?"

"I fear your brother thinks them facts," Montesquieu replied.

"Make no mistake, landholders," Stearne said. "Mrs. Webster will not rest till she hath hacked off the witch-fighting arm of the Christian religion. Were Satan to grant her the power, she would amputate all demonology from Holy Writ, impounding every Bible in Europe and America and tearing out Leviticus page by page." He flung open his Scripture, leafed his way eastward from Eden, and declaimed with a passion worthy of a Molièrean player. " 'A man also or woman that hath a familiar spirit, or that is a wizard, shall surely be put to death.' " He snapped the Bible shut and pivoted toward the bench, black cape swirling. "The Crown would now make its case in the particular."

"Proceed," Hathorne said.

"We call to the witness-stand Mr. Abraham Pollock, magistrate of Mount-Holly."

Rage boiled up in Montesquieu's every vein. *"Pardonez-moi,"* he said, rising abruptly. "By your leave, Judge Hathorne, the defense will make an opening argument."

"Mr. Stearne hath provided the jury with all the preamble it requires," Hathorne said. "Find your chair, Baron, that the trial may continue."

Montesquieu resumed his seat, moving with a sluggishness that aspired to impertinence. "In France I would be heard," he muttered.

"If you wish to return home, Monsieur, the Court will not stop you," said Hathorne.

As Abraham Pollock climbed into the witness-stand, the audience snorted and grumbled its discontent with Hathorne's ruling. We have sustained a Pyrrhic defeat, Montesquieu thought. If we lose many more such battles, we shall surely win the war.

Stearne and Pollock now commenced a protracted dialogue, demonologist to demonologist, during which interval they established why four particular tests—swimming an accused Satanist in a pristine current, pricking her suspicious excrescences, noting her commerce with dumb beasts, and requiring her to recite the Lord's Prayer—enjoyed such prestige amongst witchfinders.

The luncheon recess followed. Montesquieu marched directly to the food stalls, purchased a mutton pie as puffy and fragrant as a courtesan's pillow, and delivered it to Madame Crompton. Despite her dire circumstances, she retained a hearty appetite, devouring her portion in less than a minute.

At one o'clock the demonologists renewed their conversation. Magistrate Pollock discoursed extensively on how the Delaware River had spurned Rebecca Webster's body, how his pricking needle had failed to bloody her Devil's mark, and how the *Pater Noster* had crumbled on her tongue. Beyond this plethora of evidence lay the fact that a half-dozen cats currently inhabited the defendant's barn, each displaying indications of Satanic ancestry.

Hathorne thanked Pollock for sharing his expertise, then offered Dunstan Stearne a conspiratorial smile. "I realize that the Crown hath barely begun to construct its case, and yet the hour grows late. Might we defer your next witness till the morrow?"

Stomach twitching, Montesquieu leapt to his feet. "Before the Court adjourns, I would question Mr. Pollock."

"His testimony hath been discussed in full," Hathorne replied. "Mr. Pollock, you are excused."

Heedless of the crowd's indignant murmurs, the Mount-Holly magistrate left the witness-stand and strode out of the hall.

"Charles, we must not let this moment pass," Madame Crompton muttered.

"*N'ayez crainte, mon amie.*" He lingered briefly at the defense table, long enough to give his client's shoulder an obliquely amorous squeeze, then dashed toward the jury-box. "Good Philadelphians, I beg that you consider Magistrate Pollock's testimony in the light of Reason. If you study the bailiff over there"—he gestured toward the man called Broom—"you will note a black wart on his left nostril."

Jurors, journalists, and spectators engaged in a collective contemplation of the bailiff's nose. The man turned scarlet and cringed.

"Baron, you seem unaware that we are about to adjourn," Hathorne said, reaching for his mallet.

A hissing spread through the hall, as if the trial had attracted an audience of vipers.

Hathorne stayed his hand and scowled. "Lest a cry of favoritism be raised against the bench," he said to Montesquieu, "I shall permit you to waggle your tongue for a short interval."

The hissing ceased.

"I was speaking of the bailiff's wart," Montesquieu continued. "Tell me, honorable landholders, shall we now apprehend Mr. Broom and prick that suspect blot? For such is our sacred duty by Mr. Pollock's logic." He returned to the defense table and, opening his portmanteau, dumped out a bronze basin, a tin flask, and a leather bottle bulging with water. He seized the flask and struck it with his knuckles, producing a hollow bong. "Consider this container. Empty as a drunkard's mug. I bid you now imagine that my vessel"—he filled the basin with water—"is the lung of an accused sorcerer." He stoppered the flask, set it a-float, and carried the demonstration to the jury. "See how it swims? Do we therefore call this vessel bewitched? Or do we simply admit that it obeys the law of buoyancy, the same principle as raised Rebecca Webster from the Delaware?"

"Baron, you will finish this absurd presentation within one minute," Hathorne said.

Montesquieu retrieved the flask and laid it on the floor. "Now watch how easily I make the enchantment disappear, a mere matter of purging the lung in question." He inflicted his boot heel on the flask, rendering it as flat as a *centime*, then picked up the squashed vessel, held it over the basin, and dropped it in the water. The flask sank instantly. "Look, gentlemen, the vessel founders! The spell is broken!"

"And hence the Court is adjourned!" Hathorne shouted, hammering on the bench.

"Each time a supposed witch is launched upon a river," Montesquieu yelled over Hathorne's frantic cadence, "we learn little about the condition of her soul and much about the status of her lungs! Purged, she sinks! Full, she rises!"

"Purged, she sinks!" echoed Ben Franklin. "Full, she rises!"

"Adjourned!" John Hathorne cried.

"Purged, she sinks!" shouted Barnaby Cavendish from the front row. "Full, she rises!"

"Adjourned!"

"Purged, she sinks!" insisted the tallest of Franklin's youngbloods, the Indian John Tux. "Full, she rises!"

Now the whole gallery took up the cry. "Purged, she sinks! Full, she rises!"

Montesquieu experienced a sudden rush of admiration for Pennsylvania's yeomen. They might lack the nuances of a civilized people, but their instinctive love of *la liberté* was most inspiring.

"Adjourned!" roared Hathorne.

As Montesquieu strode back to the defense table, Franklin stood up, blotted his scribblings with a sponge, and came forward. "Congratulations, sir," he said, clasping the Baron's hand. "Despite Judge Hathorne's sophistry, you have carried the day."

Montesquieu said, "Tomorrow Dunstan Stearne interviews Rebecca Webster's supposed victims—a marvelous opportunity to acquaint the jury with the sufficiency hypothesis."

"And an equally marvelous opportunity for Ebenezer Trenchard to declare that the mirage called *maleficium* is passing from the world," Franklin said, "and 'tis time we blamed our troubles on ourselves."

BY GOADING HIS MARE to her swiftest gallop, Ben Franklin managed to reach Philadelphia as twilight fell upon the city, covering Market Street in a caul of mist and murk. No sooner had he reined up before the printing-house than his writerly imagination wrought from the surrounding gloom the opening sentence of Ebenezer Trenchard's next essay. "At the start of the Webster trial, the Baron de Montesquieu disclosed how our species might finally escape the shadowy slough of superstition to sport upon the sun-drenched plain beyond."

He entered the shop. Characteristically, he was the first man on the scene, but as the hour progressed the other journalists arrived, and ere long the collective scratchings of five pen nibs filled the press-room, none moving faster than Ben's. Beyond the Trenchard letter, the incipient edition of *The Pennsylvania Gazette* would feature William Parsons's unsympathetic report on Dunstan Stearne's preamble, Hugh Roberts's scalding critique of Abraham Pollock's witch-tests, Philip Synge's paean to Montesquieu's tin flask, and John Tux's general lament over the toll the cleansers had taken on his Indian brethren. Only Nicholas Scull's quill was unemployed, for he had elected to set his article—an attack on Hathorne's irrational rulings—directly in type, so pure was his outrage and supreme his self-confidence.

At eight o'clock the shop's foreman, Ned Billings, arrived with his six journeymen, each eager to assume his respective duty as compositor, framer, inker, washer, breaker, and spindle-man. Ben handed his essay to the trusty Billings, bid his colleagues farewell, and headed homeward, happy in his knowledge that, like two great ovens baking loaf upon loaf of nourishing bread, the Blaeu presses would that night yield five hundred copies of the *Gazette*, as they had done each night for the past eighteen months.

Though normally an early riser, Ben experienced difficulty quitting his bed the next morning, as this meant trading a pleasant reverie about Amakye-Isle—he was catching eels in Copernicus Cove—for the waking nightmare of Jennet's trial. The more alert he became, the lower his spirits fell. He wished he owned some sort of time-traveling carriage, the crowning product of his philosophic pursuits, that he might vault across the remainder of the week and land unscathed in Sunday.

Through a sudden surge of will he abandoned the sheets and, leaning over the warm cavity from which he'd emerged, kissed his drowsy Deborah on her cheek. He shuffled to the dresser, surprised his face with a splash of cold water, and climbed into his breeches. Almost as useful as a time-traveling carriage, he mused, would be a machine that performed your morning ablutions for you.

He stepped into the nursery, expecting to find William asleep, but the boy was sitting on the floor playing with his birthday present from Barnaby Cavendish, a mahogany Noah's Ark cradling a cargo of ten animals whittled from fir blocks. In theory William knew only what he'd been told— his mother was standing trial on a false accusation of witchery, the best lawyer in the world was defending her—and yet he seemed aware of more than these raw facts. It would be pointless to mislead William, painting Jennet's future in rosy hues, for the prism of his mind was aligned to pierce all such adult deceptions.

"Be thee well, son," Ben said, embracing the boy. "I'm off to Manayunk."

From his little ark William removed a wooden tiger and placed it in Ben's hand. "For Mother."

" 'Tis a bonny gift."

"Tigers are *brave*," William said.

"Indeed," Ben said.

"Tigers are *strong*."

"Quite so."

As if she'd fallen victim to a melancholia of the very sort that afflicted Ben, the mare transported him at a torpid pace, and he arrived in Manayunk later than he'd intended, entering the courthouse just as the marshals were seating Jennet. He noted with satisfaction that two jurymen and at least thirty spectators were reading that morning's *Gazette*. Pulling the tiger from his pocket, he approached the defense table, mysteriously overspread with a microscope, a horseshoe, a Von Guericke sphere, a dish of phlox petals, a phial of milk, a bowl of grain, and, most peculiar of all, a wire cage containing a distressed rooster.

"William presents you with his bravest beast"—Ben pressed the tiger into Jennet's palm as respectfully as he would Isaac Newton's epochal apple—"that you might draw courage from it."

"Tell our son I've ne'er received a better token."

"Prithee, call your first witness," Hathorne instructed the Purification Commissioners.

Abigail Stearne rose from the prosecution table and, black cape billowing like a window-drape in a thunder-gust, glided toward the judge's bench. "The Crown summons Michael Bailey," she said.

After settling behind the journalists' desk, Ben opened his valise and retrieved his writing supplies. He trimmed his quill, transmuted into Ebenezer Trenchard, and made ready to report on the day's events.

Mr. Bailey, a gorbellied harness-maker who seemed to be storing turnips in his cheeks, heaved his bulk into the stand. Questioned by Mrs. Stearne, he lamented his decision to slam the door in Rebecca Webster's face one evening when she'd come begging for a jug of cider. His regret traced not to his uncharitable behavior, however, but to the fact that Mrs. Webster had evidently retaliated by afflicting his wife with dropsy.

Spurious Connection 'twixt Webster and Wife's Illness, Ben wrote.

As the morning progressed, sufferer after sufferer stood before the Court, each attesting to how he'd spurned the defendant—apparently she'd habitually sought to share her neighbors' victuals and borrow their tools—and consequently endured some hardship or other. The jurors heard of butter that declined to come, dough that neglected to rise, hens who failed to lay, a baby who rebuffed the breast, a wound that wouldn't heal, and flax turned rotten in the field.

Feeble Attempt to cast Misfortunes as Maleficium, Ben wrote.

The first seven witnesses occasioned no reaction from the defense, but then Mrs. Stearne interviewed Bethany Fallon, a comely but morose goose girl who told how, two days after she'd refused to let Mrs. Webster roam through her henhouse collecting eggs at will, twenty of her flock had died of an enchantment. When Miss Fallon added that the birds' death throes included running in circles and pecking at rocks until their beaks shattered, Jennet and Montesquieu sat up straight and exchanged urgent whispers. The instant the Crown finished with the witness, Montesquieu proposed to cross-examine her.

"The Court hath heard quite enough of this girl's benighted geese," Hathorne replied. A sound emerged from the gallery, a shrill moan suggesting the synchronous whimperings of a hundred ill-treated dogs. "Howbeit, let it not be said I failed to accord the defense every leeway."

Like a priest bearing a communion cup to a celebrant, Montesquieu approached the witness-stand carrying his bowl of grain. "Mademoiselle Fallon, may I offer a conjecture concerning your geese? I believe they succumbed not to bewitchment but to a natural illness."

"Aye, a natural illness contrived by the Widow Webster," Bethany Fallon said, gesturing vaguely toward Jennet.

"More likely your geese grew sick from eating rye seeds such as these." Montesquieu thrust the grain before the witness. "You will note that some are brown and normal, though others appear black as tar, a sign of fungal infection. This corrupted food sickened your geese with the disease called ergot, also known as St. Anthony's fire and *infernalis*. Its cause was established fifty years ago by my countryman Monsieur Dodart, a Paris doctor with a special knowledge of molds and mushrooms. Speak truly—did you feed your flock on rye seeds?"

"I have always given 'em such."

Ergot caus'd by Fungus not Fiends, Ben wrote.

Montesquieu revisited the defense table, seized the wire cage, and bore the unlucky rooster toward Miss Fallon. Never before had Ben beheld so sorely afflicted a creature; his thoughts turned to Jennet's accounts of *skishauonck*, the small-pox, murderer of her first child. When not throwing itself against the walls of its pen, the rooster bobbed its head in all directions and tore out its own feathers. Unless it died first, the wretched fowl would by day's end be as naked as if plucked for roasting.

"Last evening I fed this rooster contaminated rye seeds, and now it displays a manifest case of the ergot," Montesquieu said. "Tell me, *s'il vous plaît,* whether my bird perchance reminds you of your own stricken flock."

"Aye, 'tis so," the girl said. "But did not Mrs. Webster mayhap bid Lucifer taint my grain with the mold of which you speak?"

"Any experienced farmer will tell you that a fungi may thrive without benefit of occult powers. *Écoutez-moi, Mademoiselle.* To save your geese from future plagues, you must purify their food. Use a sieve to filter out the larger black bodies, then drop the remaining seeds in a tub of saltwater. The lesser black bodies will rise to the surface, where you may easily skim them off."

"Thus sparing my birds this madness?" she asked, pointing a milk-white finger toward the dying rooster. "Then verily I shall do't."

"*Vous êtes très intelligente.* I have no more questions."

Montesquieu returned to the defense table, whereupon Hathorne decreed a recess for the midday meal. As the interval began, Jennet prevailed upon Ben to put the rooster out of its misery. He carried the cage behind the courthouse, took out the bird, and grasped its tattered body by the neck. Closing his eyes, he twisted the head round and round as if removing the cork from a wine bottle.

A brief trip to the Wissahickon Creek yielded two bucketfuls of stones, which he piled one by one atop the feathered witness, and soon the cairn completely obscured the rooster's earthly remains. He set the final stone in place, then offered up a succinct but sincere eulogy, for such commemoration was surely due any creature sacrificed in counter to the demon hypothesis.

Later that day, cued by Abigail Stearne, a fresh parade of *maleficium* sufferers told their stories. After disregarding the initial four victims, Montesquieu elected to cross-examine a wizened flax-planter named Zebulon Plum, whose crop had sustained a blast of Heaven's fire and subsequently burned to the ground. The Baron began by cluttering the stand with the horseshoe, the Von Guericke sphere, the dish of phlox petals, and a copy of *The Sufficiency of the World*. He turned the crank, set his palm against the equator, and thereby made a squall of petals fly to the sphere and stick to its surface like ants mired in a trickle of sap.

"Mr. Plum, I show you the force called electricity, supreme amongst those energies with which God has suffused the world." Montesquieu halted the sphere, causing it to shed the petals. "Now observe what happens when I cause an electric charge first to accumulate within my body and then to find release in iron." He gave the ball a vigorous crank, placed his left hand against the sulphur, and extended his right index finger, bringing the pad to within an inch of the horseshoe. A tiny crackling thread shot forth. The Baron flinched. "Tell the jury what you saw, Monsieur."

" 'Tis hard to describe. A kind o' thin, cold spark."

"*Exactement.* Just as the great Sir Isaac Newton discerned a general gravitation stretching to the very edge of Creation, so has Philadelphia's own Benjamin Franklin postulated a universal electricity."

Ben blushed to hear his name mentioned in the same breath with Newton's, though he allowed that the parallel was not without merit. *Montesquieu advocates for Universal Electricity over Unseen Elementals,* he wrote.

Flourishing Jennet's book, the Baron faced the jury-box and locked his eyes on Mr. Hocking. "To the curious amongst you I recommend the account of Mr. Franklin's work found in J. S. Crompton's admirable treatise, *The Sufficiency of the World,*" Montesquieu said. "If the Franklin hypothesis is correct, the spark I just now made leap betwixt flesh and metal differs only in degree"—he turned and fixed his gaze on Mr. Plum—"from the celestial torch that destroyed your flax."

"A spark is not a lightning-bolt," Mr. Plum protested. "A whelk is not a whale."

Montesquieu answered the witness's complaint with an insouciant flip of his hand, then strode toward the twelve landholders, staring at each in turn. "Perhaps these fiery blasts come forth as our planet rubs against its envelope of æther. Perhaps they form in the arcane depths of maelstroms and then ascend to the clouds, returning to Earth during thunder-gusts. But I swear to you, good jurymen, there is no more deviltry in a lightning-stroke than in the blooming of a daffodil or the hatching of a swan's egg."

To Ben's great satisfaction, Montesquieu now employed the very tactic the situation demanded. He approached the witness-stand, cranked the sphere, and instructed Plum to unfloor his feet, explaining that otherwise the planter might receive a nasty jolt. He set Plum's palm against the spinning sulphur. The remaining petals hurled themselves against the ball.

"Behold!" Montesquieu cried. "Zebulon Plum is a Christian man who has never once met Lucifer, and yet he fashions the electric force with his very hands!"

"No deviltry in lightning!" Barnaby Cavendish yelled.

"No deviltry in lightning!" Nicholas Scull echoed.

"No deviltry in lightning!" insisted the thoughtful young magistrate Herbert Bledsoe.

"Silence!" Hathorne screamed, pounding the bench with his mallet.

Von Guericke electrifies the Court, Ben wrote.

The next two witnesses—a glassblower who held Rebecca Webster responsible for his last eighty bottles turning brittle, a cordwainer convinced that she'd ensorcelled his glad-adder—inspired no cross-examinations from Montesquieu. But then Stearne put Wilbur Bennet on the stand, a swart dairyman who'd declined to lend the Widow Webster his plow horse, that she might clear a tree stump from her property. Two days later, he'd lost forty gallons of milk to curdling.

Upon receiving Hathorne's permission to question Mr. Bennet, Montesquieu marched to the stand bearing the microscope and the milk phial. "Can you tell me the purpose of this instrument?"

"Methinks 'tis a kind o' magnifier," Bennet said.

"*Vraiment.*" Montesquieu placed a white droplet on the stage, directed Bennet to peer through the eyepiece, and bid him describe what he saw.

"It looks to me a herd o' worms," the witness said, scrutinizing the specimen, "itchin' and twitchin' like they've contracted the chorea."

Montesquieu told the Court that the microscope's optical components were the handiwork of Anton Van Leeuwenhoek, the legendary linen-draper who could grind lenses so powerful they revealed "the very stitchery God employed in sewing the fabric of the world." In his letters to the Royal Society, the Baron continued, Van Leeuwenhoek had described, amongst other wonders, the tiny creatures he'd seen swimming about in pond water, tooth scum, and fecal matter. By the lens-grinder's report, sweet milk was free of these animalcules, whilst sour milk contained them in abundance.

"Would you not agree that Van Leeuwenhoek's beasties account for your ruined milk far better than does the demon hypothesis?" Montesquieu asked the witness.

"I would not," Bennet said, giving the specimen a second glance. "Your microscope tells me only that Mrs. Webster implored some demon to spoil my milk with foul-tastin' wrigglers."

"But if they're like other creatures—the ant, the moth, the field mouse—then these wrigglers generate themselves, and we need not posit wicked spirits to explain their propagation."

"The wrigglers generate themselves!" Barnaby Cavendish shouted, and instantly his cry was taken up and chorused, first by Nicholas Scull, then by the rest of the Junto, then by scores of spectators.

"You will be silent!" Hathorne demanded.

Bennet stole a third peek at the animalcules. "Baron Montesquieu, ye do not study the evidence closely enough. This puddle swarms with the squirmin' progeny o' the very serpent who deprived us all o' Paradise."

"You have a vivid imagination," Montesquieu said, packing up the milk phial and the microscope.

"These be the Devil's descendants, I swear't."

"I should be astonished to find in Europe even one natural philosopher who might corroborate that conclusion. You are excused, Mr. Bennet."

Lens-grinder sees through Witchfinders, Ben wrote.

"The dinner hour is upon us, and so we shall adjourn," Hathorne said. "Prithee, *Monsieur le Baron,* I would examine that milk myself."

Montesquieu glowered but obediently bore the microscope and the phial to the bench, setting them before Hathorne. The judge closed one eye and with the other peered into the milk's darkest reaches. He turned the focus knob, clucked his tongue, and let loose the least spontaneous laugh Ben had ever heard.

" 'Tis just as Mr. Bennet claims!" Hathorne told the Court. "A hundred tiny demons cruise these white currents! All praise Anton Van

Leeuwenhoek, whom history will remember as the man who brought Satan's invisible empire to light!"

※※

THE AUTUMN SUN BURNED that morning with an unseasonable intensity, warming the air and inspiring the larks to praise in song the world's sufficiency, but to Jennet that same world seemed bleak, sterile, and unworthy of such music. Making her fettered way to the defense table, she endured a queasiness in her stomach, as if she'd just consumed a quart of Ben's revolting nostrum for *mal de mer*.

By the Baron de Montesquieu's reckoning, the Commissioners would attack her from two sides today, indicting not only the odd behaviors she'd exhibited whilst living on the Sumac Lane farm, but also the presumed blasphemies entailed in her denial of demons. The odd behaviors were easy to explain. As for the blasphemies, she hoped to answer them by drawing upon the previous evening's tutorial with Montesquieu, during which he had offered up his illuminating translations of those Old Testament verses in which that most horrible of heresies, the willing substitution of Lucifer for Christ, was supposedly anticipated and then denounced by the Hebrew prophets.

Invited by Hathorne to continue the Crown's presentation, the Reverend Samuel Parris bestirred his creaking bones, stretched himself into wakefulness, and contemptuously discarded that day's edition of *The Pennsylvania Gazette*. Ebenezer Trenchard's column had begun with an observation Jennet thought especially pithy. "Just as Rye Seeds infect'd by Fungus must be cast aside lest they afflict Geese with *Infernalis*, so must Statutes infest'd with Superstition be struck down ere they send more Innocents to the Hangman."

"The Crown calls Rebecca Webster," Mr. Parris said.

A chorus of sympathetic murmurs filled the hall as, wrist chains clanking in a discordant carillon, Jennet assumed the witness-stand. She reached into her pocket as far as the manacle permitted and closed her hand around William's wooden tiger.

"Mrs. Webster, this Monday past the Court heard from Abraham Pollock, Magistrate of Mount-Holly," Mr. Parris said, hobbling toward the stand bearing the same fat Bible that Dunstan had employed during his opening address. "He attested to the presence of six cats in your barn."

" 'Tis as natural for a widow to solicit a community of innocuous cats," she asserted, "as for a marooned sailor to befriend a troop of wild monkeys."

"I did not ask you to opine upon the character of your cats. That is the jury's prerogative." Mr. Parris offered the landholders a labored wink and a sly grin, then faced Jennet again. "As Foreman Hocking's worthies go about their job, I know they will recall the scriptural passage Mr. Stearne read to us on Monday. 'A man also or woman that hath a familiar spirit, or that is a wizard, shall surely be put to death.' "

"When next you return to the original Hebrew," she said, employing what she hoped was a scholarly tone, "you will notice that the phrase 'a woman that hath a familiar spirit' is best translated as 'pythoness'—a seer, that is, such as the Oracle at Delphi. The word 'wizard,' meanwhile, should be rendered as 'diviner' or 'knowing one.' 'Tis baldly obvious the author of Leviticus speaks not of Satanism."

"Ah—we have a philologist in our midst!" Parris sneered.

"I'm no philologist, Reverend, but I say there be far less demonology in Scripture than the King James translation leads a person to believe."

"And have you likewise refurbished Exodus 22:18 for us? 'Thou shalt not suffer a witch to live.' "

"The problem with the usual rendering of Exodus 22:18 is that it makes a hash of the distinction betwixt executing a person and denying him a livelihood. A superior translation of that notorious verse would read, 'Thou shalt not patronize a fortune-teller."

"Superior in your *estimation*," noted Parris in a caustic voice. "Alas, Mrs. Webster, I fear you give us but the dabblings of a dilettante—and thus I am obligated to put your erudition to the test. Tell me, how do you translate the Hebrew word *kaphar?*"

Jennet blenched. Neither she nor the Baron had imagined that Parris might himself be competent in Hebrew. "I don't know."

"It means 'atonement.' Now will you please translate *eliyl* for the Court?"

She squeezed the wooden tiger so hard she felt the vein throbbing in her thumb. "My vocabulary lacks that word."

"It means 'idol.' What are the English words for *zanah, goy,* and *asham?*"

"I've ne'er made a formal study of Hebrew," she said, trying not to wince, and wincing in consequence of trying.

"*Zanah . . . goy . . . asham*—what do they mean?"

"I cannot say."

" 'Whoredom,' 'heathen,' and 'guilty.' The Crown is disappointed in your Hebrew, Mrs. Webster. Now let us consider your Greek. By your lights did the framers of the King James Bible abuse the Gospels as badly as they did the Torah?"

"My knowledge of Greek is minimal, Mr. Parris. Howbeit, I am not alone in my opinion that our Savior hath no sympathy for the cleansing trade."

"Do you say we encounter no wicked spirits or fallen angels in the New Testament?"

"We encounter no wicked spirits of the sort you prickers imagine you're fighting."

"Truly now?" Parris flung open the Bible. "Mark 1:34, 'And he healed many that were sick of divers diseases, and cast out many devils, and suffered not the devils to speak, because they knew him.' Luke 4:33, 'And in the synagogue there was a man, which had the spirit of an unclean devil—' "

" 'Tis one thing to speculate that diabolism may cause disease, and quite another to say Christ bids us murder every midwife who garbles her *Pater Noster.*"

"I am not finished, Mrs. Webster. 'Which had the spirit of an unclean devil, and he cried out in a loud voice, "What have we to do with thee, Jesus of Nazareth?" ' "

For the next two hours the minister assaulted her with the New Testament. He employed not only the Gospels for his truncheon but also Acts, Galatians, Ephesians, Second Thessalonians, First Timothy, and Revelation. As interpreted by the Reverend Samuel Parris, Christ's biography was essentially a chronicle of war: the Messiah's beatific brigades versus Lucifer's demon legions.

At noon Parris unleashed his final quotation, Matthew 25:41, "Then shall the Son of Man say also unto them on the left hand, 'Depart from me, ye cursed, into everlasting fire, prepared for the Devil and his angels.' " He slammed the Bible shut and pivoted toward Foreman Hocking. "Good jurors, I bid you recall Mrs. Webster's statement of earlier this morning: 'Our Savior hath no sympathy for the cleansing trade.' Evidently she believes the Gospels want for accuracy. She thinks Matthew a mountebank, Mark a charlatan, Luke a liar, and John a fraud."

A tremor of unease, subtle but palpable, rumbled through the courthouse.

"Reverend, you must not put words in my mouth," Jennet said, glancing every whichway. The twelve jurymen and a score of spectators all wore emphatic frowns.

"Even as *you* put words in the *saints'* mouths?" Parris retorted, facing the witness-stand. "This interview hath ended, Mrs. Webster, for I can no longer abide the presence of one who smears offal on Holy Writ."

Jennet, Ben, and Montesquieu spent the lunch recess tallying the morning's losses. It was now clear, the Baron conceded, that they would never win their case on Scripture. Whether rendered in Hebrew, Greek, Latin, or English, the Bible belonged to the enemy. Instead they must rely on a concept with which the Hebrew prophets and the Christian saints were apparently unfamiliar.

"Nature," Montesquieu said.

"*Exactement,*" Ben said.

"We must plant in each juror's brain a vision of Nature so rich and rarefied as to make demonic influence seem the silliest of ideas," Montesquieu said.

"I fear we do not address the twelve brightest men in Pennsylvania," Jennet said.

"Jesus had a similar problem," Ben said. "Oft-times his disciples found his parables opaque, and yet those poor bewildered pilgrims finally grasped his message."

When Jennet returned to the witness-stand, she saw that Dunstan would now assume the Inquisitorial rôle. He came at her flourishing a stack of papers as a Northman gone a-viking might brandish his battle-ax.

"The Crown hath collected sixteen depositions from your Manayunk neighbors," he said. "Four such reports tell that your grounds are congested with monk's-hood, thorn-apple, henbane, and other such hideous growths, all tumored and deformed as if sprung from Eden's malignant twin."

Jennet raised her arms, separating them as far as the chain allowed. "I have cultivated my garden as a philosophic laboratory, that I might learn what plants will breed one with the other. 'Tis but simple curiosity waters their roots. In other words, I seek to investigate those laws of Nature that have lately inspired so many valuable Baconian treatises"—she gestured toward Montesquieu, who flourished the demon disproof as proudly as a crusader advancing his king's banner—"such as J. S. Crompton's *The Sufficiency of the World*."

"Methinks this curiosity of yours be not far removed from necromancy," Dunstan said, pitching his voice toward the jury-box. "As for the entity you call Nature, it seems to me a peculiar locus for a woman's religious devotions." He stroked the depositions. "Another six honest citizens aver that you have oft-times launched silk kites during thunder-gusts."

"Had my neighbors spied more closely, they would have noticed how, after leaving the kite, the fly-line descends to Earth, coils about a mooring post, and enters a glass collection jar."

"A philosophic experiment?" Dunstan asked haughtily.

Jennet nodded. "I share Mr. Franklin's supposition that Heaven's fire, once captured and caged, will reveal itself as a variety of electricity." She gesticulated in the ragged pattern of a lightning-stroke arcing betwixt sky and ground. "After the initial explosion, the collateral sparks converge upon a stiff pointed wire atop the kite, then travel unimpeded along the wet twine—water, you see, facilitates the electric flow, an important finding of Mr. Franklin's. Finishing their journey, the sparks spill down the mooring post and enter the jar."

"And what amount of lightning have you harvested in this fashion?"

"Thus far . . . none."

"None?"

"Aye. None."

"Evidently God would keep His fire from the hands of self-appointed sages." Dunstan slapped the depositions. "According to six upright men of this community, you are given to building stone mounds and dancing around 'em in a lascivious manner. Enacting such a spectacle doth not strike me as befitting a Christian woman."

"And *watching* it doth not strike me as befitting a Christian man," she said, thereby eliciting sniggers and guffaws throughout the hall.

Dunstan rubbed the scar on his forehead. "Tell me what manner of philosophy is served by your Dionysian dancing."

"My dancing's no experiment, kinsman. 'Tis merely how I express my awe as I contemplate Nature's glory."

Under her brother's relentless and protracted questioning, she now reiterated the purposes behind her gardening, kite flying, and dancing, carefully explaining how each endeavor differed categorically from the worship of fallen angels and the solicitation of obscene agencies.

"Mrs. Webster," he said at last, "I believe there be but one name for your attitude to so-called Nature. Can you imagine what name I mean?"

"I cannot."

" 'Tis paganism."

"I would ne'er use that word to describe my enthusiasms."

"Prithee, inform the jurymen, yea or nay, whether you practice pagan rites."

She shut her eyes and again grasped William's wooden tiger, rubbing her thumb across its backbone. "Kinsman, I am here to tell the Court how o'er the past three centuries many a blameless person hath gone to noose and stake for activities no more nefarious than growing herbs, delivering babies, and leaping in adoration of the universe."

"I shall ask the question once again. Do you practice pagan rites?"

"I believe God hath gifted His creatures with two great books, one called Scripture, the other Nature. As you cleansers would have it, Scripture admonishes against the manipulation of demons, but when we study the *Codex Naturæ*, we find that these demons don't exist."

"Demons don't exist?"

"Save in the human mind."

Dunstan released a triumphant cackle and swerved toward the jury-box. "Faithful Philadelphians, you heard the words fall freely from her lips. Mrs. Webster hath just branded herself a Deist at best and a heretic at worst." Turning, he fixed his gaze on Jennet. "This interview is ended, sister—likewise the Crown's presentation. May our Savior forgive you for renouncing Him."

"I have not renounced Christ! I have not!"

Hathorne brought his hammer down hard against the bench. "Enough, Mrs. Webster! Enough! You are finished!"

Jennet stood and trudged back to the defense table, her fingers still clamped around William's tiger. She glanced toward the jury-box. The landholders looked variously sodden with sleep, benumbed by ale, and transfixed by boredom. It seemed fair to suppose they'd understood nothing of what she'd meant by Nature's laws. Instead they'd found in Rebecca Webster a woman so impious and arrogant that she'd routinely attempted to make Heaven's fire submit to her

❦

Will the war of the worldviews eventually cease? Will the Armageddon of ideas in time run its course? I doubt it. Since my advent I've been waging my lonely little campaign against rationalized irrationality, day and night, rain and shine, all seasons, all epochs. The *Principia Mathematica* versus sixteenth-century astrology . . . seventeenth-century demonology . . . eighteenth-century Gothicism . . . nineteenth-century spiritualism . . . twentieth-century New Age hogwash . . . twenty-first-century apocalyptics.

Now, it would be disingenuous of me to claim I have no taste for the fight. Over the centuries my struggle against the *Malleus Malefi-carum* has provided me with an exhilaration that my more pacific endeavors—my steam locomotives, suspension bridges, geosynchro-nous satellites, moon landings—could never rival. When I learned three nights ago that my recent truce with the *Malleus* had disinte-grated, I shed no tears. Instead I sallied forth to the vacant Manhattan lot we'd selected as our battlefield and took command of my biblio-phagic army.

By the terms of our agreement, should my enemy's troops triumph tomorrow, I must permit them to invade the University of California Press warehouse in Ewing, New Jersey, and devour all three thousand copies of my thirtieth paperbound printing. By contrast, should my soldiers carry the day, they will advance unharried to the Dover Publi-cations warehouse in Mineola, New York, there to consume the seven hundred copies of the *Malleus* currently on the shelves. Not since the Achæans sailed off to Troy has a war promised its victor such desirable spoils.

As I write these words, twilight descends. Our armies face each other across a terrain strewn with cigarette butts, candy wrappers, beer cans, and broken bottles. Beyond his two divisions of silverfish and three reg-iments of bookworms, the *Malleus* has recently acquired an air force—five tactical groups of paper-eating Cambodian wasps summoned to the scene by the collected works of Deepak Chopra. I have allies as well. At the beginning of the week, *The Origin of Species* joined my side with three companies of pulp chiggers, and the following day *The House of the Seven Gables* showed up with a brigade of termites. Alas, even after I add these reinforcements to my two regiments of booklice and my dozen squadrons of Indonesian moths, Revelation will still outnumber Reason by a factor of two to one.

Last night I read *The House of the Seven Gables* for the first time, seek-ing to learn exactly why it has come to my aid. I already knew that its au-thor, the estimable Nathanial Hawthorne, great-great-grandson of John

Hathorne, was so ashamed of his ancestor's rôle in the Salem Witch Trials that he'd severed the connection with a strident *W*. Only upon negotiating the text, however, did I realize that among its several villains is a
nineteenth-century judge named Jaffrey Pyncheon, clearly meant to
evoke the seventeenth-century Salem magistrate.

The story unfolds in 1850. The opening pages disclose that Judge
Pyncheon's family tree includes the unsavory Colonel Pyncheon, who
built the seven-gabled house on a Salem property he'd confiscated from
Matthew Maule, a poor man executed as a wizard during the notorious
persecutions. At the moment of his death, Maule called down a curse
upon the Pyncheons, saying that God would give them blood to drink.
Before the novel ends, Judge Pyncheon dies of apoplexy, blood pouring
from his mouth—the same fate suffered by two previous Pyncheons. We
subsequently learn how thirty years earlier this depraved jurist tampered
with the evidence surrounding his uncle's death, sending his kinsman
Clifford Pyncheon to prison for murdering their relation (though the
uncle actually died of natural causes), then claiming the entire inheritance for himself. The baroque plot comes to a happy conclusion when
Mr. Holgrove—a lodger in the seven-gabled house and the fiancé of
young Phoebe Pyncheon—reveals himself as a descendant of the murdered wizard. To wit, Phoebe and her children will bear the name of
Maule. The Pyncheon line is dead.

On the whole, I thought it was a pretty good novel, and a long time
will pass before an author gives us a more unflattering portrait of John
Hathorne. It's too bad the judge never lived to see himself so famously
skewered, but the bastard was a hundred years dead when the first edition of *The House of the Seven Gables* rolled off the presses.

We attack at dawn. Fear throbs in my soul. Terror creeps along my
spine. Part of me, I must admit, wants to take possession of a human
pyromaniac. In this guise I would rush to the Dover warehouse and
put the *Malleus* inventory to the torch. But that is not how we decided
to settle our differences—and, anyway, should I stoop to incarnation,
my enemy would do the same. Still, if a box of wooden matches suddenly appeared on the battlefield, I would be tempted to appropriate

New York City's most accomplished firebug, wherever he now resides.
Given my heritage, of course, I can hardly imagine the mind of such a
man, so easily enthralled by the sight of flame, so readily
aroused by the crackle of combustion,
so reliably excited by
the smell
of

Smoke
rose from
John Hathorne's
clay pipe, spreading outward in
gossamer curls as he seized his mallet and
called the Court to order. The tobacco stench made Montesquieu
sneeze. If there were any actual devils in the New World, he decided, one
of them was the man behind the bench, Hathorne with the acrid fire
fixed in his jaw and the hot vapors pouring from his nostrils. "This
Boston Judge is hardly the Reincarnation of King Solomon," Ebenezer
Trenchard had noted in that morning's *Gazette*. "If a newborn Babe were
to be brought before Mr. Hathorne along with two distraught Women,
each claiming to be the Mother, I shudder to imagine how he might rule.
Mayhap Hathorne would bisect the Infant with an Ax, then turn to the
Women and declare, 'Now let me observe who's the more aggriev'd, for
she shall have both Halves!' "

"*Monsieur le Baron*, you may open your case," Judge Hathorne said.

Montesquieu stretched to full height and gestured toward the Purification Commissioners. "The defense will interview Dunstan Stearne."

Gasps of surprise and murmurs of dismay reverberated through the
hall.

"Sir, I cannot permit you to abuse the Crown's advocate in this fashion," said Hathorne to Montesquieu.

Monsieur Stearne gained his feet, fired by an eagerness all too familiar to the Baron: the day before, the cleanser had shown a similar zeal in
making Madame Crompton admit to Deist sympathies. "By your leave,

Excellency," Stearne said, "the Crown's advocate will submit to the proposed interrogation. This Frenchman hath no power to perturb me."

"Would that I could say the same," Hathorne grumbled.

As Stearne settled into the witness-stand, Montesquieu flashed him the most sardonic smile in his repertoire. "Monsieur, if you had to give the Court two reasons why demons exist," the Baron asked, "may I assume that the first would be scriptural?"

"Verily," Stearne said. "Ephesians 6:12, First Timothy 4:1, and a plethora of other passages."

Portmanteau in hand, Montesquieu approached the Crown's advocate. "And the second reason—what might that be?"

"I know that demons exist because, over the years, hundreds of divinely empowered courts have found thousands of witches guilty."

" 'Over the years.' 'Thousands of witches.' Might we attempt a greater specificity? Do you agree with me when I say the epic European witch-cleansing lasted nearly three centuries, an era that saw upwards of eight hundred thousand persons burned, hanged, or beheaded as Devil-worshippers?"

"That's quite possibly the total thus far," Stearne said. "The great hunt's not yet done."

"And would you also agree that most of those eight hundred thousand persons admitted to Satanism shortly before they were executed?"

"Aye."

"Then would it be correct to say that, biblical passages aside, demonology derives its authority from eight hundred thousand signed confessions of heresy?"

"It would."

"If those documents did not exist, might not a reasonable man question both your prosecution of Mrs. Webster and your aggression against the Massachusetts aborigines?"

"But those documents *do* exist."

"Indeed they do, Monsieur. Indeed they do. Something puzzles me, however. Since a confession was unlikely to save his life, why would any self-respecting Satanist give his persecutors the satisfaction of a signature?"

"By putting his name to a confession, the heretic seeks to purge his soul of the blackest sin imaginable."

"Mr. Stearne, is it not true that the majority of sorcery confessions were elicited under torture?"

"As Judge Hathorne remarked on Monday, torture hath ne'er been used in an English witch-court."

"Let us disregard England—a mere two thousand cases at best. I speak of the momentous Continental cleansing."

" 'Tis a pity that pricking and the other reliable tests of Satanic allegiance have enjoyed so little favor outside His Majesty's realm," Stearne said. "Continental law frames witchcraft as an invisible phenomenon and hence a *crimen excepta*, an exceptional crime, so difficult of proof that the ordinary rules of evidence must be suspended."

"And the ordinary rules of civilization as well?"

The witness shuddered, temporarily dismayed, then mocked the question with an audible snort. "Because the Devil himself would ne'er appear in a courtroom and testify against his own disciple, my Continental counterparts have reasoned that torture is the best way to expose a witch."

"I'm sure you are aware, Monsieur, that in most Continental sorcery cases the executioner continued the torture well past the moment of confession. Can you explain this seemingly irrational practice?"

" 'Tis well known that Satanists perform their execrable rites in assemblies. Through torture, an executioner induces a witch to name her accomplices."

Montesquieu asked, "Is your education such that you might describe for us the five stages of torture employed during the Continental cleansing?"

"I have indeed studied the traditions underlying my profession," Stearne said. "The first stage was called preparatory torture."

"What did that involve?"

Before Stearne could answer, the Reverend Samuel Parris scrambled to his feet and cleared his throat. "Excellency, the Crown's advocate hath already stated that English witch-courts eschew torture. The Baron's question enjoys no relevance to this case."

"I cannot make a proper defense of Mrs. Webster," Montesquieu retorted, "unless I demonstrate what the witness means when he avers that his enterprise rests on eight hundred thousand confessions."

Hathorne scowled fiercely before making his pronouncement. "In the name of fairness, we shall allow a brief discussion of this unhappy topic."

"We were speaking of preparatory torture," Montesquieu reminded the witness.

"This required the executioner to squeeze the prisoner's thumb or toe in a metal vise," Stearne said.

As Parris settled back into his seat, Montesquieu opened his portmanteau and removed a device that to a naïve eye might have seemed intended for cracking walnuts. "Whilst visiting the European capitals last year"—he held the machine before Stearne—"I found myself moved to collect and catalog several dozen torture instruments of the sort once used by Continental executioners. Would you call this a typical thumbscrew?"

"I would."

"I have heard that the executioner often supplemented the thumbscrew with a larger vise—"

"The Spanish boot, aye."

"—using it to pulverize the prisoner's foot until the marrow spurted forth."

The Reverend Parris leapt free of his chair. "Excellency, I see no merit in this line of inquiry."

"Eight hundred thousand confessions!" Montesquieu shouted.

"Eight hundred thousand confessions!" Ben Franklin echoed.

Hathorne sucked contemplatively on his clay pipe. One puff, two puffs, three. "The bench will graciously permit a display of torture instruments, but only the most *pertinent* torture instruments."

"I would like you to tell the Court about stage two, ordinary torture," Montesquieu said to the witness.

"Also known as *strappado*, 'to pull,' " Stearne said. "The prisoner's feet were hung with weights and his hands tied behind him with a rope threaded through a pulley on the ceiling."

From his portmanteau Montesquieu retrieved a great iron pulley, large as a melon. "A pulley such as this?"

"Aye. The executioner raveled up the rope, lifting the witch into the air. After several such hoistings, the prisoner became highly inclined to confess his diabolism and name his confederates."

"And if he remained stubborn . . . ?"

"The executioner proceeded to stage three, extraordinary torture, accomplished through *squassation*."

Elaborating, Stearne revealed that, as with *strappado*, the accused witch's hands were tied and his feet weighted. After hoisting him to the ceiling, the executioner would release the rope, then abruptly grab it when the prisoner was within inches of the floor, causing him to jerk violently. With repeated applications, *squassation* normally dislocated a person's arms, hands, legs, and feet.

"I am told that the agony of *squassation* is beyond imagining," Montesquieu said.

"Hellfire is far worse," Stearne said.

Montesquieu spun the rollers of the pulley, sending a high barbed screech coursing through the hall like the cry of an enraged cock. "Far worse. No question. *Oui.* But may I surmise that whereas *strappado* sometimes failed to produce a confession and a list of accomplices, *squassation* nearly always turned the trick?"

"Quite so."

"Then what purpose was served by the *next* two stages?"

"Stage four, additional torture, figured in cases where a judge wished to punish a witch for a particularly horrific act of *maleficium*."

Returning the pulley to his portmanteau, Montesquieu removed his steel pincers, fanged like a serpent, then waved them before the witness. "Punish him, for example, by ripping out his fingernails?"

"For example."

"Stage five—occasional torture—was that likewise punitive?"

"Punitive, but uncommon. 'Twas inflicted only on a witch of the worst sort, one who could ne'er be called back to Christ."

For the next hour Montesquieu prompted Stearne to present the particulars of additional torture, which was subject to regulation, and occasional torture, which knew no limits. The jurymen learned of gouged eyes, severed limbs, flesh torn apart with tongs, bowels dislocated by ribbons of swallowed cloth, feet slit open and immersed in boiling lime, and diets of salted herring unmitigated by even one drop of water. Throughout the witness's testimony, Montesquieu surveyed the courtroom. With the exceptions of Judge Hathorne, Samuel Parris, Abigail Stearne, and a handful of depraved rustics in the audience, everyone seemed on the point of either fainting dead away or breaking into hives.

Hathorne now declared a luncheon interval, though Montesquieu doubted that anyone felt favorably disposed toward a hearty meal. His intuition proved accurate. Although most of the jurymen and spectators patronized the food stalls, they returned with portions far smaller than ordinary. Franklin brought Madame Crompton an apple tart, which she succeeded in consuming only on her third attempt.

"Hear me now, Charles," she said. "For all you have made a potent presentation, I believe 'twould be unwise to continue spoiling the jurymen's appetites."

"Have no fear. The Court has seen the last of my vises, pulleys, and pincers."

At one o'clock Hathorne reconvened the trial and publicly forbade the Baron to solicit any more grisly particulars concerning torture.

"I am pleased to comply, Excellency, for the real issue before the Court is how we should *interpret* the use of torture in the classic witch-trials." Montesquieu turned and gestured toward the mottled white mass on Stearne's brow. "I see your face is scarred, Monsieur. I hope you've not been tortured."

"Many years ago I rushed into a raging fire set by Nimacook savages, that I might rescue my father's cleansing license. The pain of my burns was severe"—Stearne bobbed his mutilated head toward Madame Crompton—"but not so severe as to make me repudiate God."

"Do you say that if accused of witchcraft you would cleave to your innocence no matter how terrible the torture?"

"I do."

"Most admirable." Montesquieu enacted a wince. "I promise you, Monsieur, if you subjected *me* to *squassation,* I would confess to sorcery and name my confederates not because I was a wizard, but simply to stop the pain."

"Stop the pain!" Franklin cried.

"Stop the pain!" the spectators echoed.

"Silence!" Hathorne screamed.

"Consider this narrative," Montesquieu said to the witness. "I arrest a woman on a false charge of Satanism and torture her until she names seven accomplices. Next I apprehend these supposed witches and torture each into naming another seven. By torturing the forty-nine, I acquire three hundred and forty-three new names. I perform the operation once again, flushing out an additional two thousand four hundred and one presumed heretics, and still once again, bringing in a harvest of sixteen thousand eight hundred and seven. In short, my Lord Witchfinder, the question is not, 'How could the courts have elicited eight hundred thousand false confessions?' but rather, 'Why did they not elicit *ten times* that many?' "

"I have ne'er heard such specious reasoning," Stearne said.

"Your quarrel is not with me, Monsieur, but with the multiplication tables."

"I can compute as well as you."

"Then tell me if I am correct when I compute that your organization makes an annual profit of two hundred and forty English pounds."

" 'Tis not so."

"*The Pennsylvania Gazette* reports that you indict and execute twenty supposed witches each year at twelve pounds a head."

"The Baron confuses profit with income."

Having broached the subject of Stearne's finances, Montesquieu now faced the jurymen and proceeded to argue that cleansing could not be understood apart from its economics. Because the courts were empowered to seize the property of convicted Satanists, he explained, witch-hunting had until recently ranked amongst the world's most lucrative industries, commensurate with ship-building, rum-running, and the slave trade. The enterprise was as circular as it was remunerative. As the number of trials increased, the more the courts needed money, and the more the courts needed money, the more they needed witches.

"Money for the judges, money for the lawyers, money for the bailiffs," Montesquieu chanted, glancing from one juror to the next, "money for the constables, money for the gaolers, money for the executioners." He swerved toward the witness-stand, reached into his waistcoat and, like an apprentice ambassador practicing a bow, made a great show of pulling out a scrap of paper. "During my recent European tour I came upon a German document dated the twenty-fourth of July, 1628, which I copied by hand from the original, then translated into French and English. Right before he was burned for a wizard, Johannes Junius, Burgomaster of Bamberg, wrote his daughter a letter, which the gaoler agreed to smuggle out of the prison. I would ask that you read the passages marked in red."

"I assumed the witness-stand to belie your philosophy, Baron, not to become your puppet," Stearne said.

"As you wish," Montesquieu said, slipping on his spectacles. He unfolded the transcription and positioned it a foot from his nose. "Herr Junius begins, 'My dearly beloved daughter Veronica, innocent I have entered this prison, innocent I have been tortured, innocent I shall die.' Junius proceeds to recount the testimony of the prosecution's witnesses, one of whom claimed she heard him abjure God as he danced upon the moor. 'And then came also the executioner, and he put the thumbscrews on me until the blood spurted from the nails, so that for five weeks I could not use my hands, as you can see by my writing.' Junius goes on to describe his ordeal of *squassation*. 'I thought Heaven and Earth were at an end. Eight times did they draw me up and let me fall again, so that I suffered terrible agony.' Next the prisoner reports on a remarkable conversation betwixt himself and his tormentor. 'Sir, I beg you, for God's sake, confess something,' the executioner says, 'even if it be false, for you cannot endure the new tortures to which you will be put. And even if you do bear them, still the judges will not free you, but one torture will follow upon another until you say you are a witch.' After pondering his hopeless situation, Junius accepted the executioner's logic and confessed. He told the judges how he fell under the enchantment of a succubus named Füchsin, who appeared to him first in the guise of a dairymaid, later as a goat, and persuaded him to reject Christ, worship Satan, and participate in Sabbats. 'Now, sweet daughter, here you have the story of my confession, and it is all sheer lies and fabulation, so help me God. Fare well, dearest child, and remember me in your prayers, for you will never see your father Johannes Junius again.' "

Montesquieu refolded the transcription, slowly, deliberately, and returned it to his waistcoat. A ponderous silence descended upon the courtroom.

"Monsieur, might you tell us your reaction to Johannes Junius's letter?" the Baron asked the witness.

" 'Tis probably a forgery," Stearne replied. "Or if this Junius truly wrote the thing, then he lied to call his confession a fraud. A succubus named Füchsin who is also a were-goat—that's certainly not something a person could simply invent out of his head. I believe this Junius was a wizard."

"*Merci*, Mr. Stearne. I have no more questions."

ON THE MORNING following Dunstan's testimony, the local readership of *The Pennsylvania Gazette* opened their newspapers to find an essay by Ebenezer Trenchard that in Jennet's opinion easily eclipsed everything the Seaman Scholar had written thus far. Trenchard asserted, "The Crown's Case turns on the Assumption that an innocent Man would never confess to Witchcraft even if you tore out his Fingernails." He concluded, "The Baron de Montesquieu hath shown the whole Witch-Cleansing Industry to be a corrupt Castle built upon degraded Sand."

The rising sun sent shafts of light through the courthouse windows, each beam as glorious and golden as a flying buttress pressed against the weightless wall of a heavenly palace. Hathorne puffed languidly on his clay pipe, removed the stem, and coughed.

"*Monsieur le Baron*, you may interview your next witness."

"The defense calls Rebecca Webster," Montesquieu said.

Opaque as stones, phlegmatic as clay, the twelve landholders collectively returned Jennet's gaze as she crossed the hall and settled into the witness-stand. What she most wanted at that moment was a mechanics of human consciousness, a *Principia Mentis* by which she might study each juror's deportment and consequently learn his thoughts.

"My first question is simple," Montesquieu said. "Mrs. Webster, are you a witch?"

"I am not."

"Have you ever met the Devil or written in his alleged register?"

"I have not."

"*Très bien.*" From his portmanteau Montesquieu obtained his copy of *The Sufficiency of the World.* "As a devotee of J. S. Crompton, I was gratified to hear you evoke his formidable treatise when Mr. Stearne interviewed you on Wednesday."

"I find Mr. Crompton's book to be an irrefutable disproof of demons," Jennet said.

"A provocative statement, Madame. Your lawyer would have you elaborate upon it."

Cued by Montesquieu's questions, Jennet spent the next three hours explicating the sufficiency hypothesis. She began by arguing that English experimental philosophy was of a largely Neo-Platonist bent. Because various preternatural beings logically lurked behind Plato's famous Veil of Appearances, this perspective went hand-in-hand with the demon hypothesis. On the Continent, meanwhile, René Descartes's followers had cast the world as a vast clocklike machine. But here, too, spirits both benign and malign were permitted, nay, *required*, since the universe's dynamic phenomena—magnetism, acceleration, elasticity, and the rest—necessarily employed immaterial entities as their agents, many doubtless corresponding to the demons, devils, and fallen angels of biblical revelation.

Both views, she explained, suffered from the defect of being untrue. Poised against Platonism was William of Occam's famous parsimony postulate: God had situated his creatures in a real universe, not the shadow of a real universe, and there was no need to muddy this circumstance with Eternal Ideas and Perfect Forms. As for the dead Cartesian planet, J. S. Crompton had persuasively replaced it with a pulsing, blooming, sufficient world. Why posit genies and vortices when Nature's algorithms could account for all the motions that matter enacted, all the shocks to which flesh was heir?

Hathorne decreed a recess, whereupon Jennet consumed an enormous luncheon. She could recall no time in her life when rabbit pie had tasted more delicious, cheese more savory, pease-bread more filling, ale more satisfying. Despite everything—despite Bella's death and Rachel's abduction, Dr. Halley's reproof and Tobias's reproach, the rout of Aristotle and the wreck of the *Berkshire*—she had finally brought forth an *argumentum grande* and given it to the world.

Fortified, she threw herself into the labors of the afternoon. Thus far she and Montesquieu had provided but the bones of the sufficiency hypothesis. Now they must give it muscle, meat, and skin. Under the Baron's direction, the marshals dragged the defense table to within ten feet of the jurymen, then erected on its surface a six-foot inclined ramp scored with two parallel grooves. Though handicapped by her chains and manacles, Jennet grasped a pair of spheres, one of lead, the other of straw, and set them on the starting line.

"Intuition says the heavier object wins the race," she told the jurors, "but behold what happens when I perform the experiment." She released both spheres, rolling them along the grooves. "Your eyes did not deceive you, gentlemen. Lead and straw reached the finish line at the same instant." Twice more she demonstrated Galileo's law of uniform acceleration, first pitting a ball of wire against a ball of yarn, then a sphere filled with cider against one containing grass. Victory eluded each and every sphere. "As you have seen, good jurymen, Nature cleaves to her own rules, heedless of our petty expectations."

No sooner had Montesquieu flourished his lodestone than a cry of uncertain origin and uncanny timbre shot through the courtroom, a piercing "Aaaaiiiieeee!" A second such scream sent scores of faces turning toward the prosecution table, where Abigail Stearne was rocking to and fro like a victim of the ergot.

"The witch sends forth her demons!" Abigail released a third shriek, lurched to her feet, and vaulted into the aisle. " 'Tis Hell's worst minions make those spheres move so contrarily!"

The spectators began chattering amongst themselves, a cacophony admixing confusion with fright.

"I send forth no demons," Jennet insisted, managing an outward tranquility even as she seethed within.

"Silence, spectators!" Hathorne commanded.

"I'Christ, her goblins are loose within me!" Abigail cried, limping toward the judge's bench. "They gnaw upon my stomach and bowels! Call 'em back, witch! Call thy demons back!"

"Oh, my dearest wife!" Dunstan wailed.

"Darling niece!" Mr. Parris yelped.

From Abigail's throat came a sound suggesting the death rattle of a rabid lynx. "Her demons choke me! They rob the breath from my lungs!"

It was the same old Abigail, Jennet realized. The decades since Salem had not weakened by one whit her powers of prevarication.

Arms outstretched in a pose of crucifixion, Abigail halted before the judge. "Excellency, there be but one way I may lift this curse." Like a Roman conspirator preparing to assassinate Julius Caesar, she slid a glittering silver bodkin from her dress. "I must release a drop of the witch's blood."

"This woman plays you false," Jennet calmly informed John Hathorne. "She played you false at Salem, and now she plays you false again."

Twirling around like a weathercock in a gale, Abigail sprang upon Jennet and embraced her as she might a lover. The bodkin flashed in the afternoon sun. Abigail snarled, and suddenly the blade was glancing along the edge of Jennet's jaw, leaving in its wake a stinging wound.

"Lying slush-bucket!" Jennet cried. "Filthy vixen!"

The spectators' jabber grew louder yet.

"Be quiet, all of you!" Hathorne ordered.

"The spell is broken!" Abigail shouted with manufactured exuberance. She restored the bodkin to her dress and made her way to the prosecution table, slowly, uncertainly, like a lost traveler staggering through a blizzard. "Broken," she gasped, collapsing into her chair. She folded her elbows, rested her head on the fleshy pillow, and appeared to fall asleep. "Broken . . . broken . . ."

"Good Philadelphians, you must not believe Mrs. Stearne's play-acting," Montesquieu said, placing his handkerchief in Jennet's grasp.

"*Merci.*" She raised her manacled wrists and pressed the white silk against her bleeding jaw.

The Baron turned his palms outward and beseechingly approached the jury-box. "She has merely mimicked a woman possessed."

"*Monsieur le Baron,* 'tis not your place to tell these dozen worthies what they may and mayn't believe," Hathorne said. "Prithee, finish your dumb-show, that the jury might begin its deliberations on the morrow."

"Mrs. Webster, do you feel prepared to continue, despite this outrageous attack upon your person?" Montesquieu asked.

"Aye," Jennet said, passing the Baron his blood-soaked handkerchief.

She proceeded to illustrate the law of magnetism, making first a watch-fob, next a key, and then a musket-ball fly across the table and adhere to Montesquieu's lodestone. Abigail slept soundly through all three collisions, but she stirred slightly during the fourth: the noisy meeting of the magnetite and a steel stirrup.

"The Gilbertian force is woven into the very tapestry of Creation," Jennet told the jurymen. "Magnetism follows its own God-given principle, unimpressed by human will or demonic desire."

For the next presentation she charged the Von Guericke sphere and drew a range of substances—eider-down, sot-weed granules, wig powder—to its surface.

"Though natural philosophers still have many questions concerning universal electricity," she said, "they know better than to give their ignorance the name of *demon.*"

Her climactic presentation had her placing a pentahedral glass prism on the defense table. She allowed the setting sun to strike the prism and send a full spectrum, red to orange to yellow to blue to indigo to violet, cascading across the jury-box, then employed a second prism in restoring the rainbow to a stream of purest whiteness.

"The phenomenon of refraction belongs to Nature alone. 'Tis not the plaything of hypothetical spirits. And God said, 'Let there be—' "

"Aaaaiiieeee!" screamed Abigail, leaping up like a boulder launched from a catapult. "I'Christ, her devils find me! Her refraction demons pound a prism into my heart! Aaaaiiieeee!"

The spectators abandoned their benches, their collective mutters reverberating off the walls and rattling amongst the rafters.

"Sit down, every one of you!" Hathorne cried.

To a man, to a woman, the spectators remained standing.

"Her electric imps set my bile aboil! Her magnet-spirits fill me with Golgotha's nails!" Abigail ran toward the defense table, gathered up the philosophic tools—ramp, lodestone, sulphur ball, prisms—and hurled them in all directions. "Sayeth the witch, 'Let mine enemy eat of the iron that locked Christ to His cross!' The nails! The nails! I must purge myself of the unholy nails!"

"Darling Abby, methinks this bride of Lucifer means to murder thee!" Dunstan shouted.

Bending in two, Abigail clutched her stomach, slapped her cheek, and opened her mouth. Against the grain of common expectation, four iron nails spewed from her gullet, clanking and clattering as they rolled across the table.

"Heaven protect us!" Foreman Hocking shrieked.

"I cannot believe it!" Hathorne gasped.

"Deliver me, Lord!" Abigail spat up two more nails. "God have mercy!" Another nail came forth. "Aaaaiiieeee!"

It seemed to Jennet that a tremor of unease now passed through Montesquieu. For one small second, the sliver of an instant, he apparently thought he might actually be defending a witch.

"Spectators, find your seats, or I shall have the marshals drag you from the hall!" Hathorne shouted.

Regaining his wits, Montesquieu bounded toward the jury. "Honorable landholders, heed not this woman's mendacity!"

"Oh, my Savior!" Abigail strode away from the spiky vomitus and, lurching upright, spat an eighth nail into her open palm. She rushed to the jury-box and held the nail before Mr. Hocking. "Good sirs, you must refuse to set yon witch upon the world!" She pivoted toward an open window and hurled the nail through the aperture. "In Christ's name, you mustn't loose her!"

Now Barnaby joined the tumult, quitting the gallery and dashing toward the judge's bench. "Excellency, these seeming wonders are but an illusionist's tricks!"

"The raven!" Abigail cried. "The raven! She torments me with Beelzebub's spectral bird!"

Ducking and cringing, she gestured as if to catch and crush a pesky midge, when suddenly a large black raven feather materialized in her grasp. She swatted the air a second time, thus plucking another feather from the invisible bird.

"More tricks!" Barnaby shouted.

"She shan't defeat me!" Abigail snatched a third feather from the æther. "I love Christ even more than the witch adoreth Satan!"

"Abby, save yourself!" Dunstan insisted.

"Scratch the witch!" Mr. Parris advised.

"Save myself, aye!" Abigail dropped all three feathers and pulled the bodkin from her pocket. She stepped toward Jennet and froze abruptly, whereupon her bodkin arm jerked outward, twisting and twitching like the tail of a storm-tossed kite. "Oh, sweet guardians of grace, she turns my dagger against me!" Her bodkin arm reversed direction, pushing the blade deep into her side, directly below her rib cage. "The thrusting lance! Our Savior's precious hurt!"

"Damn thee, Jennet, thou shalt cease this assault upon my wife!" Dunstan, rising, pounded his fist on the prosecution table. "Desist! Desist!"

Abigail yanked the bodkin free. A thread of blood jetted from the lesion, staining the floor with a sinuous red line. Her eyes crossed, her tongue snaked forward, and she drove the blade into her left breast.

"Witch, thou canst not conquer me!" she screamed, lactating blood. "Christ's mercy is my armor and shield!"

"Sit down, spectators!" Hathorne shouted. "Sit down!"

Barnaby dropped to his knees, pressing his right hand against Abigail's shed blood as if sealing a seed within a furrow. He lifted his palm and licked it clean.

"Excellency, this gore be sweet, not salt like true blood!" he informed Hathorne. "I swear 'tis naught but cherry pulp!"

Abigail tore the bodkin from her breast and, dashing toward the defense table, cut an invisible slit in the air and then a palpable gash in Jennet's scalp.

"She seeks to fool us with cherry pulp!" Barnaby shouted.

Again Jennet availed herself of Montesquieu's handkerchief. Even as the wound stopped flowing, Abigail pocketed the bodkin and strutted down the crowded aisle, the perplexed mob parting around her. With a final ghastly shriek Abigail entered the foyer, kicked open the front door, and leapt into the gloomy dusk.

"The Court is adjourned!" Hathorne cried.

"Cherry pulp!" Barnaby screamed.

"Are you deaf, sir? Adjourned!" Hathorne pounded the bench so violently that his tool snapped in half. The disembodied mallet-head spun like a child's top. "Adjourned! Adjourned!"

❆

MATTHEW KNOX SUPPLIED JENNET, Montesquieu, and Barnaby with a splendid meal that night, a succulent fellowship of roasted pork, boiled cabbage, and Syracuse salt, then capped the feast by rolling a cask of ale into the gaol-cell and pouring full tankards all around. As he started to leave, the turnkey mentioned, diffidently but earnestly, that he'd heard rumors of a bewitchment in the courtroom, whereupon Jennet invited him to join their colloquy. If Barnaby could convince this simple gaoler that Abigail's antics did not portend Satanic intervention, it followed that he might convince the jury as well.

She downed her portion of ale in one colossal gulp, thereby achieving considerable relief from the lacerations in her jaw and scalp. "Good curator, do enlighten us," she instructed Barnaby.

"My knowledge of the magician's art goes back some twenty years, when I joined forces with a crystal-gazer and an illusionist to create *Le Cirque de la Lune*," Barnaby told his audience. "The latter wight, one Feizunda, taught me the rudiments of legerdemain—the same rudiments as were employed against our Jenny this afternoon." He turned to Mr. Knox. "Friend, did you know your brain is home to a member of the insect race?" No sooner had a frown gathered on Mr. Knox's face than Barnaby reached forward and retrieved a large black cricket from inside the gaoler's left ear. "Behold the source of the music you hear each night as you fall asleep."

"Monsieur Cavendish, vous êtes d'une adresse stupéfiante," Montesquieu said.

" 'Tis a magnificent trick," Mr. Knox agreed.

"The same trick by which Abigail Stearne seemed to pluck feathers from a spectral raven today," Barnaby said. He presented the cricket to Jennet, who set it on the floor that it might hop to freedom. "As you may have heard, Mr. Knox, the Stearne woman also vomited forth eight iron spikes. Speaking of which, I am reminded that my noonday meal was an uncommon tart, filled with . . ." He pressed one hand against his stomach. "I'Christ, those acorns confound my digestion! 'Twould seem a purgation's in the offing!"

Clamping his free hand across his mouth, Barnaby staggered groaning and retching toward Jennet's writing-desk, then abruptly disgorged five greenish-brown acorns. They bounced off the brass ink pot with short, sharp reports.

" 'Steeth!" Knox exclaimed.

"I would imagine such sleight-of-hand demands many hours of practice," Montesquieu said.

"Aye," Barnaby said, "but once he's mastered the illusion, a person can appear to purge himself of everything from hickory nuts to Christ's own nails."

"*Hélas*, Madame Webster, I must confess that when I beheld Abigail Stearne spew that iron, a wave of faithlessness washed over me," Montesquieu said.

"I saw it in your countenance, Charles," she said. "But know that I absolve you, as I have ne'er seen so persuasive a deception."

"For her third trick the insidious Abigail stabbed herself with a bodkin," Barnaby informed the turnkey, "just as I now stab myself with my own digit."

He unbuttoned his day-shirt and, pulling back the placket, drove his thumb deep into the flesh beyond. A dollop of blood rolled down his naked chest.

"Marry!" wailed Knox.

"Be not alarmed," Barnaby said. "This blood's mere cherry pulp, burst from a leather pouch concealed within my hand."

" 'Twould appear you've poked your thumb into your heart!" Knox gasped.

"A simple matter of folding it into the palm of the same hand." Barnaby yanked the digit free of his chest, then wiped away the mock blood with his handkerchief. "Were we to examine Abigail's bodkin, we would discover that on encountering resistance the blade slides into the shaft. No doubt the flick of a lever converts it to a normal dagger."

"A question, Mr. Knox!" Cyril Turpin cried from the adjoining cell. "When this conjurer finishes entertaining you, might he bring his tricks to *my* abode? I would be a most appreciative audience."

" 'Tis not my job to arrange amusements for chicken thieves!" shouted Knox.

"I'm a horse thief, sir, and I shall thank ye to address me as such!"

The turnkey gathered up the residue of their meal—platters, utensils, tankards—and let himself out of the cell, locking the door behind him. By way of a parting remark, he proclaimed that Barnaby's magic would surely dazzle the judge, flabbergast the jury, and set Mrs. Webster free. Montesquieu and Barnaby were less confident, however, and for the next two hours they rehearsed their presentation.

At ten o'clock, yawning and bleary-eyed, Barnaby shuffled off to his lodgings in Mount-Airy Lane. Montesquieu lingered, writing out his final remarks to the jurymen, a moving and cogent paean to Nature's laws, nine pages long. He performed it aloud for Jennet. Her body felt wholly depleted, but her brain remained alert as, sprawled on her mattress, she savored the Baron's eloquence and drank in his sagacity.

It was not enough, of course. How could it be enough? What breed of eloquence could nullify Abigail Stearne's numinous crucifixion nails, what species of sagacity could prevail against her preternatural feathers?

"Compared to Abby's phantom raven," she told the Baron, "Reason's a feeble fowl indeed, its wings clipped, tail shorn, flesh rotten with ergot."

"And yet come morning we shall make it fly," Montesquieu declared, rolling his address into the semblance of a telescope. "We shall send it kiting clear to Heaven."

⁂

ALTHOUGH HER MATTRESS WAS SOFT and her fellow prisoners quiet, sleep eluded Jennet that night, and the next morning she entered the courtroom in a benumbed and bedraggled state. Someone had restored the defense table to its former location, but the aftermath of Abigail's rampage, the bits and pieces of the previous day's philosophic demonstrations, still lay scattered about the hall like corpses on a battlefield. Montesquieu sat hunched over the nine pages of his speech, shielding them with the fervor of a biblical scholar protecting a newly unearthed Gospel. He seemed no less dazed than she, peruke askew, eyes bloodshot, waistcoat only half buttoned, but he managed an energetic smile, and in receiving her from the four marshals he briefly lifted her, chains and all, off the floor.

Settling into her chair, she apprehended that an atmosphere of dread now permeated the courtroom, not unlike the palpable terror that had suffused Haverhill prior to the Nimacook attack. Each time she looked toward the gallery, most of the spectators glanced away, as if they feared bewitchment. Only the Franklin faction—the journalists and the Junto members—willingly returned her gaze. At the prosecution table Dunstan studied his notes whilst Mr. Parris read his Bible. Abigail was evidently still at the prickers' inn, nursing her illusory lesions.

"*Voilà!*" Montesquieu said, unfurling that morning's *Gazette* before Jennet. "Ebenezer Trenchard at his finest."

Her eyes alighted on the last paragraph. "Watching Abigail Stearne pretend to expel iron Nails from her Stomach this Friday, I thought of Exodus 7:11, wherein Pharaoh commands his Masters of Legerdemain to make Serpents of their Scepters in mocking Imitation of the divine Miracle the Courtiers have just witnessed: the one true God transforming Aaron's Rod into a slithering Reptile. But Jehovah has the last Laugh, for the holy Snake immediately devours those of the Egyptian Magicians."

Hathorne seized his mallet, now repaired with spirals of copper wire, and smacked it against the bench. In a striking deviation from their customary contrariness, the spectators grew instantly silent.

"Yesterday in this hall we all beheld a frightening wonder," the judge began. "We saw Mrs. Webster's demons attack Abigail Stearne with crucifixion nails, a spectral raven, and, deadliest of all, a steel bodkin. Mr. Stearne informs me that, thanks be to God, his wife will not die, though her wounds are sufficiently grievous to keep her abed."

"Excellency, the defense knows a *second* way to interpret this so-called attack on Mrs. Stearne," said Montesquieu, rising.

"Sit down, *Monsieur le Baron*," Hathorne said. He faced the jury-box, slamming his mallet repeatedly against his palm like a cook tenderizing a mutton chop. "We cannot doubt that the Court of Oyer and Terminer is now under siege from Lucifer himself. I must perforce instruct you worthy landholders to begin your deliberations anon, that this trial might cease ere all Hell's agents come against us."

"The defense calls Barnaby Cavendish to testify," Montesquieu declared.

Barnaby jumped to his feet.

"Your memory fails you, *Monsieur le Baron*," said Hathorne, "for you examined your last witness yesterday." He slid his clay pipe from his robe and pointed the stem toward Mr. Hocking. "Good Foreman, you will take your eleven to the antechamber."

Hocking abandoned his chair, removed his felt hat, and gestured the jury to a standing position.

"Your Honor, you must permit me to address the Court!" Barnaby cried, storming the judge's bench. "I am the very Dr. Cavendish whom the Baron wishes to interview!"

"Then you are the very Dr. Cavendish who will not be heard today," Hathorne said.

"Give me but a moment's preparation, Excellency, and I too shall make hobnails fly from my mouth!"

"Be seated, sir."

Barnaby flourished his blood-pouch. "I can show the Court how Abigail Stearne seemed to stab herself! 'Twas all legerdemain!"

Hocking led his colleagues out of the jury-box in a solemn parade.

"Dr. Cavendish, the Court can no longer abide your noxious interruptions!" Hathorne set the unlit pipe betwixt his lips and blew into the stem as if playing a fife. A staccato, birdish *tweet* emerged from the bowl. "Marshals, you will escort this demented spectator into the yard."

"Abigail Stearne hath deluded you!" Barnaby cried.

The four marshals lurched out of their niches and, rudely taking hold of the curator, bore him down the central aisle by main strength.

"Tell your minions to unhand that man!" Jennet screamed toward the bench. "He's but a frail and harmless philosopher who will not survive a mauling!"

"Mrs. Stearne vomited no nails!" Barnaby shouted as the marshals dragged him toward the foyer. "No nails! No nails!" And suddenly he was gone.

"Excellency, you must at least suffer the Crown's advocate and myself to make our closing arguments!" Montesquieu protested.

The jury foreman halted his eleven before the antechamber door.

"Mr. Stearne," said Hathorne to Dunstan, "what think you of the procedural issue the Baron hath raised?"

"In the interests of delivering this Court from the Dark One, the Crown relinquishes its privilege of a summarizing speech," Dunstan replied.

"Then it seems only fair for the defense to relinquish that privilege as well," Hathorne said, "and I so rule."

Montesquieu dashed across the hall and, planting himself before Hocking, made a heroically hopeless attempt to distill his nine-page address into a handful of compacted clauses. "Good landholders, this day you can bring low the odious Witchcraft Act of James the First! In framing your verdict, you must remember that God allows no demon to confound His design!"

Mr. Hocking shepherded his eleven out of the hall, the last juror slamming the door in Montesquieu's face. The bailiff inserted his key and activated the lock.

"Call those jurymen back!" Nicholas Scull demanded.

"Call 'em back!" Ben cried.

"This Court is adjourned!" Hathorne shouted, punctuating the pronouncement with his mallet. "When the jury hath reached its verdict, the tower bell will ring seven times!"

Jennet's mind became a fractured scrying-glass, a shattered gazing-crystal, each shard reflecting a facet of the commotion. John Tux stomping his feet and screaming, "Call 'em back!" Montesquieu shouting his abridged address at the antechamber door. Hathorne crying "Seven bells!" whilst hammering madly on the bench like a man shingling a roof in a hurricane. Ben brandishing the *Sufficiency* and challenging all within his hearing to read it. The spectators rising in clusters and stumbling toward the foyer, doubtless headed for the food stalls.

"Nature does not submit herself to Satan!" Montesquieu cried.

"The day is at hand when Occam's razor will cut the noose from the neck of every convicted witch!" Ben insisted.

"Mr. Hathorne, thou art no friend to justice!" Herbert Bledsoe declared.

Montesquieu projected a final sentence toward the antechamber—"Insult not the world with fables of wizardry!"—then returned to the defense table and explained to Jennet that any further unsolicited oratory would do their case more harm than good.

"You made a noble effort, Charles," she said.

"Against an ignoble judge," he muttered.

Adjusting his opulent wig, Hathorne gained his feet and lit his pipe. He puffed twice, stepped into the alcove behind the bench, and vanished through the door, a twist of smoke coiling behind him like a boar-pig's tail.

❦

THE GREAT WAITING stretched from ten o'clock till eleven, and then from eleven till noon, Montesquieu, Ben, and Jennet huddled together at the defense table like wayfarers gathered before a tavern hearth. Jennet's lawyer attempted to alleviate his anxiety by contriving chapter titles for his projected *magnum opus*, which he planned to call either *L'Essence du Gouvernement Civil* or *L'Esprit des Lois*. Ben passed the time by drafting potential headlines for the next morning's *Gazette*. Evidently his choices failed to please him, for he'd crossed them all out, including JUSTICE CRUSHED AT WEBSTER TRIAL and JUDGE HATHORNE'S SHAME and PILATE IN PENNSYLVANIA.

Jennet decided that she could best endure the immediate future by contemplating the ruins of her philosophic apparatus. Before the jury-box sat the Galilean ramp, now split down the middle. Nearby lay the lodestone, broken in two. Wrapped in shadows, the Newtonian prisms rested forlornly beneath the prosecution table; the little glass wedges seemed peculiarly alive—a species of marine creature, she imagined, spawned in a luminous sea but now tossed upon a nocturnal beach, where they lay suffocating for lack of light. Fissured but still whole, the sulphur-ball cast its shadow on the floor. The black oval evoked for Jennet one of Aunt Isobel's favorite stories from the history of natural philosophy.

"Some eighty generations ago the great Eratosthenes, director of the Library of Alexandria, joined two facts that had ne'er been yoked before. What were they, dear child?"

"At noon each year on June the twenty-first," Jennet told her tutor, "a stick set upright in the ground casts no shadow at Syene, whereas in Alexandria on the same date, at the same time, such a post throws a substantial shadow."

"Eratosthenes made an inference from this seeming impossibility . . ."

"He concluded that the Earth could not be flat. He decided 'twas in fact a sphere."

"And then?"

"And then he measured the length of Alexandria's noontime shadow. One of Euclid's finest theorems, the equality of alternate interior angles, told Eratosthenes that the distance from Alexandria to Syene must be seven-point-two degrees of the Earth's circumference: the fiftieth part of a circle. Because Eratosthenes knew that four hundred eighty miles lay betwixt Syene and Alexandria, the simplest arithmetic revealed that a bird encircling our planet would make a trip of some twenty-four thousand miles."

"Darling Jenny, you have learned your lesson well!"

Shortly after striking one o'clock, the tower bell tolled again—seven times. Judge Hathorne reassumed the bench. Foreman Hocking led his fellow landholders to the jury-box. The spectators pushed and shoved their way back into the courtroom, packing it from wall to wall.

"Oyez! Oyez!" the bailiff cried, bringing his pike against the floor with the pounding regularity of a Newcomen steam pump.

A hush settled over the hall.

"Mr. Hocking, hath the jury reached a verdict?"

"Aye, Excellency."

"How goes't with the defendant? Be she guilty or nay?"

Jennet recalled Aunt Isobel's old *experimentum magnus*, the teacher and her pupils searching for microscopic diabolism in the tissues of supposed familiars. To minimize its suffering, Isobel had ordered each animal strangled prior to dissection. But in a witch-court no such compassion obtained. Mr. Hocking slid—"By way of preventing further *maleficia*"—his knife into Jennet's side—"such as were visited upon Abigail Stearne"—firmed his grip on the shaft—"we are decided that the defendant"—and twisted the blade—"is guilty"—ninety degrees.

A strange wind blew through the courtroom, a howling amalgam of outrage and incredulity, and now the separate *No*'s burst forth, a "No!" from Ben, a "No!" from Montesquieu, a "No!" from Mr. Scull, a "No!" from Mr. Bledsoe, a "No!" from John Tux. A score of Manayunk spectators likewise expressed their dismay, unleashing sounds such as Jennet had not heard since the whooping tawnies had descended on Haverhill.

The marshals hauled her quivering body before the bench. She struggled to stand up straight, commanding each relevant part of herself to make a proper contribution to the effort, neck and shoulders, spine and hips, knees and ankles, and by the time Hathorne spoke again she had achieved a dignified posture.

"Prisoner at the bar, have you anything to say ere sentence is passed?" the bailiff asked.

"May God strike down the Witchcraft Act of James the First," she cried, "and all its abominable brethren!"

"Let the record show that in her final statement the prisoner added sedition to her list of offenses," Hathorne said. He paused briefly whilst the bailiff outfitted him with the black silk cap. "Rebecca Webster, the jury hath found that you did sign a pact with the Devil, a crime for which no punishment may be considered too severe. Come Wednesday morning a company of His Majesty's soldiers will bear you to Walnut Street Prison, where at the noon hour you will be brought into public view, stood upon the horse-cart, and hanged by your neck until you are dead."

"*Eppur si muove,*" she said.

"What?"

"Still, it moves."

The judge glowered and took up his mallet one last time. "The Court of Oyer and Terminer is hereby dissolved."

The

Twelfth

❧❧❧❧❧❧❧❧❧❧❧

*In Which Truth Acquires
the Clothes of Science,
Justice Assumes the Shape of Lightning,
and the Narrator
Finally Runs Short of Words*

❧

A s she lay atop her pallet, inhaling the stench of the straw and
shivering whilst the dungeon's chill invaded her flesh, it came to
Jennet that above all else she wanted to see the stars once more.
She'd been without them for two months, her trial having occurred entirely by day and her incarceration beneath Manayunk Gaol-House being
in essence an entombment. A glimpse of Orion would satisfy her, or Cassiopeia, Lyra, Gemini—or even a bright planet: scintillating Venus, crimson Mars, banded Jupiter, locked in their Keplerian ellipses.

It had not been Herbert Bledsoe's idea to make her final three days on
Earth a Draconian ordeal of cold, hunger, encumbrance, and solitude. He
had enjoyed no choice in the matter—or so he claimed. Shortly after the
jury delivered its verdict, Governor Gordon had informed Mr. Bledsoe
that any coddling of the Satanist would probably cost him his appointment. Thus it was that the magistrate appropriated Jennet's feather
mattress along with her woolen blanket. He removed her writing-desk,
impounded her books, reduced her suppers to stale bread and gray beer,
and forced her once again to wear the burlap smock. To Jennet each such
privation seemed as harsh as the sting of a scourge, but one cruelty in
particular she found intolerable: Bledsoe's decision to allow her just one
visitor per day, one hour per visit.

On Sunday afternoon she expended her allotted interval with
Montesquieu. Standing outside her cell, the mournful aristocrat

❧❧❧❧❧❧❧❧❧

leaned against the dormant brazier and poured out his heart whilst her fellow prisoners pretended not to eavesdrop. He pledged that upon his return to La Brède he would commend her treatise to every Continental court and legislature, so profound was his respect for her, so deep his adoration.

"*Vraiment*, Madame Crompton, the British Conjuring Statute has found a new adversary," Montesquieu said, "a weasel-faced male satirist this time rather than a beautiful female *philosophe*, but a person no less dedicated to the fight."

For all the Baron's passion, his oath sounded hollow to her, artificial as Hezekiah Creech's jaw. She hoped that her analogous promise of forty-two years earlier had not chimed so untruly in Aunt Isobel's ear.

"*The Sufficiency of the World* will outlive you," he continued. "It will outlive us all. Your masterwork is destined to join Dante and Chrétien amongst the world's imperishable things."

"If only my soul could make the selfsame boast," she said.

He ran a gloved finger along the brazier's clay chimney. "Do you not believe in the promise of eternal bliss?"

"I would not wager Pascal's last thruppence on that possibility, and neither—let us speak candidly, Charles—and neither would you. Like Shakespeare, we hold death an undiscovered country, if 'tis even a country at all."

It occurred to her that she'd managed to invent a novel sort of martyrdom. Jesus Christ, St. Stephen, Giordano Bruno, and Jeanne d'Arc had all sacrificed themselves because in their various white-hot opinions the world was *not* sufficient. By Christ's calculation, the given required a supplementary phenomenon called the Kingdom. For Stephen, it needed an organized Christian Church. For Giordano, the world must have endless mystic duplicates of itself. For Jeanne d'Arc, the world became complete only upon intersecting the plane of Heaven, the better to bring the voices of departed saints within earshot. But until the Passion of Rebecca Webster, no one had ever martyred herself to the idea that God had gotten it right the first time. Until the Webster hanging, nobody had used her own execution to argue against populating the universe with angels and spirits and other immaterial entities, so miraculous was the accessible, so wondrous the mundane.

"How I wish you could behold the commotion outside the gaol-house," Montesquieu said. "All sixteen prosecution witnesses are collected on the lawn, screaming for vengeance against Rebecca Webster as an opium-eater might cry for his next phial."

"Why would I want to see such a spectacle?" she asked.

"Because your sympathizers are gathered on those same grounds, and their number is twice as great, their voices thrice as loud. Believe me, Madame, when the executioner shows himself on the scaffold this week, the hisses and howls will deafen him."

"And will your own hisses and howls be amongst 'em?"

He bobbed his head, saying, "Forty pounds sterling has persuaded the captain of the *Fleur de Lys* to keep his ship in port another week."

"Then I shall ask a boon of thee. In my life I've witnessed two public executions. My aunt died screaming at the stake. Giles Corey kept crying, 'More weight!' I do not fear the undiscovered country, but I dread the painful portal by which I shall enter it. When the noose closes round my neck, you and Ben must come forward and ally yourselves with universal gravitation, pulling me earthward that my end might come more quickly."

"*Mon Dieu!* I cannot imagine committing such violence against you."

"You must."

"*Ce n'est point possible.*"

"Prithee, Charles. Tell me you'll do't."

The dungeon reverberated with Matthew Knox's boots clomping down the spiral staircase.

"Monsieur," the turnkey said, "I fear your hour hath elapsed."

Montesquieu abandoned the brazier and, reaching through the bars, squeezed Jennet's hands betwixt his own. "I promise to intervene as you desire. But know this. Should the rope break, I shall forthwith carry you to safety."

"Spoken like a true cavalier!" Mrs. Sharkey called from her cell.

"Baron, thou hast the soul of a knight!" Mr. Turpin shouted.

"Give no thought to heroism, Charles," Jennet said, "for't can only end in a storm of musket-balls."

"Monsieur," said Mr. Knox again.

"*Au revoir*, my brilliant advocate," Jennet said.

"*Au revoir*, my mad and glorious friend," Montesquieu said.

He turned his back and, one measured step at a time, mounted the stairs, wheezing and moaning as would an accused wizard chafing against the mask-o'-truth.

Jennet's hour with Ben occurred on Monday morning. He arrived bearing sorrowful but entirely expected news. The previous afternoon Major Patrick Gordon had summoned him to his office in Broad Street and explained that his administration was obligated to reject *The Pennsylvania Gazette*'s latest attempt to influence Rebecca Webster's fate—a formal petition, signed by over two hundred citizens of the colony, requesting that she be pardoned.

"He said to me, 'Mr. Franklin, you must realize that His Majesty's statutes apply as forcefully in the Provinces as in Piccadilly.' "

"How are we to explain such callousness from a man whose star your journal did so much to brighten?" Jennet asked.

"I cannot prove my suspicion," Ben said, "but I believe your brother hath fallen upon a means of blackmailing Mr. Gordon. And hence we are forced to pursue some other path to your reprieve."

"There is no other path."

"Then we shall hack one out."

"Do not entertain false optimism, dear Ben."

"Do not embrace specious despair, sweet Jenny."

They passed the remainder of the visit discussing their son, until at last they reached a wrenching decision: there must be no final reunion betwixt Jennet and William. Seeing his mother in a dungeon cell, shackled like a West African slave, jaw scarred, scalp shorn, whilst outside the gaol-house a mob of her supposed victims wailed for her blood, William would immediately understand that she was destined for the gallows, and this knowledge might plunge him into an incurable melancholy.

"Tell him I died of a prison-fever," she instructed Ben. " 'Tis a plausible narrative, with naught of the shame attaches to having a witch for a mother."

"Splendid idea!" Mr. Turpin shouted.

"Let the boy remember ye as ye were!" Mrs. Sharkey called.

Punctual as always, Mr. Knox came tromping down the staircase.

Ben seized a bar in each hand, as if making ready to bow the iron and pull Jennet through the gap. "Brave lady, I fear I'm about to lose my wits."

"You foresaw this disaster," she said. "You would be within your rights to look me in the eye and say, 'If only you had listened to me . . .' "

"I would ne'er be so ungracious."

She continued briefly on the subject of Ben's prescience, then bound him to the same pledge she'd extracted from Montesquieu. The moment the horse-cart pulled away, leaving her to dangle, he must come forward and lovingly abet the breaking of her neck.

"My arms and legs shall honor your wish," he said, "though my mind and heart will fight 'em every inch of the way."

The turnkey cleared his throat conspicuously. "Mr. Franklin."

Ben climbed the stairs backward, that his gaze and Jennet's might stay fused as long as possible.

On Tuesday afternoon Barnaby Cavendish descended into the depths of Manayunk Gaol-House. He arrived bearing his latest acquisition, preserved in an alchemist's flask, which he set on the floor outside her cell.

"The Globe-Boy of Baltimore," he explained.

"No other epithet would do," Jennet said, for the fœtus was marked with lines suggesting meridians and blotches resembling continents.

"A rumor hath reached me from German-Town. It tells of a stillborn babe with a brow so ridged as to resemble a crown of thorns. On the morrow I shall acquire this wondrous Christ-Child, and when I combine him with my Baltimore Globe-Boy, then add the two freaks who survived the shipwreck, I'll have the matrix of the Jennet Stearne Crompton Museum of Wondrous Prodigies."

"I am flattered by your choice of name—but now let me ask of you another beneficence." She gestured toward the thing in the jar. "I would have the loan of yon Globe-Boy, for I believe he will succor me in the hours ahead."

"The sufficiency of the world?"

"Indeed."

"I shall instruct him to watch o'er thee most tenderly."

For the balance of his visit Barnaby told tiresome and protracted tales drawn from the nonexistent archives of the Jennet Crompton Prodigy Museum. She didn't mind. Only by playing the rôle of carnival charlatan might her friend manage to endure this final reunion without dissolving into a blubbering puddle of woe. He related how the Lyme Bay Fish-Boy had once foiled an assassination plot against the Spanish king, how the Bicephalic Girl had become trapped in an endless disagreement with herself concerning the Eucharist miracle (Papist transubstantiation versus Protestant consubstantiation), and how the Baltimore Globe-Boy had recently rolled all the way to Florida and there discovered the Fountain of Youth. No sooner had Barnaby finished recounting the contrarian ministry of the German-Town Christ-Child than Mr. Knox began his descent.

"I'm told the babe's palms have tiny holes at their centers," Barnaby said. His face was so time-ravaged that the tears reached his jaw only after trickling through a labyrinth of wrinkles, grooves, and wens. "Being a doubting Thomas, however, I'd have to see the marks myself ere I called 'em crucifixion wounds."

After Barnaby was gone, she sprawled on the cold stone floor and stared at the Globe-Boy. Catching the feeble torchlight, the fœtus's lidless green eyes glinted like sunstruck emeralds. The stain below his left shoulder distinctly resembled Great Britain: each nation was there, even little Ireland, circumscribed by seas of skin.

"All flowings and fallings, all flappings and snappings, all swingings and springings, all splittings and flittings . . ."

Her chains scraped against the bars of her cell as she extended her hand, caressed the frigid glass, and prayed to the bottled monster that she might again behold the stars.

❦❦

THROUGHOUT THE DEMONOLOGISTS' homeward voyage on the *Ignis Fatuus*, the Son of Man and the Father of Lies battled one another, each seeking to determine the future of American witchfinding. The fact of Christly intervention became apparent to Dunstan when, shortly after the sloop dropped anchor off Manhattan-Isle, Abby removed her dress and permitted him for the first time to cast an eye on those places—left breast, right side—where Jennet's demons had inserted the dagger. The lesions were completely healed. It was as if they'd never existed.

"Praise God, I see no sign of the bodkin," he said, pulling off his day-shirt.

"Our Savior's lips have kissed my wounds away," Abby said.

He removed his breeches. " 'Tis a miracle, plain and true! Now let me put my own lips to those very spots, that my passion might complete thy cure."

But Lucifer, too, had reserved a berth on the *Ignis Fatuus*. As the sloop blew across Long-Island Sound, a raging fever took hold of Mr. Parris, causing him to convulse as violently as any were-wolf or epileptic. For thirty-five terrible hours he thrashed about in his bunk—hemorrhaging from his mouth and nose, spitting up bile, screaming like a victim of the Spanish boot—until at last he lay quiet in his niece's arms.

Within minutes of the minister's death, Captain Morley came to Abby and Dunstan, all grief-struck as if he too were kin to the deceased. After bemoaning the loss of "a tireless and brilliant general in the war against demonic insurgence," the captain regained his stalwart self and addressed a practical matter. Mr. Parris's remains, he explained, might harbor the seeds of a contagion, and prudence demanded that they cast them over the side.

The burial ceremony occurred at noon, the entire ship's company standing silently on deck whilst Dunstan read from the Book of Ezekiel.

Balanced on the larboard rail, the corpse lay inside a canvas sack weighted with a length of anchor chain. " 'And when I looked, behold, a hand was sent unto me, and, lo, a roll of a book was therein,' " Dunstan recited. " 'And he spread it before me, and it was written within and without: and there was written therein lamentations, and mourning, and woe.' "

" 'Lamentations, and mourning, and woe,' " Abby echoed.

"Oh, Goodwife Stearne, my heart goes out to thee." Captain Morley tipped the sack toward the waves until it slid free of the rail. The bagged corpse, spiraling, drilled through the surface of the sea and vanished.

"He was ne'er a particularly loving uncle," Abby said, "but as a witchfinder he'll prove difficult of replacement."

"May God rest his soul," Dunstan said.

"Ere I became a woman," she noted, " 'twas his wont to beat me nightly with a willow wand."

The *Ignis Fatuus* put to port the following morning. Although Dunstan had vaguely hoped that a welcoming committee organized by the Calvinist clergy might greet them, no one amongst the scurrying multitudes on Clark's Wharf took much notice of the cleansers as they disembarked. Perhaps the news of their victory had not yet reached Boston—perhaps the *Bible Commonwealth* reporters were still in Philadelphia, their quills poised to set down the visual, auditory, and olfactory particulars of Rebecca Webster's gallows dance.

Eager to collect their two hundred pounds, and more eager still to tell their sponsor of the jurymen's verdict, Dunstan and Abby proceeded directly to the Governor's mansion in Treamount Street. Splendidly attired in a red silk waistcoat and feathered turban, a manumitted Negro named Simeon ushered them past the snootish Mr. Peach and into Mr. Belcher's august presence.

" 'Tis my sorrowful duty to report that yesterday the eldest amongst us, the Reverend Samuel Parris, died of a fever," Dunstan said, addressing the Governor with a deferential bow. "Our bereavement is somewhat compensated, however"—he lifted his head and offered Belcher a sizable smile—"by the felicitous outcome of the Philadelphia trial. To wit, Excellency, Rebecca Webster meets the hangman two days hence."

"Prithee, accept my sympathy on the death of your fellow pricker," Belcher said, clucking his tongue. "Concerning Mrs. Webster's imminent execution, 'tis not exactly news round here, as this office subscribes to six different provincial journals."

Dunstan strained to purge his voice of pride. "Ah, but didst know the jury deliberated a mere three hours?"

"I did," Belcher said with an inamicable snort.

The Governor's manner perplexed Dunstan. Surely the salvation of the Parliamentary Witchcraft Act, once a matter of imperial concern to Belcher, merited a greater show of enthusiasm. "In my letter to the Privy Council," Dunstan said, "I shall fully credit you with the deft maneuvers by which John Hathorne replaced Malcolm Cresswell as chief jurist."

"Your scheme was a masterstroke, my Lord Governor," Abby added. "Hathorne displayed even more theological acuity in Philadelphia than at Salem forty years ago."

From the tea-chest beside his desk Belcher retrieved a half-dozen issues of *The Pennsylvania Gazette*. "Both *The New-England Courant* and *The Bible Commonwealth* reported on the case, but 'twas Mr. Franklin's pithy periodical supplied the fullest account. For all I hold it a seditious paper, methinks there be wisdom in these essays by Ebenezer Trenchard." He tapped the topmost issue with his index finger. HATHORNE COERCES GUILTY VERDICT FROM JURY, ran the headline. "Mr. Stearne, I am sorely vexed. Why did you neglect to tell me that the Baron de Montesquieu, not to mention Mrs. Webster herself, would make such puissant points against the demon hypothesis?"

"There be no more truth in Trenchard's narratives than in sailors' tales of selkies and sea serpents," Dunstan said.

"If milk will curdle in consequence of animalcules," Belcher said, "and geese go mad from ergot, 'twould seem the world hath need of neither demons nor demonologists."

"Every word Mr. Franklin prints is a falsehood," Dunstan said.

Propping his elbows on the desk, Belcher made a steeple of his fingers and leaned toward Abby. "According to Mr. Trenchard, you pretended Mrs. Webster unleashed a band of wicked spirits against you."

"That were no pretending, my Lord," she said. "Her goblins drove a dagger into my side."

Belcher set his palm atop a ragged stack of papers. "Yesterday I received a petition from our House of Representatives. They, too, admire the Trenchard letters, and so they ask that for the nonce I restrict your Commission's activities—"

"Restrict 'em?" Abby said.

"Restrict 'em, aye, until such time as His Majesty's advisers have sorted through the arguments advanced in Mrs. Webster's favor."

Dunstan stared out the mullioned windows. Sheets of rain descended on Boston, thick as the smoke from John Hathorne's pipe, heavy as the fumes of burning Haverhill. "I did not realize our Governor was so beholding to his legislature."

"Every so often I must lend an ear to the rabble," Belcher said. "It makes me appear fair-minded."

"I beg your pardon, Excellency," Abby said, "but the Massachusetts House enjoys no power o'er the Purification Commission, and neither— forgive my bluntness—and neither do you."

"Wrong, Madam, wrong—for your charter hath no validity without it displays the signature of the man who occupies this mansion. B'm'faith, I cannot recall setting my name to any such paper."

"You did sign it, sir, three days after you took office." Opening his valise, Dunstan withdrew the Commission's charter from its customary place betwixt Question Five and Question Six of the *Malleus*. He passed the paper to Belcher. "See how your name adorns the bottom, plain as a button."

The Governor grunted, grinned obliquely, and proceeded to perform an action so audacious that in Dunstan's view it would have shamed even the Baron de Montesquieu. Removing a scissors from his desk drawer, Belcher blithely punctured the charter and clipped out a rectangular fragment bearing his signature. The snippet drifted free of the blades and, as the Witchfinder-Royal gasped and shuddered, glided to the floor like an errant autumn leaf.

"Examine your charter more closely, and you'll see it wants for ratification," Belcher said. He smoothed the gelded document across his desk, and for an instant Dunstan imagined he intended further mutilation—but instead the Governor folded the paper in half, securing it beneath his ink pot. "You may now follow Simeon back to the antechamber, where Mr. Peach will present you with your two hundred pounds. As for your charter, I stand prepared to sign it once I hear that the Privy Council hath found no merit in Mrs. Webster's case. But until I take up my quill for such purpose, you must not imagine that you enjoy the slightest authority to hunt so-called witches in this province."

Dunstan said, "Had you seen Abby vomit forth those iron nails, you would not be thwarting us so."

"Trenchard insists 'twas legerdemain made the nails appear," the Governor said. "He compares the event to the trickery of Pharaoh's court magicians."

"They were Christ's own nails flew from my mouth," Abby said.

"Demon-carried through time and distance, all the way to Philadelphia," Dunstan added.

"Demon-carried?" the Governor said.

"Aye," Dunstan said.

"Through time and distance?"

"Indeed."

"Spend your two hundred pounds wisely, Mr. Stearne, for many a year will pass ere I suffer you or any other witch-pricking mountebank to draw a single shilling from the Royal Purse."

※

THEY TOOK A ROOM at the Red Parrot in Hannover Street, a wretched establishment presided over by a bovine woman who, upon learning that her customers were Rebecca Webster's prosecutors, treated them with a deplorable surliness. They rose the next morning at eight o'clock, discovering to their dismay that the rain had not slackened, then broke their fast with eggs and salted veal in the tavern-room. All during the meal Abby ministered to Dunstan's melancholy, reminding him of the difficulties his father had faced during the dark days following the

Salem hunt, when Sir William Phipps had presumptuously reprieved nearly fifty convicted Satanists.

"The Province's original Witchfinder-Royal did not allow Phipps's defection to discourage him," she said, "and I know you will endure Belcher's treachery with equal fortitude."

"Thy faith is most gratifying," he said, heaving a sigh.

At two o'clock they boarded a day-coach heading west, sharing the compartment with a wig-maker off to visit his sister in Natick and a tallow-chandler seeking to borrow money from his uncle in Marlborough. The rain continued to fall, drumming on the windows with a monotonous cadence that set their fellow passengers to dozing.

"Our next course of action is clear," Abby whispered in Dunstan's ear.

"How so?"

"Let us grant the nefarious Governor Belcher six weeks in which to collect and ponder the Privy Council's findings," she said. "If he ratifies our charter, we shall bless him and return to our trade. But if he withholds his signature, we must betimes cry him out."

A vile discomfort spread through Dunstan, as if in digesting the morning's meat his stomach was now encountering a poisonous green morsel. "Cry him out? Dost mean . . . for sorcery?"

"Aye."

"I'Christ, 'tis the boldest proposition I've yet heard from your lips," he said, pressing a hand to his belly. "Can you truly believe Belcher practices the dark arts?"

"He reeks of Perdition."

"But the man's a governor."

"And Lucifer's a prince. I was ne'er a person to be dazzled by rank."

The rain went soft in Needham, turned to a swirling mist in Natick, and vanished completely by the time they reached the Merry Alewife in Framingham. As dusk descended, leaching the world of its nuances and hues, they collected their valises and headed south down Badger Road, moving into the teeth of a frigid wind.

Dunstan had imagined that their crossing of Waushakum Pond might be impeded by ice floes, but so far the freezing air had wrought upon the water only a delicate crystalline crust. They removed the pine-bough cloak from their dinghy and dragged the craft into the shallows. After retrieving his fishing-pole from the stern, he upended a flat rock and took hold of the large gluey slug beneath. They clambered aboard. Whilst Abby worked the oars, Dunstan impaled the slug and tossed the hook into the pond. The iron easily pricked the ice, bearing the slug netherward. As the last light faded, a solitary star blazed white in a lapis sky, but he took no pleasure in the vista. He was cold, and weary, and worst of all nauseated, as if a regiment of Van Leeuwenhoek's wrigglers were mustering in his stomach.

By the time Abby had rowed them to shore, he'd hauled their supper from the pond's murky bottom, a corpulent catfish with long elegant whiskers. Docking, they disembarked and followed the dirt path toward the house, Dunstan holding the fish suspended before him so that it oscillated on its line like a Satanist dangling from a swimming-rope.

Two ragged pieces of paper lay nailed to the front door. The top fragment read, HEREIN DWELLETH THE MURTHERERS OF BLAMELESS SALVAGES. On the lower scrap was scrawled a familiar Gospel verse. O GENERATION OF VIPERS, HOW CAN YE, BEING EVIL, SPEAK GOOD THINGS?

"Mayhap we could be doing a better job of explaining ourselves to our neighbors," he said.

" 'A prophet is not without honor,' " Abby recited, " 'save in his own country.' "

The demonologists passed the next hour in silence, stumbling about the house like exhausted beasts of burden whilst they lit the candles, ignited the lanthorns, swept the floor, aired out the bed-chamber, and set a fire in the hearth. Presently Dunstan's thoughts turned to preparing the cat-fish. He searched through the utensil box and, finding no knife of suitable sharpness, opened his wife's valise and retrieved her dagger.

"I mourn him, I truly do," Abby said as she greased the great iron skillet. "I did not love my uncle, but I mourn him."

Dunstan winced. How might he speak to her of his apprehension? What words would make sense? After testing a dozen preambles in his mind and judging none adequate to the task, he finally blurted out his succinct but anguished opinion. "Goodwife Stearne, methinks you bring too much ardor to your designs against Mr. Belcher."

"You perplex me."

"You name Belcher a wizard, and yet we've not submitted him to a single proof." He laid the drowned fish on the dining table, brought a lanthorn close, and made ready to remove its head.

"Lucifer hath beguiled the Governor," she said. " 'Tis as blatant as blood on snow."

He set the tip of her dagger an inch behind the fish's unblinking eye, then pushed. The blade failed to pierce the scales but instead retreated into the shaft. "We've neither swum him, nor pricked him, nor—i'Christ, Abby, your bodkin doth break!" He lifted the dagger free of the fish. The blade shot forward. What sorcery was this? Again he pressed the knife-point against the scales, and again the blade retreated, leaping outward when he jerked it away. "There be some imp within!"

"Can it be you've ne'er held a pricker's bodkin before?" Abby said.

"Pricker's bodkin?"

"To secure the blade, you need but throw the lever in the shaft."

"Pricker's bodkin?!" His heart crashed against his ribs like a pent and raging beast. Lurching toward Abby, he held the dagger before her gaze. "Speak truthfully. Is this sham blade the same as pierced you Friday?"

" 'Twas clever of you to wheedle Hathorne to our side"—she lifted the skillet to her breast as a Christian knight might raise his shield against a Turk—"and no less clever of me to seal our victory with my gift for legerdemain."

"Legerdemain? So Trenchard spoke the truth? Legerdemain? Is this why your flesh bears no wound?"

" 'Tis time you cleaned our fish."

"Raven feathers, our Savior's nails—illusions all?"

"When you married Abigail Williams, you espoused a most artful cleanser."

"My sister goes to the gallows in consequence of *tricks?*"

"Nay, Goodman Stearne, she goes in consequence of signing Satan's ledger. Now let us curtail this dreary discussion of bodkins and prepare our supper."

It seemed that all his earthly possessions had surrendered their solidity. The hearthstones, door hinges, windowpanes, wall-planks, floorboards, roof-beams—these things were fluid now, molten, pouring into one another like metals roiling in a crucible. When he attempted to speak, he could find no words save the pronouncements of St. John Chrysostom, most renowned of the Desert Fathers and prime amongst the objects of his own father's secret admiration for the Roman Church.

" 'What else is woman but a foe to friendship, an inescapable punishment, a desirable calamity, a domestic danger, a delectable detriment, painted in fair colors?' "

"Husband, thou art exceeding spleenful tonight."

The manner of her departure, he decided, must be biblical yet abrupt, dramatic yet merciful. With an anguished howl he tore the skillet from her grip and, raising its iron mass high, smote her on the brow. Samson battering the Philistines. Jael spiking down Sisera's head. Her skull broke open like an egg, and she fell insensible to the floor.

" 'No wickedness approaches the wickedness of a woman'!" he cried, quoting the Book of Ecclesiasticus. " 'Sin began with a woman, and thanks to her we all must die'!"

Later, after he'd set down the skillet and prayed for her soul and mopped up the matter of her intellect, he took the Commission's tool-kit in hand and walked through the damp woods until he reached the dock. Crickets and cicadas sang all about him. The pond soughed against the shore. Opening the calfskin satchel, he retrieved the short pricking needle and hurled it toward the dark pond. Next he rid himself of the long needle, next the magnification lens. He tied the mask-o'-truth to the shaving razor and threw them both into the water.

As the night thickened there descended upon the former witchfinder a tranquility such as he normally experienced only when drawing landscapes or reading Scripture. Each second followed upon the next like the divine and perfect strokes of an angel's wing. He wished that he might just then take hold of Heaven's pendulum and bring it to a halt, stopping time forever, locking the moment in place, no incipient sunrise or insistent noon or ineluctable dusk.

What was a deposed cleanser to do with his life? How could he best put his wisdom to use? Who might his next sponsor be?

Slowly a strategy congealed in Dunstan's brain. On the morrow he would slip into the forest, deeper, ever deeper, beyond Framingham, beyond all the English settlements, and from that day forward he would live as had Chrysostom and the other Desert Fathers, sustaining himself on fried locusts and raw honey.

All five implements remained submerged—testament to their holiness, proof of their kinship with martyrs' bones and saints' fingers.

Dunstan of the wilderness. But that would not be the end of him, for on certain rare occasions he would quit the forest and appear before his fellow Calvinists, heralding the Great Antisatan, Suedomsa—Asmodeus inverted—the angel whose shoes he was unworthy to loosen and whose hem he was unfit to kiss: Suedomsa, supreme pricker, divine cleanser, descending upon Massachusetts Bay in a chariot of fire and driving Lucifer from the New World forever.

He reached into the tool-kit one last time, drew out the Paracelsus trident, and flung it into the night. The device followed a lovely flowing arc, a curve more perfect than any a geometer might inscribe, and as it reached its apex the moonlight glinted off the tines, so that the trident became a skyborne lanthorn, a celestial beacon, an Oriental comet, pointing the way toward Bethlehem.

ON WEDNESDAY AT SIX O'CLOCK, as two raw-faced, ill-scrubbed lobsterbacks brought her out of the dungeon and into the dawn, Jennet saw that the Baltimore Globe-Boy had received her petition favorably. She would not die ere seeing a stellar object. Directly ahead lay the morning star, Venus, coruscating above Martsolf's Mill. Though her flesh was numb with dread, her mind now embarked on speculation. Had the Prime Mover brought forth living forms on Venus? What manner of creatures were the Venusians? Did they suppose that demons made their world go round?

Crimson coats muted by scrims of fog, a full company of soldiers encircled the tumbrel, each man keeping an uneasy watch on the two factions in the prison-yard. She recognized the commanding officer, the same gaunt and ashen Captain Wilcox who'd led the attack on the West-Indies pirates. The crowd had apparently changed its disposition since Montesquieu's report, for whilst her admirers indeed outnumbered the sixteen prosecution witnesses by a factor of two, the latter group was much the noisier. On seeing their nemesis, Jennet's putative victims showered her with imprecations and rotten vegetables. Michael Bailey, the harness-maker who blamed her for his wife's ague, hurled a turnip. The root's decayed matter spattered against her forehead. Daniel Morris, the glassblower who imagined she'd bewitched his bottles, attacked her with a squash. The sloshy spheroid struck her shoulder and disintegrated. From Wilbur Bennet, the dairyman who believed she'd soured his milk, came a cabbage, its putridity exploding across her chest.

A solitary horse, gray and stippled as the moon, stood ready to bear Jennet to the gallows. Hunched in the driver's box, Matthew Knox offered her a flaccid smile. As the rising sun glinted amongst the trees, washing Venus from the sky and igniting the dew on the lilac bushes, Herbert Bledsoe stepped from his office. He grasped her chain, guided Jennet into the tumbrel, and seated her directly behind Mr. Knox. After easing himself onto the opposite bench, he applied his handkerchief to her brow and cheeks, wiping away the vegetable residue. From his coat he procured a glittering object that at first she thought a pocket-watch.

"Every drop's for you." Mr. Bledsoe passed her the small copper flask. "Brandy nauseates me."

"Merci." Accepting the flask, she made a mental effort to forgive the young magistrate his part in making her last days of imprisonment so gratuitously miserable, but her labors came to naught—under present circumstances, evidently, such magnanimity was beyond her. *"Merci beaucoup, Monsieur Bledsoe."*

She pulled out the stopper, tossed back her shaven head, and pressed the flask to her lips. Her wrist-shackle clanked against the copper. The fiery stream trickled down her gullet and spread across her stomach. In a matter of seconds the brandy entered her brain, but instead of producing the desired insensibility it merely made the people swirling around her seem as swollen and grotesque as anything Barnaby Cavendish had ever put in a jar.

Captain Wilcox shouted incoherently, and the Redcoats fell in on both sides of the tumbrel, twenty men per file. The drummer pulled two mahogany sticks from his belt, set them against the sheepskin head, and rattled out three tight rolls followed by two single beats. He repeated the cadence. A second shout from Wilcox, and the soldiers began to march, even as the horse, feeling the bite of Knox's whip, released a tremulous whinny and started off toward Walnut Street Prison.

Whilst the prosecution witnesses rushed to the head of the parade, Jennet's admirers clustered around the tumbrel, their ranks as ragged as the Redcoat formation was orderly. She gulped down a second dose of brandy, then a third. Her brain seemed to rotate on its axis. To spare herself the noose, she realized, she would gladly burn all existing copies of *The Sufficiency of the World*—burn them then and there, burn them into oblivion, burn them as resolutely as John Flamsteed had immolated his pathetic *Historia Cœlestis Britannica*.

The procession advanced down Ridge Road. An expansive farm rolled by, its hills a-swarm with bulbous and oblivious sheep. Apple trees raised skeletal branches toward a sky the gray of the Globe-Boy's pickled flesh.

After perhaps a half-hour the tumbrel reached the edge of Manayunk and drew within view of the Wissahickon Creek Bridge, a graceful arc of sandstone. Reaching into her smock, shuddering as the wrist-shackle touched her breast, she retrieved the wooden tiger. She passed the carving to Mr. Bledsoe and secured his promise to return it to her son on the morrow, whereupon a wholly unexpected event occurred.

With the suddenness of a thunderclap the woods flanking Ridge Road erupted with a noise she'd not heard since the burning of Haverhill: Nimacook battle cries—if not Nimacook, then some equally contentious tribe. Scores of Indians plummeted from the trees and landed on the backs of the Redcoats, two braves for each soldier, dragging them down with the predictably lopsided success of wolves falling on lambs.

The drum cadence stopped. Knox halted his team. Bledsoe yelped in fear. Jennet steeled herself and drained the brandy, soon finding within the depths of her bewilderment a lucid thought: a quick death at the hands of a tawnie was far preferable to a slow strangulation on the gallows.

In the mêlée now unfolding, the Indians did not scruple to press their advantage. The instant Captain Wilcox freed his sword from its scabbard, his collateral savages knocked him senseless with their tomahawks. Every time a soldier attempted to fire his musket, his appended Indians thwarted him by wrapping thongs around his wrists and ankles. Soon the entire Redcoat company lay rolling about on the ground, trussed and disarmed, so that a wayfarer coming upon the scene might have surmised that a committee of witchfinders was about to swim forty accused Satanists *en masse*.

A second commotion drew Jennet's attention to the Wissahickon Creek Bridge, where the Rebecca Webster faction and the *maleficium* sufferers were assaulting each other with improvised armaments—rocks and clods, sticks and fists, feet and teeth. The impetus clearly lay with her apostles, and ere long the prosecution witnesses retreated bleeding and moaning into the forest.

She surveyed the victorious Indians. There was something most peculiar about them. With their silly feather head-dresses and ridiculous war-paint, they would have looked more at home in the King's Theatre than here in a Pennsylvania woodland.

A barrel-chested savage clambered into the tumbrel and offered Bledsoe an amicable nod. "Prithee, hand over your prisoner to my stalwart Junto clan," the Indian said, repositioning his cockeyed feathers, "that we might bear her to a less hostile clime."

"Mr. Franklin?" the astonished magistrate groaned. " 'Tis really you?"

"My name's Chief Ephemeron," Ben said.

"Dearest Ben," Jennet gasped.

"Chief Ephemeron," he corrected her.

Bledsoe pulled an iron key from his coat and, sliding the blade into the lock above her left wrist, popped open the shackle as efficiently as a serving-wench turning the tap on a keg, then with equal dexterity un-cuffed her right wrist. The bracelets thudded against the tumbrel floor, quite the most agreeable sound she'd heard since William first took suck at her breast.

Now Nicholas Scull, the youngblood through whose initiatives the citizens of Manayunk had been moved to demand Mrs. Webster's arrest, appeared from out of nowhere, sporting an Indian disguise only slightly less outlandish than Ben's. He scrambled into the driver's box and snatched the reins from Knox. Addressing the turnkey in a morbidly jocular tone, Scull informed him that if he wished to avoid "the piquant unpleasantry of a scalping" he must forthwith surrender his seat. With the frightened agility of an adulterer responding to the cuckold's unexpected return, Knox leapt from the tumbrel and sprinted north along Ridge Road.

As far as Jennet could tell, the sham Indians' raised tomahawks and flashing knives were keeping the Redcoats in check, and it gradually came to her that she probably wasn't going to Walnut Street Prison this morning, or the next morning, or any morning in the immediate future. Dame Fortune and the Junto had plucked her from the gallows.

"Mrs. Crompton, I wish thee Godspeed." Bledsoe placed the wooden tiger in her palm, then jumped to the ground and rushed to join Knox.

Scull urged the speckled horse forward. The wagon rattled across the bridge and continued down Ridge Road, Jennet's partisans all the while celebrating her deliverance by applauding like satisfied playgoers and crowing like ecstatic roosters.

"Oh, Ben," she said, "I've ne'er seen such a marvelous display of derring-do—but I cannot imagine the next step in this audacious caper."

"You will be spirited to safety," he responded.

"Over two hundred miles as the crow flies, three hundred as the carriage rolls, till you reach the Hoosic River," Scull elaborated.

"To wit, you are escaping to the bosom of your Kokokehom kin," Ben said. " 'Tis high time you fulfilled your *pittuckish*."

At the Hunting-Park Road intersection, Scull set the horse on a northeast path, in eternal divergence from Walnut Street Prison with its expectant crowd of public-execution enthusiasts.

"Three hundred miles," Jennet sighed. "You may call it an escape, but it sounds more like an exile."

Ben scratched both cheeks simultaneously, his war-paint having evidently begun to itch. "As a woman convicted of witchery and suspected of sedition, you shan't this day elude the noose without antagonizing many an agent of the Crown, from Governor Gordon taking bribes in Locust Street to the Lord Chancellor shooting quail in Marylebone Park."

"To put it crudely," Scull added, "instead of a rope around your neck, you will soon acquire a price upon your head."

"Believe us, darling Jenny, the Nimacook village is your one true haven," Ben said.

"Your reasoning's persuasive, but you must suffer little William to come with me," she said.

"I think not," Ben said, "for such a gambit would surely place him in deadly peril."

Betimes the tumbrel reached the Henry Road intersection, where the Baron de Montesquieu's coach loomed out of the morning mist, the driver's box occupied by another Junto youngblood, the brawny Philip Synge, dressed in tawnie trappings. The Baron's team of matched black geldings anxiously stomped the ground, tossing their heads, steam gushing from their nostrils. As Scull pulled back on the reins, halting the tumbrel, Montesquieu and his footman stepped out of the coach. Jennet half expected to see them disguised as Indians, but instead they wore their usual powdered perukes, silk waistcoats, and perfumed neckcloths.

"*Madame Crompton, vous êtes sauvée!*" an exultant Montesquieu cried.

At Ben's urging, Jennet vaulted free of the tumbrel, regaining her balance as a second coach came clattering out of the fog. Juxtaposed with Montesquieu's lordly equipage, this newly arrived conveyance was a shabby affair, lamps broken, curtains torn, paint as mottled as the Turtle of Tewkesbury's skin, and yet it seemed roadworthy enough, pulled by as sturdy a team as Jennet had ever beheld. Commanding the horses was

Montesquieu's customary driver, the phlegmatic Herr Strossen, and no sooner had he decelerated the coach than the passenger door flew open to reveal the first real Indian of the day, John Tux, who promptly hopped to the ground.

Now Ben abandoned the tumbrel. "Herr Strossen hath agreed to transport you and Mr. Tux safely to the Hoosic," he explained to Jennet, "a task for which he will receive two hundred guineas plus this venerable coach, both incentives supplied by *Monsieur le Baron.*"

With a snap of his whip, Nicholas Scull got the tumbrel moving again. He continued down Hunting-Park Road, vanishing anon into the spectral embrace of the fog.

"We shall travel the entire western shore of the Delaware," John Tux said, "and thence to New York, and finally to Massachusetts—a five-day journey by my calculation." He pointed to his bulging purse. "Thanks to your French patron, we are supplied with funds sufficient to sleep in whatever inns suit our fancy, trade up our horses should an injury befall them, and seal the lips of any magistrate who looks upon our party askance."

Jennet approached the Baron and kissed his brow. "*Mon cher Charles,* 'twould appear I am profusely in your debt."

"I merely financed this madness," Montesquieu said. "The scheme itself was entirely of Mr. Franklin's design."

John Tux extended his fluttering hand and gestured toward the open compartment. "The faster we leave Philadelphia, Waequashim, the greater our chances of seeing the morrow's sun come up."

" 'Twill not be long ere the Redcoats break their bonds and come charging onto the scene," Ben added urgently. "I shall give you till the count of five."

"How can we know the Kokokehom will take me back?" Jennet asked John Tux. "My long-ago departure was accomplished most discourteously."

"One!" Ben cried.

"They will take you back," said John Tux with prodigal confidence. "The rules of *pittuckish* require it."

"You must tell William his mother will always love him," Jennet instructed Ben.

"Two!" he barked. "You have my word," he added.

"*Mon ami grand*," she moaned, throwing her arms around the Baron.

"*Hélas*, we've no time for farewells, Madame," Montesquieu said.

"Three!"

She turned and hugged the love of her life. "My bonny Ben."

"Four!" he shouted. "My dearest Jenny," he gasped. "Five!"

Uncoiling her arms from Ben's heroic rotundity, she allowed John Tux to hoist her into the decrepit coach. As the Indian climbed up beside her, the Baron's footman slammed the door, Herr Strossen cracked his whip, and the wheeled monstrosity lurched onto Henry Road and headed north. Leaning out the window, Jennet stole a final glance at Ben standing firmly beside the Baron's equipage, enshrouded by the dust of her departure. His absurd feather head-dress was all askew, its cockeyed angle evoking Newton's periwig or perhaps a drunken earl's peruke.

Her sweetest swain. Her bonny Ben. One day that remarkable young
man would be known throughout the Colonies, for surely
fame must touch a person so skilled at scheming
and adept at deception, even though he
made a thoroughly
preposterous

❧

Indian
disguises were by
far the most common subterfuges
employed by dissident American patriots during
the Colonial era. The stratagem through which Ben rescued
Jennet foreshadowed the several pseudo-Mohawk and faux-
Algonquin raids that occurred as the winds of insurrection blew from
Boston down to Charleston. As far as I can determine, the Colonists'
goal was not to implicate any actual Indians but rather to lend a general
mood of chaos and indeterminacy to the struggle against British rule.

A typical such action was the *Gaspée* affair. In 1772, while chasing a smugglers' ship, this British customs schooner ran aground at Namquit Point near Providence. At nightfall a wealthy Rhode Island merchant named John Brown led eight boatloads of patriots dressed as Indians out to the *Gaspée*. They shot the captain, routed the crew, and burned the vessel. The official inquiry failed to identify a single perpetrator.

Then, of course, there was the legendary Boston Tea Party, sparked by the Royal Governor's refusal to let the *Dartmouth* and her two sister ships leave for England with their unwanted tea until the Colonists paid a duty on the entire cargo. On the evening of December 16, 1773, several dozen "Mohawk braves" rowed out to the vessels, ripped the lids off 342 crates filled with the vexatious leaves, and dumped the containers into the bay. "Many Persons wish that as many dead Carcasses were floating in the Harbor," John Adams wrote at the time, "as there are Chests of Tea."

As we all know, Jennet was right about Ben. He did become famous, not only in America but throughout Europe, largely in consequence of his 1751 treatise, *Experiments and Observations on Electricity Made at Philadelphia in America,* and its two sequels. (Among their many insights, Franklin's electricity papers clarified that lightning bolts do not descend from the sky like hailstones—even Jennet, as we have seen, labored under that common misconception—for these flashes manifest a reciprocal discharge between cloud and ground.) Now, I can't really blame my father for treating Franklin so cavalierly during the four hours they spent together in 1725. How was Newton to know that this cheeky kid from Philadelphia, who seemed almost as unbalanced as his demented half-sister, would amount to anything? How could he guess that, by the turn of the century, scientists would be routinely referring to Franklin as "the Newton of electricity"?

Naturally I'm more interested in Ben's genius for experiment than his talent for expedience, but let me here acknowledge the man's political gifts. A loyal British subject at heart, he was truly aggrieved to see the Empire sundered, but when the time came to consecrate the American Declaration of Independence, he signed it with the same species of aplomb Jonathan Belcher had displayed invalidating Dunstan's witchfinding charter. "We must all hang together," Ben said, taking pen in hand, "or assuredly we shall all hang separately."

Whenever I ponder his many diplomatic achievements, I am especially moved by Ben's success in convincing the French government to supply the American patriots with firearms, foodstuffs, ships, troops, officers, and, above all, money. Consider his inauspicious circumstances. He lands in Auray on December 3, 1776, proceeds to Paris, and meets secretly with the French Foreign Minister, the Comte de Vergennes, three days after Christmas. Our hero is seventy, exhausted, and still mourning his Deborah, now three years dead. He has come to Paris as the envoy of a dubious rabble in rebellion against a legitimate European king, and somehow he must persuade an absolute Catholic monarch, Louis XVI, to aid the very sort of Protestant insurgents who for a century and a half have been his country's worst enemies in the New World. It's like inviting Francis of Assisi to go duck hunting. And yet, through a combination of wit, charm, and bald propagandizing, not to mention his *je ne sais quoi* with the ladies (who wield considerable influence in French government circles at this time), Ben brings it off. In February of 1778 a treaty is signed at Versailles, and soon afterward millions of *livres* are flowing into the Yankee treasury. I would not claim that Ben won America's war of independence with that treaty—he certainly didn't win it apart from George Washington's military prowess, Thaddeus Kosciuszko's knowledge of fortifications, and Baron von Steuben's ability to mold brigades from bumpkins—but I cannot imagine the Colonists' victory without the Franco-American alliance.

Yesterday my own war of independence, my lifelong struggle to rid myself of the *Malleus Maleficarum*, likewise received a boost from Benjamin Franklin. Throughout the long and bloody Battle of Fortieth Street, the pendulum of victory swung to and fro. The first engagement found my booklice outflanking and subsequently decimating the *Malleus*'s silverfish, but then his Cambodian wasps strafed my termites, sending them into retreat. When my Indonesian moths retaliated by firebombing the *Malleus*'s bookworms, his remaining silverfish grew so enraged that they massacred my pulp-chiggers. But then, suddenly, like Blücher at Waterloo, *Poor Richard's Almanack* swooped onto the scene leading a corps of Madagascar papyrus beetles, and the tide turned in my favor. Once I'd hurled those five thousand carapaced berserkers into the fray, the *Malleus's* doom was sealed.

My arthropod mercenaries were quick to claim their prize. Shortly after two o'clock they departed a field strewn with legs, wings, antennae, and proboscises, subsequently crossing the East River in a coal barge, hitching a ride to Mineola in a garbage truck, and marching into the Dover Publications warehouse. At 4:30 P.M. the rationalist bacchanal began. With the same caliber of zeal the Colonial dissidents brought to the Boston Tea Party, the insects descended buzzing and singing upon the nearest carton of Witch Hammers, chewed off the lid, and sunk their mandibles into the epistemic obscenities.

Only after my soldiers were well into the second carton did I perceive, and immediately repent, my error. My God, I thought—my God, I've become that vilest of creatures, a biblioclast. I am no better than those misguided Greeks who consigned the works of Protagoras to the flames; no better than Diocletian building a pyre from any and all volumes pertaining to Jesus Christ; no better than the Emperor Shih Huang-ti ordering the destruction of every book published before his ascension (so that human history would appear to begin with his reign); no better, even, than Joseph Goebbels supervising the incineration of more than twenty thousand volumes—Freud, Steinbeck, Zola, Hemingway, Einstein, Proust, Wells, Mann, London, and Brecht among them—in the streets of Berlin on May 10, 1933.

"Cease!" I told my insect hosts. "Cease and desist!"

But, alas, I no longer controlled the bibliophages. Instead of heeding me they continued feasting, and by dawn Dover's entire *Malleus* inventory lay in their digestive systems, the air filling with the sound of burping pulp-chiggers and cooing booklice. And so I must beg your sympathy, gentle reader. Now that I've regained my senses, I see that the best counter to a malicious idea is a *bon mot*,

not a bonfire; I see that the correct reply to a corrupt text is a true
one, not a termite corps; I see that the proper way to defeat the
agents of darkness is not to burn down their houses
but to rip away their shutters,
open their doors,
and let in
the

❀❀

Sunlight
dancing on the
mist above Cutshausha Falls,
fashioning a rainbow even as it corroborated
refraction's eternal laws. Snowflakes sifting down from
the winter sky, each crystalline wheel a marvel of Euclidian precision.
Rivulets rushing along the thicketed slopes, eager to feed the swollen
river in accordance with ancient hydraulic principles. *Nux*, yes, no question: here on the shores of the Hoosic, here amongst its beasts and fish
and fowl, the sufficiency hypothesis obtained in full.

An ample valley, a robust forest, a place in which Jennet had found—
not happiness exactly, not bliss, nor even satisfaction: the word, she decided, was *tranquility*. For the first time since receiving her commission
from Aunt Isobel, she enjoyed an inner equipoise, her soul's pendulum
describing an arc neither too long nor too short. Her body grew firm and
muscular. Her barren scalp, so brutally shaved by Abraham Pollock's sisters, again yielded its shock of hair, the auburn now inlaid with silver.
Her curiosity became keener than ever, eventually finding a worthy object
in the countless species of spider thriving near the Indian village. Why
didn't these daughters of Arachne get tangled in their own threads? Were
they Platonists at heart, spinning their webs in reference to an unseen
ideal? Was a spider's bite always a calamity, or might the poison be a secret medicine? The Kokokehom had noted her obsession. Waequashim
Ashaunteaug-Squaw, they called her. Waequashim the Spider-Woman.

Owing largely to John Tux's correspondence with his sagamore
mother, Quannamoo, an exchange in which he'd cast Jennet as the

heroic enemy of the Indian-killing witchfinders, her return to the clan had occasioned much festivity. Shortly after Herr Strossen's coach had clattered into the village, Quannamoo arranged a welcoming ceremony, a *wopwawnonckquat.* In form the custom was rather like running the gauntlet, though in spirit it was the opposite: instead of assailing the initiate with whips and cudgels, the assembled Nimacooks honored her with praise and caresses. As Jennet moved down the line, familiar faces appeared before her, each a bloated, shrunken, or otherwise unfaithful reflection of the memory she'd been carrying in her head. Thus did she experience a grand reunion with Hassane, no longer a rascally young medicine-woman but a middle-aged *taupowau,* well on the way to cronehood. Likewise waiting to greet her was Kapaog, the brave she'd suckled as a babe following his mother's death from the flogging sickness, his frame now towering over six feet, his legs as strong as saplings, his broad hands holding a bead necklace: a gift, he explained, offered in gratitude for her milk. But the acme of the *wopwawnonckquat* was the moment in which Pussough, her Lynx Man, stepped forward and, cupping his hands beneath her jaw, tilted back her head until their eyes met.

"*Askuttaaquompsin?*" he asked.

"*Asnpaumpmauntam,*" she replied. Yes, I am well.

From the pocket of his deerskin coat Pussough withdrew the largest raven feather Jennet had ever seen, larger even than the specimens Abigail had disgorged during the trial, a quill that, crisply trimmed and dipped in venom, would have been worthy to record her most wicked thoughts and scandalous fancies.

"I found it in the wayside cavern to which we guided you after the Haverhill raid," he explained.

"A strange place for a bird to shed its plumage," she said.

He slid the feather along her scalp, lodging it in the thickest of her nascent locks. "Mayhap it comes from the very raven who blessed us with the first maize seed."

"Then I shall wear this token with great respect, and never let it far from my sight."

After the *wopwawnonckquat* celebrants had dispersed, Jennet's Nima-

cook mother-in-law appeared, the ancient Magunga, now dry and shriv-
eled as a corn husk, bearing the news Jennet most dreaded to hear. The
rumors were true. Okommaka had been sorely wounded whilst leading
a foolhardy raid on the English settlement at Springfield. Taking Jennet's hand, Magunga guided her toward the plaza, where two more Nimacooks joined their company, nimble young braves whom Magunga
introduced as her grandsons, Wompissacuk and Chogan. The solemn
procession continued to the village's largest wigwam, its walkway planted
with trilliums—his favorite flower, Jennet remembered.

"*Pausawut kitonckquewa,*" Magunga said, pausing at the threshold. He
cannot last long.

"One bullet he carries in his side," Wompissacuk elaborated, "another in his chest."

"At first the fight went our way," Chogan added, "but then a company
of lobsterbacks arrived."

Jennet stooped before the doorway and stepped forward, abandoning
the blazing sunlight for the gloomy wigwam. It was a fœtid place, foul
and swampy as Aunt Isobel's anatomization theatre at the height of the
experimentum magnus. Speckled with sweat and taut with pain, her *wasick*
lay on a sleeping mat, eyes closed, mouth gaping, his quavering flesh
swathed in a woolen blanket. A woman of middle years crouched beside
him, the lissome mother of his strapping sons, soaking a wad of sphagnum in an earthenware bowl filled with water.

Okommaka's two wives exchanged hasty glances. "I am glad of your
arrival," Maansu told Jennet. "He speaks of you often."

As the squaw rubbed the dripping moss across Okommaka's brow,
Jennet dropped to her knees and took his fevered hand in hers. His eyes
flickered open. He smiled.

"*Waewowesheckmishquashim?*"

"Aye, my husband, 'tis your wayward Waequashim, home at last."

"I am sensible of the destiny that took you from us." A sudden spasm
rippled through his frame. He clenched his teeth and groaned. "Your
noble war on the witchfinders."

"Methinks we are not the luckiest of persons, you and I," Jennet said.

"The bold Okommaka lost his battle with the Redcoats, and the be-nighted Waequashim failed to defeat the demonologists."

"But we fought well, did we not?"

"Aye, husband. We fought well."

"Then perhaps we are not so unlucky."

She bent toward him and kissed his lips. "Do you think of her?"

"*Nux.* Yes. Almost every day."

"I would fain visit the mound beside the Shawsheen," she said, "but I fear there would be naught left of 't."

Once again Maansu saturated the sphagnum. She caressed her husband's face with the cool spongy mass.

"Has the night come?" Okommaka asked.

"Not yet," Maansu said.

"Ere the moon rises," he said, "I shall fly to the mountain of Kautan-touwit, who will then bear my soul to Keesuckquand. And after I am gone a month, dearest wives, you must look to the sun, and you will see Pash-pishia and her father, sitting by the council fire."

Okommaka did not die that night. Instead he lingered for three more days, succumbing to the bullets on a drear and drizzly afternoon, Thurs-day by the English calendar. At first Jennet felt nothing at all, and then she felt entirely too much, a knife in her heart, a nail in her gut. It was only through the greatest effort that she succeeded in applying a mask of soot to her face, paddling a canoe across the Hoosic, and joining the cir-cle of mourners.

From noon until dusk the grieving Indians sat around the grave, and for even the most stoic warrior there was no shame in letting his tears fall like rain. When at last the weeping was accomplished, Hassane came for-ward and erected the soul-chimney, the *cowwenock-wunnauchicomock*, atop the mound. Carefully she canted it to the southwest, so that Okom-maka's spirit might more easily find its way to Kautantouwit's abode.

At that precise moment Jennet's prime impulse was to march up to the soul-chimney and kick it to pieces. She wanted to grind the foolish thing into the dirt. She desired nothing more than to subtract it from the world.

But the Hammer of Witchfinders did not destroy the soul-chimney that day, nor would she destroy it the following day: Okommaka's *cowwenock-wunnauchicomock* was evermore safe from her philosophy. Instead she went down to the river and climbed back into the canoe, and as she guided the vessel toward the far shore an alarming thought entered her already troubled brain. When summer came she would occasionally lift her eyes to the blue and cloudless Hoosic Valley sky, fixing on the sun's corona. And one fine day—despite everything, despite sufficiency, despite the burning of Isobel Mowbray and the trial of Rebecca Webster—one day she would see them both, Okommaka and Pashpishia, laughing together and warming themselves by the council fire. The idea flooded Jennet with a deep distress, deeper even than her grief. It brought a chill to her blood and a hoarfrost to her veins, and she began to paddle furiously, as if in flight from the Dark One.

❦

OKOMMAKA'S REMAINS WERE NOT A WEEK in the ground when Wompissacuk and Chogan embarked upon a scheme by which they hoped to ameliorate their grief whilst simultaneously bestowing a boon on Waequashim. Their intention was to build her a private wigwam, siting it in the enormous oak tree that flourished on the lee shore of the Hoosic. Completed in the space of a month, the dwelling proved a veritable mansion, a splendid assemblage of birch bark and cedar planks, subdivided into four discrete rooms, rather like the Market Street garret in which Jennet had first frolicked with Ben. The northwest chamber she devoted to dining, whilst the adjacent area became home to her spider experiments and rock specimens. In the southeast sanctum she erected her sleeping platform, an amenity that she oft-times shared with the passionate Pussough. Most sacred of all was the remaining space, the one in which she gathered and read and lovingly stroked her books.

The source of this literary abundance was Ben. Every spring and again in the fall John Tux would employ Herr Strossen to bear him to the Hoosic, the young Nimacook having decided that he owed his mother such constancy, and he always hauled along a gift-crate from the ambitious editor of *The Pennsylvania Gazette*. By the end of her third year in exile, Jennet had accumulated a substantive library. Her trove included an especially nourishing shelf of Shakespeare, a credible collection of Milton, and a half-dozen quartos from Alexander Pope. "All are but parts of one stupendous whole, whose body Nature is, and God the soul"—a reasonable enough sentiment, though she preferred Rica's evocation of Spinoza in Chapter Twenty-nine of *Lettres Persanes:* "If triangles had a god, it would have three sides."

Beyond its bibliographic treasures, each Franklin crate included a hodgepodge of clothing, tools, and news-clippings. In the accompanying letter Ben would offer amusing accounts of William's adventures, and he also narrated his own accomplishments—his election as Grand Master of the Masons, his establishment of a public subscription-library in Philadelphia, his inauguration of America's first German-language newspaper, his definitive demonstration, via kite and collection jar, that lightning-bolts and Von Guericke sparks were in essence identical—but he always began by reporting on the aftermath of the Webster trial, which had evidently wrought a greater measure of justice upon the Earth than Jennet would have dared imagine. "As you can see by the enclos'd Clipping from *The New-England Courant*," he wrote in the spring of 1733, "Governor Belcher hath depriv'd the Purification Commission of its Charter, quite clearly in Consequence of your Testimony." Six months later: "According to this Day's Issue of *The Bible Commonwealth*, quote, 'His Majesty's American Witchfinders have temporarily ceas'd their Activities, mayhap pursuant to Governor Belcher's ill-conceived Injunction, more probably that they might mourn the Passing of their guiding Light, the Reverend Samuel Parris.'" The spring of 1734 brought the most heartening news of all: "I scour the Pages of every Colonial Journal to reach the Printing-House," Ben wrote, "and I find no Evidence that your Brother and his Wife are abroad in the Land. Is it too much to hope we have seen the Last of them?"

Not every message from Ben was cause for celebration. Scarcely a month went by in which Governor Gordon neglected to declare that he still regarded Rebecca Webster as a convicted Satanist and a fugitive from justice. A bounty of fifty pounds sterling lay upon her head, and Gordon fully intended to prosecute her the instant she was brought before him. Another unhappy dispatch detailed the attack of pleurisy, attended by a suppurating lung, that Ben had suffered in the summer of 1735. Still another sad bulletin disclosed the demise of *Das Philadelphische Zeitung*. But the most terrible letter from Pennsylvania concerned Deborah and Ben's first-born son, Francis Folger Franklin, dead of the small-pox at age four. "Shortly after we interr'd that good and loving Boy in the Yard of Christ Church," Ben wrote, "I was mov'd to reverse a long-standing Prejudice of mine, and in consequence our William is now inoculat'd against this Pestilence."

When not contemplating the mysteries of arachnid architecture, Jennet pursued a construction project of her own, an enclosed veranda extending along one side of her tree-hut. She took a particular pride in the window curtain, which she'd made by attaching colorful pebbles and shiny snail-shells to three-foot lengths of twine. It was shortly after she'd hung the last curtain-strand, on a congenial August afternoon, that a loud greeting came wafting through her oak. "Hallo, Jennet Stearne!" John Tux? No, this was a different sort of voice, less musical, more hearty. "Hallo, dearest friend!" Nor could her visitor be Pussough, whose tongue boasted a distinctly Nimacook cadence. This man sounded entirely English.

"Hallo!" she called back.

"Is it true a brilliant philosopher dwells up there, and will this same sage entertain a wayfarer from Pennsylvania? For he brings most glorious news!"

"Oh, my bonny Ben!" she cried, unfurling her rope ladder.

Five minutes later they stood together on her veranda, locked in a protracted embrace, at the end of which she stood back, pressed Ben's hand betwixt her palms, and offered her condolences on the death of little Francis.

"This life oft-times seems to me a squall of scalding tears," he said, "and they ne'er burn deeper than when a parent must bury his own child."

"I know too well the despond of which you speak," she said.

He brushed his fingers along the curtain, wringing a soft carillon from the pebbles and shells. "Let us think on happier matters, dearest. I cannot say what miseries the morrow may bring you, but *today*, J. S. Crompton—*today* every rose in Christendom blooms in your honor, every lark warbles your praises, and Dr. Halley's comet dances to an air called 'The Song of Jennet.' " Dipping into his waistcoat he withdrew a news-clipping. "Behold an article from *The London Journal* of this past July the first concerning a parliamentary act to be henceforth known as the Witchcraft Statute of George the Second."

Jennet snatched away the clipping. She rushed past the introductory paragraphs, lingered briefly on a sentence identifying the new law's initiator as an alderman named Heathcote, then plunged into the heart of the matter.

I. Be it enact'd by the King's most excellent Majesty, by and with the Advice and Consent of the Lords spiritual and temporal, and Commons, in this present Parliament assembl'd, that the Statute made in the first Year of the Reign of King James I, entitl'd "An Act against Conjuration, Witchcraft, and Dealing with Evil and Wicked Spirits," shall, from the 24th day of June next, be repeal'd and utterly void and of non effect.

II. And be it further enact'd that from and after the said 24th of June, the Act pass'd by the Parliament of Scotland in the ninth Year of Queen Mary entitl'd "Anentis Witchcraft," shall be and is thereby repeal'd.

III. And be it further enact'd, that from and after the said 24th of June, no Prosecution, Suit, or Proceeding shall be commenc'd or carried on against any Person or Persons for Witchcraft, Sorcery, Enchantment, or Conjuration, in any Court whatsoever in Great Britain.

" 'Repealed and utterly void and of non effect,' " she said, voice trembling. " 'Repealed and utterly void . . .' " Her tears hit the clipping with soft silent collisions. "Oh, Ben, you must promise me these words come not from the pen of Ebenezer Trenchard, for I could ne'er abide such a hoax."

"Even Ben Franklin places certain matters beyond jocularity. Read on, Jenny. The best is still to come."

She dropped her gaze to the final paragraph, scanning it through the watery veil.

In voting to overturn the Conjuring Statute of King James I, some several Parliamentarians allud'd to a Treatise with which we Journal *Editors were heretofore unfamiliar, Mr. J. S. Crompton's* The Sufficiency of the World. *In the Words of William, Duke of Newcastle, "This noble Tome offers a Rationale, rooted in the most rigorous Newtonian Experimentalism, whereby ev'ry thoughtful Christian might see how the supposd'd Crime of Witchcraft is an Impossible Thing."*

"My book's been read by Newcastle himself!" she cried.

Now Ben was weeping too. " 'Some several parliamentarians,' it says. *'Some several.'* " He patted his eyes with a corner of his handkerchief, then passed the cloth to her. "And now I must tell you of yet another blessing. Right before John Tux and I departed for the Hoosic, Governor Gordon made public his intention to lift the bounty and pardon you in full. To wit, my dearest love, you are a free woman, heir to the same rights enjoyed by all British subjects this side of the Atlantic Ocean. Shall I save you a place in Herr Strossen's coach?"

"On first principles, the answer requires no thought." She twisted the handkerchief into a taut cord of silk. "And yet there be riches on these shores."

As if cued by Jennet's remark, a red-tailed hawk took flight from a nearby chestnut tree, gliding past the veranda in a majestic parabola.

"The grandest telescope in America hath lately come into my possession," Ben said.

"I have my lofty house and my humble library. My industrious spiders and my beauteous rocks. I have my tranquility." She returned the handkerchief to Ben. " 'Repealed and utterly void and of non effect.' Did a Lutheran hymn e'er boast a more beautiful refrain?"

"Certainly not," he said.

"Did Shakespeare e'er write a better line?"

"Not more than once or twice in his whole life."

"Bear me to Philadelphia, bonny Ben, that I might peruse the *Codex Naturæ*, study the Galilean satellites through your new telescope, and watch our son grow to manhood!"

❦

FORESEEABLE AS THE PHASES of the moon, predictable as the pull of charged sulphur on chaff, Pussough's reaction to the news of her imminent departure involved no surprises, few nuances, and much lamentation. He moaned and keened and stamped his moccasined feet. He declared that he wanted to die. They spent the night together, alternately quarreling and swiving, and by morning her Lynx Man had found within himself a proper measure of gallantry. Of *course* she must return to Mr. Penn's province. No question. *D'accord.* Her child needed her, and moreover she was a philosopher at heart, far less Waequashim of the Kokokehom than J. S. Crompton of the *argumentum grande.* She belonged in Philadelphia.

And so it was that Rebecca Webster, née Jennet Stearne, ended her exile, allowing Herr Strossen to bear her and Ben back to the Colonial capital.

It was not long after their arrival that a typically Franklinesque obsession took hold of Ben. He wanted the reading public of America and Europe to know that the author of *The Sufficiency of the World* was in fact Rebecca Webster, vindicated witch, who was in turn Jennet Stearne, natural philosopher, a revelation he imagined making in either *The Pennsylvania Gazette* or his newest publishing venture, *Poor Richard's Almanack.* Once Mrs. Webster's true identity was known, he argued, Jennet might earn a handsome income touring the great cities of Europe, lecturing on how she'd brought the English Parliament to its senses.

But Jennet had no interest in eminence. She wanted only to pursue a modest philosophic life, designing and executing experiments spun from her intuition that magnetism and electricity, like lightning-bolts and Von Guericke sparks, shared a common heritage. Though it was not at first obvious how she might support herself during these investigations, she eventually solved the problem by selling the Chestnut Street townhouse to a Dutch shipbuilder named, strangely enough, Van Leeuwenhoek, a distant relation to the father of microscopy.

A succession of brief visits to Ben's Market Street residence convinced her that her son's real family consisted of his distractible but doting father and his dull but affectionate stepmother. If she wanted to serve William's happiness most fully, she would play a rôle analogous to that which Aunt Isobel had assumed in her own upbringing. She would become the child's secondary nurturer, his deputy mother, introducing him to Newton's optics and Virgil's epic, to Shakespeare's lovers and the Nimacooks' lore, to the glories of geometry and the satisfactions of swimming—but, alas, she would not be the one to dry his tears, wipe his nose, prepare his supper, bandage his abrasions, tuck in his bed-clothes, or comfort him when phantoms troubled his sleep.

Ignoring the counsel of Ben, Barnaby, John Tux, Nicholas Scull, and everyone else she knew in Philadelphia, she seized the opportunity to purchase, for a fraction of its worth, the Sumac Lane farm, a property that, owing to its reputation as the home of a convicted sorceress, had found no tenants since her flight to the Hoosic Valley. Her friends all agreed that the Witchcraft Statute of George II, with its unequivocal rejection of the demon hypothesis, had implicitly turned the Manayunk villagers into objects of ridicule, which meant they were certain to variously shun and harass the woman who'd brought this humiliation upon their heads. And yet something like the opposite occurred. Not long after her return to the farm a delegation of her neighbors, some twenty in all, gathered outside her door bearing home-brewed ales and piquant apple pies. This committee of the contrite owed its formation to Bethany Fallon, the goose girl who'd once fed contaminated rye seeds to her flock, though now she was Mrs. Markley, a brewer's wife with a brewer's child in her belly.

"We have sinned against thee, Mrs. Webster," she said, stepping onto Jennet's stoop. "We wronged thee no less than Judas wronged our Savior."

"My trial brought to light a wicked judge and three corrupt prickers, but I see no such malefactors here," Jennet said.

"We always remove the black bodies from our seeds ere we feed 'em to our geese," Mrs. Markley said, "and so far our flock's been free o' the ergot."

Next to speak was Mr. Plum, the flax-planter who'd told the Court how a lightning-bolt had burned his crop. "Now that Parliament hath endorsed Mr. Crompton's opinions," he told Jennet, "I am pleased to call electricity and Heaven's fire the selfsame substance."

"Sir, you must ne'er accept a scientific principle simply because it boasts the weight of authority," Jennet said. "Accept it rather because it enjoys the blessing of evidence."

The blessing of evidence. As her neighbors drifted away, the euphonic phrase lingered in her brain, mocking her aspirations. The blessing of evidence was exactly what her magneto-electric hypothesis could not claim. It was just that, a mere hypothesis, trapped in the foggy valley of conjecture, miles below the towering crag of fact.

Throughout the spring of 1738, whenever a thunder-gust seemed about to break over Manayunk, she would assemble and launch a silk kite surmounted by an upright wire. The fly-line terminated in a lean-to sheltering a collection jar in which stood an iron horseshoe, the surrounding area ringed by twenty hobnails laid flat on the grass. To guide the wire directly into the clouds, she always detached the kite from the mooring post and steered it by hand, but only after putting on boots outfitted with paraffin soles and equipping the fly-line with a water-repellent leather bridle.

By the summer solstice she'd seen a dozen storms rip apart as many silk handkerchiefs, and still not a single lightning-bolt had found its way to the collection jar. But then, one turbulent evening in July, she managed to pilot a kite directly into a burst of Heaven's fire. As the collateral sparks contacted the wire, electrified the wet twine, and entered the jar, the hobnails stirred and shivered—but they did not leap toward the encased horseshoe. Did the hobnails' agitation trace to a brief moment of magnetism, she wondered, or had they moved simply in consequence of the celestial explosion itself?

She retrieved the horseshoe and passed it over the hobnails. No movement. Not the slightest quaver. The shoe was evidently inert. Ah, but did this mean that her magneto-electric hypothesis was wrong, or merely that the collection jar had not stayed charged long enough to magnetize the iron? She couldn't decide.

The following Sunday, whilst Ben, Deborah, and William attended their dreary little Presbyterian church in Pine Street, and Jennet with equal devotion pruned her cherry tree, the vivid noon sun vanished abruptly behind a mantle of slate clouds. A thunder-gust was coming, she surmised—a new opportunity to imbue a horseshoe with the Gilbertian force.

Methodically she set the stage for the experiment, positioning the horseshoe inside the collection jar and encircling it with hobnails. This time she rested the jar on a slab of paraffin in hopes that the glass would thereby remain charged for a significant interval. She rushed into the house and laid out the necessary materials—handkerchief, cedar sticks, pointed wire, tail-cloth, skein of twine, leather bridle—on the parlor worktable. Within ten minutes she'd fashioned the wooden cross and affixed the wire. A thunderclap rolled across Manayunk, and then came another. She glanced through her front window. Myriad chestnut leaves vibrated on their twigs. The rosebush shivered as if experiencing dread. It was going to be a magnificent hunt.

As the thunder boomed a third time, her front door reverberated with a frenzied, desperate pounding. Her immediate thought was that, contrary to her wishes, Ben had revealed the Widow Webster's identity as J. S. Crompton, and now some local oddfellow wished to waste her time expounding upon the moon's inhabitants or presenting his disproof of uniform acceleration.

She abandoned the worktable and marched to the door, her humor worsening with each step. "Who goes there?" Silence. "Tell me your name!" More silence, then renewed pounding. "I receive no visitors today!"

"You will receive *me!*"

The door swung open, and a rangy man of some sixty years lurched through the jamb, clad in a shredded linen smock and, about his legs, pieces of blanket tied with thongs. He shoved past Jennet and scuttled into the parlor. It took her several seconds to recognize the intruder, so broken was his form and weathered his face. Bits of dead leaves and flecks of moss clung to his arms and shoulders. He'd lost a third of his weight, much of his color, and most of his teeth.

" 'Sheart," she muttered.

As if no longer yoked to one another, Dunstan's eyes flickered madly behind his brass-framed spectacles. "Hallo, Jennet Stearne."

"I am Rebecca Webster."

"Thou art Jennet Stearne, convicted witch, whom Providence saw fit to deliver from the gallows. As for your brother, he is now a voice crying in the wilderness, preparing the way for the divine cleanser Suedomsa." He darted to the couch and, doffing his torn felt hat, eased himself onto the bolster. Splotches of dirt covered his fire-scarred brow, making each wrinkle look like a wheel-rut. "When the messenger heard of your reprieve—he sees a newspaper but rarely—when he heard, he was glad in his heart. He started south betimes. That was . . . two months ago, three mayhap."

"If you aim to rekindle our affection for one another, you will not succeed." She sidled toward the worktable. "I'll show you no hospitality beyond a piece of cheese and a night's lodging in my barn."

" 'Leave there thy gift before the altar, and go thy way,' " he quoted. " 'First be reconciled with thy brother, and then come and offer thy gift.' "

"I am sensible of the sermon you evoke. 'Tis my recollection the Savior was reproaching those who spurn their siblings without cause. I have cause, Dunstan. I have cause."

"Suedomsa's messenger saw you draw down the lightning-fire. Why hobnails? The hobnails are perplexing." Reaching into the deerskin pouch on his belt, he filled his palm with bits of stale acorn-bread. He brought his hand to his open mouth as if concealing a yawn, then jammed the crumbs inside. "Explore your western woods—you'll find the messenger's hut, his cooking pots, the bones of twenty hares. So many bones in the world. Bones upon bones. Abby's bones still lie in Massachusetts."

"Abby's bones?"

"The messenger's wife. Abigail Stearne. Her bones."

"Were I a better Christian, this news would sadden me."

"Murdered."

She released an involuntary moan. "Murdered?" Swallowing hard, she smoothed out the green silk handkerchief, then laid it atop the cedar cross.

"Murdered, aye."

"As she nearly murdered me with her mendacity."

"Murdered by parties unknown." Dunstan devoured another handful of bread crumbs. He jerked up from the couch and limped to the work-table, casting the handkerchief aside as he might a filthy nose-rag. He seized the cedar cross, and, bringing it to his mouth, kissed the axis. "The messenger acknowledges but one authority in the matter of de-monology, and 'tis not the English Parliament. This day Suedomsa will either press the cup of martyrdom to his prophet's lips, or he will allow that cup to pass."

"To give the name of martyr to your hideous little life is to soil a noble word." She took the cross from him and, retrieving the handkerchief, tied each corner to a separate node.

Now the rain arrived, large steady droplets pelting the chestnut leaves and making them crackle like spitted meat on a slow fire. Dunstan rushed to the hearth and, for reasons not immediately apparent, re-moved the glass-chimneyed lamp from its peg. " 'Every valley shall be filled, and every mountain and hill brought low,' " he quoted, tearing the cork stopper from the fount. He lifted the lamp high, inverted it, and—

much to her astonishment—showered his head with the fuel, so that the glistery beads rolled down his cheeks like tears. Whale-oil fumes wafted through the parlor, raw and briny, layered like Barbados rum. "The messenger needs another draught."

"Dunstan, you mustn't do this."

"Another draught of chrism."

"I shan't permit it."

"Another draught."

A familiar voice broke upon the scene, rising unbidden through the strata of her brain. "Prithee, do as he commands," Isobel Mowbray said.

At first Jennet wondered if the voice might indeed be her aunt's, drifting in from some hinterland of Heaven, but she soon decided the specter enjoyed no reality beyond her skull. Marching into the kitchen, she resolved to revel in this felicitous ability to delude herself, and so she bid other ghosts join Isobel's.

"Bring him what he wants," Susan Diggens's shade commanded in tones evocative of rusty hinges.

"I shall," Jennet said, approaching the pantry.

"The man needs his chrism," said Bridget Bishop of Salem-Village.

"God forgive me," Jennet said.

"Baptize him with fire," Rebecca Nurse said.

Jennet took down the earthenware jug. "I did not imagine it would end this way."

"More oil," Giles Corey said.

"As you wish," she replied.

"Do it in remembrance of my father," said Veronica Junius, daughter of Johannes.

※

AN UNCERTAIN INTERVAL ELAPSED. Perhaps she lived amongst the *revenants* for a minute, perhaps a month—she couldn't say. She experienced a flying sensation, as if astride an enchantress's besom, and the next thing she knew she was back in her parlor, clutching the earthenware jug.

Dunstan still stood by the hearth.

"Whether a man be Papist or Protestant," she said, setting the jug before him, "self-slaughter's a sin."

He unstoppered the jug, flung the cork to the floor, and, like a priest of Apollo pouring a libation on an altar, drenched himself with the rendered blubber. " 'Thou anointest my head with oil.' " The dark flashing rivulets spilled down his arms and soaked his frock. " 'My cup runneth over.' " Stinking of whale juice, he returned to the worktable and attached the tail to the kite.

"If you mean to fly that thing, you must add the leather bridle and put on paraffin boots."

"When the messenger and his sister were but children, seven years old, eight years old, their father took 'em to a splendid fair in Ipswich." He tied the twine to the juncture of the sticks, then bore the kite into the anteroom. "A harlequin had come up from London, bringing with him a trained African baboon."

"I remember. You drew the ape's portrait."

"It danced for all the children. You laughed most joyously." He opened the door and stepped into the rain. "I'faith, Jenny, your brother loved you that day. He loved you more than love allows. He thanked the Almighty for giving him a sister."

She followed him across the lawn, the wind whipping her hair, the rain peppering her cheeks and brow, then rooted herself near the mooring post. He continued another twenty paces, stopping beside the lean-to. She shut her eyes and attempted to revive Aunt Isobel's voice, Susan Diggens's specter, all the desires of her mind. Apparently the urge to contact occult entities and do other witchy things lay deep within every person's soul—even those who knew such communion to be impossible.

She waited. No voices. No visions. Her brain had run through its catalogue of phantoms. She blinked, staring toward the lean-to, until at last a legible image emerged from the blur. Defying the elements, scorning the odds, Dunstan had gotten the kite aloft, his hands wrapped around the saturated fly-line. With icy determination he aimed the device at an immense storm cloud.

" 'And now also the ax is laid unto the root of the tree'!" quoth Dunstan as the kite dove into the nebulous black mass. " 'Every tree therefore which yieldeth not good fruit is hewn down and cast into the fire'!"

A blinding white bolt came forth, cleaving the innermost of Aristotle's crystalline spheres. Dunstan fell to his knees, fingers interlaced in prayer, the wet twine still locked betwixt his palms. A second bolt cracked the celestial dome. The great Aristotelian globe shattered. Contacting the pointed wire, the sparks jumped to the fly-line. All along the twine, the hempen filaments stood erect like the fur of an enraged cat.

Dunstan laughed. The sparks spilled into his praying hands. He simultaneously cried his Savior's name, released the kite, and burst into flames. The kite shot away like an arrow. Jennet moved to cover her eyes, but the tableau transfixed her. For a full twenty minutes she studied the oily, burning, screaming heap, the raindrops hissing as they met the fire, the fleshy embers orbiting the lean-to, until the last of the sodden ashes settled to earth, and she saw that all goblins were gone, all demons dead, all spirits fled, and there were no more witches in the world.

SHE SPENT THE NEXT DAY scrubbing the remaining corpuscles of Dunstan from her life. By tramping through her western woods, setting and resetting her course in an ever narrowing spiral, she eventually located his hut, a rude structure suggesting a wigwam assembled by the inmates of Bedlam. She smashed the thing to pieces with her hatchet, then appropriated her brother's cooking pot and gathered up his three-volume library—*La Démonomanie des Sorciers*, the *Malleus Maleficarum*, the Holy Bible.

That evening she dug an irregular and unsightly pit behind the barn. She hesitated to inter his Scripture, but everything else went into the hole, his charred pocket-watch, melted spectacles, carbonized bones, malignant books. She shoveled back the dirt. The situation seemed to demand a kind of inverse eulogy, and for a moment she considered reciting one of Barnaby's favorite imprecations (*May your sins consign you to a pit so deep 'tis yet your address after Hell's been sold to Rome*), but in the end she decided that a witchfinder was not worth even the breath required to curse him.

Three days later, as she meandered through her garden uprooting weeds and trimming vines, she was startled to observe a squat man in a grimy tan surtout making his way toward the farmhouse, a leather valise protruding from his spine like Robert Hooke's hump. She intercepted him at the midpoint of the flagstone path. Their transaction took but a minute. The mail-carrier strode away whistling, a half-crown gratuity in his pocket.

She scurried back into the house, shredded the envelope, and, scattering the bits of paper across the floor like a grass-maid seeding a park, unfolded the letter from Paris.

4 April 1738

Ma Chère Maman:

As you well know, my sweet pathetic Father view'd Postal Carriers as the most heroic of Persons, and so I shall honor his Memory by assuming my Words will reach you ere Autumn comes to Pennsylvania.

This Letter is occasion'd largely by my Acquaintance with a remarkable Englishman, Jonathan Belcher, former Royal Governor of Massachusetts Bay. Upon retiring from his administrative Post, Mr. Belcher spent several Years touring the European Capitals, and his Fondness for Tragedy and Comedy inevitably brought him to the Théâtre Français, where he oft-times observ'd my Portrayals of Corneille's Heroines and Molière's Ingénues. Shortly after seeing me in *Le Médicin Malgré Lui,* Mr. Belcher became the Patron of my Career, supplying me with such Funds as I required whilst awaiting a new Rôle. Lest your Imagination run to lascivious Fancies, let me assert that my Dealings with this Gentleman have been altogether free of improper Conduct. Our Connection is essentially in the Nature of a Friendship, Nothing more, though surely Nothing less.

'Twas through Mr. Belcher I learn'd of your Part in the Philadelphia Witch-Trial, which at the Time was much discuss'd here in Paris. Not long into his Account of the Proceeding and its Aftermath, Mr. Belcher mention'd that the Defendant was Blood-Sister to the Prosecutor, one Dunstan Stearne. Knowing Stearne to be your Maiden Name, I soon deduc'd that the Crown's Advocate was my Uncle Dunstan, the escap'd Enchantress my own Mother. As you are mayhap aware, your Testimony in Philadelphia inspir'd Mr. Belcher to enjoin the Massachusetts Cleansers from practicing their Trade, which Action doubtless prevent'd the unjust Executions of many heathen Savages.

And so it happens that my Attitude to you hath of late undergone a Revolution. I cannot forgive your Treatment of me, but neither can I shake my Admiration for you. You are still my Nemesis, and yet you are also my Idol. Mr. Belcher avers that such Ambivalence is not a terrible Thing. He says 'tis better to go through Life in thrall to Paradox than indentur'd to Regret.

For the Moment this is All I have to say, chère Maman. I harbor a fond Hope that you will wish to continue this Correspondence, as I am curious to learn just how astonishing we might become to one another.

> *Tous mes amitiés,*
> *I remain your affectionate*
> *Rachel*

It was a good letter, she decided, as pleasing a product as might ever issue from the Great Jovian Storm that was their relationship. True, she would rather have achieved the status of *mother* in Rachel's eyes than the designation *idol*. But *idol* was adequate. *Idol* would do.

The following morning she slipped her daughter's letter into her jacket pocket and took the day-coach to Philadelphia, subsequently consuming a noontime meal of broiled shad and fresh-water mussels at the Black Horse Tavern. At one o'clock she ambled down Market Street to Franklin and Meredith's Printing-House.

No sooner had she stepped into the shop, her entrance heralded by the famous brass bell, than Ben and William, huddled over the older

Blaeu press, together pulled the spindle lever, rolled back the bed, and peeled the fruit of their industry from the type-form. The boy waved the wet broadsheet through the air as exuberantly as an explorer about to plant his nation's flag on a newly discovered continent.

"Mother! Mother! Look what I made!"

"Ah, I see you've taken up your father's trade," she said.

"I did it all on my own," he said. "Compositing, framing, inking, printing. Father helped only a little."

"This man pursues the noblest calling in the world," Jennet said, kissing Ben's cheek. "I think of a remark once spoken by our friend the Baron de Montesquieu. 'I have never known any distress that an hour's reading did not relieve.' " She passed Ben the pages from Paris. "Look at this."

As Ben unfolded Rachel's letter, William placed the broadsheet in Jennet's hands.

"Take care not to smear it," the boy admonished her.

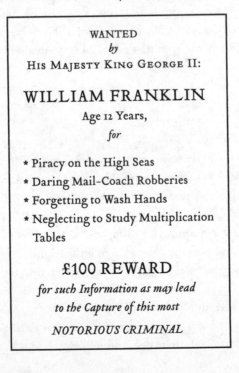

WANTED
by
HIS MAJESTY KING GEORGE II:

WILLIAM FRANKLIN
Age 12 Years,
for

* Piracy on the High Seas
* Daring Mail-Coach Robberies
* Forgetting to Wash Hands
* Neglecting to Study Multiplication
  Tables

£100 REWARD
*for such Information as may lead
to the Capture of this most*

NOTORIOUS CRIMINAL

"I've heard of this fugitive Franklin," Jennet said. "Is he not the lad robbed the Royal Mint last year, making off with two king's ransoms and a sack of shillings?"

"That'd be he, ma'am," William said.

"My son, thou art surely the second most skillful printer in Pennsylvania."

With the back of his hand Ben gave Rachel's letter an emphatic swipe. " 'Tis the very rock on which a reconciliation 'twixt mother and daughter might be built," he told Jennet. "You must reply anon."

The midday sun blazed like a hearth fire, sending trickles of sweat down everyone's temples and raising red blotches on their cheeks. "I shall draft a letter to Rachel this evening," she said, fanning herself with William's broadsheet. "However, I am dubious concerning the ultimate efficacy of such a correspondence."

"You've ne'er shared my affection for optimism," Ben said. "There be no need to start now."

She cupped her palm around William's shoulder. "Son, methinks the two of us should go down to the Schuylkill, that we might gain some relief from this uncivilized heat."

A smile as wide as Hezekiah Creech's, and high as the Maw of Folkestone's, appeared on the boy's face.

They arrived at the riverbank shortly after two o'clock. William stripped himself down to his underclothes, and then she guided him along a ramp of sand and into the water, one cautious step at a time. The current lifted her skirt to the level of her hips, fanning it outward like the petals of a lily.

Placing one hand against his neck, another under his rump, she gradually tilted his body backward—a Deist baptism, she mused, observed with regal apathy by the Cosmic Clockmaker—until the Schuylkill lapped at his sides and touched his ears. When he voiced a fear that he was about to sink, she proceeded to instruct him in Mr. Boyle's buoyancy principle, explaining that if a swimmer kept his head low and his lungs nearly full, he could not but remain on the surface. Heartened by this knowledge, William inhaled, held his breath, arched his back, and, sensing that he was waterborne, asked his mother to step away. She withdrew her hands, and he forthwith found himself a-float, ready to embrace the aquatic life as joyfully as any otter.

"And now you are evermore immune to drowning," she said.

" 'Twas considerably less painful than becoming immune to the small-pox," he said.

For the balance of the afternoon they played at nine-pins and fished without success for perch and suckers, then watched the westering sun dip toward the unseen reaches of the wild continent. The waters evaporated from her skirt, leaving behind subtle dots of mud and delicate threads of moss that, depending on one's attitude to fashion, looked either appallingly untidy or appealingly primeval.

As dusk settled over the Schuylkill, mother and son started east toward the Godfrey mansion, eating their way from one Market Street stall to the next. William stuffed himself with venison pasties, gooseberry tarts, almond puddings, and corn fritters, washing it all down with apple cider and unfermented syllabub.

At seven o'clock she delivered the satiated boy to his door. Sour and stubby Deborah Franklin greeted her stepson with an extravagant smile and a firm hug, a ritual that evidently drained her reserves of cordiality, for she neither asked after Jennet's welfare nor invited her into the house.

"Farewell, dear William," Jennet said. "Next time I shall teach you how to swim beneath the water."

"Beneath?"

"Holding your breath."

"How far might I go before I must have air?" he asked.

"From one bank of the Schuylkill to the other," she replied.

"Hurrah!" His face glowed like a night-crier's lanthorn.

"That sounds dangerous," Deborah said.

"Young William was born to the beat of the tide and the crash of the surf." Jennet stepped off the stoop and started into the darkening mist. "He shall always count the water his friend!"

The coming of night failed to cool Philadelphia, and so once again she went down to the river. Betimes she came upon a willow tree, as stately as the one that marked Pashpishia's grave, and there she shed her garments, securing them beneath a stone. She followed the shore to a place where the Schuylkill ran deep. She pressed her palms together and, leaning over the bank, bent her knees and jumped. The water received her. Rolling onto her back, she worked her legs in a flutter kick, her arms as if making an angel in snow. She moved against the flow. How far north, exactly, might she travel via this medium? To New York? Unlikely. To Massachusetts? Certainly not. And yet her great desire that night was to swim to the Kokokehom, seek out Pussough, and take him to her bower by the Hoosic.

A full moon rose over Philadelphia, the great Quanquogt *wampumpeag* bead. In nine hours the Delaware would be at flood, and the high-masted ships would leave for Port Royal, Havana, Bridgetown, Bristol, Gravesend, Lisbon, and a dozen other cities. She spun around, surrendering to the current. Her gaze roamed from Venus to the other planets to the fixed stars beyond and . . . was it possible? Had a nomad entered the summer sky? She couldn't be certain, of course, not until she'd caught the object in Ben's telescope, but it seemed that a soft glimmering comet lay just below Orion, due east of the Great Dog. Perhaps Giordano Bruno was right. Perhaps the cosmos throbbed with an infinity of worlds, which meant there were surely other thinking creatures in the heavens, pursuing their lives, charting their dreams, devising their sciences. And if you believed in the laws of probability, as
Jennet did, then one of these creatures had recently dived into
a soothing river, and she was at that moment
happily contemplating distant
constellations whilst
swimming

❧❧

Naked
came I from
my author's brain, I,
Principia, a quivering precipitate of
heretofore unthought ideas, a plasma compounded
of geometry and inspiration, celestial mechanics and lucky guesses.
The midwives of my advent, those skilled printers and diligent binders,

incarnated me with their ink, fixed me with their paper, secured me with their adhesives, and clothed me in their leather. And somewhere along the line I acquired passions commensurate with your own.

You will not be surprised to hear that my Jennet spent her remaining years endeavoring to establish a connection between magnetism and electricity. Early in these investigations she concluded, quite correctly, that to magnetize a horseshoe she must subject it to a steady electric stream, not simply jolt it with lightning sparks. Her attempts to wring a continuous flow from static Von Guericke discharges proved bootless, however, and after six months she had nothing to show for her labors except the largest collection of sulphur balls in the New World.

Eventually it came to her that she was going about the problem backwards. Rather than trying to generate first electricity and then magnetism from a rotating Van Guericke sphere, she must instead start with a lodestone, spinning it via a Newcomen steam engine. A coil of copper wire placed near such an apparatus would soon, logically enough, become home to an electric current. Alas, my goddess never realized that she should have put the coiled wire *inside* the spinning lodestone, thereby exploiting its magnetic field—or else she could leave the surrounding stone alone and spin the wire instead. And so it was that the principle of electromagnetic induction had to wait another seventy years for its definitive demonstration, which occurred courtesy of Joseph Henry in 1830 and Michael Faraday in 1831.

Throughout this period of futile experimentation, Jennet wrote long letters to Rachel, and her child reciprocated, but the exchange failed to have the effect the women desired. Rachel never managed to comprehend her mother's obsession with lodestones and copper wires. Jennet was equally confounded by her daughter's liaisons with a series of French writers both famous and obscure. At one point Rachel even attempted to fill the void that was visited upon Jean François-Marie Arouet de Voltaire by the premature death of his dear friend, the talented young actress Adrienne Lecouvreur, but she soon tired of vying with a ghost, and Rachel and Voltaire went their separate ways.

Although electromagnetic induction and maternal satisfaction both eluded Jennet, her final years were far from empty. One bright and brittle October morning Pussough appeared at the farm, accompanied by a large wolfish dog whose sienna coat suggested a patchwork quilt made of periwigs. A woman living alone might do without a birch canoe, her Lynx Man explained, or a stew pot or even a sleeping platform, but a guard dog—never. She gladly accepted the gift. The dog's name was Ahanu. He Who Laughs.

Before old age carried him off, the ebullient Ahanu watched over Jennet for seven years. Pussough stayed for roughly the same interval, learning about steam-powered magnets to a degree that far exceeded his curiosity, until a winter chill turned to pneumonia and took him to the mountain of Kautantouwit.

The longer she lived, the more the sufficiency hypothesis became for Jennet not simply an abstract principle but a personal creed, and in time her neighbors realized that a wise-woman dwelt amongst them. They appeared on her doorstep at odd hours, and unless they'd awakened her from a particularly diverting dream, she always received them courteously. While her clients had never heard of either Hassane or Isobel Mowbray, in truth she'd become at once a rationalist edition of the Kokokehom medicine-woman and a philanthropic version of Mirringate's mistress. My goddess set broken bones, lanced boils, delivered babies, dispensed herbs for preventing pregnancy, prescribed simples against quinsy and the gout, bent young minds toward contrariness and doubt, and convened philosophy salons in her front parlor. Jennet Stearne, the Witch of Manayunk.

I must decline to provide the details of her death. How could I bear to set them down? Let me merely state that she lived to the impressive age of eighty-three, whereupon her heart's Cartesian mechanism ceased to function properly. Lying abed in her farmhouse, she slipped into the undiscovered country on July 4, 1761, watched over by Ben, William, John Tux, Nicholas Scull, Bethany Markley, and Zebulon Plum, exactly fifteen years before Ben would sign the Declaration of Independence. Among her Philadelphia friends, only Barnaby Cavendish did not help Jennet out of the world, for two decades earlier he'd collapsed and died while lecturing on his newest acquisition, the Argus of Providence.

She had never joined a church, and so Ben buried her behind Manayunk Courthouse, scene of her astonishing presentation of the sufficiency hypothesis, not far from the tomb of the ergot-ridden rooster. Six months later, Ben, William, and the Junto conducted a memorial service in Nicholas Scull's drawing room, temporary home of the Free Library of Philadelphia. Rachel sailed all the way from France. Montesquieu did not attend, having died in 1755, his deathbed utterance baffling everyone who heard it: *"La vermin se reproduit"*—the wrigglers generate themselves. At the climax of Jennet's funeral Ben recited the whole of Milton's *Lycidas*. " 'Yet once more, O ye Laurels,' " he read, " 'and once more, ye Myrtles brown, with Ivy never-sere, I come to pluck your Berries harsh and crude, and with forc'd Fingers rude shatter your Leaves before the mellowing Year . . .' "

I think about her every day. I think about her intelligence, her energy, her impatience with consecrated nonsense. Naturally I retain fond memories of her struggles to comprehend me, and also of our lovemaking, which I accomplished by inhabiting Pussough during her exile among the Kokokehom. My soul bleeds for Jennet Stearne. I grieve for her now, and I shall grieve for her when my Four Hundredth Anniversary edition rolls off the presses in 2087.

Ben ultimately attained Jennet's age, then added one more year, succumbing in 1790 to yet another attack of pleurisy. He lived to see the birth and ratification of the American Constitution, surely one of our planet's worthier documents. (Vibrating with mutual if qualified respect, *We the People* and I play contract bridge in cyberspace every Saturday night, partnered respectively with *Poor Richard's Almanack* and *L'Esprit des Lois*.) Throughout his entire adulthood, Ben never stopped being rational. One month before his death, he wrote to the Reverend Ezra Stiles, "As to Jesus of Nazareth, my Opinion of whom you particularly desire, I think the System of Morals and His Religion, as He left them to us, the best the World ever saw . . . but I apprehend it has receiv'd various corrupting Changes, and I have, with most of the present Dissenters in England, some Doubts as to His Divinity."

Concerning William Franklin, the less said about that creepy little Tory bastard the better. Most historians would concur that he inherited neither his mother's breadth of vision nor his father's generosity of spirit but received instead his maternal grandfather's mediocrity. On September 4, 1762, William married Elizabeth Downes in London, and five days later he accepted a commission as Royal Governor of New Jersey. Throughout the pre-Revolutionary period, William strove mightily to thwart the dissidents' cause, alternately breaking his father's heart and rousing his wrath. At the risk of sounding vain, I would say that, while disagreeing with my illustrious progenitor on many points, ethical and theological, I have been a better son to Isaac Newton than William Franklin ever was to Ben.

I cannot take leave of you without mentioning another actor in Jennet's life, her great legacy, the Witchcraft Statute of George II. To be sure, that particular law cannot be called the beginning of the end for European witchfinding. The *Zeitgeist* was radiant with skepticism long before the British Parliament weighed in against the demon hypothesis. It was more like the end of the end. And yet I count its passage a triumph. As late as 1768, the English evangelist John Wesley, founder of the Methodist Church, wrote in his journal, "The giving up of witchcraft is in effect giving up the Bible," and two years later he publicly complained, "The infidels have hooted witchcraft out of the world." Were it not for the Act of George II and the *argumentum grande* that inspired it, Wesley might very well have found an audience for his lament.

After 1740 there is almost nothing for a witch reporter to report. Yes, in May of 1749 the Inquisition determines that Sister Maria Renata Sänger von Mossau, a Würzburg nun, has signed the Devil's book and bewitched the other members of her convent, but it's a throwback case, and everybody knows it. Sister Maria is nevertheless beheaded the following month and her corpse tossed onto a bonfire of tar barrels. Four years later a vigilante mob in Hertfordshire swims a suspected witch named Ruth Osborne, performing the test so crudely that she chokes to death. But times have changed, and at the next assizes the ringleader, Thomas Colley, is convicted of willful murder and condemned to the gallows. And then at long last, on April 11, 1775, the final legal execution for witchcraft occurs in the Western world, when a deranged serving woman named Anna Maria Schwägel is decapitated in Kempten, Bavaria, having confessed to copulation with Satan. And suddenly it's over. *Finis.* The infidels have hooted witchcraft out of the world. In 1821 even the pious country of Ireland succumbs to the Enlightenment, and its lawmakers repeal the Conjuring Statute of 1587.

The optimists among you will argue that the witch universe is gone forever. You're probably right. Still, let me take this opportunity to detail the diaspora of *The Sufficiency of the World,* quite possibly the rarest published treatise on our planet. Forget about the Internet. The rare-book websites won't know what you're talking about. At present two copies reside in the British Museum, one in the Bibliothèque Nationale, one in the New York Public Library, and two in the Library of Congress, while a seventh graces the Franklin collection of the American Philosophical Society in Philadelphia. True, it's unlikely that Western Civilization will ever again have need of Jennet's remarkable work, but I thought you ought to know where to find one, just in case.

Before we part company, I invite you to journey with me to the convivial community of Maplewood, New Jersey, for I have just now discovered an opportunity to connect—obliquely but meaningfully—with my goddess. Join me as I climb inside the mind of Inez Maldonado, an idealistic educator, sauntering toward fifty, who teaches eighth-grade arithmetic from an historical perspective. The postulates of geometry were not handed down from Olympus, Inez tells her students. They were devised by human beings. When Euclid's nose itched, he scratched it. When Pythagoras heard cicadas thrum their abdomens, he reveled in the music.

On Tuesday afternoons Inez meets with the eleven members of the Rocket Club in Room 332 of Maplewood Middle School. She would prefer coaching the chess team, but Fred Maltby, an aging geography teacher, has captained that activity since time immemorial. Nevertheless, in recent years Inez has developed a fondness for the Rocket Club, which so obviously nourishes the socially inept youngsters it tends to attract.

It's Saturday morning—launch day. The spacious grounds of the soccer field swarm with the rocketeers, many of their parents, and several students too cool to have signed up but too curious to have stayed home. The April sun is warm and mellow. Bluejays, robins, and bumblebees are on the wing.

At the moment the main object of Inez's concern is twelve-year-old Juliet Sorkin, who has designed and built a sleek, magnificent rocket named the Golden Comet. A prodigy of sorts, Juliet has a bad habit of lecturing to her classmates using big words, and in consequence they pick on her. Our teacher's pet is sweet-tempered, distractible, and like many bright people mildly dyslexic, her cherubic face sprinkled with freckles and three ripe pimples. Although Juliet has recently won second prize in the Maplewood Science Fair—for an exhibit about human cloning centered around her cousin's discarded collection of Barbie dolls—she remains an outsider.

From the viewpoint of my *Principia* self, one fact about Juliet Sorkin eclipses all others. She is a direct descendant of Jennet Stearne, Hammer of Witchfinders. Were Juliet to become curious about her ancestry, she might succeed in tracing her line back ten generations to Stéphane Crompton, born November 11, 1746, the bastard son of Rachel Crompton and René Duvic, a professional cad specializing in Voltaire's former lovers. But Juliet doesn't strike me as harboring a genealogical bent. She's a forward-looking sort of misfit.

The Golden Comet is ready for its maiden flight: parachute secure, igniter snugged against the propellant, alligator clips in place. At a signal from my Inez self, the students draw back from the launch pad—fifteen feet, that's our rule. Juliet takes the controller and inserts the safety key, arming the system. The warning bulb lights up.

"What engine?" asks Danny Ginsburg, who is forever sneaking his chameleon into school.

"A D12-9," Juliet replies proudly. Most of the kids still use pathetic B's and C's.

"That means twelve Newtons of thrust, huh?" says Danny's best friend, Raoul Pindar, who has a crush on Juliet but doesn't quite know it.

"Eleven point eight, actually," says Juliet with a touch of pedantry, then counts down from ten to zero.

She presses the controller button. At the speed of electricity the current rips along the wires, charges the alligator clips, and heats the igniter. Now comes that delicious microinstant between the igniter combusting—you can tell by the smoke, the sizzle, the little flame—and . . . liftoff! A circumscribed explosion spews sparks and cinders onto the steel disk, and Juliet's ship rides up the launch rod, leaves the pad, and zooms skyward with a thick emphatic hiss. The spectators clap and cheer. Twenty Newton-seconds elapse as the Estes engine and my father's Third Law carry the vessel five hundred—eight hundred—twelve hundred—fifteen hundred feet into the heavens! In the entire history of the Maplewood Middle School Rocket Club no ship has ever risen fifteen hundred feet.

Propellant spent, the Golden Comet glides for nine seconds, a tiny apostrophe in the sky, and then the ejection charge detonates. The nose cone pops off, the shock cord pays out, and the parachute opens like a blossoming orchid.

But now disaster befalls the flight. The ship is soaring so high that the wind gets under the chute and bears the whole assemblage far beyond the soccer field. With sinking heart and foundering spirits, we all watch as the Golden Comet floats toward the pine groves of Memorial Park and passes from view. I glance at Jennet Stearne's descendant. She is wincing. Her lower lip trembles. When gravity reasserts itself and the ship plummets, the chute lines will catch in the treetops, and Juliet will lose her masterpiece.

"I'm going to get it back!" she informs her teacher.

"Good luck," my Inez self replies.

But it is my *Principia* self who empathizes most fully with poor Juliet. For a protracted moment we stare into each other's eyes, and, romantic that I am, I allow myself to imagine that my goddess has been restored to me.

Oh, yes, it's she all right. We are back in Colonial Salem. Crouching by the banks of the Merrimack, she removes the iron hook from the trout's mouth, then glances across the river. A beautiful young Indian brave gathers marsh marigolds on the far shore, oblivious to my presence in his mind and body.

This time Jennet and I enjoy a brief conversation. In halting English, I tell her that she will come of age not in Salem but in a Nimacook village. This heritage, I insist, will figure crucially in her demon disproof.

"How can you possibly foresee such a thing?" Jennet asks.

"I know not." I set the marigolds on the shore, a gift for my goddess, then slip into the New England woods. "It's just one of those secrets of the universe."

As my reverie evaporates, Juliet, Raoul, and Danny go sprinting across the field and disappear into the pine groves. Inez Maldonado admires their ambition, their optimism. She wishes she could be like them. This is not a good time in her life. Her cholesterol count is too high. Her husband has mentioned a divorce.

We are helping Hejong Kim and Peter Gorka prepare their ships for launch when the recovery team bursts out of Memorial Park, and we've never seen a more entrancing tableau All three youngsters are jumping up and down, and there— there in the lead—there strides Juliet Sorkin, cradling the Golden Comet, nose cone and parachute included. Her smile is as big as a boomerang. Reaching the launch site, she tells her teacher that Raoul spotted the rocket at the base of a pine tree. This makes little sense to either Inez or me. Why didn't the branches snag the chute lines? For a full minute we ponder the question, and then we resolve to worry about it no longer. We give Juliet a hug. It's simply a mystery, we tell ourselves. It's just one of those secrets of the universe.

Acknowledgments

THIS BOOK ABOUT BOOKS draws its historical framework and thematic tissue from dozens of volumes. Of particular value to my project were *Masks of the Universe* by Edward Harrison, *Thinking with Demons* by Stuart Clark, *Malleus Maleficarum* by Heinrich Krämer and James Sprenger, *Witchcraft in Europe: A Documentary History*, edited by Alan C. Kors and Edward Peters, *Religion and the Decline of Magic* by Keith Thomas, *The European Witch-Craze* by H. R. Trevor-Roper, *A Trial of Witches* by Gilbert Geis and Ivan Bunn, *Les Sorcières: Fiancées de Satan* by Jean-Michel Sallman, *A Delusion of Satan* by Frances Hill, *The Devil in the Shape of a Woman* by Carol F. Karlsen, *Age of Enlightenment* by Peter Gay, *The Unredeemed Captive* by John Demos, *Women's Indian Captivity Narratives*, edited by Kathryn Zabelle Derounian-Stodola, *The First American: the Life and Times of Benjamin Franklin* by H. W. Brands, *Franklin of Philadelphia* by Esmond Wright, *Isaac Newton: The Last Sorcerer* by Michael White, *A Portrait of Isaac Newton* by Frank E. Manuel, *Franklin and Newton* by I. Bernard Cohen, Benjamin Franklin's *Autobiography*, and, last but not least, *Mathematical Principles of Natural Philosophy* by Sir Isaac Newton.

The Algonquin words and phrases in *The Last Witchfinder* are generally authentic. My characters normally speak the Narragansett dialect as recorded by Roger Williams in his remarkable linguistic treatise of 1643, *A Key into the Language of America,* the first of its kind published in the New World. Williams is better known as the founder of the settlement that became Rhode Island, an enterprise that consumed him following his expulsion from Massachusetts in 1635 for "new and dangerous ideas."

I would like to thank those friends, relatives, colleagues, and Benjamin Franklin impersonators who offered me their reactions to the novel as it evolved: Joe Adamson, Linda Barnes, Michael Bishop, Ginger Clark, Shira Daemon, Margaret Duda, David Edwards, Gordon Fleming, Merrilee Heifetz, Nalo Hopkinson, Philip Jenkins, Michael Kandel, Kirk McElhearn, Bill Meikle, Carolyn Meredith, Gregory Miller, Christopher Morrow, William Pencak, Alis Rasmussen, Elisabeth Rose, Bill Sheehan, James D. Smith, James Stevens-Arce, and Michael Vicario.

My gratitude also goes to my wife, Kathryn Morrow, for her endless emotional and intellectual inspiration; to my agent, Wendy Weil, for so skillfully navigating the shoals of contemporary publishing; to my editor, Jennifer Brehl, for befriending a formidable manuscript; to my neighbor Londa Schiebinger, for her insight into the Royal Society's female skeleton; and to my cousin Glenn Morrow, for offering me many fruitful challenges and supplementing my research with dozens of compelling facts.

About the author

About the book

Read on

Insights,
Interviews
& More . . .

My Literary Hero

MANY STRANGE AND TASTY INGREDIENTS have gone into the mulligan stew of my fiction-writing career, but none was more significant than the World Literature course I took in tenth grade at Abington Senior High School. To this day the teacher, a brilliant and dynamic *enfant terrible* named James Giordano, remains my primary literary hero, and I'm grateful for this opportunity to spend a few paragraphs praising "Mr. G," to use his preferred moniker, and by extension all teachers who go above and beyond the call of tenure to lead their students into the universe of ideas.

Mr. G's syllabus was a wonder. Here we were, a bunch of callow kids from the Philadelphia suburbs, fourteen years old, fifteen years old, becalmed in the doldrums of public education—and suddenly, bang, this astonishing curriculum appeared in our lives, implicitly telling us that we possessed sophisticated minds capable of handling complex literature. We read Kafka's *Trial*, Camus's *Stranger*, Voltaire's *Candide*, Dostoevsky's *Crime and Punishment*, Flaubert's *Madame Bovary*, Sophocles's *Oedipus Rex*, Homer's *Iliad*, Dante's *Inferno*, four plays by Ibsen, and a half dozen other vital works.

Although he had no interest in critiquing his students' personal religious and political beliefs, Mr. G invited us to approach this heady menu on its own adult terms, and he clearly delighted in telling us about the freethinking birds and the godless bees. Indeed, I'm sure that for Mr. G a person

Meet *James Morrow*

Didier Leclerc/Atelier N89

JAMES MORROW is the author of eight previous novels. He lives in State College, Pennsylvania, where he spent seven years working on this book.

couldn't honestly teach *Candide* or *The Stranger* without navigating these treacherous waters. And in me, at least, he found an eager acolyte. The novelist as contrarian, eternally at odds with the received wisdom of his day: yes, I thought, that's certainly a myth to live by—sign me up.

As that amazing school year of 1962–1963 went on, a second overarching theme emerged in Mr. G's class. Enduring fiction evidently occupied some indefinable domain where intellect and feeling met and fused, fueling an eternal conversation about the mystery of it all. The most valuable novelists, poets, and playwrights didn't simply tell stories; they didn't just solicit our vicarious involvement in imaginary adventures. Fiction writers had *something to say.* They were on fire with *ideas.* But the novelist wasn't essentially a philosopher. *The Trial* and *Madame Bovary* got at truth obliquely, subjectively—emotionally. Although Mr. G. didn't spend much time touting Kafka and Flaubert as producers of marvelous artistic effects, it was obvious that he loved these books, and that their ultimate value for him lay in the domain of passion.

Many years after leaving Mr. G's English class, I had the opportunity to pay him tribute—in my sixth novel, *Blameless in Abaddon*. The plot revolves around the efforts of Martin Candle, a magistrate whose jurisdiction is "Abaddon" (read "Abington") Township in Pennsylvania, to put God on trial for His seeming indifference to human suffering. Martin's energy and inspiration trace largely to a World Literature course he had in high school, taught by the iconoclastic "Mr. Gianassio." For *Blameless in Abaddon* I altered the syllabus somewhat and transferred the hero's experience to his senior year—who would believe tenth graders reading Dostoevsky?—but there is no question which humanities curriculum and what teacher are being celebrated in those pages. ༗

The Origins of
The Last Witchfinder

I GREW UP IN A HOUSE suffused with the spirit of Benjamin Franklin, that admirable soul who came to personify the Age of Reason on this side of the Atlantic.

My maternal grandfather, Charles Develin, who lived with us during his final years, was a lithographer by trade and a painter by choice, and his proud daughter, Emily Morrow, decorated our suburban Philadelphia residence with his work, including a watercolor of Ben Franklin that he'd synthesized from existing portraits. Franklin was the patron saint of printers and lithographers, and I can still see my grandfather's interpretation of Ben's countenance, aglow with the same "smile of reason" that the sculptor Houdon had bestowed on Voltaire.

Years later, as an English teacher living in Westford, Massachusetts, I periodically encountered a very different dimension of the Colonial American psyche—the fear-crazed world of the Puritan minister Cotton Mather—when various friends and relatives, visiting from out of state, would request that we drive to nearby Salem and patronize the museums commemorating the Witch Trials. Invariably I found these trips depressing. Despite a decided affection for the macabre, I learned more than I wanted to know about the "prickers" who in 1692 traveled from Boston to Salem with their steel needles, probing the skin of accused witches in search of the insensate "Devil's mark" with which Satan supposedly branded his disciples.

But ultimately these Salem forays, like my hours spent in communion with my grandfather's portrait of Franklin, planted the seeds of *The Last Witchfinder*. Puritan Boston versus Quaker Philadelphia, the rage of Mather versus the Age of Reason, the scowls of the Calvinist prickers versus the smile of my Enlightenment printer: for years these contrasts beguiled me, and then one afternoon, shortly before my thirty-eighth birthday, while reading physicist Edward Harrison's marvelous history of human thought, *Masks of the Universe*, I came upon an astonishing sentence that made me realize there was a novel in all this. The prickers' enterprise, Harrison argued, was not simply a phenomenon—it was a worldview, a zeitgeist, a "witch universe" that would have "destroyed European society but for the intervention of science."

Eventually I worked up the nerve to attempt my epic, and I started composing the story of Jennet Stearne, born and educated in Restoration England, who makes it her life's mission to bring down the Parliamentary Witchcraft Act of 1604. Although *The Last Witchfinder* required much research, I would periodically reinvigorate myself by returning to Salem, drawing inverse inspiration from the prickers' ghosts, as well as to Franklin's beloved Philadelphia, where I had gone to college—to the University of Pennsylvania, in fact, the school founded by Ben himself. As the project grew, so did the scope of my travels. I spent a week in England, following in Jennet's footsteps as she encounters Robert Hooke at Cambridge University, witnesses Aunt Isobel's execution behind Colchester Castle, and tracks down Isaac Newton in London.

My grandfather's watercolor of Franklin is no longer in my family's possession. He gave it to a neighbor, William Sharkey, another printer, now fifteen years deceased, his worldly goods scattered to the winds. But I like to believe that, if *The Last Witchfinder* is close to what I intended, then it has served to widen the smile on that particular Franklin portrait, wherever it now resides. ༄

James Morrow
A Self-Interview

Book reviewers have categorized your previous novels as wild Vonnegutian satires full of fantastical and even surrealistic events. Why this sudden leap into straight historical fiction?

The leap was a long time coming. As I mentioned in my essay called "The Origins of *The Last Witchfinder*," about twenty years ago I had a mind-boggling encounter with a single sentence in Edward Harrison's *Masks of the Universe*: his audacious assertion that the coming of science prevented the "witch universe," the zeitgeist of the late Renaissance, from obliterating European society. And I said to myself, "Good God, what a great subject for a novel!" Even if Harrison was overstating the case, I simply had to explore that astonishing idea, the near destruction of a civilization at the hands of its own theology.

So you spent twenty years researching and writing The Last Witchfinder? *You have a long attention span.*

Not the past twenty years, no. I kept deferring the project, daunted by its scope, and composed other sorts of fiction instead. But I never stopped thinking about Harrison's riveting sentence, and then about eight years ago I took the plunge and committed myself to writing a *magnum opus* about the shift from the "witch universe" to our modern, scientific world-picture. Before long I realized that a woman born around 1678—don't ask me why, but I knew the main character had to be a woman—would have lived through the great Revelation-to-Reason transition.

Why did the main character have to be a woman?

I've always enjoyed creating strong female protagonists. My fourth novel, *Only Begotten Daughter*, recounts the adventures of Jesus Christ's divine half sister in contemporary Atlantic City. By placing a woman at the center of *The Last Witchfinder*, I believe I made the death throes of the "witch universe" more engaging than if I'd used a male protagonist. Obviously a woman would face an uphill battle convincing the world that she'd discovered a scientific refutation of the "demon hypothesis." And I thought there would be a certain poetic justice in having a heroine, as opposed to a hero, put the witchfinders out of business, since women endured a disproportionate amount of persecution during "the burning times." Indeed, the main reason Jennet goes on her quest is that, early in the novel, her beloved aunt Isobel is publicly executed as a Satanist.

Jennet Stearne is a formidable heroine: brilliant, sharp-tongued, courageous. But why would even the cleverest seventeenth-century woman imagine she had the intellectual and political resources to destroy the "witch universe"?

Throughout her quest, Jennet takes heart in a kind of talisman bestowed on her by Aunt Isobel: a letter from Isaac Newton in which he implies that a "demon disproof" lies hidden between the lines of his scientific masterwork, the *Principia Mathematica*. Jennet comes to believe that, by studying the *Principia*, she'll uncover an argument that will persuade the English legislature to overturn the Witchcraft Statute. After several false starts, she manages to write a persuasive treatise, but then she faces an even bigger problem: convincing Parliament to read it. And so, in a daring move, Jennet puts herself on trial for witchcraft in Colonial Philadelphia, using the attendant "media circus" to publicize her argument.

Is Jennet based on a real person?

No, though numerous women of this era were passionately involved with the new mechanical science—or, as it was called then, "natural philosophy"—of Descartes and Newton. The recent epochal exhibit at the New York Public Library called *The Newtonian Moment* featured a gallery of "Newtonian Women," among them Laura Bassi, Diamante Medaglia Faini, Maria Gaetana Agnesi, and Voltaire's celebrated collaborator, Madame du Châtelet. In the 1750's Oliver Goldsmith, noting the phenomenon of women wedding themselves to natural philosophy, remarked that a man "who would court a lady must be capable of discussing Newton and Locke."

So Jennet is your own creation, but many actual historical figures parade through the novel: Benjamin Franklin, Isaac Newton, Robert Hooke, Cotton Mather, the Baron de Montesquieu. ▸

James Morrow: A Self-Interview *(continued)*

Beyond Edward Harrison's inspiring sentence, the most important catalyst in the development of *The Last Witchfinder* was my discovery of an obscure historical fact. In 1725 the young Benjamin Franklin, age eighteen, traveled to London on a mission for the royal governor of Pennsylvania and eventually penetrated Newton's inner circle, hoping to meet the genius behind the theory of universal gravitation. But Newton saw no reason to waste an afternoon talking to some cheeky kid from Philadelphia.

But in The Last Witchfinder *Newton and Franklin really do meet.*

I realized that I could use these fascinating characters as symbols of the two universes: Newton the avatar of the Renaissance, as pious a man who ever lived, versus Franklin the quintessential Enlightenment skeptic, eternally playful and irreverent. When they finally cross paths in my novel, they have nothing to say to each other. Newton wants to talk about the great preoccupation of his dotage, biblical prophecy, and Franklin wants to talk about electricity. The problem isn't just that they're from two different continents and two different generations. They're from two different universes.

Extreme cases to be sure. But wouldn't it be fair to say that most people during this period lived in both universes at the same time?

Indeed. That's what makes the worldview of early modern Europe—and its counterpart in Colonial America—so compelling. For Jennet's generation, demonology and the new mechanical philosophy were not *ipso facto* incompatible. We tend to think of witchcraft as a mere superstition, belonging largely to the Middle Ages or even the Dark Ages, but the theology of Satanism was actually quite sophisticated, flowering fully only during the Renaissance. For nearly a century, the Age of Demons and the Era of Demonstrations overlapped. Many members of the Royal Society, most famously Robert Boyle, believed that evil spirits were a fact. And, of course, the various "proofs" of Satanic compact were ostensibly "scientific." It stood to reason, for example, that the Devil endowed his disciples with special teats for suckling their animal familiars, and so the witchfinder would search the suspect's skin until he found an unusual excrescence, then prick it with a needle: if the "nipple" failed to bleed, this confirmed its demonic nature. It was equally plausible to assert that pure water, the medium of baptism, would reject a disciple of Lucifer: hence the practice of "swimming the witch"—tossing her into a river and then, if she floated, declaring her a Satanist.

This large theme of yours, the clash of Renaissance theology and Enlightenment science—for some prospective readers, it may sound a trifle dry.

Or even dull?

Or even dull. And yet The Last Witchfinder *is a rollicking, satiric, picaresque, and sometimes bawdy adventure. As the plot progresses, Jennet runs afoul of Indians, pirates, whores, scoundrels, charlatans, and hurricanes.*

My models included those juicy, spirited, comic novels of the eighteenth century—Laurence Sterne's *Tristram Shandy*, Henry Fielding's *Joseph Andrews*, and, of course, Voltaire's *Candide*—that people still read today with pleasure. I especially enjoyed juxtaposing the scientific and the erotic, as when Jennet and Ben Franklin seduce each other while performing an experiment with a rotating sulfur ball. They're diligently determining the degree to which a human body can conduct static electricity, and before long they're sparkling and crackling with mutual desire, and next they're swiving on the mattress in Ben's garret.

Swiving?

It rhymes with driving.

You mentioned that the encounter between Newton and Franklin never really happened—but many of the events in the novel are historically accurate, yes?

I was continually delighted by how much real history I could incorporate into *The Last Witchfinder*. It seemed as if all these ▶

James Morrow: A Self-Interview *(continued)*

glittering shards of the past were lying around in a field, and all I
had to do was glue them together into an urn of my own design.

Almost as if the book were asking to be written?

Exactly. At one point the story line required Jennet to be abducted
from her home in Haverhill, Massachusetts, by Algonquin Indians.
Well, it turns out that the Abenaki tribe really did attack Colonial
Haverhill in 1696. When Jennet puts herself on trial for witchcraft,
I thought it would be interesting if the Baron de Montesquieu—
another personification of the Enlightenment—came forward to
defend her. So naturally I was pleased to discover that, not only had
Montesquieu denounced the conjuring statutes, he was a world
traveler and could easily have landed in Colonial Philadelphia at
this time. Even the climactic courtroom battle has a rough historical
counterpart. Shortly after he took over the editorship of *The
Pennsylvania Gazette*, Franklin reported on a witch trial that had
supposedly occurred across the Delaware River—in Mount Holly,
New Jersey. As I mention in the Author's Note at the beginning of the
novel, the article was almost certainly a hoax, but I think it's telling
that demonology was evidently very much in the air as late as 1730.

We began by talking about The Last Witchfinder *as your foray into
straight historical fiction. But the novel has one frankly fantastical
dimension. The narrator technically is not James Morrow but rather
Newton's* Principia Mathematica. *From the first sentence onward,
you give us a world in which books have minds, souls, and a passion
to write other books.*

I'd always envisioned *The Last Witchfinder* as a qualified defense of the
eighteenth-century Enlightenment. And yet these days, I've noticed,
the Age of Reason has few friends. The religious right detests the
Enlightenment because it leads to secularism; postmodern academics
reject the Enlightenment as the presumed progenitor of an oppressive
scientism; and the New Age fringe invites us to regard Reason as
Spirituality's feeble and overrated shadow. So from the instant
I started composing chapter one, I wanted to incorporate a
contemporary perspective—not only to give the anti-Enlightenment

argument its due, but as a way to avoid the bane of historical fiction: characters who are implausibly aware of what their lives will mean to their descendants. At first I tried to achieve this distance by having Aunt Isobel compose a long, prophetic poem in which she foresees the French Revolution and other disasters accruing to the apotheosis of Reason. But it didn't ring true, and so I tried an even stranger ploy: turning the narration over to Newton's *Principia*, a sentient book living outside the bounds of time and space.

Your Principia *narrator invites us to regard the witch-persecution era as a mirror of our present age. Do you see* The Last Witchfinder *as an allegory on the contemporary problem of faith versus rationality?*

If satire is what closes on Saturday night, allegory doesn't even get into the theater—nor should it. The last thing I had in mind was inflicting an uplifting lesson on the reader. That said, we're obviously living in an age when theology is again leading people down some very dark paths indeed. Whether we're talking about the rise of jihadism or recent attempts to cast "intelligent design" as commensurate with Darwin's theory of natural selection, the shadow side of religious faith is haunting the West. So if I had to tease a message out of *The Last Witchfinder*, I would paraphrase Winston Churchill and hold forth as follows: Reason is the worst possible mode in which to negotiate the world—except for all the others. ᘒ

The Godhead Trilogy

Read on

JAMES MORROW'S GODHEAD TRILOGY
was called "one of the wildest series ever
written" by the *Denver Post*. Based on the
audacious conceit that the Creator of the
Universe has not only incarnated himself
but subsequently passed away, leaving
behind a two-mile-long cadaver, the three
books in the cycle—*Towing Jehovah,
Blameless in Abaddon*, and *The Eternal
Footman*—acquired a cult following as they
were published during the 1990s. Several
critics saw in the Godhead Trilogy a
demented updating of Dante's *The Divine
Comedy*, but whatever their ancestry, these
novels stand among the most engaging
works of humanist satire in recent memory.

"Morrow understands theology like a
theologian and psychology like a psychologist,
but he writes like an angel."
—Richard Elliott Friedman, author of
The Hidden Book in the Bible

"Move over Kurt Vonnegut. James Morrow
has put on the mantle of America's best
satirist." —James Gunn, University of Kansas

TOWING JEHOVAH

Anthony Van Horne, a supertanker captain disgraced by an oil spill, is given an opportunity to redeem himself by transporting God's outsized corpse to a tomb in the Arctic. Eager to atone for his environmental sins, Anthony sails out of New York with the Corpus Dei in tow, soon becoming involved in a series of adventures involving ravenous sharks, a militant girlfriend, an estranged father, sabotage both natural and spiritual, a crew on (and sometimes past) the brink of mutiny, and greedy hucksters of petroleum, condoms, and dubious ideas.

"If Salman Rushdie had had Morrow's light-handed sense of satire, he would be in demand for all the right reasons."   —*Chicago Tribune*

"This is a book that should make everyone—from atheist to devout believer—think about things they may never have considered before."
                                        —*San Diego Union-Tribune*

The Godhead Trilogy *(continued)*

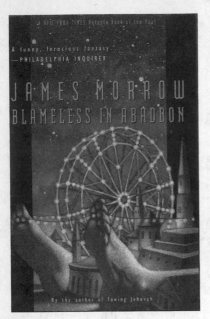

BLAMELESS IN ABADDON

Martin Candle, a small-time and sore-afflicted Pennsylvania judge, vents his rage at the cosmos in a most unusual fashion. He undertakes to bring the corpse of God before the International Court of Justice, indicting the Almighty for His indifference to human suffering. In his quest to counter the world's great theodicies, Martin embarks on an astonishing journey through the mind of the Creator, where Lot's wife proves a most convenient way of salting a margarita, early hominids debate Augustinian doctrine over jasmine tea, and Job keeps an eternal vigil atop his dung heap.

"Morrow hilariously joins the ranks of the great satirists and skillfully adds a serious critique of two thousand years of Western theology."
—*Denver Post*

"Best of all, Morrow chooses not to leave us with the smug nihilism such an effort could easily have produced. . . . Diverting, entertaining, sober, and demanding, all at once."　　　　　　　—*Philadelphia Inquirer*

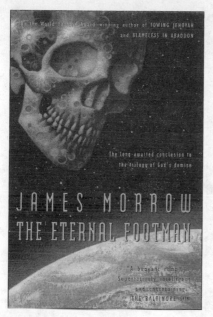

THE ETERNAL FOOTMAN

God's corpse has self-destructed and His skull is now in orbit directly above Times Square, causing an epidemic of "death awareness" across the Western hemisphere. In this plague-ridden world, two people fight to preserve life and sanity: Nora Burkhart, a schoolteacher who will stop at nothing to save her only son, and Gerard Korty, a brilliant sculptor struggling to create a masterwork that will heal the metaphysical wounds caused by God's abdication.

"It's all in a package that will rock you back in your chair and make you take notice on almost every page."   —*San Diego Union-Tribune*

"A buoyant romp . . . superlatively intelligent and entertaining."
                                                              —*Baltimore Sun*

More Fiction by James Morrow

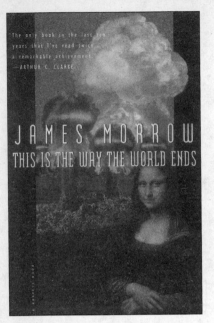

THIS IS THE WAY THE WORLD ENDS

Content in his life as a tombstone carver and a family man, George Paxton lacks only one thing: a fashionable "scopas" survival suit to protect his daughter in the event of thermonuclear war. Then, through a twist of fate, George secures the coveted garment for the price of a mere signature. Unfortunately, what he signs is a confession of his complicity in the arms race, and as the war that could never happen happens, George is whisked into the past and the future to face the consequences of his guilt.

"Astute, highly engaging, and finally moving."   —*Los Angeles Times*

"The most affecting account of nuclear devastation I have ever read in a work of fiction."   —*Newsday*

"Begins where *Dr. Strangelove* ends . . . utterly dazzling and memorable."
                                                        —*Philadephia Inquirer*

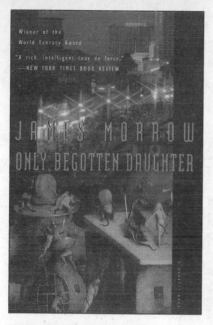

ONLY BEGOTTEN DAUGHTER

Call it a miracle. Call it an accident at the sperm bank. But Murray Katz, the celibate keeper of an abandoned lighthouse near Atlantic City, has been blessed with a daughter conceived from the union of his own seed and a holy ovum. Like her half brother Jesus, Julie Katz can walk on water, heal the blind, and raise the dead. But then her life gets really complicated, as God's daughter undertakes a fantastic odyssey through Hell, a seceded New Jersey, and her own confused soul.

"A rich, intelligent tour de force." —*New York Times Book Review*

"Sort of a Catechism-22 . . . delightfully devilish." —*Philadelphia Inquirer*

"Morrow unerringly targets the nerve endings most readers won't know they have until he zaps them." —*Washington Post*

More Fiction by James Morrow *(continued)*

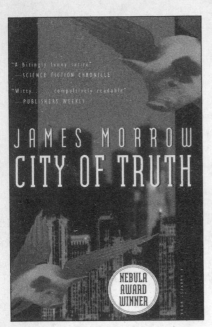

"A bitingly funny satire"
—SCIENCE FICTION CHRONICLE

"Witty... compulsively readable"
—PUBLISHERS WEEKLY

JAMES MORROW
CITY OF TRUTH

NEBULA AWARD WINNER

Don't miss the next book by your favorite author. Sign up now for AuthorTracker by visiting www.AuthorTracker.com.

CITY OF TRUTH

Jack Sperry spends his days diligently destroying "mendacious" works of art in Veritas, a city where people have been brutally conditioned to always tell the truth. But then one day Jack's beloved son, Toby, is bitten by a rabbit at Camp Ditch-the-Kids and contracts a rare illness. Suddenly our hero must somehow learn to lie—the only way, he believes, to give Toby sufficient hope to conquer his fatal disease.

"A quick and delightful read, with a sharp, unmerciful edge that would have pleased old Jonathan Swift." —*Minneapolis Star Tribune*

"Morrow's satire is funny and sad, and increases our ability to see little bits of truth in our own world." —*Denver Post*